PhotoPlay

To Barbara
my favorite scene
partner!

Daniel
Will-Harris

Thanks

To my friends and family who were there for me during the pandemic. This book was a delightful place to escape, but I would have gone mad without (in geographical order, including, but not limited to): Debra, Celeste, Max, Tim, Dora, Fred, Susan, Jennie, David, Phil, Howard, Lorenzo, Bruce, Lisa, Loren, Ocea, Ari, Violet, Jett-Jeff, Mike, Jack, and David. Thanks to my writing group who kept me going and kept it real: Robert, Greg, Christopher, Jeremy, and Karin. And Erin!

Finally, I'd like to thank Herb, Myron, Glenn, Pat, Kitty, Iris, Tiger, Esther, and the rest for telling me their stories. Writing is all about getting out of your own way and *listening*.

1 ⟫⁺ Five tigers in the Bronx

Five tigers were let loose in the Bronx today. They were leaping around like kittens on their own little island in the zoo, separated only by a moat. No bars between them and me.

It was thrilling—something from the movies. But back at home, life wasn't anything like the movies—and that was the problem. I figured the hospital made a big mistake 17 years ago and I was living the wrong life with the wrong parents. When my Pa knocked me out cold on my birthday I knew I had to get out.

Maybe my real Ma was Ginger Rogers. I saw women like her on the Upper East Side. Pretty pink dresses, pretty blond hair. "Shiksas" my dark-haired Ma, in her dark clothes, would call them.

I needed to live in a world that looked like the movies, so I finally set out to find it. I jumped the subway turnstiles and rode into Manhattan. I snuck into the movies to see "A Star is Born" with Janet Gaynor and Frederic March. This poor farm girl with a terrible name goes to Hollywood, changes her name and makes something of herself while her movie star husband is a drunk, like Pa. She wins an Academy Award and he walks into the ocean.

I wanted to be like her but was afraid I'd become like him.

2 ⟫⁺ Tailoring

Pa changed jobs a lot. Or, as Ma said, "Nobody's gonna hire a lush like you, now wadda we gonna do?" I was in the bathroom at the end of the hall and I could still hear them through the walls. After coughing a lot, he yelled, "And what're you doing to earn your keep, bitch?"

Later he said the same thing to me, replacing "bitch" with "bastard." I said, "If I'm a bastard then I don't have a father which means you can't tell me what to do." He threw a lamp, but, like me, he didn't have good aim and it just crashed on the floor.

I felt sorry for him. My Pa, the loser. I felt sorry for myself that my Pa was a loser. No wonder I didn't have a room and had to sleep on the sofa.

I wasn't gonna let that happen to my kid. I knew there was more to the world than my poor, sad parents in our dirty old basement apartment.

I always remembered that, just a few subway stops away, was a gleaming city, mostly clean except on garbage day, filled with non-loser fathers and beautiful mothers. I went there as often as I could, which was less often now that I got myself a job. I told ma and pa I wanted to help. I just didn't tell them who I wanted to help.

Truth is, I always helped them. Before I had the job I had chores, and once I got a job I always gave them money. I could help them out, but I couldn't help them out of the quicksand life they'd sunk themselves into. I just couldn't stick around to get stuck myself.

My first job was a delivery boy for Shapiro's tailoring shop. I was always nosing around there anyway because I liked the fancy clothes. Myron, the nice young man who worked there, let me try things on. He'd say, "Come out and show it to me, boychik," in his light voice.

Myron seemed old to me, but once Mr. Shapiro snapped at him, "you're just 19, what do you know?" so only by two years.

After the shop closed Myron would take me in the back and show me a book that had big photos of sheep in Scotland and explained this is where wool came from, which was surprising, because I never thought about it. All those rich people walking around wearing sheep? It made me laugh to picture it. It also made me want a suit, so bad.

He took me to the garment district where they had used clothes and found me a nice suit that mostly fit for $3. He paid for it himself, and said he'd take up the shoulders and sleeves, then he took me to lunch at Schimmel's Deli and made me wear a napkin so I wouldn't spill soup on the suit.

Then he tried to kiss me... right there in the alley next to Schimmel's. Well, he did kiss me. I didn't know that's what he was doing, I thought I had food on my face or something but, no, he just leaned right in and put his lips on mine. I'd never been kissed before, and it wasn't bad or anything but I thought boys were only supposed to kiss girls.

I said, "Myron, thank you for the suit and I had a good day with you but I don't think I'm allowed to be in love with you so you shouldn't kiss me." I mean, kissing meant you were in love, right? "We can hug if you want, you're a pal."

"Oh, yeah, right, sure, sorry, I just..." and then he started to cry. This made me feel bad and I almost wanted to kiss him just to make him stop crying, but instead I hugged him.

He sniffled, "I'm really sorry, Herbie. I'm really sorry. I'm not right, is all."

"You don't seem sick or nothing," I said, patting his back, pal-like.

"I had a doc tell me I needed shock therapy to get better and I did it and it really hurt and it didn't change nothing. You can stay away from me, it's OK, I'm a freak but I won't do 'nothing. Just don't tell anyone OK, because Mr. Shapiro would fire me for sure and I need this job."

"You're good at your job," I said, still not understanding what all this was about except that he was really upset. "I like you, Myron, I really do. That was a nice kiss. And you're nicer to me than anybody else. Don't worry, I won't say 'nothing, and we can still be pals, OK?"

"Look, Herbie, I won't do that again, I promise. I'm just lonesome and you treat me like..."

"Like somebody who knows stuff," I said.

Back at the shop he drew on the shoulder and sleeves with some chalk and started to sew. He took off his glasses and squinted close at his stitching which was so fine I could barely see it.

I liked watching him sew, then I looked up from his small hands and noticed that without his glasses, I could see his beautiful green eyes. Almost goyish. I kind of wanted to kiss him back.

3 ➺ Night
on the town

Near Year's Eve, 1938 going on 1939.

"Let's sneak out to the Paradise," Ma said, not even bothering to whisper because Pa was out like a light, having celebrated with an entire bottle of his best friend Smirnoff.

Ma loved Loews Paradise theater on the Grand Concourse because inside it looked like a Spanish town under a blue sky with moving clouds. "It's a holiday, just a few stops north!" she'd say when she felt particularly blue.

I liked The Paradise, too, but not tonight. "Let's go to Times Square! We can get all dressed up!"

"All the way down there?" she said, her face lighting up.

"It's just a few stops more than the Paradise, and it's actual paradise! It was, in fact, my favorite place in the whole world. Sometimes I'd jump the turnstiles and take the D train all the way down just to see the lights and come right back. I'd never even thought to go there to see a movie! "And after the picture, at midnight, we can watch the ball drop!"

I hadn't seen Ma smile this big in too long. "I'm putting on my blue dress!" she giggled. Her blue dress was only for special occasions, weddings, funerals... and now our glamorous New Years Eve on the town!

I'd outgrown the suit Myron bought me, so I bought one of my own at the Temple Beth Shalom tag sale. The fancy label inside said, "Made for Melvin Goldschpeigel by Bloomingdales."

Everybody liked Mel. I went to his funeral. He worked at his cousin's jewelry store and was quite the snappy dresser—and ladies man. His wife, Rivkah, didn't think much of that, especially when he flirted with the other ladies at the temple. Mel got hit by a taxi, but I wasn't the only one who thought maybe she pushed him in front of it. He'd be happy his special suit was going to have a special night.

Ma slammed the front door as we left, and we skipped down the sidewalk to the subway. She used to be like this most of the time, and only went to her dark place once in a while, but lately she was there more. I blamed Pa, but then, I blamed him for everything, including my curly hair. I wanted straight hair, like the goy boys. I'd flatten it down with water but the curls would pop up again. Even Brylcreem couldn't hold it down so I stopped trying.

We took the subway to 42nd where everything was aglow, including Ma, who looked young and happy and pretty, as if the past 20 years hadn't happened.

I was determined to give her a treat. "We're going to the Automat!" I said, pulling her up Broadway to *Horn and Hardart,* the black and white restaurant from the future. I'd seen it in movies but this was my first time inside. The walls were covered with gleaming chrome boxes full of food of all kinds!

I put two nickels in the slot and opened the chrome door. She reached in and, like magic, pulled out a hot chicken pot pie. The next wall said, "Dessert Caravan," with rows of chrome boxes filled with treats from around the world! I knew she liked coconut cream pie and got a slice for her, and chocolate pudding for me. We sat at an empty table.

"Pudding's not enough for my growing boy," she said.

"I was so excited I forgot dinner, be right back!" I got an egg salad sandwich and returned to the table where Ma was still looking around at all the people and all the food. "Come on, Ma, you gotta eat."

She'd been getting skinnier. She'd make dinner for Pa and me but didn't eat much herself. "I don't have much of an appetite these days," she'd say, nibbling a slice of bread and margarine and not even finishing that. Some days I'd bring home a Baby Ruth bar and leave it in the utensil drawer where Pa never looked. The next morning it'd be gone and I hoped she ate it.

But we didn't talk about these things, we didn't talk about anything, really. We pretended everything was fine. I loved going to the movies with Ma because then, at least, we could pretend—together. Tonight she cleaned her plates, letting out a big sigh, looking content.

It was almost 9, time for the movie. *Broadway Melody of 1940* with Fred Astaire and Eleanor Powell. One poster outside called it a "Miracle Musical" and another said, "It's as big as Broadway and twice as gay!"

I bought our tickets and sat in the first row of the balcony so nobody's head would block her view. The lights went down, the silver screen lit up and the rest of the world was gone. I watched Ma, watching the screen. It made me happy to know that for the next two hours she'd be happy.

All that singing. All that dancing. Astaire and Powell in sparkly white clothes, dancing on a shiny black floor to *Begin the Beguine.* They made glamour look so natural, I was sure that someday that would be my life, too.

The movie let out and Times Square was already crowded. We pushed into the throngs of merry-makers. All these people. All this noise. All the lights.

Suddenly the neon signs went dark. Everyone gasped. A giant ball lit up on top of the triangular Times building and a deep voice blasted from a speaker, "10, 9, 8..." thousands of people joined in, "7, 6, 5, 4..." Ma joined in, so did I, "3, 2, 1... *Happy New Year!*"

The cheering made the world feel like it was going to crack open, revealing a bright new year.

I looked over and Ma had a tear in her eye. "You OK, Ma?"

"I forgot what it was like to be happy," she whispered in my ear.

The signs turned back on, the crowd drifted away. Ma and I were still standing there, looking at this shining world. "Shall we dance?" I asked her. We spun around the sidewalk, feeling like Fred and Eleanor, tapping our feet to 42nd street, laughing.

4 ➻ Reality

We were still laughing when Ma unlocked our front door. The laughing stopped when we saw Pa, standing there in his undershirt, his face red. "Where have you two good-for-nothings been?"

Ma was still smiling, "Herbie took me to Times Square for New Year's eve. We had dinner at the Automat, I had pie, and we saw a movie..." he pushed her aside and shoved his face up to mine, exhaling hot liquor breath up my nose.

"Mister Moneybags, are you now?" he hissed at me.

I looked at Ma, hoping she would stop him but she backed away. "I earned it!" I protested. He had me pinned against the wall.

"You? You're nothing."

He grabbed my shoulders and spun me around, reaching into my back pocket and pulling out my wallet.

"That's mine, give it back!"

He tore it open, practically ripping in half. I'd hidden a five dollar bill inside the secret slot in the back but he knew right where to look and pulled it out. "You think you're something, don't you? You're not even worth five bucks. You're worthless" he said, tossing my empty wallet out the window onto the street.

I leaned out the window to see where it landed and felt him grab my ankles and push me out the window, onto the sidewalk. "YOU'RE NOTHING" he yelled, before slamming the window closed behind me.

I picked up what was left of my wallet. Nothing.

Ma slipped outside in her nightgown and whispered, "You know how he is, he'll forget it all in the morning."

"I won't," I said, tasting blood on my lip.

"He's unhappy, Herbie," she said, shivering.

"But we don't have to be."

"Where would you have me go? She said, sadly.

"Goodnight, Ma, you better go in, it's cold."

I waited to see the lights go out, then snuck in, got my coat and the few clothes I'd bought myself and left. I was nothing and I had no place to go.

5 ⟫ Real Life

Real life was a let down.

I wouldn't go home again.

I slept in the back of Shapiro's, nestled between bolts of fabric. It wasn't my room, but at least it had a door.

I graduated from High School. I was 18.

6 ⟫ Deliveries

Myron still avoided me. Every once in a while I'd ask him, "Can't we be friends?"

"No, Herbie..." he'd say, turning away. I wondered if there was something wrong with me. Today he hid behind a stack of packages, neatly wrapped in brown paper and secured with red ribbon with the words "SHAPIRO" on it in gold letters.

Myron placed the packages on the counter and muttered, "Here," then turned away.

I grabbed his arm.

"Hey. Are you mad at me or something?"

He froze that way for a bit, with my hand holding his arm, then he slowly pulled away.

"'Course not, Herbie. I thought *you* were mad."

"I never said that. I thought *you* were."

"Nope," Myron said, looking down and making it sound like "Yup."

I looked at my next delivery... What was this? A delivery in Manhattan?

7 ⇒ UWS

I loved riding my bike to Manhattan even though the subway was a lot faster. But on a clear, sunny November afternoon, with the trees changing colors, riding over the Harlem river was like going on vacation.

I'd never been to Broadway and West 73rd. The Upper West Side seemed like a step up from my neighborhood, and maybe someplace I could live myself if I could get a real job doing something... But I didn't know what.

When I'd watch movies, I'd see what the guys were doing, like being spies or generals or international playboys. Those all sounded good, so maybe I just needed to hang around where spies and generals and international playboys hung around.

Suddenly I realized I'd forgotten to look at the street signs, and I was already at W. 70s. I had to turn around and go back up three blocks... when I did. Yowza. I mean full on YOWZA.

This was no mere red brick apartment building, this was a full on palace. I counted 16 stories and at the top were turrets topped with church-like steeples. There were round windows and all sorts of fancy railings and stuff. I sat on my bike, gawping at it.

8 ⇒ The Ansonia

"The Ansonia" it said on the green awning right on the Great White Way! There was an actual theater, the Beacon, just a block away, the subway just two blocks away, and at least three pizza parlors between them. Basically heaven.

I rode into the alley and changed into my city clothes because this was far too nice of a building to enter in short pants. I changed into a white shirt with wide blue stripes I bought at Loehmann's discount basement, and dark blue pants Myron showed me how to cuff.

As well as my good clothes, I put on my good posture before the doorman could see me. I smiled, without teeth, the way I'd seen sophisticates smile in the movies, and nodded. He held his hand out in front of me and I admired the gold braid on his cuff. I'd have to ask Myron how to get some of that.

"May I help you, sir," He said, and I liked that he called me, "Sir."

"I have a delivery for one Miss Rose in apartment 1616," I said, lowering my voice to sound as professional as I could.

I thought I saw him roll his eyes, then he said, "You can leave the parcel with me and I will deliver it."

I looked at him looking at me. No, no, no, this would never do. I was supposed to deliver it personally to the customer. I mean, what if this doorman took the package and said it never arrived and then wore it himself... no, in this case he might give it to his wife or girlfriend. No.

Besides, I really, really, really, really, really, really, really wanted to see inside this palace.

"I'm sorry, my employer insists that I make deliveries personally in case there's any issue with the goods." I held my breath to see what he'd say.

"Fine. 16th floor," he said. "Better bring your bike inside or it'll get stole for sure."

I went around the corner, got my bike and wheeled it in. "I'll keep my eye on it, kid... Sir," he said, opening the iron gate. I walked inside and there was a park, right in the middle of the building, with some big black cars parked. I looked around for the elevator.

A hand tapped my shoulder and the doorman's gold braided sleeve pointed to the right, "The lobby is that way... sir."

I hurried off and now there was another doorman who opened the door and nodded. Inside there was a lobby with black and white checkerboard marble floors, a trickling fountain and a grand staircase. Yet another man in a fancy coat was standing behind the desk.

"May I help you, sir," he said.

"I'm here to *personally* deliver this package to Miss Rose in 1616."

Did he roll his eyes, too? "I can deliver it for you," he said. Not this again.

"No, my employer insists all parcels be *personally* delivered."

He shrugged and pointed to the elevators. There were six of them. Six elevators. In one building. That was enough elevators for six buildings!

A uniformed elevator operator waved me in and I said, "1616, please."

"Yes, sir," he replied. Why was he smirking?

It was a long ride. The elevator door opened on a hallway wider than my parents' living room. I could have lived in that hallway, with its black and white marble floors and fancy chandeliers.

"Your floor, sir," he said, holding the door for me.

"Thank you, kind sir," I replied and he gave me a funny look. Maybe I wasn't supposed to call him "sir."

The door closed behind me and I wandered down the hall. 1601. 1602... it was a long hall. Each door had a number, and a little brass plaque with a name on it. This one said, "1616, Miss Katherine Rose."

I knocked. Nobody answered. I knocked again. Finally I saw a button next to the door that said, "Bell." I liked pressing buttons, so I pressed it and heard a pretty chime.

I saw an eye looking through the peephole just above my head.

9 ➻ Heaven or Hell

"Who's there?" a young woman's voice asked.

"I'm Herbie... Herb... Herbert from Shapiro's Tailor Shop, here with a delivery for one Miss Rose."

The door opened, stopped by a chain. A cool breeze wafted at me as I saw her fabulous face for the first time.

"Oh, OK," she said, removing the chain and opening the door.

I nearly fainted right there. She was like one of the statues in the Met, come to life. Only a couple of years older than I was... and perfect. *Perfect.* Wearing this pink... thing. I'd never seen anything like it because I could see clear through it... It was so short I could see her knees, and so thin I could see... things I had never seen before and didn't even have names for. Breasts, yes, I knew that word but I'd never seen any in person. They were beautiful!

"Well don't just stand there, good-looking, come on in," she said.

As soon as I crossed the threshold it felt like walking into a movie screen. I had goosebumps, but then it was also surprisingly cool inside, like an air-conditioned movie theater—or maybe it was just the sight of her.

"What 'ya got for me, boy?" she said, impatiently but sweetly. Oh, so sweetly. Her voice was like... I couldn't even compare it with anything because I'd never felt like this before. I could just lay down and die a happy boy. I was shaking as I handed her the package.

She unwrapped it carefully, keeping the ribbon to tie back her long black hair.

"Sit down, baby, I'm gonna try this on, just in case. Oooh, it's pretty, ain't it?"

I sat down on a white satin chair that seemed to want to eat me as I sank into it. I didn't care. Let it eat me while I watched this... wonder.

She took off what little she was wearing and put on the black sequined dress from the package. I'd never seen anything like this from Shapiro's.

"Myron is a miracle worker," she said, admiring herself in a big mirror. She turned around with her backside to me. I hadn't even noticed her backside before and it was... breathtaking. I literally couldn't breathe.

"Zip this up for me, honey, won'cha?"

I had a hard time getting out of the chair, then almost tripped on the carpet, it was so thick. She must have thought I was stupid or something as I stumbled over to her.

"Just up the back, baby" she said, again in this voice that sounded like a breeze with words.

My hands were freezing and I wasn't sure I could move my fingers and when I tried to hold the zipper pull I slipped and touched her back... oh... my... God... her back felt like... satin? Velvet? Words couldn't describe the feeling.

She giggled. "You're so sweet."

I finally grasped the pull and zipped it, slowly, so as to enjoy the view along the way.

"Fagela's are the best dressmakers. They don't oggle me... she said, spinning in front of the mirror and admiring her own reflection. "But you sure do, big boy! I can see you're all man under those pants."

What was this creature? What was happening? Where was I? Why was it cold and why did I have a stiffie, the likes of which I usually only had when I woke up in the morning?

"I could just eat you up, baby," she said. "I hope this makes me look older and more sophisticated."

I had lost the power of speech and just kind of grunted.

"I feel very glamorous. I want to look 21." she went on while I'm pretty sure my mouth hung open.

"I just love the strong silent type," she said, taking my cold hand in her warm one and running her other hand through my hair, "Such cute curls!" She sparkled, like a fish, like a mermaid.

"It's nice to be with a well-built boy, baby, it's been too long. The old guys, they got money but not... well, what you got right there in your pants."

For a moment I thought I'd gone blind. I couldn't see anything. Then I realized my eyes were closed and when I opened them her face was very close to mine. A face so beautiful... even sitting down I felt like I was going to faint.

"Oh, honey, you look like you need to lie down..." she said, taking my hand again. I didn't know if I was frozen or feverish.

She opened a pair of doors with shiny chrome knobs and led me into the bedroom, all white. There was just one small round window, but somehow the room was full of light from above. I looked up and saw blue sky and clouds through a window in the ceiling. A window in the ceiling! Who'd ever heard of such a thing?

I had clearly died and gone to heaven. It was the only explanation for all this. Maybe I got hit by a taxi and I was dead and that was A-OK by me.

She touched me lightly and I sat on the bed. She knelt down and untied my shoes, and touched me again and I fell back. Absolutely, positively dead. No bout adout it. I meant, no doubt about it.

I was always told Jews didn't have a heaven, but clearly they were wrong. And what a heaven it was. Kitty lay down beside me. Thank you, God, for letting me into heaven. I wasn't sure I'd get here. I was always a good boy but wow.

"You're very sweet. I remember a boy like you when I was just a girl... His name was Billy and he was my first. Have you ever... never mind, I'll show you."

And then she kissed me. On the lips. A lot like Myron, but a lot better. Softer. Smelling like roses.

Then her hand touched my chin, down my neck, down my chest... I was simply covered in gooseflesh. Her hand slid into my pants. I didn't have the power or will to stop her even though I couldn't imagine what she was doing. I didn't care either.

I'd seen people kiss in the movies but then there'd be a picture of the fireplace and in the morning they'd be dressed and so I waited to see a fireplace.

Instead I felt her soft hand wrap around my hard pecker.

That's when I started to cry.

"First time, huh?" She said, sweetly, never loosening her grip. "You're adorable," she said, pulling her hand away.

"I almost forgot you'll shoot in no time," she whispered in my ear, her warm breath making me shake.

Then she unzipped my pants and pulled them down.

"Big man!" she said and she did the strangest thing. She got on top of me and then I felt this incredible warmth and I started to shake and then cried out and felt myself explode bigger than I'd ever felt before. It is wonderful and terrifying.

I was so embarrassed.

"I'm sorry," I managed to say. She just kept sitting on top of me, smiling.

"What you lack in stamina you make up for in power. We'll work on it."

Then she got up and I heard the water running and I just lay there, naked.

She came back and rubbed me with a warm washcloth.

"I needed that, baby—To know I still have that power over a good looking young man. You're very sweet, a lot like Billy, only nice. Kind of like a very handsome puppy, too, which is good, 'cause grown men are dogs."

I just lay there, looking at the sky through the ceiling. I fell asleep.

When I woke up, I saw stars through the ceiling. The angel girl was shaking me.

"Time to get up puppy boy, my sugar daddy called and he's on his way. Won't be as much fun as you but he pays for the place. Come on, get your pants on."

I didn't understand a word of what she was saying, but she pulled me out of bed and straightened it up and I felt embarrassed to be naked and put my underwear and pants on.

There was a knock at the door.

"Oh, baby, it's too late. You're gonna have to hide."

"I really have to pee," I said.

"No time now, sweetie... go into the bathroom and hide in the shower, and you can pee there if you have to, just be quiet about it."

The bathroom was all white marble as befitted heaven and she pushed me into the shower and closed the glass door with a white swan painted on it/ She whispered, "Don't make a sound or he'll kill you, or me, or both of us."

I was afraid my peeing would make a sound so I just held it. I heard her open the door and a man's deep voice was talking but I couldn't hear what he was saying.

Now I wondered if I might be in hell and he was the devil. I'd somehow failed in my test with the angel and now he was here to drag me to hell. Well, it was good while it lasted.

The man grunted, "And then she said, 'I want a divorce,' and I said, 'you can't leave soon enough,' and she called me a bastard, can you even imagine, what a witch."

The angel said, "If you get divorced then…"

The devil said, "I can't afford to get divorced, the money's from her family. I'll fix it up, I always do."

Then it was quiet and I really, really, really needed to pee. But I didn't. I thought I might explode but maybe that would save me from going to hell, so I held it.

"I'll send her some flowers and a bracelet and go down on her and profess my love… love. It's a chore, not like with you."

The angel laughed but didn't sound happy.

Then they stopped talking and he started moaning and she made weird squeaky noises.

I couldn't keep my eyes open. I'd ridden my bike and seen a naked girl and done more than just see her and the more I tried to stay awake, the heavier my eyes felt until they closed.

I woke up when I saw the sun through another window in the ceiling and realized I'd wet myself. But at least I wasn't in hell.

The angel came back in. "I'm so tired of hearing about that bitch, his wife," she said, opening the shower door.

"Oh, you poor baby, you were fast asleep when he left and I didn't want to wake you. I'll call the concierge and he'll get your pants cleaned."

I took off my pants and she wrapped them in a towel.

"I liked knowing you were here, it made me feel safe," she said, picking up the telephone... In the bathroom. A white telephone in the bathroom! At home we had one downstairs in the hall for the whole building and she had one... in the bathroom.

"Cleaning please, 1616, it's a rush. And my usual breakfast but for two, thanks." She hung up. Wear my robe for a while till they get back," she said, handing me a white satin robe that felt like I was wearing water.

I felt compelled to follow her... yes, like a puppy. I would happily be her puppy. I didn't know this was an option!

Next to her front door was a closet door she opened and put the pants in. I heard a bell tinkle and she said, "They've got 'em. Give 'em a half hour. You must be hungry."

I sat on the sofa with her and she petted me, like a puppy. I lay back with my head on her lap and looked upside down through the round window and saw we were right up next to the roof. My stomach rumbled.

"You're not by any chance rich, are you, baby?" She purred.

"I think I had two dollars in my pants..."

"Don't worry, they won't take it. But it won't go very far in this neighborhood. You from the Bronx?"

"South... Yes... ma'am..."

She stopped petting me. "Me, too. Oh, don't call me 'ma'am,' makes me feel old. Call me 'Kitty,' it's my stage name."

"Yes... Kitty."

She ran her fingers through my curly hair again. "It's so cute when you say it, like you're the puppy and I'm the kitty. You make me feel so young again, not like the '20-year old maid,' my mama calls me."

"I like you," I said without thinking, but it was true, I liked her. And not just because of how she looked or what she did to me, but because she seemed nice.

"It gets lonely here by myself and I have to be at his beck and call. I used to love to go out and do my shows and dance and now I just have to wait around..."

"Wait around for what?"

"For David."

"I don't understand," I said, and I didn't.

"Sometimes neither do I. I got tired living in a cold water flat with 4 other girls... These stage door Johnnies smell swell and give nice presents and I thought it would be.... I dunno, easier."

"I don't understand," I said again.

A bell tinkled by the front door. She got up, opened the closet door and pulled out a silver tray full of dishes covered with silver domes.

"No reason you should, baby. Hey, what're you doin' today?" she said, lifting the domes to reveal plates full of food: scrambled eggs, sausages, hash browns, fried tomatoes. I looked on in wonder at this magical breakfast that appeared from the closet and was still steaming hot.

What did she ask? Oh, right, "I got more deliveries from Shapiro's I guess."

"I'll call Mr. Shapiro and tell him I need you to help me, it'll be fine."

"You can do that?" I asked.

"With what David spends there on me I can tell him anything, boychik."

We sat in front of the little round window and ate our delicious breakfast.

She opened a little bottle of pills and swallowed one. "Bennies," she said, handing one to me. I took it. It tasted bad, but the food was so good!

She perked up, "I heard there used to be a farm on the roof of this building. They raised chickens and plants and pigs and stuff."

This didn't look like New York at all. Maybe I'd taken a wrong turn and ended up in Oz. I saw that movie, twice, with Ma. Only this looked more like that movie I saw, "Paris Rain" with Cary Grant and Ingrid Bergman as this couple in love only he was taken away by nasty Germans and she had to become a nun and when he got out and found her she's already found God and so they had to say goodbye. I cried.

I hadn't noticed that Kitty had left the room until she floated back in.

"I called Saul and he said you're mine all day!" she giggled. "I want to ride the carousel in the park. David would never do that. He doesn't know how to have fun, besides, he couldn't be seen with me. When your pants get back, let's go!"

There was something so familiar about her.

I heard the little bell ring again and watched her open the closet next to the front door and pull out a package wrapped in tissue paper.

"Here are your pants, sweetie, let's go!"

What a magic closet! There were my pants, all clean and soft and pressed. I took off the robe and pulled on my trousers. Suddenly, I felt like a man. Not the "just turned 18 year old," kind, but like a real adult kind of man. I'd changed in one night.

And I had so much energy!

She changed, too, into a white dress with red cherries on it, and red shoes. She looked like a movie star... and I was her man... at least for the day.

She held my hand all the way down the hall and even down the elevator where I saw the operator look sideways at me.

"Not a word of this," Kitty said to him, pulling a quarter from her shiny red purse.

Out through the big lobby. "They tell me there used to be live seals in the fountain here, but that was long before I moved in. Musta stunk."

When we got outside it was hot—like when I got out of the movies where they had "scientific air cooling" and I'd forget it was hot outside.

"Get us a taxi, Max," she said to the doorman, who flagged one down.

10 ➻ A walk in the park

I opened the taxi door for her.

"Ooh, a real gentleman. I knew it when I first saw you... what was your name again"

"Herb...ert. Herbert."

"I like that name, it sounds Europeanish. To the central park carousel please, garçon."

And off we went, my first time in a car! The back seat was like a sofa and we sped along, until there was traffic and we just sat there. But it was still comfy. Plus, Kitty smelled good, like flowers.

When the car didn't move for a while, Kitty said, "We'll walk the rest of the way," and handed the driver some money and we got out. "It's not far and it'll be a pretty walk by the lake. It's nice here, peaceful," she said, taking my hand again as we walked in the shade of the trees and then by a big lake with people riding around in little boats.

I heard some music, like a monkey grinder and Kitty started to run, "We're almost here!" she cried out in joy and I followed her, hot on her heels. She stopped with her arms open wide. "I'm going to ride the big white horse!" she cried as I raced after her. She handed a man a dime and we jumped on.

"Here, help me up, doll," she said, and I held her hand and she got on the horse. She was so happy. I got on the black horse next to her. I'd been on a carousel before, of course, the little one at the Bronx zoo where all the animals were bugs. I liked the praying mantis best because it was the biggest and a shiny green with red jeweled eyes.

But this horse was shiny, too, and had a real hair mane and blue jewel eyes. Everything started to move... not just around but also up and down! The air smelled like grass and the breeze felt cool and she reached out and took my hand.

I felt like I was in that movie, "The Sword of Stanstead," with John Wayne as a knight in shining armor winning the heart of his lady fair, Irene Dunne. I liked that movie, it was in color. Everything today looked especially colorful. Kitty's red shoes and green eyes and the sparkling jewel eyes of the animals. There was music playing, too, just like in the movies, only this was better than the movies, this was real, even if I might be dead. No other explanation came to mind for how this was happening.

The music stopped, the carousel slowed and she handed me a silver dollar, "Give this to the ticket man and tell him we're staying on for a while."

He laughed when I told him and said, "As long as you and your sister like, kid."

What? She wasn't my sister, she was my lady fair. What did he know, he didn't even have gold on his jacket.

Other people got on and off but we just kept riding, the wind in our hair.

11 ➟ Dizzy

Finally the ticket man said, "You gotta get off now, we close at 3."

I felt dizzy and had to hold onto the horse's mane to keep from falling down. Kitty just drifted off towards a cart with candy floss as I stumbled along behind her.

She bought two, a red one for her and a purple one for me. I didn't really like candy floss, I had it once at a carnival and it tasted like sweet sand, weird and gritty, but it would have been rude to refuse... this one was still oddly crunchy but softer, and it tasted like grape soda.

"What does pink taste like?" I asked her. She put hers in front of my face, "Take a bite, baby." It was strawberry. I handed her mine and she tore off such a big bite it trailed down her chin to her chest. I took out my handkerchief and wiped a purple spot from her breast.

She wrapped her arm around me, "You really are the sweetest boy. I might just steal you away from Mr. Shapiro."

"Please," I said, and she laughed, sweetly.

The rest of the day was a dream, like the part of a movie where music plays and the happy couple is walking by the shore, then they're in a restaurant, then they're sitting on a bench... we did all that. We ate hamburgers. "David never wants normal food, it's always frou frou frenchie this or la la something fancy I can't even tell what it is because the restaurants are always so dark. He makes us go to the outer boroughs where nobody will recognize him. This is nicer, right in the city, with you, Herbert."

When she said my name... it was the first time I actually liked it. She made it sound classy.

I reached over and took her hand, and she smiled. We sat that way, eating our burgers and fries with one hand and holding the other.

I was in love.

Now I understood those movies where two people stared at each other for a long time and didn't say anything. Before I found that boring, but now, it was the most beautiful thing in the world. Especially looking at Kitty.

"I love you," I said.

She gasped, dropped her burger on the plate, put her hand over her mouth and started to cry.

"Oh, my little love," she sniffed and I handed her my handkerchief. "I've waited so long for a boy to say that to me. David's never said that. Not once."

We sat there quietly. She finished dabbing her eyes and handed me my handkerchief.

"I love you, too, Herbert. You're a sweet boy... man... gentleman. This has been the nicest day I've had in a long time."

We finished eating without talking, which was OK because I didn't know what else to say as we took a taxi back to the Ansonia.

"I guess I better go home now," I said.

"I'm gonna be so lonely without 'cha," she sighed, fluttering her eyelids. "You can stay the night, can't cha? Or you got somewhere better to go?"

There was no place better to go. Not in the whole entire world. Not even to a Shah's palace with tigers.

"Course not, I mean of course not, m'lady."

She giggled. "David won't be back for a few days, he has to be good to that witch… so maybe you can be good to me?"

"I will do anything you want," I said, and meant it.

She wanted some things I never would have imagined.

12 ❧ The Light of Day

The sun was streaming in my face from the ceiling window. I turned to see Kitty, still looking like a movie star. I wasn't sure if I was dead but didn't care. I thought of that song, from Porgy and Bess, but with, "Kitty, you is my woman now."

After everything we did last night, things I once again had no names for, I was surprised to discover I was hard and wanted more. But I figured it would be ungentlemanly to awaken my lady this way, so I got up quietly and went to the bathroom where even the toilet was a throne fit for a king!

I ran the shower carefully so as not to run out of hot water, but it was hot immediately, and there was so much pressure! It felt like standing in tropical rain. The soap smelled of roses—and made so many bubbles I got soap in my eyes, and didn't see when Kitty joined me—but I felt it, her slipping around me.

"For a puppy you're an animal!" she whispered in my ear as her hands slid all over me.

I was about 100% sure I was the luckiest man on the entire planet, harems and tigers be damned! I turned around to face her and she even looked beautiful wet. She was magic. I was magic. Everything was magic—and the world would always be magic from now on!

I was clearly dead. Thank God.

We lathered each other and rubbed our bodies against each other and before I knew it I was inside her again and her tongue was inside my mouth and I stopped being me. That's what this felt like, I was no longer Herbie, the mensch, I was Herbert, the animal!

The shower water never got cold.

Once we finally rinsed off, she wrapped herself in a fluffy snow white towel, then handed me one. It was soft and dry and warm, not having been previously used by both parents and left on the floor of the shared shower at the end of the hall...

"Why me?" I asked her while I shaved. If, by some miracle, I was actually alive, I'd probably have to go back to reality today and just wanted to know what I did to deserve all this, in case I might be able to make it happen again.

"Why not?" she whispered, sweetly.

"Why not?" I thought. "Because this isn't my world," I heard myself say.

"You think it's mine?" she replied, combing her hair.

"It is yours, Kitty, this is your place."

"I come from the South Bronx, too, baby."

"Is that why you like me?"

She looked into my eyes, her green eyes so familiar, "I like you because you're like me. You want to get out of the Bronx, you want more outta life. And—you didn't want to take anything from me."

But I had. I had taken her body and her heart... and given her mine.

"I love you," I said, for maybe the fifth time since last night.

"You gotta be careful with those words, baby, or you'll get your heart broke."

"I'll always love you," I said, believing it with all my not yet broken heart.

"I believe you will, love. You will always have the only little soft spot in my heart, too."

She picked up the white bathroom phone and asked for flapjacks and bacon and toast. I loved this breakfast ordering phone! By the time we got dressed, the little bell tinkled by the front door and she opened the closet to reveal a silver tray full of covered dishes.

Everything was still hot and delicious and we sat by the little round window and looked out at the blue sky and white clouds.

Then the kitchen phone rang and she answered. Her face immediately changed, little lines forming between her perfect eyebrows. "Today? Oh, I... Noon, fine."

"And so the dream dies," she sighed, popping a little white pill and handing one to me.

"Why? What happened?"

"David's coming over at noon. I have to see him, he makes all this possible."

I still didn't understand how that worked, but I did know I didn't want to hide in the shower again.

"Look, sweetheart, you gotta go. But I like having you here. You're sweet and good company and I'm not used to that. Mr. Shapiro won't let me have you indefinitely—yet. Call me later, like 8. If David's gone you can come back tonight."

Then she gave me the softest, sweetest kiss, right on the lips, and said, "I love you, too." and I almost fell off my chair.

When I got down to the lobby, the doorman looked at me and said, "Hmm, sir" Then I got to the outside doorman who handed me my bike and said, "Hmm, sir."

And I rode uptown, over the river and back to Shapiro's. When I came in Mr. Shapiro was waiting. "Hmm, boy. You gonna make a habit of that nonsense?" he asked, sternly but with a smile.

"I sure hope so!" I said, seriously, but with a smile.

"Don't mention it to Myron," he said, turning and going into the back room.

Myron emerged with a load of packages. "You feeling better, boychik?" he asked me?

"Never felt…" I started, before figuring out Mr. Shapiro musta told Myron I was sick yesterday. "…so bad, I honestly thought I was gonna die yesterday but today I'm OK," I said.

He patted me on the shoulder, "I wouldn't want anything to happen to you," he said, in a sweetly familiar tone.

Today's deliveries were all local. Three shirts for a short, wide man on the ground floor who gave me a quarter so I liked him. A sabbath schmatta for an old lady who gave me a nickel… which might have been real money in her day. A Rabbi's suit, delivered to the temple. I didn't expect him to give me anything but Rabbi Schmule gave me a silver dollar and said, "I sense great things in you, young man." I thought this was very classy and vowed to remember it.

I sensed great things in myself.

I was hot and smelly when I was done with deliveries at 4pm. I headed north to the Crotona Pool, one of great President Roosevelt's gifts to us citizens. It was big and clean and had nice showers and only cost a nickel, including a clean towel.

I had a slice at DaVichi's on E. 150th, and I thought about my life, just on the other side of the Harlem river. I'd have to get a job down there, maybe another delivery job, or, better yet, a spy. But I would make it work, because I was Herbert, the animal!

Maybe I could work in a zoo? I'd keep my options open, and then I could have Kitty and tigers, too.

13 ➼ Cherry Pie

I called Kitty at 8 on the dot.

"Oh, hi baby," she cooed. I instantly felt like a man again. "All clear. Come back to mama."

I rode like the wind towards the Oz of the Ansonia. Max, the doorman from earlier, looked me over, "I'll take your bike, sir," and I gave him a quarter. "Ah, a gentleman, I see," he said, smiling. Yup, if I was going to be a man I would have to tip like one. The inside doorman got a quarter, and so did the elevator operator. After the price of my pizza and coke, I'd just finished off the Rabbi's dollar, and I'm sure he would have been proud of the way I spread it around.

When Kitty opened the door she looked sad. "Come on in, baby."

"You OK"

"Just tired, sweetheart. I need to get some sleep tonight."

I kissed her cheek, "I want you to have whatever your little heart desires," I said, cribbing a line from a Fred MacMurray movie.

"Ain't you sweet," she said. "I like having you here with me so I'm not all alone with only the radio."

"I like the radio," I said, looking for one. "Where is it?"

"Right there, on the table."

All I saw was this round blue mirror... with knobs. That was a radio? I tuned it to WNEW and dance music wafted into the room. I put my arms around her and we danced for a bit, then I stepped on her foot and apologized and she said, "I'm tired, baby."

"I'm sorry, I've never danced before but I wanted to, with you. She sat on the sofa and I took off her white furry shoes and put her perfect feet up on the cushion. "What can I do for you?"

A single, beautiful tear ran down her face, taking a streak of black with it. "Everyone else tells me what to do for them."

"Not me, I want to take care of my lady fair."

"I'd really like some cherry pie. David won't let me eat pie, says I'll get fat."

"I'll go to the store and get you some..."

"Just call, they'll bring it up. Ala mode."

"I called for two cherry pies, ala mode."

"Would you massage my feet, baby?" she asked, and of course I would, she had beautiful feet. I'd never really paid attention to feet before, except my own when I'd stub my toe or pull out something from under my toenail that smelled like Parmesan cheese. But her feet were like those statues at The Met.

I heard the bell ring and opened the closet door and there were two full cherry pies, each with four scoops of vanilla ice cream. She laughed, sweetly. "You didn't say 'slices', but that's OK, I love pie for breakfast and we can get fat together!"

I'd never thought about getting fat, but that would make me look like a rich man.

I sliced the pie in the kitchen and put it on plates. Since the ice cream was going to melt, I put it all on and handed her the plate.

"I'm gonna need a napkin, baby, I don't want to spill cherry on white satin!"

I got her a napkin and she put her plate on the glass table between the sofa and chairs. We sat, side by side, eating pie and listening to Ramon Rodriguez and his rooftop orchestra till I was so full of pie and ice cream it was harder to breathe.

"You're going to have to carry me to bed," she giggled.

I picked her up, and, both a little sticky with ice cream, we kissed. I carried her to bed and tucked her in, the way I saw Maureen O'Hara do for Shirley Temple.

She took another little pill from a bottle by the bed. I lay down beside her and watched as her eyes closed... she gave out a little toot. I didn't know ladies did that. I liked it.

14 ➤ It's Just Sex

The phone ringing woke me up. Yes, there was another phone, this one by the bed. I reached to pick it up before Kitty woke up, but she grabbed it out of my hand and put her finger to her lips.

"Morning, David. Oh, how... nice. Yes, I'll be ready." She hung up the phone. "Never answer the phone here. Never. Got it?"

"Yup, sorry, I didn't know."

"It's OK. I gotta get ready. David's taking me to the Catskills for the weekend... in the off season. Nobody goes in the off season, which is why we can go. That means you have the place to yourself all weekend, baby, and I'll see you here on Monday."

"OK," I said, kissing her. "Can you ask you a question, Kitty?"

"Sure, kid, anything you want."

"What do you do with David?"

"Oh, That. I don't love him, if that's what you want to know. It's just sex."

"But isn't that what you do with me?"

"Naw, baby, we make love."

"That's OK then," I said, relieved.

"Just call for anything you need, you know the drill," she said, heading to the shower. I ordered us breakfast, bacon, eggs, hash-browns, and toast. She ate, looking sad, then packed a suitcase with a lot of pretty things.

I tried to make her feel better, "You don't have to go if you don't want to."

"Ah, sweet pup, you're wrong about that. I have to go. A girl's gotta do what a girl's gotta do to take care of herself, that's all. But I'm glad you'll be here when I get back."

There was a knock at the door and the elevator operator was there for her bag, and her. She turned back and blew me a kiss, then she was gone.

The place wasn't the same without her. But now I would have the entire weekend to try to get a job here. I unpacked the garment bag I'd borrowed from Shapiro's and looked for an empty drawer. There were none. Half had her clothes, half David's I guessed. I put mine on the floor of the closet.

I thought about her having sex with him. I didn't like the idea, but I guessed it was her job, like Betty Grable in that movie, "Dance Hall Dolly," so it was OK.

I went downstairs, though I didn't have enough to tip all those uniformed men every time I went in and out of the building, that'd be crazy, but I smiled, with my mouth closed and nodded, so they knew I appreciated their effort and I'd tip them... once a week? I'd figure it out.

I rode around the neighborhood looking for "employee wanted" signs. There were a lot of them. Older guys had already started enlisting so I had my choice. Delivery boys. Stock boys. Shoe salesman (more ladies feet!). I kept riding, hoping to find an opening for a spy.

That's when I saw "Grossman's Detective Agency," had a sign in the window, "Detectives wanted, we will train." I just kept getting luckier.

I went inside and an old lady with bright red fingernails and lipstick was smoking and reading a magazine.

"Whaddya want, kid?" she said, in a Brooklyny way.

"I want to be a detective."

She laughed, smoke pouring out of her gaping mouth. She coughed and yelled, "Yitzhak, get your ass out here, you gotta see this!"

I didn't know what there was to see, other than me, and I was turned out quite professionally in a blue shirt and red tie and my nicest brown shoes.

This old guy came from the back, wearing a wrinkled suit and smelling like tobacco. He looked at me, shook his head and grunted, "What do you want, putz?"

I did not like his tone one little bit.

"I am here to learn how to be a detective, sir," I said, firmly.

"Interesting!" he said. She exhaled smoke like a dragon.

"Go home, schmuck, your mama is looking for you," she sighed, taking another long puff on her cigarette.

"I'm here to see Mr. Grossman, madam."

That got her attention. She shot him a look and he cocked his head.

"I'm a fast learner. Clean. Conscientious.. I'll do you proud!" I said, convincingly, I thought.

"You got chutzpah, and nobody would ever suspect you. You good on fire escapes?"

"Yes, sir, I can climb six stories without getting winded," I added, helpfully.

"Small frame, you could slip into a lotta places I couldn't. Come with me," he said, pointing to the back as the woman raised her hands and shook her head.

His office was dark and smoky. He sat behind a desk and pointed to a chair. "Sit," he said, and I did.

"Sherlock, Chan, or the Thin Man?" He asked.

I replied without thinking, "The important thing is the rhythm. Always have rhythm in your shaking. A Manhattan you shake to fox-trot time, a Bronx to two-step time, a dry martini you always shake to waltz time."

He nodded. "Thin Man, good man. You got manners. But you got any idea what we do here?"

"Catch murderers?"

"Adulterers."

I didn't know what those were. "Adult murderers?"

He laughed. "Naw, kid, men dicking around on their wives."

"It's just sex," I said.

"Trust me, I'd have one on the side if I could afford it and my lovely bride, Ruth, wasn't sitting out front, watching me like a hawk. She'd murder me. She'll kill me eventually, anyway. But that ain't the point. Ladies hire us to see if their husbands are being unfaithful so they can get divorced and a new husband."

I nodded as if I understood what he was talking about. I mean, I understood a little bit, from movies, like Cary Grant and Irene Dunne in *The Awful Truth* where they got divorced and then got back together at the end but we didn't see what we did, we just saw a cuckoo clock.

"So we follow the schmucks around and get photos and get paid. You got a camera?"

I shook my head, I did not have a camera. But I remembered seeing a Brownie at a pawn shop.

"Get yourself a camera and a roll of film and come back tomorrow and we'll start your lesson."

"Excuse me, sir, how much do you pay?"

"Wow, kid, pushy ain't ya? How much are you getting paid now?"

"A quarter a delivery at Shapiro's."

"I'll give you a quarter for a clear photo and 5 cents if it's fuzzy. I try to get at least five clear ones, but it might take you a couple of days to follow the guy."

"A couple of days for a quarter? No thanks," I stood up to leave.

"Good—you're not as dumb as you look."

"I'm not dumb... and I can get photos you can't," I said, thinking about fire escapes.

He flipped a coin between his fingers. "OK, cocky, let's see if you can deliver. $1 for a clear photo and 50 cents for a fuzzy one."

I could make five bucks for a day? Just for taking pictures?

"That sounds swell!" I said, I'll be back tomorrow with a camera! And I was.

15 ⇒ Double Exposure

8 am. At the Grossman Agency front door. Knocking. Nobody there. I waited around a half hour, then finally spotted the little clock face that said, "Be back at 10." OK. Rode to the Ansonia and ordered a big breakfast, waffles and eggs and bacon and a cup of coffee, because I was going to be a detective and they all drank coffee in the movies, or booze, and I didn't want to be a drunk like my old man.

Coffee tastes horrible! How did people drink this stuff? I put a bunch of sugar and cream in it and it tasted less horrible, but still. Why? Next time I'd order hot cocoa.

I checked my Mickey Mouse watch and his little big arm was at the 9 and his little arm was almost 10 so it was time to go.

I was back at Grossman's at 10 and still, nobody was there. I inspected my genuine brown leatherette Brownie Boy Scout camera. I'd never been a Boy Scout but it felt very official.

I read the "Simple Instructions for Use": "To take a photo in sunny weather, press the shutter bar." Yup, easy. Oh, wait, I just took a picture. "Always remember to advance the film before taking the next photograph or you will have what's called a double-exposure." OK, so turn the key till I see #2. Stop.

"Lever A keeps the shutter open for low-light indoor photos, hold and count 1, 2 3..." might need that. "Lever B controls the aperture from f/16 to f/8". Don't know what that means. Oh, "f/16 for sunny days f/8 for overcast."

Suddenly I was in a big shadow and looked up to see Mrs. Grossman, glowering.

"Oy. Don't sit on the curb like a bum, come inside." she said, unlocking the front door. She smelled like onions. I wondered why Mr. Grossman would have married this creature.

I re-read the camera instructions and heard the bell tinkle above the door. Mr. Grossman shuffled in, putting his hat and coat on the rack and squinting in the darkness. He finally noticed me.

"Oh, he's back."

"With a camera, no less," the Mrs. said.

"Come into my office, kid."

I did as I was told.

"Where'd you get that piece of dreck?"

"Morton's pawn on 112th. Cost 50 cents."

"You were robbed."

"It's a genuine Boy Scout model... sir" I defended it.

"Are you a Boy Scout?"

"No... sir."

"I rest my case. Ruth always said I should have gone to law school. She was right."

"I know how to use the camera, sir."

Grossman sunk into his chair, opened a drawer and pulled out a flask. He took a swig and handed it to me, "You drink?"

"No... sir."

I didn't know whether to look serious or smile so I looked serious which seemed more adult.

"OK, so here's the schmuck, Christopher Wood, 165 E. 89th street. Nice neighborhood. Wife thinks he's schtupping some chippie. If you get pictures, you get paid. If you don't, you don't. Oh, wait, I gave you the wrong address, that's the wife. The chippie is at 350 w. 112th street, 6th floor, he was there last week at noon. I followed them but couldn't get up the fire escape. You can. Be quiet and take pictures with them in flagrante delicto."

I didn't know what that meant but it sounded like an Italian dessert.

"You know what that means, kid?"

"Um..."

"Screwing, when they're screwing. You know what that is, right?"

I certainly did, though I just nodded.

"Good, you're gonna need to photograph a lot of it. Bring your film back here, I'll show you how to develop it in the back. If you take it to a photo store they'll arrest you for pornography and I'll pretend I don't know you. If you get caught, I don't know you. If you get killed, I never met you."

I looked at Mickey. Almost 11.

"I'm on it, sir!" I said saluting."

"Oy vey is schmear. We don't say 'Good luck,' we say 'come back with both balls.'"

"I will, sir!" I said, turning briskly and leaving, only to run into Mrs. Grossman's wrinkled outstretched arm.

"I never met you either," she coughed.

16 ➻ Triple Exposure

Outside the sun was blinding. I put the camera in the basket on my bike, tied the handle down with a Shapiro ribbon and headed uptown.

I felt like I was in a movie, complete with background music courtesy of radios in the brownstones I passed. I avoided the avenues and took the crosstown streets, in case I was being followed. I was already good at this.

I found the address. Found the fire escape. Pulled it down quietly. Climbed up to the top, looking in windows along the way, just in case there was any screwing. But I didn't want to waste film, because each clear shot was worth a dollar and I had 15 more on the roll. Wait, there was a pretty girl in the shower... maybe just one shot... *Click*.

At the top landing I hid next to the brick wall and waited for someone to come into the room. I almost fell asleep, then heard laughing. An oriental woman came in, holding the hand of a white man! Wait, was this white slavery? I'd seen something like it in the Charlie Chan feature, "Charlie Chan and the Deadly Laundry," where poor American girls were drugged and dumped into laundry baskets and smuggled to Shanghai where they were made to sit on the laps of old Oriental men. Insidious!

She wasn't American, but he was so I thought I might need to save him, but then he unbuttoned her dress and slid it off and he looked happy to be there. She was skinny, not a figure, like Kitty, and from the back she didn't look Oriental. Interesting!

I moved slowly and held the camera at the edge of the window. Since it was dark inside, I pulled lever A then clicked the shutter counting "1, 2, 3" Oh—the shutter was surprisingly loud. I leaned back away from the window and the fire escape creaked. They were making their own noise and didn't seem to notice.

Pretty soon they were all at it and I learned in, pressed the camera to the window and took some more shots. It was only then I realized I'd forgotten to advance the film... so I did and started over. *Click*. Film. *Click*. Film. The film was used up and the winding key just turned and turned and I looked up to see...

The man turning to the window. "You little shit, I'm gonna kill you!" he screamed. I turned my head so he couldn't see my face, then clambered down the fire escape. He followed, naked, "Stop, kid, I'll pay you double," he yelled, reaching his long arms out to me.

The last two floors I just grabbed the railing and slid, jumping to the ground, the camera falling out of my hands and breaking open. "Oh shit!" I grabbed it, hopped on my bike and rode south as fast as I could, sweating and panting.

Then I stopped. He'd pay me double? Maybe I'd... no, I wanted to do this job right. I rode back to Grossman's. It was noon. The door was locked. The sign said, "Back at one!"

I was hungry, and hot, so I went to the park by the lake and got a hot dog. Sitting there, where I'd sat with Kitty, I thought about her, with David. She wouldn't need him much longer. I'd make enough money for both of us.

I looked at the camera and thought about all the pictures I'd take of Kitty... and our kids, playing in the park, boating on the lake, living among the swells.

I was snapped back to reality when a bird crapped on my head. I wet my napkin in a drinking fountain and cleaned myself off. I wasn't going to let the world shit on me.

I rode back to Grossman's and went in.

"Yitz, the kid's back," Mrs. Grossman yelled, turning the pages of a movie magazine with Dolores Del Rio on the cover—she had shiny black hair, like my Kitty.

"I'm taking a dump, he can wait!" was the reply.

"Dolores Del Rio is a great beauty," I started a conversation with Mrs. Grossman.

"I was a great beauty. Once. My Yitz was better looking than you, kid. See what the years have done. My advice, 'die young.'"

"Um... thanks?" I replied, trying to be a gracious recipient of her clearly hard-worn wisdom.

"OK, I'm done. Bathroom's back into a darkroom. Come 'ere." Grossman yelled from the back.

I went into his office. He sat. I sat.

"So? Got both balls?"

"I got the goods... sir."

"You're a fast worker, I'll say that, but are they any good?"

"I think so, sir."

"I'll be the judge of that, here, gimme," he said, reaching for the camera. "Did you use the whole roll? You should always use the whole roll. You don't want two schmucks on the same film, I did that and confused the hell out of a lady in Westchester. "Who is this naked man!" she screamed, like she'd never seen one before. "Sorry, wrong schlong," he laughed.

"I took 'em all, but then he chased me and I dropped it."

"All part of the job, boy. As long as you rolled up the film at the end it's OK. Come into my darkroom. It's OK, I lit a match."

I followed him into the cramped toilet. It smelled like a sewer mixed with ammonia and something that made my eyes burn."

"Darkroom Rule #1, always knock, like you should do for any shitter. If someone opens the door while you're developing a film it's ruined and you're out the cost of Kodak."

"Got it," I said, eager to see the magic.

"Turn off the light and turn on this little red light. Now, you roll the film onto this spool. Put it into this metal can. Pour in the developer. Shake. Gently."

"Like a good martini," I added.

"Oy. Check your watch. Give it a good five minutes. Better a little longer than shorter, otherwise the pictures are too dark."

We stood there in silence for five minutes, while I watched Mickey's glowing hands move slower than I thought was possible.

"OK, pour out this shit, run water in the sink so the pipes don't get eaten up and we have to call an WOP plumber who'll gyp us." Rinse with water. Shake... like a Martini... then you pour in the fixer. Another five minutes."

After about a minute, I needed to talk, "So, your wife was a great beauty?"

Even in the dim red light I could see Grossman's face change. "That she was. We were so in love. Fucked like bunnies. Happiest time of my life. All downhill from there."

"Um... that's nice," was all I could think to say.

"Oy, time goes by quick," he said.

"Three minutes," I replied, time crawling.

"Forty years. She's a good woman even if she's become her mother. Still a rabbit in the sack."

More than I needed to know, but encouraging nonetheless.

"Time!" I said.

"Empty the fixer, back into the bottle, you can reuse it. Rinse again. Now, we'll unroll and see if you got anything at all, which I sincerely doubt."

He unrolled the wet film and it dripped on my arm.

"Well, fuck me. You got some pictures here, kid! Sharp! What a whang, hung like a racehorse. Mind you, size doesn't matter, Ruth and I got three kids."

I looked at the film. It was hard to figure out because everything was backwards, what was light was dark and what was dark was light but it started to make sense.

"Yeah, that's the guy," I announced, proudly.

"Who else would it be, kid? Gotta hand it to you, nice and sharp... good, you got his face, I forgot to mention that's important... wait..."

"What?" I asked, excitedly.

"Who the fuck is this?"

"I forgot his name. You told me."

"This ain't Wood, he's got a stache."

"I dunno, maybe he shaved"

Grossman threw open the bathroom door and rushed to his desk, rifled through some papers and pulled out a picture. "Here, this is Wood. Blonde. Your guy's some Goomba with black hair... and an X-scar on his ass..."

Grossman froze, then whispered, "Oy."

"I'm sorry, sir..."

"What floor were you on?"

"The top, like you said."

"I said sixth."

"I thought that was the top."

"If you tell me that lady was an Oriental I'm gonna shit myself, then kill you."

"Um... well..."

"Was she?"

"Yeah. But she didn't look Oriental from the back!"

Grossman sank into his chair and put his hands over his eyes. "I'm not gonna have to kill you, he's gonna kill us all."

"I'm sorry, what'd I do?"

He was practically crying, "Oy Gevalt! Oy Vey iz Mir! That's Marco DiMorte. We're all dead!"

Grossman dropped the film like a hot potato, then pulled scissors out of his drawer and cut it up into little pieces. I jumped up to stop him.

"Those are my pictures!" I cried.

"They're your death warrant, kid. You said he saw you?"

"From a distance... He chased me. But he was naked and I rode fast... It's OK, he said he'd pay double."

Grossman laughed, then coughed. "He'd have snapped your neck and left you dead in the street. Wouldn't be the first time. Or the 10th. Nobody's supposed to have pictures of him, not even the fucking FBI."

"I'm sorry, I didn't know!"

"All dead," he sighed. He jumped up and went out front, and I followed. "Ruth, my nightmare, your dream, call the movers, we're going to Miami."

She turned her head slowly towards me. "Schmuck. If we survive this I'll send you a postcard."

"Get out kid, we're closed. Forever," Grossman panted.

Mrs. Grossman slyly smiled, slipped me a $20 bill and whispered, "Take this and never ever come back here again. Don't even ride down this street, you hear me? In fact, ditch your bike, buy another one."

I'd never even seen a $20 bill before!

"Yes, ma'am. Sorry, sir."

Mrs. Grossman held her husband's hand, sweetly. "Or, you can die young, maybe not a bad idea, but then you'd miss out on a sweet life... in Miami beach!"

"GO!" Grossman yelled, in anger or happiness, I wasn't sure which, I just ran. I grabbed my bike, wheeled it down to the corner and left it there.

As I walked back towards the Ansonia I spotted a shiny red bike in a window. An almost like-new ruby red Schwinn Rocket Auto Cycle De Luxe. It cost $10 and made me feel like Flash Gordon.

And I still had $10. This wasn't such a good first day!

17 ➻ Kitty First

I slipped Max, the outside doorman, a shiny new 50 cent piece as I handed him my new bike.

"Flashy," he said, "I'll keep it safe," he said, giving me a wink.

Sam, the inside doorman, got a quarter, and so did Ellis, at the elevator.

It was only when I got back to Kitty's that I remembered she wasn't there. But I could still smell her. I took a shower and put my clothes in a bag and dropped them in the front door closet to be washed. This was the life!

I took a nap and had a terrible dream...

...I was reading the New York Post and on the cover was a grizzly photo of a boy, strangled with a red ribbon. Bright red in the otherwise black and white paper. The ribbon said *Shapiro's* in gold letters. I dropped the paper, looked up, and through the round bedroom window saw DiMorte screaming, "You little shit, I'm gonna kill you!"...

...My scream woke me up. It was dark outside. I heard the front door rattling. I froze. Terrified. Couldn't move until I slid off the edge of the bed and hid under it.

Footsteps coming closer. I almost screamed again, but I heard Kitty, talking really loud, "Yeah, sure, don't I always forgive you? Now I really gotta pee," and then close the door behind her. I ran into the bathroom, just in case I needed to hide.

I heard her walk slowly into the bedroom. "Babycakes, you here? It's OK, I'm by myself."

I slunk out of the bathroom and saw her looking small as she sat on the edge of the bed.

"I'm beat," she said. I moved towards her and she put her arm out, "Not too close, baby, I must stink."

She was wearing a scarf around her head covering the right half of her face, and even that way she looked pretty in the moonlight. "I'm sorry, let me give you a kiss," she said, reaching out for me and giving me a sweet peck on the cheek. "Be a good boy and order me an ice tea with plenty of ice and extra teabags, OK?"

I picked up the phone, "In the other room, sweetie." I went in the other room and ordered, then I heard the shower running.

The little bell by the front door rang and there was a tray with tea, tea bags and a bowl full of cracked ice. I put them on the sofa table and turned on the radio, then switched it off. I didn't want to hear any news about any possible dead boys. I turned it back on to WOR to listen to a band playing.

"Bring the tea in here, will ya?" Kitty called from the bedroom. She was in bed, with the covers pulled part way over her face. She reached out her hand for the tea, then held the glass against her face. "I got something to tell 'ya." She slid the sheet down her face to show a big shiner.

"I was clumsy's all, I fell," she said, dunking a tea bag in the drink and holding it against her eye. "Don't worry, I'm OK."

I leaned in and kissed her bruise, gently. "I'll take care of you," I whispered.

"I know, that's why I wanted to come home early." She took a big swig of tea and put another teabag on her eye. "You'd never hurt me."

"Never... wait, did David hurt you?"

"He didn't mean to, it was an accident."

"He *accidentally* hit you?"

"Don't get jealous. He was jealous."

"Of me?"

"He doesn't know about you, baby, and hopefully he never will. He said he smelled another man on me and I told him he was crazy."

"It was my fault! I'm so sorry, Kitty!"

"Don't go gettin' jealous, and do anything stupid. Please, baby, please."

"OK, but I'm still sorry."

"Me, too, baby. Me, too."

"I got a job today."

"That's nice," she said, sleepily.

"And I got $20 and a new bike."

"We both had big days, didn't we? Night night, little love."

Her eyes closed and I rearranged the teabags on her face then lay in bed beside her. If that goomba guy was going to kill me, at least I could save Kitty first.

18 »+ Pinnacle Depths

I lay awake all night, looking at her. Or maybe I just dreamed I did because the phone rang and my eyes opened. I knew better than to answer it. Kitty reached across me and picked it up, then sat bolt upright.

"Thanks for letting me know, Sam, you're a doll!" She hung up. "You gotta get out right now, baby, David's on his way up."

I'd fallen asleep in my clothes, so I only had to jump out of bed and put on my shoes.

There was a knock on the door, then the sound of a key. Kitty frantically pointed to the little round window, then ran over and unlatched it. It twisted open from the center, leaving a small gap on either side. My camera was on the ledge so I took it with me as I squeezed my way through, then grabbed onto the green copper parapet that ran across the width of the roof. Kitty blew me a kiss, then waved me away.

The view from the roof was wondrous, like I was in the Wizard of Oz's balloon with the city spread out before me! The roof itself was an ornate sea of green copper with fancy metal railings all around. I climbed up a thin ladder leading up to the very top... or what I thought was the top, because there was still more! Two tall spires, one of this very corner, the other across the wide, deep crevasse between the two parts of the building.

I took the spiral stairs to the very top of the spire and reached the pinnacle. This is where I wanted to be—at the top.

I felt a little dizzy from the height and excitement and the fact that all my dreams were coming true.

Then I remembered Kitty. Downstairs. Alone. With David. I knew it wasn't enough to stand at the top, I had to stand for what I believed, I had to stand up for the woman I loved.

I snapped some quick photos from here, so I could remember this feeling, then I went down the spiral stairs, down the thin metal ladder to the narrow ledge outside Kitty's round window.

I kept hold of the ladder with one hand and peered in carefully so as not to be seen, knowing if I was I'd not only risk my own life, but Kitty's as well.

She sat on the side of the bed with her head in her hands. He handed her a little box, then took out a necklace and put it around her neck. I couldn't hear them, but she looked OK—for now.

I don't know what possessed me but I took a picture of them—even before the image set in the film, it had seared itself into my head. She would never be mine as long as he was around. She would never be safe. He was like some evil king or even a wizard who had her under his spell... and I was going to break it.

But, like all true knights, I would do it not through mere strength, which I didn't think I had, but through purity of heart, which I was pretty sure I had, and cunning, which I knew I had.

I thought of "Sword of Hades," with Errol Flynn and Olivia de Havilland where poor Errol had to endure the terrible trial of following Olivia to hell! There, despite it being really hot, especially in his armor, he screwed up all his courage to sing so sweetly that the Devil let them both escape, only realizing he'd been duped once they were gone and the singing stopped.

I couldn't sing. At least I'd never tried, and it didn't seem like the time. For now, my trial would be to watch and wait.

I thought waiting would be the hard part, but no, it was the watching. Kitty had said, "It's just sex," but what I saw them do together looked just like what we did together. Kissing, undressing, screwing... He was taking my place. She was letting him.

My heart broke.

19 ➤ Click

I'd never had a broken heart before. But it had been so full one minute, and so empty the next. I couldn't bear to watch and couldn't take my eyes away. Or my camera. *Click. Click. Click.*

I made sure to get a photo of his face. Kitty saw me through the window and blew me a kiss—*Click*—Then made a "get outta here!" gesture.

I reached the end of the film, rolled it up, and scurried back up the narrow metal ladder to the roof, then to the spire, then down the spiral stairs, down the fire escape, down the elevator to the lobby, where I waited.

"You OK, Herb?" Sam asked, seeing me winded.

"Because of you, I am, thanks, pal," I said, getting out a quarter to tip him.

"Naw, it's my pleasure. I see how you look at her. I get it," he said, patting my shoulder. I'd never really looked at Sam before. I'd seen him, but as a fancy coat, not as a person. I'd never thought that he was looking at me, either.

He was a lot older than I was and looked tired, but kind. He patted me on the back, which set me off crying. He sat down next to me and put his arm around me, until some lady was at the door and he had to jump up and open it, then he sat back down next to me.

"First love?" he asked me. How did he know?

"Uh huh," I sniffed.

"My first one was a chorus girl, too. Almost as pretty. Heloise. Sweet. Married a Wall Street guy," he said, handing me his handkerchief. I wiped my eyes.

"Sorry."

"It's OK. That's what she wanted. Then I found my wife, Sally, and *I* was what she wanted. It's better that way."

"I feel stupid," I said, noticing he was wearing thick glasses. I'd never noticed he wore glasses.

"Comes with the territory, kid," he said, jumping up again to open the door for a mother and daughter taking a pile of packages from Max, which he handed to Ellis in the elevator.

He sat back down with me again, "Not dumb. Foolish. Like all us men."

Now Ellis sat on the other side of me, "Girl trouble?"

"Ain't it always?" Sam said.

"You know what they say about herding cats," Ellis continued. I didn't know what they said. "Can't be done, and your Kitty's a pretty wild one."

I didn't believe him. But it was nice to know these guys were looking out for me when I didn't even know they were looking.

The elevator bell rang and Ellis sprang up. A buzzer at Sam's desk went off. "He's on his way down, kid."

"Who?" I asked.

"David. Ya don't want him to see ya."

He was right. I gave him a quick salute that shot out the front door, got my bike in the courtyard and wheeled it around into the alley. I saw David ask Max to call him a cab, but didn't give him a tip. Cheapskate bastard.

I got on my Schwinn Rocket and followed David's cab up Broadway, along the 79th Street traverse through Central Park. It stopped at a five story white stone townhouse at 83rd near Madison. Once again I didn't see him tip the driver.

I stood across the street, watching as he swaggered into the shiny black front door and slammed it.

Now, how could I get this film developed?

I drove back through the park, down the street past where Grossman's. I know Mrs. Grossman told me never to come back but I couldn't take these shots to a photo store. I stopped at the place where Grossman's was and everything outside was gone. No awning. No sign. Yet inside, it was like nothing had changed.

I went down the alley and the bathroom/darkroom window was still open, so I pulled it down and squeezed in. The chemicals were still there. I turned out the lights, developed the film, felt like I was gonna puke—and did.

20 ➺ The Other Cheek

I rode back to the Ansonia, gave Max a quarter and a smile. I really looked at him this time. He had red hair and pudgy hands. I gave Sam a quarter and he tried to give it back but I saw the smile behind his thick glasses.

"Hey, Sam, I need to get some photos printed. Some sensitive photos. Know anybody who can handle it without getting in trouble?"

"I thought you was a smart one, Herb. Sure, my buddy, Glenn, at Fine's Fotos, Columbus and 66th. Tell him Sam sent you."

I gave him a big wink and handed Ellis a quarter. Ellis had a lazy eye.

Kitty was flitting around her satin robe, arranging pink flowers. "I missed you, baby!" she said, throwing her arms around me. I looked down at her neck and saw she wasn't wearing the necklace. Good.

"You OK?" I asked.

"Yeah, sure, of course. He was sorry. Always is. I'm sorry you had to dash like that. What'd you do?"

"Went to the top of the roof and took some pictures. Rode my bike." All true, if not all the truth.

"I'm kinda tired, I wanna stay in today," she sighed, sweetly. I'd forgotten how sweet she was.

"Sure, baby. Whatever you want. I got a couple of errands I gotta run."

"For your new job?" she asked, yawning.

"Yup. Can I get you anything before I go?"

"A kiss?"

I took her hand and led her to bed, tucked her in, and gave her a little kiss. It wasn't just the bruise, but her face didn't feel quite the same.

21 ➻ Fine's Fotos

On my way through the living room, I spotted the necklace: a gold heart lying in a little blue box. I picked it up and put it in my pocket.

I rode up a few blocks to Fine's Fotos, a dusty store stuffed with cameras of all kinds. The young but somehow old looking guy behind the counter was short and stout, with curly black hair.

"I'm looking for Glenn," I said.

"Who's asking?" he said in a low voice.

"Sam sent me."

"Ah, hold on a sec," he said, waddling to the front door, rolling down the blind and flipping over the little clock sign to the side that said, "Back in 15 minutes."

"I'm Glenn Fine. What can I do you for?"

"I need some sensitive photos printed."

"Nudie magazine?"

"Detective stuff."

"You come to the right place. I do nudie photos, too, if you ever want to sell yours."

"Good to know, but not today."

He motioned me to the back. "I consider myself something of an artist with nudies," he grinned, opening a cabinet to display a wide selection of what I immediately thought to be quite artistic nude photos of girls almost as sexy as Kitty. Girls on rugs. Girls on beds. Girls with whips.

"The human body is art, ya know, like in a museum. Nothin' dirty." he said, quietly hiding a shot of a couple screwing since it did seem kinda dirty.

He held out his hand. I gave him the film. "Ya shoulda let me develop this, you coulda got yourself arrested," he warned.

"I know, I did it myself."

He stopped and looked at me, curious, impressed. "Where'd you learn that?"

"Grossman."

"Cheap old bastard. I heared he moved to Florida."

"Nobody's supposed to know," I whispered.

"I know everybody's business, yours included now, too. But your secret's safe with me. I'll be your go-to guy."

Then he did a weird thing with his hand, sticking out all five fingers, then making a fist, then pointing his index finger out, then up, then pointing to his nose, then a forehead salute, ending with pointing directly at my head.

"Do it," he whispered.

"Do what?"

"The secret handshake. So guys know you're in the know."

I tried to do it but didn't remember. He showed me again. I did it and this time our fingers touched.

"Welcome, fellow B.A.T.—to the Benevolent Association of Tits!" he said, officially.

He unrolled the film. "Nice shots. What'd you use?"

"A boy scout Brownie."

"Piece of shit. You need a Leica or a Rolli. How much do you got?"

"$10."

"Don't make me laugh, man. Come back with another $10 and I'll start you out with a Kodak 35 Anastigmat Special. F3.5 51mm gear-coupled RF—almost like new."

He closed the door and now there was just a red light.

He put the film in a metal holder and placed it into a tall machine with a light on the top that projected the picture onto the base.

"It's an enlarger, to make prints," he explained. "You sure you don't want to sell these? She's one hot tomato! I'll do the rest of the work for free in trade for one shot"

"Naw, can't, I work for her."

"Your loss. Maybe next time?"

The picture disappeared and he put a piece of blank paper where it was. He set a timer, turned on the enlarger light, waited till the timer buzzed, then turned off the light. He put the paper into a tray of clear liquid.

Then, like magic, Kitty... and David started to appear on the paper. I felt queasy but luckily didn't have anything left in my stomach. He took the photo out of the first tray and placed it in the second. "Stop bath. Stops it from overdeveloping." I heard him counting to 15, then he put it in the third tray, "Fixer makes image permanent," and counted to 30. He turned on the faucet in the sink, ran water over the picture, then used two clothespins to hang it up.

"So what's the story?" he asked.

I didn't want to tell him. "Just a dame with a guy she wants to get rid of."

"I know guys who know guys who could get rid of him for good," he offered, generously.

"Naw, don't need that."

"Blackmail?"

"*Persuasion.*"

"Classy," he said. The next shot was fuzzy. "Don't bother." The next, a clear shot of David making an ugly face. "Good one!" Then one that made Glenn grunt and whisper, "Yeah, sexy!" This was hard to watch.

And finally, one of David on his back, Kitty on her side, facing away from him towards the window, seeing me and blowing a kiss. I hadn't noticed one of her perfect breasts was exposed.

"Oh, this one is artistic man. I really want it. Sell it to me."

"Sorry, can't."

"I'll trade you the Kodak 35 for it."

"Naw, can't... betray a client."

By now the prints were hanging and he turned on the light and did the funny handshake again. I repeated it back to him. "You got morals, like me. I respect that. You are always welcome here, my friend."

He pulled a Snickers bar out of his pocket, bit off half and handed me the other half. I ate it. He held a hair dryer up to the prints, loudly hitting them with hot air and yelling over the noise, "OK, so you owe me two bucks to cover the prints and my silence. But remember, anytime you want to sell that last art shot, you promised it to me first."

I nodded as I chewed, even though I had no intention of ever selling that picture of Kitty. He slipped the photos into a manila envelope and closed it with the metal clasp. I gave him two dollars and a one dollar tip.

"I could tell you was a quality guy soon as you come in," he said, handing me a fresh roll of film, "For your next batch that I'll handle now that you know what I like. Gimme your card, case I need to get hold a you," he asked.

"I just have one from Grossman's."

"I'll print you some new ones," he said, "on the house since we're new besties. What's your name?"

"Herbert." I said, without thinking. I had to learn to be more discreet.

"Last name?"

I wasn't about to tell him, besides, Horowitz sounded too Jewish. I looked at his watch, it was a Hamilton. "Herbert Hamilton. Hamilton Agency, ANsonia 1616."

"Sw-wanky!" he said, sticking little metal letters into a small press, running an inky black roller over them and pressing them down onto a small card. He held it up, blew on it and handed it to me.

I was a real detective now.

Glenn printed up a dozen and put them in a little white bag with the words "Fine's Fotos" in green. "Use 'em in good health, or at least come back with both balls."

He walked me to the door, pulled up the blind and flipped over his sign. One more funny handshake and I was off. Nice guy.

22 ➤ Special Delivery

I went into the alley and pulled out the prints. They were even more awful in the light of the sun. I took out the last one, tore it in half to get David away from Kitty. I threw his picture down and ground him into the pavement with my foot. I folded up the part with Kitty and put it in my wallet.

I put the incriminating photos in my pocket and rode furiously back across the 79th Street traverse then up to 83rd and stopped at David's townhouse.

I took a deep breath and knocked on the shiny black door. A young woman answered, wearing a black and white maid's uniform.

"What can I help you with, young mister?" she asked with a strong Irish brogue.

It was only then that I realized I didn't know what I was going to say. I didn't have a plan. I gulped. "Um, sorry... this is my first day..."

"It's OK, lad. We all gots to start somewhere. You sure you're in the right place?" she asked, kindly. She had a round face with pink cheeks and was pretty in her own way.

"I have a delivery... for Mrs. David Cooper." I said.

"Next time, come round the back to the tradesman's entrance. But hand it over and I'll give it to her," she said, reaching out her hand.

"My employer... new employer... requires me to deliver it personally."

"Are you sure? That's not the way it's done." she replied, eyeing me.

I took the blue box out of my pocket. "It's a necklace... from David," I said.

"Ah, Tiffany's!" she exclaimed, I didn't know why. Who was Tiffany? The box didn't have a name on it.

"She'll be delighted!" she exclaimed. "Wait here, lad."

She closed the door and I stood there, sweating. She opened the door again, and a very classy lady appeared wearing a blue velvet dress. She was maybe as old as my ma, but looked so soft.

"I hear you have something for me, young man?" she asked, with an accent that sounded almost foreign, like Katherine Hepburn.

I held out the box. "From Mr. David," I just barely managed to say.

She gingerly took the box from my hand and opened it. She looked confused, then delighted. "I was sure I'd lost this!"

The maid chimed in, "We all looked everywhere, ma'am!"

"David must have had a duplicate made. How very sweet!" Then she opened the two halves of the heart and looked inside. "Yours, David!" she exclaimed.

Now I was confused. I didn't think she'd be happy about this.

"David! Oh, David! It's so sweet!" she cried out into the house. "This was the first gift he ever gave me... to have another one made touches my heart so!"

The maid helped her put it on and I could hardly see it behind her strands of pearls. She turned and threw her arms around him. "You lovely man! I'm getting all teary eyed," she said, holding him tight.

He glared at me over her shoulder. "I'm so glad you like it, my love. Please excuse us, I want to have a private word with the... delivery boy... to thank him."

The lady gave me a girlish wave as she went back into the house, followed by the maid.

David stepped outside, very tall. He closed the door behind him with one hand and grabbed my lapel in the other, practically pulling me off my feet.

"I don't know what your game is, but I'm gonna beat the shit out of you," he whispered so close I smelled his hot alcohol breath, like my Pa.

"If you hurt me your wife gets photos of you and Kitty," I choked out.

His grip loosened and for a moment he looked scared. I thought I had him, but he pulled me closer and hissed, "Don't threaten me, kid, nobody can find out about me and that little freak." His hands were around my neck now, my feet clean off the ground.

I used my last bit of breath to say, "Marco DiMorte," and saw his face change. In that second I knew I had a chance—I kicked wildly until I landed one right in his balls. He fell over, taking me with him.

I jumped to my feet, grabbed the photo envelope out of my pocket and threw it at him. "She's not a freak, she's perfect," I spat at him. "Leave her alone, but keep paying for her place."

He grabbed the envelope, looked inside, frowned and shoved it into his pocket.

Just then, the front door opened and the maid looked shocked. "Oh, my heavens, what's happened here?" She gasped.

"I dunno, he musta had an attack of something!"

"Good thing you were here, lad. Help me get him inside."

He angrily shooed me away and crawled back in, squinting at me as tears ran down his cheeks.

The maid reached into her apron and pulled out a silver dollar. "I'm afraid to think what mighta happened if you weren't here, lad." She reached back into her apron and pulled out two more silver dollars. "You're a wee angel, you are!" she said, smiling, as she closed the door.

I felt something liquid running down my pants. Hopefully sweat. I pocketed the coins, got on my bike, and rode away.

I stopped, right in the middle of the park, panting. I got off the bike and lay down on the grass, my heart still pounding.

I did it! I beat my rival. I didn't know if I could, but I did! I looked down at my hands and they looked stronger. My legs, longer. My knees, now a deadly weapon, like Douglas Fairbanks in "The Black Pirate" when he saves Billie Dove from kidnappers and she reveals herself to be a real princess!

23 ⇛ Caterwauling

"You did what?" Kitty howled.

"I protected your honor," I said, pulling off my pants, soaked to the skin. It was sweat.

"You've ruined everything!" she sobbed.

"I've fixed everything!" I insisted.

"He'll come back."

"Max and Sam won't let him in. Sam's changing the locks."

"He'll kill me."

"I won't let him!"

"Why, because little Herbie told him not to?" she looked at me, her eyes angry and sad at the same time. "He's not going to listen to you."

"He'll listen to Marco DiMorte."

She stepped away from me.

"Oh, no. No! And I thought you were a sweet kid..."

"I am. I am sweet!" I screamed.

"Not if you're mixed up with DiMorte. Oh, I'm such a dope. A soon-to-be-dead dope!" she started sobbing again, her hands over her ears. "I'm gonna have to leave town!" she gasped.

There was no getting through to her, other than to hand her tissues which she filled with snotty tears and threw on the floor.

Finally, when she seemed too exhausted to cry, I put my arm around her. She pulled away. I pulled her closer.

"I took care of you. He's not gonna hit you again. I made sure of it."

"You little idiot," she sighed. "Sweet, stupid idiot."

"I'm not stupid. He knows I got photos of him with you. And I met his wife."

Kitty pulled away from me. "You met that bitch, Clara?"

"She was very nice," I said.

"Don't tell me that. Why'd ya have to say that?" she started crying again. "It's easier when I can think of her as a witch."

"He didn't deserve you."

"He liked my kind and he could afford me."

"I love you," I said, taking her red, puffy face in my hands.

"Oh, baby. That, and a nickel, will get you a cup of coffee."

I didn't understand it. Why wasn't she happy?

24 ⇛ Front Page

She went to bed, closing the double doors behind her. I lay on the sofa and looked up through the window in the ceiling and fell asleep...

...I dreamt I was holding another newspaper. This one had a photo of me on the front page, standing at the top of the spire on top of the building on top of the city. I was looking up, pointing to something in the distance.

Then the sun fell out of the sky.

It landed in the Hudson River, with a small puff of steam and suddenly it was a black, starless night...

...Just as it was when I opened my eyes again and looked through the ceiling window.

25 ⇛ Shortcake

The next time I opened my eyes the sun was in them. Yesterday felt like a dream. The last week or... how long had it been? It all felt like a dream. Yet I was still here, knowing Kitty was just behind those doors which I quietly opened. I watched her sleep. As beautiful as she always was, she was most beautiful asleep. Like an angel. When she was awake, I started to notice something just under her forehead, behind her green eyes. Something nervously unfamiliar. Something she was hiding.

I felt lucky to be there, in her world, but I wasn't just a visitor anymore. I was part of it. I was her protector. I wanted to touch her face so she could feel me take away the worry behind her eyes. But I didn't want to wake her.

I took a shower and called for breakfast. Strawberry shortcake with whipped cream. When it arrived I carried it into the bedroom, set it down on the sill, then kissed her lightly—on her still angelic forehead.

"Good morning, my love," I whispered and her eyes shot open. She looked confused, the fear behind her forehead instantly apparent.

"You're still here?" she said.

"I'll always be here." I replied.

She smiled, sadly. I brought the strawberry shortcake tray to the bed.

"Sweets for my sweet," I said, another line I cribbed from at least one movie.

For a moment the worried look went away as she dipped her finger in the cream. "I'm sorry I was mean yesterday. I'll be your good girl," she said, in an odd way, licking it off.

"I'm sorry I upset you." I said, sticking my own finger in the cream. She reached for my hand and put my finger in her mouth.

"I guess I'm yours now," she said, kissing my fingertip.

"And I'm yours," I laughed because it tickled.

Then I saw her eyes dart around, as if she'd just realized something. "I haven't heard that one before," she said, mysteriously.

"What one?"

"That you're mine. It's never worked that way."

"That's how love works."

"Love. Right!" she said, blooming into a smile, then batting her eyes like a vamp.

She didn't make any sense to me.

"So what're your plans for me?"

"For us."

"Us!" she giggled but I still couldn't tell if she was happy. "Am I allowed to tell you what I want?"

"Always. Please."

"I want to dance again. How do you like that?"

"I love to dance with you," I said, feeling better.

"Dance on stage, again. I miss it."

"Then you shall dance on stage, m'lady."

"Really? You're OK with that?"

"I've got a job and you can have a job if you want."

"I want to earn my own keep again. Speaking of which, what exactly is your job... with DiMorte?" she asked, the worry creeping behind her brow again.

"I don't even know him... just saw him once. But I figured everybody's scared of him, so I used him to scare... you know."

"You can say his name."

"I used him to scare David." Her eyes searched around the room again, then a smile crossed her face.

"I don't know how this is gonna work out, baby, but I admire your moxy."

"I did it for you. I'll do anything for you."

"I don't know if I'll ever get used to that," she said, leaning in to kiss me, sweetly, on the lips. She tasted like strawberries and cream. My girl.

26 ⟫⁺ Workday

Her bruise was almost all healed up, and what little was left I watched her cover up with makeup until she looked perfect again, "fixing myself up," as she called it.

"I'm going down to the club and see what I can do to convince Frank to give me my old job back," she announced. "What're you doing today, love?"

I liked when she called me "love" because it meant she could see what I felt.

I didn't know what I was going to do now that I was a detective with my own business cards. "I gotta get some clients, I guess. I'm not sure where to go to meet rich ladies."

"Oh, so you're going to replace me already?" she teased.

"Never. As clients. That's what Grossman told me, rich ladies want to know who their husbands are screwing."

"Oh, I know who they're screwing all right." she said, darkening her eyelashes with a little fuzzy brush.

"You do?"

"Yeah, all my friends. I'll introduce you at the club." She was full of surprises.

"So I can save them the way I saved you?"

She put down the little brush, held my face in her hands and pressed her lipstick red lips on mine.

27 ➺ Photographic Arts

I followed her out of the apartment. She turned left towards downtown and I turned right and rode up to Fine's Fotos. The shade was down and the "be right back" sign up, but when Glenn saw me through the window he opened up and introduced me to an older man in an old-fashioned suit.

"Roger, this is Herb Hamilton, that photographer I was telling you about."

I shook his hand, very soft for a man.

"Pleased to meet you, very impressive work," he said, sounding like James Mason as he looked me right in the eye.

"Thanks?" I said, almost like a question because —what work?

"Roger's a fellow BAT. Yeah, I showed him your stuff from yesterday. That last shot's killer."

They both gave me a thumbs-up.

"I'll give you $25 for it," Roger said.

"Don't take a penny under $50," Glenn suggested.

"I told you it's not for sale... how'd you even see it?"

"You left the negatives here, Herb, but I've got 'em in safe keeping."

I felt really stupid. "I'm gonna need those back," I said, firmly.

"You sure?" Glenn asked, heading to the back of the store.

"I see great potential in you, young man," Roger said, reminding me of the Rabbi, only clearly goyish with his neat goatee and pointy mustache. "Photographic Arts are the future, my boy." He handed me his card which read, "Roger Reed: Photographic Arts Magazine for Men." It had a small photo of a woman's profile made out of little black dots I could feel when I ran my finger over them.

"Thanks, sir."

"Where do you find your subjects?" he asked. His accent wasn't from here, it was royal-like.

"She's a dancer," I said, not knowing what else to say.

"Ah, like Degas!" he said, excitedly. I had no idea what he meant. "What a wonderful approach. Much more artistic than the normal harlots." I still didn't know what he was talking about.

Glenn came out with the negatives. They were cut into little squares inside a whitish envelope. "Here, Herb. If you're sure you want them. You gotta keep em in a cool dark place, and I've got a fire-safe vault here for protection."

"You really should have them in a vault, my boy, you don't want anything to happen to your masterpiece," Roger added, taking the envelope and holding it up to the light. "That would be a terrible loss."

"You don't mind?" I asked Glenn.

"Happy to," he replied, pulling the negatives out of Roger's hand.

"Your boy tells me he's shooting dancers now," Roger said to Glenn.

"I tole you he was an artist," Glenn said, proudly.

"Call me first when you get more art, boys," Roger said, lighting up a cigar as he floated out.

"He's classy," Glenn said. "And he thinks you're good, so let me get you a better camera."

"I still only got ten bucks," I said, "and I'm taking my girl out tonight."

"How's about this," Glenn said, reaching up on the shelf for a black and yellow box. "Alls you gotta do is give me one photo a week I can use and you can use this sweet baby."

He opened the box to reveal a gorgeous thing, silver metal and black leather with knobs and gears and levers. It looked like the real life spy camera I saw in, "Darkness before the Dawn," where Frederick March plays a spy following Joan Bennett who's another spy and they fall in love and she finds out who he is and doesn't kill him so he doesn't turn her in and they move to Tangiers and change their names.

I loved the way the camera felt. Solid. Cool, smooth metal and "nice grippy leather," as Glenn called it. "Good for low-light, with the all-new KodaMatic silent shutter that won't wake a baby."

Glenn showed me how it worked, explaining what all the numbers meant. The shutter speed, the faster the better but you had to go slow indoors. The f/stop, the smaller the better inside. I loved turning the knobs and feeling them click into place.

I looked through the rangefinder and saw how it worked—I saw two images, then turned a knob until they came together into one. Neat!

"You'll need a light meter, too, at least at first, then you'll just kinda know," he said, opening a blue and orange box containing a brown leather case with a strap. He opened the case, revealing something from Buck Rogers: a curved brown Bakelite contraption with a big knob and a little window. The knob had four wheels of numbers around it. The window showed a thin needle which jumped back and forth across an arc. "You set this dial for the film speed, turn the dial for the f/stop, then follow the needle to the number on the dial."

I tried to take it all in.

"You break or lose 'em you'll owe me..." he said, "...a lot. I'll throw in film 'cause I want you to take a lotta shots for me to choose from," he said, putting the camera strap around my neck like I was getting an award. He slipped the light meter into my coat pocket. "Looks complicated, but you'll get the hang of it."

28 ⮕ Rangefinding

He patted me on the back as I left the shop in a daze. I couldn't wait to try the camera, so I stopped on the sidewalk. I held up the light meter like he showed me. It read: 1/250th at F16. I set the camera and looked through the rangefinder, turning the focus dial until the two images aligned.

I shot down Columbus Ave, taxis and trees and big puffy clouds. *Click.*

Back at the Ansonia, as Max took my bike I saw his white gloved hand reach for the shiny brass knob of the gate. "Hold it!" I said, leaning in to take a shot, then realizing I hadn't used the light meter.

"What're you doing?" he asked.

"Just foolin' around,"

"I don't need no photo of my hand, but my wife always says she'd like one of me in my uniform."

"Sure, Max!" I said. "Keep your hand there, and I'll stand back." Max smiled so big I could see his broken front tooth. *Click.* "Got it!"

Inside I showed Sam my gear and thanked him for introducing me to Glenn. "I thought you guys'd get along, both go-getters," he said.

"Lemme try an indoor shot," I said, holding out the light meter and turning the dial. f/3.5 at 1/25th of a second. "Hold up a key or something," I suggested. He held it up and looked at it as it swayed. *Click.*

"Oh, almost forgot, got a message for you from Kitty." he said, handing me a pink piece of paper that had been skewered on a metal rod. "She got the gig and needs to rehearse today. Meet her at the

Copa, 8pm, stage door. Tell Joey you're with her," he finished reading, then added, "Leave your suit by the door and I'll get it cleaned and pressed."

I reached for a quarter, "I want that photo instead!" he said, waving me on.

Ellis opened the elevator door, "Point left down the hall," I said. *Click.* "Very handsome!" He blushed all the way to the 16th floor.

29 ⟫⃗ Backside

I put my suit in the service door and called to have it cleaned and pressed. It came back with a white carnation in the lapel.

I played with the camera and took some shots of spoons on the kitchen table, some of Kitty's clothes, laid out on the bed, without her. I had the strangest feeling like they didn't belong to her, even though I'd seen her wearing them.

I finished the roll by taking some pictures of myself in the bathroom mirror. I'd never had a picture took of me, and I saw myself differently. I could see what other people saw.

Tall. Dark, light brown curly hair, unlike David's balding gray. Husky with a flat belly, unlike his ugly gut. Plus, I'd seen his pecker and it looked weird, like something was wrong with it. Mine was... well, Kitty liked it.

I used the two mirrors to see what my backside looked like, because I'd never seen it!

How had I gone through life never having seen half my body? OK, so maybe I would now, though the magic of the little self-timer lever on the lens. I finished the film and rolled it up, then put in a fresh roll.

I was excited about seeing Kitty dance tonight. I missed her already!

I took a shower and a nap and ordered a pastrami sandwich on rye and some fries. It just seemed natural now to pick up the phone, tell Sam what I wanted and have it appear as if by magic though the dumbwaiter, not even needing someone to carry it up.

I'd almost forgotten my life wasn't always like this: clean, modern, efficient, luxurious. I had a flash of where I grew up, sleeping on the sofa, using a damp dirty towel in the cold shower. That was old Herbie. I was the new, modern Herb...bert. Hamilton. This was me now and there was no going back. Ever.

30 ⮞ Mr. H.

Putting on my clean, pressed suit, with that carnation, felt like putting on a suit of armor. I dabbed a little of Kitty's lavender toilet water behind my ears.

I decided to take the subway to the club so I could escort my dancing lady back home after the show like a real gentleman would.

I put the extra film in my pocket and camera and light meter around my neck. Sam was already off and the night desk guy... I didn't know him. Tall. Skinny. Dark eyes, dark hair, slicked back. "Tony," I saw on his name tag and said, "Evening, Tony," and he said, "Evening, Mr. H."

I liked that.

I turned around and asked, "Mind if I take your picture?" He stood tall and smiled. The room was on the dark side so I fiddled with the meter, then needed to hold the shutter open for 2 seconds. "You look fine!" I said, saluting as I left.

Max's night man was Stan. He already had my bike, but I thanked him and said, "The subway," and gave him a quarter so he'd know I appreciated his effort.

The evening was chilly, but nice as I walked two blocks to the 2 train, south to Columbus Circle. Back up on the street, I walked along the south edge of the park on 59th. On one side were glowing apartment windows, on the other, dark sky and the lonely trees. I took a picture and thought about how they'd have leaves in a month or so and I'd take another one to see the change.

I passed the stately Sherry Netherland hotel and turned right on 60th. I went down the alley and found the stage door. There were some guys already milling around outside, older guys in tuxedos, waiting with flowers and boxes of candy. I felt special walking right by them and opening the stage door. I was hit with a wall of smoke, sweat and so many kinds of perfume at once it was like I'd fallen into a tropical flower house.

The old guy at the top of the stairs reached out his arm to stop me and I said, "I'm here with Kitty, she told me to talk to Joey."

"I'm Joey, and what're you, her brother?" he asked, moving his arm and letting me pass.

I slipped downstairs into a bustling world of waiters and wonders. Lots of girls, as tall as me, flitting about in tight shiny costumes, white with silver flowers and feathers in their hair. They were all gorgeous blondes—so close they brushed by me.

I followed a flock of them into a dressing room and watched as they stripped off their costumes like I wasn't even there, wiping themselves with matching pink towels and fanning off with silk fans like the oriental courtesans I saw in *"Charlie Chan: Dangerous Money"*

The room was filled with light and color, skin and sequins, feathers and lace. I stood there, staring, until somebody's hand covered my eyes and I jumped.

"This ain't the floor show, baby," Kitty said, turning me around and giving me a big smooch on the mouth so all the other girls could see. "Ladies, meet Herbert. Don't go getting no ideas, he's mine," she announced, which made me feel so proud.

She had a blond wig on, too, but still looked so different from the others who waved at me and then got back to their mirrors, changing into red wigs and black costumes with red feathers.

"Shoo, now" Kitty whispered, pushing me out of the door and closing it behind her.

The hallway was dim and drab, gray concrete walls and a lot of hissing pipes. I wandered towards the bustling kitchen, bright fluorescent lights and steam. The waiters scurried about, picking up plates and piling them on trays they held high then carried through swinging porthole doors, padded in white leather.

I tried to stay out of their way, pressing myself into a corner, taking out my light meter to get a reading, then setting my camera.

The camera was like a magic lantern, because when the cooks or waiters would see me point it at them, they'd stop, pose with a big smile, wait for me to take a shot, then hurry off.

Everybody wanted their picture took.

I heard a Latin band playing on the other side of the swinging doors and slid through them. I was in yet another world—all white— walls, ceiling, waiters, band... a grove of magical white satin palm trees held up the ceiling, with lights glowing inside of frosted glass coconuts.

It was like stepping into a movie. Even more so when I saw Peter Lorre sitting at a table. I was nearly scared to death, he always scared me, but now he was laughing with Mary Astor, almost like a normal person, as if they could possibly have been normal people.

Everywhere I looked there was somebody I recognized. There was Joan Blondell chatting with Una Merkel! They looked as beautiful as they did in the pictures and the whole place swirled in a mist of smoke and Latin rhythms.

It was only when I was almost knocked over by a waiter carrying a bucket of champagne that I pressed myself up against the shiny white wall, carved to look like monkeys. I checked my light meter again, focused the rangefinder and took it all in.

Click. I pressed the shutter and the image was locked into my brain. Light and white and smoke and bodies in black. Peter Lorre. *Click.* Ida Lupino. *Click.* Both stopped and smiled for me then went back to drinking. It was easy, just raise the camera, they'd stop and pose, and... *click.*

The coconut lights dimmed, the stage got brighter and the bandleader made his entrance in a silver tux with sequin lapels! The room got quiet. Two girls in the red and black costumes skipped out, arm in arm, stopping front and center.

They announced, "Ladies and gentlemen, may we have your attention please! Monte Prosser's World-Famous Copacabana is proud to present a bright new star to the New York firmament. Please welcome Senorita Carmen Miranda!"

The band leader lowered his hands and a drumbeat began. The lights went out and suddenly there was an explosion of color spinning onto the stage like a human tornado.

The spinning stopped right in time with the music, and there was this... creature. Ruffles of all colors, and, on the top of her head, an entire fruit salad shining in sequins.

The spotlight reflected off of her, filling the room with sparks of light. *Click.*

She started singing very fast, moving her arms and feet and undulating her hips in a way I found so hypnotic I could barely hold the camera still. *Click!* When she was done, the audience jumped to their feet, clapping and shouting and I wondered how long I'd been holding my breath. I joined the ovation which went on so long my hands hurt.

The señorita took a long, deep curtsy, waved and put her hand to her mouth, shyly. The audience settled down and she began to talk and I couldn't understand a word she said. It didn't matter.

A man with a guitar got down on one knee, and she sat on his other knee and sang something quiet about "Mi mamita," as the audience started to drink again, even to start talking. I wanted to shout, "Be quiet, she's singing!" but nobody seemed to care.

Then, after a short bow this time, four men with big drums ran out in a circle and lined up playing a jungle beat. That's when I saw Kitty, leading the line of girls in black and red dancing in, her limbs flying and her face aglow. *Click.*

Every click was a memory I'd never forget.

And I would never forget the way she danced. All the girls were pretty and leggy. But there was something different about Kitty, something bolder. She didn't try to fit in with the others, in fact, she did everything just a little bit bigger, stronger. Higher kicks, faster arms, bigger smile. Even with Miss Miranda in front of them, I still couldn't take my eyes off Kitty. *Click. Click. Click.*

31 ➡ Miss Miranda

I took countless pictures of Miss Miranda, the Copa Girls, and the glittering audience. I didn't even keep track, I just kept changing the film until I was on my last roll and thought I'd better be more careful.

Suddenly I felt this big hand on my shoulder, and a tough guy in a white tux turned me around, "Now I got 'ya! Come with me!" he demanded, smelling like spearmint and pulling me through the kitchen doors.

I thought the jig was up. "Benny said he sent a new guy and you shoulda reported to me," he said, dragging me by my heels across the slippery kitchen.

"We gotta have these shots for the morning papers," he said, pulling me into a dressing room where everything was bright red.

And there, on the red velvet sofa, was Miss Miranda, wearing a white lace robe.

"Olá bebê!" she cooed. "Você não é um pratinho... oh, pardon me, aren't you a little dish!" She crossed her legs and leaned back so I could take her, from feathers to feet and every little and not so little bit in between.

CLICK.

She lay on the sofa, leg swung seductively over the back. *Click.* She rolled onto her front, head on her hands, delicate feet pointing up. *Click.*

I held open the shutter while she moved, hoping to show the human blur she could be. Then I ran out of film.

"Done so soon? Such is youth!" she cried playfully, kissing me on the cheek, her hand on my back guiding me out even before I could figure out what happened.

The brute in the tux grabbed me again. "I need prints by 3am to make the morning papers," he demanded, pushing me up the stairs. "I'll be here, you betta be."

Before I knew it, I was out on the street, the cool air hitting me in the face like the night's cold kiss. I literally ran down 59th, hopped the subway then hightailed it over to Fine's, ringing the buzzer and pounding on the plate glass door.

I saw a light go on inside, and made out the round figure of Glenn in striped PJs shuffling to the door. "Whatcha doing, it's 2am for chrissakes!" he moaned, opening the door a crack.

"I gotta get prints back to the Copa in an hour for the morning papers!" I said, pushing my way in.

"You don't waste time, do ya?" Glen yawned, locking the door behind me.

"I shot all the film you gave me at the Copa and they have a new star and...." I rattled on while Glenn got the film ready.

"This better be good, Herb, I was having a really hot dream..." he said, while all six rolls were developing. He proceeded to tell me the dream, in too much detail, and the thought of Glenn and some Princess of Persia together made me momentarily forget what I was even doing there.

Then Glenn unrolled the film. "Holy shit, Herb." and I thought, "Oh, no, I set the camera wrong and they're all blank!"

"Look at those bazoombas!" Glenn said, happily. Roger's gonna eat these up!"

"We've only got a half hour to make prints!"

"Why'd you take a picture of your ass?" he asked.

I was embarrassed. "I'd never seen it."

He handed me the negative. "Not much to look at. But—boy—there are so many hot ones here, Herb! Geez, she looks like a real live Vargas girl!"

"Print the ones of Miss Miranda, then I'll come back and we'll…" and he already had the negative in the enlarger, with Miss Miranda looking larger than life. Her onstage, fuzzy with motion. Her on the sofa, looking like a pin-up girl.

"That's one hot tamale!" Glenn panted, print after print. This time, after developing, he put them, face down, on a big silver drum. The paper made one pass around, then he peeled them off, revealing a glossy finish.

"Always put your name and number on the back, but gently on the edge cause you don't wanna crease the print.," Glen instructed and I wrote, "Mr. H, ANsonia 1616," stuffed them in an envelope and rushed back downtown.

Joey let me right in and the club was still booming. I found the angry guy in the white tux pacing outside Miss Miranda's dressing room, checking his watch. He grabbed the photos out of my hand, rifled through them and nodded his approval. "Nice work, kid, I'll hand them out to the columnists."

My stomach rumbled and I nabbed some fries off a silver tray, then went looking for Kitty.

"Just finished the last set, baby, you're a doll to wait around for me!" she squealed. She wriggled out of her costume, toweled off, patted herself with a big powder puff, slid into a white dress and pulled me back through the kitchen.

"Now it's time for us to dance—together!"

"I don't know how to dance!" I strained over the music. But it didn't matter. All I had to do was stand there and sway while she Conga'd circles around me.

It was the first time I'd been still tonight—even as the world continued to spin around me.

32 ➺ Photo Credit

Kitty practically skipped home while I dragged behind her.

"Wasn't that the best? That's living, that's what it is. All those eyes on me..."

Back at the apartment she got in the shower, "Come on in, the water's fine!" I heard her giggle as I fell asleep on the bed in my suit.

The phone woke me up. I didn't answer it. Kitty's arm reached across me to get it. "Thanks, Sam," was all she said. She shook me awake. "Sam says you gotta lotta calls but knew we was out late and didn't want to bother us earlier."

I smelled like smoke and sweat and fries. I emptied my pockets then dropped my clothes in the service door and shuffled naked through the living room back to the shower. My feet hurt. My eyes were so dry I could hardly open them and my mouth tasted like soot.

The hot shower washed it all away. I came out feeling better, but still beat. I put on the first pants I saw and a white shirt, then answered the bell at the front door.

Sam was there, with a stack of pink message slips. I fished around for a quarter.

"You made some splash last night, 'Mr. H.'!" he said, handing them to me. I didn't know what to make of all this.

Then he reached to his side and grabbed a big stack of newspapers. "Times, Post, Mirror, Newsday, and the Herald." One by one he pulled them from the stack, riffled through and opened them to a page featuring either a big photo of Miss Miranda, splayed out on her sofa as she was just a few hours before, or a cool, fuzzy one, showing her in motion.

It took me a few seconds to look below the picture, to the small type that said, "Photo by Mr. H."

Sam patted me on the shoulder, "I'm proud a ya!" then flipped the quarter in the air as he sauntered back to the elevator. Sam turned around, "I wanna see that pic you took a me!" he laughed as Ellis gave me a thumb's up.

I pulled the papers inside and covered the floor with them. Kitty came in, "What's this mess" she said, then, "Oh, good press!"

"I... took... I... took..." was all I could manage to say.

Kitty picked up a paper and studied the picture. "She's a little old but these make her look good," she said, casually dropping the paper back on the floor.

"I... took... these... pictures!" I eked out.

She leaned down and looked at the paper again. "So you're 'Mr. H.' now? I can hardly keep up with you! Why'd you never take pictures of me like this?" she whined.

"'Cause I never took pictures like that!"

"Well, now I want one," she said, before picking up the phone to order eggs and sausage and pancakes with whipped butter and maple syrup, and something called a "prairie oyster."

I wolfed it all down, except the prairie oyster, which turned out to be a raw egg with Worcestershire sauce that Kitty downed in a gulp and announced, "Hangover be gone!"

I looked through the stack of pink message sheets. Sam's handwriting was very neat and one stood out: the word "LOOK!" circled three times.

Kitty pulled the message slips from my hands and looked at them, "Mokambo club... no... Latin Quarter... don't make me laugh, Cotton... hell no..."

I tried to grab 'em back but she wouldn't let me. "Just ignore those, baby, you work for the Copa now and there's no better club in the city, maybe the entire world."

"But..."

"No sense arguing with me. Frank knows you now—he wouldn't even let you work anywhere else at night," she handed me the one that said LOOK. "You can do what you want during the day, like I do."

"What're we doing today, Kitty?"

"A girl needs her beauty rest!" she trilled as she tiptoed back into the bedroom.

I looked in the bedroom and she was already beautifully asleep, so I got my camera and light meter and headed out. Sam caught me in the lobby and shook my hand, "Remember, I want to see that pic you took of me!"

"I remember, Sam, I'll get it from Glenn."

33 ≫→ LOOK

Fine's was locked when I got there and I rang the bell. I heard some yelling from the back and waited, checking the light meter and taking a shot through the window so you could see "Fine's Fotos" and the wall of cameras.

Glenn came to the door, looking neat, but beat. "What took you so long?"

"For what?" I asked.

"LOOK magazine, of course, Sam called me. This is the big leagues, bubby."

"I don't even know what they want..."

"I do, and I've spent all morning printing all your shots—except the one of your own butt."

"Have you ever seen your own?"

"No, and I don't want to. Don't worry, I took it out."

He handed me a big box that said, Kodalure Glossy Photographic Paper, tied up with an emerald green Fine's Fotos ribbon. "Contact sheets and proofs. Take it."

"What're contact sheets?"

"You're kidding me? They're made by putting the negatives directly in contact with the photographic paper to create a single print showing the whole roll at once."

"Oh, right," I said, pretending to know.

He held a smaller box that said, Kodalux Negative Film. "I got the negatives in glassines, that's what he'll really want but I didn't want to take chances."

"How do you know..." I said, noticing he was wearing a tight, well-pressed charcoal pinstripe double-breasted suit that made him look a bit like Orson Welles.

"Look, Herb, and I mean *Look*. I sell to magazines all the time, I know how they operate and you don't. So say 'hello' to your new agent, Glenn. I handle negotiations, productions, and archiving for 25%. Shake on it."

I shook his slightly sweaty hand and we headed down into the subway. I took a picture of the turnstile bars.

"So you've worked with *Look* before" I asked?

"Not exactly. Lots of magazines with one-word names. Girlies. Jugs. Butts. "

"Oh, good," I said, as we sat on the 1 train going downtown.

"This Pat guy is just another photo editor, they all want basically the same thing—he'll want to know what you know."

"What do I know?"

Glenn explained, "Just remember these three names, they're classy photographers. City: Alfred Stieglitz. People: Alfred Eisenstaedt. Nature: Ansel Adams."

"Alfred Adams?"

"Ansel."

"Is that even a name?"

"Yes, remember it. Oh, and Henry Cartier-Bresson, street photography."

"He took photos of streets..."

"People on the streets. Pictures that tell stories."

"Ah, I see."

We changed to the crosstown bus—I didn't even know where we were going.

We got off and I looked up and saw it, my favorite building. That gleaming crown of chrome, shining in the sun. The Chrysler Building. Why'd I never thought to come on my own? I checked the light meter and took a shot up the tall, narrow skyscraper so that the tip looked like it was touching the morning sun.

"Hurry up, for heaven's sake," Glenn pulled me through a crowd of men in army uniforms who were also looking up and gawking.

We pushed through the revolving doors into a lobby that looked like a movie set, but in color—all honey-colored light and stone. I looked up again, and the ceiling was painted with a view of the building itself, with it's famous crown gleaming gold against golden clouds, circled by silver biplanes.

This was clearly the center of the world. Right here where I was standing. I felt Glenn tugging at my sleeve towards elevator doors that looked like frozen fountains of wood and steel.

"I'll do the talking, Herb, but if he asks you something just say the names I told ya," he said, pressing a button marked "50."

I felt my ears pop!

The elevator doors opened onto a wall with the word "LOOK" in glossy metal letters. I looked and would have touched if Glenn wasn't still pulling me along to a young woman in a bright red dress, sitting at a shiny black desk, once again with the word "LOOK" on the front.

"Mr. H here to see Pat Whyte, we have an appointment," Glenn said, his voice sounding lower than usual. The young woman got up and led the way.

"Pat's very busy so I suggest you keep it brief," she informed us, stopping at another desk with a young woman, this one wearing blue. "Pat's 10am," she said, turning to leave.

"You're on time, good. Please sit down."

Glenn plopped right into one of the black leather chairs but I was too nervous to sit. I was glad he knew what he was doing because it just hit me that I didn't.

Then I heard this little voice coming from inside my head, "That's never stopped you before, Herb," it said. I turned to see who said it, but nobody was there. Glenn was on my other side, carefully rifling through the negatives.

The phone buzzed and the woman in blue motioned for us to follow her. I wasn't expecting what I saw.

34 »→ Second Look

First, there was the room itself, with windows on two sides... windows higher than I'd ever been. I thought I'd been high up at the top of the Ansonia, but this musta been what it was like to be in an aeroplane. Sky and clouds and a long view down to the river. I felt dizzy.

Behind the desk stood a tiny... woman. Shorter than Glenn, even. She was about the size of a slightly pudgy 12 year old boy if he was a full-grown lady. She wore a gray wool suit jacket and long skirt, white shirt and a scarlet tie. I wanted to take a picture of her.

Glenn reached his hand out across her wide, white-glass desk. She was wearing white gloves and waved his hand away. "Which one of you is Mr. H?" she asked. I raised my hand, sheepishly and she pointed at Glenn, "Then who are you?

"His agent," he replied, clearing his throat.

"Oh," She sighed. "Sit, boys," she commanded, and we did. She pointed to the desk and I put down the box of prints and fumbled to unwrap them. "Negatives," she said, and Glenn handed over the box, taking off the top like he was revealing a treasure for King Tut's tomb.

Pat flicked a switch and the entire top of her desk glowed white. "This is a lot, I'll take the contact sheets after all," she said and Glenn opened the paper box and took them off the top like he already knew what she wanted.

She leaned over the contact prints, using a big magnifying glass on a round clear base to stare at them, took a red grease pencil and started writing, right on them, first x-ing out the entire page of Miss Miranda on the sofa. "Cheesecake. Not us. Know your market. We want action and story."

"It's here," Glenn said, sliding more contact prints towards her.

"Better. Doormen. Real life. Good," she stopped to find her cigarette and take a puff, then immediately looked down again.

She turned over the contact sheet and started to write something, then abruptly sat down, exhaling smoke. She stopped and looked at us for the first time, glancing at the back of the print, then me, then Glenn. She put down her pencil, turned around in her chair and looked out the window. She looked at her watch, spun around, shrugged her shoulders and focused on the photos.

"You're always very well organized, Mr... Fine. I'll give you that."

Suddenly an image in the contact print caught her eye and she circled it in red and sighed "Yes." She kept studying the contact sheets and talked without looking up, "So who are your photographic influences, Mr. H?"

Glenn prodded me. "Um... Alfred Stieglitz. Alfred Eisenstein. Alfred... I mean... Adams."

"Uh huh. And for your candids?"

I couldn't remember, so Glenn started, "Henry Cart-ier Bresson."

"Henri," she corrected. "Good." She circled more pictures and wrote their numbers on another piece of paper.

"Get me roll A 1, 2, 3. B, 12, 15, 19. C 1, 7, 8, D 11 and 17 and 18," she ordered as Glenn carefully pulled negatives from the box and laid them on the glowing table.

She stopped on a photo of Kitty. "And who's this charming creature?" she asked.

"My girl. Kitty."

She nodded and circled it. "I'd like to see more of her. Around town. Eating ice cream. Tasteful." She looked at the picture for a bit longer, then stood up to look at us.

"So here's the deal, boys, we pay $5 for a 90 day exclusive hold on the selected photos. If we use one, and that's a big if, we pay $25 if it's under a quarter page, $50 if it's over half page, $100 for a full page, $250 for the cover—highly unlikely. If we use a shot, we own the negative and retain world rights."

"You get North American rights for one year. We own the negative and copyright," Glenn said, flatly.

Pat stopped, looked him up and down, slowly, taking another puff of her cigarette, "Agents. Fine, Mr. Fine." she said, respectful but amused. "Consider yourselves lucky boys. We're behind on the issue and that action image of yours in the Post got noticed. Mr. H... do you have a real name?"

"Herbert," I said. "Horo... Hamilton."

"Horohamilton? That's an odd name."

"Just Hamilton, sorry, My throat is dry from the height."

Now she actually smiled, her teeth both menacing and beautiful. "Before you go I'd like a word with Mr. Fine and think Mr. Hamilton should know what he's getting himself into."

She stood up and placed both hands on her glowing desk. "I almost threw you and your boy out of her, Mr. Fine. Do you know why?"

Glenn shook his head and started to sweat.

She flipped over a contact sheet and pointed to the stamp on the back, Fine's Fotos. "I've seen this stamp before, Mr. Fine. On photos that convinced the judge to grant my divorce petition. While I am grateful for that, most of the editors in this building are men, and might very well have found themselves on the other side of your service. If any of them saw this you'd both be blackballed in this business."

I saw Glenn's mouth trying to form words but nothing came out.

"I'm taking a chance here because I see something in the kid and I like to encourage talent. But if I so much as see that name or stamp again I'll drop you both like hot potatoes. The men who work here might think of this as their magazine, but I know it's mine. A clean, wholesome, family magazine. So, Mr. Fine, as for any other, shall we say, 'artistic' publications to whom you peddle, I will not allow so much as the hint of that here. Keep your nose clean or you'll be out on your plump little ass."

Glenn was frozen like a statue.

"Finally, Herbert, next time you're here... if there is a next time, I'll want to see a portfolio of more than just nightclubs. There's a great big city out there full of stories you can tell with your camera. Maybe I'll buy them. Maybe. Surprise me."

She slid a piece of paper across the desk to me. "Give this to my girl, Louise. She'll have papers for you to sign then will take you to accounting for a check. You may go," she announced.

"Thank you very much, ma'am," I said, since Glenn wasn't talking. He was stuck to his seat. I grabbed his sleeve and he stood up, wobbly, taking the box of negatives and holding it in front of himself. I took the box of prints and bowed to her, twice, then felt relieved to leave.

"Oh my God, oh my God," Glenn whispered.

"It's great, huh," I whispered back, closing the office door behind me.

36 ➠ Small Fortune

"Holy cow! I've never had a woman talk to me like that!" Glenn gulped, turning to look back at the closed door.

Just then Louise arrived carrying a clipboard with a stack of papers and said, "Sign everywhere you see an X," handing me a fountain pen with the cap already removed.

I wasn't sure who to sign it as and decided to use my new name, "Herbert Hamilton." I signed it page by page, over and over, until the word "Hamilton" started to look natural.

When I was done, Louise said, "Follow me, gentlemen," leading us into the hallway, then the elevator, down to the 35th floor where she handed the note and stack of signed papers to a young woman in yellow. "Beth'll cut a cheque," she said, turning on her heels and heading back to the elevator.

Glenn was shaking. We sat in the green leather chairs right next to a window that still felt awfully high.

"You OK?" I asked him.

"Yeah. Sure. It's all good. Better than good. Fine. I'm fine. We're fine." he said, not sounding fine. "I'm sorry, Herb."

"You did great, I couldn't have done it without you."

Beth returned, holding out an envelope. Glenn's hand was trembling, so I took it. "We'll send over copies of the final contract if any of your photos are used. Thank you, gentlemen."

Glenn got up, forgetting both boxes on the windowsill. I picked them up and followed as he shuffled to the elevator. Once inside I opened the envelope. It said, "Pay Sixty and 00/100 to the order of Herbert Hamilton," with $60 embossed right into it. I'd never had so much money.

I showed the cheque to Glenn. "Very pretty," was all he could say.

"$15 of that is yours," I told him, proud that I'd made money for the both of us.

"We gotta work with this broad again," he said.

In the lobby I saw a sign for the 'First National Bank,' the same name on the check. "Maybe I can cash this here," I suggested as he continued to follow me in a daze.

I went inside and the room was all black and white and chrome, like a nightclub of money. I'd never been in a bank before. They were for rich people. Now I was rich.

I got in line with the other rich people and when I reached the front I handed the cheque to a mustachioed man who sat behind chrome bars like he was in his own tiny jail. "I'd like to cash this, please."

"May I see some form of identification?" he asked, staring hard at me in what I thought was a rather rude way. I took out my wallet and showed him my business card, "Hamilton Agency."

"Yes, sir," he replied, stamping the check hard, then scribbling my phone number on it.

"May I take your picture?" I asked him.

"What? Why?"

"Because you look very... classy..." I said, not adding "behind bars."

He looked around, then sat up straight and said, "Thanks. Sure."
Click. I took a couple more of him counting out 12 crisp new $5 bills,
then fanning them out. *Click.* "5, 10, 15, 20, 25, 30, 35, 40, 45, 50, 55,
60," he counted.

"Thank you, sir," he said, smiling with crooked teeth.

"Thank you, sir," I replied, scooping up the small fortune that lay
in front of me.

37 »→ Thanks, Sam

I handed three of the $5 bills to Glenn, who almost dropped them.

"I gotta go take a cold shower," he said, as we headed into the
revolving door. Out on the street it was sunny, F.16 at 250th of a
second bright. "Come back with me and I'll give you more film, then
you can take shots for the portfolio."

"I don't know what that is," I admitted.

"A lot more pictures, in a binder. I've got a binder." Ah, good,
that'd be easy.

I felt uncomfortable walking around with that much money but
Glenn was with me. We stopped at Fine's and he gave me a dozen rolls
of film then waved, still shaky, as he went inside, pulled down the blind
and flipped the "closed" sign.

I went next door to the newsstand and bought a Coke because I
felt shaky, too. Buzzing, really. Right under my belly button. The coke
settled my stomach and I walked slowly back to the Ansonia, taking
pictures of the manhole covers I'd never noticed before.

Max opened the front gate and I gave him a silver dollar.
"Somebody had a good morning!" he said, saluting.

Sam opened the next door. I sat down on the bench and he sat
next to me. "I owe you, Sam."

"You don't owe me nothing, Herb."

I pulled a $5 bill out of my wallet and handed it to him.

"Naw, I can't take that much."

Then I reached into the photo box, which I'd forgotten I was still clutching, and fished around for the photo I took of Sam holding the key. He was sharp, the key blurred with motion.

"This I'll take!" he said, admiringly. "I never had a movie-star picture like this."

"You're a good man, Sam." I said, handing him the $5 bill again. "I want you to have this."

"Gee, Herb. I've always liked you." he said, blushing.

"Friends take care of each other," I added.

"Kinda like the son I never had," he said, proudly, patting me on the back.

Ellis got a silver dollar and bowed, smiling up all 16 floors.

Kitty was still asleep. *Click.* She looked so innocent. *Click.* Tasteful. *Click.*

I took the money out of my pocket and fanned it out on the window sill, trying to make it look the way the bank man had. *Click.*

Then I left, quietly so as not to wake her.

38 ➻ A Boy and a Duck

"Portfolio." That sounded kinda intimidating. But Glenn had said it was just pictures in a binder, so I'd take the pictures and he'd supply the binder.

I rode my bike down to the park. When something caught my eye, I'd hold up my camera and click while I was moving. I liked the fuzzy motion pictures, and remembered that Pat had circled some from the club.

It was such a beautiful day that I just wanted to lie in the cool, green grass, so I did, looking up at the puffy white clouds. *Click.*

There was an ant on a blade of grass. Couldn't get it in rangefinder focus. *Click* anyway.

Through the blades of grass I saw a boy's foot, dirty toenails. A piece of dried corn landed on his toenail. *Click.*

He picked it up. *Click.*

He walked to the nearby duck pond. *Click.*

He sat with his feet in the water and tossed corn at the ducks who excitedly swam to eat it. *Click.*

They fought with each other over each piece. *Click.*

He looked at them, sweetly. *Click.*

He stepped out of the water and walked to the grass, dropping a piece of corn every few steps. *Click.*

Ducks followed in a line, white, brown, blue. *Click.*

He sat down next to a tree and picked up a brown burlap bag. *Click.*

Then he swiftly pulled the bag over a white duck duck and scooped it up. *Click, Click.*

He picked up the bag and slammed it against the tree. Wait. *Click.*

The bag started to turn red.

I couldn't press the shutter as he walked away, waving the bag. He turned and smiled. *Click.*

I sat there, stunned. I had stopped breathing and gasped for air. The other ducks returned to the pond.

I thought about what was now in my camera, and in my mind's eye. I didn't like it. I thought about opening the camera back and exposing the film, as if that would make me forget. But I wouldn't forget.

Who would do that? Why? Maybe his family was poor and it would be dinner? Or maybe he was just a murderer and in a few years I'd go to the post office and see him on the FBI's most wanted list.

I tried to distract myself with a group of little girls carrying balloons. *Click.* One of them stepped in chewing gum and cried trying to get it off her shoe, then stuck what was left in her mouth.

I bought a strawberry ice cream cone and watched as it dripped down my hand. *Click.*

It was red and didn't taste good. I dropped it on the grass. *Click*. A squirrel ran up and started to eat the cone. *Click*. I liked squirrels. I took more pictures of it as it licked at the melting cream. *Click*.

On my wrist, Mickey said it was still only 1pm but I felt dog-tired. I got back on my bike and pedaled back up to the Ansonia.

"You look beat, Herb," Max said while taking my bike.

"I feel beat. Too much excitement for one day, maybe."

"Yeah, I have days like that," Max started, "Like yesterday, Mrs. Meyerwitz made a funny face then fell down, fell down right in front of me before I could catch her. I thought she was dead. Called an ambulance. She hasn't come back. Maybe she is dead," he trailed off.

"Seems to be going around," I signed, shuffling into the lobby. Sam was on the phone but looked up to wave. Ellis was as cheerful as ever and didn't seem to notice I wasn't. He told me he had plans for my silver dollar and was taking a girl for pizza and to the movies that very night. I tried to smile at him but it didn't feel right.

Kitty was still asleep. I let my clothes drop to the floor and fell into bed. I had another dream....

... There was a big storm cloud coming—so dark it made day look like night. I was in the spire on the top of the building and the wind picked up so hard I had to hold onto the spiral stairs to keep from being blown off the roof.

Lightning struck the spire, so bright I couldn't see, so hot I thought I would dissolve into ash. I felt the electricity burn through my body and I couldn't let go.

Then, suddenly, a brown burlap bag was over my head. I wanted to scream but nothing would come out...

...Kitty shook me, "Baby, you're having a bad dream," I heard her repeating but I couldn't open my eyes. Couldn't wake up until I felt the water she threw on my face. My eyes opened and she looked scared and fragile.

"You look like you're going to be sick," she said.

I was.

39 ➠ 7-up and Saltines

"You musta drank too much last night, I know I did," Kitty said when I staggered back from the bathroom. She looked at the mess I'd made, closed the door and said, "I'll call housekeeping to clean up," she added.

"I didn't drink anything."

"It's a lot of excitement, takes getting used to," she said, now quite chipper. "*I'll* take care of *you* today!" she announced happily. "I'll get you some soda crackers and 7-up to settle your stomach. My nana drinks it for the lithium which settles her mood, too."

I lay back down in bed. This morning everything had felt so good and now everything felt so bad. I'd never seen anything killed before. Right before my very eyes. Right inside the camera, still.

I kept remembering that boy's smiling face.

Kitty brought the crackers and 7up on a silver tray. "Here baby, eat a few of these and drink this all down." The salt tasted right. The 7up was sweet and the bubbles felt good. She brought a cool washcloth and put it over my forehead.

"You'll get used to it," she said. I wasn't so sure. "When I started at the Copa I was sick almost every morning. But I got used to it. Now I love it. I'm so happy to be back at the club."

My stomach felt better, and seeing her green eyes flash with happiness made me feel better, too.

Nothing had really changed. I was still here, with Kitty.

40 ➤ Unreal beauty

I fell asleep, the kind of sleep where I woke confused. Was it Morning? Afternoon? The sky was still blue. I looked at my wrist but my Mickey Mouse watch wasn't there. I looked in the pile of clothes on the floor and found it inside my shoe. Little hand on his right hip, big hand over his head. 4pm.

Kitty was lying on the sofa, listening to Bing Crosby while leafing through a magazine called "Bazaar." There was a lady's face on the front, half of it covered with a giant green butterfly, the spot on its wing looking like a mask over her eye.

What a beautiful photo. I sat next to her and looked closely at it. How did you take a picture like that? Were there really butterflies that big? How'd they get it to sit still long enough? Wasn't the lady scared of a giant butterfly on her face?

It musta been some kind of trick. I'd ask Glenn about this, he'd know for sure.

I liked this idea that photos didn't have to be real. They could just be beautiful.

41 ➤ Windows

"I'm gonna take a beauty rest before the show. You go do whatever it is you're doing and we can go to the club together at 8." Kitty drifted into the bedroom.

I leafed through her magazine, stopping to look at the photos of pretty women in pretty clothes. They made me feel better. One image stood out, a page covered with green leaves, with just a hint of something behind it. It was an advertisement for Saks Fifth Ave, so that's where I'd start.

I rode my bike south on Fifth Ave, watching people and occasionally stopping to take a picture of someone particularly interesting. An old woman feeding pigeons in front of St. Patrick's Cathedral, a building that felt too old to be in this new city. A pigeon landed on her head. *Click.* I left before she could do anything to it.

Then there was Saks, a full block long. *Click.* Rows and rows of American flags flying from it, all those stripes and stars. *Click.* It made me feel proud to be an American.

The sidewalk was lined with big windows like I saw in the magazine. The glass was covered on the inside with green leaves, leaving only small gaps you had to stop at if you wanted to see inside. People lined up to take turns peering at the mannequins wearing fancy dresses in bright colors, red, yellow, orange. It was like looking through summer and seeing fall in the future.

I held my camera up to the window but couldn't get a clear shot inside. Instead, half the view was covered with the fuzzy closeup of a leaf, and the mannequin in the background wasn't quite in focus. It wasn't a picture of something, it was just shapes. *Click.*

I changed my angle so I could see a young woman in a black hat pressing her nose against the glass. *Click.*

I moved slightly so half her face was covered by one of the leaves, like a mask. *Click.*

Then I saw something unexpected. A soldier was looking through an opening in the leaves right next to her. From where I stood it looked like they were looking at each other through a hedge. *Click. Click.*

Now there was a story. *Click.* Exhale.

I pulled away from the window and let someone else look and saw the photo I just shot in my head. Two lonely people. Separated by so much, yet longing for each other. Blink.

A man pushed me aside to look in the window. I saw the back of his head crowned by leaves like a native. *Click.*

I walked up Fifth with the crowds of well-dressed people. A man in a bowler hat, carrying a white cat. *Click*. A woman and little girl in matching hooded capes, holding hands. *Click*. A big man walking three small dogs and tripping over their tangled leashes. *Click*.

A group of Marines, in sharp khaki uniforms, lined up staring into a window full of ladies underwear, hands pressed against the glass. *Click*.

Then something that made me laugh. Windows full of life size animals, made out of clothing fabric. A gray pinstripe horse. If I moved just a little to my left, I could see it and the reflection of a Marine looking like he was standing next to it. *Click*.

Down on my knee, now there were clouds reflected, too. *Click*.

A unicorn covered in fancy blue and silver fabric, and the reflection of the little girl in the cape reaching up to touch it. *Click*.

The photos in my memory from earlier began to fade.

The world was beautiful again.

42 ➥ See What I Saw

Eight rolls in my pocket, I rode back uptown to Fine's. The door was open and Glenn was talking to Roger.

"Just the man I wanted to see!" he said.

I handed the eight rolls to Glenn. "Portfolio," I told him.

"Anything in there for moi?" Rogers eyebrows danced.

"Everybody's got their clothes on, if that's what you're asking. I don't do nudes anymore."

"Oh, more's the pity," Roger said, disappointedly. "So many delights at that nightclub. It would be an artistic tragedy for those lovelies to go unseen."

"Pat wouldn't like it," I explained.

"Who's this Pat fellow and why are you working with him and not me? I thought we were friends."

"Pat Whyte, at *Look* magazine," I said and then immediately saw Glenn shaking his head "NO!"

"I know her quite well. Quite. Unlike her, I deal in real art: Beaton. Capa. Evans. Kurtz. Call me when you get over being a hack." he said, loftily as he swept out.

"Don't mind him. He's still miffed you won't sell that girl in bed or those showgirls. He knows his stuff, but he's a stuffed shirt. Oh, and don't mention Pat to nobody or she'll kick my ass, which I'd like but it wouldn't be good for you."

"OK, Glenn, sorry."

"It's OK, Herb, let's see what you got here," he said, taking the film into the back. I told him about the magazine cover and the windows and the people. "Yeah, I saw that butterfly cover shot, too. Crazy good photomontage. That's a dark room trick where you combine a couple of images into one, in case you didn't know. Put together by this mod-ren Swiss guy, Herbert Matter—hey, another Herbert!"

We sat and waited for the film to develop. The room was dark and warm and I found myself drifting off, waking up when I heard the water running as Glenn rinsed the film.

"Holy crap, Herb, what the duck!"

I thought I'd forgotten it, but it all came back. "I dunno, it was all nice until it wasn't."

"Like life," he said. "Shots like that make you a photojournalist." Then he held up one negative and said, "Whew—with this one you're an artist," he said, showing me the photo of the girl looking through the leaves at the soldier. "Pat's gonna eat this up with a spoon!"

"I don't know what I'm doing, Glenn. I just know I love doing it."

"You're good, and a good guy, I'm awfully glad we met, Herb."

"Me, too, Glenn, you're swell."

"Let's print up some of these and stick 'em in a binder and go back and see Pat. In the meantime, come with me." he said, leading me back out front.

He pulled a red box with a white circle from under the counter, opened the box and gently lifted a silver and black camera. Smaller than my Kodak. Sleek, rounded, like a silver speedboat.

"Best you can get. Leica IIIa. 50mm, fast f/2 Summar lens," he said, stroking it in a way I'd seen him touch his nudie pictures. "The lens retracts so it can fit in your pocket! Quiet. Stealthy. Thing of beauty, ain't it? Can't get 'em from Germany anymore. Maybe never again when they lose the war. My uncle worked there."

"Yeah, it's a beaut," I said, wanting to touch it, but he wouldn't let it go.

"You need this more than I do," he said, finally handing it to me. "I'm not gonna use it 'cause I'm a twin-lens Rolleiflex guy," he said.

I'd seen one like it in "The Most Dangerous Game," where a rich big game hunter, played by some English guy, goes to a private island where he hunts people (in this case, Joel McCrea)! The rich game hunter had it around his neck to take pictures of his victims but in the end McCrea escapes with Fay Wray.

"I dunno," I said, stroking it.

"Best in the world. Uncle Otto snuck it over for me hidden in a tin of butter cookies when Leica helped him get outta Germany. The cookies were tasty."

"I'm doing fine with the Kodak," I told him, still running my fingers around the smooth curves of the camera.

"This is what the pros use. Pat sees this and she knows you're legit."

"Why are you doing this for me?" I asked.

"Because you're the real deal—and we're like brothers, I never had a brother."

I couldn't help myself, I started to tear up, then quickly wiped my eyes with my sleeve.

"You can buy it from me someday when you're rich and famous and I'm 25% rich and famous."

Click. No film, though. I just liked how it felt.

"Let's go make some art!" he said, and I followed him, the new camera around my neck.

He printed glossies of the girls and balloons, the squirrel, the girl in the window, people on the street and soldiers and funny animals.

The past few days piled up in a stack of shiny black and white prints. Glenn pulled a binder from the shelf. "Let's get these in some kinda logical order... maybe by place..." he slid them, one by one, into the clear sleeves, starting with the club.

"No, wait, she's already seen these, let's lead with something new," he said, putting the girl in the window in the first sheet. "I like this one, too," he said, about the fuzzy one that was just shapes. "Artsy." He closed the binder, then reopened it with a flourish. "Let's see what we got here."

"It's funny," I said, flipping the pages. "I saw them all in my head, took them, and now here they are, looking like a real book."

"Yup, I see them, too. That's what you do, let people see what you see."

43 ➽ Taking

Kitty. I wanted her. I took her. She gave herself to me, as if something came alive inside her. As if something died inside me. Someone nice breaking open into someone strong. It hurt. It felt good.

She was mine. Was I hers?

Click. I took naked photos of her, wide awake, looking into the lens, uncovered, unashamed. She took naked photos of me, erect, unafraid. *Click.*

It felt like the most natural thing in the world. It felt dirty. It felt necessary.

She curled up next to me, like a baby. I held her, like a man. We slept.

...

The phone rang. I answered without hesitation.

It was a wake-up call from Sam. I lifted Kitty from the bed, carried her into the shower and had her again, a wet echo of moans.

I couldn't tell if those were tears on her face. I kissed them off anyway.

...

I devoured a steak, green beans, baked potato with sour cream, and chocolate cake. I fed her bites knowing she didn't want to eat too much before her show.

She looked at me in a new way, as if she could see what I saw.

44 ➠ Different

How long had it been since I delivered that package here? It seemed like a lifetime ago. I was a different person. No, I was the same —I just saw things differently.

45 ➠ Momma

We got dressed for the club. I finally opened the ex-David's drawers and found ties and cuff-links and socks and shirts and pants. The clothes were too big, and there was something ugly about them I didn't care to take on. But there was a Tuxedo. Double-breasted, midnight blue silk, with rounded satin lapels. The fabric had wide vertical stripes that were just slightly smoother, that made it look like a skyscraper. The pleated pants were lined with white silk.

The seams of the coat and pocket were edged in satin, and there was a bold stripe down the side of the pants. There was a satin edged belt in the pocket.

I put it on. It was too big and too long, but I wanted it anyway. I put it in the bottom of my drawer.

Kitty wore a long pink dress, and high silver shoes. She was glowing. I was sorry I only had my gray suit but at least it was clean and pressed, and looked spiffier with my new leopard print tie I chose. I'd found a dark red tie in David's drawer, but I saw it had a wild lining, turned it inside out, and now it was mine. I put the new camera around my neck, my pockets filled with film.

Kitty eyed me up and down and sighed. "Well, I'll be."

I took her arm and even Ellis raised an eyebrow, impressed, so did Tony at the desk. Max, at the gate, whistled as we walked away.

I couldn't take my eyes off her at the club. Every time she talked to someone, I felt jealous. Especially if it was a man. I'd watch her go onstage and perform, then watch her come back offstage and change costumes. I watched so hard I forgot to take pictures.

I followed her. There she was, with Frank. His arm around her waist. I didn't like it. They were talking but I couldn't hear them through the din of clattering dishes. He popped a piece of gum in his mouth, then guided another piece into hers.

He said something. She laughed, big, her mouth wide open, then she pointed at me. Frank gave me a look then crooked his finger at me and I wanted to break it off.

"Hey, kid, not much action here tonight, but Kitty's one smart cookie. Had a fine idea of how youse can make yourself useful."

"And stay outta my hair a bit," she added, taking my arm and leading me down the hall. "Look Herb, you're smothering me. I can't have you following me around like a... a... G-man. I'm working here and there are things a girl's gotta do to keep her job, like making nice with Frank."

"You don't need this job."

"I *want* this job, baby," she said, rubbing her nose against mine. I wanted her to have what she wanted.

"OK. Sorry."

"Look at this as a favor for Frank, it's always good for him to owe you something, understand? That's how it works."

"Yeah, I get it."

"It's just a little babysitting."

"What?"

"His momma. Sweet old lady. Her deaf nurse is sick and he brought her to the club. You just gotta watch her so she don't wander off and talk to strangers."

"Sounds boring."

"It'll get you on Frank's good side."

"OK. I'll do it for you."

She kissed me deeply, her tongue pushing the spearmint gum into my mouth. "So you smell as sweet as you are. Just one thing—don't listen to nothin' the crazy ol' bitch says. She's old and doesn't make sense. And, whatever you do, don't breathe a word of it to anybody else, OK?"

"I guess so," I said disappointedly.

She opened a dressing room door and there, sitting on a brown sofa was a giant baby. At least someone dressed like a baby, with a bonnet.

"Hi, momma Maria," Kitty cooed.

"Whaddya want?" the baby grunted, turning to reveal the face of a very old, wrinkled woman.

I stepped back in shock. Kitty pulled me forward.

"Frank's got a friend for you tonight!" she said in a sing-songy way.

"Frankie? Come here, baby! Sit down next to momma!"

Kitty pushed me towards her and motioned for me to sit, "Call her momma," then closed the door behind her.

Momma pinched my cheeks. Soft little hands. Hard little grip. "My sweet bambino!" she said, with a toothless smile... like a baby. "Get momma a drink. You know what I like."

I looked around. "A coke?"

She cackled. "You always was a funny boy. Four Roses. Neat. I can smell it over there." she said, waving towards the long makeup table surrounded by little white lights. Sure enough, there was a bottle of Four Roses Bourbon.

I had to get a picture of this. I quietly lifted my camera, checking the light meter. *Click.*

Maria's head turned fast. "What was that?"

"Just opening the bottle... momma." I poured the drink. She held out her hands and I made sure she had a grip, with both hands. She downed it in a swig.

"Smooth," she croaked, patting the seat next to her again. "It's been too long since we talked."

Her feet were in Mary Janes. *Click.* Her white stockings came up to her knees. Her hands were bony and wrinkled. *Click.* Her face was surrounded by the bonnet. *Click.*

With each click, her white eyeballs moved around. "I hear a mosquito, kill it, KILL IT!" she yelled.

I slapped my hand hard. "Got it... momma."

"I hate those Jewish bloodsuckers." she said, wiggling her fingers around her face. "Now, answer me this, did you take care of Lansky like I told you?"

She wasn't making any sense.

"Answer your momma or I'll give you a whopping you won't forget, stronzo!"

"Um..."

"Do what I tell you, boy!" she demanded.

"Yes... momma."

Her face turned hard, the toothless mouth now a gaping black hole through which I could see her tongue moving, wordlessly." *Click.*

"KILL HIM!" she yelled.

I slapped myself again. "Got 'em."

"Weak, like your father, God rest his soul. 57 years and I always had to tell him twice, three times. See where it got him. I don't want to outlive you, too."

She grabbed my hand and dug her fingernails into it.

"I can smell their shit a mile away. Anastasia. Campione. Especially that Jew bastard Seigel. Kill them." Her grip got tighter till my hand hurt and my eyes were watering. Her grip softened and she patted my hand, "Like the bugs they are."

"Yes, momma," I said, standing up to get away from her.

"Another drink, sweet bambino!" she said, sweetly. I got her another drink which she downed in a gulp and held her hand out for another.

"I can smell that Kitty creature on you. She gets around. I don't trust her."

I almost dropped the bottle.

I watched as her eyes closed and her head tilted back, mouth wide open in a loud snore. *Click.*

Frank opened the door. "Beat it, kid," he said, sitting down next to his momma and holding her hand, tenderly.

46 ⇒ Good Boy

It was a slow night at the club. I didn't recognize any famous faces. Just a lot of people who looked drunk, tired and sad. *Click.*

A woman in a purple dress leaned on her hand, looking at the man next to her and let out a sigh. He was looking at a pretty young girl in green at another table sitting with an older man. She pretended to smile. *Click.*

Waiters collected glasses, sometimes knocking back whatever was left in the glass. *Click.*

I went through the kitchen doors to the dressing room where a redhead was completely naked. *Click.*

"Oh, sorry," I said.

"Take all you like, cutie, just gimme copies for the stage door Johnnies," she whispered, too close.

Even Kitty looked tired with no makeup. She smelled like Listerine. "How was momma," she asked, taking my arm and heading up the stairs to the stage door.

"Creepy,' I said.

"What'd she say?"

"You told me not to listen."

"Good boy."

47 ➺ Dodge and Burn

The next thing I knew the phone was ringing. It was Sam. "I know you was out late, but they said it was important. Mr. Whyte's office at *Look*. Needs you to sign some papers, pronto."

My eyes were dry. I smelled bad. Kitty was still fast asleep. I got in the shower. I loved this shower, really loved it. Hot water and a fresh bar of soap every single day. Clean white towel.

I ordered waffles with bacon, then called Glenn. "*Look* called. Need me to sign stuff and I got more pictures for the portfolio."

I heard sniffling at the other end. "Aw jeez, of all the luck."

"Be right there."

I wolfed down the pancakes and bacon, maybe too fast. Made me feel kinda queasy. Or was I nervous?

Got to Fine's and handed Glenn yesterday's film. He was still in his PJs and looked like hell.

"Sorry, Herb, I got a cold... from a girl..." he said, smiling.

"We're seeing Pat."

"And it pains me to miss it, but I don't want her seeing me like this."

"You look fine. You're my agent, I need you there."

"We already agreed to terms. Lemme develop and print this, then you go."

He was so sniffly I thought he was gonna get snot on everything, but he kept his hands clean and I kept my distance.

He checked the negatives. "Woah, what's with the big baby?"

"I'm not supposed to talk about her."

"This is terrific, grotesque!" he said, projecting them onto the paper. "A little light there, a little too dark there, I'll fix it" he said, waving his hands between the light and the photo paper below, then using a piece of cardboard with a hole to focus the light around Maria's bonnet.

"Dodging and burning, brings out the details. I made her mouth lighter so you can see her tongue, and her hair darker around the hat thing."

"You mean you made her even creepier."

"Guiding the viewer's eye where you want it to go." He developed the pictures and put them on the glossy drum.

"OK, boychik, go make me proud. Keep the Leica around your neck so she sees it."

I already had it around my neck.

"I'll let you know what she says." I put the portfolio under my arm.

"And remember to say 'hello' to Pat from me!" he said, blowing a kiss, then sneezing.

48 ➺ Birds of a Feather

I clutched my portfolio on the subway, then the bus. I wanted Pat to like my pictures.

The Chrysler building. Just seeing it made me feel better. The lobby still felt like being in a movie.

I was in a movie! My own personal movie. "Boy from the South Bronx finds love and fame in Manhattan." A classic American success story, and I was the hero! I stood up straighter and took the elevator to the 50th floor, feeling my ears pop.

"I'm here to sign papers for Louise and see Pat," I told the young woman at the front desk, now wearing blue. She was pretty, with big pink cheeks.

"He's here," she said into the phone. Louise came out, wearing green. "I apologize for making you come all this way back, there's just one more release you have to sign."

"It's OK, I brought the portfolio Pat asked to see."

Louise handed me a clipboard and pointed to where I needed to sign.

"Oh, she can't see you now, she's busy putting the issue to bed. That's why we needed your signature."

I signed. "I'll wait."

"She probably won't have time."

"I do."

Louise disappeared back into her office. I sat in the green leather chair and waited, occasionally opening the binder and leafing through the first few pages. I remembered taking them. But they also felt like distant memories.

A big group of men wandered out, talking and laughing and not noticing me, though the one with wild red hair briefly turned and looked back.

Louise followed them, "They were done early, unusual consensus. Come."

I followed her into Pat's office, once again impressed but no longer dizzy from the view. She was wearing another suit, this one dark blue check, like a man's, but with a skirt down to her ankles where she wore bright red shoes.

"Sit," she said. "Where's your husky little friend?"

"He's got a cold and didn't want to give it to you."

"Thoughtful."

"But he said to say 'hi'"

"Cute. I'm glad you're here because I wanted to tell you this in person." She looked at me and I couldn't tell what she was thinking. "We're using all your photos. That's very unusual. Rarely happens. Don't get used to it."

"Wow." was all I could say.

"Everyone agreed... again, doesn't usually happen that way," she said, sliding a big piece of paper across the desk. The top half of the page had the word LOOK in big letters. Behind the letters "OO" were Carmen Miranda's eyes, and below that, her body spinning in motion. I thought it was so clever how they put her eyes in the O's, like glasses, that it took me a second to realize it was my photo.

"Wowie!" I said.

Now she laughed, "You're such an old soul I forgot you're a kid... young man. You got lucky. With the shot. It happens. With us wanting to use it."

"I'm very lucky," I said.

"Agreed. But you can't count on luck. You need to know that we might not ever buy another photo from you."

"Did I do something wrong?"

"No. It's just the way it is. I don't want you to get the wrong idea about how this all works just because you hit a home run right out of the box."

"I appreciate you telling me that. You've been very kind."

"Ask any of the men who were just in here, I'm not kind. I'm smart. I hope you are, too."

"Thank you. I brought my portfolio like you asked."

"Smart. Let's see." I put it on the table and slid it over to her. She took a breath and opened the cover. She didn't move, just looked, sat down, closed the cover, and spun her chair around so she was facing away from me to the windows.

I didn't say anything because I didn't know what to say. She spun her chair back, slowly, opened the cover again, slowly, and looked at the first picture: the girl peering through the leaf window at the soldier.

"When did you take this?"

"Yesterday."

"Saks?"

"Yes."

"Do you know how many photographers have come in with photos of that display?"

"No."

"Over a dozen."

"Oh."

"Do you know how many of those I thought were worth the paper they were printed on?"

"No."

"None."

"Oh," I said, trying not to sound disappointed.

"Until yours. It's exquisite," she said, quietly.

"Oh?"

"This tells a story. Everything I need to know in a single look. I was right about you."

"That you may never buy another photo from me?"

She laughed, "No, wrong about that. Right that you have an eye. Let's look at the rest, shall we?" she said, picking up the book and moving to the red velvet sofa. She put the book on top of a bunch of magazines on a low glass table. "Come, sit." she said, patting next to her.

She looked at each image and asked me questions. Where was this? Why'd I take that particular picture? What was I thinking?"

I told her I looked around and clicked the shutter when I saw something that stuck in my brain.

She stopped at the photo of the bank teller behind bars and laughed. "Where did you study?"

I felt my face twitch as I tried to figure out something to say. "I've always had to look out for myself?"

"School of life. Best teacher. The photographers you mentioned the last time you were here, do you actually know who they are?"

I shook my head, "No."

"Thank you for your honesty. It's refreshing. You'll be my tabula rasa."

"Is that a good thing?"

"Very," she said, turning the page... to the boy with the duck. I didn't know it was there!

"I honestly don't think you'll want to see these..." I said, closing the book.

"I want to see them."

"I... don't."

"Now I want to see them more than ever," she said, gently prying my hand off the cover and opening it, studying each image, then turning the page. "Nice progression, almost like a storyboard. Cute boy. Cute ducks. Not outstanding, but pleasant..."

Then she turned the page to the bag hitting the tree and the bloody bag. "That's quite disturbing."

"I'm sorry," I said, feeling my face get hot and turn red.

"I'm not. It happened and you told the story. That's brave."

"I hate those pictures. Glenn musta slipped them in."

"Photos are powerful. That's the point. It's what we do, tell the story of the world."

"I don't want to tell this story."

"But you did. Now you get to decide what happens to it."

"I'm going to cut them up."

"Or you can sell them to me. They are a perfect metaphor for the world right now and what's happening in Europe—the hideous joy in cruelty and disregard for life. Millions of Americans are ignoring it because it's too big. But they will relate to the story of one boy."

I thought about all the pictures I'd seen in magazines and how I remembered the faces. "I don't want people remembering him."

"They need to."

"I don't know."

"Think about it."

I felt myself tearing up. "I don't like to even think about it. I like pictures that look better than life."

She reached over and held my hand, softly. "I do, too, my boy. But sometimes we have a mission to do more."

"I don't get scared and this scared me and I don't like it," I said, looking at her bright red fingernails. They matched the color of her shoes. She smelled really nice, like fresh laundry. We just sat there and she patted my hand.

"Herb... I understand. I do. Your pictures have such love because you think the best of people. I hope you always do." she said kindly, but sadly. "I used to. But in this world, people can disappoint you and make you... Mean like them. You have to work double hard to put good into the world..."

"That's what I want to do," I said, looking up at her. She had light blue eyes, like some gray dogs I'd seen in the park.

"The world's a dark place now and getting darker. Every week I put out a happy family magazine, but I need... We need... to start showing our readers the truth. Those men who were in here, don't understand, so I have to sell them a story... this story. May I?"

I thought about it. "Yes."

"Thank you." she said, leaning her head on my shoulder. I watched while a tear rolled down from her icey blue eye, carrying a line of black makeup with it that dripped on my shirt, spreading like a storm cloud.

She sat up, "This is not like me at all. They call me the cold-hearted she-boss. I'm sorry."

"I'm not."

"We're birds of a feather, Herb, and nobody's going to make us into that duck," she said, wiping her eyes. "OK, where were we?" she said, turning the page to... Momma, then laughing. "Oh, my heavens. It's almost too much for one day. Almost," she said, turning the page.

I told her about babysitting and she laughed. "Gothic. Charming."

I told her the story about the mosquito and the killing and the names she mentioned. Pat closed the book and leaned away from me.

"What is this woman's name?" she asked.

"Maria Costello."

"At the Copa? Frank Costello's mother?"

"That's her!"

"Burn them," she said, closing the book.

"Excuse me?"

"Burn them. Tell Glenn to burn the negatives, no, I'll call him and tell him. You don't want to get yourself mixed up with these people."

"She's just a crazy old lady," I explained.

"With a crazy young son. You're really that naive?"

"I guess so."

"That's wonderful. It makes me worried about you—and breathless with wonder at what you'll show me next."

She opened the book again and slid out the duck pictures, placing them in a neat pile. Then she slid out the momma pictures and tore them into little strips, then tore them again into tiny pieces she threw up in the air. I watched while they floated down, like confetti, a shower of black and white on the white rug. "I've never done that before."

"I won't make you do it again."

"No, please do," she said, getting up, pouring two glasses of water and handing me one. "You're just what I've been looking for. I've got an assignment for you."

I drank the entire glass of water.

"We need stories that show people from different countries uniting to work together to create 'The World of Tomorrow.' That's happening in Queens now, at the World's Fair."

"Oh, I've wanted to go!"

"Good! Show the world the good you see in people, Herb. Make the world look beautiful. For me. For yourself. For the future. Remember, we are shaping the future, people like us—Making memories that people never had—and will never forget."

I understood. I could make the world a better place by showing the world I saw!

There was a knock at the door. "Back from accounting," Louise said, handing me a check.

$1,000. One. Thousand Dollars. I handed it to Pat.

"It's yours. You earned it."

"A thousand dollars?"

"Yes."

"A thousand dollars?"

"Yes."

"A thousand dollars!"

I saw Pat and Louise look at each other and laugh.

"Go to the fair. Show me what you saw."

"A thousand dollars."

I must have said thank you and goodbye, it would have been rude not to but I had no memory of it. I just kept looking at the check and all those zeros. What was I going to do with all this loot? What could I buy Kitty? Oh, right, 25% was Glenn's, he'd like that...

49 ➻ Banking on it

Next thing I knew I was inside the bank, standing in front of the same moustachioed teller behind bars.

"Good afternoon, sir. How may I help you today?" he said.

I couldn't say anything. But I remembered his picture and opened the book to show him. He grinned. I pulled it out of the sleeve and handed it to him.

"Thank you, sir, most generous of you. I like it very much." Then I remembered the check and placed it on the counter. He looked impressed. "A photographer for *Look*, no wonder it's such a fine image. With a sum of this size let me introduce you to a personal banker."

He gestured for me to follow him. "Mr. Clarke, this gentleman is a very successful photographer for *Look* magazine with a high-income and deserves special attention," he said, placing the check on the desk, then bowing slightly and returning to his cage.

Mr. Clarke, balding with a goatee, adjusted his vest and long gold watch chain. He looked down at the check and his eyes widened. "It's a genuine pleasure to meet you, Sir. Kindly allow me to explain how I can help you," he said.

"I need to cash this, but I don't want to carry around this much."

"No need, sir. We can keep these funds safe for you yet easily available by bank draft or cheque. Let me open an account for you ," he said, and started to ask me questions, like my name, address. "Do you, by any chance, have a Social Security number?"

I shook my head, "No."

"Most people still don't, but I can file a form and get you one," he said, scribbling something. He slid the papers to me and pointed where I needed to sign. I wished Glenn was here to check this but it was a bank, and they had to know what they were doing, at least after FDR.

"When you need to pay someone, you simply write it down on a cheque. The money is withdrawn from your account and credited to them."

"What if they need cash?"

"Then their bank will provide cash. Convenient and safe."

Mr. Clark handed me a little stack of blank cheques, then leaned over and showed me how to fill out one. "First, one enters the date, then your name at the top. It is best to print rather than use cursive. Next, the name of the payee. On this line you write the total amount, spelled out as words with cents, finally in Arabic numerals. At the bottom you write your account number, which I have noted on the back of the book for easy reference."

"I need to write one right now," I said.

"Allow me to demonstrate, sir. To whom is it to be paid?"

"Glenn Fine," I said, he wrote. "Glenn with two 'n's"

"Amount?"

"$250..." he wrote "Two Hundred and Fifty Dollars and 00/100s" in beautiful handwriting, then wrote the number, then the account number. "Sign here, please, a cheque is not valid unless you sign it." I signed. He tore it from the book and handed it to me, then wrote down -$250 in a little blue book, and wrote $750 in the total column.

"And I need $20 cash," I added. He handed me four $5 bills and changed my total to $730.

He placed both the checks and the little book in a small buff envelope and handed it to me. "I have enclosed your bank book. Please notate the checks you write so that you might keep a running total of your funds. We don't want to overdraw as there is a $10 fee for returned checks. If you need anything please do not hesitate to call me at this number," he said, sliding his business card into the envelope and closing it with a silver metal flap. "I am at your service, sir."

The sun hit me through the window, blinding me. I squeezed my eyes closed, then open. Everything was still here, including the envelope in my hand. *Click.* Damn! "Uh, I'd like to take a picture of the check, please."

"I've already stamped it and that's not necessary."

"It's for me." *Click.*

I put the envelope in my pocket and headed back to Glenn's.

50 ⇒ Holy Moly

Glenn was still in his PJs. "I heard! Congratulations!" he said, unlocking the door.

I handed him the check.

"Holy Moly!" he said, stepping back to sit on a stool. "That's huge."

"And that's just your part of it."

"Pat called me. Said, 'your boy got the cover!' Then told me to burn the old lady."

I told him how she liked the whole awful duck thing and wanted me to go to the fair.

"I hear they gotta lotta ladies without tops in the amusement zone, you'll want to see them first!"

None of this felt real. Except the picture I took of the check. That I could clearly see in my head.

I stopped back at the Ansonia and slipped the envelope under the mattress where Kitty was still sleeping. I had the only topless lady I needed right here.

I wanted to do one more thing before I left for the fair. I pulled out Mr. Clarke's card and went into the living room and closed the bedroom doors so as not to disturb Kitty.

I dialed. "Mr. Clarke? This is Mr. Hamilton."

"Yes, Mr. Hamilton, what a pleasure to hear from you so soon. How may I assist you?"

"Can I send someone money without them knowing it came from me?"

"I can draw up and send a bank draft for you, sir," he said as if it was no problem at all. I gave him the information.

"$100 to Mrs. Rita Horowitz... yes... address... I shall post it today, too. Please deduct it from your total in the book. Thank you for your business, sir."

And it was done. I wondered what Ma would do it with. Hopefully not tell Pa.

I made sure my pockets were full of film before I took the subway to Queens.

51 ⇉ World's Fair Play

I loved the subway—all those people. I liked to try to guess who they were, what they did, how they were related to each other. I'd see a man and woman sitting next to each other in the crowded car and wonder if they were friends, colleagues, or married?

The Leica was so small and quiet I didn't even need to put it up to my eye, I just aimed it at someone interesting and—*click*. A woman holding a bag of groceries with an egg carton teetering at the top. *Click*.

The man and woman directly across from me. They looked like strangers: he was tall and dark and well-dressed, she was small, blond and rumpled. He was reading a book and her head was nodding. *Click*. Her drowsy head fell onto his shoulder, and he looked at her, sweetly. *Click*.

It was warm and I felt drowsy, too. I closed my jacket around the camera, as if protecting my baby and fell asleep...

...I dream that Kitty is with me as we go to the 'world of tomorrow,' together. Everything is bright and sunny and full of color, not just black and white. She's beautiful, and so are our two children, a boy who looks like me and a girl who looks like her.

We stride, hand-in-hand, into this gleaming city of the future. A city where dreams come true. Everyone is clean and happy with money in their pockets. The world of wonders is so close we can touch them. Our house is all white and modern, with big windows and a big car in the driveway. Kitty cooks while I work in the darkroom, watching the future develop before my very eyes...

...I woke at the end of the line, looked out the window, and that world was already here.

People swarmed onto the platform and I took in the view from the Empire State Bridge—clean, white and modern as far as the eye can see. At the very center, beckoning me on, stood a tall white spire next to a giant sphere—the Trylon and Perisphere. *Click.*

There. *Click.* Was. *Click.* So. *Click.* Much. *Click.* To. *Click.* See!

I didn't know where to start! I paid 75 cents to get in, and 25 cents for the official deluxe program with its colorful cover. I was going to see the future, here at the fair!

I headed towards the Trylon and Perisphere to see *"Democracity, a vision of America's future in 2039."* But as I passed by the Science Building, I was struck by something in the window. A giant eyeball.

I'd never thought about my eyes. Even when I took pictures, it seemed to happen inside my head—like a movie projected on the back of my skull.

But there was this giant eyeball, taller than I was. I looked right through it, past the lens and iris that got bigger and smaller (like the f.stop thing in the camera!) and saw a little boy through a hole at the other end. *Click.*

I didn't know why, but this shook me up. I had to sit down on a bench while the crowd swarmed around. I felt confused about... sight. Before this moment I just looked and saw and now... I was thinking... Eyeball then brain then viewfinder then finger then shutter then film then development then printing...

And an assignment, I'd never had an assignment. Where did I even start?

No, it was too much to think about. There wasn't time. I closed my eyes. Opened them. Look. A woman holds a baby up to the giant eye. See. *Click.*

I closed my eyes again, like a shutter.

OK, I'm fine. *Look. See. Click.*

As I left, I was stopped by the sight of an entire wall of tubes bubbling with clear red liquid. Above it, the words, "ALL THE SAME UNDER THE SKIN." *Click.*

The "activated mural" showed three human outlines filled with spiraling tubes of red liquid going up and down their bodies.

A panel lit up with the words, "*Science proves we all come from the same seeds, the same place.*" The next panel read, "*Geography has caused our bodies to adapt to climate.*" *Click.*

And finally, "*A Scottish terrier doesn't hate a Great Dane, nor a German Shepard feel the need to dominate a Polish blue hound...*"

Click.

52 ➤ Trylon & Perisphere

The majestic Trylon and Perisphere. It was impossible not to take pictures of them. As modern as anything I'd ever seen. Smooth. White. With only shadows as detail. *Click. Click. Click. Click. Click.*

Oh, wait, I didn't get any people in the pictures.

At the base of the Trylon was the entrance with a long long line of people. *Click.* Up the "World's longest, tallest escalator," I looked back down at the long line of people. *Click.* I walked across a bridge into the Perisphere.

Inside was a vast open globe space, like being in the center of the earth. A pretty girl in a blue and orange uniform pointed to the right and I followed a line of people walking around a row of tall chairs built into the wall then sitting one by one.

The lights dimmed. The floor vibrated—we started moving!

A choir of angels sang from above. I looked up and saw clouds parting to reveal the words "YOUR WORLD OF TOMORROW!" *My world.*

A deep voice told us we had left the world of 1940 and were in a time machine hurtling 100 years *into the future!* I could feel my heart racing.

"To the world of 2039. A world of peace and plenty! No poverty or war. Science has given us all health and happiness... as you can see..."

The bottom half of the sphere started to glow, illuminating a city at our feet, as if we were flying high above it. Higher, even, than Pat's office.

It's the city of the future! All neatly arranged in a circle of towers, then houses, then farms and factories, spread out like a sunburst, connected by ribbons of highway and tiny moving cars!

Night fell and the buildings lit up!

"*A brave new world built by united hands and hearts. Here brain and brawn, faith and courage, are linked in high endeavor as men march on toward unity and peace! As man helps man, so nation helps nation, connected by 10,000 roads of commerce, art and human aspiration. Listen! From office, farm, and factory they come with joyous song: Hand in hand, side by side, and tomorrow, and forever, comes the great rising tide!*"

A bright flash of white light. Silence.

I felt tears of joy running down my face—yes! This is the future I want!

A softer voice now intoned, *"You have visited 100 years in the future, and yet only 333 seconds have passed in the present. Welcome back to your world, but remember, the future is made of your dreams!"*

At the exit I squinted from the sunlight as a young uniformed woman handed me a blue and orange pin that said, "I have seen the future!" I pinned it, proudly, to my lapel. I looked up and saw I was on a long narrow ramp, high above the fairgrounds, feeling as if the future was still everywhere I looked. *Click.*

A world full of people. It was only then I realized that 100 years in the future, not a single person was shown, only buildings and machines. Was that why the future looked so orderly?

I stopped and took a deep breath. I'd never see that world. Unless some miracle of science let me live to be 118, I'd be long dead. Or maybe all humans would be—Maybe we'd all be killed in this great war, replaced with machines.

Next stop, the Westinghouse building... and what did I see? A giant machine of a man, a robot named Electro, the Moto Man. He could walk and talk and smoke a cigarette! Were we being replaced already?

Of course, my camera was like a machine for my eye, but it didn't replace my eye, it amplified and literally enlarged it. That was different. The Kodak exhibit showed how images could be enlarged to the size of a billboard! I'd never seen photos so huge!

I thought about what Pat had said, about how we can show the world what we're seeing and feeling so more people recognize the problem—we enlarge and repeat it until a whole country can see it!

I had the chance to do that. Maybe to save humanity! I had work to do!

53 ➻ Human Heroes

The world of smell surrounded me as I walked down the long ramp. Hot dogs and waffle cones, bread baking from the Wonder Bread building and coffee and flowers and fresh paint. It made me hungry, especially the hot dogs, so I bought one with mustard and relish from a cart. No time to stop—I ate it as I walked, careful not to let it drip on the camera.

I heard an announcement that *Billy Rose's World Famous Aquacade,* starring Buster Crabbe, was starting in 20 minutes. Buster Crabbe! Flash Gordon himself! He was always flying through space, saving the galaxy—a real human hero!

I followed the crowd through the gates of the "Amusement Zone," to an enormous amphitheater that said it had 10,000 seats! Tickets were 40 cents or a dollar... I'd brought $20 and only spent, let's see, $2? I decided to go for the good seats and handed over a whole dollar. The good seats were closer for a better view and came with a deluxe program I could show Kitty to get her to come back with me.

Just a few feet in front of me was the biggest pool I'd ever seen—as big as a lake. Suddenly, fountains shot up all along the front, making a cool mist, then opening, like a curtain, to reveal a man on a high diving board. It was Buster! In person and swim trunks!

Buster raised his arms and ran off the end, seeming to float in space, twisting and turning before entering the water so perfectly he hardly made a splash. I was amazed and forgot to take a picture! I quickly cleaned my camera lens with my tie in time to capture Elenor Holm, who I'd seen in "Tarzan's Revenge," do her own graceful dive off the board and into the water. *Click.*

She and Buster quickly swam the entire length of the pool as a bevy of beauties dove one by one from the side, while an army of men dove from three levels of diving boards and soon the pool was full of people, making circles around Buster and Eleanor who magically rose from the water on a platform covered in firework sparklers, maybe the most impressive thing I'd ever, ever seen! *Click. Click. Click!*

Then everyone disappeared from the pool without even getting out. Where did they go? And there were more ladies on a stage, this time wearing long blue and white dresses with big silver stars as hats. A curtain rose in the back showing a whole live orchestra and chorus, singing about "America, the land of the free, the home of the brave!"

How brave and beautiful they *all* were. Not just Buster and Eleanor, who, as movie stars, had to be beautiful, but every single woman was beautiful and every single man was handsome. *Click!*

Here were people of today who looked like people from the future! Tall. Fit. White. In fact, it was hard to tell them apart. It didn't matter, as they dove and swam and formed patterns in the water like an aqua army... like little pieces of... a machine. Oh.

After the show I went up to a guard and told him I was a photographer for *Look* magazine doing a story about the fair, and I needed to take pictures of the performers. He looked me up and down, then saw my Leica camera and waved me backstage where the swimmers were taking showers and wrapping themselves in towels.

A beautiful couple was clearly enamoured with each other. *Click.* A young woman was shivering. *Click.* Buster strode by... *Click*... but I only got a picture of his backside.

A scowling red haired woman came up to me, "Excuse me, young man, but you can't be here."

"I'm here shooting a story."

"For what, kid, your high school paper? Scram. Damn kids, trying to sneak in..."

"No, I work for *Look* magazine."

"Oh, tell me another one, get out."

"I really do," I showed her my press pass.

"Who'd you steal that from?" She was mean!

"I got it from my editor."

"Yeah, sure. What's his name, then? Better answer right or I'll have you out on your ass."

"Pat. Pat Whyte!" I said as fast as I could.

"How is he?" she stared at me.

"Pat's a she."

She blushed quite pink. "That was a trick question and you passed... What's your name?"

"*Mr.* Hamilton."

"Sorry, Mr. Hamilton. We have kids sneaking back here all the time... what can I do for you?"

"I'm looking for heroes, for people working together," I said.

"That's what we do here at the Aquacade, Mr Hamilton. Once again, I apologize. I'm Carol Weber, at your disposal, at least until the next show in one hour."

I looked up. "I'd like to take some photos of divers at the top of the diving platform."

"Of course, I'll arrange it, please wait right here."

Burly hands moved large scenery pieces. *Click.* Women wheeled racks of costumes. *Click.* It was a well-oiled machine backstage, too.

Mrs. Weber returned with four women and four men who somehow seemed even better looking than all the rest. "Follow me, please," she said, walking briskly to the base of the diving tower where a staircase spiraled up and up and up.

She led the way, followed by the divers, followed by me. It was a lot of steps.

The others thought nothing of the height or narrow railings but I was careful to stand in the very center of the long, narrow board. I directed one of the men to stand at the very end, facing me.

He did look heroic from here, surrounded by nothing but sky and clouds. "Can you jump facing me like this?" I asked.

"A backflip, of course," the man said. "Tell me when."

I made sure the camera was ready with it's fastest shutter speed, 1/1000th of a second. "Now!"

"To GRAVITY!" he yelled, raising his arms, hopping up then flipped over backwards. *Click.* Wind the film. *Click.* Wind. *Click.* As I shot him flying through space I didn't even realize I'd nearly walked off the end of the board, only to be pulled back by another man grabbing my belt.

"Gotcha, sport!" he said, playfully patting my butt and winking.

From now on I sat on the board while the others took turns at the end, posing like Greek Gods and Goddesses.

A dark haired man yelled, "To FALLING!" then lept in the air, hanging weightless, then plunging down into the pool.

And finally, a blond woman who seemed the most relaxed (and shapely) of the bunch gave me this slightly bored look, yelled "TO FLYING!" like it was the most normal thing in the world, then simply fell into the air like a languid bird.

When it was just me and Mrs. Weber, I crawled back to the stairs and followed her down.

"I do hope you got what you needed, Mr. Hamilton."

"I think... yes, I did, thank you, Mrs. Weber."

"My pleasure. I will have the publicity department send additional information to your publication. Please send her my regards to Pat," she said, leading me out as the stage door closed behind me.

54 ⇻ Real people

My head was full of images of people in flight like beautiful birds. Perfect people, as if minted from the same mold.

I checked to see how much film I had left, plenty. I was strangely hungry again, maybe from a lovely BBQ breeze. I followed the smell to a rustic place that looked like returning to the present.

Long wooden picnic tables filled with people of all shapes, sizes and ages. Roustabouts, policemen, and people in native dress from all over the world: dark African men and women in grass skirts, blond Swiss people in lederhosen, small Japanese men and women in robes, American Indians with painted faces...

All sitting together. Eating together. *Click.*

A brave new world built by united hands and hearts...

"Excuse me, do you speak English?" I asked an African man who had a bee on his shoulder.

"I'ma from Tennessee," he said in an accent that was hard to understand.

"I'm a photographer from *Look* magazine…" I said, maybe too loudly, because people started to approach me. The Japanese were from Bayonne, New Jersey. The Swiss from Brooklyn. The Seminole American Indians from Florida. They were all excited to have their pictures taken but their lunch break was almost over and they had to get back to work.

"We get off at 6," a Japanese woman told me, with a Jersey accent. The others all nodded.

"Meet me at the Trylon at 6:30!" I said, as they waved goodbye.

Soon everyone else was gone, and I was the only one at the picnic table, enjoying the best plate of ribs I'd ever eaten.

I wandered around, looking, so many signs vying for my attention. Oh—there was the Seminole village! I paid a quarter to get in and sat in the bleachers for their show. One of my new friends came out, dramatically posed as if he was looking for something. *Click.*

He pointed! An alligator! Even the men in the audience gasped! He snuck up behind it, then leapt on it! *Click!* He threw his arms around the great monster's mouth (*Click!*) and they wrestled in the stream, twisting and flipping! *Click!* It was thrilling, though I was worried that he'd be eaten and I'd have to take pictures of it. But it didn't happen. He subdued the beast and dragged it off by the tail. The audience applauded wildly. An announcer said, "The brave savage has saved you! Take a picture with him after the show!"

And people did, lining up for a photo of themselves with the brave noble warrior. *Click.* Two nice ladies and a savage! *Click.* A mother dragged her crying daughter towards this strange man who made a funny face at her until she laughed. *Click.*

On their way out, a squaw shook a tip jar that said, "Thank your native friends!" half-filled with quarters, smiling as people dropped in more coins. I dropped a silver dollar and she gave me a thumbs up.

Just over there was the parachute jump! 25 stories tall! *Click.* A boy and girl are kissing on the way down. *Click.* It looked terrifying but I bought a ticket and held tight! Zooming straight up! *Click!* Swaying in the breeze at the top, a great view of the fair. *Click.* And falling, sickeningly!

Oooh, my stomach. I ran to a trash can and heaved, then lay on the grass for a few minutes, watching the clouds and falling asleep...

...I am one of the last few people on earth. Just me and the Seminoles and Japanese and Swedes and Africans I'd met. We're all standing on top of the Perisphere, cold, barren, alone, like on a giant snowball. It's windy and slippery and the only way to stay alive is to stick together, to work together, to hold onto each other for dear life. And we do...

55 ➥ Around The world

Now it was off to Japan. How beautiful everything was here. Orderly. Even the gravel neatly raked in patterns. Little trees and big fish. Beautiful people in colorful Kimonos, seeming to float in their wooden sandals. It smelled of clean wood and smoke and there was soft flute music in the air.

I saw the woman from Bayonne, nodding and taking tickets for a tea ceremony. I bought one and she smiled but didn't speak. I followed the others and sat silently on my knees on grass mats, while the woman carefully made tea. It was very slow, but that gave me plenty of time to lean left and right and arrange her in the viewfinder so she was centered in a window with a view of the sky, like with the divers. *Click.* The simplicity was startling.

Then she poured the tea. *Click.* Gestured to show us how to pick up the cups with both hands. *Click.* The tea was green and foamy. *Click.* I took a sip. Bitter! I looked up at her and smiled. She cupped a pink little candy bird in her both hands. *Click.* She handed it to me and pointed to my mouth. *Click.* I popped it in and it was sweet, then I took another sip of the tea. Ah, now it tasted good!

Back outside in the garden, even though the gravel looked perfect to me, a man in a blue robe gently swept it with a bamboo broom, picking up every little pine needle. *Click.* He walked backwards, pulling a wider broom until everything was perfectly smooth. *Click.* Then he pulled a big rake, making lines in the rock that circled bigger rocks like waves in the water. *Click.*

I was mesmerized. I lay down and shot up at him holding the rake against the sky, the clouds now reminding me of rocks. *Click.* It all made me feel very calm.

I bowed to my new friends, the way they had bowed at everyone, and was off to Switzerland.

The Swiss building reminded me of the Japanese in its simplicity, but all very modern, stone and steel. The sign at the entrance said, "Welcome to the oldest democracy in the world, established 1291."

As soon as I entered the building I was hit with the smell of cheese! Yum! I heard a trio of musicians, one being the man I met earlier. They wore leather shorts with suspenders. One was playing an accordion in an oompa style while another man played the bass and a third sang something fast that went up and down a lot like when my voice was changing. I got down low and shot up, with the doorway framing the sky like in Japan. *Click.* The singer made a funny face. *Click.*

Now, where was that cheese! I found it in an exhibit set in a log cabin. The ladies wore red dresses with white aprons and walked with milk buckets on their heads. *Click.* They poured it into a big copper caldron with a fire under it. *Click.* Two more women stirred the boiling milk. *Click.* A milkmaid led us through ceiling-high stacks of "the world's biggest wheels of cheese!" she said.

We wound up in a room that looked like it was outside because the entire wall was painted with a picture of the alps. A man with a very long horn played it like a trumpet. *Click.*

A pretty girl handed me four bite-sized samples of genuine Swiss cheese made in the real Switzerland. *Click.* She explained the one aged 4 months was a baby cheese, sweet and chewy. The 2 year one, still a baby to me, was harder and "nuttier," at least that's what she called it. I liked 'em all!

The exit went through an exhibit of Swiss watchmaking. "Rolex, the best time pieces in the world," the sign said, but I was kinda partial to my Mickey Mouse watch, which told me it was 5pm and I still had to visit Africa!

The dark continent cost 50 cents to get into. *Frank Buck's Jungleland* had wild animals brought back by Frank 'Bring 'em-Back-Alive' Buck. First stop, Monkey mountain, an 80 foot tall mountain of boulders teeming with 3,000 chimpanzees and orang-utangs. That was a lot of... smelly... monkeys! *Click.* Laugh. *Click.*

I spotted my new friends dancing around a fire while the crowd watched. *Click.* The drums kept pounding faster and faster and the jungle instinct made it hard not to dance myself!

I crouched low and shot up, the sky and clouds once again a heroic background. I wanted to catch their incredible fast and rhythmic motion, so I closed down the aperture to f.32 and set the shutter to a slow ½ a second. *Cliiick. Cliiick.* I could see the action blur in my head.

Then opened the aperture to f.4 and set the shutter to 1/250th of a second to get a sharp shot. *Click... Click... Click.... Click... Click...* No matter how fast I shot I could still see all the individual images inside my head.

When I was done, my friend came right up to me, arms out, big smile. *Click!*

He gestured for me to join the dance circle, along with other audience members and we mimicked their movements. I didn't know what I was doing but it didn't matter, the drums made me move. All of us, African and Americans, joined hands in a circle—though I had to let go with one hand to take pictures. *Click!*

An old grandma in a flowered dress swayed her hips like the dark woman with flowers in her hair. *Click!* A little boy in a Mickey Mouse t-shirt was raised into the air by a tall African with two clumps of hair on his head that looked like Mickey Mouse ears. *Click!*

The drums stopped. I was winded and my feet were sore! My friends rhythmically shook the tip jar full of quarters with a sign that said, "Thank your native friends!" and I dropped in another silver dollar. They smiled. I pointed to the Trylon and they nodded, "Yes!"

Now I had to sit down! I put my feet up on a bench and they pulsed. I felt like I'd walked around the entire world! I went through my film and made sure the exposed rolls were neatly rubber banded in my left pocket, while the fresh rolls, I only had 2, were safely tucked in my right.

I walked back to the Kodak exhibit to buy more film. I saw the "Hall of Color" where giant screens wrapped around the inside of the building with photos and music and narration from the whole world. Beautiful! My favorite was a series that followed the life of a boy from birth through marriage and a honeymoon at Niagara Falls—a life in pictures!

Back to the Trylon and Perisphere, I shot them with growing shadows. My feet were hurting again, so I took off my shoes and socks, rolled up my pant legs and cooled them in the pool at the base. *Click.*

56 -In Their Hands

The Japanese were the first to arrive at 6:30 on the dot. They rolled up their robes at the waist, tucked them under their wide belts and cooled their feet in the water, too. The lady brought a sleeve-full of little candy birds and shared them with me. They were sweet and tasted like flowers.

Next, the Swiss arrived, bearing a paper bag full of cheese. I took a handful, so did the Japanese. We thanked them for the delicious food. They were already wearing shorts, so they just removed their shoes. We all talked about how good the cool water felt.

The Africans arrived with hot dogs for all of us, the hot dog vendor being a friend of theirs who gave them away at the end of the day. Finally, the Seminoles, with strips of what they said was alligator jerky. It was tasty.

This was the nicest picnic. I walked a few steps further into the shallow pool and looked at them all happily eating and chatting. *Click.* They took turns holding up the different foods. *Click.* They put their arms around each other and literally said, "cheese!"*Click!*

I took the African's hand and signaled for everyone to follow me. Together we waded to the base of the Perisphere. From a distance, the giant sphere looked like it was floating on the fountains. Up close, I could see it was supported by columns covered in mirrors.

I guided each friend to stand by a column so the 8 of them were reflected into dozens. *Click.*

Just then, powerful electric lights turned on under the water, illuminating the people from below, making them even more dramatic. *Click!*

I asked them to all reach out towards each other, their arms not quite touching. *Click.*

I had them stand, arms linked in unity, around the front of the Perisphere. *Click.*

Finally, they all stood, arms raised as if they were holding the giant sphere aloft.

Click! Click! Click!

They were holding the whole world in their hands. *Together.* Smiling. *Click.* Laughing. *Click.* Then, as if it was planned, they all looked straight at me, with serious, strong expressions.

CLICK. Tears, first from me, then them. *Click.*

For the first time, I turned the camera on myself with them in the background. This moment was etched into the back of my skull, but I wanted to see it on film, too.

Then they all hugged and jumped up and down. *Click!* I joined them, holding the camera as far away as I could from all of us and pointing it back. *Click.*

I loved these people. I wanted us all to have this beautiful future together.

Two security officers told us we weren't supposed to be in the water. I apologized and mentioned *Look* magazine and took their pictures shaking hands with the people of the world. They were smiling. *Click.*

Everyone said their goodbyes and luckily I thought to stop and asked them to give me their names and addresses so I could send the magazines—if the pictures made it in because that wasn't my decision.

The Japanese were Grace Keiko Kelly Fujitami and Hiro Yatsumoto. They took the train back to New Jersey every night and gave me their address. I wanted to hug them but they bowed and smiled and shuffled away, silhouetted in the sunset. *Click.*

The Swiss were Oscar Pappan and Sophia Zbinden. They were sharing an apartment in Queens with four other Swiss people who worked at the fair. I got their address. We hugged. More silhouettes. *Click.*

The Seminoles were Holata (which meant alligator) and Haiwee (dove). They lived in their huts at the fair because they didn't like sleeping inside. Big, happy hugs. I whispered "Thank you, my beautiful friends" into their ears. They turned back and held their hands up to wave. *Click.*

The Africans were James Madison and Christmas Jones. Frank Buck had a dormitory in the compound where they lived so I could send the magazines in care of him. Christmas gave me a warm hug, then strode away proudly. *Click.*

James and I sat there, looking at the fading sky and glowing sphere. This was all so beautiful I was sad to see it end.

"You touched me," he said, turning to look at me.

"You all touched me," I said.

"I mean..." he looked away. "You held my hand. No, white men ever has," he said, head back, looking at the sky. "Never."

"Oh. I'm sorry."

"I liked that you did," he said, turning back to me, then reaching out for my hand. I took it, and he led me back into the water, through the fountains, to the very base of the giant sphere, just a few feet above us.

He leaned in close and whispered so I could hear over the rush of the water. "You are like me." I could feel his warm breath like a bee's lazy buzzing, and feel his soft lips next to my ear.

"Yes, I like you," I whispered back, my lips brushing his ear.

He wrapped his arms around me and we stood, nose to nose, eye to eye... lips against lips, tongue against tongue—love for my fellow man.

We shared a desire. A need. Not about completion but connection.

"I see you," I said.

"I *feel* you," He whispered.

Then the lights went out. The fountains stopped. All was dark and quiet. I could only see the outline of his face in the glow of the moonlight.

He took my hand again and led me out of the pool.

"We will not see each other again, but I will always remember this. Always." He said, tears glistening on his cheek.

"Why" I asked.

"There is a proverb... 'only walk forward so you do not fall behind,'" he said.

I reached out to wipe away his tears but he brushed my hand aside and shook his head. He kissed his fingers then touched them to my forehead. "Always," he said, walking away with long strides.

It was so quiet I felt like I could hear the buzz of the stars.

57 ➻ Babies in my Pocket

My feet were cold. I put on my socks and shoes and rolled down my pants. I checked my film and added rubber bands to keep it safely wrapped. I thought about how much I liked rubber bands. I thought about how I felt full and happy. I thought about anything other than what just happened.

The exhibits were closed but I could hear music coming from the Amusement Zone. Back in my shoes, my feet hurt again and I didn't want to walk anymore. My focus was on this film. Protecting it, as if I had a dozen babies in my pocket that just had to be born. They just had to be.

It was a long way to the train, so I flagged down a pedal car and paid a whole dollar to ride it back to the station. The buildings glowed, white at the center, stronger colors towards the edges. I smelled doughnuts and pizza and hamburgers and something exotic.

It felt luxurious to glide along, the wind in my hair, thinking about this extraordinary day—And James.

I wouldn't tell Kitty, even if she might understand.

58 ➻ Fellow Man

I called her from the train station.

"25 cents, please," the operator said. I dropped in two dimes (chime) and nickel (a different chime). "I'll connect you."

"Hey, baby, where are you?" she asked.

"Still at the fair, taking pictures for Look.... I threw up."

"Ah, poor thing, you're always so excitable," she said softly, like she was thinking about something else.

"I don't think I should go to the club tonight."

"Frank wouldn't want you near the kitchen if you're puking, I'll tell him now."

"Thanks, baby."

"It's a weekday—nobody important'll be there anyway. See ya later!" she whispered, then hung up.

I had so many pictures stuffed into my head it was hard to stay awake on the train but I kept both hands in my pockets, holding onto the film.

The train came to the end of the line at Grand Central and I woke up. Luckily this is where I changed from the 7 train to the 1. My feet felt like lead all the way up the stairs. I never realized how many stairs there were here.

I waved at the outside doorman but didn't look up. Then at the inside one. Max? Tony? I couldn't remember their names. James.

I went to the bathroom, peed and ran the bath. I dropped my clothes by the bed and sat in the hot, soapy water, leaning back and slipping my head under, holding my breath as long as I could.

I dried myself a little but felt too tired and lay on the bed, feeling the heat rise off me. Indians. Japanese. Swiss. Africans... African.

Was that queer? Or just love for my fellow man?

59 ➽ Still Life with Glenn

I didn't even hear Kitty come home or take a shower. I didn't feel her get into bed with me. I just felt the sun on my face and woke up. My entire body felt stiff. *All* of it. I rolled out of bed, stretched and went to pee, then looked at myself in the mirror.

I looked like a nice enough person. Kinda like the person I'd always been. Kinda not. Scruffy, I needed to shave.

Kitty shuffled into the bathroom, her eyes half closed. She sat on the toilet as if I wasn't even there. I'd never seen her pee before. I'd never even thought about her having to pee. I watched her, eyes closed, touching her neck while tinkling.

I thought about the first time I saw her, how mature she seemed. And now, how like a little girl. Made me a little embarrassed to think of the things we'd done together. She got up, kissed me on the back of the neck and went back to bed.

My stomach rumbled. I called for some oatmeal and peaches ala mode because it sounded soothing. 6:00 am. Too early to call Glen, but I was so excited to see the pictures, and even a little worried for every minute they went undeveloped.

Bell. Breakfast, pretty with the sun streaming on it. *Click.* Delicious. I took a shot of the empty bowl—abstract. *Click.*

Might as well use up the rest of the roll. Kitty could sleep with the sun on her face. *Click.* How pretty she was without makeup. *Click.* Her soft arms over the sheet, exposing her breast. *Click.* Like she was carved out of marble. *Click.* Somehow untouchable now.

Was that a hickey on her neck? Had I given it to her? *Click.*

The room felt stuffy. I checked the vent and it was blowing cold air, but I went to the window anyway to open it, stick my head out and breathe the warm, humid air.

7am. I didn't care. I called Glenn. No answer. I'd go over and pound on his door.

"Morning Ellis." He yawned back at me. "Morning Sam," I said, holding up a handful of film. "Morning Max," I said, fetching my bike myself.

I felt bad waking Glenn, but not that bad—he was my agent! I knocked on the glass door. Nothing. Louder. Nothing. I yelled through the letter slot, "Get up, you sloth!" then saw his striped PJs and bare feet shuffle to the door.

"Aw, Herb. Why can't you just jack off and sleep in like a normal guy?" he said, grumpily unlocking the door.

"Sorry, Glenn, but I got so much film and it's really important!"

"There'd better be at least one boob."

"There's one—a really good one."

"In that case, come in."

"We're gonna save the world, Glenn," I said excitedly.

"One boob at a time?"

"No, I mean it. World unity!"

"Jesus, you're serious."

"I got 16 rolls, we better get started."

Glenn pulled out all his developing tanks. I told him everything that happened... *almost* everything that happened... sometimes he nodded and sometimes I thought he'd fallen asleep but that was OK, the timer went off and he woke up.

He unrolled the first batch of wet film and spotted the shots of Kitty from this morning.

"Damn fine boob, thank you. Your Kitty's an unusual girl. I looked at those shots you took before, she's got something odd down below..."

"What're you talking about?" I protested.

"OK, OK, don't get worked up... besides, I can retouch it."

While I didn't like someone else looking at her, I knew many had and somehow it didn't bother me as much as it might have before. "She's perfect!"

"Yeah, in this picture, she is. Skin like a peach!" He looked at more shots. "What's with all them foreigners?"

"That's the whole point, it's what Pat asked for."

"Who am I to question the great and powerful Pat Whyte? If she asked for it, then it must be important. Let's start the next batch," he said, sounding awake now.

I finished extolling the virtues of the fair and the wonders of its people.

"Now I feel like I don't even need to see the pictures," he said, yawning again as the timer hands seemed to move in slow motion. I looked at the negatives, hanging, and was relieved to see that they showed what I remembered. The subway people. Escalator people. Divers, hanging in space. Not just imagined. Not just in my brain. But on film.

The timer went off and we rinsed the next batch of 8 rolls. Seminole. Switzerland. Japan. Africa. Perisphere.

Glenn held up a loupe and studied them up close. "I'm sure glad I lent you the Leica, these are beautiful, man. Wow, I love the framing. The sharpness of the Zeiss lens. What was that, 1/1000th of a second?"

I nodded.

"If Pat doesn't love these then she's not the dame I think she is. Roger would buy the entire diver series from you, even with them wearing swimsuits and all. Gorgeous ladies and you can see their nipples."

"Is it always about boobs?"

"Not always, but you can't fault a guy for looking."

"Can I use your phone? I want to call Pat."

"Be my guest. I'll dry these and put 'em in glassines for you. But I'm holding onto the ones of Kitty!"

"I wouldn't want Pat to see them anyway."

I called Pat's office. Louise answered. "Hello Mr. Hamilton. I'll check her schedule. She has a 1:15 if that works for you."

"Yes, thank you, Louise."

"Thank you, Mr. Hamilton. See you this afternoon.

Suddenly I was nervous again. Glenn laid the negatives out on a light table and we took turns looking at them. He couldn't keep his eyes off the divers. "These are art, man!"

I couldn't keep my eyes off the group holding the world in their hands. "But don't you think these are... I dunno, more important."

"They're just normal people, Herb."

"Exactly!"

"People of the world, unite, right?" he seemed unsure.

"Exactly!"

"Me, I like the pretty stuff. I like the textures and contrast, the way the sun hits their skin, how half her body is in shadow against the sky. How the cloud seems to caress her."

I looked again. Yes, it was pretty. I liked it, too. But it was just shapes, not stories.

"And this one you got here, shadows of the Perisphere. It's not even like a photo anymore, it's like a painting. This is pure abstract modern art!"

I looked at it again. I had to admit I did like that. It wasn't the thing, but the effect of the thing— the mark it made, no matter how temporary, frozen in time.

They all were—moments, frozen in time. Like memories.

Glenn's stomach rumbled. "I need some cereal."

"Naw, I'm gonna take you out for the biggest breakfast you ever had."

That's how we ended up a few blocks away at Barney Greengrass, whose slogan was "If you can finish your meal, we've done something wrong."

"Corned beef hash, crisp, eggs sunny side up, bagel schmear—for both of us." Glenn ordered.

"What if that's not what I wanted?" I asked, surprised.

"You want it."

"Yeah, as soon as you said it, I wanted it." And I did. The shadow of the water glass made a series of ripples on the table. *Click.*

"So what goes on inside that head of yours, Herb?"

"What kind of question is that?" I asked, mid-bite of a dill pickle.

"Like that you just took. What'd you see?"

"It was right there, you saw it, too. Shadows."

"I need to set up something and study it. A still life, really look at it. In the studio," he said, staring at the table. "You see everything."

"Nobody sees everything."

"I wish I had x-ray vision so I could see through clothes. I bought a pair of those spiral glasses from the back of a Bat-Man comic and they didn't do shit."

The waitress slid dishes onto the table. It all looked so good. It all tasted so good, but Glenn just sat there, staring at it so I stopped eating. "What's up with you?" I asked.

"That check you gave me."

"What about it?" I asked, not being able to resist the crispy edge of the hash.

"I feel bad. That's more than I make in a month and you just gave it to me."

"You earned it. You're my agent."

"Yeah, some agent," he sighed, poking at his eggs till the yoke spread over the hash.

"Damn right, some agent! You taught me about cameras and what a portfolio was! I didn't know what she was talking about with the business stuff."

"Yeah, OK, I know some things. But I'm supposed to be the lensman."

"All you've ever shown me was your nudie stuff. It's very artistic, but..."

He blurted out, "I shoot flowers. That's why. Who wants to see pictures of flowers?"

"People who love flowers? I mean, everybody loves flowers."

"And fruit and vegetables."

"I like fruit. Some vegetables."

"Well, now you know," he said, finally taking a bite of his breakfast. "Damn, this is good."

We ate in silence. I couldn't finish all mine but Glenn just plugged away, eating all his and cleaning my plate, too, mopping it up with a bagel.

"Next time you should show Pat your work. I'll bet she likes flowers. And fruit. And vegetables. A lot."

"Yeah, maybe." he said, eking out a smile. "Sorry, I know I can get moody. Thanks for breakfast."

"Thanks for helping me."

My feet still hurt as we walked back to Fine's Fotos.

Glenn showed me some of his photos of flowers and fruit. The lighting was so beautiful it was like my eyes could *smell* them, *feel* them. "These are gorgeous, Glenn. I never saw flowers this way. Or grapes. Or squash."

"You don't have to say that, Herb."

"I mean it. I remember seeing paintings like this at the Met."

"Dutch masters, yeah, I love 'em." He pulled out another print, this one of a woman's hand holding a piece of jewelry, a spiral of diamonds that sparkled into the lens—scattering circles of light like speeding stars in Buck Rogers.

"Wow. That's... like magic."

"Naw, it's just a kicker light, but I like the way it turned out."

"OK, so how about this deal: I'll be *your* agent and take 25%!"

"You gotta deal," he said, shaking on it.

"I'll talk you up to Pat, she's gonna love these."

60 ➤ Green Eyed Monster

I biked back to the Ansonia. Kitty was still asleep. I wanted to wake her up and screw her, even after what happened last night. Instead, I just watched her sleep.

Then I thought about how she sounded distracted on the phone. Why was she whispering?

A memory picture flashed up from the back of my head, her laughing with Frank. His arm around her. The way she touched his lapels. She was just kissing up for her job, that's all. Being nice to the boss. That's all.

And then the hickey.

Why'd I care so much? Did I love her? Did she love me? The more I knew her the less I knew.

The phone rang and I grabbed it so it wouldn't wake her up.

"Mr. Hamilton? This is Louise at *Look*. I'm sorry for the late notice but Pat needs to push your meeting back to 4:30. I hope that's not a problem for you."

"Oh, no, I mean, of course not, that's fine. Thank you for calling."

I was disappointed but glad she could still see me today. What was I going to do all day? I was tired... I took off my clothes and got in bed. Ah, that felt good. Kitty rolled over and snuggled up to me, feeling all soft and warm. I got all hard and hot. She reached around and wrapped her hand around my cock.

"There's my big boy!" she whispered in my ear.

61 ➺ Sex. Saks.

All was forgotten as she guided me inside her and clung to me tightly until we merged.

I slept like a rock.

Woke up at 2:30. Plenty of time. Took a shower.

Looked through the negatives and thought about sorting them in order of what I thought of best... but then I thought, "Maybe I should save the best for last." So I kept them in the order I took them. I thought Glenn removed the shots of Kitty, still, I'd better double check as I didn't want Pat to see them.

But *I* could still see them in my head. Glenn called her a peach. Maybe that's why I wanted them this morning—and her.

Now that I was a man of means it seemed like a good time to buy some new clothes so I could wear something sharp for this meeting.

I put a bunch of rubber bands around the box of negatives to keep it closed, then tried to figure out where to go to buy a new suit. There was really only one person and place I knew would do the best for me, Myron at Shapiro's. But it was in the opposite direction and there wasn't time right now.

Maybe a new shirt and tie. Macy's? Gimbal's? Bloomingdales? No, it was Saks' windows that helped me get here, so that's where I'd go.

The windows were still there, people leaf peeping at the colorful mannequins. I didn't even take another picture here. I took the elevator straight to the fifth floor, the men's department.

"How may I help you, sir?" asked an older man in a perfectly-fitting dark suit with a long jacket that made him look like a butler.

"I have an important meeting and require a new shirt and tie."

"Of course, sir, we have the finest selection in the city, it will be my pleasure to serve you," he said, extending his arm and pointing the way. He went behind the counter and looked me up and down. "16 regular. Do you prefer an oxford, pinpoint, poplin, broadcloth or stripe, sir?"

He slid them out of their cellophane so I could see and touch them. "Do you have something in blue?"

"Of course sir," he said, pulling out a selection of shirts so light blue they were almost white.

"I want a stronger blue?" I asked. He grimaced the tiniest bit (it was comic and I would have taken a picture if I could). Then he walked from behind that counter and crossed the floor. I followed. The sign above this department said, "Hot Mikado."

"Our newest line for the... young... adventurous spirit," he said, as if the words tasted bad in his mouth. But the shirts were beautiful, bold hues of blue and orange, the colors of the fair! I remembered seeing signs for the Jazzy Hot Mikado musical at the fair. Wide stripes and big polka dots! Wow, I really wanted one of these.

The salesman pulled out a tray of ties in likewise bold colors, but one stood out—cream silk with a watercolor painting of the Trylon and Perisphere. I pointed to it. "A... fine choice... sir, hand painted."

I pointed at a bold blue shirt which reminded me of the color of the sky yesterday. "Will Sir be wearing these today?" he asked, sounding more like an order.

"Yes, thank you." I went into the changing room and put them on —though never taking the Leica from around my neck. Oh, the color! I felt... adventurous! *Click.*

"To complete the..." he cleared his throat, "...ensemble, might I suggest a suitable bag, such as this jaunty hunter green canvas stowaway bag trimmed in fine Italian saddle leather. Large enough for your golf shoes... or boxes... tucks into its trim canvas envelope between times."

Isabel gingerly placed the necklace in the box, then inserted the box into a clear pneumatic tube that whisked it away with a loud suck!

I wrote "Twenty six dollars and fifty cents," much easier this time, and signed with a flourish!

There was a pop in the pneumatic tube and a gift wrapped box appeared as if by magic. Isabel presented it to me, metallic silver paper with midnight blue flocked stars, topped by a wide blue satin ribbon bow. I unbuckled my new bag and slipped the package in.

Everything fit so neatly, so elegantly.

Including me.

63 ➤➤➤ Pride and Shame

4pm. A half hour to get to Pat's. A beautiful blue sky. A beautiful blue shirt. I felt straight and tall as I walked down Fifth Ave with the other fashionable people. I saw people looking at me. I imagined them thinking, "Who is that man in the blue shirt with the green bag, he must be *somebody*!"

I *was* somebody. I was a successful photographer, walking to meet my editor, the famous Pat Whyte!

It was only when I reached 42nd street that I stopped and felt myself sweat. No, no, no, I can't sweat in this shirt! I had on an undershirt, of course, but no. I stood over a subway grate and let the air shoot up into the cuffs of my pants and under my arms.

I stood there, looking around at the big buildings all around, at the people all around.

I was back in reality. Where had I been? My own little world where it was all about me. About shirts and ties and dueling pistols and necklaces... It was like I'd been under the spell of shopping. I looked at the bag in my hands, still beautiful with its leather trim., my shirt, still deep blue and tie, with its symbol of the World of Tomorrow. It all looked good—and I felt bad. $22.50 and $26.50. Almost $50. More than a month's rent in the Bronx.

I felt ashamed. And, worse, I felt happy. Happy these things were mine. I remembered that I'd sent Ma $100, twice what I'd spent on myself—and spent more on Kitty than on myself, too.

A scowling man in a black trench coat shoved me off the grate so he could stand there. I was back at the corner of Fifth and 42nd.

I turned left onto 42nd and looked up at the Chrysler Building, that shining beacon.

64 ➽ Framing the Narrative

I got to the office early. The 50th floor didn't seem so high anymore.

Louise smiled as she asked me to wait. "Spiffy!" she said, assessing my outfit.

"Thank you, Louise," I replied, smiling back.

I unbuckled my bag and looked at the starry silver package for Kitty, the shiny pistol lighter for myself. Maybe I'd have to take up smoking. That would look artistic and sophisticated.

"Pat can see you now," Louise said, opening the door.

Pat was standing, wearing a gray plaid suit jacket and shirt, white shirt with blue tie and blue shoes. She walked up to me and shook my hand. "Good to see you, Herb. My, don't you look natty!"

"Thank you. So do you," I offered.

"Let's see what you've got."

I lifted the negative box out my bag and placed it on her desk. She put on her white gloves, flipped the switch to light up her desk top, then laid negatives out over the whole surface.

"They're in the order I took them," I added, in case she was wondering or in case it mattered, I didn't know.

"I see. On the way to the fair... good candids if not special... Trylon and Perisphere, nice shading but there are a million like these... I like the shots of the boy through the eyeball," she said, pulling it to the left edge of her desk. "I haven't seen this 'all the same under the skin,' mural. Good background image and pull quote."

She started stacking the images of Democracity and the robot in a new pile, "These are all fine, but they just retell someone else's fictional narrative and we want to tell our own story. That's not a criticism, simply words of advice."

She leaned into the look at the divers under her magnifying glass. "Diving. Lovely images. A bit anodyne." I didn't know what she meant.

"Thank you?"

"Beautifully shot... but, dry, no pun intended."

"None taken," I said and she looked up and smiled, and put the divers in another pile and moved them to the left with the eyeball negatives.

"Still, something the other editors would go for. Ah, but these at the picnic... such varied and interesting people. Indians! Yes! Crocodile... or is that alligator? And this one of the natives and a grandma, all smiles. charming. Good." She slid a few more to the left.

"Japan, beautiful... oh, I see what you're doing now. You saw the divers as heros but these are the real heroes."

"Yes!" I was so excited that she understood.

"I can see it from the framing and sky, like the divers. Ah, the Swiss... We'll see how that neutrality works for them against Hitler. Still, I like the images, especially the singer making a funny face. Reminds me of my ex-husband."

She slid that one image to the left. "Monkeys, cute, but no. Africans, yes! Movement, yes! A motion series, yes!" she scooped them up and slid them left. "Mickey Mouse boy and native... fine juxtaposition. These are good, Herb."

Now she was at the series of my friends coming together at the Perisphere. She studied them, not saying anything. She swallowed, hard, and sat in her chair, tears in her eyes. "I am at a loss for words."

"They're really nice people!" I said.

"I can see that. More than that, I can *feel* it. That's why I do this. That's what this is all for." She stood up and walked towards me. "I could just kiss you," she said, reaching her small arms around me and giving me a hug. I wasn't sure what to do, should I hug her back? I did.

She let go and I let go and she went back behind her desk. I handed her the list of their names and addresses which I'd tucked into the box. "I got all their names and said if you used the pictures maybe you could send them a copy."

"Good for the captions. Of course we'll send them copies." She put them all in a pile and slid them to the top left of her desk. "I like the one of you with them, too. You're part of it. Good."

"I wrote down a proverb that the African man... James... told me, 'only walk forward so you don't fall behind.'"

"I rarely say this... except maybe to you... but you have exceeded my expectations, young man."

"Thank you!"

"So, no more freelance work for you."

I was confused. "But if I did a good job..."

"Great job—Great."

"Then why no more work..."

"No more *freelance*. I'm putting you on staff with a weekly salary."

"Oh, I didn't understand. Wow. I'm already working at the Copa..."

"Really? You'd rather do that?"

"No, of course not, I just have to quit... though I was never really hired, I guess."

"I'll have Louise draw up the papers for... speaking of which, where is your cute little agent man?"

"Oh, you like fruits and flowers, right? And vegetables?"

"What? Yes... why?"

"You should look at his portfolio because he does beautiful still life work. Fruits, flowers, jewelry and stuff. Like old Dutch Masters and I'm not just saying it."

"I take your word on it. Have him set up an appointment with Louise to review your contract and to view his work."

"Thank you, Pat. Thank you for everything. I feel like I have a reason now. For being."

She arranged the negatives. "You absolutely do. *We* do, together. I have plans for you. I need to know I can trust you, completely."

"Yes! Of course."

"I'm working on something... secret. I'll need you to sign this confidentiality agreement. It says that there are some things we talk about that you will not reveal anyone else. That means Glenn. That even means Kitty," she said, sliding a paper across her desk.

"I'm good at keeping secrets. I've seen a lot of spy movies..." I read the two paragraphs which simply said, "I, the undersigned, agree not to discuss, reveal, write or otherwise communicate anything I discuss, learn, discover with anyone outside the office of Pat Whyte or her specified associates."

"I agree that by doing so, I could cause serious harm to all parties involved, including myself, as well as the government, and that I will be held personally responsible in every legal way, including potential incarceration. I enter into this agreement willingly and any information shared while this is active will now, and forever be kept secret and confidential."

"Thank you for trusting me," I signed it. Willingly.

"Thank you for signing it. For your first assignment. I need you to go back to the World's Fair. There are a few specific photos I need at the British Pavilion. One is of a German parachute used to drop mines in the English Channel."

"That sounds terrible."

"It is. Your photos show the happy side of world unity. I also want to show our readers what's already happening when we hate instead of connect."

"I want to show that, too."

"Good. You need to be there tomorrow, July 4th, in the afternoon. I've heard whispers that something might happen at the British Pavilion, something the world should see. Something you can show them. You must be outside, at a safe distance by 4pm. I want to make it clear that this could be dangerous. Is that clear."

"Yes, at a safe distance by four."

"This is not just about you and me. It's bigger than all of us. You understand that?"

"I understand."

She spotted one last negative lying flat in the bottom of the box and put it on the table.

It was Kitty, in bed! Oh, no! Glenn had forgotten it! Oh, no! Pat leaned in. Luckily it was just Kitty's face.

"Um, sorry, that was just for me... it's my girl, Kitty."

"I remember her from your first set. Lovely. Unusual. This gives me an idea for a framing device."

"You want to frame her?"

"A narrative framing device. A way for our American readers to enter into this story, to see it from her point of view. Pretty girl, goes to the fair, meets all these lovely people... a sweet sugar coating. An easy sell to the male editors and the readers will eat it up. Have her interact with the same people if possible, but don't recreate anything you've already done. I seem to remember she had a dress with cherries on it, that would work, and sensible all-American girl shoes. Would she do that?"

"I'm sure she would if I asked."

"We'll pay her a modeling fee, too, of course. But remember, you cannot tell her anything else. And make sure she's as far away from the British Pavilion as she can be."

"I cross my heart, hope to die."

"I hope you don't. Thank you, Herb. I know you will live up to my trust."

I leaned over her desk and shook her hand. "I don't know what I did to deserve this..."

Pat smiled and looked me right in the eye, "You started with an open heart, and that opened your eyes." She picked up the phone, "Louise, please send a staff photographer contract to Mr. Hamilton's agent and set up a meeting with him to review it... and his own portfolio," she winked at me.

She pointed to the negatives on her desk, "I'll hold onto these for now," and I nodded. "Bring the film with your girl to me tomorrow night, we'll develop these in house. "

I wasn't sure what to make of all this, except I felt a level of excitement I normally only felt during a movie! I picked up my green canvas stowaway bag, the genuine leather handles felt good in my hand. I turned around to Pat, "Thank you.... I... Thank you."

65 ➻ Unbelievable

I went straight to Glenn and told him about the contract. I realized I never asked how much I was getting paid.

"I can't believe it!" he said, his voice sounding high.

"It's true—And she wants to see your portfolio!"

"I can't believe it!" his voice was even higher.

"It's true!"

He just kept shaking his head. "I don't know which one is more unbelievable!" he squeaked.

"And Pat wants Kitty to be my model at the fair..."

"Now, that I believe." His voice was low again.

"You'll believe it when you call Louise and set up an appointment."

Glenn didn't waste a second, he picked up the phone, almost panting. I heard Louise at the other end and Glenn, now very calm, said, "This is Glenn Fine calling to schedule an appointment with Pat Whyte... yes, tomorrow at 10am works for me, thank you. I will bring it along. Thank you, Louise." He hung up, paused, looked satisfied, then screamed at the top of his lungs, "I BELIEVE!"

"OK, Herb, I've got a lot of work to do before I meet with Pat, I'm going to reprint all of these... and I need a haircut and shave..." He seemed off in his own little world.

"I'm going home to tell Kitty the great news," I said, without him taking much notice.

Outside, I looked through the windows and watched him jumping for joy.

66 »→ Horror and Joy

I brought in the three newspapers outside Kitty's door. She was still asleep, so I had time to read the papers rather than just looking at the pictures.

"The passenger ship Arandora Star was heading for Canada transporting German and Italian internees and prisoners of war when she was torpedoed and sunk west of Ireland by a German submarine. 865 lives were lost."

I was shocked, even more so when I read for the first time, about Buchenwald, a concentration camp... for Jews... who were no longer considered French citizens...

This had been going on for three years and I hadn't known? I felt ashamed. But I wasn't alone in having not seen it. That's what I was helping Pat with... even though I couldn't talk about it.

Tomorrow was Thursday. Kitty wouldn't have a late show on Wednesday so we'd go to bed early and wake up early. Otherwise she'd sleep the day away. Like now, when I have so much to tell her! And not tell her!

And, oh, her present!

I ordered lunch, a Reuben on Rye with fries and a Coke—and a slice of chocolate cake to celebrate! The bell rang. The food appeared in the dumbwaiter on a silver tray. I carried it into the bedroom and waved the cake near Kitty's face until a little bit of frosting stuck to the tip of her nose. Her little pink tongue licked it away, then her eyes fluttered open, looking around.

"What're you..." she whispered, then, "Oh, cake!" and opened her mouth. I guided a forkful into it and she licked it clean. "Good morning to you, too, baby!"

"I've got great news—for both of us!"

"Another bite, baby." I gave her another. "Sweet way to wake up."

"I'm now an official staff photographer for *Look* Magazine!"

"More..." She took the plate and fork from my hand and took a big bite. "That's wonderful news, congratulations, baby."

"And you're going to be my model at the fair tomorrow!"

"I'm going to get my picture in a magazine?"

"Yes!"

"You done good, boy!"

"I did, didn't I? And I've got a present for you!"

She put the cake plate on the bed and held out her hands, expectantly and closed her eyes. I dashed into the living room and brought back the silver package covered in blue stars, placing it in her waiting hands. She kept her eyes closed and felt the package, shaking it.

"What is it?" She asked.

"Open it and see."

She tore at the wrapping like a tigress, shredding the silver paper and blue stars with her fingernails, sending flecks flying. Inside was a black box with "Saks Fifth Ave" in silver script.

Off flew the box top, pink tissue paper filled the air like clouds, landing softly on the bed until... there it was—the necklace—Five red stones on curled chrome.

She was momentarily frozen. "This is... this is... gorgeous. Something for a real lady!"

"You are *my* real lady, Kitty!"

She lifted it from the box and looked closely, then smelled it. "It even smells fancy."

"It's from Austria."

She held the necklace up with one hand and watched the light sparkle through the stones. Her eyes lit up, "I saw Joan Crawford wearing this very necklace last week at the club!" she exclaimed, so excited she put her other hand right into the chocolate cake. She started laughing, reaching out to me with her cake-covered hand.

She grabbed my neck and pulled me close, kissing me and covering me with frosting. It was sweet. The frosting. And Kitty. We made messy, chocolate covered love, slept, then shared the Reuben, cold fries and a shower.

She was still drying off when I placed the necklace around her neck and watched her cheeks glow as the stones reflected up from the chrome. She dropped her towel and stood there, naked, but for the necklace. "Take a picture," she said.

CLICK.

I was sure the picture couldn't possibly have looked any better, though we kept trying, with one of her lounging on the bed, the sunlight sending sparkles shimmering through the stones that lit up her breasts—that took the cake!

67 ➺ Bulb

That night, everything that had seemed so exotic about the Copa felt so familiar. The doorman, the stairs, the smoke and perfume, the hallways and dressing room and greasy kitchen floor. Even seeing the Wicked Witch Margaret Hamilon laughing with the always affable Guy Kibbee didn't strike me as unusual. *Click.*

I found Frank behind the bar, checking receipts.

"Excuse me, Mr. Costello, I need to talk to you."

"Yeah What?" he said, without taking his eyes off the papers.

"I gotta quit... sir."

"Why?"

"I got a job... at a magazine."

"Just so long as it's not another club."

"Nope. Never."

"Whata we owe you?"

"Oh, I don't... it's me who owes you, sir. Thank you."

"Momma'll miss you," he growled.

"Um, yeah, me, too..."

I backed away, hitting a waiter, and feeling a drink spill down my back. Frank looked me in the eye and smiled.

A drumbeat started, then trumpets, as the line of girls shimmied onstage, led by Kitty. *Click.* They snaked through the crowd, the girls teasingly playing with the men's hair as they passed. *Click.* Smoke and smiles and a pounding beat made the place come alive.

Yet I felt strangely quiet. People swirled around me. I was still. I set the camera's aperture down to f.16 and put the shutter on "bulb," where it would stay open as long as I held it down. *Cliiiiiick.*

I let the world dissolve into a blur. The camera would see more than the moment, it would capture the passing of time and people. Our little paths from here to there leading... where?

Paths around me. Passing, but not intersecting. *Cliiiiiick.*

And me, in the middle, hurtling towards who I wanted to be, who I would be... who I really was.

Later I sat in an empty dressing room, closed my eyes and just listened—listened to how it all looked.

68 ➺ Ready

I felt a hand shaking me. "I'm ready." It was Kitty, taking my hand. I looked up at her face and smiled, then felt sad.

For the very first time, I wondered if I was seeing something for the last time.

69 ➥ Higher

She went right to sleep. I watched her. I looked up at the stars. These rooms, which had felt so cozy and safe, now only felt a tiny part of a big menacing world—one ominous sky covering us all...

...I dreamed I was in the *Explorer* helium balloon that went higher than anyone had ever gone before. I watched through the porthole as the earth grew small below me, keeping my eye on the spot where Kitty was. The world looked like the model city at the fair, then a patchwork of green and brown squares, until it looked like a modern painting in a museum.

I'd lost track of the point where Kitty was. There was no way to find her in this big world made small.

Then I heard an explosion and looked up. The balloon was in flames and I was falling, plummeting back to earth...

I woke up, sweating. Kitty was still next to me. Smiling in her dreams.

70 ➥ Early Bird

Morning hit me in the face. Kitty wasn't in bed. I heard the shower running. A breakfast tray was sitting on the bed. Eggs and pancakes and bacon and bagels and coffee. I was so hungry I pulled it onto my lap and ate in bed, happily letting the egg drip down my chin to my chest.

Kitty emerged from the bathroom, wrapped in a towel like Jean Harlow in "Goddess, Mine," where she uses a love potion to make Clark Gable fall in love with her so she didn't have to go back to the past.

"Hurry up, sleepy head," she teased me, messing my hair.

I mopped up the last of the eggs with the bagel and gulped down some cocoa, forcing the big lump of bagel down my gullet. 8am? I jumped in the shower and by the time I was out Kitty had finished her makeup.

"How do I look?" she asked.

"Always beautiful!" I said, leaning in to kiss her. She turned her face and pointed to her cheek, so that's where I kissed. I'd kiss any part of her.

"I thought we'd get an early start so you can get plenty of shots of me looking fresh!" she patted my butt and pushed me out of the bathroom.

I scrambled through the drawers, trying to figure out what to wear to look suitably professional. I knew I would wear a hat today, to proudly display my official blue and orange press pass! But I needed to wear more than that! I'd wear my gray suit with my blue and orange diamond tie! Drat! The pants were getting a little short. I rolled down the cuff and flattened it out. There.

I looked up and saw Kitty, in her familiar white dress with the cherries. Yet today she looked especially glamorous. I reached around her waist and held her very tight.

"My God!" she said.

"My Goddess!"

71 ➡ 4th of July

It was hard to see anything but Kitty as we headed towards the fair. The subway was packed with holiday makers but it felt like everything in the world was merely a backdrop for her. The song, "I only have eyes for you," was playing in my head.

"Oh, pretty!" she exclaimed, stepping out on the platform, pointing at the gleaming Trylon and Perisphere. I saw the sunlight shining off her hair and joy on her face as she cheated towards the camera. *Click.*

Last night she'd been a showgirl. This morning a Goddess. Now she was a wholesome All-American girl.

As we walked towards the Trylon, she stopped, pointed and laughed. *Click.* All carefully posed yet seemingly candid. She sat on a bench and shook a pebble from her shoe. *Click.* She bought a pretzel from a moustachioed vendor, then took a big bite (and handed me the rest).

She coyly licked an ice cream cone while letting the cream run down her fingers. *Click.* Then tried handing it to me but I didn't want to touch it because I couldn't have sticky fingers! She turned and handed it to a little boy behind his mother's back. *Click!*

We visited Japan and were told my friends no longer worked there. That seemed odd. But Kitty liked dressing up in a Kimono *(click)* and learning how to use a Japanese fan *(click)*.

The swiss showed her how to blow one of the long Swiss horns *(click)*. She was always beautiful but these shots were boring.

It was off to the Seminole Village where her look of utter horror at the Alligator was all too real (*Click!*). Holata and Haiwee were both there and happy to meet Kitty. They wrapped a giant python snake around her (carefully holding its head and tail). She wasn't scared, it was all smiles and snakes *(click)* until I asked her to act frightened and suddenly she was Fay Wray in King Kong *(click)*.

Next we visited *Frank Buck's Jungle Land* where James and Christmas spotted me and ran over.

"Hi, James, this is my girl, Kitty," I said, preemptively.

James gave me a penetrating look, interrupted by Christmas holding up a finger with a gold ring on it. "James and I got engaged!" she laughed, and it was my turn to stare at him.

We both shrugged, then gave each other a big hug. It was lunchtime, so we went to the BBQ place and ate and talked and laughed like two normal, happy couples. Because, maybe this was normal. I didn't know from anything else.

Back in Africa, James triumphantly held Kitty aloft over his head. I comically tried to lift Christmas... She ended up carrying me like a baby *(Kitty clicks)*. More hugs all around. I hoped we could stay in touch.

Kitty napped on the grass in the triangular shade of the Trylon. *Click.*

I checked the time. 3:30pm.

"I've got to go take some dull pictures of fair officials. That won't be any fun for you, so this is a good time to get in line for *Democracity*—then the *Futurama*—you don't want to miss seeing the future!"

"Oh, but I wanted to have a real English tea, in Merry Ole England!"

"You can't! No, I mean, it's not a good idea." I desperately tried to dissuade her by making up a story, "I read that the English don't have refrigerators so their cream can go bad and you can get food poisoning and puke for days!"

"That can't be right, Herb. Let's go have a fancy tea!"

"No, I can't do that now, and you have to promise me you won't, either, OK? I mean, really promise you won't go anywhere near there, please, please promise me!"

"You're being very odd, baby."

"Promise me!"

"Very odd. But I promise."

"Good... I just... I just have a feeling... I don't want you to miss out on the future!"

"Yeah, I would like to see the future, after all, it's where we'll be spending the rest of our lives," she said, giving me a sweet, soft kiss. "OK, you go take your boring photos."

"I'll meet you back here... at 5. OK. Right here."

"Right here. Mr. Mystery. You're not meeting another girl here, are you?"

"Girl? No. Don't be silly. There's no other girl for me. Go have fun—in the future!"

She walked away, turned and blew me a kiss. *Click.*

I walked to England and stood outside the pavilion, my heart pounding.

72 ➣ Blowup

I didn't even know what I was supposed to be looking for, other than danger. But how did danger look? Like Greta Garbo as "Mata Hari," the exotic dancer accused of spying for Germany during World War I? Or did it look like "Confessions of a Nazi Spy," where Edward G. Robinson was an FBI agent investigating the espionage activities of the German-American Bund? I didn't know—I didn't see the Nazi spy movie because I wasn't interested at the time.

I sat on a bench a safe distance away from the British Pavilion and kept my eyes peeled. I felt my eyelids get heavy. Oh, no, I couldn't be sleepy now. I was excited and worried, scared... and sleepy!

I yawned, and when my mouth finally closed, I saw a cluster of men—running. One was carrying a canvas workman's bag, the others had formed a circle around him.

My nerves instantly jolted me to attention and I chased after them, keeping my distance. They ran past the former Polish pavilion, closed after Germany invaded.

The men stood in an empty plaza and spread out under a large maple tree. An ambulance arrived and a nurse got out. A policeman made me back away. I showed him my press pass. Didn't matter. "Stay back," he told me. *Click.*

Two men inspected the bag. "It's the business," I heard one say. *Click.* BOOM.

A bright flash of light and choking smoke—my ears rang, my eyes stung.

I rubbed my eyes. The smoke cleared. The men were gone. *Click.* Disappeared. Like a Houdini trick. All that was left was a big hole in the ground. *Click.* Another man was flat on his face, his back covered in blood. *Click.*

People were frozen in shock. My eyes searched for some sign of the two men. There was nothing but black around where they were, even the tree that was in bloom was now black and bare... except... for a charred human arm, dangling from a branch, just under a blackened American flag.

No. I couldn't. I looked away.

Then I remembered why I was here. I forced myself to think back on the boy and the duck. The camera felt so heavy. I lifted it. *Click*.

77 ⇝ Sparks

More police arrived from the 'Bomb and Forgery Squad.' They put up ropes and cleared the area. I pointed to my press pass, but a cop said, "Nothing to see here, keep moving."

It was only now that I could feel how hard my heart was pounding and how I sweated through my shirts. I watched while two, or three men died—those images burned into my brain, forever. Men with lives and families one second, then completely gone in the blink of an eye.

Who could have done such a thing? The same heinous villains who were planting mines— The Nazis. Those two men gave their lives to save the hundreds of innocent *American* people having tea in the Pavilion. Kitty would have been one of them!

Nobody was safe.

I felt very, very small, and yet... I also felt a spark ignite inside me. Maybe, just maybe, my spark could help light a larger flame of hope and justice.

I felt the weight of the world yet simultaneously lighter. I took off my jacket, tie and button down shirt and lay in the grass cooling off in my undershirt.

I closed my eyes. Birds. Laughter. Breeze. It all sounded so normal. I felt something on my left hand. A bee. In the past I would have swatted it away but I'd never had a bee sting, so I just watched it's little dance as my eyes grew heavy.

I fell asleep, awoken by a fair policeman tapping me lightly with his stick. "Hey, buddy, put your clothes on, there are families here."

"Oh, sorry, sir," I said, putting on my shirt and tie, now cool and dry. What time was it? Almost 5! I hurried back to meet Kitty.

5:05. 5:15. 5:25! Where was she!

Finally, she practically skipped over and gave me a kiss. "You were right, I wouldn't have wanted to miss the future, it's so pretty!"

"See, I know what you like."

"You look tired, baby. You've always been so easily overwhelmed. I'm tired, too, and my feet hurt!" Together we hobbled back towards the train.

I was just about to hail a pedicab when I saw them, marching towards us in formation. A group of young men in brown shirts, black shorts, tall khaki socks... and red arm bands, with Swastikas. All very neat and tidy. My blood was starting to boil, but I didn't want to upset Kitty.

"This way," I said to her, changing directions away from them. They changed directions, too, until they were standing in front of us, blocking our path.

"Pretty girl," the tallest blond one said to Kitty.

"Thank you," Kitty said, tensely. "We were just leaving, thank you."

He reached around her waist and pulled her to him. I was instantly enraged.

"Take your hands off her!" I said as calmly as I could, which wasn't very calm.

"No. When the Führer successfully exterminates this nation of filthy Jews—like you—it will be girls like this with whom we breed the next generation of pure Americans!"

I reached back to punch the bastard in the face, but someone grabbed my right wrist, then my left, and held them behind my back.

Kitty grew calm, too calm, her face like a mask. "Then you definitely need a picture with me so you can find me later," she said, flatly to him. Then gently to me, "And you will definitely want to take this picture, Mr. Hamilton."

The tall boy nodded and whoever was behind me released my right hand. I moved it slowly towards the camera.

I squirmed but couldn't escape his grip, so I forced myself to watch in disgust as his hand moved up from her waist towards her breast. *Click.*

I was surprised when *her* hand moved down *his* leg, then to his inner thigh. *Click?*

His big, ugly, long-toothed grin turned into a wide-mouth smile. His long arm reached up and out in a Nazi salute. "Heil Hitler!" *Click.*

Her smile hardened. *Click.*

His smile turned into a grimace of pain as her fingers tightened around his balls like a vice. *Click!*

He doubled over and she rammed her knee into his face.

"YO, FDR!" she screamed, giving him the finger! *Click!*

She transformed into the very picture of masculine fury. There was nothing pretty about this creature. "ANY OF YOU LITTLE BOYS WANT TO FUCK WITH THIS JEWESS??? I WILL FUCKING TEAR YOU APART WITH MY BARE HANDS AND SUCK THE MARROW FROM YOUR BONES!" She kicked wildly and roared like a raging tiger!

The other brown shirt boys backed away in fear.

I felt a shadow creeping over my shoulder and my left hand being freed and watched as a brown shirted boy flew over me and landed on the other boys like so many bowling pins. *Click.*

Suddenly, James and his friends walked past me holding sticks and snakes. *Click.*

What had been a group of brown-shirt bullies dissolved into a pile of crying little boys, scrambling to run away... *Click... Click...* Kitty still roaring and kicking.

A policeman approached and yelled, "Hey—You niggers get away from this girl!"

I pushed the cop back, "Leave them alone, they saved us!" I screamed.

"I SAVED YOU!" Kitty shrieked. "I SAVED... myself..." she panted, her face red.

I threw my arms around her. I'd never felt her body so hard, unyielding.

James' big hand squeezed my shoulder, softly. "Women are stronger than men," he whispered to me, the warm buzz of his breath giving me gooseflesh. One last look and he and his friends were gone.

I stood there, holding her. Her eyes were vacant. I was afraid.

73 »→ Fireworks

I finally felt her soften. A tear rolled down her cheek. She quickly brushed it away.

"I'm fine, Herb. Let's go."

"I'm not," I whispered. "I wanted to protect you."

"I've always had to take care of myself, and my little brother, too."

"I couldn't..."

"Did you get the pictures?"

"Yes."

"Then you did what you needed to do."

"But..."

"I don't *need* to be protected, Herb. I don't *need* to be *saved*. Ever again. Do you get that?"

"OK."

"I'm not going to be told what to do anymore. Not even by you."

"I don't tell you what..."

"No, you're the only one of my fellow men who never did. Thank you," she said, leaning in and kissing my cheek with hard lips. "I need to see the fireworks tonight. I want to watch things explode. You can go home if you're too tired."

I'd seen enough things explode for one day. But I felt her hand wrap around mine.

We turned away from the sunset and walked towards Fountain Lake.

74 ➠ Fountains and Fire

Neither of us spoke for a long time. I watched her watching everyone around us as if they were possible threats. Her breathing was shallow, each exhale sounding like a small gut punch.

We sat on a bench facing the large pool that ran towards the Persiphere. The water reflected its glow, like an earth-bound moon.

I felt Kitty shiver and instinctively started to take off my jacket to give to her, but I remembered what she said earlier and instead whispered, "It's getting chilly..."

She cut me off, "...I'm fine, Herb."

The bell tower started ringing. A cloudy mist rose from the water as a full orchestra started to play stirring music. Blasts of water were perfectly timed with the tympany, then trumpets.

Jets of water flew higher than a skyscraper. Walls of water like Niagara Falls, yet dancing to-and-fro like Carmen Miranda. Colorful lights so bright it could be confused with daytime.

Suddenly, flames, like volcanoes, erupted right from the water! Somehow the water and fire co-existed together!

Here in the future, man had control over all the elements of nature!

Except his fellow man.

An announcer told us the dancing waters were depicting "The Garden of Eden," with two white jets representing Adam and Eve. Between them, a wriggling green-lit "serpent" of water enticed them to come closer together—when the two white fountains touched, they blushed pink.

Fireworks exploded overhead, sending silver and gold shimmering down like metallic rain. With each explosion I felt Kitty's body stiffen, her fingernails digging into my hand, then softening a bit more.

The wind changed, and now we were in the path of mist and smoke just in time for the frenetic finale.

Kitty looked up into the sky—fireworks illuminating half her face, the other half obscured in darkness. *Click.*

The music stopped. The sky grew dark. The water, calm.

She leaned her head against mine yet we felt worlds apart.

75 ➪ Development

The subway was packed with sleeping people on their way home after an exhausting day of fun. Kitty and I were wide awake but said nothing. Did these strangers know what was going on in the world? It hadn't been that long ago when I didn't.

I felt like I could still see a sweaty handprint on Kitty's dress where that monster touched her. I hoped she'd throw that dress away.

The ride seemed endless and stifling. We finally changed at 42nd. I was going to walk her home, but she walked away and didn't look back.

I walked down 42nd street. The top of the Chrysler building still shone like a beacon of hope, but the lobby was dark. Inside, there was a guard at his desk. I knocked on the chrome and glass door. He walked over and opened the door a crack.

"Closed," he said with an accent. Was that German? He was blond.

"I have an appointment with Pat Whyte."

"At this hour? I gotta call." He went back to his desk and picked up the phone, then came back to the door. "OK."

I walked past him and took the elevator to the 50th floor. The view out the window at night was sparkling, silent, sad.

Pat was waiting, her door open. "I heard what happened. How're you? Kitty?"

"I don't know."

"But you got the shots?"

"Is that all you care about?" I asked, bitterly.

"No, but we need to care about it."

"I saw two men die."

"I'm sorry," she said.

"I am, too."

"But it could have been hundreds of people. Now it might be millions. That's what I care about."

"I care about... you'll see."

She led me across the hall through a long room with rows of desks, then into the big darkroom with a dozen enlargers. I handed her the rolls I'd taken.

She pressed a glowing red button and a machine hummed to life. She fed the end of the film into a slot, which pulled until the film unrolled. She fed it all in, one roll after another. There was nothing but whirring for a while, then the processed film emerged from another slot, completely dry and flat.

She clipped each roll onto a tall vertical lightbox on the wall. Once all the film was out of the processing machine, she turned on the backlight and looked through a loupe.

First were all the posed, happy, pictures of Kitty, looking like a completely different person this morning.

"Cute. Good. These will work just fine, Herb."

"Those are crap."

"No, they're not. They're fluff, but necessary. Think of them as an aperitif that helps people digest what's coming." She continued looking down. "The shots with the Africans show unity, there's a message there."

"They're made up, not what really happened..."

"Sometimes you have to make a story happen."

I scoffed out loud. "They're not real," I sighed.

She put down the loupe and looked at me, seriously. "It doesn't matter."

I swatted at something flying around me. I felt my face get hot. I wanted to shout but stopped myself. Even so, my words still came out, heated. "What side are you on?"

She took a step back. "What?"

"How did you know?"

"About the bombing?"

"No, about Kitty eating ice cream. Yes, about the God damned bombing. Jesus! I don't know anything about you, lady, and here I am, doing your bidding. I have the right to know. Are you a Nazi?"

She put down the loupe and leaned against a table. My body tensed. If she said yes I was going to grab the film and run, out of the darkroom, out of the building, to the New York Times and hand it all over to them. Hand *her* over to them.

"Why would you..." she said, but was unable to finish. She closed her eyes and took a long breath. "I'm sorry, given what you've... I understand you asking."

"Are you?"

"No. I am not. I will never be. Even if they attack us, and they will. Even if they land on our shores, and they might. I may be small, but I am determined, and I am trying..." her voice broke, "I am trying, with your help, to do everything in my power to stop them before it's too late."

I could tell she meant it. "Thank you. I'm sorry I asked."

"It's something we all have to ask today. Because you can't tell what's in someone's heart by looking at them."

"So how did you know?"

"Let's just say I have friends in high places. A bomb threat was called in two days ago and that person wanted to make sure it was covered. Was there any other press there?"

"Not that I saw."

"That's why he called me and I called on you."

"Because the world has to see this."

"Our country needs to see this. Too many people here think this is just something happening in Europe. We have the entire Atlantic ocean between us. But I know, and now you know..."

"It's already here."

"It's already here." She picked up the loupe and kept looking—at the group of men running. At the empty plaza. At the two men... the blackened hole and tree... the arm.

"Oh, Herb."

I didn't have to see the film to see it, repeating over and over and over, like a sick cartoon, two men, then a hole, two men, then a hole.

"I'm sending these over to the Times right now."

"I don't want my name on them."

"They'll need it for their files but I'll ask them not to print it." She picked up a phone, "Phil, I need you to deliver something to Robert Gardner at the Times ASAP." She cut out the shots and put them in an envelope with my name and the words "No credit."

Then she turned back to the next roll. "Wait, what's this?"

It was the Nazi youth. It was Kitty breaking. It was a knife in my brain, tearing a slit between what was and what would be.

There was a knock at the door. "Come," she said. "He's waiting for you," she told Phil, who took the envelope with negatives she handed him. "Go—now." Phil ran. She leaned into the photos. "Barbarians," she whispered.

Then she saw the rest of the images and gasped, then laughed. "You've got quite a girl."

"I don't think she's a girl anymore."

"And you're not a boy."

"No."

"She'll be OK," Pat put her little hand on my shoulder and I had to resist shrugging it off.

"You don't know that."

"No, I don't. But I know she has you."

"I was no help."

"Yes, you were. You can show the world."

"For all the good that will do," I said, hopelessly.

"Yes, for the good it will do." She looked at her watch. "It's almost 10 and... I know you must be exhausted but you asked what side I'm on... come with me."

"Where are we going?"

"Up."

76 ➠ View from the Crown

Pat pressed the top-most button in the elevator: 66 with a silver label that read "Cloud Club." It was a short ride to the top.

We got out into a dimly lit, two-story space. At first all I saw was the view of twinkling city lights through triangular windows. I imagined this is what it was like to be in a great airship. Then my eyes adjusted and I could see the sloping ceiling painted a fluffy white as if it was perpetually piercing a cloud, hence the name.

"Wait here, Herb," she said, walking towards a grand chrome staircase at the back of the room, "I'll be right back."

I sat down next to one of the triangle windows and looked out at the shining city. What day was this? I couldn't remember if all this had taken a day or a week or what. I had flashes of the pictures I'd taken— Kitty smiling and James and a black hole in the ground and the Nazi boys and Kitty's transformation into a tiger... It was too much for one day...

I needed air. I twisted a lever on the bottom of the window and a breeze blew in with such force and chill it woke me up.

There, struggling, against that torrent of air, 66 stories up in the sky, was another bee. Or was it the same one from earlier? It landed on my left hand, right between my thumb and forefinger. Even in this light the yellow and black stripes looked downright regal. A queen, yes.

She settled down and I watched as she pressed her tail against my hand. I felt her stinger pierce my skin. It stung for a second then stopped like getting a shot from a hypodermic needle.

I looked closer, right into her eyes, she looked right back at me—and I understood. I was being knighted. I felt... honored, and scared, wondering if I could live up to this.

She proceeded to turn in circles until she'd pulled out the stinger, then flew up to my face as if to tell me something, then back out the window again. I looked at the small red mark on my hand. It felt hot but didn't itch.

Pat tapped me on the shoulder. "They're ready to meet you. One thing: we only use first names here." she whispered, taking my hand and leading me upstairs into a small private dining room with a long silver table.

The walls were covered with black glass panels, etched into a mural of heroic workers on a car assembly line, strong men with gears and drills and wheels. Along the top of the walls, right near the ceiling, were the words, "Truth, Honor, Integrity, Justice, Democracy."

Like any New Yorker, I immediately recognized the small man of huge stature at the end of the table—mayor Fiorello La Guardia. He smiled and nodded. Next to him, a tall man... where had I seen his face... that's right, a portrait in the lobby of this very building, Walter P. Chrysler. Next to him, another small man, I'd seen him in a magazine... movie director Frank Capra, who directed one of my favorite movies, "Mr. Smith Goes to Washington." And one more man I remembered from another portrait... in the bank downstairs... but I didn't know his name.

And finally, a man in a beautiful tweed suit. I had no idea who he was.

Pat announced, "Gentleman, this is the photographer, and young patriot, I told you about." they all nodded and smiled... though Mr. Chrysler... Walter... was only able to smile with half his face.

Fiorello stood up, walked to me and shook my hand firmly and brisky. He looked at me like I was the only person in the world. "Thank you for your important and courageous work. It's young men like you who are the light in this dark time."

My hand started to itch.

"Welcome to the Free League of Storytellers," Frank said.

"I don't think much of that name," Walter managed, using only half his mouth.

"It's a working title," Frank replied.

"What happened to 'Voice of Democracy?'" Walter asked.

"We agreed this is about *freedom*," Fiorello said in his famously high, sharp voice.

"Then 'Freedom League,' don't you agree, Junior'?" Walter asked, clearly frustrated that he was no longer in charge in his own building— or of half his body.

"Let's be plain, gentlemen, this is the 'Propaganda Patrol,'" said Junior who looked to be about 80 years old.

Frank slammed his hand on the table, "No! What *they* do is promulgate propaganda. We tell the *truth*!"

Arguing ensued. Pat stood up, though it didn't make her much taller than when she was sitting. Still, they all immediately quieted down.

"Gentlemen. This is no time for arguing. Herbert here watched two men get killed today. Just a few minutes ago he summed it up with the words, 'They're already here.' We know they are. Not just a few of them, not just Germans, but a large, organized following of people who consider themselves 'Patriotic Americans for Hitler.' They think they're right. It is our job to open their closed minds again."

She sat. Silence.

Now the tall man in tweed spoke, with a crisp English accent like Ronald Coleman. "Miss Whyte is quite right. Mr. Churchill sent me here to take action, and this is why I convened you. Herbert, I have seen your work and am pleased someone of your generation understands that the future is in your hands. It takes an army of hands and minds to change hearts."

"Thank you, William," Pat said.

"To change hearts, we need to change dreams," I said, scratching my hand. I was so tired now that my words tumbled out without thought. "Dreams are like clouds—we see in them what we want to see. But we can help arrange those clouds in people's minds. We here, in the Cloud Club, are the *Cloud Rangers*." Then I felt sleepy and couldn't remember what I'd just said.

"Yes!" yelled Frank.

"An excellent code-name," William agreed.

"Do we get decoder rings?" I asked.

They looked at me, befuddled.

"Gentlemen, I wanted to assure Herbert whose side he was on and for you to meet him. That said, it's late and he has experienced a traumatic day. I'm sure you will remember the first time you saw a man die. I know I do. One of you please call him a taxi, then we will continue our discussion anon."

The men took turns shaking my hand and Pat led me downstairs, and accompanied me in the elevator.

"I'm very proud of you, Herbert. Remember, not a word of this to anyone. We will not even speak of this in my office. Do you understand?"

"Yes, I understand," I said, feeling the elevator drop like the parachute jump at the fair. I rubbed the red spot on my hand as it faded away.

77 ➻ Glenn

The phone woke me up and I didn't even remember getting home.

"Herb? Glenn. I need you to come with me."

"What day is this?"

"What do you mean 'what day is this?' It's Friday."

"I'm really tired..." I looked around and Kitty wasn't there.

"I'm meeting with Pat to go over your contract and show my portfolio and I need you to come with me."

"I don't feel good," I said, looking around for my watch to see what time it was.

"I don't feel good, either, but I still have to go and now you're my agent!"

"I was just joking about that..."

"Just get your ass over here, now, Herb. I've been there for you and you need to be here for me." He hung up. I called for some oatmeal with brown sugar, cinnamon and hot chocolate...

I got in the shower. The water felt especially wet. Why did I smell honey?

I heard the bell and got the food. It was nice and sweet. I dropped yesterday's clothes in the cleaning box and put on my dark blue pants and Saks blue shirt... but not the Trylon and Perisphere tie, I couldn't even look at it. I wore a yellow one with blue stripes.

I could only mumble to Ellis and Sam and Max, who just rolled his eyes. I didn't think I could balance on my bike so I walked.

Glenn was waiting, his door uncharacteristically open. "You look like shit," he grimaced. "We need to talk."

I sat on one of his chrome stools with the sparkly green vinyl padded seats. The light coming through his window was too bright. I realized I hadn't brought my camera with me for the first time in... I don't know.

"Your contract is for $250, is that OK?"

"$250? A month? That's crazy. I never dreamed..."

"A week, Herb. $250 a week."

"Naw, you musta read it wrong."

"No, Herb, I'm not the zombie here this morning, that's you. The contract says 'a week.'"

"You did a great job, then, Glenn. Wow."

"I did bupkis, bubbe. It also says they'll be handling all film developing and archiving. So I can't take 25%, Herb, it's not right."

"It is—for getting me that much in the first place."

"Nope. I'll take 10%, a normal agent's percentage. That'll still be $100 bucks a month for doing nothing, like a normal agent."

"Whatever you want, Glenn. I think I'm gonna puke, so do you want me to do it here or back at my place?"

"Do it here, Herb." he said flatly, handing me a bucket. "Then you're coming with me to meet Pat because I'm too nervous to go by myself."

It seemed like too much trouble to puke. "You'll be fine. Pat already told me she loves fruit. Do you have a 7-up?" He did. I drank it in two long sips and burped for what seemed like a minute, immediately feeling better. "Thank you."

"I've never shown those pictures to anybody, but you. I got a few more I want you to look at, too."

"Not nudies, I hope," I said, followed by a short, but impressively loud burp.

"Jesus, Herb." He handed me his portfolio. It started with the fruit, then the hand and the piece of jewelry, then there were a bunch of portraits of people I recognized, like the waitress from Barney Greengrass, and the wrinkled old man who ran the newsstand next door and the crazy lady who wandered the street always wearing at least six sweaters, including one wrapped around her head like a turban. Finally, an old man in shadow, one eye closed, the other eye illuminated and enlarged with a little magnifying-glass like lens.

Like the fruit, he made them all beautiful in their own way, the light caressing their skin as if you could touch it.

"Wow, Glenn," I said, rubbing my finger along the surface of the print, surprised I couldn't feel the texture I saw. "I don't even know what to say other than I can feel these."

"I don't know, I had more fruit and I thought, 'this is too much fruit,' so I put in some squashes and I thought 'nobody really likes squash,' and I thought, 'maybe people would be better,' but I don't know!" His normally low voice had become squeaky.

I put my hand on his shoulder. "I think they're beautiful, Glenn. Really. I think Pat will think so, too. I'm here for you, buddy."

"Thanks, Herb. I gotta pee and change my shirt because I sweated through this one. Thanks," he said, scurrying off to the back. I looked at more of the people in his pictures. They were so different from the ones I took. So simple. Just a face or head and shoulders on a plain background. That's it. Yet, I felt like I knew these people just by looking at them. Like I could see what they were thinking. They weren't stories, like mine, they were... statements."

Glenn came out in a clean, pressed shirt and an emerald green tie. "I put on baby powder... and maybe too much bay rum... "

"How do you take these, Glenn?"

"I've got a 4x5 in the studio and..."

"I mean, how do you show what's inside them? I think I can only show the surface."

"I just get them to talk about themselves. Everybody wants to talk about themselves. Mine just show a second, yours tell stories. Ready?"

I nodded. We headed back to the Chrysler building... wasn't I just there? Last night? This morning the silver spire seemed awfully sharp.

78 ➻ Fineline

Louise waved us right into Pat's office. Pat looked different today, wearing a beige linen jacket and skirt, white shirt and orange string tie and matching shoes.

She smiled, "Come on in, gentlemen. It's been too long, Glenn, my don't you look dapper and smell... nice." Glenn grew visibly pale as we sat. "Did our boy Herb tell you all about yesterday?"

Glenn looked confused, "No, in fact, he didn't tell me anything."

"Excellent! Then let's move onto business, shall we? First, I hope the contract is acceptable."

I piped up, "Yes, more than... acceptable. Except Glenn's only taking 10% now."

"Really? A mensch, too? Then why don't you sign that now and get it out of the way?"

She handed me a beautiful red marbleized bakelite fountain pen and I went through, page by page, and signed on the dotted lines.

"Welcome to the *Look* family, Herb. I have an assignment for you but we can get into that later. After your effusive praise, I'm eager to see Glenn's work."

Glenn was clutching his portfolio tight to his chest. I tapped his hand and tried to pry it away from him. He let go and it went flying and landed on the floor behind him.

"I was just going to suggest we sit on the sofa, better light for prints," she said, graciously picking it up and placing it on the glass table. We swiveled our chairs to face her.

She opened the cover and her mouth was open in surprise, until she remembered to close it. She said nothing for a long time, but, like I had, she ran her finger over the print as if to feel the texture of the fruit. She turned the pages, slowly, and I watched her eyes move, taking in each image, studying them.

"Light. Texture. Composition."

"They remind me of the Dutch Masters at the Met," I chimed in.

"Yes, they do."

She got to the portraits and raised her eyebrows. "Who are these people, Glenn?"

He swallowed, "Just neighborhood people, I liked their faces. The last one's my Uncle Otto, worked at Leica before they helped him get outta Germany."

"They're exquisite. Technically, of course, but deeper than that. I feel they're telling me who they are, inside. Herb was right about you."

"Thanks," Glenn still looked confused.

I shook his arm and whispered, "She loves them!"

"I have one question. These are such accomplished prints I'm wondering why you didn't crop the background, so we don't see your studio on the edges of the frame."

"I do that on purpose. I don't want any pretense that these are anything but photographs. This way, the viewer first sees the face, but they're also aware how it was made."

"You're full of surprises. I'm glad I didn't throw you out of my office that first day!"

"Yeah, I am, too, also, as well," Glenn stammered.

"I've got an assignment for you now if you've available."

"I am. Available. Anytime. Always. Whatever you want me to do." It was sweet to watch him, gobsmacked by her. Did she like him, too?

"I need portraits of our men and women in uniform... that aren't about the uniform, they're about the men and women." She looked at me, "the brave human beings putting their lives on the line for us." She continued, brisky, "Two photos of each, one in their uniform, one in their street clothes, I might use one or the other or both. We'll arrange for the people and send them to your studio...

"That'd be swell..."

She stopped, "Oh, wait. You're not still "*Fine's Fotos* are you?"

"Um, I..."

"No," I jumped in. "Fineline Studios," says so right on his window in gold and everything.

Glenn shot me a look, then looked at Pat, then nodded, a little too vigorously. "In gold and everything."

"Good. Wasn't it my lucky day when you two landed in my office?"

"It was a *beautiful* day!" Glenn sighed.

She called through the still open office day, "Louise please take Mr. Fine to legal. I'll hold onto your portfolio if you don't mind, there are some people I'd like to show it to."

Louise breezed in, "Follow me, Mr. Fine.".

I turned to Pat, "Thank you. Thank you. Thank you."

"I should be thanking you," Pat smiled as Louise led Glenn by the elbow. "For your work, and for bringing Glenn. He's quite a character."

"Really good, isn't he?"

"Yes," she got up and closed the office door. Then she went to the bookcase and put on a record... some frenetic classical music... Oh, I recognized it, *The Flight of the Bumblebee.* "Just in case anyone's listening." She turned up the volume, sat beside me and whispered in my ear.

"I need you to shoot a rally at Madison Square Garden. It might be difficult for you."

"It's not hard to get there," I said.

"No, it's not just any rally, it's the *German* American Bund."

"Germans..."

"Nazis. Claiming they are the *true Americans.*"

Did I just hear her right? My stomach tensed. She whispered something else I couldn't understand. My mind was buzzing with the classical music and the memory of the horrible boys in uniform... I squeezed my eyes closed and put up my hand. "STOP!"

She got up and turned off the music.

"I can't," I said.

"Can't shoot the rally?"

"No, I couldn't hear you! Did you say they're the *True Americans*?" I yelled, only then realizing the music had stopped.

"That's what *they* call themselves," she answered, quietly.

I was so angry I felt my hands start to shake. "They're the complete opposite!"

"Yes, and it's something our *democracy-loving* Americans need to see. But you'll be there as part of *Look* magazine. You can't cause any trouble."

"Then I won't bring Kitty," I said, sarcastically.

"You're only there to take pictures. Even... look like you're sympathetic."

"They'll know I'm Jewish."

"Keep your hat on and your head down. Smile. Show them you're not scared."

"I'm not scared. I hate them."

"You can't show them that, either. It's enough to shine your light on the darkness. Show them for what they are—ignorant, blind, afraid."

"I won't let you down."

"I know you won't. But do be careful." She handed me an official Press Pass. "Keep this press pass in your hat and they shouldn't bother you. Come back here directly after so I can see the shots right away."

Then she did something surprising, she leaned in and kissed my cheek. I thought I saw something fly away.

79 ➺ Gold leaf

As I left Pat's office I felt around for my camera, naked without it. Then I remembered I'd left it at home. Glenn was sitting next to Louise's desk, looking over his contract. I tapped him on the shoulder.

"How's it look?" I ask.

"Uh... nice... good... nice!" he whispered, loudly.

"Congratulations..."

"We gotta get back and change the... you know. Right away." He sprang up. "Thanks, Louise, you're a peach!" She smiled.

In the elevator he said, "I owe you $25."

"Not this again."

"Yes, 10%. $250 for five portraits. But I'm gonna take more shots and let Pat choose."

"OK, you can apply it to what I owe you for the Leica."

"You're keeping it?"

"What're you crazy? Of course I'm keeping it."

"It cost $400," he told me, tentatively.

I'm shocked, "What're *you* crazy?"

"No, that's really how much it costs."

"I'm crazy then, and I'm keeping it. I'll write you a check..."

"Hold on, hold on. You basically already paid me $300, or thereabouts. Plus you got me this job. We can call it square."

The elevator reached the lobby. "No, Glenn, you knew what I needed and made sure I had it and now I want to know I paid you fairly for it."

"OK, Herb. If that's what you want. How's about this, you can start out by paying for the new sign... in *gold letters!*" He laughed.

"Sure, buddy. My pleasure!"

We raced back to his place, took out the yellow pages and searched for "Sign painter." There, on page 468, was an ad with beautiful hand-lettering and the words, "Your Name In Gold!" That was it.

A half hour later, Lazlo DiSilva arrived, looking every inch the artist—happily drooping face and mustache, white overalls covered in paint and flecks of gold. He was cheerful, if hard to understand.

"And I tella Rosa, no more Il Duce, we must go to the New World!" And we here two years' now, is wonderful country, thank you very much!"

"How long will it take to..." Glenn started to say.

"In old country, I am gold leaf master. Gilding churches and paintings, thank you very much. Here, names on doors and windows. So American—wonderful! What you want it to say?"

"Fineline Studios."

"How many letters that?"

"I dunno... 1...3...6...12... 15."

"And how big you want them is?"

Glenn looked at me. I looked at the window. "Big. Like..." I stretched my hand on the glass, "Yea high."

Lazlo's finger tapped his nose as he calculated. "Okey dokey. $25."

"Okey dokey," I replied, handing him $25.

"No, after you like, OK? Write down words, per favore." I wrote them on a piece of paper and handed it to him. "You Mr. Fineline?" he asked me. I pointed to Glenn. He shook his hand, "Good to meet you Mr. Fineline, thank you very much!"

"Glenn, I want to take pictures of this momentous occasion... can you lend me a camera?"

"I think I have one or two around here..." he said, reaching behind the counter and pulling out my old Kodak 35. "I hope this is nice enough for you now!"

Lazlo went up to the glass. First, he took a razor blade and scraped off the old sign's black letters. *Click.* Then he used a grease pencil to sketch out the letters in a fancy way that looked like the "New York Times," then another set that were big, bold and modern. "Which kinda you like?" he asked.

I pointed to the big bold ones. "Perfecto!" I said, not knowing why I added the "o" onto the end.

"Perfetto," he replied, rubbing off the fancier letters.

I went outside and shot him through the window as he leaned in and drew a fine black line around each letter.

"I should probably get a sofa," I heard Glenn saying inside. "For people who are waiting. I've never had anybody wait. Fruit doesn't need a seat."

I popped my head back inside. "You've got stools, that's fine."

"This place is a mess, I need to call a cleaner," he said, as if he'd never noticed the dust on everything and the schmutz on the floor.

"Call Sam at the Ansonia. He can probably send someone over."

Lazlo had a sure hand. His straight lines were simply straight. The sunlight made his brown eyes shine, right next to his glossy black paint brush. *Click.*

I pulled back from the camera and looked at him through the window. It wasn't the same. I saw the world differently through a viewfinder. The rest of the world went away and I could focus on one small rectangle of space. Take it all in. Understand it.

Now, the end of his mustache looked like the end of his brushes, both thick dark hairs. *Click.* Once the letters were all outlined, he brushed a clear liquid over them, then took out a wide flat brush and a little white book. He ran the brush across his hair (click), then opened the book and used the static electricity to lift a piece of gold as if it was weightless. He moved it towards the glass and it floated from the brush to the glass like magic!

He repeated this till the letters were all covered with extra gold on the outside of them. Oh, I liked that! Not the clean, refined letters I saw everywhere, but sharp letters with a slightly messy, chaotic but artistic layer of gold rectangles behind it.

"Now, must dry, then I trim," Lazlo said, wiping his forehead.

"It's beautiful the way it is," I said."

"You joking! Too messy!"

"Not messy, modern. The rectangles look like the shape of photographs."

"No, no, no, people think I crazy."

"We won't tell anybody."

"Then how I get word of mouth?" he protested.

"I'll pay you double."

"OK, so now *you* crazy. Not bad crazy—American crazy!" he said, rolling his eyes, but smiling and applying a layer of varnish to seal the gold.

"Glenn, get in the window with Lazlo so I can take your picture together!"

He looked at the lettering, "Shouldn't we wait till he trims the gold?"

"I told him not to, it's cool this way, think of the gold squares as photographs."

"It's certainly... different."

"Artistic!" I yelled. There they were, in profile, looking at each other from each end of the words. *Click.* Then looking at me, like I was crazy, and sticking out their tongues in unison! *Click!*

Lazlo handed me his card, embossed, in gold. "Don't tell anyone I made this mess," he whispered, handing a card to Glenn, too. "Let me put your name on the door, nicely, my gift to you, OK?"

"OK, thank you," Glenn said, and Lazlo made quick work of it "Glenn Fine Photographer" in crisp letters across the glass door.

"You like?" Lazlo said when it was done.

"Very much," Glenn said. I counted out $50 cash and handed it to Lazlo.

"This door, you can say I do that." He said, pointing, as if we didn't already know.

Glenn and I thanked Lazlo and shook his hand. As he walked away he turned, shook his head *(click)* and went down the street into a shadow *(click)*.

"Sam's sending over a cleaning lady... I'd better lock up the nudies before she, or anybody else stumbles on them. Oy, they could be anywhere..."

"Need my help?"

"Naw, 'cept maybe I should put curtains up in the window? Whaddya think?"

"I think you're crazier than I am."

"Green. Velvet." He mused. "It'll make the name stand out nice. I got a thing for green... my ribbons, the stools. It was my grandfather's last name... I'll talk to Mrs. Segal, down the block, maybe recover the stools, too. Want it to look nice if more people are coming over."

It was so good to see him happy that I forgot what I was going to have to do, or that I was still carrying the Kodak as I headed back home. I felt better with a camera in my hands.

80 ⟫ Top-o-the Charts

Kitty still wasn't home. I called Sam, "Did Kitty say where she was going?"

"Nope, but she was wearing dungarees, which I thought was kinda funny," Sam said.

"Maybe she had a rehearsal? She said they were getting a new headline act..."

"Glenn told me what you did for him. You're a good guy, Herb."

"Look who's talking. You introduced me to Glenn, he helped me get the job at *Look*..."

"I remember the good guys. If there's anything you need..."

"Thanks, Sam. Actually, I could use a club sandwich and a coke!"

"Done and done! Oh, Kitty just came in... It's Herb on the horn, wondering where you was."

"Men, always so jealous!" I heard her say. A minute later she opened the door, her hair freshly cut, short, like a boy.

"Oh! Your hair!" I said, shocked.

"It's cute, isn't it? You like it?"

She looked so different. Handsome? "Yeah, sure, of course, you're always beautiful!"

"It's for my new number..." She breezed past me to the bathroom and slammed the door.

"I ordered a club sandwich, I'll save you half." I knocked on the bathroom door. "Or do you want me to order you something else?"

"Just leave me alone for a bit, can you?" she yelled over the running water.

"Sorry," I mumbled. My sandwich arrived and I ate half, just in case she wanted half... then I thought about what she told me at the fair and I wanted to eat the other half but I didn't want to in case she might want it.

I turned on the radio. "And now, for the first time ever, Billboard Magazine's 'Top-o the-Charts' presents the countdown to the number one record of the week. At number four, here's Glenn Miller's 'Fools Rush In.'" I loved Glenn Miller.

> *"Fools rush in*
> *Where angels fear to tread*
> *And so I come to you my love*
> *My heart above my head*
> *Though I see*
> *The danger there*
> *If there's a chance for me*
> *Then I don't care"*

Since Kitty was in the bathroom, she couldn't hear me, so I sang along, loud!

> *"Fools rush in*
> *Where wise men never go*
> *But wise men never fall in love*
> *So how are they to know*
> *When we met*
> *I felt my life begin*
> *So open up your heart and let*
> *This fool rush in"*

I closed my eyes and thought about Kitty. "At number three, Glenn Miller's *'Imagination.'*"

> *"Imagination is funny*
> *It makes a cloudy day sunny*
> *Makes a bee think of honey*
> *Just as I think of you..."*

I stopped singing because I couldn't remember the rest of the words... But I hummed the melody! "At number two, Jimmy Dorsey's *'The Breeze and I.'* It was moody and sad, not one of my favorites. Still, I closed my eyes and crooned.

> *"The breeze and I are saying with a sigh*
> *That you no longer care*
> *The breeze and I are whispering goodbye*
> *To dreams we used to share..."*

Kitty sang along as she came in the room. She'd never sung to me before.

"Ours was a love song that seemed constant as the moon
Ending in a strange, mournful tune
And all about me,
they know you have departed without me
And we wonder why,
The breeze and I."

I felt my tears before I opened my eyes. She sat down next to me and dabbed my eyes with the satin belt of her robe, then pulled my head to her shoulder like I remembered doing for her.

"And now, the first ever top-o-the-charts, Tommy Dorsey's *'I'll never smile again!'"* I had a lump in my throat too big to sing through. Kitty held my face in her hands and sang right up close to me, like they did in the movies.

"I'll never smile again
Until I smile at you
I'll never laugh again
What good would it do?
For tears would fill my eyes
My heart would realize
That our romance is through

In my mind, Kitty was Ginger Rogers, I was Fred Astaire and we were dancing circles around the roof.

I'll never love again
I'm so in love with you
I'll never thrill again
To somebody new
Within my heart
I know I will never start
To smile again
Until I smile at you.

The world seemed OK, again. Even when I opened my eyes and saw tears in hers. I kissed her, so sweet, yet with a hint of salt.

81 ➺ Bewitched

The kiss lasted a long time, our tongues intertwined, then slowly separated. I felt her newly short hair, and looked into her emerald eyes.

"I'm sorry I was a bitch," she said, turning off the radio.

"I'm sorry I..." I didn't know what I was sorry for, but I was sorry, too. "I've been working too hard and not coming to the club to watch you."

"Oh, I don't want... don't expect you to watch me every night. Frank gave me a new solo spot and I don't want you to see it until I feel I'm ready."

"That's exciting. And it works out because I have an assignment for tonight."

"Speaking of which, how'd it go at the magazine?"

I thought back... so much had happened and I didn't want to say anything I shouldn't... "Pat *loved* your photos! I'm pretty sure they'll get in the magazine."

"Imagine that," she said dreamily. "Me, in a magazine."

"Then the whole world will know how beautiful you are." She smiled. I felt good I could do this for her. I wished I could tell her everything, too, but knew *not* telling her made her safer. "I'd do anything for you, Kitty."

"You're the only man who's ever told me that. They've said 'I'll *buy* you anything you want,' but never 'I'll *do* anything.' I will always remember that, Herbie. Always. No matter what."

"Always," I said. Then silently to myself I heard, "No matter what?"

There was a knock at the door. Sam's voice: "I've got a package for Miss Kitty."

She danced towards the door. "Thanks, Sam!" He handed her a package tied up with a familiar red ribbon. She gave him 50 cents. I waved.

She tore open the package and used the Shapiro's ribbon to tie around her head like a headband. Inside was a black tuxedo.

"I've always wanted a tux!" I said, jumping up and taking it from her. It was beautiful, with wide peaked satin lapels. I tried to put on the jacket but it was way too small. "I guess I'm bigger than the last time I worked there…"

Kitty gently took it off me. "No, silly, it's for me… for my… specialty spot." As she took it away I spied a red tag inside that said, "Made by Myron."

"Oh, I forgot you know Myron."

"Since we was kids. Here, tell me how it looks!" She dropped her robe and wasn't wearing anything underneath. Where was my camera?

She slipped into the jacket and buttoned it. It fit like it was made for her, because it was. Perfectly taut across the chest, the curve of her breasts just visible in the V-shaped opening where the shirt should go.

She put on the pants and stood there proudly, her hands on her hips.

"I start out looking like a man, singing like Dietrich," she sang, with an unexpectedly low voice.

> "*Falling in love again*
> *Never wanted to*
> *What am I to do?*
> *Can't help it*
> *Love's always been my game*
> *Play it how I may*
> *I was made that way*
> *Can't help it*
> *Men cluster to me like moths around a flame*
> *And if their wings burn, I know I'm not to blame…*"

Her voice lightened, "Then I take off the pants, then the jacket..." My mouth must have been open, because she added, "Don't worry, I'll be wearing a sparkly bodysuit underneath. And now I sing..." Her voice was high and sweet.

"*I'm wild again, Beguiled again*
A simpering, whimpering child again
Bewitched, bothered and bewildered am I"

She was bewitching. I was bothered.

82 ➤ A Night at the Garden

"I've got to get to the club early and rehearse with the band," Kitty said, garment bag over her shoulder. "Tell me the truth, do you like my number?"

"Beguiling."

"You're so sweet. I hope the audience thinks so. Frank promised there'll be a Hollywood talent scout in the audience tonight!"

"Break a leg, baby."

"From your lips..." she said, leaning in to kiss mine, then slinking out the door.

The music in my head went from major to minor. Why was it every time I looked at her I felt like I saw someone different?

I put on my white shirt, gray suit... I needed a new suit... something with bigger lapels... what tie? Simple. Invisible. Black.

I filled my pockets with film. Cleaned my camera lens, and in one mental "click" pictured myself, safe, back in the darkroom at *Look*.

If I could see it, it had already happened.

I took the 1 train to 50th street. I kept checking that my press pass was in my hat. My hat band felt loose and I didn't want it to fall out. There was a hat shop in the station, so I bought a new hat band, a wide, black grosgrain ribbon which the old gentleman in the shop cut, sewed together then fitted, tight. I slipped in the pass. It felt secure. He asked for a dollar. I gave him three.

I emerged on the sidewalk, not scared—prepared.

It was a warm, humid night. The air felt heavy. I could already hear the noise a block away, a mass of people outside Madison Square Garden. There was a line of mounted police trying to control the crowds. *Click.* Normal looking men yelled at the police "stop blocking the future!" *Click.* The policemen looked uncomfortable. *Click.* So did the horses. *Click.*

The marquee said, "Pro American Rally," followed by "Hockey Tuesday, Rangers vs. Detroit."

People crowded through the doors. I merged into the mob, holding my camera above my head to show how this all felt. *Click.*

Once inside, there were rows of men in brown uniforms. *Click.* There were young men and women, matching white shirts, brown pants, and black sashes, looking like carbon copies of each other, standing guard at the doors. *Click.*

I could smell meat frying.

I pressed my way through the lobby looking for something familiar... ah, George Washington! He was *everywhere*. On banners, on signs that said, "True Americans Unite!" *Click.*

Then I saw a familiar face. Mrs. Weber from the aquacade, sitting alone behind a table with a sign that said "VIP." I pulled my hat down.

"Hello, Mrs. Weber, I'm here for *Look*." I smiled.

She couldn't have been nicer. "Mr. Hamilton. How lovely to see you here! I'm glad you found me, I'll get you a personal escort to make sure you get a front row seat for the festivities."

"That's very kind, I'd appreciate getting a close look, but I don't need an escort as my Uncle Otto said he'll introduce me to some of his friends," I lied.

"Ah, another True American, that's so heartening when so much of the press is run by Jews. I mean, sometimes you can tell just by looking at someone but you have a very nice nose."

I'd never paid much attention to my nose except when it was in the way of my camera. Then again, I'd never paid much attention to anybody else's nose, either. Mrs. Weber had a small, sharp nose. "You have a fetching nose, too," I said, stupidly. She touched her nose with her finger, covering a shy smile and blush.

"Oh, Rolf!" she said, waving at a blond man in a uniform. "You remember Mr. Hamilton, the photographer from *Look*."

Why would he remember me? I didn't recognize him, but it was hard to see past the uniform and hat. Ah, the diving board. He was the one who grabbed my belt and kept me from walking off the edge. "Hello, sir! It's good to see you again! It's fine to see a member of the press who isn't a…"

I knew what he was going to stay and stopped listening. He looked like a nice guy. She looked like a nice woman. Happy. Smiling. Helpful. But I remembered Pat's words, "You can't tell what's in someone's heart by looking at them."

Mrs. Weber explained, "Please come see me after the rally and I will be honored to introduce you to our leader, Fritz Kuhn. We like to think of him as our home-grown Hitler! We'll have plenty of food. After all, there's nothing more American than a frankfurter and hamburger, both German!"

"Right this way, sir," Rolf said. I wondered how old he was. Probably older than I was and he was calling me "Sir." I followed.

I'd never been in Madison Square garden. It was gigantic. Thousands of chairs, filled with men, women and children, all dressed in their Sunday best. "Rolf, how many… True Americans… will this place hold?"

"20,000, and we expect it to be full, more people than can get in. We're all here because we believe Fascism is what our founding fathers intended for our future!" His face lit up when he said it, and I focused on his nose, which dipped in the middle, then turned up.

I noticed noses everywhere. A blond family all shared small ones, right down to their cute little girl, sucking on a lollipop. *Click.* Her older brother yanked it out of her mouth. *Click.* It was in the shape of a swastika. *Click.*

Another family stood next to a life-size cutout of Hitler for a happy photo. *Click.* Some of the kids had Hitler mustaches stuck on their upper lips. *Click.* A wholesome looking couple carried a mustachioed baby. *Click.* Not a good shot.

"Excuse me, may I take a picture of your beautiful baby?" I asked, smiling.

"Of course!" they said, posing the baby's face forward for the camera. *Click.* I gave them the "OK" sign and they smiled.

I followed Rolf as he walked briskly down the long aisle. At the end of the arena was a stage with a three-story tall glowing painting of George Washington. On either side of him were tall banners with stars, stripes—and swastikas. *Click.* I almost tripped over my own feet.

"Right here, sir," Rolf pointed to a group of seats cordoned off with red ropes which he lowered to let me in. I sat on the aisle so I wouldn't feel trapped. Men in expensive suits pushed past me, joined by other men in uniforms with a lot of medals. I tried to be as casual as possible taking pictures of them, not even holding the camera up to my eye. It could be useful for the Cloud Rangers to know exactly who these men were.

The aisles started filling with what looked like endless rows of identical men in uniforms in this row, young men in uniform in the middle row, and young women filling the third. All looking so powerful in their conformity. But I knew, just under their uniforms, they were just big babies like the boys at the fair. Still, there were so many...

There was no escape now. I pulled down my hat and made sure my curly hair wasn't sticking out and giving me away.

The audience was cheering as more men in uniform filled the stage. Then a man with the most medals, the widest pants and biggest boots climbed onto the podium and started to shout in a heavy German accent.

"I pledge undivided allegiance, to the United States of America, and to the Republic, for which it stands, one nation, with liberty and justice for all White Christians!"

The crowd joined him, hands on hearts. Then he thrust his arm into the air in the Nazi salute, and I looked around as 20,000 Americans, men, women, children, raised their arms, too. I lifted my camera, more as an excuse to not raise my arm than to take a picture, but no, I was disgusted and a picture must be taken. *Click.*

The Nazi continued speaking with his heavy accent, "Ladies and Gentlemen. American Patriots. I am sure I do not appear before you tonight as a complete stranger. You have all heard about me through the Jewish controlled press, as a creature with horns and a cloven hoof and a long tail."

The audience roared with laughter, unable to see that this was who he really was—but I could. I closed the aperture and took a long exposure so the camera would capture his evil expressions. *Cliick.*

"We must denounce the 'campaign of hate' being waged against us in the press, the radio, even the cinema through the hands of the Jews!" More cheering.

"We, with true American ideals, demand that our government shall be returned to the American people who founded it!" Wild applause and cheering. "George Washington understood the power of a strong leader. When he was only 15 years of age, he rode a horse to death because it would not give in!" The crowd gasped and cheered. "Nor shall we!"

"If you ask what we are actively fighting for under our charter, first, a socially just, white, gentile ruled United States. Gentile controlled labor unions free from Jewish Moscow-directed domination!" Cheers. Another long exposure, to expose their savagery. *Click.*

"We all know the cancer in this great nation, headed by so-called President Franklin D. *Rosenfeld*, and his '*Jew Deal.*' We are fighting shoulder to shoulder with patriotic Americans, like you, to protect

America from a race that is not the American race, that is not even a white race ... The Jews are enemies of the United States!" More wild cheering. *Cliiick.*

"The true great Americans, Father Coughlin, Henry Ford, Charles Lindbergh, they all know our true enemy—the Jews!"

Just then, a man rushed the stage and lunged at the speaker. Before he could reach him, a dozen men in uniform surrounded him, beating and kicking him. Twelve men against one lone protester. The young boys on stage jumped up and down, excited like dogs with raw meat. I held down the shutter to melt their monstrous motion. *Cliick. Cliiick.*

The crowd booed, which sounded like "Jew, Jew, Jew!" I spun around, *click, Click, CLick CLIck CLICk CLICK,* capturing their contorted faces, haunting, their humanity overwhelmed with hate.

The protester's clothes were torn away and he was thrown off the side of the stage.

The speaker was hurried off the other side of the stage, replaced at the podium by a woman who started singing the Star Spangled Banner in a loud operatic voice as the band played and the audience joined in more screaming than singing.

I felt the need to go somewhere, anywhere. I went to see what happened to the protester and found him, crumpled in a heap, bloodied. unconscious. *Click.*

A man lifted a little girl towards the protester. *Click.* She spit in his face. *Click.*

"What do we say?" the man holding her asked, seriously.

"Dwirty Jew!" she laughed, innocently. *Click.*

I grabbed a New York City policeman. "You've got to help him!"

"We're taking him down to the station. He's under arrest for disturbing the peace," he said, with an Irish accent.

"*He* is?" These policemen and their uniforms—pretending they made them stronger. All you had to do was focus on their faces—Scared little boys or frightened big ones. That's why so many covered their eyes with hats or sunglasses. Hiding their last feeble bit of humanity. I saw right through them.

The man's arm was bleeding. I yanked off my new hat band and used it as a bandage.

"I'm press and I'm going with you to make sure he's taken care of. Unless, of course, you want to see your name in the paper as having let him die, Officer O'Hara."

83 ➤ The Station

"You'll have to ride in back with him," the officer barked.

"That's fine. Just know I have my eye, and my camera on you," I replied, coldly. I'd never been in a police car and it took me a minute to realize there was no handle on the door. *Click.* My fellow passenger had slumped over onto my shoulder. *Click.*

The West 47th Street station was only four blocks away. Office O'Hara opened my door and scowled at me. *Click.* He waved his hand as if to knock my camera away and I wanted to punch him one. But I knew better. "Don't you dare touch this camera... or me," I barked.

He took the protester and led him into the building. I followed, closeup of his hand on the man's neck. *Click.* We went from the dark night outside into a glaringly lit station.

"Disturbing the peace," he told the man at the desk.

"The Nazi's had already disturbed it," I added.

"You want we should book you, too, loudmouth?" the desk sergeant asked me. I flashed my press pass. "I don't give a shit if you're royalty, you're in my house now."

Officer O'Hara shook the protester. "What's your name, buddy?"

"Izzy... Isadore Greenbaum... sir."

"OK, Greenbaum, what you got to say for yourself?"

"I went down to the Garden without any intention of interrupting. But being that they talked so much against my religion and there was so much hate against us I lost my head, and I felt it was my duty to talk."

"Don't you realize that innocent people might have been killed?" the Sergeant asked while I stared at him in disbelief.

Izzy replied, "Do you realize that plenty of Jewish people are already being killed with their persecution? Imagine if it was your people, sir?"

"Yeah, well it ain't. You gotta choice. 10 days in jail or a $25 fine."

"$25? That's a month's rent!" he said, shocked. "I don't have that."

"Then 10 days in jail."

I opened my wallet. I had $40 cash. "I'll pay it."

"And who are you, exactly."

"I'm the press."

"'The Press?" He mocked. "What, like some superhero bullshit? Where's your cape?" they all laughed.

"Take. The. Money." I said, trying to contain my anger but not quite caring if a little showed.

"Keep. Your. Pants. On. Missy." The Sergeant grabbed the cash out of my hands and handed me a receipt and $15. "And now he's your problem, get him out of here."

I helped Izzy outside and hailed a cab. I drove with him back to Brooklyn and had the cab wait. I helped him up four flights of stairs and knocked on his door. A tiny woman opened the door and was aghast.

"Izzy, what happened to you?" she asked.

I told her.

"Isn't he wonderful?" she asked, kissing his face gently. "Thank you," she said to me.

The entire cab ride back, I kept seeing the loving way she looked at him. I wished I had a picture of it.

84 ⇛ Enemies

The cab let me off at the Chrysler building. The lobby guard
recognized me and let me in. The 50th floor was dark. I knocked on
Pat's door. No answer. I let myself into the darkroom.

I pressed the red button on the developing machine and heard it
whir into action, then fed my film into it and waited for it to come out
the other end. I turned on the light box and clipped the negatives to the
top so I could see them.

Then I felt something on my shoulder! Had I been followed? *I
screamed and jumped!* All the adrenaline from the night had finally
caught up with me. I stood there, gasping for breath.

It was Pat. "Sorry Herb! I didn't mean to scare you. I was asleep
on my sofa."

It took me a bit before I could talk, during which I just waved my
hands as if she'd know what that meant. "I.. it was... There are so many
of them. I even knew two. A PR woman from the aquacade, Mrs.
Weber... said she knows you"

"Carol Weber? She used to work here in advertising! You can
never trust someone in advertising."

"There were 20,000 people there. Look!" I stepped aside and she
took a loupe to the negatives.

"My God. Terrifying." She silently inspected the images. "You've
made them look like monsters."

"That's what they looked like to me."

"Showing them for what they truly are."

"And *we're their enemy*," I said, feeling a smile spread on my face.

"Indeed, we are," she said, smiling back. "The truth will out." She
took a swig from a flask, then handed it to me. My heart was only now
starting to calm down. I sniffed the flask. It reminded me of Pa, I shook
my head, "no," then had to steady myself against the light box.

"Go home. Be back tomorrow at 10. We're putting the issue
together and I want your input, also any captions or stories you have
for a writer to work up."

I followed her into the reception area. She picked up the phone, "Please call a cab for Mr. Hamilton on our account."

She patted me on the back. "Goodnight, Herb. I'm very proud of you." Luckily the elevator door was already open, because once inside, by myself, I cried all the way down to the lobby.

85 ➺ Beautiful Mess

I fell asleep in the cab. The cabbie's voice jolted me awake. Kitty wasn't home yet. I dropped my clothes on the floor and fell into bed.

Next thing I knew it was morning. My eyes were dry. I shuffled into the bathroom and splashed water on my face. I went back into the bedroom. Kitty wasn't there. I found my watch. 8am. Mickey was smiling but maybe it was time for an adult watch.

Wait, 8am? Where was Kitty?

I went to the front door to see if Sam had left a pink message slip under the door, but no. What if she'd been kidnapped? What if Mrs. Weber, who knew my name, had me followed and kidnapped Kitty? Surely she would have fought back! She could have even beaten them up... but maybe there was a gang of them! My face got red and hot and I started pacing from one end of the living room to the other.

What had I done? What could I do? Why was I so hungry?

And what was that noise at the window? I heard something tapping on the glass. Tapping. Tapping. It was a bee. That bee. *My bee.*

I moved towards the window to let it in. Just then I heard a key in the door and the bee flew away just as Kitty flew in, looking messily elegant in her tux—and the necklace I'd given her.

"Good morning, baby!" she slurred.

I was simultaneously relieved and angry.

"I was so worried! Where have you been?"

"My solo was a smash! You shoulda seen it!" she fell onto the sofa. "Then we partied with the nicest Hollywood talent Scout, Mr. Kenton. Mr. *Wallace* Kenton. Of Mr. 20th Century Fox studios, himself. You have simply *got* to try this cocaine, it's marvelous. I have some in my bag..."

And then, just like that, she was out cold. I picked her up and carried her to bed. I tried to get her out of the tux but gave up and she lay there, snoring, a beautiful mess.

She'd be out all day. I took a shower, ordered eggs, sunny side up, hash browns, bacon, a bagel with a schmear, orange juice and coffee. It arrived by the time I dried off. I was ravenous.

I looked at the newspaper delivered just outside the door. I scanned the front page for an article about the rally. There was one, but no pictures. The article mostly talked about how the police kept things in order *outside*, not what was really happening *inside!*

"'We have enough people here to stop a revolution,' the police Commissioner said jocularly." Was it a joke to him? With that attitude, would they fight, if necessary?

The article mostly talked about the protests outside... a whole 'nother story I hadn't seen. More than 800 protesters and 1,900 policemen... but who, exactly, were they protecting?

"Mayor LaGuardia ridiculed the event as an 'exhibition of international cooties' and said he believed in exposing cooties to the sunlight."

Maybe I'd eaten too fast or but all this just made me feel sick to my stomach. I wished I did have a superhero cape.

I put on my gray suit... oh no! There was blood on the shoulder from Izzy's face.

86 »→ Fair/Unfair

I headed downtown early, got off the subway at 42nd street and walked. Everyday, everything looked different.

But now this all felt routine. I almost forgot to stop and appreciate the golden splendor of the lobby. 50th floor. View. Louise. "Good morning, Mr. Hamilton, you're early. I'll let Pat know you're here."

I wasn't taking pictures so I wasn't sure what I was doing there. Pat appeared from the darkroom. "Come with me, I'll show you how it works before the others arrive."

I followed her into a conference room with a big wood table and 16 chairs. The walls were covered, floor to ceiling, with cork. Pat was pinning prints up and down and left and right all the way around the room. There was a small number in the lower right of each image. Between them were full page advertisements.

"This is how Sergei and I see the order of the issue, but things will change before it's set. The men will want their say, especially Jerry Norman, head of advertising. He'll be sitting to your right. I'll keep the editorial integrity intact, but sometimes compromises must be made. Remember that. We do what we have to, so we can say what we must. In the end, Clive has the final say."

I walked past the photos, some mine, some I'd never seen before, like dramatic photos of bombed out buildings. "Where is this?" I asked.

"London. The Germans are bombing the city every night now."

I wondered how long before they started bombing New York City. About what could happen to Kitty and the Chrysler building... and Ma. I felt a sharp pain on my hand and slapped it.

"Are you OK?" Pat asked. "Sit there," she pointed to the other side of the table. "Let the others talk first. They'll be moving the photos around, taking a lot of them off the wall. Don't let that bother you. Everything is negotiable..."

"...Everything?"

"Except the truth. Trust me, I do this every week." I did trust her. "The best time to say something is when it's most important *to you*, then it stands out. OK? And keep your camera out where they can see it, but do not take any pictures here. This process is private."

"OK."

A group of men came in, all older, in nicer suits than mine, but I was the only one there with a camera. They were carrying cups of coffee and laughing about something. They looked at me like, "Who are you?" then saw the Leica and nodded. They walked around the room, looking at the photos in order. Some didn't pay much attention, others frowned and shook their heads.

A tall man in a dull gray suit yanked a series of photos from the wall, leaving a long gap. He set the photos, face down in front of his chair, then rested his coffee cup on top of them, not caring it was leaving a stain.

A smiling man in a sharkskin suit and bright tie with a hypnotic modernist design sat next to me. "Hi, I'm Jerry Norman. Pleased to meet a budding talent!" he said, exceptionally friendly. "We're always looking for a good lensman to help our advertisers." He handed me a card. "Come see me after the meeting and we'll talk." Nobody else introduced themselves.

Every seat was filled, except for two at the ends of the table. The men quieted down with the occasional whisper to each other, things like: "always late," and "power play." Pat, meanwhile, took note of the blank spaces on the wall, looked at who had them on the table and pursed her lips.

The men went silent when the last man finally arrived, distinguished, white mustache, impeccable dark blue window-pane checked suit with a blue velvet vest and a long gold watch chain. He sat at the far end of the table. "Pat, I hear you have something very special for us, please proceed."

"Thank you, Clive, gentlemen. First, I'd like to introduce you to our guest, a talented new staff photographer who shot several series in this issue, Herbert Hamilton." She gestured at me and they applauded, politely.

She went to one corner of the room that had a beautiful photo of the Trylon and Perisphere that I didn't take. "Now, as you all know, we did an issue on the World's Fair's opening, but the world has already changed since then. Germany has invaded..."

At the mention of Germany, I saw a couple of men roll their eyes, including Jerry.

"To give credit where credit is due, it was Clive's brilliant idea that we produce a very special double edition titled 'Fair' on one cover, and 'Unfair' on the other. Yes, two covers in one issue. 'Fair' isn't just about the fair, but about the 'World of Tomorrow,' a hopeful look at what the world can be. 'Unfair' is our world of today, the war in Europe that's creeping its way over here, too. 'Unfair' is printed upside down on what otherwise would be the back cover, and the two meet in the middle with a two-page spread that reflects the turning point between these two worlds."

"Excuse me, but..." Jerry started.

"Jerry, I understand we lose the back cover ad space. Clive and I also discussed the difficulties of selling ads for the 'Unfair' side. So, in the interest of world events, Clive has magnanimously decided that 'Unfair' be pure editorial—you don't have to worry about selling ads there."

"But, in the interest of costs..." Jerry continued.

"It's already been decided, Jerry, let's move on. Gentlemen, to make it more palatable for you and our readers, I'd like to introduce..." She unveiled an easel in the corner revealing two of my photos of Kitty, one excitedly pointing at the Trylon and Perisphere, the other of her held aloft by James. One of the men whistled. "Kitty Rose, as photographed by Mr. Hamilton. Kitty is the all-American girl who'll be our guide through both worlds, making them palatable, relatable, as well as very pretty."

Genuine applause. The men clearly liked her. Even Jerry smiled, if a bit greedily. "Nice piece of ass," he whispered to me and I smiled back, bearing my teeth.

"Given that this is a double issue, yet we only have Clive for the customary time, I ask that we all work together to make this process as efficient as possible. Thank you."

The men got up and walked along the walls, making notes. Jerry sidled over to Clive and whispered something. Clive shook his head *no,* dismissively.

A slight man, maybe 35, in an unusual rough cream jacket, was unpinned and rearranged pictures. He moved gracefully, like a dancer, but with the energy of a hummingbird. His long, narrow face was topped with a small explosion of wild red hair that bounced as he moved, and ended in precisely trimmed V of a goatee.

Pat whispered to me, "That's Sergei, the art director, he's on our side but he'll make a show of arguing, it's part of the game."

A pasty blond man removed two photos. Sergei wrenched them from his hands and put them back. The blond man sat down in a huff.

"Pat, my luff," Sergei said with an accent and a touch of a lisp. "The concept is divine, of course, but the covers are banal. May I?"

"Do I ever deny you anything, Sergei?" she replied. More rolling of eyes from the other men, especially Jerry.

Sergei unpinned my photo of the people holding up the world and tore it in half. I felt my mouth fall open but closed it before anybody saw. He put it under the full photo of the Perisphere so it was clear they were holding up the whole thing.

Then he took one of my diver-in-mid-air photos, unpinned it and tore out the diver. He unpinned an advertisement for kitchen knives, tore out the knife and stuck it, blade up, next to the globe, making it into a deadly Trylon. Finally, he placed the diver so it looked like he was doing a backflip from the tip of the blade.

Pat smiled. I smiled. It told the whole story instantly on both ends. I liked this Sergei fellow—and I wanted to know where he bought his jacket.

"You can't use an advertiser's knife for this!" Jerry protested.

"Really? I thought they'd want to be on the cover for free, Jerry." Sergei teased him.

The other men started to argue, "Radical." "Off putting." "Too surreal." "Too cerebral." "Won't play in Peoria..."

They grew increasingly agitated until Clive stood up. They all went silent. "Excellent work, Sergei. Thank you. Next."

Jerry pointed at his watch and left promptly. Sergei rearranged the order of some photos and looked at Pat who approved.

Then, slowly, the tall, gray man in a cold gray suit walked up to the biggest blank spot on the wall and announced grandly, "I veto photos 36-42," he said, flipping them face up on the table. They were the series of the Nazi youth accosting Kitty.

"I second that veto," said the pudgy blond man to his right.

"Perhaps you can let the others see them first?" Pat said. I reached across the table and handed the stack to the younger man to their right. He looked, disturbed, and passed it on to his right.

"And your rationale?" Pat asked.

"Our readers will not take kindly to having their pretty all-American girl threatened like that."

I had to speak. "But that's what happened."

The pasty blond man continued, "I think what Douglas is saying is that our readers will find it upsetting."

"Thank you, Karl," Douglas said, "that's exactly what I meant."

"But it *was* upsetting. It *is* upsetting." I said, as calmly as I could.

"I imagine it was, but our readers in the Midwest are unlikely to..."

"So you're saying they'd rather be surprised when Nazis accost their daughters than to have been given a warning?"

"I don't think that's what Douglas meant..." Karl offered.

"Douglas, what exactly did you mean?" Pat jumped in before I jumped on him.

"I question the wisdom of alienating our readers of German descent."

"German or Nazi?" I couldn't stop myself, "Because it sounds like you're saying they're all the same thing." A ruckus ensued. I hunkered down and tried to be invisible, but saw Pat wink at me.

"Herb has a very good point." Pat spoke, calmly. "Those of German descent should know there's a difference and not take offense. But, as always, let's see what Clive feels about this."

Clive went through the stack and took a moment to consider. "It's a powerful series. Run it."

Sergei pinned the photos back up.

"Please excuse Karl and me as we have a phone call scheduled with the head office in Des Moines," he said as the two sulked out.

There was a brief silence, broken by one of the younger men with slicked back hair. "Um, pardon me, but I don't understand the ducks."

My ducks? I hadn't even seen the ducks! I scanned the walls for them. There, on the 'Unfair' side, the boy with the bloody bag, smiling. Followed by the little girl spitting in Izzy's face, then smiling, followed by thousands of God-fearing Americans giving the Nazi salute.

"They learn young," was all Pat said. I saw the understanding dawn on his face.

"I have a very very big problem, Pat. It simply cannot be done this way. Quite impossible"

"And what is that? Sergei?"

"It's the center spread where the two issues meet." Sergei announced, rifling through a stack of unused photos on the table. He pulled out two. On the 'Unfair' side he pinned the two policemen with the bomb. In the very center he placed the blackened crater with the arm and charred flag above. "That's where the ends, is it not?"

"Hopefully not, but you're right, it's the central image."

Clive got up and walked around looking at the order. "I agree. But we can't have the disembodied arm. Move the burnt flag down to cover it and that's our hero image."

I wanted to protest that he was changing the story... until I understood how he was making it about all of us.

The others followed behind him, suggesting, "we could use some photos from Poland, before and after the invasion. I have cousins there," and "we should include Japan's occupation of French Indochina..." "What's the page count and how long can we go?"

They looked through the unused photos and pinned more up on the wall. Pat leaned on the table next to me and whispered, "Got 'em."

Clive leaned in and inspected the rough 'Unfair' cover, patted Sergei on the back, then shook Pat's hand. "Marvelous work, Pat, thank you." Then to me, "and thank you, Mr. Hamilton. I look forward to seeing great things from you." Then, to the remaining men, "Carry on," he said, as he left.

Pat whispered to me, "Douglas and Karl are no doubt crying to head office in Des Moines even as we speak. But it won't matter with Clive firmly on our side."

"That's why you said this was his idea?"

"We'd discussed it and it partly was, besides, nobody argues with Clive. Jerry will be angry but I'll bet he's on the phone right now, too, selling full pages to companies with pavilions at the fair... If not that knife company about the back cover! He'll get over it. Now, let me introduce you to Sergei. Serg, Herb."

He squeezed my hand gently... what soft hands he had. He looked me straight in the eye. "It is my greatest pleasure to make the acquaintance of such a fine artist as yourself." He leaned over and kissed my hand.

"Serg, play nice."

"Was that not nice?"

"It was very nice, thank you, Sergei. I love what you did with the covers, and the center spread. Where'd you get that jacket, it's beautiful!"

"Raw silk from Thailand. As I suspected, a man of true taste and refinement, my dear," he said to Pat.

"Serg collects beautiful things... and people," Pat said, while Sergei bowed deeply. He stood up and took off the jacket.

"You must try it on Hugh-bear," he said.

"No, really, I can't."

"Of course you can, but if you choose not to I will be deeply offended." He handed it to me. I put it on. I was surprised at how well it fit, snug but European. Except that, being several inches taller than him, the sleeves were too short. He fussed with the cuffs. "My tailor took these in so he can let them out. It is you, maestro, you must keep it."

I immediately started to take it off. "No, that's very generous but I couldn't possibly…"

"He probably has three others just like it, don't you Serg?"

"Only two. This is the oldest. Frayed like a rag, I am almost embarrassed to offer such a schmatta but since you like it…"

I shook my head, "no."

"Consider it a trophy for your work in this issue. Wear it tonight when you come to my loft for a party of artists to whom I would like to introduce you."

"He's not going to stop until you say *yes*."

"OK, then yes, thank you. It's too kind, really."

"You will like my friends and they will like you."

"Will you be there, Pat?"

She laughed. "Once was quite enough for me. But you're young, and his friends are… interesting…"

"I seem to remember it was more than once…" Sergei teased her. She placed her finger on his lips.

Sergei reached over to me and pulled a small purple leather pad from the inside of his, now my, jacket. "I do need this. I shall write my address for you. The party starts at midnight." He turned on his thick heeled ostrich cowboy boots and strode out of the room, turning back to blow a kiss.

"What an interesting guy," I said.

"More than you know. Herb, I'm damned proud of what we've done here and what 2 million readers are going to have to confront. We're going to change a lot of hearts and minds. Who knew we'd have Carmen Miranda to thank for our meeting!"

"It's weird how the world works—and wonderful."

"Let's hope we can help it be more wonderful than weird."

"Speaking of wonderful, I can't believe he gave me his jacket."

"It suits you. He likes you. Which can be... intoxicating. Just know that he... likes a lot of people, if you know what I mean."

"I guess so."

"Seriously, listen to me, Herb—Do *not* take your Leica to the party. Some of his so-called artist friends are more con artists than fine artists."

"Oh, OK, thank you."

"I have a lot of work to do with production to get this ready. Clive's being very generous but our deadlines are the same. In the meantime, your next assignment is to figure out what your next assignment is and tell me!"

"I'll keep my eyes open, chief!" I said. She laughed.

As I left I turned back and looked at the walls. So many of my photos. It just dawned on me that this would be printed millions of times over and the world would see what I saw.

87 ⇛ The Great Wave

Kitty was still asleep. I carefully hung my new jacket, then took off my clothes and got into bed with her. She curled up in my arms. I reached down, got my camera, held it above us and clicked. I wanted to remember what this felt like. Whether or not the photo was in focus, the memory would be sharp in my mind. I fell asleep...

...We are on a raft together, floating down the Hudson river, only the river is clear and blue and there are colorful fish swimming beneath us. The shore is lined with hula girls strumming ukuleles and dancing in their grass skirts. It is paradise.

The calm is shattered by the sound of metal cracking. I stand on the raft and watch as the Statue of Liberty strains at her base, topples over and crashes into the bay, creating a tidal wave that grows and grows as it rushes towards us.

I furiously paddle the raft, thinking we might be able to somehow surf the wave, but it's taller than the Chrysler Building which disappeared under it.

Kitty's asleep on the raft and won't wake up!

I see a bald eagle flying overhead and call for it to come down and take Kitty in its talons, flying her to safety. I wonder how long I can hold my breath. The wave hits and I'm rolled over and over and over...

...Until I fell out of bed, pulling the covers with me. I whimpered and flailed until I was awake and extricated from the sheets. I stood there, naked, surprised to be dry. Kitty was still asleep on our bed, our raft. I straightened out the covers and as I tucked her in I saw bruises on the inside of her right elbow. What were those?

I leaned in to look closely and just then she turned over, her arm hitting me in the face, knocking me back to the floor.

Ow! My nose! I held it and moaned.

"What happened to you?" Kitty said, her eyes still closed.

"You did."

"What's that supposed to mean?"

"You hit me!"

"I'm asleep."

"You're talking! And before that, you pulled a Joe Lewis right hook!"

"You musta been dreaming. Go back to sleep and dream I'm blowing you, Frank."

It was like she'd punched me in the gut. I fell backwards and lay there on the cold wood floor, unable to move.

Slowly, thoughts returned to my head, like "it's only sex," one of the first things she said to me. She musta wanted that solo spot really bad and... That Hollywood talent scout... And "a girl's gotta do what she's gotta do to take care of herself."

I could take care of her. But she didn't want me to. So why'd she let someone else?

"What're you doing here, baby?" Kitty mumbled.

"Who were you expecting?"

She opened her eyes and looked around. "Only you, baby. Only you." That just made it worse. "Could you get me some bromo, I don't feel so good this morning. Thank you, baby."

I went to the bathroom, filled a glass with water and stirred in two spoonfuls of powder. But I couldn't pick it up. I left it on the counter, walked past the bed, opened one of the little round windows and climbed to the roof, naked. I stood there, letting the wind whip around me.

What else could hurt me? I'd already drowned.

88 ⇒ Different Animal

I climbed down from the roof. Threw on some clothes and went downstairs to talk to Sam.

"You always knew she was a cat, Herb. Doesn't make it easier, though, I know." Sam said, his hand on my shoulder.

"But I'd *hoped...*"

"You mean, 'you loved.' Or still love? What're you gonna do?"

"Hell if I know."

"I told you about Heloise, right?"

"Your chorus girl?"

"Yeah. And Sally?"

"Your wife."

"Them's two different animals."

"I'm really sad."

"A course." Sam's hand hadn't moved from my shoulder. It was nice just to sit there, quietly, and not feel alone.

After a while he said, "Find yourself a different animal. Or, let them find you."

89 ➻ Bespoke

I had to get away.

Everything was a sunny blur, back on my bike, gliding down Amsterdam Ave. Listening to kids laughing and moms yelling and taxis honking. Smelling pizza and pretzels and dry cleaning and diesel. Even tasting a bug in my mouth. For a little while, at least, the world felt normal. *I* felt normal.

I thought about riding up to the old neighborhood... Until I remembered what normal there was like. I'd somehow forgotten. I made a mental note to call Mr. Clarke at the bank and send more money to Ma.

I was brought back to the present when I hit the bumper of a stopped cab and had to hold on to the handlebars to keep from flying off my bike. Two women in the back of the cab turned around to see what had hit them. They both wore white hats, and between them sat a little dog with a shock of white hair. I grabbed my camera. *Click!*

Traffic was stopped for blocks. I rolled down the street, slowly, looking in car windows. People inside were in their own little worlds. In one cab, a little girl was pressing her face up against the glass, squishing her nose. *Click.* In another, a well-dressed older man was kissing a pretty young woman... Yuk. *Click.*

In another, a couple was fighting, their faces alternating between being wounded and enraged, back and forth like a poisoned game of catch. *Click. Click.*

A family, windows rolled down, heads out like dogs, ogling the tall buildings. Tourists. *Click.*

In a taxi, A young man fumbled with a small blue velvet box in his hands. *Click.* He accidentally dropped the ring and frantically fished around on the floor of the cab. *Click.* Looking horrified. *Click.* Finding it! *Click.* Putting it back in the box and the box in his pocket and sighing in relief. *Click.*

I wondered if that would ever be me.

A long, black limousine. Windows closed. A well dressed couple, him in a morning suit, her wearing a fur piece in summer. Both looking unhappy. Did someone die—or did love? *Click*. Or just mine? Trouble was, it hadn't died—I still loved Kitty.

A cabby was reading a paperback till the car behind him honked. *Click*. He drove up a few feet and started reading again. *Click*.

Another cabby trimmed his fingernails. Another ate a hoagie. One pulled a flask out from under his seat and took a swig. One was bouncing up and down... I kept moving.

I got out of the street and onto the sidewalk, walking my bike and looking in more windows. Into a hair salon where women in pink robes sat under hair dryers like pink mechanical beehives. *Click*. They looked like science fiction robots with shiny helmets which they'd lift to expose a strange assortment of metal loops attached to their heads. *Click*. Other women sat at their feet, painting their toenails. *Click*.

In a tailor shop a man was being measured for a suit. Oh, I needed a new suit! Which reminded me of Shapiro's which reminded me of Myron, which reminded me... of Kitty.

I could go back to Saks for a suit... but I could afford to have Shapiro's make me one custom. Why not? I rode over to Central Park West and up 8th to 145th and into the South Bronx.

It felt the same, but different, because *I* was different.

I went into Shapiro's. It hadn't changed. Only I had. Maybe Myron had, too, because he didn't look like what remembered, there was something more familiar about him.

He froze when he saw me. "Herbie."

"Myron."

He didn't move "Where ya been?"

"Workin'." I held up the camera. "I'm a photographer. For *Look* magazine."

"No kidding?"

"No kidding."

"Good for you, boychik. Good for you."

"I need a new suit and I want you to make it."

"No kidding?"

"No kidding." He just kept looking at me. "I want you to make it."

"No kidding."

"Why would I kid about this? I'm serious and I got money. What'll set me back?"

He stared at me for a while. "Depends on the fabric."

"Raw silk."

"Ain't we fancy? It's fine for a sports coat, but doesn't work for pants."

"Then Super 150 dark blue window pane." I took a step closer to him.

"$55. But for you..."

"$55 is fine. Maybe more. I want a fancy silk lining."

He sat behind the counter and shook his head. "I thought maybe something bad happened to you."

"No, all good. Mostly."

"We got some red Indian paisley silk, left over from Raj's wedding suit. He finally married Sapna. It was a nice wedding, but the food was too spicy. You coulda let me know you was OK."

"I'm sorry."

"Naw, it's OK. Why would you? I'm just surprised, is all. Glad you're doing so well. Mr. Shapiro is retiring so I'm head tailor now."

"Congratulations."

"It'll still be his shop, though. Can't afford to buy him out just yet. Maybe in a couple of years... Let me get Aaron to measure you..."

"I'd rather you do it."

"Naw..."

"It's OK."

"Let me get my tape measure..."

"It's around your neck."

"My new one, it's in the back... I gotta..." he went into the back. I heard him blow his nose.

I stood on a small raised platform in front of three mirrors, like I'd seen other customers do.

He came back with what looked like the same tape measure but his eyes were red. "My sinuses is bad right now, it hurts to lean over, so Aaron will measure you, he knows what he's doing. I'll pull some fabrics for you."

Aaron, short, balding at maybe 30, was a no-nonsense kind of guy. "Stand straight please. Arms down to your side." He started at the floor and measured up the outside of my leg, then the inseam, hips, waist, chest, arms, shoulder, neck. "All done. 36 regular."

"I've got some choices for you in blue windowpane check. If you're really flush, there's a special order Italian Super 150 that's better than the $200 suits downtown, and I can do it for $75."

It was beautiful, and felt very soft.

Myron asked, "You sure you didn't get into anything shady, Herbie, with all this dough?"

"No, I'm legit. Just been lucky, is all. That's a beautiful fabric, Myron."

"Yeah, I've wanted to make a suit with it. Oh, and here's the lining."

"Wow!"

"Too much?"

It was definitely too much. "I love it!"

"You always did appreciate nice clothes, I remember."

"And you were always very kind to me, Myron, I remember. That's why I wanted you to make my suit."

"Thanks, boychik. I'll need a deposit of $37.50, and it'll take two weeks... unless it's a rush."

"I was hoping to have it for tonight..."

"You're kidding."

"Yes, kidding."

"But we're not so busy at the moment. Maybe a week. I'll call you."

I opened my wallet to hand him a card, then stopped. "You can leave a message for me here." I wrote down Glenn's number. "Can I write you a check?"

"Sure."

I wrote it out for the full $75 and handed it to him.

"Naw, I only need a deposit today..."

"It's OK—You gotta order the fabric special and all."

"Thanks Herbie." He looked at the check. "Hamilton? Well, I'll be."

"Just sounded more... artistic."

"Yeah, I get it. Sounds good. And you look good. Thanks for trusting me... with your fancy suit and all."

"Hey, would you mind if I took some pictures of you at work? Maybe for the magazine?"

"Imagine that. Me, in a magazine. Could be good for business. OK, fire at will!" he said, finally smiling. A really nice smile. Soft. Guileless. I took a portrait of him reflected in the three mirrors, the measuring tape around his neck. *Click.* Putting away bolts of fabric. *Click.* Closeup on his delicate hands, marking a pattern in chalk. *Click.* Holding scissors, cutting fabric. *Click.* Holding a seam close to his face to sew. Breaking a thread between his teeth. *Click.* Finishing a padded shoulder. *Click.* Steaming. *Click.* All very calm and steady.

"Those look great!" I said. "I'll show them to my editor and see what angle we can find, like 'Old-world craftsmanship from a new generation.'"

"Thanks, Herbie, that's real nice of you."

"If you're hungry we could go over to Greenblatts and..."

"...Thanks, but I'm gonna keep working. I got some baked chicken from last night."

"Oh, OK. I'll get going then."

"Thanks for everything, Herbie. I appreciate it. It's good to see you, really. I'll call you when it's ready. We can deliver it, well, you'd know that."

"Thanks, for doing this for me, Myron. It was good seeing you again," I said as I left. I wanted to turn around and look at him but I didn't because now it was my eyes that were red.

90 ⇝ Want / Need

I wanted to go home. Wherever that was going to be now. The Ansonia had felt like home. Kitty had felt like home. So that's where I went. Max. Sam. Ellis. And Kitty. She was awake, perched on the sofa wearing my only pair of khaki pants and my white shirt while eating a steak and baked potato.

"Hi, Herb, whereya been? Hungry? Want some steak?" she said, all with her mouth full of food.

"Are those my clothes?"

"Yeah, they were just lying there in your drawer."

"*My* clothes."

"Very comfortable. You can wear mine if you want."

"I don't want."

"Steak?"

"No."

She took the last bite and some sauce dripped on my shirt. *My* shirt. "Oh, sorry," she said. "It'll come out."

At least it wasn't my special blue shirt. Still, I was so stunned I didn't know what to do. I went into the bedroom, took off all my clothes, put on her white satin robe, came back and picked up what was left of the baked potato, making sure to spill some butter on the silk. "Oh. Sorry. It'll come out."

She laughed gutturally. "I don't care. You can keep that."

I looked down at the greasy stain. What a shame, because it really was a pretty robe and the silk felt smooth and cool, but I was pretty sure it was as ruined as my shirt. I dropped the robe to the floor, then threw it towards the utility door and stood there, naked.

She tore off the shirt, two buttons flying, and unbelted the pants (which were held up with my blue and orange diamond tie!) and stood there, naked.

I was so angry I didn't so much want to screw her as control her. Yet there was something in her eyes that seemed to say the same thing to me. She leaped on me, like a tiger, knocking me onto the floor, my head hitting the edge of the sofa, stunned. She pushed me down and held my arms above my head, pinning me down and straddling me, kissing me so hard it was suffocating.

How dare she! I flipped over on top of her pressing into her. She struggled and gasped as I displayed my dominance. I felt her nails down my back, pulling me closer, wrapping her arms around me so tightly I could hardly breathe.

She wrapped her legs around me, too, then kicked at the sofa, sending us rolling across the floor. I tried to end up on top, but couldn't, we were locked side by side. She bit my lip, hard, I tasted blood. She *wanted* to hurt me! But I couldn't hurt her. I just wanted her to... wanted her to... I didn't know.

The fight went out of me. I went limp. Everywhere. I threw the game. She couldn't win if I didn't play.

She looked disappointed. I felt a tear run down my cheek.

"You're not even going to fight for me?" She panted.

"Why should I?"

"Because you love me."

"Why should I?" I asked.

"Because I know you do."

"Yeah, I do. But you don't care."

"I do care. But the world is changing," she said, looking off into space.

"I don't see a place in your world."

She stood up. "I'm going to Hollywood."

"I figured that. With Frank? Or with that talent scout guy, Kenton."

"You don't understand."

"Explain it to me. I deserve to know," I demanded.

"You couldn't understand. You haven't been with any other girls."

"So what?"

"It's not my secret to tell,"She insisted.

"Bullshit. Whose secret is it?"

"I'll tell you after I leave."

"You disgust me," I sighed.

"I used to disgust myself. Now I'm finally..." She got off me and sat in a chair. "Taking control of my own life."

I sat up and leaned against the wall. My back hurt. "That's what you call it?"

"Yes."

"Using yet another man to get what you want."

"Yes."

"What did you want from me?"

She closed her eyes and whispered. "Love."

Hearing her say that hit me hard. "I gave that to you. With all my heart."

"I'd never felt it before," she sighed.

"AND?" I demanded.

"It... was lovely, Herb... But..."

"BUT???"

"It wasn't what I needed."

I let my head fall back and rest, then began to knock my noggin against the wall, over and over, as if I could knock some sense into myself.

"Don't do that."

I kept doing it. Harder.

"Stop it, Herb!"

Harder.

She sat on the floor next to me and took my head in her hands until I stopped.

"You are the sweetest person I've ever known. You're way too good for me. And you knew it."

"I didn't."

"You do now. You also need to know that there will always be a little part of my cold, hard heart where I love you. Always."

"Just a little part."

"That's all I've got, baby. The rest is just muscle, ambition and anger."

I couldn't hold my head up anymore and let it fall into her hands. She stroked my cheeks and my hair and it was so strange to know this was over. That this woman, this person, this thing... had taken me from a boy to a man and now a broken man. No, not broken. Changed.

91 ➤ Raindrops

I watched her pack, rolling up the necklace I'd given her inside a silk scarf and slipping it in a red satin shoe to protect it. It meant something to her. I also saw her pack one of my ties... Maybe she'd remember me. I couldn't forget her.

She'd already told me she didn't want me to come to the station. "I don't want to cry and mess up my makeup," she said. She was wearing the white dress with cherries on it, "for the photographers."

Ellis got her bags and waited in the elevator.

We stood in the doorway, looking at each other. I couldn't tell what she was thinking.

"I'm gonna miss you," I said.

"Not as much as you think," she replied, rather sweetly before leaning in and kissing me, softly, but quickly. "See you in the funny papers," she said, eyes moist but forcing a smile. She turned and walked down the hallway, then into the elevator, then into my memory.

I closed the door.

I guess this was my place now, if I wanted it. I called Sam.

"Hi, Herb, you OK?"

"I dunno."

"You will be."

"I dunno."

"You should go out on the town and have a good time."

Oh, that's right. Sergei's party tonight. I'd forgotten. I already knew what I was going to wear. Raw Silk jacket, blue shirt, blue pants. And no Leica.

"Can you give me a wake-up call at 11?"

"I'll put it down for Tony, it's his shift."

"Thanks, my friend."

I couldn't do anything but get in bed. Still on "my side." I stared up through the ceiling window as the clouds rolled by, then little drops of rain started to fall...

...Suddenly it's morning and I'm reading the paper, a big photo of Kitty in her cherry dress on the front page. The headline screams, "Kitty makes Hollywood Purr!" Clark Gable is handing her a key to the city. The front page picture comes to life, like a movie, and there she is accepting her Academy Award and putting her feet in cement at Grauman's Chinese and there I am, waving at her, calling her name. She looks right at me and doesn't recognize me...

...I was back in bed at night, the rain fell harder. The steady pitter patter made my eyelids heavy.

The phone rang. It's my wake-up call from Tony. "Good evening, Mr. Hamilton. It's 11pm. Are you awake or should I call you back in 10 minutes?"

"I'm awake, thanks."

I took a shower. I got dressed. Put the old Kodak 35 camera and some film in my pocket.

Down in the lobby, I asked, "Tony, can you look up this address for me? Christopher St. at West St."

"That doesn't sound right, let me check." He pulled out a large map, ran his finger along the index at the bottom and said, "G2..." then moved his finger to that box on the map.

"West Village piers? At night? Are you sure?"

"That's what he wrote down, I was invited to a party."

"Oh, dear. I'll call you a taxi. Make sure they wait 'til you know it's the right address, you don't want to be out on the street there alone."

I didn't think Sergei would lead me astray, but now I was anxious.

"Thanks, Tony," I handed him a silver dollar. "Do you have an umbrella I could use tonight?"

"Yes, sir, we do. But you won't need one tonight, that storm has passed."

The sky was, indeed, clear.

92 ➻ The Colony

"You sure this is right?" the taxi driver asked, smelling like garlic.

"It's what he wrote down... but no."

"It's your funeral," he said, taking off south down Broadway, to 7th. There wasn't any traffic so the city flew by. With each block the buildings got darker until the entire block was dark, except one building at the corner.

"This should be it, but please wait until I'm sure," I asked, paying him. As soon as I got out of the cab he sped away, leaving me alone on the deserted street.

I heard music coming from the building with lights on inside. There was a large man sitting on a small stool outside the front door. "Name?" He demanded.

"Sergei invited me"

"He invited a lot of people. What's your name?"

"Herbert Hamilton."

He picked up a clipboard from the floor and looked down the list. "Don't see it. Go away."

"He just invited me today, I'm sure if you ask..." He held up his hand, then flipped to the last page, the last name. "See, there it is!"

"Yeah, man, I can read. Good luck there, fresh meat!" he said, opening the door.

"What?"

"I said, 'Nice to meet... you,'" he said, holding out his hand for a tip. I gave him 50 cents just for letting me in.

Inside was a large, white-washed brick room, empty except for the walls which were covered in basically the same large painting, repeated eight times. They looked like the Russian icons I'd seen at the Met, only bigger.

The backgrounds were silver leaf over geometric textures, different on each painting. Floating in the middle of the silver was the figure of a man, his arms outstretched. His body was silver, too, like armor, except for his face, hands and feet, which were painted.

I recognized Sergei's face in one of the paintings. I didn't recognize the other man, or a woman's face in the third. The other five paintings were black where the faces and hands would go.

I heard soft rhythmic music coming from upstairs and followed it. Each step was painted with line of a poem:

Let us go as bees in honey drown
  Gone before we're ultimately down
    Subsumed in sweetness
      to completeness
        sugar for our crown.
      Let us go for go we surely will
        feel the warmth before we feel the chill
        the end is always near
          climb up with me, my dear
            until it's all downhill, from here.
          Let us go as venom is expelled
            rebelling till the end when we are felled
            in service of the hive
              we won't make it out alive
                but at least we know that once
                we had excelled.

The next floor was a tall, two-story space, filled with people and smoke. Overhead were steel tracks and a yellow crane, fitted with a mirror ball that was slowly moving back and forth, bathing the room in ever changing sparks of the light.

I made my way around the edge of the room, looking for Sergei, or Pat, or anybody I knew, but they were all strangers. "Stranger" was putting it mildly. *Click.* Many wore masks, but otherwise were naked from the waist up… sometimes the waist down, too. *Click.* Their faces and bodies were painted with lines, like skeletons, and glistening with sweat… even the women. *Click.* They moved slowly, as if they were in a trance, and nobody seemed to notice me.

I made my way to the front of the building where large doors opened to a view of the river. I stood there, watching.

There was a loud buzzing noise from overhead, and I looked up to see a winged angel, all in white, hanging from the crane, floating down, towards me—Sergei.

He landed, softly, locking my gaze. He slipped out of his wings, which floated away behind him. The others froze. He took a step towards me. They took a step towards me. Another step. Another.

His nose was practically touching mine. I could smell mint on his breath. I could hear the group breathing in unison until I breathed with them.

He smiled, then leaned in and whispered into my ear. "Welcome to The Colony." His lips brushed my cheek, then my lips, then he kissed me and slipped his tongue into my mouth. I let him. I wanted to forget.

His tongue was supple, strong. I felt him push something small and hard under my tongue. A pill, bitter, metallic before dissolving, and then his minty tongue again.

I felt lightheaded. He reached around to hold me up, his hand slipping down my back, into the waistband of my pants, holding my ass tight. I wanted to let go. To be taken somewhere. To be taken.

I felt his other hand move down my chest, into my pants, into my shorts and cup my balls. I opened my eyes and saw everyone watching. I wanted them to know. To see. To see me. To see who I was and what I wanted.

I felt their hands on me, removing the raw silk jacket. Unbuttoning my shirt. Undoing my belt. Unzipping my pants. Releasing me from the constraints of clothing. Freeing me from being human. I watched as they did the same thing to him, and he emerged a furry satyr.

I reached around him and felt his fuzzy ass. It was nice. Did he have a tail? I kept feeling.

He kissed my chest, licked my nipples, kissing down until he was on his knees. I watched while he kissed my cock, then sucked it into his electric mouth with a current I'd never felt—it ran up my spine to my tongue and mouth and ears and eyes.

Was he growing horns? I thought maybe he was...

I *knew* he was glowing, filled with red light, like a cloud of incandescent poppies coalescing into human form. I wasn't imagining it, I could *see* it. Just as I could see the colors in everyone around me... Orange. Peach. Daisy. Cornflower. Fuchsia. Ginger. Rose.

I could even see the colors of people behind me, cooling in the breeze from sunflower to iris, hibiscus to morning glory.

I was filled with fresh leaf green. Moss. Pine. Pear. Pickle.

The room was ablaze with color as edges disappeared between myself, or whatever I was now, and the air, between myself and Sergei, or whatever he was. Light. Color. Energy.

All was one.

His fire was mixing with my sea and together we were becoming gold.

I felt us floating up, my feet no longer needed the floor, and we were alone, upstairs, while the others colors swirled below.

I was on my knees in front of him, marveling at his light, at the intensity of the color, my tongue wanting to taste his pomegranate red heat. There was a moment when I hesitated but the color was too compelling, and the feeling... Warm, smooth, solid yet yielding... the taste... salty sweet nourishing, life-giving... natural.

So natural. So normal. Simple. How men should be with each other. How people should be with each other. Touching. Giving. Sharing. No boundaries.

I floated down on a soft cloud bed. I watched and felt him on top of me, all that light and color and heat opening to me and gliding down my cock head and shaft, so tight and warm and right. Absolutely right.

I wanted us to be one. I wanted to feel him and know how he was feeling me as we emanated this amber light. I felt a lime coolness as he slid off of me and lifted my legs. A crimson warmth pressed against me, into me... I opened for him. I welcomed him. I felt him enter me, take me, fill me.

I was finding myself by giving. Finding, not losing.

His stinger was in me—then his venom... no, it was honey.

I once was lost, but now I am found, was blind, but now I see.

93 ➽ Baptism

Golden light oozed through the windows as a horizon of color rose inside the room. Sergei's arms were around me and I didn't want to move. I closed my eyes and went back to sleep.

I woke up later with sunlight on my face. I sat up, trying to remember where I was. I had a headache. My body was sore, my armpits itchy, my mouth dry.

There was a pitcher of water with lemons by the bed. I poured it into a glass and drank it, then another.

I heard footsteps, looked up and saw Sergei enter, barefoot... furry but human feet. He was wearing a saffron silk robe, embroidered in purple, hanging open. He carried a silver tray.

"Good morning, lover." He sat on the edge of the bed, picked up a piece of pineapple and placed it at my lips. I opened my mouth and tasted its juicy tart sweetness. "How are you feeling today?"

"Different," I swallowed.

"OK?"

"Yes."

"Good."

"I have a headache," I said, squinting at the sharp edges of everything.

"That's normal. Drink all this water, and eat, that will help."

"Itchy."

"I'm drawing you a bath."

"You're not glowing anymore." It was disappointing, though he was still quite beautiful.

"What colors were we?"

"Together we were golden."

He smiled. "I saw this, too." He placed a piece of something yellow and soft at my lips... cheese. Earthy, sharp, smooth. I looked at the tray covered with a perfectly arranged spiral of fruit and cheese, drizzled with honey, a sunflower at its center. I wanted to take a picture of it. Of him holding it.

"Where's my camera?"

"In the closet with your clothes. I took out the film from last night. We have rules about that for everyone's privacy."

"Yes. Besides, what I saw at first is not... things look different now."

"Exactly. I knew you'd understand."

His soft penis looked very strange, with extra skin at the end. I thought maybe he'd had some kind of accident. "What happened to your cock?" I asked.

"Nothing. This is how cocks are supposed to look. I'm not circumcised like Jews are."

"Oh, I've never seen one." I sat up to get a closer look. Weird. Then I glanced over the railing to the large room below. It was full of furniture now, sofas and chairs covered in bright flower colors, like the colors of the people last night. "I remember... everything... or think I do... but now..."

"What you remember is what matters." He prodded my lips with a piece of orange. It tasted especially... colorful. "Eat. Drink. You'll need more sleep, too. I hope you'll feel at home here," he said, with such welcoming gentleness that, despite the grandeur of the space, I did.

"Does that happen every night?" I wondered aloud.

"Heavens, no. It was in your honor. During the day this can be a beehive of artistic activity, but nights are usually quiet."

Another man entered, I recognized his face from the painting downstairs. He leaned in and kissed Sergei on the mouth. I must have looked surprised.

"Did you not meet last night? Hu-bear, this is Julien."

"Oh, hello, I saw you in the painting."

"Maybe you will join us there soon?" Julien said, sounding French.

"Who is the woman?"

"I told you he sees everything." Sergei raised his eyebrows at Julien.

"My wife, Claudine. She prepared this tray for you."

"It's beautiful, and delicious, thank you," I said, seeing but not understanding.

"You are still confused, I can tell. This is normal. Did Sergei tell you this is normal?"

"Yes."

"I must go and help her prepare for the lunch. I will see you again, I feel sure of it," he said, bowing, then leaving.

"Come with me," Sergei said, reaching out his hand. His skin was darker than I remembered. He helped me to my feet, but I felt dizzy. He put his arm around me. His hand was smaller than I remembered. "Take your time."

"I'm OK, now," I said, as he led me, arm still around my waist, into a small, tall room in the back. It was painted midnight blue, with arches and gold stars like a cathedral room I'd seen at the Met. It was lit by a candelabra that made the stars flicker.

In the middle of the room was a hexagonal marble tub with flowers floating on the water. It smelled of lilac and lavender. Sergei helped me step into it. I sank into the warmth and instantly felt better.

"I don't want you to fall asleep in the bath so I will stay here. Besides, I am sure you have questions. Ask. Anything."

I had so many questions and yet none would come out as the water held me. "Maybe they don't matter."

"You matter, so anything you wonder or share matters to me," he said, picking up a sea sponge and washing my back.

"I feel like I see everything but... I don't understand it."

"Still, you go with it, don't you?"

"I want to experience, and understand."

"Sometimes we can only experience." He wrung out the sponge and the sound of the water echoed off the walls.

"And that's enough?"

"Yes.

"Who is Julien?"

"We are lovers and partners."

"And Claudine?"

"With her, too."

I shrugged. "I don't understand."

"What's to understand? We love each other."

"I feel love, but don't understand it."

"Who does?" he chuckled.

"And he... they... are OK with... me?"

"Of course. We mean the world to each other, but we are not the world. One must always be open, as you are, to new ways to expand your world."

I slid my head underwater. I stayed under as long as I could and wished I could breathe like a fish. I came up and brushed the flowers off my face. It was very quiet.

Sergei asked, "Tell me what is happening in your world."

I heard myself telling him about Kitty. About her leaving. Feeling both abandoned, and somehow relieved. I hadn't known I felt relieved until just then.

Without thinking, I told him about the bee.

"She led you here."

"But isn't that weird?"

He untied the sash of his robe and let it fall to the floor. He leaned over and pointed to his right shoulder. There was a life-like tattoo... of a yellow and black bee. He smiled, "Weird?"

My stomach rumbled and I was unable to stop the torrent of bubbles that emerged and floated to the surface. Sergei laughed.

"The world is weird, Huber. Evaporation. Chlorophyll. Digestion. Shit. War. All weird. I don't claim to understand any of it. We, you and I, are queer. That I do understand. Others might think we are weird and everything else is normal. That is because they don't really see. They just 'look,' like the stupid name of our magazine. My magazine will be called 'SEE.'"

"Queer sounds bad to me, like a playground bully."

"Who is probably queer himself and afraid of it. It's a good word, meaning, off-center, eccentric. Which we are."

"I used to think I was normal."

"What is normal? To you and I it's you and I. We understand each other. It's the rest of the world that's weird." He stepped into the tub behind me and I felt his legs wrap around me. "How does this feel?"

"Queer. Normal." I leaned back against his chest and lay my head on his shoulder, looking at the bee tattoo. I wanted one.

94 ⟫ Sonar

I felt so relaxed after the bath... and sleepy. Sergei led me back to bed and now, in the light, I saw the window above the bed was a large round clock face with the backwards words "Old Colony Tea" painted on it. The time. 2:30... no, it was backwards, 10:30.

"Go back to sleep. I'll wake you for lunch," he said, tucking me in, sweetly. I looked up at him, I looked up *to* him. I'd never met anybody like this man. Exotic, yet gentle. Artistic yet just a man. Queer, yet normal.

He touched my face and I got goosebumps all the way down my side. I felt like I could breathe, underwater...

...Then I *am* underwater. Gliding swiftly forward with each strong stroke of my tail. I rise to the surface, exhale a plume of mist, inhale in an instant and dive again.

Everything looks different through the lens of the sea. I can see to the left and right of me at the same time, but not straight ahead. Yet while I can't *see* it, I sense it in an entirely new way.

I send out sharp clicks through the front of my head and feel them come back as shapes. Not flat pictures but three-dimensional models I can recognize. Coral. A tuna. A shark. A human. Sergei. His shape is distinct from the other humans swimming in the water and I can tell this at a great distance.

I can see inside his body, inside his head. His skeleton and his heart. Completely clear in my mind. Like last night, the edges aren't important, it's about the light and shading. That's what makes the shapes special.

It's a new way to see...

...My eyes opened, full of tears, swimming in the light. Everything was unclear, with perfect clarity.

I ran to the closet and got the camera, I twisted the focus randomly, closed my eyes and felt my dolphin vision guide me. *Click.* Left. *Click.* Up. *Click.* Around. *Click.* Angular. *Click.* Light. *Click.* Shadow. *Click.*

Eyes still closed: Wait, are those stairs? I peeked, yes. Down the stairs. *Click.* People shapes. *Click.*

Uh oh! I'm naked, turn and run back upstairs. End of the roll. I remembered what I saw in my head and wondered if the photos would let other people see it, too.

I got dressed and found Sergei downstairs in the tall room, painting my face onto one of the icons. He looked up and smiled.

95 ➺ Lunch Crowd

"Ah, you're awake! Let us lunch!" he said, making one last dab of paint, adding a sparkle to my eye.

"I can see with sound!" I announced, proudly.

"Like a bat!"

"A dolphin!"

"How very interesting. What does it look like?"

"Shapes. I took pictures."

"Of sound?"

"I think so. I hope so... I don't know."

"I hope so, too, Hubear."

The ground floor, which had been the gallery last night, was now packed with tables full of diners. Sergei found two empty seats at a long table and we sat.

"What's going on here?" I asked.

"Our restaurant, 'The Old Colony.' Only open for lunch on the weekend but it pays for the place. He hopped back up and went into the kitchen, carrying back two bowls of bright red soup. "Borscht, it's delicious."

"I love borscht!" I said, slicing up my hot potato into the cold soup. The red was so vivid that I closed my eyes and used my new powers to see it... hmm... a circle and some lumps... not as vivid, but now I could smell it more! I kept my eyes closed to taste it- sweet, sour, tangy, cold, but with warm creamy potato. "Mmmmm."

I opened my eyes to see Sergei staring at me. "That's what you said last night," he smirked.

"So what? You think it means I like Russian?"

"Da."

"Ha!"

We finished the soup and Sergei carried the bowls back into the kitchen and came out with two plates covered filled with Beef Stroganoff on buttered noodles. I closed my eyes again and reveled in the curling shapes of the noodles, then inhaled the onion, mushroom, sour cream and beef richness. I took a bite and the flavor filled my head. I swallowed, and moaned. "I could eat this every day."

"Not everyday, Today's Russian. Sunday's Belgian, where Julien and Claudine come from. You'll love their meatballs in cherry sauce. And waffles."

Sergei had a trail of Stroganoff on his chin. I wiped it off with a napkin and wanted to kiss him, but there were people all around. He leaned in and kissed me quickly on the mouth.

"We will go get your things and you will move in with us," he said, as if it had already been decided, even though it had yet to be discussed.

I stopped eating, closed my eyes and looked at him. I wanted to see what was going on inside his head. All I could see was how different he looked from everyone else all around, just like he did when I was a dolphin.

"OK...." I said, thinking about Sam and Max and Ellis... and, for the first time in what felt like a long time, Kitty. She had become a fuzzy, almost unrecognizable shape. What was left for me there? "Tomorrow."

I cleaned my plate, then it was my turn to jump up and take them back into the kitchen. While I was there I watched Julien flip food over the fire, *click,* and Claudine artfully arrange the plates, *click,* while the two of them did a deft dance around each other in the small, steamy space. The steam itself was beautiful, *click,* the fire, *click,* and the joy they felt being together, cooking together and watching the diners enjoy the fruits of their labor.

Labor! That was the theme for Pat! Myron and his tailoring. Julien and Claudine and their cooking. I'd find out what the diners did and follow them to their jobs. I'd shoot some with my eyes open, and some with my dolphin vision!

But first, dessert! Claudine handed me two plates of Apple Sharlotka with dollops of sweet whipped cream. I closed my eyes and leaned into the plate and felt the cream touch the end of my nose. I left it there as I carried them, joyfully, to Sergei.

I hugged Julien and Claudine when I returned the dishes to the kitchen. "That was the lightest cake I've ever had!"

"Thank you, my dear," Julien said, kissing me on the mouth. My eyes moved to Claudine to see how she felt about that, but I needn't have bothered, as she leaned in and kissed me on the mouth, too. Lovely lips! All this felt oddly... normal... Yet it would still take some getting used to.

Sergei helped clean up, along with a few of the diners who were rewarded with a free lunch and extra cake to take home.

I asked some of the diners what kind of work they did and asked if I could photograph them doing it. Fishermen. Artists. Iron workers. They all said "yes" and gave me their addresses.

96 ⟫ Labor

To save time, I took a taxi back to the Ansonia to get my Leica and a small bag of clothes.

"Tony told me you didn't come home last night," Sam said. "We were worried about you!"

"I spent the night... with a friend."

"Ah, getting back on the horse already!" Sam winked.

"I might... I'll probably be spending more time there," I told him.

"Good for you! Just keep in touch so we know you're OK!" I threw my arms around him and gave him a long, tight hug.

"Thank you for everything you've done for me, Sam. I really don't know how to repay you. But if you ever need something... even if you just *want* something. Please, please, it would be my pleasure and honor to help you. I mean it. OK?"

I felt him squeeze back and when I pulled away he had tears in his eyes. "It makes me truly happy to know I've helped you, kid.

I dashed up to the apartment. It hadn't changed, and yet, it felt so empty. I got my Leica and film and packed fresh shirts and pants and boxers in my green canvas stowaway bag. And my pistol lighter, just in case... I remembered the envelope with my bank book under the mattress. It had four $5 bills, and I put two $5 each into two envelopes. In the third, I put a twenty from my wallet. I wrote "With sincere thanks," on each.

On the elevator ride down I gave a $10 one to Ellis. "Thank you for everything, Ellis." I took another picture of him.

I handed Sam the envelope with $20... not nearly enough to repay him, but I would make sure he was taken care of. I held my camera in front of me and took a picture of us both. *Click.* Max got the final one with $10. Somehow, I still ended up feeling cheap, but it was all I had on me. They stood together outside and waved. *Click.*

I dropped off my bag at the Colony then walked a few blocks south to Pier 40. I thought I'd recognize the fisherman from lunch immediately from his red knit cap, but most of them were wearing red knit caps! *Click.* Nets full of silvery fish suspended above. *Click.* Fish pouring out into trucks. *Click.*

There he was, waving from the wire above another load of fish. *Click.* They were emptied into a truck and he climbed down. *Click.*

"Ken," he introduced himself again.

"Herb," I replied, going to shake his hand, but he held his hand up to his nose, scowled, then waved. *Click.*

"I'll show you around!" he yelled over the noise and I followed him up the gangway to the ship. It was old and grimy and stank. *Click.*

"We're all happy to be at home for a while. It gets lonely at sea," he said, showing me their cramped bunks. *Click.* "But at least we got a good cook, not as good as at The Colony but good for a fishing boat."

I followed him to the deck with its massive nets full of fish. *Click.* They were beautiful, but dead, and then I recoiled. There, among the small fish, was a large dolphin. Also dead. *Click.* I closed my eyes. Twisted the focus randomly. Felt for the shapes in my head. *Click.*

"Was there no way to save that dolphin?"

"You mean 'sea vermin'? Out there eating our catch? Naw. There are plenty more of them in the sea." Eyes still closed, I took a picture of the man. *Click.*

I pointed to my watch as if to say, I gotta go," and took a cab crosstown to the lower east side.

Clyde met me at the door of the iron works. Inside it was smokey and acrid. Red hot metal and men's faces glowing in the forge light reminded me of the colors I'd seen last night. *Click.* Sparks. *Click.*

Railings and hinges. *Click.* I took a closeup of his strong, weathered hands. *Click.*

He was a man who actually made things. Did I make things, or just pictures of things?

Next, Tamara met me at her West Village sculpture studio. A beautiful young woman, full cheeks, black hair, yellow apron, her hands black with clay. *Click.* Her sculptures were all black and looked like rocks and pebbles. *Click.* Stacked precariously. *Click.* Or melting. *Click.* I asked her if I could touch them and she said, "That's the best way to experience them!"

I closed my eyes and touched. Some were gritty, some smooth, and I saw shapes in my head while taking pictures. *Click, click, click, click, click.* I felt her hand on mine, guiding it. *Click.* I opened my eyes, focused and took another.

"They feel beautiful," I said while she peeked through a sculpture. *Click.* Her dark eyes looked like her sculpture. She smiled, shyly, and hid her mouth behind her hands.

"You're very kind."

"I don't know. I hope so. But I know what I feel." What I felt was attracted to her, but now I was with Sergei...

I got back to the Colony feeling conflicted. *Was I really capturing what I felt, or only what I saw? And what, exactly, was I feeling?*

97 ➺ Sunday

The front door was locked, so I used the windmill shaped knocker. I waited. Nobody answered. I pulled down the fire escape and climbed up. The windows were locked. I could see them inside, laughing, and heard them singing, but they didn't hear me.

It was getting dark and cold and just when I thought I should go back to the Ansonia, Claudine saw me and unlocked the window. "I'm sorry, bebe! Did Sergei not give you a key?"

I climbed in. "Thank you. I didn't know I'd need one."

"I will give him a spanking, bad boy," she teased. "You are just in time for dinner. We are having Carbonade flamande."

"I don't know what that is, but something smells good."

"It is I. Me? I. I always smell good! Come!"

Sergei was lounging on a bright green sofa playing the flute. He jumped up when he saw me, took my hand but kept playing. He danced in a circle and I followed. Julien put a tureen on the table then joined us. Claudine brought out bread, then took my hand. She did smell good.

Sergei's song ended and we plopped down in the dining chairs, each a different color velvet, daffodil and carrot, apple and salmon, plum and peacock. Sergei ladled a stew into our bowls and it smelled as good as Claudine, who handed me a plate of spice bread which might have smelled even better.

I took a bite of the stew, "Wow, this is incredible!"

"It's the beef," said Claudine.

"It's the beer!" argued Julien.

"It's the love!" growled Sergei.

Didn't matter what it was, it was delicious. And the spiced bread— gingerbread with cinnamon, nutmeg and clove. The slight sweetness combined with the dark flavor of the stew were ambrosial. I ate seconds of everything and was stuffed!

I volunteered to do the dishes but Julien wouldn't hear of it. Instead, I curled up next to Sergei who quietly played the flute while Julien played the accordion and Claudine played the musical saw. She sang a song in German and translated for me.

"...A sweet little girl from a very small town...

...met a nice little boy and they fooled aroun'...

He got her in trouble... in the family way...

So they married and have seven children today..."

"They're basically all about girls getting knocked up and either having to get married or kill themselves." Julien added, Claudine still playing what seemed like a happy tune. The song ended and she started a quiet one...

Sergei was warm and my eyes were heavy and I drifted off...

...everything was black. Someone was singing far away. I was carrying a big, heavy flashlight. The light was bright, but it didn't matter where I pointed it, the light just trailed off into blackness. I turned off the light and let the dark enfold me...

...I found myself back on the sofa. Dawn, gray, foggy, cold. I felt Sergei asleep next to me on the sofa. I had to pee and realized I didn't know where the toilet was on this floor, so I'd have to go upstairs. I shook Sergei gently, took his hand and led him to bed with me where it was warm under the covers.

When I woke again the light was different, warmer but brownish. Sergei was still asleep. I had to pee extra bad because I'd forgotten to when we came upstairs! I scurried to the toilet and felt like Niagara Falls, then ran back to get under the covers.

Sergei was awake. "Good morning, lover!" he whispered. "Other than helping out with the lunch crowd, what do you want to do today?"

I didn't know I got to help out with the lunch, I'd never done that, it sounded fun. "I thought I might go to the darkroom and..."

"On a Sunday? You can do that during office hours. This is our time."

"OK, I hadn't thought..."

"Let's get high and fuck!"

"We just did that."

"Your point?" he laughed. "It's Sunday. This is what we do."

"Sounds like you have it all planned," I said, cheerfully, though still thinking about the darkroom. I wanted to know what my eyes-closed sonic pictures looked like. But they'd be there tomorrow.

He handed me a green pill. I looked at it. "What is this?"

"LSD. It's a new thing from Switzerland."

I handed the pill back to him. "I want to be with *you*, just you. Is that OK?"

Sergei looked at me, then touched my face. "That's very sweet. It's been a long time since I... if that's what you want."

I pulled him close and kissed him. His body stiffened, then relaxed. We melted into each other, quickly not knowing where I ended and he began. There was only touch and smell and taste, and click-like flashes of eyes and skin.

I lost myself to the feelings the way I lost myself inside a camera —fully alive in a little rectangular world... the viewfinder, the mattress... contained, comprehensible.

Even the explosion at the end made sense, no turning back, no control, pure animal instinct as my eyes squeezed shut and I saw his shape in my dolphin brain, surfacing to breathe, then feeling the waves break above me as I dove back into sleep.

"We could use some help, boys," Claudine announced to the two of us, still asleep and naked. "Wash your hands first!"

Sergei's eyes blinked. His eyelashes were red. "You heard the lady," he said, groggily. I started to get up but he pulled me back. "That was beautiful. You are beautiful. Thank you, Hubear."

"We fit together."

He blushed, his cheeks turning a bright pink.

We washed our hands, put on clothes and went down to the kitchen.

98 ⇒ The Issue

"The kitchen is too small for four people," or that's what Sergei said after I knocked into him, sending a plate of Carbonade flamande flying, only to be caught, mid-air, by Claudine who then suggested I might want to play waiter for a while.

I was relieved, actually, because I didn't see what they enjoyed about the kitchen. It was hot and steamy and frantic. It was more fun to seat people (and take their picture), and then bring them food and beer.

No menus, everyone ate the same thing (which was even better today than it was last night, which is why they made it last night). I just had to carry plates from the kitchen to the table and the empty plates back to the kitchen. No checks, either, people left cash on the table, usually $2, sometimes $5, and occasionally nothing if that's all they could afford.

Lunch went from 11-1, which didn't sound like long but by the end I was beat. Everybody left and Julien, Claudine and Sergei came out front, put their feet up on the tables and drank beer. I was ready to join them (except with ginger ale) when Claudine sweetly said, "Thank you for offering to do the dishes, bebe." To me. I'd offered for last night. I looked at Sergei who just raised his eyebrows.

There were a lot of dishes and they took a very long time to wash. Just when I thought they were done, Sergei put a bunch of pots and pans next to the sink.

"I volunteered?" My feet were tired, my hands wrinkled.

"They so appreciate it," he smiled.

I did my best, but dishwashing was not my forte. I'd think a dish was clean then notice something still stuck to the front, or the back. Finally, I let the very last dish fall to the floor, just to hear it break.

"Only one broken! Good job!" Sergei brought me a broom and dust pan.

I helped him pile the tables and chairs in the back and turn the room back into the gallery of icon paintings. There was my face, surrounded by silver, next to his. Sergei captured me, the eyes even seemed to move to look at me. I leaned in closely to see how he did it, how he contoured the light and shadow to create an illusion of depth. A very good illusion, indeed.

As I hung one of the faceless paintings, I noticed the blackened oval where the face would go wasn't just a flat blank space. It looked as if there had been a face there that was then painted over in black. I tilted the paintings towards the light to see if I could see more detail, but could only see arched eyebrows. Curious.

I went upstairs and lay back on the poppy colored sofa, my feet up, looking at all the windows. The light streaming through the windows felt alive, illuminating floating motes of dust like angels. Or at least that's what I saw when I closed my eyes.

I heard the door downstairs slam and footsteps running up the stairs. Sergei was waving something above his head.

"It's here! The latest issue!" he said, tossing a copy at me and almost hitting me in the face.

I set it down in my lap, "Fair" side up. Here was a refined version of the cover he'd so quickly made in the room, my international friends holding up the Perisphere, now looking seamless, as if it was all one photo.

Sergei plopped down next to me. "The cover looks great," I told him.

"I am a genius, yes?"

"And someone here took the picture that made it possible," I said right back at him.

"Oh, you are a genius, too, Huber. Your photos fill at least half the magazine. The other photographers must hate you!"

I liked that so many of my pictures made it in, but not that other photographers would hate me. "Do they really? Hate me, I mean?"

"Just envious. That they are not a genius like you and me!" He laughed.

I opened the cover. Inside was an advertisement for Coca Cola, then a red Studebaker car. "Why are the advertisements in color and my photos have to be black and white?"

"Because they pay the bills."

"I'm going to talk to Pat about this."

"Good luck with that," he said, winking.

The next page was the table of contents. Across from it, the Letter from the Publisher, Clive Nash. There was a fine portrait of him next to his message, "We live in unprecedented times. While we would like to believe that war is an ocean away and America is safe on its own continent, the threat is ever closer. As you will see, it has already breached our shores.

"Americans have never been ones to bury our heads in the sand. We believe in hoping for the best and preparing for the worst. With that in mind, this issue shows our best hopes for unity and peace, as well as the dangerous realities facing our neighbors, friends, and yes, families in Europe. It is the hope of the *Look* family that you will find this both informative, and inspiring, so we may all work together towards a better future."

"He wrote that beautifully," I said.

"Pat probably did. She's a wonderful writer." Sergei said, his magazine already open to the center spread of the bomb hole.

I turned my page, and was hit with a full page image of Kitty, on tiptoe, pointing towards the Perisphere. I remembered that moment. I remembered all my moments with her. Just as I was reminded that she was gone.

The caption read, "Our All-American Girl, Miss Kitty Rose, invites you to join her in the world of tomorrow *Photo: Herbert Hamilton/LOOK*!" I wondered if Kitty would get a copy on the train to California. Were strangers already looking at her, asking for her autograph? I hoped she was happy.

Sergei's hand reached over and turned the page for me. "Move on, Hubear. She has." I wanted to slap his hand away. But he was right. She had.

The magazine pages felt so crisp, like a freshly ironed shirt at the Ansonia. I sniffed the clean, inky scent of the page and looked closely at the tiny dots that made up my photos, as if they'd been chopped into 10,000 pieces and put back together perfectly. When my nose wasn't pressed up against the paper, the dots all blended into what looked like my original photo. I ran my fingers across the paper and it felt smooth.

"It's called halftoning," Sergei explained. "Printing presses only use solid color, so everything is either black or white..."

"Or color in the ads!"

"...yes, but those, too, are solid colors broken up into tiny halftone dots. Most people never notice them, they just see your beautiful photos, Hubear."

"The photos do look good."

"Two million people will see them. All across the country. Does that excite you? All those people looking at your work?"

"It's hard to imagine." Pat had said it, but now it was real. There wasn't just this one copy in my lap, Sergei had one, and there was another dozen in a stack on the floor. All identical.

"It still excites me!" he said, fanning through the pages. "Worming our way into their feeble minds."

"They're not all feeble..."

"No, some are quite powerful. The White House gets over 100 copies, and Clive says FDR reads it cover to cover."

FDR? Seeing my photos? My name? Kitty? I looked away, not wanting Sergei to see me tearing up. Was I crying about the great FDR or the late Kitty?

I turned the page. Two quite beautiful photos of the Trylon and Perisphere I didn't take. Then, on the next page, James, holding Kitty over his head. Sergei put his hand on mine and guided me to turn the page again.

But there was no escaping Kitty. Yes, there were pages of my international friends, looking like heroes against the sky. But then she'd appear, the apple-cheeked American making the others look that much more exotic. Yet, there was something exotic about her in these photos that I didn't remember in person. Her eyes set just a bit too wide. She was starting to look unfamiliar already.

"I love this series, Hubear. You communicate such youthful and unrealistic hopefulness."

"Unrealistic? It was all real."

"It was a fair. None of it was real," he said in an offhand way that shocked me. Then he simply dropped the magazine. "I must have another slice of spice cake, how about you?"

"No, thanks," I didn't want to get my fingers sticky and mess up the magazine. It had all been real. The Africans and Japanese and Seminole and Swiss. James. Kitty. I was there. I *saw* it. I *felt* it. Sergei hadn't been there. All he saw was the pictures. Was that how readers were going to feel? Because I wanted them to feel what I did.

Sergei came back with a slab of cake. He took a bite, then left a big fingerprint on Kitty's face.

"This is a very good issue. I am proud. Next week it will line bird cages and cat boxes. But today, we celebrate!" he said, pressing the cake to my lips. I took a bite and all I could taste was bitter black pepper.

99 ➻ Shadow of a Ghost

I had a hard time falling asleep. The streetlight coming through the clock tower window felt too bright. Sergei's breathing was too loud. So was my heartbeat—beating with excitement about the issue, but the rhythm was off.

My eyes wouldn't close, I just kept watching shadows floating across the ceiling, like ghosts. *Click.* Ma. *Click.* Kitty. *Click.* Frank. Myron. James. Grossman. David. *Click. Click. Click. Click. Click.* All gone but I could still see them in my head.

I didn't mind the ghosts. In fact, they were beautiful. Visible, photographable. Yet not really there. They left no mark on the ceiling, like they had on my life.

I felt my camera start to slip out of my hands and set it down and fell asleep. I felt like it had been all of five minutes but it was dawn.

Monday! I felt antsy, dressed quietly and walked six blocks to the subway.

The low morning sun cast long shadows. *Click.* I knew these shadows would disappear in just a few minutes, but now they were almost tangible. The pay phone's shadow looked like it had a nose and mouth. *Click.* The curlicues of the bakery sign made a face on the sidewalk. More ghosts. Everywhere. *Click.*

The lobby guard at the Chrysler let me in when I showed him my press pass and I went straight to the darkroom to develop my film.

Even in the dim red light of the darkroom I could see shadows in the corners. Not menacing, but watching.

The shots of Myron were good, it was clear how much he loved his work. He photographed very well, handsome—almost pretty.

The next roll was entirely out of focus. They must have been my dolphin view sonic pictures but they had no shape, no composition, no meaning, much less any kind of story. Disappointing.

Then there were the kitchen photos, which were mostly fine, except those I took with my eyes closed, which, again, all looked like mistakes. The food, the diners, all fine. The docks, fisherman, dead dolphin... clearly his sonic vision failed him, too. Ironworks, sculptress... OK.

Still, I was disappointed in myself. I really thought I'd invented a new way to see, but there was nothing to see there.

Except... in the last roll... the ghosts. The shadows. Exactly what I'd seen in my head. They looked eerily alive.

I made contact sheets and blow ups of the ghosts. The weird thing about the photos of shadows was that photos themselves were shadows —shadow and light on the film in the camera and from the enlarger onto the photographic paper. They looked as real as the moment they existed even though they only existed here.

Even weirder, now that they were frozen I could see faces in all of them. Eyes, a mouth. Haunting? I had to turn off the enlarger light and remind myself they were harmless. Yet somehow I must have been printing them for a long time, dodging and burning to make their "faces" more clear, because a steady stream of people came in to do their work, and Mickey on my wrist said it was 9am.

I packed up my negatives and prints and went to Louise's desk. "I've got an assignment from Pat and was hoping she had a few minutes this morning."

"She hasn't come in yet, but she keeps a half hour open first thing for contingencies so I'll ask."

I didn't have to wait long as she strode down the hall, more colorful than I'd ever seen her, sky blue skirt, jacket and shoes, and pink shirt and tie.

"Ah, just the man I wanted to see—and congratulate. The issue sold out on newsstands and we added an extra run!"

I jumped up and she shook my hand.

"You did a beautiful job!" I said, as if she didn't already know.

"I'm very proud of it."

Louise added, "I sent copies to everyone from your list, Mr. Hamilton." I could imagine James and the rest looking at their copies.

"Thank you, Louise!"

Pat motioned for me to follow her, "What have you got for me today?"

"I needed a new suit after the rally... anyway, I went back to the South Bronx, to a tailor shop where I used to work and my friend, Myron... well, take a look."

I put the contact sheets on her desk and she leaned over to inspect them while I continued. "The theme is *labor*, about people who do and make things. For Myron it's about a new generation keeping old-world craftsmanship alive."

"Excellent photos and a good caption, too!"

I pulled away the dolphin-view image contact sheet. "Oh, sorry, these didn't turn out right."

"A whole roll? What happened here? Looks like you shot them with your eyes closed!" she joked.

"I did. I thought I could see like a Dolphin, sonic photography..."

"Oh... I forgot... Sergei's party?" she mused.

"After that..."

"Yes, it can have that kind of effect... I trust Sergei took good care of you."

"Yes, he's being very good to me."

"Being. I see. How does Kitty feel about this?"

"She doesn't... care. She went to Hollywood." I sat down, deflated.

"I didn't know, I'm sorry, Herb."

"It's what she wanted..."

"And what do *you* want?" Pat asked, sitting on the sofa and patting the seat next to her.

"How do you think people felt about the Fair/Unfair issue? About my photos in it?"

"They were moved enough to buy up every copy."

"But what did they *feel?"* Sergei said my photos were unrealistic and would line bird cages next week."

"Did he now? Our friend Sergei is very talented but can also be very cynical. It would make me sad if he infected you with that particular malady. It's a bad mindset for an artist."

"I started to have doubts."

"About?"

"What I'm doing and if it matters. About myself," I looked down to my lap and saw her reach over and take my hand.

"I'm very disappointed."

"In me?"

"In Sergei. When I first met him, five years ago, fresh from Europe, he was full of excitement about everything, like you are and I hope you continue to be. He had a love of the art as well as the craft, like you, and Glenn, too. There are few things more attractive in a man. Oh, and just to be clear, you're too young for me!" she said, smiling. "But Glenn... Anyway... I don't know what happened, maybe it was the drugs which seemed so exciting at first... he's still a very creative art director but he stopped making his own art."

"Maybe he started again, he painted my face..."

"In one of the icons?"

"Yes, he's a wonderful painter."

"Hmm. I understand how overwhelming and confusing it can feel to be the center of his attention." She said, arching her eyebrow in a way that reminded me of something... ah, the face that had been painted over.

"Oh. I didn't realize that you... Now I feel bad."

"It was a long time ago... OK, let's look at the rest of your shots." She held up the contact prints and looked closely. "The kitchen? He had you working in the kitchen?"

"Just on Sunday... I didn't like it."

"Then don't do it. Go with your guts, stick to your guns! Lord, I sound like a greeting card but I mean it. Don't fall for that," she said, looking at her hands as if they were remembering the dishes. "Julien and Claudine are still there, I see. Great chefs. But..." She put down the contact sheet.

"But what?"

"Game players."

"We haven't played any games, but we did dance."

"Different games..." she focused on the photos again. Fisherman... what didn't you like about him... ah, I see now. Just so you know, your photos do convey what you're feeling, it's very clear here. Ironmonger... hmm... can't tell who he is, just the heat and glow. Sculptor... interesting, you hardly show her face. Did you do that on purpose?"

"Really? No..."

"Yes, just her hands, and yours. Sensual approach."

"She said they were meant to be touched."

"These are good, Herb. I want more. We could make this a weekly feature." She got up and stood looking out the window down 42nd street. "About the dolphin-view photos... they don't work... but it's a good experiment, and it's important to keep experimenting."

With that I remembered the last contact sheet, which I hadn't shown her. "Here's another experiment," I said, handing her the shadows. She studied them.

"What are these?"

"Shadows. On Sergei's ceiling. In the street." I handed her the enlargements.

"I'm not sure what to make of them," Pat said. "They're beautiful abstracts... I can appreciate them on that level. But where's the story? The emotion?"

"I just started seeing them."

"What are you trying to communicate?"

"I... don't know. They felt like ghosts."

"They're fine studies in composition and shading. I admire them on an intellectual level, but I don't see the ghosts, and they don't move me."

"Then they're failures," I said, sadly.

"No—I wouldn't say that. They're a more formalist kind of art, well-done, and there's value there, but *what do you want to say with them?*"

The question stopped me. "Honestly?"

"I hope we're always honest with each other."

"Once I started to see them I couldn't not see them. I'm confused and scared. About my own life. About the world. I feel like the shadows are winning. I want people to *feel* that."

"I understand the confusion and fear, but they're not conveyed in these images. These are beautiful, but *just* beautiful. As for feeling, pure abstract art is difficult—the viewer has to willingly give it attention. To do that, the art... these 'ghosts' must first speak to them."

"I don't know what to do."

"The answer to that is simple: Take more—But look beyond the surface." She checked her watch. "I've got a meeting with Clive, can't be late." She squeezed my hand and I showed myself out.

100 ⇒ Frames

I tried to follow Pat's advice but the surface was so seductive. Shadows were literally everywhere. I'd only ever seen them as part of the thing that cast them. *Click.* Now, they were like Peter Pan's shadow, with a life of their own. *Click.*

As time passed the shadows got shorter, until, at noon, they were gone. All that was left was a clear, sunny, fall day in Central Park. Strange, I'd forgotten about the sun... And the Metropolitan Museum of Art, right there. When was the last time I'd been inside?

For a moment I thought, "Maybe my work will be here someday!" then I had to laugh at myself, which turned into chuckling, which turned into the kind of laughing you can't stop because suddenly everything is hilarious.

A guard kindly asked me to leave and I fled down the stairs and I stood behind a shrub, laughing like a loon, surely scaring passerbys until it subsided. I couldn't even remember what was so funny. I went back inside, head down, and hurried upstairs past the guard.

I saw something new, not the paintings which I remembered, but the frames. So ornate as to compete with the pictures. Underneath them, shadows, the complicated edges of which created a whole host of interesting shapes, and, again, faces. *Click*. Less ghostly, more comic, though one appeared to be screaming, like an ancient Greek mask. Kind of scary. *Click*.

Nobody else seemed to notice them—I'd hadn't either, yet they were *everywhere,* sharply defined on the smooth walls by the bright lighting above. *Click*.

There were so many that when I reached in my pocket for a fresh roll of film I discovered I'd shot them all!

On the way out there was an exhibit of old photographs by Alfred Stieglitz. I remembered that name from Glenn and entered the gallery to look at them. The frames were simple, so there were no interesting shadows, making it easy to focus on the photos.

There were a lot of old-timey pictures of New York City, some quite beautiful in the snow or at dusk. Simple, very little contrast, like paintings. A lot of a naked woman named Georgia. Not so different from Glenn's nudies, really, and one showed her privates and everything, right out in the open in a museum. They were beautiful for their own sake. Wasn't that enough?

Finally, a series of clouds, almost abstract, called "Equivalents," I loved how they were pure light and dark. But did they make me *feel?* Not really.

I left and walked through the park, still shadow hunting. Yet every time I spotted a beautiful one I was reminded I couldn't capture it and it would disappear. I felt loss and sadness... but how did I capture that feeling in my photos?

I stood outside Glenn's... now Fineline. I was happy to see the gold leaf was still spilling over the letters. The door was open. Everything was clean, with the addition of a new green velvet sofa. I walked into the studio and stood at the doorway, silently, watching Glenn work.

An older man in a naval dress uniform was sitting stiffly on a wooden chair, looking uncomfortable while Glenn adjusted the lighting, then picked up a twin-lens Rolleiflex in his right hand and didn't even look down into the viewfinder. He seemed to be checking his light meter with his left hand, but I could see he was discreetly pressing the shutter, *click,* then winding the film when he swapped the light meter from hand to hand. *Click.* The man in uniform didn't even notice Glenn had already taken six pictures.

Glenn approached the officer, very closely, and said, softly and sincerely, "Sir, before we start, I want to thank you for your service. I appreciate what you do to keep our country safe." The man looked pleased. Glenn leaned in and said, "Let me get this piece of lint off you," and removed an imaginary piece of lint. The man looked grateful. Glenn waited a moment until the man's face relaxed. *Click.*

"Tell me what you're most proud of as an officer," Glenn asked. The officer thought about it, then his expression lightened. As he spoke, Glenn then took small steps from left to right, getting different angles. *Click click click click click click.*

"I've been an officer for 20 years, and I get letters from the men who served under me. They often remind me of something I told them when they were in a challenging situation. When they say how it helped them through difficult times in the rest of their life..." He got a little choked up. *Click.* "Knowing I've been of service to my country, and specifically to my men, that's what makes me most proud." *Click.*

"I thank you, too," Glenn said, turning off the biggest studio light. The officer, thinking it was over, shook off his emotion and was even more relaxed. *Click*, half his face in shadow. "All done, you look like a leader!" The officer smiled. *Click.*

"Thank you, Sir."

"I'll send you prints in a couple of days."

As he left, Glenn finally saw I was there. "Herbie!" He hugged me. Where ya been? I saw the Fair issue. It's tremendous and Kitty is pretty as always."

I hugged him back. "I just saw what you did, you put him at ease while putting yourself in control."

"The series is turning out well, want to see?"

"Of course!"

He handed me a binder. They were beautiful, proud, strong, yet also casual—because they didn't know when they were being shot! Some were smiling, even laughing. Once again, I could feel the people in the picture. I kept turning the pages.

"Wow, how many are there?"

"Pat assigned five, but I put a little ad in the paper... I don't know, a couple dozen... I feel like I'm doing a service taking 'em for their families. I'll just show Pat the ones she sent over..."

"...No, show her the whole book, Glenn, they're wonderful. She might want to run some every week like she talked about with me."

"OK, speaking of you—what's up?"

"Um... A lot has happened."

"It's you, Herb, a lot always happens."

"Are you hungry?" I asked.

"Does the Pope poop in the woods?"

"Silly question."

"I've got another session in a half hour, let's get a slice across the street."

DeLuca's floor was slippery with grease, so was the pizza, it was great!

"I've got a meeting with Pat on Wednesday and I'm nervous. Come with me."

"Oh, stop already, Glenn. She loves your work, she'll love these shots, she even mentioned you..."

"She talked about me?"

"Yes, said you're a real artist."

"Are you shitting me?"

"No, she did."

Glenn smiled and red pizza oil dripped down his chin. I pointed to it and he dabbed it with a napkin. "What've you been up to?"

"... trying new things."

"Like always... like what?"

I thought about Sergei and didn't want to go into details. "Experimenting... I'm shooting shadows."

"Whaddya mean? We all shoot shadows."

I laughed. "You're right, but I'm *only* shooting the shadows... not the thing that makes them."

"Ah—like you did with the Perisphere, I loved that picture."

I'd forgotten that picture. "Yeah, like that, but also kinda... like ghosts."

"I don't put anything past you, Herb. I'd offer to develop them but I've got this other shoot..."

"Oh, that's OK. I miss our time in the darkroom but you'll love the one at *Look*, they've got a machine that processes your film all by itself. Just stick it in and..."

"You're doing a great job of *not* telling me what's happening with you, Herb," he said, chewing on the pizza crust and downing it with a Coke. "How's Kitty?"

"You know that picture of her you always liked..."

"The one of her in bed, waving at you, of course."

"You can have it now."

"What? Why?"

"It's yours."

"Uh oh, what's happened Herb?"

"She left for Hollywood."

"I thought she'd get modeling offers after the magazine came out but that was fast..."

"Before the issue came out. I don't want to talk about it."

He patted me on the back. "Aw, I'm sorry, boychik. But you can always go out and visit her..."

"Naw. It's... complicated."

"Another guy?"

"At least one. I'm OK, I really am. Oh, I should give you my new number."

"You moved, too?"

"Just staying with some friends from the magazine for a while."

He handed me another slice and we ate in silence, except for the radio playing Perry Como singing "I Wonder Who's Kissing Her Now." Sigh.

"You're always welcome to stay with me above the shop if the ghosts come after you!" he said.

"Thanks, Glenn, you're a pal. I'm OK... for now."

He checked his watch. "I gotta go for my next session, but don't be a stranger."

"And don't worry about Pat, pitch her on a weekly series," I said, leaving.

"You're a better agent than I was!"

101 ➠ Shadow of a Doubt

The sadness only hit me in the darkroom. It wasn't the darkness that did it, it was the light—of the shadows. They were like memories, always there, yet already gone, making me wonder if they ever really existed at all.

Did Kitty ever love me?

I loved her. Now I didn't—or wouldn't let myself. But I still remembered exactly how it felt. The wonder. Surprise. Delight. Fear. Going from happily knowing nothing to painfully knowing too much. Shit. Was it worth it to know?

I'd been so angry since she left I didn't feel the sadness underneath it all.

I'd never remember movies the same way, either. Before they'd been romantic and exciting and ultimately happy. Now I'd learned life was more complicated than I'd known.

I was glad it was dark because nobody could see me cry, but I could still feel the warm tears on my cheeks.

All around me were negatives from other photographers shooting in Europe—pictures of people whose lives and bodies were literally torn apart. And me, pathetically, with just a broken heart, I was one of the lucky ones—with the freedom to chase ghosts and take pictures of something that nobody would have missed.

No wonder Kitty left.

I had no idea what I should do, so I just did what needed to be done. I put the negatives in glassine sleeves, wrote my name along the edge just to be safe, grabbed a dozen fresh rolls of film, stepped out of the darkroom and back into the light.

102 ➺ See

I went to Sergei's office, knocked, didn't wait for a reply, and opened the door. He looked up, surprised, rushing to turn over three stacks of photos so they were face down.

"Any of those mine?"

He was startled. "Oh, Hubear. No.."

"May I look through them?"

"No. Why?"

"Just curious."

"Not now, I'm very busy..." he said, putting his hand firmly on the stacks so I couldn't touch them. It just made me more determined than ever to see them! So I sat on his lap and wiggled around.

"Close the door, at least," he whispered. "And lock it." I did, then sat on his lap again. "You little minx."

"I don't know what a minx is, but I'll take it as a compliment," I teased, turning over the stack of photos... to see a collection that looked like it came from Glenn's old nudie vault, if Glenn had been interested in men. Very naked men. Some doing things I'd never imagined.

"Oh, my! Is this the theme of the next issue? If so, why didn't you ask me to shoot any?"

"This isn't for *Look*."

"But these are office hours, aren't they?" I teased. They were very naughty photos indeed. Not artistic or well-shot, but clear—no, explicit. "Don't leave much to the imagination, do they?"

"That's the point."

"Really? Or is the point to be sexy? Because imagination is the sexiest thing," I said, moving his hand off my lap. "Anticipation. Desire. Once you get it, can it live up to what you wanted?" I looked through the photos and made my own stacks. "On the left is sexy, on the right is just sex. See? Oh, wait, are these for your new magazine, '*See?*'"

"Yes. Nothing else like it on the market now outside Scandinavia."

"Probably because it's illegal."

"It's being printed in Denmark where it's legal. Then it gets imported as medical literature, under an exemption regarding diagnosing perverse pathologies. Roger figured it out."

I jumped up as my mind jumped back to Glenn's. "Photographic Arts Magazine? Roger... Reed?"

"Yes, how do you...?"

"I met him. I thought he liked girls..."

"...He goes both ways."

"He wanted one of my shots." I remembered I still had half of it in my wallet. I unfolded it, and despite it being cracked, and now maybe because of it, it was stunning.

"Enticing, Huber. As is that man's cock beside her." David... I thought I'd torn that off! Sergei inspected it too closely.

Seeing it made me wonder why anything Kitty did surprised me. I knew who she was from the start. I took a picture of it and carried it around with me... but never bothered to open it and actually look.

"Roger's very knowledgeable about photography. A dealer in all the big names. Taught Pat everything she knows when they were married."

I heard buzzing in my ears and the room started to spin and I fell into Sergei's lap. So Roger met Glenn from the divorce photos? My mind went in circles.

I didn't even hear Sergei at first... "I understand what you mean about sex vs sexy but we need both, Hubear. We don't have much of a budget for the first issue so these shots are all from Europe where Roger picked them up on the cheap."

"Sounds very artistic. You must be proud," I said, teasing.

"I am proud to be offering erotica to our kind, Prince Hubear on his high horse. I will make a lot of money, too."

"Don't get me wrong, I think it's a good idea. I just wish they were good photographs."

"Fine, take some," Sergei pushed me off his lap.

"I'd need some models."

"I've got a little black book of boys..." he said, then realized what he said and turned pink.

"I bet you do, Sergei."

"We can shoot them at the colony. I'll art direct. It'll be fun to work together."

"It would certainly be interesting..."

Just then, the sun was coming through the window, casting a long shadow into the wall behind Sergei. His unruly mop of hair cast a shadow that looked like two horns. I laughed out loud. *Click.*

"What's so funny? What did you take a picture of?"

"Ghosts."

Sergei spun around to look for one. "Real ghosts? In here? What did you see, where? Tell me!"

"I've been seeing them everywhere, nothing to worry about—I'm probably just going crazy."

"I am terrified of ghosts. I feel them, but can't see them. I did not feel this one, but now, look, it made my skin crawl."

Poor Sergei was shaking. I put my arms around him. "It's OK, I just thought I saw something, it was only a shadow."

Sergei relaxed. "My whole life is shadows, I am not afraid of them! But you must protect me from my ghosts!"

"I'll do what I can. But I can't risk my job here."

"I'm not going to tell Pat about any of this, and what we do on our own time is our business. Besides, Pat..."

"I don't want to betray her trust..."

Sergei went from scared to scathing in a second, "Who is more important, Pat or me? Fine, you continue to be a tool of bland American capitalism and I will forge a path towards sexual freedom!"

The sun moved a bit more and now Sergei's shadow was just a blob.

"Look who's calling who a capitalist. I respect what you want to do, just not how you're doing it."

"You'll wish you had been in our inaugural issue, Roger can put a photographer on the map...."

"Or in the gutter!"

"You are such a pain in the ass, Huber. Literally. But I forgive you because you will pain me later, will you not?"

"It all depends on how good... or bad you are. I'm going to go now and pretend I know nothing about this."

"Don't be afraid of Pat. Trust me, she's no prude. Roger and I have some stories..." I put my hand over his mouth. "That's not my business."

"I'll be back at the colony before you do and I need a key."

He opened a desk drawer and there were about 20 of them. He handed me one but now it didn't feel special.

"Close the door on your way out." I did, and heard him lock it.

I took the photo of Kitty out of my pocket, tore off the last of David's bits, tossed them in the trash, then folded the rest back into my wallet.

103 ➼ Made by Light

I felt lost. Literally lost. As soon as I left the building I started seeing shadow ghosts everywhere. They fascinated me to the point where I saw little else.

I finally looked up when a woman hit me with her handbag after I leaned over to get a shadow shot and she thought I was trying to look up her dress. I wasn't, I hadn't even seen her!

Where was I? What was this street? I didn't recognize the neighborhood. Nothing. I looked up at the street signs, 35th and Lexington.

There at the corner, was the *Church of the Epiphany.* I could sure use one about now. I went inside. It was dark, the only light coming softly through stained glass windows. It was a relief not to see any shadows. I sat in the last pew and closed my eyes. I heard footsteps. Smelled candles.

I was not one to pray and I wondered if being a Jew praying in a Catholic church would cause me to burst into flames. Still, I figured it was worth the risk.

"Dear God. Sorry, is that too informal? I can't remember the last time we talked. I think I was 8 and praying for a bike and that might not count because it's more like shopping. Sorry. First, thank you for all the good stuff that's happened lately. I don't really know how I got here so I guess you played a part in it and for that I'm grateful..."

I said all that while silently thinking, "This is ridiculous. He can't hear me," and then thinking, "Maybe the church steeple is like some magic radio antenna to heaven and it helps him hear," and then I thought, "But I'm just whining and there are other people suffering who need to be heard more so maybe I shouldn't bother him right now," and then, "How do I know it's a *him*," and then, "How does anyone know anything?"

I decided he couldn't possibly hear me so I might as well say whatever I wanted. It was probably best to be honest on the off chance that he existed and all that magic was possible then he would also have seen everything I did, and I mean everything. I didn't know how he'd feel about it, except *I* didn't feel bad about it so why should he. And, if he was a he then he'd understand, wouldn't he?

"OK, God, I'm gonna cut the crap. Save you some time so you can concentrate on the people suffering in Europe, which is a bigger problem than I am, and I hope you're doing something about that, though so far I still have my doubts that you exist, so if you want to prove it you could do something good in Europe, not that you have to prove anything to me or you even care if I believe I you or not... sorry, I'm rambling.

"The truth is that I just fell into all of this. I didn't plan anything. So here I am, without a plan. I liked how it felt to be useful. To see things and help other people see them, too. But now I don't understand what I'm seeing and don't know how it can possibly help other people.

"It's like there are all these faces trying to tell me something and I can't quite hear them. Ha! I wonder if that's a little bit like being you. Hearing all of us talking at the same time and not being able to hear anything but this buzzing... like bees."

"Oh, and about that whole bee thing, I could use that again. It was weird but helpful and led me to a kind of hive... Maybe it led me to where I needed to be but I'm not sure it's where I want to be.

"Oh, wait, that's important, I'm not sure what I want. Maybe this is why people pray, so they can hear themselves think. Or maybe you planted that idea, if so, thanks.

"So I need to stop and actually *listen* to the shadow ghosts? Is that what you're saying? Not that I heard you say anything, it just kind of popped into my head, but I'm happy to give you credit for it."

I felt a tap on my shoulder. I opened my eyes and a priest whispered, "Sir, prayers here are silent and you're speaking out loud."

"Oh, I'm sorry, I didn't know..."

"New to the church?"

"First time. I'm sorry if I'm doing it wrong."

"I was listening and I'm sure God understands what I do not... Speaking of which, Might I suggest leaving a donation and lighting a candle, my son? Let there be light."

"What about the shadows?" I wondered, again aloud.

"They can only be made by the light."

104 ➽ Hearing Voices

I sat on the sidewalk outside the church, staring, and listening. At first, I heard a high-frequency noise, like the sound you hear when a neon sign lights up—so high you can barely hear it, and yet so sharp it almost hurts.

No words. No language. Just this sound that got louder when I stared at one of the shadows. The shadow faded, but the noise remained. I froze, not moving my head because I didn't want to lose the signal. I listened until it faded away. It was annoying. And fascinating.

What if the sound was the language? Maybe the voices were summoning images from my brain, knowing that's how I saw things.

A few people dropped quarters in front of me, like I was a hobo, which I thought was odd, because I was wearing awfully nice clothes to be a hobo, but then, they weren't really seeing me, just someone sitting where only hobos otherwise sit.

They weren't seeing the world as it was, just as they *thought* it was. But I wanted to see, and now hear, how it really was, even when nobody else was paying attention.

I closed my eyes and saw rows and rows of shadow faces, as if there was a contact sheet inside my head. I enlarged a single image with an imaginary loupe: One of the first faces I'd seen, a shadow cast from a frame at the Met, it's eyes wide, mouth agape, screaming like a Greek mask... or a muse.

Then I heard the words, "Photos are light." I opened my eyes and looked around. There wasn't anybody around. I closed my eyes again. "Light is time." That made sense.

But maybe this was just me, thinking. I wondered how I could tell the difference.

"What am I seeing when I see you?" I heard myself ask, out loud.

"The past."

"What do you have to say that hasn't already happened?"

"The past doesn't change. Only how you see it does."

I was never good with puzzles or riddles so this was starting to annoy me. But I was good with clouds, looking at them and seeing bunnies and tugboats and breasts. Maybe these words were like clouds and I could let them turn into a familiar shape.

"Photos don't change once you take them," I said to the voice.

"What you see depends on what's in the frame. If your perspective changes, or you crop it, you can see in new ways."

"How do you know about photography when it was invented thousands of years after you lived?" I said, still thinking of it as a Greek mask.

"I was born yesterday. I'm your muse."

My stomach rumbled. Had I eaten anything today? Oh, right, pizza with Glenn. That seemed so long ago.

Sanity seemed so long ago.

The ghost spoke so clearly I couldn't ignore it, *"Just because you can see and hear what others can't doesn't mean it's not there."*

I let the words bounce around the inside of my head like light against mirrors.

I already knew I could see, and now I could hear as well. Maybe it was real. Maybe it was my imagination. Maybe it didn't matter which it was.

105 ➻ Faith Business

I tried to stand up, but my legs were asleep, so I flailed around, guarding the Leica as I fell. The priest who talked to me earlier came to my rescue and lent me a hand. I grabbed onto him.

As I struggled to my feet, my wallet fell out of my back pocket. I leaned over to get it, lost my balance and put my arm around the priest's waist to keep from falling.

"Wallet!" I gasped, holding tighter to him.

"Oh my stars, you're mugging me!" he whispered. "I don't have much, but please, take it, take what you need, my son," he thrust his wallet at me, just as I was about to grab my own.

Now my legs felt like pins and needles, "Nooo!" I cried, reaching my wallet. "Why do people keep thinking I'm... No!" He kept pushing his wallet on me and I kept pushing it away.

I snatched up my wallet and pulled out a $20 bill. That caused Kitty's photograph to fall out, get picked up by the wind and float down the street.

"Here, please take this for your trouble and kindness, please..."

I wanted to run and get Kitty's picture but my legs still hurt, and the priest took the $20 and handed me his wallet. "No, I'm not buying your wallet, it's a donation."

"I am worried about your mental state, my son. Would you like to talk with me about it?"

"I'm sorry, Sir..."

"Father Sylvester..."

"Father Sylvester, it was a misunderstanding." I said, watching Kitty's picture sail high off the ground, flirt with a tree, then spin down the street, out of sight.

"What do you think you are seeing?" he asked.

"Love, floating away."

"Please come inside. We can talk. I have tea and cookies," he said, kindly.

The feeling was returning to my legs in pins and needles so I was still staggering. "I appreciate the offer but I'm going to go home, wherever that is."

"Wherever that is?"

"It's a long story."

"I have a lot of time."

"I had a vision. You wouldn't believe it."

"Belief is my business."

"I'm Jewish!"

"You're human. We have that in common."

I couldn't argue with that. "Tea and cookies sound good," I said, giving in.

I shuffled inside and followed him into his office. I sat in a threadbare chair and he brought a tray of hard dry little cookies and poured watery tea.

"Tell me about your vision. Before you do, I'll tell you that I envy you, I've been waiting for a vision myself."

"I am a photographer. I had been shooting people... I mean taking pictures of people, I don't shoot people... but then my girlfriend left and I followed a bee and started sleeping... that's beside the point, I started taking pictures of shadows."

"Hence what you asked me earlier about shadows."

"Yes, and you said 'They can only be made by the light,' but they're still shadows."

"In order for us to recognize the light, we must know the dark," he said, simply.

"That's beautiful... Father... but the dark is talking to me."

"You're hearing demonic voices?"

"No, I don't think so. Let me show you." I took out the glassine full of negatives. "Now, these are negatives, so the light looks dark and the darkness is light." Even as I said it, it sounded crazy, like in order to show people what I saw I first had to see the opposite?

I pulled out the strip of negatives with the Greek mask shadow.

"My, that does look like it's talking... screaming, actually."

I dunked a cookie in the tea and ate it. "The shadow wasn't very loud. It said 'The past doesn't change. Only how you see it does.'"

"How has your view of the past changed?"

"Kitty... My girlfriend... my first girlfriend... my first love... It was her photo that fell out of my wallet and flew away down the street. I didn't imagine it, I watched it happen. I mean, I watched her picture fly away, but I watched her fly away, too. Not literally fly... I don't want you to think I'm crazy, because I don't *think* I am."

"So you see her as a kind of angel—angels fly."

"She was no angel..."

"Angels are no angels. Rainer Maria Rilke wrote, 'For beauty is nothing but the beginning of terror that we are still able to bear, and we revere it so, because it calmly disdains to destroy us. Every Angel is terror.'"

"That's strange," was all I could think to say.

"And yet, the very word 'Angel' is part of the word 'st*rangely*.' We were talking about change, and again, the word 'angel" is at the heart of 'Ch*angel*ings." So angels change, and change us."

"You're good," I marveled at his meaning while still unclear as to what any of this meant.

"God wants us to change. That's why we are living this life. To suffer, and learn and change our souls for the better. So maybe Kitty was your angel, helping you to change."

"Ah, now I know what you're saying. But I don't know what I'm changing into... and that scares me."

"Does the voice you hear or the vision you see tell you to hurt yourself or others?"

"No, just the opposite. It's telling me to look and listen to people from a different perspective. May I take a picture of you, Father?" I asked, wanting to be able to see him better.

"Certainly, if you tell me what you see and hear."

The light wasn't very good here. His dark hair and coat blended into the dark wooden wall behind him. His skin and beard were dark, and the longer I stared at him, the more he appeared to disappear into the background. *Click.* All I could remember of the shot were his eyes.

I said the first thing that came to my mind, "You use invisibility to your advantage. You watch, listen, learn and share that knowledge."

"It sounds as if you are describing yourself, Herbert."

It did. I looked at him again and he came into sharper focus. I had been guilty of only seeing his clothes, not him. He was younger than I'd thought, maybe 24, with dark eyes and large eyebrows. He seemed to use his eyes the way I used my camera, inquisitive and unblinking.

"Wait—how do you know my name?" I asked, now wondering if he was an angel himself.

He just smiled, beatifically, then dunked a cookie into his tea. "Thank you for talking with me. I haven't been able to work with people very often as I just graduated from seminary. I never eat these delicious cookies by myself."

I still didn't know how he knew my name. Yet, I felt sorry for Father Sylvester and his dry cookies and tasteless tea. He'd been very kind to me.

"Why did you become a priest?" I asked, truly curious. What did he get out of all this?

He laughed. *Click.* "Most people only talk about themselves. They don't ask about me."

"Do you mind my asking?"

"Not at all. Why did you become a photographer?"

"As I said to God earlier... Oh, was it wrong to talk directly to God, I don't know the rules around here. Was I supposed to go through you?"

"No, that's how it's done."

"Being Jewish we don't believe in middlemen," I joked.

"You're talking to me now," he replied.

"I decided to take action to change my life, to get out of the Bronx. I didn't exactly know how to do it, but I knew I had to. I kept my eyes open, things happened and I said 'yes' to them and it led me... here."

"That's wonderful, you followed God's lead."

"I'm not sure I believe in God."

"But you were talking to him."

"You never answered my question."

He paused. "It is more important that you ask questions than for them to be answered."

I paused. "That's convenient, as I don't have a lot of answers right now."

"I wanted to be a priest because I want to help people. There. An answer," he said serenely.

I understood. "I want to help people, too—help them see the world."

"There, another answer."

"But now... I don't know what to show them."

"Show them your vision."

"The shadows? They don't make any sense."

"You're trying to turn them into answers when they are questions."

I felt myself exhale a sigh of relief.

"That makes sense. Thank you. You have helped me."

"I'm here to serve. So, between you and me, and God, of course, that makes me happy."

"Do you think God would mind if I took more pictures of you for a series I'm shooting for *Look* magazine about 'labor' and the work we do?"

"I can't presume to know what *He* would think, but labor is mankind's noble enterprise, so my guess is that he'd be gung ho."

"Gung ho! OK, let's go. Do what you normally do and I'll follow you around and take a few pictures."

"I feel shy about this, but the church could use a larger flock, so hopefully this will help."

I tried to be inconspicuous as he prayed at the altar. *Click.* Lit candles. *Click.* Went to nearby St. Luke's hospital and offered comfort to sick men, women and children. *Click.* He listened to confessions. *Click.* Led mass. *Click.* I thanked him and put another $20 into the donation box.

106 ➽ The Hands of Time

As I walked back to the Colony, I stopped fixating on the shadows. They were still everywhere whether I focused on them or not, but the light was everywhere too. I could choose what I wanted to focus on, just like I did with my photographs. So I took pictures of people at work, driving cabs, building walls, sweeping sidewalks.

I used my key to unlock the front door. Before, I'd always been let in and now I was choosing to let myself in. That felt better.

The icon paintings were all up on the wall, and I walked up to the ones with the black ovals where the faces would go or had been. It was hard to imagine Pat in one of these paintings, but then it was hard to imagine Pat in this place. As I looked around, it was hard to imagine myself here too. But here I was. I felt like I had come here for a reason, even if I didn't know what that was. Yet.

I didn't always have to know the answers, did I? I tried to think back to a time when I knew some. Whenever I thought I'd found an answer, like with Kitty, it was really just another question. At least I hadn't questioned the questions.

It had been a long day. I walked upstairs, reflecting on the poem written on the steps. The meanings seemed to change each time I trod them. "Let us go as bees in honey drown... sugar for our crown..." I did seem to be drowning... yet life was sweet. Go figure.

I lay down in bed and I looked up. The afternoon sun illuminated the "Old Colony Tea" glass clock face casting its shadow on the ceiling. Instead of focusing on the shadows, I closed my eyes and listened....

...I hear a whirring sound. I am standing on a clock face with the number 1839 at my feet.

The hands are sweeping around like swords. I act like Tyrone Power in "The Mark of Zorro," leaping over the rapier hands as they speed by to keep them from slicing me in half. Time is swift, and deadly!

I am trapped, endlessly jumping over the razor-sharp hands as they spin faster and faster. I try to jump out but the glass crystal knocks me back down and I have to pin myself against the face as the hands slice the air above me...

...I jolted myself awake. The clock shadow was still on the ceiling. I was relieved to be safe here in bed. Or at least here in bed....

...I blinked, and am back on a clock face—now with glowing neon hands. The minute hand is a cold cobalt blue, the hour hand fire red.

Under me I see the number 2039, and while staring at it, the minute hand sweeps by, knocking me off my feet and onto the hand. I am riding the minutes, holding tight so centrifugal force won't throw me off.

Perched on the glowing red hour hand is Sergei. We pass each other, our fingertips just touching as we speed by. Each time we pass each other he tries harder to hold onto me... but I slip away.

The next time he comes around he's carrying a Buck Rogers ray gun, spewing a red neon beam that burns through the air with a hiss. I dodge it by laying flat on the hand. More spinning. More shooting.

I'm getting dizzy, so I put my head down and see my reflection in the mirrored minute hand. Reflection! I pry up a piece of mirror. The next time Sergei shoots I raise the mirror to deflect the ray back at him.

Light is his weapon, but reflection is my power. Everything he shoots at me is reflected back to him, even more powerful as I can focus and frame and magnify.

All I need is this one thin sheet of... mirror, which turns into a negative, which turns into a print. The hands stop. The neon lights sputter out...

...The only light came from the street lights outside. I didn't know what time it was, but I knew it was just a matter of time...

107 »→ Sextet

I heard voices downstairs and looked over the railing to see Sergei come in with a group of men carrying lights, stands and reflecting umbrellas. The men moved gracefully.

"Set the stuff down here, boys," Sergei told them, "And help me set up the lights." They unfolded the tripod light stands and mounted the lights on top. Sergei made adjustments, adding the reflective umbrellas to two of the lights.

"Herb! Come on down and help!" he called out. Wanting to make myself useful, I went downstairs.

"So glad you could join us, Herb. Boys, this is Herb. He's our most talented photographer at *Look* magazine. If you're very nice we might persuade him to use his skillful eye to make you all look that much better."

The guys surrounded me, shaking my hand. They were nothing if not friendly... and attractive, all about the same height and build... Other than being different races they could almost have passed for brothers.

"Where did you find such a handsome group of men, Sergei?"

"We're in Jack Cole's dance company but he's out in Hollywood right now," said one with dark hair and a mustache.

"I hate Hollywood!" I offered.

He laughed, "I do, too... though I'd go there in a second if anybody would ask!" The others all agreed.

"So what're you still doing here?" I wondered.

He replied, "Nobody's asked! But a girl's gotta do what a girl's gotta do to make a buck!" That sounded too familiar.

The one with curly blond hair piped up, "There are worse ways to make 20 bucks. Besides, I'm never going to look this good again, so I might as well have something to remember it by!"

The man with the mustache kissed him, "You'll always be beautiful to me, baby!"

The room got very bright as Sergei adjusted the lights.

"Mr. Cole won't mind?" I asked, naively. They all burst into gales of giggles.

"We're gonna send *him* these pictures to get him to bring us Hollywood!" said the mustache.

"Then I'd better help Sergei with the lights," I said while they made themselves comfortable.

"You were right," Sergei whispered to me. "I need better photos, so I'm paying them out of my own pocket. Please, please help me out here, Hubear."

"OK, fine, but I get to call the shots."

He patted my ass, "Whatever you say... as long as I can make suggestions from time to time so they're not just arty."

"I know what you need. I'll bring the art, they'll bring the sex."

He gave me a kiss, and a few of the dancers went "ahh."

"You get their balls rolling, I'll be right back." Sergei said, disappearing downstairs and leaving me alone.

"First, please tell me your names so I know what to call you."

"You can call me *stud* like the Arabian Stallion I am!" said the mustache.

The blond laughed, "He makes me call him that, like the Swedish sissy I am! But you can call him Gene and me, Fred." He gave Gene a playful kiss.

"Hi, Fred... and Stud. Good to meet you both."

"I'm Sammy," said a young one with pink cheeks, a baby face and an Irish accent.

"Gen'ichirō, but you can call me Alvin," said the Japanese man while standing on his toes.

"Jerome," croaked a redhead with a heavy Jersey accent and beautiful blue eyes.

"I'm Bobby," said a shy but flexible southern black boy who stretched his leg till his knee touched his forehead.

There was silence. They all turned to the guy who hadn't spoken yet. He was standing with his pants around his ankles, exposing himself.

"I'm Rudy," he said in a heavy Russian accent.

"Impressive, Rudy. Good to... meet you," I said.

"Don't encourage him," said Fred.

"I want us to work together to make art here." I explained.

"I can paint with this thing!" Rudy bragged, swinging his dick around while the others shook their heads.

Luckily Sergei appeared, carrying a large tray of fruit and cheese like the one he first gave me, as well as a basket with bottles of wine. "OK, boys, on the off-chance that any of you actually eat, I brought some refreshments."

Rudy kicked his pants from around his ankles and grabbed a bottle of wine. The others swarmed around the food, variously saying, "I'm famished," and "OMG, Gouda!" and "The last time I saw a tray this tasty I was a waiter at Eugene O'Neill's opening night party."

Sergei took me aside, "So, what's your plan, Maestro?"

"When do I ever plan? They're dancers, so why not have them dance? That's sexy."

"To start, but we need sex as well as sexy," Sergei complained.

"Won't that happen naturally?" I suggested.

Half the tray was eaten in a matter of minutes while Rudy reclined, naked, on the rose-colored divan, polishing off an entire bottle of Riesling.

"OK, boys. Better stop before your stomachs are distended!" Sergei announced. "Time to get naked." They shed their clothes as naturally as a snake sheds its skin, only a lot faster.

Really, all they needed to do was just stand there looking beautiful. *Click.*

"If we're going to be naked we think it's only fair Herb and Sergei are, too," said Gene. Sergei stripped off to some polite applause. I felt a little self conscious, but what the hell, off went my shirt, pants, and boxers. One of the guys whistled and I took a bow.

I explained, "I'd love to see you all dance a bit and then we'll work together to decide what poses look the best."

"OK, boys, let's start with the *Orientale*" Gene told the others who lined up, closely, front to back in a row. *Click.* They looked forward. *Click.* They pointed their right feet. *Click.* They held their arms up. *Click.* Hands above their heads. *Click.* Moved their arms down around each other's chests. *Click.*

"We can't see their cocks," Sergei whispered to me.

"We don't have to see everything every time, besides, they're all touching each other, that's sexy!" I told him, moving around to shoot this same tableau from the back as they had very nice—no, perfect—asses. *Click.*

"OK, every other one of you turn around to face each other." This only created general confusion that was messy but made them laugh. *Click.* Luckily, they figured it out themselves and now there were three couples facing each other, nose to nose and cock to cock, though, so far, only Bobby was "excited" which also made him embarrassed. *Click.*

"Can we get some kissing, boys?" Sergei said, to which nobody protested, in fact, they all took to it so passionately I found myself getting excited.

This continued for some time which led to quite the case of roving hands. *Click. Click. Click.*

"Sorry to interrupt," I called out, "But I'd like you dancers to do a little dancing," to which they tore themselves away from each other and stood in a triangle formation with Rudy at the front, Gene and Fred in the second row and Jerome, Sammy and Alvin in the back row. *Click.* It was an impressive arrangement, made even more dramatic with some high kicks. *Click!*

Some turns, *click,* and then some seriously sexy lifts where the guy being lifted had his cock very near the face of the guy doing the lifting, *click,* which stimulated some not-previously-choreographed oral action. *Click!*

Even Sergei had to admit this was some high quality erotica.

"Move them further from the wall, there are some bad shadows there," Sergei suggested.

In a flash of inspiration, I saw exactly what I needed to do.

"Alvin, Bobby, please stand against this white wall, nose to nose," I instructed while moving one of the lights. "Fred, Sammy, please stand to the left, in front of this light, back to back."

I positioned Fred and Sammy so that they cast a shadow on the wall. It looked like it was the shadow of Alvin and Bobby, only the shadows were back to back, facing away from each other.

Now the shadows told a story! *Click!*

Next, I posed Jerome and Sammy an arm's length apart, with only their fingertips touching and their manhood at half-mast. I used Rudy and Gene as the shadows, their fully erect cocks almost touching. *Click!* Another story.

"Rudy, please sit on this table like Rodin's *Thinker.*" I chose him because even soft, even sitting, his size was impressive. "Don't point our toes please, make it natural and pensive."

"I don't know from pensive," Rudy said, annoyed.

"Thoughtful," I explained. The others all laughed.

"Rudy? Thoughtful? That'll take some acting on his part!" Fred said.

"My cock is a better actor than all of your assholes combined!" Rudy replied, resting his chin on his hand and looking to the side— pensively.

"Gene, stand in front of the light and lift Alvin over your head. Alvin, do a superman, with your arms out like you're flying."

I framed it so it looked like Rudy was imagining the shadow of a naked superman flying to him. *Click.* Another story.

"Gene, Fred, face each other and stand an arm's length apart, with your arms out. Bobby, and Freddy, copy their pose for the shadow, but with Rudy standing between you."

They did, making another story. *Click.*

Sergei whispered to me, "These are very classy, Herb, I see how we can use a shadow for the cover but now we need some smut!" He called out to them, "OK Gene, Fred, why don't you demonstrate the proper form for successful sucking." I jabbed him in the ribs.

Fred got down on his knees and complied. "For God's sake, Gene, point your toes!" Rudy chided, but Gene's toes curled instead.

I moved the camera so that they made a very clear shadow. *Click.* "Not just the shadow!" Sergei said, literally kicking my ass. They were very brightly lit, but OK. *Click.*

"Switch positions," Sergei ordered. They did. *Click.* "OK, the rest of you, pair up and show me how it's done!" They did. *Click.* "Switch positions." They did. *Click.*

There was genuine joy in all this, as well as the beauty of seeing these perfect specimens giving and receiving pleasure. I shot the couples individually, *click*, and then, in a wider shot with all three couples. *Click.*

Sergei pressed himself up behind me and could feel his excitement.

"I need to fuck or I'm gonna bust a nut," Gene announced, matter-of-factly.

"Trust me, we don't want that," Fred volunteered, lying on the table with his legs up. Somehow this suddenly felt too intimate for a picture.

"Enough of your artsy shit," Sergei roughly grabbed the camera out of my hands.

"Artsy *shit?*" I thought, feeling wounded as Sergei moved in for closeups. I watched him *artlessly* shoot these beautiful men and backed away, right into Alvin. "Oh, I'm sorry, I didn't mean to..."

"I'm glad you did," Alvin smiled. "I liked what you did with the shadows, you're a very artistic man." He pressed himself against me, put his strong arms around me and pulled me close. It felt good. I turned around—looking in the eyes of a beautiful Asian man. I kissed him.

I felt another set pair of arms around me. It was Bobby. A beautiful Black man. He joined the kiss. I didn't know three people could kiss at once, but it was easy and felt so good, our tongues exploring, or bodies pressing against each other. My right hand was feeling Alvin's smooth muscled body and straight dark hair, while my left was appreciating Bobby's round butt and tight curls.

I wondered what the world might be like if men from different continents got together like this. Focusing on what we have in common instead of our differences... Brotherly love instead of war...

That's what I wanted to show in my photos of the men. That's what I was doing here with Alvin and Bobby. I had another idea for a series! I glanced away from these two handsome men and saw that Gene had already finished with Fred.

I tore myself away and said to all, "Indulge me in one more pose. I'd like you to line up, shoulder to shoulder." They were used to being choreographed and obeyed immediately.

"Now, wrap your hand around the cock to the right." They did. "At the left end, Fred, wrap your left hand around Gene. Gene, turn your head to the right and kiss the man next to you." Gene and Fred did.

"Now, Fred, turn to your right and kiss Alvin." They did. "Alvin, turn to your right and kiss Jerome." They did. I didn't have to explain any more, they just did it, turning to their right, kissing the next man down the line until they reached the end where Rudy had no one to kiss, so Sergei leaned in, grinning, taking it for the team.

Italian. Irish. Russian. Black, White. Asian. All kissing each other. Yes, this was the world I wanted to live in.

The rest of them circled around Sergei and pelted him with kisses while I ran upstairs to get an overhead shot. *Click.* As long as I was doing that...

"OK, guys, it's Busby Berkeley time!" I didn't even have to explain it to them, they simply knew to lay on the floor, in a circular formation.

Gene called out poses and they made moving geometric snowflakes
and flower shapes as the men changed the positions of their arms and
opened and closed their legs. *Click click click click click.* Spectacular!

Bobby was the first to laugh and it spread, infectiously until the
precision melted into messy flailing, then into them rolling on top of
each other until they were an unruly and sweaty pile of arms, legs,
cocks and asses. *Click.*

I came downstairs to take closer shots that, to me, resembled kids
at play.

"Boys will be boys," Sergei smiled, taking the camera for some
closeups.

Then he motioned for me to follow him and we went to a
storeroom and dragged out mattresses and blankets. "Feel free to
spend the night, boys," he started to sing, "you've sung for your supper
so you'll get breakfast, songbirds always eat..."

The boys paired off on the mattresses and Sergei and I covered
them with blankets.

"Thank you, Herb. That was money well spent... and fun, too."

I stopped and looked at Bobby and Alvin. "It was fun.. Does it
have to end so early?"

"You look like you want to join them."

"Yeah."

"What, I'm not good enough for you?" Sergei pouted.

"It's not that..."

"Would you like it if I wanted Rudy to screw me?"

"It's only sex," I heard myself say, and thought of Kitty.

"I've created a fucking monster," he sighed, sliding under the
covers with Rudy, the two Russians together.

I got under the covers between Alvin and Bobby who welcomed
me with open arms and other appendages.

There was such a sweet playfulness about all this, like a pack of
randy puppies. The only time the smile was wiped off my face was
when my mouth was otherwise engaged. There was a lot of grunting
and groaning which gave way to delighted laughter, then snoring.

I lay listening to them all asleep. Staring at the ceiling. There were no shadows.

108 ➼ From 'Nudies' to 'Nudes'

The direct sun on our faces woke us up. Last night felt like a dream. But, no, they were all still here. What nice guys.

Sergei waddled upstairs to the shower, followed by the rest. We lathered each other and took turns rinsing off. Sergei then took pictures of the soapy studs and dudes drying other dudes. He was getting his money's worth.

Back downstairs Julien and Claudine came from the kitchen with trays of scrambled eggs, rashers of bacon, hash browns, buttered toast, bagels and cream cheese. The still-naked and now ravenous gang ate it all in under 5 minutes.

Sergei handed each one a crisp new $20 bill, and another $5 as a bonus. Big spender. I had them write down their names and addresses so we could send them copies of the magazine. I asked if they wanted to be credited and, except for Rudy, they all made up names like, "Rod Masters," "Billy Driller," and "Downtown Spunky Brown." Rudy wrote, "Rudolph Khametovich."

I thanked them for their good humor and exceptional skills! They got dressed and kissed each other, and Sergei and I, goodbye. Independent of each other, both Alvin and Bobby slipped me little notes with their phone numbers which I thought was very sweet.

Sergei was packing up the lights. "Good job, Hubear."

"My pleasure, truly. It was fun."

"We will go to the office together... you can help me carry this equipment back."

Even though he had an ulterior motive, it felt very adult to be going to the office with my... boyfriend... or whatever Sergei was. Sergei thanked Julien and Claudine for breakfast, then we got dressed and headed to the office. I made him carry the heavier equipment!

Since it was still early, the darkroom was empty. I ran the film through the developer. The negatives looked even better than I had hoped! I made some contact sheets for Sergei and brought them into his office.

"Wow, Herb, these are sensational. I know you don't want credit but I'll make sure Roger knows, he can open doors for you."

"I wish I could show them to Pat, but..."

"But nothing, show her. She'll love them. I told you, she's not..."

"I know, but she almost kicked us out when I first came in with Glenn."

"She didn't know you. Now she does."

He slid the negatives and contact sheets over to me. "Go see her now, she's always got time in the morning. Go!"

"OK," I said, even though I had no intention of showing her.

I went to her office and Louise held up a finger and called on the intercom.

"Go right in, Mr. Hamilton."

"Please call me 'Herb,' I replied because I didn't know her last name and it felt wrong for her to call me "Mr Hamilton" and me to call her "Louise."

"OK, Herb," she replied, which also felt a bit odd.

Pat was wearing pink. I'd never seen her wear pink. Pink tweed jacket and long skirt with white patent leather shoes and belt. "Good morning, Herb, you're here early! You must have something exciting to show me!"

"It is exciting, but I'd rather describe it to you..."

"Nonsense, that would be like trying to describe a Rembrandt," she said, pulling the negatives and contact sheets out of my hands. She flipped the switch on her desk, lighting up the top, then leaned in with her loupe.

"Oh, my! These men are more like Michelangelo's David!"

"I didn't mean to..."

"It's nothing I haven't seen before, Herb. Besides, as usual, you have turned it into art. Ah—wonderful, you figured out what to do with your shadows! They're telling emotional stories!"

"I want to use this shadow idea for other portraits."

"We have a feature coming up about the Broadway fall season and this idea would be perfect for the performers." Pat opined.

I took back the bottom three contact sheets which were the most explicit. "You don't need to see these, really. But this last one..." I put down the Busby Berkeley shots.

She laughed. "This would be charming for our spring fashion features! And bring back those two contact sheets, you tease." I begrudgingly set them down. "Hot stuff. Completely illegal, though it really shouldn't be. You know better than to have your name in that magazine, right?"

"Of course..."

"It wouldn't be good for your reputation as a commercial or fine artist. Still... you managed to make them beautiful. Sergei is very lucky you shot these, otherwise the stuff he had for *'See'* was garbage."

I was surprised, "You know about *'See?'*"

"Of course. Sergei's always been a terrible liar. Besides, Roger told me."

I was even more surprised. "The first time I was here you made such a big deal about this being a family magazine and..."

"It is. That doesn't mean I don't keep abreast of what's happening in the industry," she said, winking. "By the way, Glenn brought me two dozen remarkable portraits and I agreed to make it a regular feature. Is he always that nervous?"

"Only around you. He respects your opinion."

"Oh, I thought maybe he had a crush on me."

"That, too."

"Sweet. He's a talented and cute fellow."

"He's a good guy."

"OK, I'm scheduling you for the Broadway shoot, you'll meet a lot of famous actors and actresses... If possible, keep their clothes on."

"And if I can't?"

She laughed again, "Take the photos before they disrobe."

"Will do!" I laughed, too. Then I stopped and wondered who was taking Kitty's picture now. Why did I keep thinking about her?

"Before you give those negatives to Sergei, make yourself some prints of the non-sexual ones for your portfolio."

"But you said..."

"I said you don't want your name associated with that magazine. But the shadows and Busby Berkeley shots are art, which elevates them from 'nudies' to 'nudes.'"

109 ➻ Uncut

It was still early, so I headed over to Glenn's to congratulate him. The door was wide open but nobody seemed to be there.

"Knock knock," I said, loudly. "Glenn?"

He came from the back, wearing a long denim painter's smock.

"Wow, that's some getup?" I asked.

"Mrs. Weismann made it for me, said it's what real artists wear. She made one for Salvador Dali's aunt Rose who gave it to him for Christmas last year and he wrote her a letter saying how much he loved it. Whaddya think?"

"I think... it makes you look like the real artist you are!"

"Ah, thanks, Herb. Dali wears it without pants but I'm gonna keep mine on. Anyways, it's nice and loose and comfy and cool under the studio lights."

"I like it!" I said, and meant it.

"I'm gonna have her embroider the Fineline logo on the pocket so it looks even more professional," he announced proudly, while rifling around behind the counter. "Hey, I got a message for you... it's here somewhere... some guy with a high voice... about a suit..."

"Myron? From Shapiro's?"

"Yeah, that's it, now I don't have to find it. Says it's ready to deliver, just tell him where."

"I'm getting a new professional outfit, too!"

"We're both looking like artists now!" he said, delighted. "I'm shooting more portraits now, it's really fun."

"I know, I just shot some..." I wondered if I should go into details. "You still into nudes... nudies?"

"I'm not taking 'em, but of course!"

"Um... these aren't women."

"Then what are they?" he asked, confused.

"What's left? I replied.

"Dogs?"

"No... men."

"Men? Why?"

"Some people like looking at naked men, I mean, women like to."

"Huh. Who knew?"

"I took some, for a friend."

"OK, show me." Glenn was a good sport. I pulled out the contact sheets with the shadows and Busby Berkeley, but not the explicit ones. He took out his loupe and looked.

"What's wrong with these guys?" he asked.

"Whaddya mean?"

"What's wrong with their dicks?"

"They're dancers... Oh... Not Jewish."

"Poor guys... But the shadow stuff is cool, very you the way they tell a story. The overhead ones, like in the movies, those're funny."

"Thanks."

"They just look so weird. Poor guys," he said, shaking his head.

"I hear that's how they look if you don't have a bris."

"Makes me glad I had one," he said, looking down.

There was a long pause. I broke the tension, "Hey, congrats on the *Look* feature, Pat tells me it'll be weekly!"

"You're idea, boychik."

"And Pat likes you..." I blurted out.

"She likes the portraits, yeah, she told me."

"She likes *you,* said you were cute."

"What're you talking about?"

"Pat. Whyte. Told me you're cute. You should ask her to dinner or something."

Glenn leaned against the counter and his eyes darted around. "I... I don't... you mean she likes my photos."

"No, how many times do I have to tell you? She likes *you.*" I thought about slapping some sense into him the way people do in the movies.

"Mrs. Weismann said I was handsome in this smock, but I didn't wear it to see Pat."

"Why do you find this so hard to believe, Glenn?"

"Because she's... she's... her! What would she see in me?"

"Talent. Niceness. Cuteness, apparently."

"Well, I'll be. I didn't think I was her type."

"How would you know what her type was?"

"She used to be married to Roger... I'm more of an anti-Roger," mused Glenn.

"Maybe that's exactly what she's looking for—a *nice* guy."

"She's totally my type."

"I noticed. She noticed, too."

"I don't know what to do now!"

"Just tell her that you'd like to get to know her better and ask if you can take her out to dinner," I explained. Not that I'd ever done that...

"But what if she says 'no?'"

"I don't think she will."

"Don't think—or *know?*"

"Just ask her."

"I'll think about it," he said, sounding like, "I won't."

"You do that. I should go pick up my suit."

"Here comes my next portrait session."

"Ask her!" I said as I left.

110 ➵ Iris In

I took the 2 train uptown to the South Bronx, then walked to Shapiro's. The old neighborhood seemed even older, tired.

The little bell above the door rang as I entered Shapiro's. Myron came out, eating a sandwich with the crusts cut off.

"Herbie! I was wondering if you got my message. Sorry, everybody's at lunch..."

"It's OK, you eat. I love egg salad."

"Naw, it can wait," he said, setting the sandwich down on the table. "I really want you to see the suit, it turned out beautiful, and I got big news to tell you! Hold on, gotta wash my hands first."

I heard the sink running in the back, then he came out carrying what honestly was the most stunning suit I'd ever seen. The special-order Italian fabric was midnight blue with a subtle windowpane check. It had the depth of velvet, with the color-changing sheen of sharkskin. The buttons were covered in the same fabric and the whole thing just looked... rich!

"It's the best work I've ever done, Herbie," he said, opening the jacket to reveal the lining, ruby red and silver silk paisley."

"I think I should wash my hands, too," I said, going into the back and scrubbing the subway off.

"It's almost too beautiful, Myron, I'm kinda afraid to wear it... except I know you can always make me another." I took the hanger from him and went into the dressing room.

The blue wool was so soft and light it felt like the kind of fur I'd want if I were an animal! Then the lining, the lining—like a Shah! The pants were lined down to the knees and the silk felt cool against my skin. Everything fit like it was made for me... because it was.

I looked in the mirror and... I was a man. A grown man. A classy, elegant man who could go anywhere in the city and instantly be recognized as *somebody*. I stared at myself like I was somebody else.

Then I heard Myron, "Did you hear what I said, Herbie?"

"Oh, no, sorry, I was so happy with how this fits and feels." I opened the curtain to model the suit for Myron. He looked pleased.

"You look beautiful, boychik. Even handsomer than I remember."

"Thanks, Myron, it's like a dream."

"I'm glad you like it. Like I said, I can't make you another one."

"Oh, why not? Did they run out of the special order fabric?"

"No, I'm going west."

"What? Why?"

"I thought I'd be running the shop here... but Old man Shapiro brought in his cousin, Les, cheap bastard. Wants me to 'work faster.' But doing the best work takes time. I can't work like that."

"I'm sorry, Myron."

"It's for the best, I saw an ad in *The Tailor Times* and got an interview for MGM!"

"MGM? The roaring Lion MGM?"

"That's the one. Working for Adrian, their head costume designer."

"Wow, that's... great... really..."

"Yeah, I brought your suit with me when I met Mr. Adrian at the Waldorf and he hired me on the spot! Said it was 'exquisite perfection!'"

"Hollywood, huh. My girlfriend... ex-girlfriend, went there."

"I'll probably run into her, what's her name?"

"Kitty..." Myron's face froze. "Kitty Rose—oh, that's right, you know her, you made a tuxedo..."

"You and..."

"Kitty, yeah."

Myron fell into a brown leather chair, twisting his tape measure around his fist until it snapped. His face turned red.

"She's always taken... How did you meet?"

"I was delivering a dress you made her..."

"Motherfucker!" he screamed, pulling what was left of his tape measure around his neck like he was trying to strangle himself.

I was shocked. "What? What's wrong? What'd I do..."

"I can't fucking believed it. I cannot fucking believe it. Cannot. Fucking. Believe..."

"I'm sorry, whatever it is..."

Myron started gagging, choking, then slumped over and puked on the floor. He kept gasping and crying, "Why *her*? *Why?*"

"She was pretty and nice..."

"Pretty?" he choked out a laugh. "*She's* pretty," more choking and crying and laughing. "*I'm* nice. I've *always* been nice. That bitch of a sister!"

"Kitty's your sister?"

"My *twin!*" he yelled, furious, tears streaming down his pale face, from his *green eyes*... oh, how did I never see it! They had the same eyes!

"You could have fallen in love with *me!*" he cried.

"But she's a girl, and you're a boy..."

"AM I?" He wailed. "How do you know?"

"You're Myron, you've always been Myron."

"YOU DON'T KNOW THAT!" His head was in his hands and he was making no sense. His wailing sounded like a wounded cat and broke my heart.

"I'm sorry, I didn't know, I didn't know, she never said..."

"Of course she never said," he hissed, angrily. "Just one more secret... "

"When she left me she said she had a secret but wouldn't say..."

"*Her* secret, not *ours*, not *mine!*" His panting slowed, then he looked me coldly in the eye. "No, it won't be a secret anymore!" He stood up and got close to me, looking crazy. "You never noticed anything unusual about her?"

"No, she seemed perfect to me," I said, sheepishly.

"*She* was perfect? Then *I'm* perfect, too! You should have loved *me!*"

"I don't understand, Myron..."

"Don't call me that name! *She* chose that name!"

"Myr... I don't... what's happening"

"You screwed her, right?" he said, staring me down. I didn't want to answer. "You screwed her and you didn't notice... Oh, my God. Oh. My. God!"

"I'm sorry, My... I didn't know or I wouldn't have..." I was confused and scared.

"She musta been the only girl you ever been with. Was she?" I didn't know what to say. "Answer me!"

"Yes, yes, the only one."

He started to laugh—Kitty's laugh, high and sweet, but sad. "And she was *perfect*..." another laugh, sadder. "I don't know who's the bigger schmuck, me or you, Herbie..."

"You're not a schmuck..." I said thinking it would help.

"Then *you* are. If I'd only known you were then... I wouldn't have felt like a *freak* all this time."

"I never thought you were..."

"No, you never did. You were always nice to me... My God, I can't believe she did this to me— again."

I felt myself sweating in my new suit. "I'm gonna take this off and then we'll go somewhere and talk and make this all right..."

"Go, change. It's time I change, too."

I undressed quickly but carefully, hung up the suit and put on my old clothes.

When I got out, Myron was rifling through a rack of ladies dresses. "I should never have let her decide... But she was always making the decisions..." He pulled out a white dress... With cherries on it... just like the one Kitty had. "I made this for her, did you ever see it?"

"Yes, it was her favorite dress, she wore it to Hollywood..."

"Hollywood. What will I do about that now... now that Mr. Adrian has seen me like this... She's even ruined that for me..." He tore the dress off the hanger and went into the workroom. I didn't know what to do or say. I heard water running and things crashing but was scared to go see what was happening.

Then Kitty appeared in the dress.

"Kitty?" I gasped.

"Iris. That's the name I wanted," she said, quietly.

Did they have another sister... or was...

"I wasn't *always* Myron, Herbie. I was Iris."

I heard buzzing... I saw spots in front of my eyes or were those bees? My legs gave out and I landed hard on the floor. "I don't understand, I don't understand," I repeated, stupidly. Hadn't I lost Kitty? Yet, here she was...

Whoever it was in the cherry dress sat on the floor next to me. She took my hand in her small, soft hand... just like Kitty's hand.

"Dear, dear Herbie. Of course you don't understand. How could you?" This person cooed. "Kitty and I are *identical twins*."

Her grip on my hand tightened and she pulled my hand to her thigh, then under her dress. I tried to pull back but she made me feel between her legs... she felt just like Kitty.

"They didn't know what to make of us when we were born," She said, calmly.

This had to be a dream, that was the only explanation. I missed Kitty so much I made her re-appear from Myron just because they both had green eyes...

"Were we girls or were we boys? They were going to cut off... but Momma refused, said we were perfect the way God made us... perfect like you said Kitty was... like I must be, too..."

I will wake up... I pinched myself hard... It hurt but I didn't wake up.

"Daddy called me a freak. Kitty, too. Two little freaks. And one drunk nut job, Momma. He left. Momma took to her bed. Three days later she told us it was time we decided."

I thought maybe if I talked I'd wake up, so I said, "Decide what?" but nothing changed.

"If we wanted to be boys or girls. I was shy, and Kitty was bossy. So she told me, 'You're quiet, like daddy was, so you must be the boy, and I'm like Momma so I'm the girl.'

"But I liked being a girl, I wanted to be a girl. 'We can't both be girls,' she insisted, 'Why not?' I asked. 'Because I'm prettier and if we're both girls you'll be the ugly sister, you don't want that, do you?'

"I didn't care. But she did. 'You'll be Myron, after dad. I always thought you looked like a Myron anyway. I'll be Katherine, like Momma.' From then on she called me 'Myron,' and Momma started calling me that, too, and bought me boy's clothes. It never felt right, but when I'd wear Kitty's clothes Momma's new boyfriend would beat me... Yelled I was a freak... again... so I gave up. Became Myron. Only it never felt right."

"I still don't understand, who gets to decide if they're a boy or a girl?"

"If you'd ever seen another girl then you'd know, Herbie. We have both parts. Our penis is small but it's there."

"That's just how girls are, boys are bigger and girls are smaller..."

"Who told you that?"

"Kitty..."

"And you believed her."

"Of course..."

He... she laughed bitterly, then took a deep breath and said, "We're hermaphrodites."

"I don't know what that is."

"We're both boy and girl... at least on the outside. Inside I've always known I was a girl. Iris. That was my name... Is my name."

The egg salad sandwich on the desk was dripping onto the floor. "This isn't a dream, is it, My... ris?"

"No, but it sure feels like it sometimes, don't it?"

"I'm sorry for you..."

"Don't be sorry for me," Iris said. "Like you said, I'm perfect." She smiled, and looked perfect. I felt like I'd swallowed an entire hive of bees.

"I'll start fresh, in Hollywood... as Iris. Nobody knows me there. Except Kitty, and she wouldn't dare open her big mouth. Oh, Mr.

Adrian... if he doesn't understand I'll go to another studio, there's plenty of work there dressing movie stars."

I sat in silence. "Are you sure this isn't a dream?" I bleated.

"My life has been a bad dream—but I'm finally waking up."

111 ➵ Never Again

"I can't be here when they get back from lunch. I'm never going back to Myron." Iris said, cleaning the egg salad off the table but leaving the puke on the floor.

"Is there anything I can do to help... Do you need money?"

She stopped fussing and looked at me.

"You're a real mensch, Herbie, you always was."

"What do you need?" I had $80 in my wallet. I took it out and handed it to her. "Please, take it."

"Thank you. I'll pay you back."

"You don't need to."

"Then stay with me when you come to Hollywood," she said, sounding so much like Kitty saying the words I wanted her to say.

"I don't know," I put my wallet back in my pocket.

Myron... Kitty... no, Iris, held my hand in both of hers. It felt so warm. "I hope you do, Herbie. I surely hope you do." She pulled her hands away and hurried into the workroom. My empty hand felt cold.

I picked up my new suit... beautiful but infused with confusion, put it in a garment bag and zipped it up. I went to the workroom where Iris was quickly packing a bag with shears, pins and needles in a pin cushion, a thimble, chalk and other tailor's tools.

"Please write and let me know how you're doing."

She kept packing. "I will. Give me your address."

I didn't know what address to give... So I wrote down Glenn's. "You can always reach me here." I handed it to her and our hands touched again. She leaned in and kissed me on the cheek, warm, soft, familiar but new.

"Come on," she said, taking my hand and pulling me out the front door. She looked around, then down at herself, then at me. "I'm sorry, Herbie," she whispered. "Sorry I didn't do this a long time ago."

"I'm sorry, too... Iris." I said her name out loud for the first time. She looked at me, tears in her eyes, then turned away and headed down the street. I waited to see if she'd turn around. She didn't.

I watched her leave me—again.

112 ➺ Picture Encyclopedia

I was confused. Nauseous. Hungry.

I stopped at a drug store and got a roll of *Tums*. They tasted like toothpaste and chalk, which at first made me feel even more nauseous, then better, or at least like I'd just brushed my teeth.

Now I was hungry, but still didn't feel good enough to eat. So that left me "confused." But not just merely confused, so dizzily bewildered that it was easier to think about anything other than what just happened.

I'd lost Myron. And Iris. And Kitty, which is who I thought of when I saw Iris. What did she say they were? Identical twin, yes, I understood that. It was the other word. It reminded me of that goddess movie, "Aphrodite, My Love," starring Adolph Menjou as an archaeologist who digs up a statue of Aphrodite only to have it come to life as Claudette Colbert who he falls hopelessly in love with.

But it wasn't just Aphrodite... What was it? Herman Aphrodite? I think that was it.

Who could I ask about it? A librarian. I didn't go to the libraries very often, but I'd seen one next to Bryant Park when I walked from the subway to the *Look* offices. I could go there and find a book about it. I took the 2 train back downtown, got off at 42nd street, and walked a few blocks.

The library was large, but luckily there was an information desk. I asked the woman behind the counter where I could look up something, and she asked, "What do you want to look up?" and I didn't know what to tell her so I said, "Something," and she said, "That's too vague, young man, what subject are you interested in?" and I said, "I just want to look up a bunch of things," and she said, "like what? language, history, botany, geography, biology..." and I said, "That's it, biology," and she said, "Insect, Animal, Human..." and I said, "Human!" and now she sounded kinda snappy, "You know what, why don't you just use an encyclopedia so it's all there in one place. Go straight ahead to the general reading room, then it'll be along the back wall on the right side."

I thanked her and found myself in a room where the walls were filled with books that were all either brown or sometimes green with little gold letters on them. There were just too many. I saw a young woman pushing a cart of books so I asked her, "Can you point me to the encyclopedia?"

"Sir, we whisper here," she whispered.

"Oh, sorry," I said, feeling this must be like the church. "Could you show me..." I whispered.

"Which one?"

"Does it matter?"

"Yes, there's the Encyclopedia Britannica for scholarly work, the World Book Encyclopedia with a focus on technical, scientific and medical, the Compton's Pictured Encyclopedia is highly illustrated..."

"I'll take that one. The one with the pictures."

"That's on the third floor in the Juvenile section."

I thanked her and went to the third floor. Luckily one of the rooms had the word "Juvenile" right above the doors. I went in and saw a sign that said, 'Encyclopedias' on the bookcases.

I chose the book with "L-O" on it because I thought it might be under "Lady Parts" but it wasn't there. I tried E-G and looked under "female," but no. Then there was a section called "Female reproductive system" where there were only drawings, but Iris was right, girls weren't supposed to have... I set down the book, feeling stupid, but how could I have known?

I put that volume back and took out "H-K" and tried to find Herman Aphrodite but it wasn't there but I did find "Hermaphrodite" and that sounded right so I read it: "Hermaphroditism, the condition of having both male and female reproductive organs." Oh. Well, maybe this happened a lot... "Such conditions are extremely rare in humans."

I always thought Kitty was "one-in-a-million" and other than being "two-in-a-million" I was right. I put the book back. I thought about how Kitty was the best of both worlds... Iris, too.

I walked a few blocks to the Look offices and went to Sergei's office. I needed to talk to someone about this.

113 ➤ Eat it

"She had what?" he said in disbelief.

"Both parts," I repeated.

"That's crazy. I wish I'd been able to fuck her!"

"Don't say that," I protested.

"Well, *you* liked it, right?"

"But I didn't know."

"I had no idea you were such a virgin."

"I wasn't a virgin... I kissed two boys, too, except one boy is now a girl." I could see Sergei was trying not to laugh. "Please, be serious about this!"

"I'm sorry. You should fuck Claudine if you want to see what most girls are like."

"Now I'm sorry I told you!" I said, angrily. "Don't you see, I've lost both of them!"

Sergei snickered, "Doing twin sisters, or brothers, is a dream of mine..."

I threw a pen at him, "You're an asshole. But I didn't know who else to talk to."

He put his arms around me. "Come here, baby."

"Don't call me 'baby!'" Sergei held me and I cried on his shoulder. "I'll never see them again." My stomach rumbled like thunder.

"I'm going to take you to lunch at my favorite Greek place down the block," he patted my head.

We left the lobby and headed east on 42nd, then I saw a blue awning that read, *Aphrodite's Grill*. "I'm not hungry anymore, Serg..."

"Don't be ridiculous, of course you are," he said, holding the door for me. I entered and sat in a booth.

The menu was plastic covered and sticky. "The souvlaki here is great. I wanted them to cater my birthday party but Julien and Claudine insisted on cooking."

"When was your birthday?"

"This Saturday."

"I didn't know. Why didn't you tell me?"

"I'm telling you now."

"That's not much time for me to find you a present."

"My present... is your presence," he said quietly, holding my hand under the table.

"That's very sweet, but I want to give you something."

"I know just what I want," he said, placing my hand on his crotch which might have been sexy except for what happened earlier.

I pulled my hand away. "I mean buy you something. Like a hat."

He picked up a spoon and used it like a mirror to inspect his scalp, "What, you think my hair is thinning?"

"No, I thought you'd like a fedora."

"I'm only turning 30!" He jumped up and went to the bathroom. I slumped against the wall.

He came back, looking happy, "My hair is fabulous, thank you. Why cover 'all this' with a hat?"

"Please, just tell me what you want."

"I want a suit like the one you just got, it's beautiful," he said, without a hint of sensitivity.

I stared at him and shook my head. "Take it. It's yours. I don't think I can wear it."

"Seriously? It'll be too big on me... But I'm sure my tailor can cut it down."

The waitress came. She looked old and tired. "Whaddya want?"

"We'll both have the souvlaki with hummus, thanks." Sergei said. I looked at him in disbelief, then sighed.

He pulled out his purple leather pad and wrote something in it. I closed my eyes and smelled roasted meat and ammonia and closed my eyes.

"Here you go, boys," the waitress said, startling me awake by dropping the plates on the table with a thud that nearly made the food fly. Sergei dug right in. I hesitated, then took a bite and it tasted good. Really good.

"Great, huh?" Sergei said, between bites, a little lettuce hanging out of his mouth. I nodded in agreement. I thought about my suit... the only thing I had left to remember Myron or Iris, and I was already sorry I'd given it away.

114 ➻ Darkroom

I walked back to the office with Sergei then went to the darkroom. I made duplicate contact prints of the shadow and Busby photos, as well as enlargements to send to the dancers.

"Those are extraordinary," a voice behind me said. I jumped.

"I didn't know anyone else was in here..."

"Yeah, I have that effect on people... I'm Horace, I manage the darkroom. And you're...?"

"Herb, sorry... this isn't personal work, Pat asked me..."

"Hamilton? I loved your work in Fair/Unfair!"

"Thanks! Um, these aren't going in the magazine, of course, but I'm going to do a couple of shoots based on them... with clothes.."

"I like them the way they are... You can do whatever you want here."

"Thanks, that's nice." It was hard to see what Horace looked like with only the dim red safety light, especially because his skin was dark.

"Can I get you a binder to protect those?"

"Thanks, that'd be great. I need to deliver these..."

"For Sergei's new magazine, I'll bet."

"Does everybody here know about it?"

"Just a couple of us, and we're not talking." he said, opening a binder and putting the prints into protective plastic sleeves. "Do you have copies of those negatives?"

"Why would I want copies?"

"To give to Sergei."

"How do you copy a negative?"

"We've got a special negative printer, right here," he said, pointing to a machine in the corner. "May I?"

"Sure."

He took the glassine of negatives and pulled out the strip with the Busby negatives. I stood close to him to watch. He smelled good, like cloves.

"Insert the film here... he said, clamping one end into a holder with teeth that matched up to the holes in the film. Press the red button and..." the machine flashed, then made a whirring sound as it advanced the negative to the next frame. "Repeat until you're done." He put in the next strip, then the next until he'd copied the whole roll. "When you're finished, push this lever and the new negatives are placed into a cartridge you can take to the developer."

He carried it over to the processor. "Keep the originals for yourself to retain the best quality," he said, handing me back the originals before the copies emerged, developed.

"Wow, thanks, Horace. I would never have known that!"

"My pleasure. Here's my card in case you have any questions," he said, handing me his card, our fingers touching. I thought maybe he was flirting with me but I wasn't sure. "Questions... about *anything*," he whispered.

"I need to make some prints," I said as I put the negative in the enlarger and showed off my dodging and burning.

"Nice technique, Herb," he said, putting his hand on my shoulder. Yes, he was flirting. After I exposed the paper he ran it through the developer, then printed two more.

"Let's go out and look at these in the light," I suggested, leaving the darkroom. He followed. I glanced at the print, which I knew was fine, then looked at Horace. He was Middle-Eastern and reminded me of men I'd seen in "The Mummy" with Boris Karloff, not Boris, who was scary, but one of the handsome ancient pharaohs.

Horace pointed to a spot on the print where a hair had gotten on the negative. "Definitely needs to be reprinted," he said, looking me straight in the eye, then looking at the darkroom door. Sergei was walking the hall at that exact moment.

"Hands off, Horace!" Sergei said, seriously.

"I was just showing him the ropes." Horace replied.

"That's what I was afraid of. He's mine!" Sergei said, as he rounded the corner and disappeared, peeked back, then left again.

"Sorry, I didn't mean to stir up Sergei's infamous jealousy."

"This has already been a difficult day..."

"What do you call difficult?"

"My girlfriend was half boy and my friend who was a boy but could have been my boyfriend turned out to be half girl, now all girl."

"Confusing."

"And I'm with Sergei and I meet you and I..."

"Don't need any more confusion right now, I get it. My timing was bad, I apologize."

"No need to apologize, Horace. I've got a headache and a heartache and I think I'm getting a stomachache, too."

"The trifecta. I'll let you go."

"You're very kind."

"Actually, I am. Next time you're here I'll introduce you to the radioactive Staticmaster Ionising Brush that'll keep hairs and dust off your negatives."

"You just made that up!"

"No, it's a real thing. I look forward to showing it to you at some later date," he said, kindly.

"Thank you, Horace. You're a mensch."

"If I had a nickel for every time I heard that... I'd have a dime!" I laughed. He leaned in and kissed me on both cheeks. "Go home."

I went to Sergei's office and dropped off negatives... the copies.

115 ➥ I'm Flying!

I went to bed but I couldn't sleep. It wasn't the late afternoon light, or the shadows. I just kept seeing Kitty and Iris, smiling, then disappearing. At least I had photos of Kitty, I didn't have any of Iris, only Myron. I wanted to compare them, because as similar as they were, I knew they were different—Identical but individual... yet Iris kept melting into Myron. More than anything I wished I had a picture of them together I could study for clues.

Kitty had just left me. Iris had just met me—she was leaving to find *herself*. That was different. Kitty might have said she was leaving to find herself, but to me it felt like she was doing what she'd always done, but with a different man. Unless... What if *she* was different now?

I wondered if they'd be close in Hollywood. "The Rose Sisters." No, Kitty wouldn't share the spotlight like that. But how could she hide Iris when she looked just like her?

Could either of them be trusted with each other? With me?

I turned my head so I didn't have to look at a ceiling strewn with shadows. Instead, I looked out over the mezzanine railing to the living room below, empty and serene. The colorful sofas and chairs just waiting, waiting... for what? For someone to use them?

Then I saw it. Quite small. A shadow of the curly wrought iron railing onto the walkway. A shadow that looked like a face, except it had two sets of eyes. As if Iris and Kitty were overlaid on each other.

The shadow moved, slowly, and began to talk. "What do you see in me?" the face asked.

"I don't know," I thought.

"You do know, you're just afraid to admit it," the shadow spoke again, now stern.

"I don't know," I thought again.

"You can lie to yourself, but I know the truth," it said.

"If you know, then tell me!" I didn't know if I was shouting or if it was just in my head.

"Come on, admit it. You see yourself," it sounded disgusted.

"No, I'm not like her or him or her."

"You're not normal," it said, it's mouth either a grin or a grimace.

"That's not news, muse."

"What would other people think of you if they knew?"

"Pat knows and she's..."

"Not normal either. I'm talking about normal people, like your Ma."

She'd be... confused... like I am. And Pa... I didn't care what he thought. "What does it matter what they think?" I asked the shadow.

"You're right, it only matters what *you* think." The shadow mouth stretched as the sun set, opening wider.

"I only care what other people think of my pictures."

"Do you even care about that?"

"Yes, I want to make them think, or better yet, *feel*."

"You want them to see the world in your weird way so you don't feel so alone."

"That's not true," I protested as the shadow's face distorted, its eyes agog. "I want to enlighten them."

The shadow was cackling, ugly. "What makes you think you're the light... not the shadow?" it choked, before fading out of existence.

I felt myself struggling to move, as if paralyzed, then jolted, facing the ceiling, dark, with the occasional streak of light.

Which was I? The light or the shadow? Or both?

I wrapped the blanket around me and went downstairs. The colorful furniture looked gray in the dim light. I went down to the ground floor and looked at the icon paintings which still somehow sparkled. I stared at the painting of my face, trapped in that little oval. Did I really look like that? Or was that just how Sergei saw me. And were photos any different? Did they show things the way they were, or the way I made them look?

I heard the key in the lock and Sergei came in, carrying a big bag of groceries.

"Quite avant garde," he said.

"What?"

"Your sartorial sense. A plaid blanket... bold choice!"

"I'm glad you approve."

"I didn't say I approved."

"Too bad, I was planning on wearing this to your birthday with nothing but my birthday suit underneath."

"That I approve."

"But I decided it's a bit breezy."

"I'll turn up the heat..." he said, struggling with the grocery bag. "I love our witty repartee, but you need to help me with the food. I bought a selection of cheeses for our guest tonight."

"What guest?" I asked, not having been informed of a guest.

"Surely I told you, I invited Reggie DeBilt to screen his latest film, *'Death Miracle.'* His work is painfully opaque, you will adore it." I followed him into the kitchen.

"You can't watch a film without cheese?" I chided him.

"It would be too, too inhospitalière. Besides, we'd have trouble hearing his subtle soundscape over the stomach growling." He removed the cheeses from their paper wrappings and arranged them in a semicircle, "From mild to sharp," he explained, placing a pale orange translucent block of something at the end, "Quince paste," he told me.

"Where do you even get this stuff?" I picked up a knife to sample it.

"Murray's on Bleeker. Put down that knife or I will stab you with mine," he threatened with a little rounded butter knife, fanning plain crackers in a row behind the cheese.

"I want a taste."

"And you will have one when Reggie is here. I would suggest you change, but your schmatta is growing on me." He raised the cheese tray out of my reach above his head and headed upstairs. He set the tray down on the table between the two sofas and guarded it. "I know exactly where each piece of cheese is, and if anything moves..."

He walked backwards and took a small box with four buttons off the wall. He pressed the red button and the industrial hook I'd seen the first night lowered, stopping at waist level. He dashed into the storeroom and brought back a leather harness.

"Put this on, and I'll make you fly," he told me. Who wouldn't want to fly? I put it on and he tightened the straps a little too tightly around my groin. He connected me to the hook, and pressed the green button. I was whisked off my feet and into the air... where I dangled, swinging back and forth. "Now the cheese is safe," he told me. I kicked madly, which only made me swing more... It was quite pleasant.

He returned to the storeroom and came back and handed me a big bundle of white fabric. "See those hooks on the brick wall? I'll raise you up and you will hang the movie screen on them."

"Ah, so this is about more than cheese."

"I could have done the screen myself. The cheese is a bonus," he pressed the green button again and I jerked upwards, then sideways until I was forced to use the bundle to keep from crashing into the wall. I saw the grommets along one edge of the fabric and started at the corner, placing each one over the hook in the wall until the big screen hung down, kept taut by the little weights along the bottom. "Well done!" he said. I looked down and saw him slipping a cracker covered with cheese into his mouth.

"Cheese thief!" I yelled. He acted like he didn't hear me and ate another. He repeatedly pressed the buttons which swung me from side to side. I didn't show him how much I was enjoying it or he might stop.

"Don't you dare swing me around like that!" I cried, hoping my protestations would encourage him to keep doing it.

Ahh, it felt like flying! It was only when I started to giggle that my cover was blown and he knew I liked it.

"Set me down, now!" I yelled, hoping he would do just the opposite. Instead, he lowered me until my feet were just a foot off the ground, just high enough that I couldn't get out of the harness—and just far enough from the cheese that I could smell it.

"Hang around until I get back," he said, laughing, as he went upstairs. When he was out of sight, I kicked my legs until I made contact with the sofa, sending me swinging. I kept kicking until I was close enough to reach the cheese! On one swing I reached down and grabbed a large piece of blue and white cheese, then took a bite... ug, it tasted like feet smell! I wanted to spit it out but then Sergei would know, so I swallowed it fast, the aftertaste being quite pleasant. I heard him coming downstairs and tried to stop my swinging.

"Did you enjoy the Stilton?" he asked, casually, moving the cheese tray out of my reach then pressing the buttons to make me swing back and forth.

"Whee!"

"I knew you'd love it. The harness, not the cheese." With that he raised me higher. I felt like a baby bird that was just learning to fly. It was heaven.

Sergei held up a cracker and cheese and I caught it in my mouth as I flew by.

116 ⫸ Death Miracle

Hanging around was all fun and games until the harness started to dig into my thighs. "OK, Sergei, put me down now." I said, no longer able to kick the sofa and swing without causing myself pain. Sergei was nowhere to be found.

I heard the doorbell and waited for someone to answer it, but nobody did. "SERGEI, THE DOOR!" I yelled. Nobody answered.

I used my leg to drag the sofa underneath me, then undid the straps and let myself fall into it, landing so hard that my leg went right through the seat.

The doorbell rang again. I worked to extricate myself from the carnivorous chesterfield, and limped down to the front door.

I opened it and was greeted with the sight of a man who looked like a bum.

"Hello, I'm Reginald," he said, with a voice like velvet.

"Oh, hi, I'm Herb," my voice sounded like sandpaper in comparison. "Come right in, I'm looking forward to seeing your film."

"Then you're the only one," he said, smiling. "Could you help me with the projector?" he asked, pointing to a large trunk. I grabbed it by its handle and dragged it inside.

"I don't know where Sergei's gotten off to, but I do know he has a delicious cheese tray for you!"

"When you think about it, that's all that matters, really, isn't it?" Reginald proclaimed.

Just then Sergei appeared from the kitchen, this time carrying a pitcher of something red. "I call it 'Death Campari' in honor of your film, Reggie!"

I took the pitcher from him, "Let me carry this for you," I said, limping up the stairs as quickly as I could so he'd be stuck with the projector. I heard the whirring of the overhead crane and watched a trap door open in the floor so the hook could be attached to the projector crate and lifted effortlessly upstairs.

Sergei and Reggie removed it from the trunk and set it up facing the screen.

"It's very kind of you to host a showing," Reggie said, still sounding like a prince while looking like a pauper. "Nobody in the city wants to see it, not after my last film."

"Personally, I loved '*You will die*,'" Sergei announced. Then turning to me, "Stupendous artistic achievement, everything in it was dead yet it was all about life!"

"I won the Berlin prize, before it was revoked and the film burned," Reggie announced, proudly. "I shot the burning as the final scene of what would be the new cut, 1205 minutes of blackness followed by five minutes of the film on fire!"

"I told you he is a genius!" Sergei said, never having told me that.

The doorbell rang again. "Get that, won't you," Sergei said to me. I limped downstairs, my leg feeling better but holding out hope that Sergei might notice what he had done to me before he discovered what I'd done to the sofa.

I opened the door to... a mob of people, a line stretching from the vestibule to around the corner. They oozed in, right past me, then seeped up the stairs. I lost count of how many there were as it was hard to tell them apart, all dressed in black with odd hairstyles.

I waited till they were all inside and closed the door. When I got upstairs all the seats were taken, including on the damaged sofa where an emaciated young man was sunk down to his black leather jacket.

I looked in vain for the cheese tray which, I assumed, had all been consumed, including, perhaps, the tray. There was a lot of noise and chatter until Sergei stood in front of the screen and raised his arm. Silence ensued.

"Thank you all for coming tonight," Reggie said, looking shocked and delighted to have an audience. "I recognize some friendly faces from last time and I hope you enjoy this as much. A little background, 'Death Miracle' was inspired by my birth mother, who I adopted on my 40th birthday, right before she died of alcohol poisoning. This film documents the last 6 hours of her life, unedited. Enjoy!"

"Six hours?" I whispered to Sergei.

"Julien and I prepared a meal for intermission."

"I'm hungry now, where's the cheese?"

"Focus on the film," he said as my stomach rumbled.

The screen was filled with a closeup of a woman's face, unmoving, until she coughed quietly, which caused gasps from the rapt audience. "Stop pointing that thing at me, Dwayne," she said directly into the camera.

"Sorry momma," an off-screen voice said, but the filming continued. "And my name is Reggie now."

"Get me a shot of Dewar's, son," she said as she closed her eyes. We heard the sound of liquid being poured and saw a glass handed to her. Without sitting up, she opened her mouth and simply poured the drink in.

"I'm disappointed by the narrative complexity," Sergei whispered to me, "I hope this is just a prelude to his trademark minimalism."

Sergei needn't have worried, because for the next endless hours, the woman just lay there, wheezing until the protector made a sputtering sound and the screen went black. The audience was either in awed silence or asleep. There was a smattering of applause from a few, while the others hushed them.

Julien appeared at the top of the stairs. "Dinner is served," he announced. At last!

The group nearly trampled each other to get downstairs. Sergei held my hand, "This is wonderful, isn't it?" he said, loudly. He and Reggie and I walked down the stairs where the room had been transformed into a dining area.

The crowd applauded Reggie, who bowed, shyly before announcing. "The menu tonight is my mother's last meal." Claudette and Julien carried out plates of almost clear steaming liquid. The diners didn't wait to taste it, then reacted with either "umm?" or "mmm" it was hard to tell which.

Sergei pulled Reggie and me into the kitchen to plates of steaks and fries. "Thank God!" Reggie announced, tearing into it as if he hadn't eaten in days. I joined him, as if I hadn't eaten in hours! In between bites, and sometimes in the middle of them, Reggie said, "At the end. my mother would only eat consommé, and then only because I convinced her it was a cocktail with a twist of lemon."

I started to laugh but didn't want to be rude so I pretended to cough, then a bit of French fly lodged in my throat and I couldn't stop coughing until there were tears in my eyes.

"He's very sensitive," Sergei said to Reggie who put his dirty fingernailed hands on mine reassuringly, then helpfully pounded on my back until a bit of fry went flying past Julien, attaching itself to the wall.

I started laughing again, got up and excused myself.

"I can see he was deeply moved," I heard Reggie say as I crouched behind the stove until I'd composed myself. I returned, dabbing my eyes on a napkin, finishing my meal in silence.

Sergei and Reggie went into the dining room. "And now, for Act II: Her final hours," Reggie said and I heard them packing the stairs like cattle.

Now that my stomach was full, I felt sleepy and wondered how I'd make it through the next three hours.

The projector sputtered to life again, only now the camera had moved. We were no longer confronted with his mother's face, but, instead, a blank wall. Occasionally there was the sound of Reggie crying and the camera would shake, but that was the extent of the excitement. After about an hour he pointed the camera back to her face, which, startlingly, seemed to have aged 30 years in one hour.

Her eyes were still closed, only now, every little twitch became meaningful. Was she dreaming? Was this her last breath? I was transfixed.

Suddenly her eyes opened wide and she took a deep breath. "Dwayne, baby?" she croaked. Reggie's face appeared next to hers. "What, momma?" he asked. She exhaled and her eyes closed as quickly as they'd opened. Were those her last words?

No, she continued to wheeze, though shallow, and her forehead trembled as if she was thinking.

I was deeply moved and felt tears rolling down my cheeks, and heard everyone else sniffling.

Her mouth opened, then closed. Wheezing. Another hour passed. Then her mouth opened again and she whispered, "Baby..."

Silence. The credit said, "The End" but the film kept going.

She was gone. For the next hour, I stared at this face which had gone from being alive to being like a still photo.

Time had died with her. It made me wonder about my still photos, were they frozen moments or were they dead?

"It's a miracle I found you." Reggie said as he covered her face with a sheet. The sound of his own breathing was all we heard for the next 20 minutes until the screen went black.

I wanted to applaud but it felt wrong. Instead I shook Reggie's hand and whispered, "Thank you." The movie had been slow verging on tortuous, but that only made every miniscule movement monumental.

I wondered, could one image possibly capture a living person? Was that even fair? Because who chose that moment? Me? Pat? Sergei? Never the person in the picture.

I knew how I had to shoot next.

117 ⇛ Three Spoons

After the others left Sergei finally brought out the now legendary cheese tray!

"I thought cheese would be the highlight of the evening," Reggie said, "But the audience reaction was! Still, the cheese looks awfully good right now!"

Between bites of yellow cheese I said, "I'm speechless, Reggie. To be honest I was afraid I'd be bored, but it made me experience time in a new way. You're a genius."

"And I'm not?" Sergei said, grabbing the cheese knife away from me.

"It takes one to know one." Reggie retrieved the knife from Sergei's shaking hand and sliced into a creamy white cheese, spread it on a cracker and slid it into my mouth.

I wasn't even all that hungry now, just excited about how I was going to do my next shoot. Still, the cheese was delicious.

"Herb will be far too delighted when he hears you're going to grace us with your presence tonight, Reg. Emmental?" Sergei asked, aggressively placing a piece of cheese into Reggie's mouth.

"I will enjoy your company," he said, chewing the cheese which had holes in it and tasted like the one at the Swiss pavilion. "But first I'll need a fire hose, or a shower, whatever you have handy."

"Relax and get your fill of cheese—whatever we don't eat tonight you can take with you. You know where the shower is, and it's stocked with a fresh loofah, pumice, razor and scissors, as always."

Once I knew Reggie was getting the remainder of the cheese I stopped eating it, he needed it more than I did. "Thanks again, Reggie, I'd love to talk to you about capturing time on film..."

I reached out to shake his hand, but Sergei pulled me back. "OK, little fanatic, give the man a break already."

In bed, I was too excited to go to sleep, and kept extolling the virtues of the film—how the hour of looking at the wall made me focus on my sense of hearing, and then how different his mother looked when the camera was back on her and how emotional it all was.

I told Sergei about my Ma, and how she was the only thing I sometimes missed from my old life. He pulled me close and talked about his mama, and how she died in the typhus epidemic in Russia when he was only 8. He and his father escaped from the pogroms in Russia and came to New York where he had cousins. His story made me feel lucky even to have the lousy childhood I had!

I hugged him to make him feel better, and then a handsome man appeared at the door... wait, it was Reggie! He was clean, his hair cut, his beard shaped, and now he looked as good as his voice sounded.

Sergei patted the mattress next to him and whispered to me, "Don't get too excited, he's as celibate as a monk, he just likes the company."

Reggie dropped his robe, revealing a physique strong from schlepping that projector, I guessed, and got into bed next to me. "Serg is right, I believe sex dissipates creative energy that can be put in my work. You two should consider that!"

"I'd never thought of it," I mused, snuggling up to Reggie.

"I'd never consider it!" Sergei laughed, pulling me back to him.

"Your decision, boys. Still, I'm not above a good cuddle... it's nice to have human contact, again." He spooned me.

"Where have you been living?" I asked.

"With a group of folks at the base of the Brooklyn Bridge. Good people. Non-judgmental, if penniless."

"Why?" I was genuinely curious.

"Serg didn't tell you"

"I didn't know if you'd want me to."

"*Now* he wants permission!" Reggie laughed, putting his long arms around both of us. "To answer your question, Herb, because they are anonymous. Invisible, actually. I like that—it gives me freedom. You see, I grew up a Vanderbilt. Not born one... they basically bought me from my mother who'd gotten pregnant from Willy Vanderbilt. Didn't give her a choice. I don't blame her, what could she do up against all their money? I wanted to be an artist. They wanted me to work for the family's New York Central Railroad. I did, for a number of years, until I finally ran away... literally ran down Park Ave..."

"...We met when he stole my movie camera," Sergei interrupted.

"He loves to say that. I didn't steal it, I borrowed it."

"By breaking in."

"I always planned on returning it when I was done."

"And he did, which is how we met."

"I was one of the first faces you painted on the icons downstairs. Even before Julien and Claudine."

"He'd still be there if he hadn't tried to kill me."

"Serg is so theatrical. If I'd wanted him dead he'd be dead now. I merely wanted to strangle him."

"I understand that feeling," I said. I could feel Reggie laugh, then Sergei pinched me.

Reggie continued, "I'd just finished my first film, called 'Sergei, sleeping,' which was just that... have you ever watched him sleep, he's quite dramatic, all that tossing and turning and snoring..."

"I do not snore…"

"That's what he said then, too, but it was there, on film—quite beautiful. Of course Sergei was quite beautiful back then before he got so old and cranky. No, he was always cranky."

"If you had asked my permission I would have said yes."

"I asked your permission after I shot it and you said 'no,' so I put my hands around your neck to help you form the word 'yes!' But you wouldn't. So I left."

"I admitted I was wrong," Sergei said, angrily.

"Hence we are friends again."

"What happened to the film?" I wondered aloud.

"Serg sold it to the Museum of Modern Art. Without asking my permission."

"I asked after, like you had. And I sent you their check."

"Like I needed money… then."

"But isn't it wonderful to have your work in a museum?" I asked

"Not when my relatives were on the museum board and found out where I was. They had me institutionalized—and disowned me.

"I admit that was bad, but I did help you escape…"

"…hence our enduring friendship!" Reggie finished, without so much as a hint of rancor.

"Wow" was all I could say.

"It all turned out OK—I honed my aesthetic in the asylum."

"See, it wasn't all bad," Sergei couldn't help but add.

"And you're making your art," I said.

"Someday, probably after I'm dead, people will watch it. Ironic, isn't it? The world works in mysterious, if fucked up ways." Reggie said, snuggling up to me. "Thanks for tonight, boys. For the opportunity, the company… the cheese…" he trailed off.

I didn't want to wait till I was dead for people to appreciate my work. I didn't want to have to get Sergei's permission, either. And he did so snore.

118 ⇒ Cake
and Circuses

I snuck downstairs after Reggie and Sergei fell asleep and put the cheese tray on his projector case, lest he forget, along with $100 cash and a note saying if he ever needed anything to look me up.

Reggie was gone when I woke up with the uncomfortable feeling I was being watched. Sergei was lying next to me, staring.

"Do you miss your new boyfriend?" he said, meanly.

My eyes were barely even open and I didn't know what he was talking about. "Whaa?"

"Your new favorite genius, Reggie, left, he couldn't be bothered to stay and be worshiped by you."

"What's wrong?" was all I could think to say, because he was being so strange.

"I saw how you looked at him last night."

"Wait, are you jealous? We didn't even have sex, he just spooned me. Besides, how did I look at him?"

"With love!" he spat.

"What? Respect, yes, but love? That's ridiculous."

"I saw the money you left, too."

"I was being nice, and you're being crazy." I dressed silently, and went down to the kitchen.

Julien and Claudine were already busy cooking. Had I forgotten it was a weekend? No, not yet.

"Ah, so you've come down to help us prepare for Sergei's big birthday?"

"Oh, no, I came down to make breakfast. I have to go to work."

"That's OK, you can't cook, can you?"

"I can scramble eggs and make toast, but I don't think that'll help for the birthday bash."

"Claudine is baking a special Korolevsky cake, a sour cream cake with layers of poppy seeds and walnuts."

"Sounds delicious!" I said, figuring out this was code for "there's no room in the kitchen for you, clumsy little man." But it made me think—I'd been here all this time and knew so little about these two people. "I'd like to get to know you and Claudine better, how did you end up here with Sergei?"

They looked at each other and shrugged. "How much time do you have?" Claudine asked.

"Plenty... if I can lick the frosting bowl!"

"We were circus performers. I worked the high-wire, and Julien tamed the tigers," Claudine said, handing me a bowl and a spatula. The cream cheese frosting was possibly the best breakfast ever.

"Tigers?" I asked, between licks.

Julien laughed, "She was married to her high-wire partner but having an affair with me."

Claudine put her hand over his mouth and continued, "When my husband found out, he cut my wire so it would break. I fell and broke my back. Julien nursed me back to health but we needed money so he became a chef and I worked with him as his sous chef while still lying flat."

They looked at each other, adoringly, laughed, and kissed. Julien raised his arm to show five long, raised scars on his side.

"From Pasha, my favorite tiger. She was so angry when we said goodbye she tried to keep me from going," he said, wistfully.

Claudine turned out and lifted her shirt, revealing scars on her back, "I have 14 stainless steel screws holding my spine together." she said, a badge of courage.

"What an amazing story!"

"Sergei wanted to open this restaurant but couldn't find chefs who would stick around. We saw a little advertisement in the Times, cooked for a weekend and never left."

"How long have you been here?" I asked.

"Three years this month. We have seen many others come and go from the paintings and Sergei's bed... Oh, I am very sorry, that was tactless," Claudine said.

"We like you, Herbert, even if you are not good in the restaurant."

"Thank you, and I'm sorry about that."

"No need to apologize. It is not who you are. Hold on, you have frosting on your nose," Julien said, leaning in and licking it off.

"We should all have sex and get to know each other better," Claudine said, casually while whipping cream for the cake. Despite remembering Kitty's motto of "It's just sex," it still surprised me that everybody here was so casual about it.

"I've got to go to the office, let me know if there's anything I can get for the party... like some falafel?"

"Oh, Lord, he's taken you to that awful diner and told you he wanted it at his party. Ungrateful bastard!" Julien laughed. Claudine stuck out her tongue. I left.

119 ➻ Cole

Kitty... Iris... no, I wouldn't think about her. Shadows. People. Dogs. *Click. Click. Click.* The pictures didn't go together or tell a story except for the variety of the city. I didn't care, I envisioned a contact sheet of all those different images, letting the viewer decide how they connected.

I got to the Chrysler Building... a familiar part of my life now. As I passed by Louise's desk she called out to me, "Herb, I was just going to call you. I've got a list of the Broadway performers Pat wants you to photograph. I can schedule them for you if you'd like, but Cole Porter needs you to shoot this afternoon because he flies to Hollywood tomorrow. He lives at the Waldorf, and you'll need to make arrangements with his secretary, Bianca."

"I'll get right on it," I said, mesmerized by the list of famous names she handed me. Was I really going to get to meet Ethel Merman, Gene Kelly, Danny Kaye... and Boris Karloff?

But first, the famous Cole Porter who'd written so many songs I loved! "You're The Top," "I Get A Kick Out Of You," and the very racy "Anything Goes." I called Bianca.

"He'd like to have you for lunch," she said with her elegant Spanish accent.

"I'd be honored," I replied.

"12pm, sharp. Please remember, he doesn't like it when people are late... or say *no*." she said right before hanging up.

It was just a few blocks down Lex then over to Park. I cleaned my camera, got plenty of film, and a strong light and umbrella reflector to make shadows.

I wished I'd worn my nice new suit. Oh, wait, I'd left it in Sergei's office! I went in, closed the blinds, and changed. The fabric felt so good... but it also made me sad to think about Myron/Iris's delicate little hands making all these perfect little stitches that held it all together... I hoped that he... she was happy in Hollywood dressing the stars.

I left the office and Horace whistled! Louise did a double-take. "Snazzy!" she said.

Pat opened her door and gestured for me to enter. "Well, don't you cut an elegant figure, Mr. Hamilton!"

"Thank you, I want to look good for Mr. Porter."

"About Cole... remember what I said about keeping your pants on..."

"You said to keep *their* pants on, you never mentioned mine," I joked.

"Just know he has a... reputation for enjoying the company of young men."

"I appreciate your concern, but he'll never muss the crease on my blue wool pants. He doesn't stand a chance."

"'This is a Fine Romance'... Cute, but those aren't *his* lyrics, Dorothy Fields wrote them. Just be... careful. Then again, after his riding accident I know you can outrun him."

"I read about that, so I thought I'd have him on his piano bench."

"Just be careful he doesn't have you on his piano bench," she chided.

It was 11am. I wanted to get there early. I'd rather wait in the lobby than be late. Normally I'd have walked the few blocks, but since I was carrying a heavy light and didn't want to sweat in my suit I called a cab.

It was interesting to see how differently the driver treated me in these duds. He jumped out, opened the trunk and took the tripod and lamp from me, and when we reached the Waldorf he got them both out where the doormen proceeded to pick them up and carry them inside for me.

Of course, I tipped them all, which is what they had hoped for when they saw the suit, but it was still nice to be treated this way.

Once inside, I sat on a plush chair and watched the clock. A young bellhop asked if he could do anything for me.

"I have an appointment with Mr. Porter at noon." The boy smiled and asked if he could bring me a drink. "Mr. Porter likes his guests taken care of," he said, winking.

"I'll have a Coke, thank you."

"Anything in it?" he asked, obsequiously.

"Ice."

He scurried off and I checked my camera and film so I was all prepared for work. The boy returned with a glass of coke on a small silver tray. I tipped him, and saw there were two maraschino cherries in it. I liked them... until they reminded me of Kitty. How long would I keep being reminded of her?

At five till noon the bellhop reappeared. "I'll take these for you, sir," he said, picking up the tripod and light. I followed him to the elevator then to the 33rd floor. He rang the doorbell for me and an elegant woman with long dark hair answered.

"Right on time, thank you for being prompt, Mr. Hamilton," she said in her Spanish accent while the bellhop waited to be tipped. "Thank you, Dennis," she said, tipping him. He just kept standing there. "Your services aren't needed today, thank you," she said to him. He looked at me and waited, so I tipped him, too, and he practically danced down the hallway.

"I apologize for Dennis, he's usually so accommodating. Come in, please, Mr. Hamilton."

I carried my tripod and lamp into the fancy foyer, then the large living room. I thought this was a hotel, but the place was as big as a house. The walls were a soft green that echoed the view of Central Park just outside.

"Welcome, Mr. Hamilton," a cultured voice said to me, and I turned to see Cole already sitting at the dining table. "Come right in and join me, won't you?"

I put down my equipment but kept the camera around my neck. I sat in the empty chair at the table, covered with fancy linen, glasses and silverware.

"What a pleasant surprise to have a handsome young man for lunch."

"It's a pleasant surprise for me to meet such a great man as yourself," I said.

"That's a beautiful suit you're wearing, who is your tailor?" he asked.

I had to think about it. "Iris Rose, of Hollywood," I replied.

"A female tailor, how very unusual. I must look her up when I'm out there this week."

I flashed the red silk lining.

"My, not even playing 'hard to get,' are we? Shall 'we dine on my fine finnan haddie?'" He asked. I didn't know what he was talking about. "No, I'd rather bring on the beef." He rang a bell, and a butler appeared carrying two plates covered with domed silver covers. He placed them in front of us and simultaneously removed both domes with a flourish. Steak and baked potato on both plates. "I assume you like meat," he said, slicing into his steak.

"Yes, it looks delicious, thank you." It was exceptionally tender, even better than at the Ansonia.

"I have them brought from my family ranch in Indiana. But let's not talk about my beef, let's talk about yours."

"My concept for the shoot is to have you and your shadow..."

"That's a Billy Rose song, my boy."

"I didn't mean the song, I mean literally, you at the piano bench, with your shadow on the wall doing something completely different, like kicking for 'I get a kick out of you.'"

He stared at me. "I'm afraid my legs aren't equipped for that at the moment, but I have a very talented tongue," he said, sticking it out and wiggling it, suggestively.

"We can certainly use that..."

"...That's what I was hoping you'd say..."

"...In the photo, to show your sense of humor..."

"...Not as tasty as what I had in mind but possibly more tasteful, photographically. I was hoping for something from one of my lyrics, like 'Anything Goes,'" he proceeded to sing, "When every night the set that's smart is intruding in nudist parties in studios...'"

"Anything goes," I completed the line, then thought better of it and took another bite of steak.

He continued, "...If love affairs you like / with young bears you like / why nobody will oppose."

"Perhaps we should get started," I suggested.

"I thought you'd never ask!" he replied lasciviously.

"With the shoot," I added.

"Shoot!" he picked up an ivory cane and hobbled to the piano bench.

"An artist friend just told me that that sex takes away from your creative energy." I said in lieu of an explanation.

"Your friend is a fool. I've found that just the opposite is true, and I challenge you to argue that my creative output is anything other than prodigious. I believe that comes, in part, from ingesting pure male energy. I'd like to show you how it works... Let's misbehave!" he said, which I found disconcerting because I really had to get these shots, then I recognized it as the name of the song he was playing. *Click.*

He sang, animatedly, "There's something wild about you child / That's so contagious / Let's be outrageous / Let's misbehave." *Click, click, click, click, click,* I caught his many expressions: Curiosity, delight, charm, seduction.

He patted next to him on the piano bench and I sat down to get closer shots of his face. He continued singing, "They say the Spring / Means just one thing to little lovebirds / We're not above birds / Let's misbehave!" *Click, click, click, click...* I could imagine the contact sheet filled with his expressions...

Then he glared at me and sang, "I hoped that you'd be mine, inclined to be supine, dear / It would be so divine in 1939, dear."

I'd been hypnotized by Cole's cobra gaze so I didn't even see him leaning closer to me until his lips met mine. I pulled back, not because he was unattractive, no, he was handsome and certainly charming, but...

"Mr. Porter..."

"Call me 'Cole'"

"Cole, I need to get more shots first."

"As long as I get your last shot," he replied incorrigibly.

I set up the light for the shadow shot, with him sticking his tongue out, then arranged it so he was sitting, elegantly, in the foreground. Click. Click. "I'll combine the two images in the darkroom, putting the focus on the shadow with you as a silhouette in the foreground," I explained. I hoped it would convey who he really is. *Click.*

"Just a few more," I said, and he rolled his eyes (click), pouted (click), lowered the piano key cover, (click), resting his head in his hands and looked wistfully into the camera (click).

"...'Cause If baby I'm the bottom, you're the top,'" he whispered, sidling closer to me. I saw no escape from this situation, especially when I felt his hand on my leg.

Just then Bianca entered the room, "Mr. Hamilton, there is a call for you from your editor, Miss Whyte."

I extricated myself from Cole's firm grip and apologized, "I'm sorry, excuse me," then went to the phone in the foyer.

"I hope I'm interrupting something," I heard Pat say, a smile in her voice.

"Perfect timing," I told her quietly. Then I announced, loudly so Cole would hear, "Oh, no, that's terrible, I was so hoping to get to know Mr. Porter better... but I guess I have no choice other than to leave right this very minute!" I said, dramatically. He heard and put his head in his hands.

"I'm sorry, Sir, but there's a deadline I can't miss..." I said, packing up my lights which were still warm.

"Your loss, my boy, my talents are much appreciated on six continents. Perhaps we will meet in Hollywood, at your tailor," he said, resigned.

"Hollywood... perhaps," I said. He was actually a nice man. I didn't mind his advances, I was just trying to be professional here. "Goodbye and thank you for lunch."

As I left I heard him talking to Bianca, "Thank you for nothing... get Dennis up here..."

120 ➻ Contact Sheet

Pat inspected the contact sheet, "You're right, this shows who he is in the way a single image couldn't. We'll use it as-is, and the facing page will feature the shadow image with his tongue out—it's a take on Cole the world has never seen before."

I was so pleased Pat understood what I was going for. "This is what I plan to do for each portrait in the Broadway series, a contact sheet and shadows."

"Louise tells me she's scheduled the other shoots, as well as arranging for tickets to shows so you can photograph them in their dressing rooms if you'd like."

"That's so exciting, I hope not tonight, though, it's Sergei's 30th birthday party."

"Again," she sighed.

"What?"

"He's turning 30, again."

"How is that possible?"

"This is Sergei we're talking about here."

"Oh, I didn't know that." It didn't make sense. "How old is he really?"

"At this point I'm not sure even he remembers. The only way to tell might be to cut off his cock and count the rings," she laughed.

"That's not funny."

"The truth so often isn't."

121 ➽ Birthday Matters

I was excited to show Sergei my contact sheet photos and talk to him about new projects using this new format.

The colony was already a beehive of activity, with Julien and Claudine filling tables with food in the dining room. It looked lavish but something was off... one of the blank icon paintings was missing. Huh.

Upstairs, strangers were hanging a series of photos of Sergei, one per year (or just 30) from his first baby picture to the present day, all blown up to epic proportions. Finally, someone I knew, Horace from the darkroom.

"Hello, Horace! How did you make such big prints?"

"Oh, hi Herb! Look closely and you'll see each one is a mosaic of 18 smaller prints, all tiled together."

"That's very clever—and gives me ideas."

"That's what I like to hear! But I've got to get back to hanging these before the guests arrive."

"Where is the birthday boy?"

"I believe he's upstairs, engrossed in ablutions."

"I don't know what that means but it sounds serious, I'll go see if I can help."

I went upstairs and Sergei was panicking. "I tried a new skin rejuvenation serum and now my face looks like a chili pepper!"

It did. Red and shiny. "It's OK, we'll figure out something. Ice?"

"Tried it, didn't help."

"Calamine lotion?"

"Takes too long."

"Makeup. I'll go get Claudine," I said, already running downstairs to find her. "I know you're busy with the food but Sergei's face is literally bright red and he needs makeup."

She never stopped moving, carrying food from the kitchen to the tables. "And you thought of me, why?"

"Because you're a woman, because you were in the circus. You must know how to put on makeup." She looked at me as if I was stupid. "Circus? Oh, yes. If he wants to look like a clown."

"He already does!"

"Idiot."

"Me or him?"

"Both. I'll see what I can do. Julien, Sergei has fucked his face and I need to see if I can help."

Julien brought a plate of sliced cucumbers, "You'll need these." She grabbed them and dashed upstairs. I followed.

"OK, Sergei, you can relax. Remember, I was in the circus!"

"What're you talking about?" he asked as she covered his face with cucumber.

"Don't you remember, before we met you," she said, nudging him.

"No, you and Julien were on parole for murder and I..." she stuffed a cucumber in his mouth, then laughed.

"I told the boy here that we'd been in the circus so as not to scare him."

"What about the scars?" I asked.

"Knife fights," she said, disappearing out of the room.

"Sergei, is this true?"

"Murder? Yes, but they didn't kill nice people so it's OK."

"Why didn't you tell me?"

"Because it doesn't matter."

Claudine came back carrying a tray with makeup. She peeled off the cucumber, he looked better already. She glared at me, "I know you know how to blow, but this time restrict yourself to his face," she said, threateningly. I did as I was told.

"This is what I use when my face is red from cooking," she said, opening a box of green colored powder and dipped a fluffy puff into it, then lightly dabbed Sergei's face. I thought he was going to look like the Wicked Witch of the West, who really scared me, but the green counteracted the red and made him look more normal.

"You look fine now," I said, backing away from Claudine.

"I'm not going to stab you with a powder puff," she hissed at me as she left.

I pulled out the contact sheet of Cole, "I want to show you something."

"Whatever it is, it doesn't matter."

"It does matter," I said, testily.

"Things matter too much to you, Hubear."

"That's because I *care*. Like I care about my work and wanted to show you the photos I took today of Cole Porter. I'm excited about them." I pulled out the contact sheet. "Instead of just using one photo, I convinced Pat to run the entire contact sheet to show his many expressions. It's like cinema in stills!"

I held out the contact sheet for him to see but he couldn't tear his eyes away from the mirror. "Look at them!" I insisted.

"They don't matter."

"Is your face the only thing that matters to you?"

"At this moment, yes."

"What, are you afraid you don't look 30?"

"What? How old do I look?"

"How old are you *really*?" I said, heatedly.

"You little monster, what a horrid thing to ask."

"Are you afraid of the answer?"

He wheeled around and slapped me across my face. I was so stunned I dropped the contact sheet. He picked it up, glanced at it and tore it in half.

"Do you think your work actually matters in the world, Hubear?"

My cheek burned, my eyes watered from the slap, but his words hurt more.

"Yes, I've warned people about Nazis, I'm showing them Cole Porter, who brings them joy..."

"SO WHAT?" he spat, dabbing more green powder on his face.

"*So what?*" I couldn't believe my ears.

"So fucking what," he said, still staring at his own reflection. "Nothing matters. My magazine? No more, the negatives sunk in the Atlantic by a German torpedo. So what? Your little pictures of Nazis? They didn't stop that, did they? They aren't stopping the war, are they? Now you've got some pictures of a faggot songwriter, who the fuck cares!"

"I didn't know about your magazine. I'm sorry, but you can't blame me for that. I'm doing what I can."

"You're a child. Living in a dream world where you think you can make a difference."

I was speechless, then sputtered "I am trying..."

"Did he blow you?"

"What? Who?"

"Cole. I hear he's very good. Of course, it doesn't matter to me."

"Nothing seems to, except your face. And no, he didn't."

"Too bad, because now all you have is pictures rather than a real life."

I had never wanted to hit a person as much as I wanted to hit him. But I didn't want to bruise his precious face. Or did I? "I thought I might have a real life with you."

"Like you thought you had one with Kitty!" he laughed. It hurt. "So what, kid?"

"So what? Is that how you feel about me, too?"

"What does anything matter Herb? Grow up and read some Nietzsche."

"It matters to me, you asshole. It matters to people who give a damn about something other than their age!"

"OK, Baby Hubear, how old do you think I am?"

"Twice as old as I am!"

"Fuck you!"

"I let you—but that doesn't matter to you, does it? *I* don't matter to you! For once in my life I need to matter to somebody!"

He turned around, the anger making his face red again.

"Good luck with that, child."

"Thank you. I'll need it." I swallowed hard to keep from crying, stuffed my stuff into my green bag, then got very calm and stood close next to him.

"What are you doing?"

"I need to apologize, Sergei?" I said, sweetly, as I sidled up to him. "You're right, you're always right and I've been a bad boy."

"You certainly have."

"I'm going to make it up to you,' I whispered, running my hand down his leg to his inner thigh. A smile spread across his face... turning into a grimace of pain as my fingers squeezed his balls, hard.

"You little motherfucker!" He cried, dropping the box of powder which hit the floor, exploding in a great green cloud. He pulled back to hit me, but I swung my bag and blocked him, punching him as hard as I could—in the eye—where it would show.

I ran, leaving him coughing from the powder. Downstairs past 30 giant pictures of Sergei staring down at the room, down to the ground floor, where the missing icon painting was now back on the wall—with Horace's face painted on it.

I picked up a knife from the cheese tray and attacked the painting of myself, slicing out my face. It was *my* face. Sergei couldn't cover it over with his black paint!

Then, standing behind a roast beef, I saw Julien holding a sharp chef's knife. He was carving the meat but I wasn't going to take any chances.

I reached into my bag and pulled out my lighter pistol and pointed it at him! "Stay back or I'll use this!" I kept it pointed at him as I backed out of the building and hit the street, running as fast as I could for six blocks, looking back to see if he was following me. I didn't see him as I dashed down into the subway station where a train was waiting. I jumped on and kept looking around.

122 ⇒ Don Voyage

I dashed out of the subway at 72nd and walked to the Ansonia, still looking behind me. Nobody was following me. Hell, I probably didn't matter enough to Sergei to have Julien follow me.

It was a relief to see Max standing outside. "Hey, Herb, good to see ya, where ya been?"

"Doesn't matter, I'm back."

Inside, just seeing Sam made me feel safe. "Herb! I've been thinking about you—I saw *your* magazine... you took so many beautiful photos!"

"Thanks, Sam. I've missed you."

"I missed you, too. But before you go upstairs I need to tell you something." He looked concerned.

"What's wrong, Sam, what can I do to help you?"

"It's not about me. It's the apartment. Syd, in accounting, told me it's only paid through the end of this month."

"That's OK, I can deal with it."

"It's a lot, Herb."

"How much?"

"$250 a month, plus extras, like food and cleaning... last month cost $375."

"What? Wow. I had no idea. How much do I owe?"

"Nothing yet, but the end of the month is Monday, so if you stay longer than that..."

"I need to think about it, Sam. It's expensive... and there are all those memories of Kitty."

"Yeah, I wondered about that. In case you need a place, Sally and I got an extra room in our apartment in Queens..."

I hugged him. I knew he was someone I mattered to.

"Thank you, my true friend. I can't imagine Sally would want a third wheel around."

"I told her about you, she'd be fine..."

"...You're too kind. Let me see how I feel and I'll get back to you tomorrow. OK?"

I patted him on the arm and went to the elevator. I didn't recognize the elevator operator. "Where's Ellis?" I asked.

"Moving up in the world! Tony left so he's Sam's night man now."

"Everything changes. That's great for him. What's your name?"

"Diego."

"Good to meet you, Diego. I'm Herb. I don't know how long I'll be here for."

"Good to meet you anyway, Herb. Let me know if there's anything I can do to help."

I handed him a silver dollar and walked down the elegant hallway. I unlocked the door and looked at the apartment. It seemed so much smaller than I remembered it.

This place had felt like a cocoon, one where I transformed from a boy to a man.

Now it felt like a tomb.

I turned up the fan so cold air would blow through the vents, then stuck my head out of the round window. Didn't matter, I found it hard to breathe here now.

I called Glenn. "Hey, can I ask a favor?"

"Sure, buddy, anything you need."

"Do you still have a room above the store?"

"Your new place didn't work out?"

"That's putting it mildly."

"Don't worry, I got room and you're welcome to stay as long as you'd like!"

"Thanks, Glenn. I'll be over tomorrow night if that's all right."

"Of course—it'll be fun to have a roomie!"

"Thanks, Pal."

I was hungry so I picked up the phone to order... but how much would that cost? I had no idea.

I looked around. I had more clothes than would fit into my small bag. I needed a real suitcase.

I went downstairs to the lobby to talk to Sam.

"Sam, that apartment doesn't feel like home anymore."

"I figured."

"I appreciate your kind offer but Glenn's got a room above his store... it's closer to work."

"Sure, and you two photo-nuts'll have a lot to talk about."

"What I need now is a suitcase for my stuff."

"Go to *Don Voy-age* on 68th and Columbus. Ask for Don Voytovych. Tell him I sent you and he'll give you a deal."

I walked down Columbus and saw the blue and white striped awning of Don Voyage. Inside, I was overwhelmed with the choices, so many sizes and colors and materials.

A salesman came up to me, "Hello, friend, we got a special today on Samsonite, let me show you..."

"I'm looking for Don, Sam sent me."

"Sam is a mensch. In that case, you don't want the Samsonite, it's crap. I'll take good care of you, where's ya going? Ship? Train? Plane?"

"Right now I'm just moving and need a place for my clothes... but might as well get something that works for a train or boat, too." I said, admiring a bag covered in alligator.

"So what price range? I got cheap, but I see you appreciates quality."

"I like this one."

"You got a good eye—that's top of the line Pullman case. Pricey. But I've had it way too long, so I can make you a deal. Made in Italy from genuine Australian alligator. Solid oak frame. It'll last a lifetime. Pure English brass locks. Violet Italian moiré silk lining with Dutch elastic compression bands to hold your belongings in place. Even a secret compartment, under the lining."

"It looks perfect, how much?"

"Now, remember, it's made by Mark Cross, the very best you can get."

"OK, how much?"

"Mind you, at Saks or Bergdorf this bag would set you back $200..."

"How much for a friend of Sam?"

"I'm not going to make a penny on this, but I need to make some space for stock that'll move... $95. Today only. That's a steal. No, don't take it, I'm robbing myself. That's what I paid for it two years ago and it's still sitting here..."

"Fine, can I write you a check?"

"You want it?"

"Yes..."

"Nobody wants this. I was crazy to buy it in the first place. Who needs such an expensive bag? You don't want this."

"I do, it's beautiful and I'm probably going to be living out of it for a while, so it's basically an apartment."

"It costs as much as one... Now I know you're crazy, does Sam know you're crazy? You can't fit inside this, where are you gonna sleep?."

"Can I write you a check?"

"I feel bad selling you something so crazy. Look, I've got a heavy-duty leather-like bag here for $20, very nice quality..."

I took a check from my wallet, picked up a pen from the counter and wrote, *Ninety Five and 00/100*. "Who do I make it out to?"

"Cash."

123 ➳ Stuffing the Alligator

As I carried the suitcase up Columbus, the $95 made me feel like a million bucks. I justified it by reminding myself that I hadn't had to pay any rent all this time! Plus, I was helping Don because nobody else wanted it. But I wanted it—I loved the way it felt, even the way it smelled. And it would last a lifetime, right? I wouldn't want to pack my beautiful $85 suit in a crappy suitcase, right? How would Myron... Iris feel about that?

No, I wasn't going to think about them or Kitty or Sergei... I was just going to think about my beautiful suitcase, made from one of those terrifying alligators. This bag has probably saved the life of some unsuspecting native—that's right, I helped save a life with this bag. I started to feel better.

Back at the Ansonia Max eyed the new bag, "Wow, Herb, that's rich!"

Inside, Sam inspected it, "What did Don soak you for that?"

"He said they were $200 at Saks but he gave it to me for $95."

"$95? For a suitcase? You gotta be crazy. I could buy a new living room set for that! I hope they pay you good at that magazine so you're not eating macaroni for months. But it's a beaut of a bag, Herb, it really is. Like something a rich Park Ave swell would have. And it's not like you had to pay rent here!"

"That's exactly what I thought, Sam! I know it's expensive, I know I'm nuts, but..."

"I get it. I bought a $25 pair of shoes once. Most beautiful shoes I'd ever seen that weren't on someone else's feet. Wore them for my wedding. But then they were so beautiful I was afraid to wear them so they sat in the closet until I didn't even know they were there and the leather got dry and cracked. I shoulda just worn 'em, so if it makes you happy you should use this extravagant, beautiful thing."

"Thanks, Sam,"

Diego appreciated the bag, too, "That's a very handsome suitcase, Herb. I hope to someday have something like that."

"You can. It wasn't that long ago I couldn't even imagine all this, now I have it."

It felt like the apartment was getting smaller each time I came back. I couldn't wait to leave. I put my shoes in pillowcases and placed them on the bottom. I emptied my drawers into the bag, Socks, boxers, ties.

I took my pants and shirts off their hangers and folded them neatly. Finally, I placed my beautiful new suit on top. It was a tight squeeze, but I sat on top to press it down, then clicked the locks shut. Done.

Did I even want to spend one more night there, or should I go over to Glenn's now? I called Glenn. "I'm all packed, could I come over tonight?"

"Sure, I'll get a pie from DeLuca's for dinner!"

I was happy to leave this place, but sad, too. I gave it one last look around, then carried my new suitcase and my stowaway bag with my camera stuff. I thanked Diego and said I probably wouldn't be seeing him again and gave him a dollar.

Sam was on the phone, leaning over to look up something in the phone book. I put $20 on the spike where he kept his messages so he couldn't try to give it back to me. He stood up and saw me, smiled, reached out to shake my hand, mouthed, "thank you" then turned around and left before he could see me cry.

Because my bag was heavy I asked Max to get me a taxi, then gave him $5. As I got in the cab, I looked back at the building where so much had happened. All that was past. Now I'd be a new man.

124 ⟫⟶ Chrome
and Glass

Glenn's place was lit up like a Christmas tree, not that I'd ever had one, but I'd seen them in shop windows. I didn't even have to pound on the door, Glenn was standing there, smiling.

"Welcome, roomie!" he yelled, genuinely pleased, as I got out of the taxi. He even ran out to help me with my bag. I paid and tipped the cabbie then went inside. "Is that a Leica in your pocket or are you just happy to see me!" he joked. I looked down to make sure I wasn't excited in that way... nope. I wondered if he knew about me... didn't matter, it was nice he was happy I was there.

"Thank you for letting me stay here, Glenn."

"My pleasure! Stay as long as you need, and do not insult me by offering me money. After all you've done for me I want to do this for you."

"You're a true pal, Glenn," I'd never been upstairs and when we got to the landing I was shocked. The walls and floor were painted black and the chrome and leather furniture seemed to float in space, lit by two studio reflector lamps.

Over the fireplace was a large photographic enlargement, an arresting image of a woman's wrinkled face behind a black lace veil. It drew me to it and had Glenn's signature style of texture so fine it felt palpable.

"Wow, Glenn, this is a beautiful room!"

"What were you expecting, hand-me-down furniture and orange crate bookcases?"

"No, I didn't mean that..."

"Because that's how it looked two weeks ago! Now that I'm making good money from *Look*, thanks to you, I went out and bought the furniture I always wanted. Hired a professional painter to paint the room. 'Welsh Charcoal' is the name of the color even though it looks black."

"It's very impressive. And what a gorgeous photo!"

"Thanks, it's my momma."

"You made her look like a movie star!"

"That's what she said, so I made her a big print for over her fireplace, too. Her friends are so jealous!"

"I'm going to have to learn some of your secrets for my series of Broadway stars—I just shot Cole Porter."

"No shit! Lemme see!"

I opened my green bag and pulled out the box of contact sheets. "He had so many expressions they couldn't be caught in a single image, so Pat's gonna run the entire contact sheet, as is, along with a full-page enlargement of one of the photos."

Glenn studied it, his head tiling left and right.

"I'm also playing with shadows, they're small here, but I combined two in the darkroom so his shadow is sticking out his tongue while his foreground figure isn't."

"I love these, Herb, they're so lively. Mine feel so stiff," Glenn said, now looking at the combined shadow shot.

I shook my head, "I love the light and texture of your work. Mine feel so rough."

"Now that we're living together we can teach each other what we know! But first, I waited to eat with you, go sit down!"

The chrome and glass table was set with shiny white plates and ultra-modern chrome forks and knives. In the center was a silver vase holding a single red chrysanthemum, the only color in the room! I sat on the chrome and white leather chair. It felt cold but its shape made it bounce which was fun.

Glenn carried the hot pizza, and set it down on chrome trivet. He used a big serving fork to put a slice on my plate. "You're my first guest for a fancy dinner!" I could tell he was enjoying this.

Normally I'd have just picked up the pizza with my hands, but I used the hard-to-hold chrome knife and fork to cut and eat it.

"Oh, I forgot drinks!" he said, rolling a chrome bar cart to the table. "Coke, 7-up, Dr. Pepper, Nehi Grape, Orange Crush?" I pointed to the Orange Crush and he opened the bottle and poured it into a modern cut glass tumbler. He poured himself a coke. "Enjoy!"

"I've never eaten pizza with a knife and fork before, it's very classy," I said between bites.

"Fun, isn't it?"

It was fun. Glenn had no agenda. He wasn't playing me. We were simply two photographers, two friends.

I ate till I was full and there were still two pieces of pizza left. If they were there in the morning I was going to have a slice for breakfast!

"Let me show you your room" Glenn picked up my suitcase. "Only you'd have a suitcase covered in dinosaur."

"It's alligator."

"Same thing."

We walked down a narrow hallway."This is my bedroom, this is the bathroom." Standing at the last door he explained, "Now, Herbie, ya gotta know, you didn't give me much warning. I store photos in this room and I only had time to clear the portfolios off the bed so there are a few file cabinets we can move to the basement if they're in your way.

He opened the door and the "few" file cabinets were about 20, lining every wall and leaving barely enough space to get around them to the bed. "I hope this is OK," he said, squeezing by and putting my suitcase on the bed.

I followed him, but then realized it was only wide enough for one of us, so I backed into the hallway so he could get out. "It's fine, very cozy. And nice to know I'm surrounded by photographs!"

"The good news is that the radiator is under the bed, so you'll be toasty with just a quarter turn, but don't turn it more than that 'cause that could damage the negatives."

"I'll be fine," I said cheerfully.

"I emptied out a file cabinet for your stuff," he said, pointing to a battered blue one in the corner.

"That's nice, thanks, Glenn."

"If you need anything you can knock on my door any time. I'm a heavy sleeper but if you pound hard enough I might wake up. If it's really urgent you can come in and shake me. It can help to wet a toothbrush and flick a little water on my face while singing the "Beer Barrel Polka," that's what my momma used to do... I hate the Andrews Sisters."

"Got it."

"And I snore. Sometimes the people next door complain so I got you the same ear plugs I got them just in case it bothers you."

"I'm used to snoring."

"Abbott and Costello are on the radio at 8 if you want to listen with me, but you don't have to."

"I'd like to, thanks!"

"Maybe you want a little lie down till then, I mean, you can do whatever you want, even if you want to have a girl over or something, that's OK."

"I don't think I have time for a girl before Abbott and Costello," I joked.

"I didn't mean right now, though if you wanted to right now that'd be OK, too. If you want to eat something in the middle of the night just take whatever you want, though I was hoping to have a piece of pizza for breakfast."

"Me, too. You can relax, Glenn, it's only me."

"I know, I just want you to feel at home."

"I appreciate everything, thank you."

I unpacked my boxers and socks to the bottom file cabinet drawer. Pants in the middle drawer. Shirts and ties in the top. I hung my suits from the cabinet handles. I lay down on the bed and it was fine. Not as soft as the one at the Ansonia, but springier than Sergei's.

I looked out the window above the bed. It faced the backs of the buildings and I could see into some of the other windows. I opened it for some air, which was chilly but nice. I heard radios playing, smelled stuffed peppers and cherry pie, and saw the silhouette of a man and woman kissing.

I heard loud music coming from the living room and heard, "Abbott and Costello, time to laugh, with the Ipana Troubadours playing 'I'm nobody's baby'..."

Glenn was squeezed, somewhat uncomfortably, on one of the chrome sofas. It was too short for him to lay flat, and too low to lean back on, so he was in a kind of fetal position with his head sticking to the black leather cushion on the side.

"That's a beautiful sofa," I said.

"It's more comfortable than it looks, give it a try."

He had two identical sofas, so I lay down on the other one and he was right! Not as uncomfortable as it looked.

We listened to Abbott and Costello... It felt so good to laugh.

125 ⇛ Take a Shot!

Glenn's place felt homey. The mattress was already warm from the radiator below it, and I kept the window open a crack because I liked the fresh air, the smells, and sounds. I closed my eyes...

...Everything grew bright. The buildings outside turned into a stage set, and the people took turns singing from their windows—new love songs, old torch songs. The buildings split apart and slid away making room for scores of dancers dressed in sparkly rhinestone versions of everyday outfits, like all-white bakers, blue-plumbers (complete with crack) and cleaning ladies with fluffy, candy-colored marabou feather dusters.

Glenn made a grand entrance in a sequined version of his artist's smock, singing a song called "Take a Shot!"

While he sang his photos came to life with pale, mostly naked girls emerging from the pictures, and dark African girls coming through the negatives. Glenn was surprisingly graceful and took turns dancing with the nudie girls.

The world is too vast
And progress too fast
If you want it to last
Take a shot.

There's too much to see
With places to be
So take it from me
Take a shot.

You simply take aim
At what's in the frame
And give it your full attention

You might find acclaim
Or meet a new flame
For pleasures too hot to mention!

No matter the spot
If you're on a yacht
Atop Montserrat
Tied up in a knot
Like it or not
Before you rot
Give it all you got
TAKE A SHOT!

The song reached a fever pitch and ended with the girls in the photos turning into photos again—except for one where Pat Whyte leaned out of the frame and gave Glenn a big kiss to triumphant applause....

...I bolted awake, not knowing where I was. It took a minute to recognize the moonlit file cabinets, and Glenn's jack-hammer-like snoring.

I looked out the window again, most of the lights were out. Just one was on, the shade drawn and the silhouette of a woman, naked. I picked up my camera from the floor and—*Click.*

I tried to go back to sleep, but the combination of the dream and the snoring kept me up. I got the ear plugs from off the top of a file cabinet and they helped. So did the image in my head of the naked woman in the window... and the song running through my head.

I awoke with the sun as sounds of running water and clanging pans shook my ears, while the smell of eggs and bacon, sardines and toast assaulted my nose. It was a lot of stimulation this early in the morning. I put the covers over my head and lay on my side so I could breathe through a little opening I left.

I didn't hear snoring so I took out the earplugs and heard movement downstairs. Glenn must already be up. Did I need to get up this early now? Would there be any pizza left for breakfast?

I got out of bed, put on some clothes and looked in the fridge. There was one slice left but I wasn't hungry just yet. I went downstairs and Glenn was in the darkroom.

"I had a big musical dream last night, about you and Pat! How're things going with her?"

"Great—As well as the weekly portraits, she also assigned me to shoot still lifes of Christmas presents."

"That's great. Did you ask her to dinner?"

"She never looked hungry."

"Are you kidding me, Glenn?"

"No, you've seen her, did she ever look hungry to you, Herbie?"

"It's not about being hungry! It's about getting to know each other."

Glenn took a bite of cold pizza, then a long, slow, swig of Coke.

I remembered the song in the dream, and said, "Before you rot, take a shot!"

"I don't know how. You tell me—How'd you meet Kitty? I'm sorry, I didn't mean to mention her... how about this other mystery person... no, that didn't work out, I'm sorry, Herbie," he looked down at his feet.

He was right. I met Kitty at *her* apartment. I met Sergei at the office. I didn't have a date with either, I just moved right in. Now that I thought about it, maybe it wasn't normal. Or smart. "Sorry, Glenn, what do I know."

"No, I didn't mean it to sound like that, Herbie, I don't want us to fight."

"This isn't fighting. There's no screaming or hitting or knives..." I started to laugh. Glenn laughed, too.

"I got a thing for Pat but when I see her I clam up."

"I got an idea! Let's have a housewarming party! Then you *can* invite her and your friends, and any respectable people you work with, the people you photograph, other artists... like that."

"I could do that. Get some food from Mrs. Miers at the bakery who's always trying to set me up with her daughter."

"I don't think you want to do that when Pat's here."

"Right, that's dumb, but it's a good bakery. I know, my momma can cook."

"It might be a little soon to introduce Pat to the parents."

"See, I get stupid when I think about this."

"I know two really good cooks but they might murder us."

"Not good when Pat's here," Glenn joked, and we laughed again. "There are plenty of restaurants in the neighborhood, I can get some trays of food. Plus you'll be here to tell me what to do"

"Yeah, I'll be here... but I'm not going to tell you what to do."

"But you could, if I asked, right?"

"If it makes you feel better, yes."

"I'm kinda nervous already."

"It's just a party. Let's set a date!"

"What if she doesn't want to come?"

"I'll ask her if you'd like."

"Really, you'd do that for me, Herbie?"

"I'd be happy to do that for you, Glenn. It'll be fine. It'll be better than fine, it'll be fun."

126 ⇒ Love's for Suckers

I was excited about a breakfast of cold pizza and going to see a matinee of *Panama Hattie* starring Ethel Merman. I'd heard her trumpet-like voice on the radio and she was constantly in the papers as, "The Toast of Broadway." The first time I heard that I wondered why "toast" was such a big deal on Broadway, surely they all had toasters! Then I learned it was the kind of toasting you do with champagne and that sounded even less appealing.

I had what Louise called "house seats" in the third row, center, and an appointment, after the show, to meet "Miss Merman" (as I'd been warned to call her) in her private dressing room.

I wore my best suit, which still felt much too nice to wear in the subway so I took a taxi to the 46th Street Theatre. The audience was mostly old ladies. I couldn't figure out why so many of them had blue or purple hair. It was pretty, but odd, especially because in all other respects they were well turned-out. They wore fur coats or fur pieces, including the scary kind that still had their little animal heads, only with a metal clip in their mouth to bite their own tail and stay around the old ladies' neck.

The few men were older, too. They either looked like they'd been dragged there unwillingly by their oddly colorful wives, or they were unusually natty, with wild ties that reminded me of my leopard one.

This second type of man tended to be handsome with perfectly pomaded hair, neatly trimmed mustaches and goatees. They smiled at me and I smiled back.

I took my seat and to my right was one of the dapper men. He wore a light gray wool suit with gray suede shoes that exactly matched the shade of the suit. He smelled of bay rum.

On my left was a little girl who couldn't even reach her arm rest. She wore a red velvet dress with a white bow and held her mother's hand. Her mother glanced at me and said, "Don't worry, she loves the theater and is always very good."

"I wasn't worried," I replied. "I wish I'd been able to go to the theater as a child."

The mother laughed, "You basically still are!" I scowled and she added, "Wait till you have a child, then you'll feel really old."

"You don't look a day over 21," I said, quoting a line I remembered Cary Grant saying to Katherine Hepburn.

"Aren't you sweet," she said, blushing.

"Aren't you a charmer," the man on my right said, flashing his perfect teeth. "You don't look a day over 21 yourself."

"I'm older than I look," I replied, again cribbing another line from the pictures, only after I said it I thought maybe it had been said by Shirley Temple.

"I wish I could say that," he sighed.

"You're quite debonair. I've never seen shoes that so perfectly match the pants."

"You have a good eye, and a wonderful suit. Is it Italian?"

"The fabric? Yes. Good eye yourself. The lining is Indian," I said flashing a bit of the paisley.

"Charming," he said, feeling the fabric on my cuff between his thumb and forefingers which he then ran down the back of my hand. "I should introduce myself, I'm Willy Smith, Miss Merman's agent."

I shook his hand, "Pleased to meet you. I'm Herb Hamilton, I'm photographing her for *Look* magazine after the show."

"I know, that's why I'm here. It's a pleasure to meet you, too. I wanted to make sure you were well taken care of," he said, his perfect gray suede shoes nudging my imperfect black ones.

The theater lights dimmed. "I'll take you backstage after the show," he whispered, so close to my ear it tickled.

The orchestra started playing bright, swingy music and I was excited already! The curtain rose on a nightclub with chorus girls (like Kitty, which made me momentarily sad), and boys singing about Hattie. A spotlight—there she was at the top of the stairs, Ethel Merman, singing "Visit Panama!" her voice like a fog horn with perfect pitch.

The show was silly, but the songs were smart, and it was only when I looked at the program during intermission that I saw they were written by Cole Porter! I was going to tell Mr. Smith I'd met Cole, but he wasn't in his seat. I'd have told the little girl to my left but I doubted she'd care.

The show started up again with more orchestra music, then another big dance number. My favorite part of the show was Miss Merman singing a ballad, "Make It Another Old-Fashioned Please," about how her dream castle in the air had crashed. I thought of Kitty and Iris and felt my eyes welling up with tears. I didn't have a proper handkerchief, just my fancy red silk pocket square which would have to do for my eyes but I wasn't about to blow my nose on it!

After the show Mr. Smith reappeared, "I trust you enjoyed the show."

"It was great, and that old-fashioned song made me cry."

"You must tell Miss Merman, she'll love that. Follow me, please."

We walked down the row of seats, then up the aisle to a small door to the right of the stage. He knocked, the door opened a crack, then all the way.

I'd never been backstage before—the space was so high, painted black and filled with ropes and wires and set pieces I'd seen onstage. From the audience it looked like magic. Backstage it looked like a machine.

"Watch your step," he said before I almost tripped on a thick pile of cables on the floor. We reached a door painted shiny black with a big gold star and the words "Miss Merman." He knocked on it and a loud voice bellowed "Come on in, boys!"

The dressing room was all pink, with a pink satin sofa. She was sitting at her dressing mirror, looking smaller than she seemed onstage. She got up, extended her hand to shake mine firmly, then kissed Mr. Smith on the mouth.

"Ethel, dear, this is Mr. Hamilton, the young photographer from *Look* magazine."

"It's a pleasure to meet you kid," she said, her voice loud even when she was just talking. "I see you've met my agent, and husband, Willy."

"Ah, yes, he's been very nice," I said, surprised.

"Cole said you did a swell job with his photos."

"I'm so glad, I wasn't sure he liked them."

"I'm sure he liked a handsome young man like you, I hear he's quite the cocksucker!"

I'd never heard a woman say that word aloud, much less this loud. "I wouldn't know," I said, feeling myself blush.

"Your loss, I'm sure! I've been told I'm good at it, too," she winked, "That's not an offer, as I'm a married woman... though I'm not sure for how long, so check back with me in a few months and I might be willing as well as able." She laughed loudly. "You can run along, Willy, if Cole couldn't land this tasty boy I'm sure I can't, either."

Willy smiled a tight little smile. "I'll be back in a half hour to make sure Mr. Hamilton hasn't worn out his welcome."

"Yeah, yeah, I can take care of myself," she said, shooing him away.

"Miss Merman, it's a great honor to meet you."

"I'll bet. Wouldja like a whiskey?"

"No... but thanks, I need to set up my light."

"Don't bother. I know exactly the shots I want. Do what I tell you and nobody'll get hurt." She explained she liked the way the makeup lights had a soft glow and instructed me to sit on the makeup table and shoot from there while she pretended to get ready for the show. She put on lipstick. *Click.* Primped her hair. *Click.*

"So, whaddya think about Willy?" she asked, cocking her head. *Click.*

"He seems very nice," I said, concentrating on the viewfinder.

"That's what I'm afraid of, too nice." She scowled. *Click.*

"He sat next to me during the first act..."

"Where the fuck was he for the second?" She looked angry. *Click.*

"Could I get you to sing the 'Old-Fashioned' song? I want to get shots of you singing, and the way you sang it made me cry."

"Aw, that's awful sweet kid. Sure." *Click.* This time, she sang it soft, sweet and sad, "Once high in my castle, I reigned supreme / And oh what a castle, built on a heavenly dream / Then quick as a lightning flash, that castle began to crash / So, make it another old-fash-ioned, please." *Click, click, click, click, click.*

There were tears in my eyes. "Thank you," I sniffled.

"I'm glad it got to ya, but you gotta learn not to be a sap. Cole wrote a lyric for me after the last schmuck who fucked me:

"Love can sound so good in song
Till all those other motherfuckers
Lie and cheat and it goes wrong
That's why, my dear, true loves' for suckers."
Click. Click. Click.

She handed me a tissue. "You're quite a dame," I said, trying to sound like Cagney.

"Don't I know it, kid. OK, Now scram. Where's my soon to be ex-husband?"

128 ➡ The Invite

I walked the six blocks to the *Look* offices, developed the film and made a contact print. Miss Merman knew what she was talking about because the lighting and angle on her was great! Lots of good facial expressions. It was only then I realized I didn't get a chance to shoot any shadows, and, when I made an enlargement, I could see myself in the mirror behind her! I could always burn that out while printing.

I asked Louise if Pat had time and she said, "She always has time for you, Herb," which I thought was nice. Louise opened the door. Pat was on the phone and pointed to the sofa. I sat, looking at the photos. What I liked best was that they looked the way it felt being there with her, so I'd be sharing that feeling with the readers.

I listened to Pat's conversation, she was arguing with Jerry, the head of advertising.

"Maybe you should have read his contract, Jerry. We only have North American rights to his photos for 12 months. After that you'll have to negotiate with his agent, a ruthless SOB..."

Glenn, ruthless SOB?

"He's in my office right now. I'll send him over to talk to you, but you'll still have to get through his agent, Fine. It's your funeral." She hung up. "Jackass."

"What's all this about Glenn being an SOB?"

"I wanted to scare Jerry, that's all. He wants to use your Broadway photos for advertisements, like Cole for Chesterfield cigarettes. You can get him to pay you top dollar for them since editorial contracts are separate from advertising."

"That's awfully nice of you, Pat, thanks."

"It's my pleasure to help you, Herb."

"Then I hope you'll come to a housewarming Glenn and I are having."

"You and Glenn? No more Sergei?"

"No... I don't know what to say other than..."

"No explanation necessary. Are you OK?"

"Yeah, I avoided getting Julienned," I joked.

"So are you and Glenn an... item?"

"Oh, no! We're just friends. He likes *you*. After I left the colony I didn't want to go back to the place I shared with Kitty. Glenn graciously offered to let me stay with him."

"He's a mensch."

"Absolutely. He just redid his place, all very modern, and I suggested we have a housewarming..."

"So he and I could get to know each other?"

"Yeah, didn't fool you for a minute."

"Not for a second. It's very sweet, thank you. When is this soiree?"

"We were thinking this Saturday at 8... if you don't have theater tickets or anything. Because if you do, we can change the date." She checked her calendar book.

"I have..." she crossed out something in the book, "No, I'm free. I'll pencil you in. Can I bring anything?"

"We're going to have food, so you don't need to."

"Does Glenn like champagne?"

"He doesn't drink. Well, he drinks water and Coke and stuff like that, of course, but not alcohol. Neither do I."

"What a couple of teetotalers! I'm not used to that in this business. OK, I'll see you on Saturday at 8," she said, jotting it down in her calendar.

"It should be fun."

"I look forward to it. Now, what do you have to show me?"

"Ethel Merman. They're a little different, because she insisted..."

"I've heard she's difficult. Did she give you any trouble?"

"Not exactly, I think they turned out good but I wasn't able to do the shadow thing."

She took the contact sheets from me and looked at them through the loupe. I showed her an enlargement. "I didn't notice at the time, but you can see me in a mirror in the background, but I'll burn it out."

"No, it's interesting—adds a sense of reality to the backstage world. I like the whole contact sheet again, so we'll use it, like with Cole. Who're you shooting next?"

"Gene Kelly, a dancer, then Noël Coward, he's a writer or something."

"*Or* something? He's a world-renowned actor, singer, songwriter, and one of the funniest and most sophisticated playwrights in the world! Like Cole, he's quite the charmer if you know what I mean, and you do." She pressed the intercom button. "Louise, please have research pull a bio and articles about Noël Coward for Herb, ASAP. Thanks." She turned back to me. "Go see Jerry and Louise'll have photostats for you when you get back."

"As always, thank you, Pat."

"I'll see you, and Glenn, Saturday night."

129 ➟ Sales Job

Jerry's secretary was quite the dish, big hair, and big breasts almost spilling out of her tight red dress.

"Hi, I'm Herb Hamilton, Jerry is expecting me."

She looked in her book and her squeaky voice had a heavy Brooklyn accent. "Nope. I don't see ya here Mr Hamburger."

"Hamilton."

"Not that, neither."

"Pat Whyte was just on the phone with him."

"That broad, nothin' but trouble," she whined, pressing the intercom button.

"Some guy named Hamburger is here to see you."

"Miss LaRue, do you mean 'Hamilton?'" Jerry's voice crackled back.

"Yes," I said.

"I dunno, I'll ask," she said.

"What's your name again?"

Jerry opened the door. "Sorry, Herb," he said, waving me into the office. "You'll have to excuse her, she has a bad cough and has been drinking a little too much cough syrup," Jerry explained, unconvincingly.

Jerry's office was bigger than Pat's and more colorful. One sofa was royal blue with orange cushions while the other was orange with royal blue cushions. There was a bar built into one wall and an aquarium built into the other, containing what appeared to be a single small shark. Jerry sat in an imposing black leather chair behind a nearly invisible glass desk.

"I'll get right to the point. We'd like to use your celebrity portraits for endorsement ads. Chesterfield already signed Cole Porter, and they want to bag Merman too with the line, 'The favorites of stars and smokers!' Cole loved the pictures you took and wants us to use them, that's easy, isn't it?"

"Could be," I said, warily.

"Let's get down to brass tacks, Herb, what do you want?"

"Wow, that's very direct, Jerry."

"Despite what Pat might have told you, I'm not the enemy. I know your work, it's good, I want to use you."

"So the question is whether I want to be used."

Jerry stood up. "No, the question is 'do you want to be of service to your country.'" he said, seriously.

"Of course I do."

"Have you taken the time to study our advertisements?"

"In color, yes."

"Full color is coming soon. We'll have it and editorial won't. I remember from the Fair/Unfair issue meeting that you want your work to do something important. Am I right?"

"But you're just selling things."

He walked closer to me and leaned on the edge of his desk. "That's like saying the editorial department only prints pretty pictures. You have to look deeper. We do creative work. Important work. Without us, there'd be no *Look* magazine because subscriptions don't cover even a quarter of production costs. Advertising pays the bills."

Jerry, who had seemed merely superficial before, grew increasingly passionate, "What's more, we fuel the engine of consumer consumption that drives the economy, and now, the war effort. We need creative communicators, like you, to help *Look*, the country and the world."

"You're very persuasive."

"That's my job. And yours."

"But cigarettes?"

Jerry stood up, as if at attention. "The tobacco industry employs tens of thousands of hard-working Americans in agriculture, production, distribution and retail. The vital, nourishing tobacco plant is the only natural source of vitamin N, essential nicotine that gives people energy to do their work, and relax when they're at home. People have been smoking plants since time immemorial and top quality brands like Chesterfield help promote American values around the world!"

"I never thought of it that way."

He leaned down to me, "We're also preparing a pro bono series for military enlistment, War Bonds and public awareness about how rationing is a vital way we can all support the war effort."

"That's important."

"You may not know this, but our studies have found people actually *enjoy* our advertising. They tear out pages for future reference. We provide a valuable service for 2 million Americans."

"OK, I'm sold."

He stood up and briskly walked behind his desk. "Good. We'll need world-wide rights in perpetuity."

"But I retain the negative and copyright. And $250 per image."

"That's steep."

"And worth it."

"We'll have access to any celebrities you photograph, with their permission, of course."

An idea popped into my head. "One more thing. I want a photo credit."

"In the advertisement? That's simply not done."

"It's what I want."

"Have you ever seen an advertisement with a photo credit?" Jerry asked, incredulously.

"Have you ever seen an advertisement with photos like mine?" I replied.

He sat down abruptly. "That's quite presumptuous."

"It costs you nothing."

"It distracts from the advertiser's message."

"Or, it lends prestige."

Jerry laughed. "Nobody in the general public can name a photographer!"

"Yet."

"You're impertinent—and impressive. I'll need to sell that to the Chesterfield excs. I can't promise they'll bite."

"My name is something you can offer that the other magazine's can't."

Jerry sprang up and bounded around his desk. "You audacious little asshole!" Then he reached out his hand, "I like you!"

We shook on it. He smiled, a sharky grin.

"I'll get you a contract."

"Let's hope Miss LaRue gets my name right."

"That's not where her talents lie," he chuckled, leading me out of his office with his hand on my back, then closed the door behind me.

I walked out the elevator, wondering if I'd been sold a bill of goods.

130 ➤ Pizza Again

I told Glenn what I'd done.

"Without your agent?" he frowned, in mock sadness.

"Only because I learned it all from you."

"Sounds like you made a good deal. The part about a photo credit is crazy, I'd never have asked for it."

"He was such a good salesman, it gave me the idea of having my name associated with celebrities. He told me they were doing ads for military recruitment, so you should approach him with your military portraits."

"Good idea. I've been thinking of enlisting myself."

"No!"

"What, you think I couldn't do it?"

"Of course you... I meant 'no, don't do it.'"

"I woulda thought with all the shit that's going down you'd want to serve your country, too, Herb."

"I do, but I'd make a lousy soldier—I don't take orders very well! Besides, I can help through photos, like I did in the *Fair* issue."

"Yeah, that's what made me think about enlisting."

"You have that same power of persuasion, too, Glenn! Let the strong farm boys go to war and do what they're good at. We need to do what we're good at."

"I'm strong. I carried the new furniture upstairs by myself!"

"I know you're strong, I'm just saying that your vision is your strength. You and I can do more when we use our particular kind of strength."

He thought about it. "Yeah, I see that."

"Oh, and I almost forgot to tell you the big news."

"Bigger than that?"

"Pat's coming to our housewarming party!"

"No shit!"

"She checked her book and everything and she'll be here. She asked if you wanted some champagne."

"I hope you told her 'no' because the last time I had that stuff it gave me a headache and made me puke."

"I told her no, without the gory details."

"We've got to start getting ready now. I'll call the Carnegie Deli... and Mrs. Miers' Bakery but I won't mention her daughter."

"Glenn..."

"...what, it's the best bakery!"

"It's your party, get what you want. For tonight, let me know what you want for dinner and I'll go get it."

"How do you feel about pizza?"

"We just had it last night!"

"So?" He had a point. "Last night was pepperoni, tonight can be totally different—meatball."

I went across the street and ordered a large pizza. Glenn was right, who'd ever heard of too much pizza? Between bites Glenn had a flash, "Oh, I just remembered, you got a postcard."

"Really, from who?"

"I didn't read it, that would be illegal."

"It's a postcard, it's right on the back!"

"I'll go down and get it." Glenn put down his pizza and went downstairs. He returned with the card, picture side up. "I still didn't read it."

I read it, "Hollywood is wonderful. I've got a sweet bungalow in Culver City. Come visit anytime. Iris." There was a lipstick print after the signature.

"Who's it from?"

"A friend in Hollywood."

"Come on, you can tell me, it's Kitty."

"Very close."

"You gonna go see her?"

"Me? Naw, I hate Hollywood."

"Why? You love the movies. Seems like it'd be awful nice. Besides, she sent you a card..."

"...I don't want to talk about it, Glenn."

"OK, OK, I get the picture. Sorry!" He stuffed a big bite in his mouth and looked down. We ate in silence.

After dinner we listened to Charlie Chan, then Raymond Raquello and his orchestra which put me to sleep until Glenn's jackhammer snoring woke me up. I shuffled down the hall, squeezed by the filing cabinets, and lay down in my cozy little bed. I looked at the postcard again. *"Greetings from Hollywood!"* it screamed in red and blue, each letter filled with: Orange groves, Palm trees, Pagodas; Grauman's Chinese theater, Search lights! The Pacific Ocean! The HOLLYWOODLAND sign! The always sunny, glamorous home of the movies I loved. I'd always wanted to go, but now... it meant something else. I put the postcard under my pillow and fell asleep.

131 ➽ Ghost Light

The next morning I went into Glenn's darkroom. "Hey, Glenn, I'm shooting a dancer this afternoon and want to know how I can use a fast shutter speed inside."

"You need a lot of light, Herb. I've got a Speedotron strobe 300 watt pack and head."

"I don't know what that is but if you say it's good I believe you."

"It's big and heavy but you can shoot 500th of a second and freeze pretty much anything."

He showed me how to use it and packed it up in a sturdy black case. I called a taxi and gently put it in the trunk myself.

I arrived at the Ethel Barrymore Theater at noon. Scotty, the stage door man, let me in and once again I was amazed at how big the stage area was. I looked around to find some angles, but what looked best was right in the middle of the empty stage with its one bare light on a stand that Scotty called a "ghostlight" and told me not to touch.

"You probly wanna know why it's called a ghostlight." he said, without my ever asking. "Lots a people got lots of reasons. If you ask me, and you did ask me, I say it's there so the ghosts can perform while everybody's gone. Keeps 'em from cursing the theater or messin' up a show. Long time ago, I worked a play called "September Morn," where somebody, not me, forgot to leave the ghost light on. The next night a backdrop fell and almost hit the leading lady, one Salome Swenson, who quit and never performed on stage again. She still swears she saw a ghost right before it fell and tells that story all the time and I know 'cause I married her and now she knits sweaters for rich ladies and sick babies."

"Wow, that's quite the story." Since I'd seen the shadow ghosts myself I didn't doubt this.

"You ain't heard nothing, yet, I gotta million of 'em. One time, I come into the theater on a Monday, when it's usually dark. I swear, and Salome will back me up on this, that I saw two ghosts dancing on stage. They were all white and I could see right through 'em and they were doing an old-fashioned waltzy dance but there weren't no music and when they saw me they started to fly right through the air at me and I ran like the dickens right outta there and quit the show that very day. Ask Salome. That was the old Beckworth Theater on 44th. Had to be torn down 'cause nobody would play there. Then there's the story of…"

Luckily he was interrupted by Mr. Kelly who bounded in. "Hey Scotty, you're not talking this poor fellow's ear off about ghosts, are you?"

"'A course not, Mr. Kelly, just wanted to make sure he didn't fool with the ghostlight, is all, for obvious reasons, you know don't want nothin to happen to you or Miss Segal, cause you know what they say…"

"I do, in fact, know what they say. Thanks, Scotty, I appreciate you keeping us safe! I'll take it from here," he said as Scotty shuffled back to his stool by the stage door. "Sorry about that," he whispered

"He was telling me about some dancing ghosts…"

"Oh, he was just getting started. Before you leave, tell him you've got an appointment, otherwise you'll hear about Salome's run-in with Great Bluebeard's ghost, and, trust me, nobody should be subjected to that. Speaking of time, I've only got an hour then I have to get ready for the show."

"I'm quick, Mr. Kelly."

"Call me Gene, and thanks for doing this—I'm here to promote *Pal Joey*—Rodgers and Hart at their best. OK, so what do you want me to do?"

"I noticed the posters outside don't show you dancing, I thought you were a dancer."

"I am a dancer!"

"Then let's get shots of you dancing!"

"OK, but they'll be blurry, that's what am lousy lensmen told me."

"I've got a special light that'll let me freeze you in mid-air."

"Hopefully it won't upset the ghosts," Gene joked.

"That gives me an idea, let's get some ghosts in the pictures!"

"They don't scare me, but whatever you do, don't tell Scotty!"

"I wouldn't dream of it!"

"I don't have room in my dreams, they're all about dance."

"That's it!" I was excited to get an idea. "I saw a bed backstage. I'll shoot you like you're sleeping and you'll be dreaming of yourself dancing in mid-air and I'll combine the shots in the darkroom."

"That sounds super."

The bed was on casters so it was easy to roll onstage. Scotty asked, "Need some help with that?" and Gene and I both yelled, "No, we're fine!" Gene lay down in bed and I took some shots of him pretending to be asleep.

Gene said, "As long as we've got the bed here, it's got a trampoline in it for a trick I do during the 'Our own little den of iniquity' song. I can jump ever so high on it."

I set up the strobe. "We may have to do this a number of times so I can get the shot just right."

"That's fine, it's easy... and fun," he said, starting to jump. Each time he rose in the air he hit a different pose, his arms up and legs out *(flash/click!)*, doing the splits while touching his toes *(flash/click)*, or twisting to make a sideways 'V' *(flash/click)*.

I could see the flash freeze him in my head, and hoped the camera was catching it, too. I unplugged the flash and changed my shutter speed to ¼ of a second to capture blurry movement. These would be the ghosts. "Do those same movements again."

He kept jumping *(click)*, splits *(click)*, 'V' *(click)*, without the flash I could imagine the movement. "Now, be a ghost!" I whispered loud enough for him but hopefully not Scotty to hear. He leaped and put his body in grotesque shapes *(click)* while making horrible faces *(click)*. "Got it!"

His bouncing slowed and when he was back on earth I asked him to give me as many facial expressions as he could *(click, click, click, click, click)*. "You're great, I think I got everything I need."

"That was fast, Herb, thanks!"

"As long as I've got film left, is there anything else *you* want?"

"Actually, yeah, I want some of me leaning casually against the pipes on the back wall of the theater. Simple, gritty to show I'm a man's man, not one of those sissy dancers." I took the shots he described and they looked elegant, his white shirt and socks contrasting against the black wall.

Then I saw the ghostlight again. "One more quick idea. I think it'll look good *and* appease any spirits we might have stirred up. I want you to hold the ghostlight like a partner and dance with it."

He laughed, but did it perfectly, holding it tenderly and dipping it so elegantly the light started to take on a life of its own. *Click!* Then finally one more shot, where he's looking into the light, lovingly in profile. *Click!*

"There are so many great shots here my editor's going to have a whale of a time choosing one!"

"It was a pleasure," he said, patting his pocket for a cigarette.

"Please, take one of mine," I said, handing him a Chesterfield I'd never smoke but bought for just such an occasion. He lit it up, the ghostlight illuminating the smoke in all its ghostly grace. *Click.*

We shook hands and I was so excited to see the shots I didn't even stay for the show.

132 ➤ Ghost Dark

Back in the darkroom I developed the film and could tell I had gold. The shots of Kelly, isolated in mid-air worked like magic—he appeared to gracefully float n total stillness. They were stunning, shockingly static.

The "ghost" images were wonderful, too, the blur revealing his path and movement compressed into a single image.

I combined an image of him "sleeping" with a mid-air dream shot above him and it told the whole story. I made double-exposures of him mid-air with the ghosts, showing both clarity and movement.

Still, even after all that darkroom magic, it was the simple photos of him dancing with the ghostlight were the most captivating—the light making him glow against the black background. And the cigarette smoke! Woah! Even in the negative I could see a face in it and it gave me goosebumps all down my arms. It must have been the ghost of the light! But luckily, it looked quite happy to have a living dancer finally take it for a spin. I made prints for Pat and took the smoking one to Jerry's office, where, conveniently, Miss LaRue wasn't at her desk and his door was open.

"Hey, Jerry, I've got something to show you," I said at the door.

"Come on in, you little SOB," he said, nicely.

"You're welcome," I said, plopping the smoke image on his desk and pointing to the end of the cigarette that said, *Chesterfield.*

"Well, I'll be. I'm meeting with them this evening. Armed with this, your outrageous proposal just might have half a chance."

"It'd be a shame if they couldn't use this image, wouldn't it?" I pulled the image away from him until he grabbed it back.

"Don't press your luck."

"I'm not, I'm pressing yours."

"You've got chutzpah, I'll give you that."

"And I deliver the goods. You gotta give me that, too," I said, walking out the door and across the hall that separated editorial from advertising.

Louise wasn't at her desk, either. I pressed the intercom button, "Hey, Pat, it's Herb, I've got something to show you."

"Come on in," she said.

I opened the door and the room was filled with women in colorful dresses, Pat in red, Louise in blue, Miss LaRue in pink, Alice from accounting in lime, and others I didn't know in a rainbow of hues. It was a beautiful sight, like a flock of exotic birds. Why were men always so drab?

"Ladies, this is Herb Hamilton, one of our star photographers, and newly single, I might add." Pat announced, and they flocked around me. They smelled really good.

"I'm sorry to intrude on the festivities."

"We're just having a shower for Miss LaRue. She's found herself a nice little millionaire from Texas."

"Congratulations, Miss LaRue."

"Thank you, Mr. Hamburger," Miss LaRue said. "The only part I don't like is having to ride them cows, boy."

"I think she means 'ride 'em cowboy' but no matter." Pat added, winking. "What've you got to show, Herb?"

I temporarily forgot why I was there, then saw the photos in my hands. I set them on her desk and the women huddled around, oohing and ahhing. They admired the dream images. They liked the mid-air shots even better, handing them around. Pat liked the combined mid-air ghost shots, but then I knew she liked movement.

When she uncovered the shots of him dancing with the ghostlight the room got quiet and the oohs and awws turned into "Ohs" and "I wish he was dancing like that with me."

"I think we have a winner, Herb. Have a cupcake." Pat handed me a pink one with jimmies. "Now you must leave us so we can continue our secret mission to take over the world."

"Would the secret society like a photo before I leave? I'll keep it all very hush-hush."

"OK, ladies, everyone group together by the sofa," Pat directed. The others crowded around, some sitting on the coffee table, others on the floor.

"Smile!" I announced, then felt stupid, I never asked people to smile. They all smiled. *Click.* Click. *Click.* I surprised myself by saying, "Now make a funny face," and they all did, including Pat who frowned and crossed her eyes. *Click.* "Beautiful, got it!"

134 ⇒→ Still Life

I showed the Gene Kelly shots to Glenn. He was partial to the simple frozen-in-mid-air shots. "The strobe worked great. Nice idea about the dream but you don't need it. Same with the ghosts, though I like the motion images by themselves. The ones of him dancing with the light are the winner, though, don' cha think?"

"That's the consensus, but I'm disappointed people like them better than the complicated shots."

"Just be glad they like 'em!"

"Yeah, but it's so simple. I guess there's a lesson there."

"The lesson," Glenn said solemnly," is to keep doing what you're doing. Shoot a lot, then be happy when one's a winner. How do you feel about pizza?"

"Three days in a row?"

"Yeah?"

"Works for me." I went across the street and got a garlic pizza which we, once again, ate fancily with knives and forks.

Glenn showed me what he'd been shooting—luscious flowers... studded with ants and earthworms and bees and butterflies... and diamonds. "Pat wanted still life shots of jewelry, so I went back to the original still life paintings which usually had flowers and sometimes bugs."

"They're gorgeous..."

"... but you're thinking ladies will be put off by the bugs?"

"No. You're such an artist I wish I could see these in color."

"Funny you should ask, because I felt that, too. The colors were too tasty not to capture so I shot 'em in both but had to send the color out to a lab, too complicated to process here."

"Jerry says that the ads will get full color soon, so show these to him when you're pitching your military portraits." I kept looking at his prints. "People like my photos, but I love yours, they're so... artistic."

"Are you doubting yourself?" Glenn asked sincerely. "I always do."

"The more I learn the more I know I don't know."

135 ⇒ Noël

Maybe the ghosts had been angered after all. I read that Pal Joey's songs had been banned from radio across the country (along with all music represented by ASCAP, the American Society of Composers, Authors, and Publishers). No airplay, no hit songs. No hit songs, no ticket sales. I hoped the ghosts weren't after me, too.

I couldn't worry about them this morning, I had to get down to the Pierre Hotel to photograph Noël Coward. I'd read the press clippings from *Look* and knew enough about him to be intimated.

He was a playwright, songwriter, director, actor, singer and painter, famous for his wit, style, cheek and chic. How could I possibly be stylish, witty enough? The only thing I knew for sure is I'd be wearing my fancy blue suit, which would at least make me *look* stylish.

But a blue suit and a green bag? If I'd had time I would have gone to Saks and bought a blue one to try to match the suit, but I had to be at the Pierre at 9am—sharp.

I'd walked past the hotel many times when going from the subway to the Copa, so once again I was reminded of Kitty... which reminded me of Iris. I wished I could forget them, and needed to, at least for the next hour or so.

The Pierre's lobby had a black and white marble floor in a checkerboard pattern. Walking on it made me feel like a life-size game piece. Was I a pawn or a king?

I was surprised to see "William," the perfect English gentleman from the Cloud Rangers, get out of the elevator and glide across the floor like a Rook.

"Hello, Herbert, grand of you to come."

"Hello, William, I didn't expect to see you here."

"I arranged for this shoot. Noël's new play doesn't open till fall, so he's here as part of the war effort to help persuade the American government and public to help Britain."

"Oh, I had no idea."

"Nobody does, old boy. Pat shared some of your lighthearted photographs and I wanted to make sure you kept in mind that this is quite a difficult time in England. Please take a sober approach to your photography of Mr. Coward."

"Thank you for letting me know, William."

"Good chap. I must run. I imagine I'll be seeing you soon in London," he said, tipping his hat as he walked briskly away. I didn't know what he meant, but looking at my watch I didn't have time to worry about it. I got in the elevator and told the operator, "Forty-first floor, please."

I took slow, deep breaths as we shot upwards, and rummaged around in my pockets for change to tip the operator, but I found none. Instead, I offered a sincere "thank you," and felt like a cheapskate.

Suite 41A had a set of double doors, painted cream, with a large brass knob in the middle of each. I was about to knock when I saw a small doorbell button to the right and pressed it, hearing a set of gongs that sounded like a church at noon.

A butler in a morning coat answered the door. "Good morning, sir, how may I help you?"

"I'm Herbert Hamilton, here from *Look* magazine to photograph Mr. Coward."

"Yes, we were expecting you," he intoned. "Please do come in."

I followed him into a suite so big and fancy it made the Ansonia look like a tenement. It felt like a French king's palace hoisted 41 stories into the air overlooking Central Park. The walls were a shade of yellow so light it made butter look garish. The floors were a starburst of dark wood, and the furniture was even more luxurious than the silk lining of my jacket.

Noël was sitting, as elegant as the articles suggested, perfectly framed by the window, his long cigarette holder held as if he was an art deco sculpture. He turned, slowly, and seeing me, rose from his chair with such grace as to seem like levitation.

He reached out his hand, "My dear Mr. Hamilton, it's a pleasure to meet you, I've heard such wonderful things about you." His grip was exceptionally firm, yet his hands exceptionally soft.

He made me feel like I was the only person in the world and I was rendered speechless that he would have known who I was, much less heard things about me. "Hello," was all I could manage to stay for a moment, until I swallowed and managed, "It's an honor to meet you, sir."

"Don't call me 'sir,' duckie, call me Noël."

"Please call me Herb," I said, somewhat stupidly as he could call me anything he liked. "I saw William in the lobby, and he told me..."

"Yes, I am working with Mr. Stephenson on the war effort and I can only imagine what he told you. Ignore it all, my dear boy."

"But..."

"He's a rather serious chap, and I am famously not. Should I suddenly appear too serious I might arouse suspicion."

"OK..."

"We can, of course, appease Stephenson and Churchill with a few weighty portraits, though please don't make me look weighty or portly. I adored your photographs of Coley."

"Thank you. Coley?"

"Cole Porter, my dear friend. By the way, did you manage to escape from that old queen with your virtue intact?"

"I'd been warned, yes."

"Have you been warned about me? Because I tend to succeed where Coley fails. In life as well as art."

"No, I wasn't."

"Good. But first, you must have *your* way with *me*, photographically of course."

"Speaking of songwriting, could I have you sit at the piano and sing one of your favorite songs?"

"Let's see... 'You're the Top.' Or did you mean one of *my* songs?"

"Whatever you'd like to sing."

"Ah, in that case, certainly nothing Porter, although I have written filthy lyrics for 'you're the top' if you'd like to hear them.

> *"You're the top*
> *Not, wait you're a bottom*
> *Gone to pot*
> *Till the world forgot 'em*
> *You're a flaming queen*
> *With Vaseline*
> *To slop*
> *Cause if baby you're the bottom*
> *I'm the top!"*

As he sang his expressions ranged from mock shock to devilish delight to blasé sophisticate.

Click, click, click, click, click.

"Don't tell William I sang that, I'm sure he'd be horrified, though Winston laughed his ass off when he heard it."

"I thought it was very funny."

"Coley hates them, then again, you should hear his parodies of my songs. He turned my 'Someday I'll Find You' into a vulgar and unimaginative 'Someday I'll Fuck You.'" He said this while staring deep into my eyes with such intensity I felt a little weak.

"I... um... you..." I cleared my throat, which seemed to make him smile. "When I came in you were framed by the window and I'd like to take a shot of that."

"Of course, let me get another fag first." My expression must have told him I was shocked. "Fags are what we call cigarettes in England, dear. Tell me, are *you* a faggot?"

Nobody had ever asked me that and I didn't know the answer so I stopped and thought about it. He watched me, motionless.

"To be perfectly honest, Mr. Coward... Noël... I don't know if there's a word for what I am. My girlfriend used to say 'it's only sex.' My boyfriend said I'm 'queer.' But my girlfriend turned out to be part boy and her brother turned out to be his sister and I'm not sure which one I have a thing for."

A sly grin grew across his face. "I have no idea what you just said but I loved every word of it."

"Even I'm confused."

"Love is always confusing, dear boy. Good for you for playing both sides. I myself tried that when I was young before I found that I much prefer the cricketer's bat. As for your beau/girl, why do you think you're in love? Is it like in the cinema? Or my plays? If so, then it isn't real. Trust me, I've learned this the hard way."

"I feel haunted by her."

"How interesting you should say that. In my next play, *Blithe Spirit*, a man is in love with his late wife's ghost."

At the mention of the word 'ghost' I almost dropped my camera, but luckily I had the strap around my neck.

He stared into space, sadly. "It may be perfectly preposterous, but I believe true love never dies."

"I've photographed ghosts—and spoken with them. Do you believe me?"

"Just because you can see and hear what others can't doesn't mean it's not there," he said, seriously.

"That's exactly what the ghost said!"

"That's why artists must see and hear them. What else have they told you?"

"The past is the only thing that doesn't change. Only how you see it changes.'"

"Very wise ghosts." He exhaled a cloud of smoke. *Click.*

"Let's see if we can call one in for a photo with you," I said, thinking about the ghostlight smoke.

"How perfectly ghastly, and charming!" he exhaled another cloud of smoke, but it didn't look ghostly to me.

"I have another idea. Let's go somewhere dark."

"Why my dear young man, are you trying to seduce me?"

"I thought that was *your* job."

"Touché. The third bathroom doesn't have a window, so it will be dark if we turn out the light."

"I'll need your butler to accompany us," I specified.

"Kinky."

"Practical."

"How disappointing. Giles, please accompany us into the bathroom." he said. Giles and I followed him into the large black marble bathroom.

"Noël, please stand in the shower."

"You do know my Anderson & Sheppard suit is dry clean only?"

"We're not turning on the water. Giles, please stand by the light switch. Noël, first, I'll take a shot of you with the lights on. Then I'll turn off the light and take a long exposure of you drawing a ghost in the air with your glowing cigarette. It'll be like painting with light."

"This is either tremendously clever or completely idiotic!"

"Let's find out which!" I set the camera to "bulb" so the shutter would stay open for as long as it was pressed and set it on the sink so it would be stable. "Giles, lights off." *CLICK OPEN*. The room was pitch black. "Noël, draw your ghost and tell me when you're done." He waved his cigarette around in a curvaceous pattern.

"Done."

"Giles, lights on!" The lights came on and I released the shutter. *CLICK CLOSED*. "Let's do that a few more times so there's a better chance of getting something good."

"Are you taking the mickey out of me?"

"I don't know what that is. Giles, lights off." *CLICK OPEN*.

Noël drew in the air with his cigarette... a simple shape of three circles.

"Giles, lights on." *CLICK CLOSED.* "I know you drew Mickey Mouse."

"So we're even."

"Let's try it a few more times, please." We did. Lights off, *click open,* cigarette drawing, lights on, *click closed.*

"Giles, you can go, my ciggie's gone out." he said, his cigarette having grown dark. Giles left and I pulled out my pack of Chesterfields and handed him one.

"I see you come prepared, thank you," he put the cigarette into his long holder and looked at me, waiting. "Light?"

I remembered my cigarette lighter pistol and pulled it from my bag. Much to his surprise, I pointed it directly at him and pulled the trigger, producing a flame from the end.

"For a moment there I wondered if you were a German spy... then I realized I'm not that much of a threat to anyone. Where did you get that horrific thing?"

"I'm sorry it upset you."

"Quite the contrary, I'd love to frighten my friends with it."

"Then it's yours," I said, handing it to him.

"You're much too kind, I simply couldn't. But I may very well use this charming idea in a play. 'Don't introduce a pistol in the first act if it doesn't go off in the third,' and all that."

"I'd like you to have it."

"That's very generous, my boy. What can I do for you in return?" He said, stroking the barrel.

"Let's take some photos with it—for William!" I smiled.

"How wonderful, he'll be utterly mortified!" He held it at an angle in front of his face like he was blowing into the barrel the way they do it in westerns. *Click.*

"You make a very fine spy," I said, dreamily.

"I learned everything I know from my friend, Fleming." Noël pointed the gun at me and made serious 'spy' faces, clearly relishing the game. *Click. Click. Click.*

"I think that's all I need."

"Really, how terribly disappointing. I was sure you'd need me," he purred.

"Trust me, I am very tempted."

"As Oscar Wilde said, 'I can resist anything except temptation.'" He reached out his hand, "Grab every scrap of happiness while you can."

I took his hand and he leaned in to kiss me. He smelled slightly of orange and smoke. He tasted sweetly of sugar and tobacco. It lasted what seemed like a long, lovely time.

Our lips parted and he spoke, "You kissed me because you were awfully nice and I was awfully nice and we both liked kissing very much. It was inevitable." My knees were weak and I sat next to him on the window seat. "I very much enjoyed that, thank you." He said, putting his hand on my cheek and lowering it to his shoulder. "But that, my delicious young man, is as far as we shall go. How could it get any better than that? Besides, you know what they say in show business, 'always leave 'em wanting more.'"

I did want more. But I was content to sit next to him, feeling his warmth and smelling his scent.

"What a sweet boy you are. I do want more, but I'm feeling old and tired, and in this ugly world it's best not to look too closely."

"That's what I do, I look closely—and share what I see."

"That must be difficult for you. People don't want to see the truth during these difficult times. They need fantasy and beauty to carry them through."

"But don't they need to be shown the truth?"

"We have enough truth. What we need are the sweet lies of hope. I'd rather leave you with an evergreen reminiscence of what might have been, than a desiccated memory of what was."

I'd always remember our kiss, and sitting with my head on his shoulder.

"Now, it's best that you go before I change my mind and we share a momentary pleasure in this world of pain." He lifted my head off his shoulder, held my face in his hands and looked me straight in the eye. "As for your girl/boys —never miss an opportunity for love. Never. They don't come around often. Love's sweetness is worth any bitter aftertaste." There was a tear in his eye.

He kissed me lightly on the mouth, "Now, go—to her... him... them... never let love pass you by, sweet boy." He patted my cheek then pulled his hands away and picked up his cigarette again. He turned to look out the window. I walked towards the door. Now the tear was in my eye.

136 ⇛ Go West, Young Man

What a charming man. He looked so handsome in the photos... and the ghost photos were startling. He had drawn a perfect woman's figure: head with eyes, nose and mouth, breasts with nipples, narrow waist, wide hips and shapely legs.

It's like he'd made his own ghost, which made me wonder if I did that, too. Were Kitty and Iris haunting me because of a picture I'd drawn in my own mind? They had no real sway over me, they were 3,000 miles away... yet I felt their pull.

I had to laugh at his Mickey Mouse drawing and marvel at how he understood camera angles and maneuvered himself in the most attractive pose. The simple shots of him singing at the piano were spontaneous and those framed by the windowsill were elegance incarnate.

I made some enlargements of him smoking for Jerry, and some of the others for Pat. I realized I used to let her choose and now I was showing her the ones I liked best.

I went to Jerry's office. Miss LaRue was gone—to Texas. I pressed the intercom button and tried to imitate her nasal Brooklyn accent. "A Mr. Hamburger here to see you, Mr. Normal."

"How many times do I have to tell you it's 'Norman!'... wait, who is this?"

"It's Mr. Hamburger," I said in my own voice.

"Get in here, you little asshole."

I laughed as I walked through the door. He seemed less amused, arms crossed.

"Can you believe Miss LaRue chose Texas over Manhattan, it's insane."

"Fifty million cattle can't be wrong."

"My next secretary's going to be a dog."

"French poodle I presume?

"Enough with the Noel Coward banter, let me see the pictures." I handed them to him.

"You'll notice he's smoking Chesterfield."

"Duly noted. And now you need to remember that it was *me* who convinced the advertisers to give you photo credit in the ads. Dumb bastards thought it was such a good idea they want you to photograph movie stars."

"I love the movies..."

"In Hollywood."

"Yeah, sure." I sat, shaking my head, he was such a jerk.

"I'm serious. All expenses paid."

I couldn't believe it. "I don't know..."

"You can't be such an idiot that you'd turn down this plum assignment?"

"I'd have to ask Pat..."

"Pat, schmat. Of course you'll go." His pressed the intercom button, "Arrange for train tickets for... oh fuck. I'm not doing it myself. When I get a new secretary I'll tell her."

"Woof woof."

"Get outta here, you beautiful bastard!"

I left his office, happy I was getting a byline but disturbed that Jerry, of all people, liked me. Did that mean I was as bad as he was?

I walked across the elevator hall to Pat's office. Louise was crying.

"What's wrong, Louise?"

"Nothing."

"It must be something."

"My fiancée, Jim, was called up in the draft."

"Oh... He'll be A-OK," I said, grasping for something to say.

"You can't know that," she said angrily. "Please excuse me, I don't know heads from tails at the moment." She got up and scurried down the hall.

I knocked on Pat's door.

"Come in."

Pat looked somber, dark gray suit, shirt, shoes, black cardigan and string tie. "Louise is very upset."

"I saw that."

"Have you registered for the draft?"

She pointed to a chair and I sat. "I didn't even know I was supposed to."

"Your draft notice was probably sent to your old home address. You need to register, but the group you met upstairs knows you're doing vital war work and can get you an exemption." She took a notepad out of her desk drawer and made a note in it.

"Here are the photos of Noël." I laid the contact prints on her desk, along with the enlargements.

She pulled out her loupe and studied them. "Lots of excellent work here. Wonderful expressions, framing... what are these?" She looked closer.

"His next play is about a man in love with a ghost, so..."

"...How did you make this effect? Did you draw on the negative?" She looked closely at the enlargement.

"I took a long exposure of him drawing with his glowing cigarette."

"It's enchanting, Herb."

"Thank you, Noël is an enchanting man. Oh, I saw William before meeting Noël and he mentioned meeting me in London. What's that about?"

She made notes. "That's the vital war work I mentioned. You're to go to London to cover the bombings. It's another way to get Americans more involved..."

I stood up. "No."

"What?"

"I'm not going to London. I'm going to Hollywood."

She dropped the notepad. "What on earth has possessed you, Herbert?"

"Chesterfield cigarettes."

"Don't tell me you've gotten involved with Jerry!"

"I don't know what you mean by 'involved' but it's just business."

"This is more than business, Herb, and I thought you understood. We are doing important war work here."

"Since when are photos of Cole Porter important to the war effort?"

She stood up, imposing for such a small person. "Broadway stars are morale boosters, and this is simply a short assignment."

"Hollywood stars are bigger morale boosters!" I said petulantly.

"I don't know what Jerry's said to you, but you know better."

"Better than what, Pat? Noël Coward inspired me to follow love..."

"Kitty?"

"Um..." I didn't want to have to explain, "Yes."

"Oh, Herbert. This isn't the time for frivolity."

"Is love frivolous?

"Of course not, but..."

"But nothing, Pat. Noël said 'Never miss an opportunity for love. Never. They don't come around often.'"

Pat sat back down and looked at her hands. "I'm very disappointed in you, Herb."

I sat down, feeling deflated. "I'm sorry. I don't want to let you down..."

"...It's not about me, Herb. It's about the future. It's about life or death."

"So is love."

"I know that's how it feels at your age..."

"...that's how it feels *to me*."

Pat was silent for a time. Three minutes, I know because I watched Mickey's hands the whole time. "You're sure about this?"

I didn't wait three seconds to reply, "I don't have a choice."

"You always have a choice, Herb. But you must always be sure that choice is *yours*. It breaks my heart, but I will cancel your contract as of today."

I stopped breathing. "What?"

"You made your choice."

"But..."

"Do you want to change your mind?"

I thought about it. "No. I'm sorry."

"I still hold out hope that when you read the newspapers you'll want to do your part for the war effort."

I looked down at my feet and saw her come closer. She put her arms around me and I thought I heard her cry. I couldn't tell, because I was crying louder.

137 ➺ Housewarming

I didn't want to put a damper on his big night, so I didn't tell Glenn what had happened.

"I'm thinking this is a housewarming for the studio as well as my home, so I thought I'd wear *this*," he said, putting his denim smock over his charcoal pinstripe double-breasted suit.

"Uh... both are one too many."

"So the smock?"

"I think Pat would prefer the suit."

"Of course, how stupid of me," he said, wriggling to remove the smock.

"You look very smart, Glenn. You're just nervous. You need to breathe."

"Did I stop breathing?" he said, nearly panting.

"Calm down."

"Herb, what if she doesn't like me?"

"What are you talking about, she already likes you."

"I feel like I'm 12 and looking for my first pubic hair," Glenn said, smock tangled on his head.

"Why the hell would you say that? Do not say that to Pat." I helped extricate him.

"Is Pat here?"

"No."

"Then I'm saying it to you," he said, smock finally off. "How's my hair? On my head."

"Glenn, I swear, you've got to relax. What makes you relaxed?"

"Not something I can say around Pat."

"Oy. Maybe a little alcohol would help."

Glenn arranged his hair in the mirror. "I hate the way it tastes and I don't have any."

"You're having a party and you don't have any alcohol?"

"Why would I?"

"For *other* people."

"I didn't know that. Did you tell me that? No, you did not tell me that. Why are you telling me that now?"

"I'll go to the liquor store and buy something, even though I don't know what people drink I'm sure they'll want to drink something... Oh, Pat mentioned champagne, so I'll buy some of that."

I ran down the street, wanting to get back before Pat did, just in case Glenn fainted or something worse. I saw the sign for Zelda's Fine Spirits two blocks away and went inside.

"I need champagne," I said to the elderly man behind the cash register.

"Nobody *needs* champagne, boychik. Except my late wife, Zelda, God rest her soul. You've never seen such a petite person down three entire bottles, by herself, have you?"

"Uh, no, I haven't."

"My Zelda was special. A real conna-sewer, that woman. God, I miss her."

"What kind of champagne did she drink?"

"Anything. If it was in a bottle and still had bubbles my bubala would imbibe—straight from the bottle. Never saw anything as impressive in my entire life."

"Did she have a favorite?"

"Of course. Me. I was always her favorite from the very first time we met at the Yiddish theater downtown. It was after the play, she played Ophelia in the Yiddish version of *BethMac*... no, that's not right. *Hamlet.* We used to laugh and call it *Omelette*, so we could make ham kosher."

"I really need to get to a party and I need... how much champagne should I get for 12 people?"

"If they're like Zelda you'll need 6 cases... but there was never anyone like Zelda. Here, look at her punim," he said, pointing to her portrait which hung right behind him. She looked like an elderly elf with especially sparkly eyes.

"How much champagne for 12 non-Zeldas?"

"Six bottles."

"Give me six bottles of Zelda's favorite."

"This is *real* champagne, Moët & Chandon, from France. It's expensive, $10 a bottle."

"Fine, give me six bottles."

He shuffled around, "Let me see, I haven't sold one of these in so long... and maybe Zelda drank them all... Ah, wait, I'll check in back."

I was getting franc. What if Pat arrived and Glenn made a fool of himself? No, he wasn't a fool, just nervous. What if he talked about his... Zelda's widower emerged from the back room with five bottles.

"I'm sorry, this was all I could find. I don't get much call for this and I buried several bottles with her, so..."

Luckily I had enough cash, which I handed him.

"Zelda would have liked you, young man. Come back any time, I have more pictures of Zelda drinking champagne on our honeymoon, for New Year's, and at her father's funeral..."

"Thank you!" I yelled as I ran back to Glenn's.

I had to stand outside for a minute to cool off before I went inside.

I heard talking coming from the darkroom. Not just talking, laughing.

"You're so talented, Glenn!" I heard Pat say. I peeked through the crack in the darkroom door and she was standing very close to him, one hand on his shoulder, the other running across one of his prints. "And cute."

"Naw"

"Yes."

"Naw!"

Her voice got softer, "Yes. A real mensch." I saw her hand move from touching his print to touching his hand, then up his arm, neck, to running little circles around his ear.

He stammered, "I... don't... I mean, I can't... I want... you are so... I don't know what to say."

"Words are overrated," She whispered in his ear., her lips grazing his cheek then meeting his mouth. He stood there, like a statue, finally putting his arms around her and drawing her close for a long kiss.

They pulled back, looked in each other's eyes, smiled, and kissed again.

It was nice and all but felt a little like watching your parents kissing. I took the bottles upstairs where there was exactly nobody and went downstairs again to greet the guests... of which there continued to be exactly none.

I hadn't invited anybody. Who was I going to invite? Glenn? Kitty? Iris? Sergei? Horace? Oh, I could have invited Louise but last time I saw her she was in tears and a party would have seemed callous. I sat on the green velvet sofa in the storefront with the door open, waiting for somebody, anybody to arrive.

I waited. And waited. My head grew heavy...

...I was on the Super Chief "train of the stars," headed west to Hollywood, along with Joan Crawford, who scared me, Cary Grant who interested me, and Clark Gable who couldn't be bothered with me.

Joan knocked me aside to get to Clark who was more focused on his steak than her. Cary winked at me so I went to sit with him, but just then Irene Dunne arrived and he kissed her and looked at me like I was in the way and I left them alone.

I slunk back to my compartment where it was as hot as hell. I opened the window, and the rush of air sucked me right out of the train. I flew through the air, tumbling into a cactus, its spines piercing my backside. As I lay there, painfully trying to pull them out, a snake slithered up to me, it's tail rattling and sounding like "Kit-ty, Kit-ty, Kitty" while it's tongue hissed, "I-ris, I-ris, I-ris."

It's mouth gaped open, terrifying fangs dripping venom in the moonlight...

...I was shaken awake. "Hey, Buddy, wake up, wake up, you're having a bad dream."

I looked up at Glenn who was wearing his pajamas. "You can't wear that to a party!" I slurred at him.

"Party's over."

"I missed everybody?"

"What everybody? It was just Pat."

"But the plan was to have a housewarming with other people so there wouldn't be any pressure."

"Yeah, I thought about it, but that seemed like a lot of bother so I just invited her."

"You two seemed to have had a good time," I said, surprised.

"Yeah."

"Good for you."

"We've got a lot of leftover food, she wasn't very hungry—I told you she never looked hungry."

My eyes were sticky and my neck was sore. "I'm glad you two got along..."

"Like gangbusters. She told me she liked me the first time we met."

"Then why'd she act like she *didn't* like you?"

"You don't understand women, at all, do you, Herbie?"

"I think I've proven that."

"She offered me a contract!"

"That's wonderful, Glenn, I'm so happy for you." If I didn't have one, I was glad he did.

I went upstairs, ate a cheese Danish off the bakery tray (Glenn was right, it was a very good bakery) and went to bed. I was happy for Glenn—and Pat. And worried for myself.

138 ➻ Tickets

I got a call from Jerry's new secretary, "Mrs. Goldfarb," that he needed to see me. Great, Hollywood had probably fallen through and now I'd have nothing...

I took the subway, then walked. It felt like a long time since I'd taken photos without having to make them happen. A little girl was licking a store window. *Click.* An old man holding a fishing pole sat on a box in front of a subway grate. *Click.* A pair of twins about 80 years old wearing matching red capes with white fur trim. *Click Click.*

Speaking of fishing, and 80 years old, Mrs. Goldfarb was too busy maneuvering a long fork in a jar to retrieve some gefilte fish to notice me walking past her into Jerry's office.

"Is she dead?" Jerry asked.

"Fishing."

"I'm not fishing, I'm coming right out and asking."

"I didn't put a mirror under her nose, but I've never seen a dead person stab a gefilte fish, so I'd say 'no'."

"What're the advertisers gonna think when they see her?"

"If they're kosher, probably 'Bubbe.'"

"I keep forgetting what an asshole you are. Why do I keep forgetting that? Because the advertisers love you. That's why."

"I'm not an asshole, Jerry."

"Oh, yeah? Let's see what the bubbe thinks." He pressed the intercom and heard a lot of clinking. "Mrs. Goldfarb, please come in here." There was more clinking. He released the intercom button. "I'm pretty sure she's deaf."

The door opened and Mrs. Goldfarb entered holding a steno pad in one hand and the gefilte fish jar in the other. "What can I do you for, Jerrila?"

"Do you think my friend Herb here is an asshole?" Jerry asked her. She looked quizzical, put down the jar and walked around me in a circle.

"What a thing to ask a person. If anyone could spot an asshole, it'd be you. Oy. Enough already, I'm going home. I never wanted this fakakta job for a schmuck goy in the first place, but after my Sidney died, my daughter Selma said I should do something to fill up my time... like matzo balls make themselves."

Her kvetching reminded me of someone... Zelda! "Do you like champagne?" I asked her.

She looked at me like I was a halfwit, "Do I like... of course I like... I could drink it for breakfast, what kind of question is that, everybody's meshuga here."

"I suggest Zelda's Fine Spirits on 63rd and Amsterdam, best selection in the city and a proprietor I think you'll like."

"Thanks, Yenta." she said, leaving without the gefilte fish jar.

Jerry rolled his eyes and handed me a folder. "Your train tickets for tonight."

"Tonight?"

"You got better plans? 6pm. 20th Century limited to Chicago, then the Super Chief all the way to LA. Reservations for a bungalow at the Beverly Hills Hotel so you can shoot in your room. You'll want to rent a car when you get there."

"This all looks swell... but I don't know how to drive."

"For Christ's sake don't tell them that at the car rental place. Just ask for an Oldsmobile with a hydramatic so you don't have to shift. That's what I do. I'll cable your shooting schedule once you're there. Get yourself some traveler's cheques and go."

"Your charm knows no bounds."

"Thank you," he said, his back to me.

"It wasn't a compliment."

"What part of 'go' did you not understand?" He said, and I tried to think of a snappy answer, but got distracted looking at the shiny silver tickets for the 20th Century Limited. "All of it, apparently, go." He sat, looking down at some papers.

I waved and skipped out of the office, grabbing the jar of gefilte fish on my way. I almost ran smack dab into Mrs. Goldfarb, handed her the jar, and practically floated to the elevator.

Louise saw me and waved. It felt like goodbye.

139 ➡ Traveler's Cheques

I stopped at the bank in the lobby. Mr. Clarke was there, so I asked for a thousand dollars in cheques.

"It's a wise decision to carry American Express traveler's cheques. They're accepted like cash, but if they're lost or stolen you can get a full refund at the nearest American Express office. Where, might I ask, are you traveling? Domestic or international?"

"I'm going Hollywood," I sang like the Bing Crosby song.

Mr. Clarke's face appeared frozen. "Then US dollars should suffice. If you please, I need you to sign each one of these individually in my presence, sir." It was a lot of signing and my hand got tired so the later signatures didn't look at all like the earlier ones.

"I'd also like you to anonymously send $100 a month to my mother, Rita Horowitz, you have her address."

"Certainly sir."

Mr Clarke made note of the withdrawal in my bank book. Even with eleven hundred dollars removed, my account still had $2,925 in it. I could buy a house in Hollywood with that!

"If you have any financial transactions while you're there, our West Coast branch is downtown. Bon voyage, sir." I tucked the cheques into my breast pocket and walked down the sunny street feeling safe carrying my fortune.

No sooner did I get back to Glenn's than he accosted me with questions.

"Did she say anything about me?" Glenn asked, nearly breathless.

"I didn't talk to her today... I have something to tell you."

"Oh, no, she doesn't like me after all!"

"Come on, Glenn, she liked you just fine last night."

"But this morning?"

"Call her. Talk to her. I'm sure it's fine."

He exhaled and plopped down on the sofa, wincing because he'd forgotten this wasn't the kinds of sofa you plopped onto.

I continued, "What I need to tell you is that I..." I didn't know what to call it. I didn't exactly quit, did I? "I'm not going to be working for Pat anymore."

"What? No! Oh, No! This is all my fault! I'm so sorry, I'll talk to Pat, I'll fix it up."

"Glenn, no. It was my decision and had nothing to do with you or Pat. I have great respect and fondness for you both."

"Then why would you leave?"

"I have to follow my heart—and go to Hollywood."

"But you've told me you hate Hollywood. Why would you... Oh. Oh. Oh. Kitty. Of course."

"It's not Kitty exactly..."

"Ah, Herbie. I get it, and I want you to be happy..."

"Thanks, Glenn..."

"But I'm not happy about it. I've never had a pal like you," He rubbed his eyes with the back of his hands and sniffed. "I'm gonna miss you, Herbie. Who am I gonna talk to now?"

I sat down next to him, "You can talk to Pat."

"You know what I mean."

"I'll miss you, too. But they have telephones in Hollywood, you know," I consoled.

"Yeah, I know, but I never made a long-distance call."

"I'll call you so you won't have to pay for it. I'll come back... sometime."

"Sometime?" his voice got high the way he did when he was upset or excited.

I put my arm around his shoulder. "You changed my life, Glenn. I... I can never thank you enough." Now it was my turn to rub my eyes and pretend I wasn't getting weepy. "I know we'll see each other again."

"You been like the brother I never had, Herbie," he sniffed.

"I never had a brother, either, till you." We were both fighting the waterworks. "I'll call you, Glenn, as soon as I get there... in four days. I have to leave tonight."

Glenn looked sad. "Tonight? No time for pizza or cake or a going away party? Damn, Herbie this is hard on a fella." We sat quietly together until the sniffling stopped. "OK, boychik, you go get your girl."

"And you get yours."

I headed towards my bedroom, "I gotta go pack."

"I gotta buy condoms."

"What???"

"Better safe than sorry, my dad always used to say. Him being sorry is how I got here."

"But if he'd had condoms you might not exist!"

"I never thought of that. Didn't you use protection with Kitty?"

"I didn't know I was supposed to."

"She didn't say nothin'?"

"Nope. I guess she wasn't worried about getting pregnant... oh, of course she wasn't." It was all making more sense... Sometimes I wondered if I was especially slow.

"Loose lips sink ships!" Glenn whispered.

"I don't even know what that means."

"Yeah, I'm not sure it was the right thing to say, but I liked the way it sounded."

I left the room and started packing. Once again I was glad I'd bought the alligator bag. It would look good on the train, in a taxi, at the hotel. Besides, it meant there was one less of those man-eating beasts.

I decided what to wear on the train. Not my best suit, but my gray one, white shirt, blue tie, gray fedora—dapper yet not too flashy. I'd wear my raw silk the day I arrived in Los Angeles. I tucked my cheques safely in the suitcase's secret compartment, neatly folding my clothes on top of it.

I packed my green stowaway bag with my camera equipment. I'd keep the Leica around my neck, and the bag would be full of film, lens cleaner, and the special "Ilford Pitch Black bag" Glenn gave me as a going away present. I'd put exposed film in that to ensure it didn't get fogged by light if the suitcase fell.

If I needed any other equipment I was sure I could buy it in Hollywood.

I looked at the handsome bags. My entire life fit into two bags. Not completely, I had a lot of negatives now but Glenn had those for safe-keeping. Otherwise, I was "Two Bag Herb." I could go anywhere in the world. Not Europe right now, but anywhere else. I didn't want to go to London... the point was, I was free as a bird, about to ride the rails to the other coast!

If I was so happy about this, why was I starting to cry?

140 ⇛ 20th Century Ltd.

It was quietly snowing as I hailed the cab and told the driver, "Grand Central Station, New York Line." I looked at the streets, blanketed in white, at once familiar and strange. *Click.* I'd be back in a couple of weeks, right? Or maybe I'd never see it again, so I looked especially hard at it. *Click.*

I'd never been outside of New York. I'd never been on a train (unless you count the subway). I'd only ever been *under* Grand Central Station, but now the taxi dropped me off at the entrance to the great hall. Sunbeams illuminated the colossal room where the ceiling was painted with celestial bodies in the night sky. *Click.*

Track 34. That's what I was looking for. I saw 33 other tracks, and then... a blue and silver gate, a red carpet with the streamlined 20th Century Limited logo. Men in blue uniforms stood at silver podiums, checking tickets.

"Good evening, sir. You're booked in Roomette 3901, conveniently located near the Century Club car where dinner is served from 6:30 until 11pm. Breakfast is served from 5 till 7:30am and you'll arrive in Chicago's La Salle Street Station at 9am."

He handed me brochures about the train, its services and dining cars, then leaned in and placed a carnation boutonniere in my lapel.

"The New York Central Railroad wishes you a most pleasant journey on The 20th Century Limited. If you should require anything on your trip, please feel free to ring for your coach porter, Lionel."

Lionel, a black man in a red-cap, bowed. "At your service, Sir. I'll take your very handsome bag here. Folla' me to your coach. Should you be needin' anything cleaned or pressed, jes' let me know." He put an elastic tag with my room number on my bag's handle, bowed again, and started walking briskly down the long red carpet that ran the full length of the train. I followed, looking in the windows of the cars to see men and women settle into their hotel rooms on rails. *Click.*

"It's a long walk," I said to Lionel, looking down the length of the train. *Click.*

"Shore is, Sir! Train's almost as long as the Empire State Building's tall! But that cain't move at 60 miles per hour ta get ya to Chicago in only 16 hours!"

"This is my first time on a train."

"You're starting on the best, sir!" He gestured for me to step aboard before him. I climbed three stairs and found myself inside a modern marvel, smartly done up in shades of blue, gray and rust. Lionel opened the door to 3901 and welcomed me with a sweep of his arm.

"May I take your photo, Lionel?"

"Most certainly, sir," he said with a big photogenic smile. *Click.*

I entered the compact but well-appointed room with two wide deep blue mohair seats across from each other next to the large window. The walls were curved metal painted in two-tone blue and gray. Lionel placed my bag on a ledge opposite the sofa and pointed out the features of the room. "Your personal toilet is hidden under this seat here. A worsh basin folds down here under a lit mirror. At night you folds the bed down from the wall and it's already made up. May I hang your coat in the closet?"

"I'll keep it on for now, it's rather chilly in here."

"Yes, sir, this whole train's air conditioned from end to end. We'll be leaving in about five minutes, if ya need anything else jes' let me know."

"Thanks, I'll settle in."

"One mo' thing: Dinner service starts at 6:30. Ya might wanna gets there early 'cause later there'll be a wait. But you can get a nice cocktail in the lounge."

Lionel turned to leave, and I was so impressed with everything I almost forgot to give him a tip! I gave him two silver dollars.

"Thank ya kindly, sir!" he said, saluting. "Anything you need, anything at all, you just ask me."

I took a few shots of my room. But I *was* hungry and if I didn't want to wait in the lounge *not* drinking a cocktail I'd better go.

I opened the door and ran smack dab into a fair man with reddish hair. He looked me up and down, slowly, then put on an almost convincing smile.

"Yes—it really is me!" he said, raising his eyebrows and tilting his head as if this meant something.

"It really is me, too," I said, for lack of anything better to say.

He didn't move. "But *I* am..." he paused as if I was going to fill in the blank.

"I am, too," I tried to get around him but he wouldn't move.

"You honestly don't recognize me, young man?"

"I honestly don't recognize you... man."

He pouted. Slumped. Sulked. Everything he did was deliberate and theatrical, as if he'd practiced it countless times in front of a mirror.

"Excuse me, I'm trying to get to the dining car before the rush."

"As luck would have it, that's where I am headed, too. I don't mind if you join me." If a person could trot on a train that's what he did, down the narrow hallway, looking back at me. "Come, come, or we'll be late."

I followed, mostly because I had no idea which direction the dining car was in and he seemed to know. "Seemed" being the operative word, because he reached the end of the car, turned around, squeezed by me and trotted the other direction. "Just testing you!" he said, his melodic voice going high.

We passed through two more sleeping coaches before reaching the lounge, all brushed metal and chrome. It looked as fast as the landscape moving outside.

The maître d took one look at the man with me, stood taller and said, "Right this way, Mr. Kaye."

"You see, most people recognize a star when they see one," he said, shaking his head in a parody of disgust. I sat across from him.

"Mr. K... Is that an initial or your last name?"

"Heavens, boy, you're one comment away from buying your own dinner."

"I can afford my own dinner, Mr. K... not Danny Kaye?"

He rested his chin on his hands and batted his eyes. "The one and only. Aren't you today's lucky fan... besides, I hate to dine alone."

"Oh, I'm so sorry. I was supposed to shoot you back in the city."

"Then I guess I 'dodged a bullet.'" he said, trying to be cute. "I do hope you're not going to shoot me now that you've landed your prey." He said everything as if he had an audience.

"Since I didn't know you were here, I could hardly..."

"...Oh, drop the charade. You've clearly followed me, which is flattering if frightening. I appreciate my fans but not when they intrude on my private space."

"You're the one who invited me here." The waiter brought him a big martini without having even been asked. "I'll have a Shirley Temple," I told him.

"Yes, sir," the waiter said, stifling a smile.

Danny sipped slowly. "Only because you clearly arranged for it to happen, which I give you credit for."

"I guess I could try shooting you on the train..."

"How alarmingly Agatha Christie!" he squealed. "Here I was, afraid the next four days would be a bore with only June Allyson for company. Have you met June? She has absolutely no talent whatsoever, except in bed, that's how she gets all her roles, and I have absolutely no interest in her whatsoever. But let's talk about you..."

The waiter slipped a Shirley Temple in front of me and winked.

"You don't look like a child, boy. Exactly how old are you?"

"I'm 17½"

"Oy. And across state lines, too."

"I really was supposed to shoot you—for *Look* magazine," I gestured to the Leica around my neck.

"So you're a photographer. A photo shoot on a train would be novel. Did I mention dinner's on me, you lucky sod? Just don't order the lobster."

The waiter stood at attention with his pad looking at Danny, not at me. "I've already put in your standing order, Mr. Kaye. What would your companion like?"

"Just a cup of consommé..." Danny said before I interrupted.

"I'll have the New 20th Century Dinner with braised celery hearts, fresh deviled lobster and banana shortcake with whipped cream." Danny's eyes turned to slits. I'd never had lobster before and didn't even know if I'd like it, but who did he think he was ordering for me—and just broth! "We'll have separate checks, please." I smiled at Danny.

"You must be very pleased with yourself," he said.

"No, that would be you," I said in a way even I thought was rather rude but I wanted to enjoy the train and he wouldn't stop talking. My celery hearts arrived and I was relieved that they didn't involve actual hearts. They were cooked and covered with cheese, so what was not to like? I looked up to find Danny studying me like I was an animal.

"Would you like a taste?" I offered.

"Not of that," he said, ignoring it.

The waiter gingerly placed a plate in front of Danny. Filet Mignon, tomatoes, Brussels sprouts, and cute little baby potatoes. I pushed aside the celery to make room for the main event and the waiter slid my plate in front of me.

It had two large reddish tails like from a big hard fish. Inside was some pinkish stuff I assumed was lobster, since that's what I ordered. If I didn't like that, there were a lot of tiny little peas and tiny french fries.

I dug my fork into the lobster and it was already in little pieces in a sauce... like tuna salad? I took a bite. It tasted a bit like tuna salad, only not so tuna-y, creamier, better, and the sauce was a little spicy. I could eat this!

While I was focused on my plate, Danny was somehow eating yet never taking his eyes off me. It was creepy, but he was famous, which I was starting to think was a good excuse for bad behavior.

I temporarily forgot about him as I devoured my delicious dinner. I finished the lobster and the banana shortcake with whipped cream arrived. This was maybe the best dessert I'd ever had, so good I licked the plate, then looked up to see Danny studying me again. "My dinner was excellent. How was yours?"

"It's always delicious. Now you will come back to my compartment for a little game of Parcheesi."

"I don't want to play games."

"Do you not like me? That can't be it, everybody likes me... whatever your name is."

"Herb."

He said in tongue-twisting rapid-fire, "Basil, bay, and caraway, chamomile and comfrey... dill, and fennel, feverfew, garlic, ginger, ginseng, too..."

"Herbs, I get it."

"It's from a Cole Porter show I did. My character's name was Herb. You're quite the enigma, Herb, if that is actually your name. ¾ of the people in this car would be honored to keep me company tonight."

I paid the bill. "Then I'm sure you'll have no trouble finding company when I say goodnight. Goodnight."

I was quite proud of how I handled him, until I stood up— somehow the tablecloth was stuck in my belt buckle and I would have pulled everything off the table if Danny hadn't grabbed it. "Thanks," I whispered, feeling dumb as ¾ of the people in the car watched me leave.

Back in my roomette, I changed into my PJs and pulled down the bed, only to realize the bed covered the toilet which I needed to use. I pushed the bed back, did my business, pulled the bed down and got in. I left the window blind open so I could watch the lights glisten on the water, (*click, click, click*) and the motion and sound soon put me fast asleep.

141 ➽ June

The next thing I heard was a knock on my door. I woke up with the landscape blurring by, a grimy dawn of stockyards and the occasional shack.

I heard Lionel, the porter, from the other side of the door. "Good mornin', Mr. Hamilton. Breakfast is served in the dining car. If you're hungry you wanna get there early and avoid the rush."

My stomach rumbled, I slid out of bed and pushed it back up into the wall, jumped into my clothes and headed to the dining car, keeping one eye out for Danny to make sure he wasn't going to try to eat with me again.

In the dining car the maître d' said, "We have one seat left if you don't mind sharing a table sir."

"I don't mind at all, thank you."

He led me to a table where an elderly woman sat, looking a little like a fluffy white dog. I sat down and said hello.

I felt a hand tug at my arm and thought, "Oh, no, he's found me." When I turned around there was a perky young woman with a low voice and a high forehead.

"There you are, brother dear!" she said to me in a gravelly voice. "Come sit with me!" she said, as she pulled me away. I followed her to her table where she gestured for me to sit in the chair across from her.

I told her, "You must have me confused with someone else."

"I'm sorry to be so forward, but I'm in danger—and you look like the kind of strong man who can protect me."

"I'm always happy to protect a damsel in distress. But it would help to know what I am protecting you from. Is there a fire-breathing dragon on board?"

"'Fire-breathing,' that's a good description of him. 'Dragon...' He does like drag. If he sees me engaged in conversation with someone else he'll leave me alone."

"Who is the person so that I'll know him if I see him?"

"You don't know him, he's an obnoxious redhead."

"Danny Kaye? He had me for dinner last night... or at least he wanted to."

"Holy fuck! It doesn't surprise that he tried to lure you into his web. He no doubt made low implications as to my morals and gossiped that I slept with anything in pants or even a skirt..."

"He didn't mention the skirt..."

"Did he also tell you that he was married? No? That shows you what kind of liar he is, so you can ignore anything that he said about me. We're going to MGM together but he's only getting a screen test and that doesn't mean shit in Hollywood. Hello, I'm June," She smiled, sweetly and held out her hand.

I shook her small but strong hand. "Pleasure to meet you, June."

"Charmed, I'm sure. As for Danny, don't waste your time with him —he's just an actor. He can't and won't do anything for you. He's the lowest rung on the totem pole. *I* have a part in the new MGM musical, 'Too Many Girls,' starring Ziegfeld Girl Lucille Ball."

"Didn't I see you in *Panama Hattie*?"

"Yes, how sweet of you to remember! I'm a working actress, but you don't have to worry about me trying to seduce you because I can tell you're not a producer."

"How can you tell?"

"Why don't you tell me who I have the pleasure of breaking bread with this morning."

"My name's Herb. I'm a photographer for *Look* magazine."

"Magazines are so important for an actress' public image. That makes you a semi-useful person. Is this your first time in Hollywood?"

"Yes, yes it is."

"Aren't you a dear! You'll be my protector and I'll show you the ropes so nobody hangs you with them. You won't have to worry about me trying to seduce you because as adorable as you may be, you're simply not important enough. Lesson number one: everyone in Hollywood is judged by how useful they can be to your career. Take

Danny, for example, I'm afraid that the better he gets to know me, the more dirt he'll have on me. But I can tell a sweetheart like you would never do that, would you?"

"Never, cross my heart."

"Danny probably said I'm a slut—I'm not—I'm strategic." She waved for the waiter, then whispered to me, "Don't order the sausage. Normally. I'm a big sausage fan. I like the feeling of it in my mouth. The firmness on my tongue. The juiciness down my throat... But on this train, stick with the bacon."

She turned her attention to the waiter. "I'll have scrambled eggs, bacon, extra-crisp, and toast dry."

"I'll have what the lady's having, but with a bagel and a schmear." The waiter scribbled in his pad then turned on his heels and left. I turned to her, "I'll protect you."

"You're a good kid. Back to lesson one: how to be selective in Hollywood. To be clear, 'selective' means only sleeping with people who can do something for you. Either they can do something for you, or they're worthless. Take worthless actors, like Danny: They only care about themselves and have no power to get you hired. All an actor will ever give you is a social disease."

I made mental notes.

"The next least important person up the useful ladder is the writer. On Broadway, the writer is king, but in Hollywood he's not even a pauper. Out there anybody can be a writer. Don't get me wrong, writers are charming. They're funny. They're alcoholics. But, and trust me on this, even if you make them fall in love with you they're useless. They'll say 'I've written an Oscar winning part for you, baby!' then you'll watch someone else get the part and the Oscar. Remember, writers have no power whatsoever."

Hollywood was sounding stranger and stranger.

"One step up from writers are directors—they're egomaniacal, mean, and alcoholic and/or fags. I should add some of my good friends are fags, they're the best makeup, hair and costume people and great fun. Directors have more power because they can *suggest* you for a part, even *lobby* for you if they want you on set to service them between takes. But they don't have the final say."

How lucky was I to have her explain all this, because I always thought the directors were in charge.

"Then there are studio executives—they change like the weather—ignore them. Which takes us to the upper echelon of the 'they can do something for you' ladder—the producer. They're at the top because money talks. They can hire whoever they want, and what they say goes. So—when you're looking around for someone to have an intimate and productive relationship with, you want to find yourself a producer."

"How do you spot a producer?"

"I'm glad you asked. I'm going to give you this tip because you're no competition for me. In fact, if you get in good with a producer, I'm sure you'll put in some nice words for sweet little June. First, they always have gray hair. By itself that's not enough because drunken writers, mean directors and useless studio execs can have gray hair, too. The secret: *shoes, and watches.* Producers *always* have expensive shoes and watches. In New York if you're rich you dress like you're rich. But in Hollywood the rich like to dress like teamsters. I don't claim to understand why, but that's how it is.

"When they're on the set they'll be dressed in a fine English suit and they're easy to spot because they make everyone around them sweat. But in their off hours, they wear dungarees and polo shirts. The polo shirts may even appear dirty so they look like they play polo, but they never do. You don't want to make the same mistake that I did the first time I was in Hollywood and confuse an actual polo player for a producer. No, no, no.

"But no matter what else they wear, their shoes are always expensive and Italian, usually spectators or loafers. Easy to spot once you know what to look for in fine men's footwear. Their watch will either be a Cartier or Rolex. Period. Full stop. I should also say that producers are all men, but not all of them are interested in women, and that's where you come in. Oh, here's breakfast—See, I was right about the bacon."

142 ➽ Chicago Morn

Breakfast was good, as was June's lesson—it was helpful to know the pecking order. I walked her back to her room.

"Now, my handsome squire, it's time to pack so we can change trains. I assume you're continuing on the Super Chief and I look forward to seeing you on board!" A quick peck on the cheek and she pulled back and closed the door. She was nice.

I went back to my roomette and Lionel had already packed my bag. "When we gets to Chicago, many travelers like to take a room and bath at the Ambassador East for the day to take a bath and dine at the Pump room. Would you like me to make arrangements for ya?"

"That sounds excellent, thank you, Lionel."

"Thank you, sir!"

I put my feet up and watched the landscape go by...

...Suddenly I'm in Hollywood. Orange trees everywhere. Pretty girls and handsome men in costumes of all eras; Egyptian outfits, Grecian togas, knights in armor, Wild West cowboys and saloon girls, 1920s flappers and dandies.

A big lion saunters towards me, walking on his hind legs. He's wearing a dirty polo shirt, Italian loafers and a big shiny watch. "I'm glad you're here, Herb!" he growls with long white teeth. "What would you like me to do for you?"

He seems like a nice lion and I'm not afraid. "I'm here to see Kitty and Iris Rose."

"Iris works in my costume department, that's where I got this shirt. Lovely girl. But Kitty? I can't say as if I've met anyone by that name."

I follow him to a station wagon with wooden sides and he gets in the passenger seat. "You need to drive, Leo's not allowed," he says. I get into the drivers' seat but don't know what to do other than what I've seen in the movies. I turn the key and the engine roars to life.

I find myself on the bustling highway, trying desperately to avoid hitting anything. There are orange trees in the middle of the road. People reach out of their car windows to grab fruit right off the tree.

I try it myself, but it causes me to lose control of the car and careen off a bridge. The car is falling, spinning, the roof tearing off, the lion flying away on wings. Someone new is sitting beside me. It's a man who looks like Myron, but tougher. He laughs in my face and I hear a loud, high, painful squealing sound...

143 ↠ Present Tense

...I wake to hear the squealing of the train's brakes. My excitement has turned to fear and sadness, but there's no turning back now. Outside are endless enclosures full of cows. *Click*. P-U, it stinks!

Lionel knocks on my door. "We're almost at the station. I'll see your bag gets to the Super Chief, and I'll reserve your room at the Ambassador."

The idea of renting a hotel room for a few hours to take a bath seems silly. I tell him, "I think I'd rather see the city, if that's OK."

"A-course it is, sir. I'll take care of it. Don't you worry 'bout a thing. Dearborn station is just hop, skip and a jump from State Street for shoppin' and eatin'. Ya gotta see the Art Institute, too, just a couple blocks north from there. I love me the Art Institute, 'specially them 'pressionists!"

I clean my camera lens and put rolls of film in my pocket. Finally, the train comes to a stop.

"We're here. Your train leaves at 7:15 from Track 1. You gotta be here by six thirty. The *Super Chief* waits for no-one, not even Gary Cooper. So's you knows, you gets a Santa Fe line porter for the rest of the trip. It's been a pleasure servin' you, Mr. Hamilton." He takes my bag.

"Thanks, Lionel." I give him a five dollar bill and he gives me a big smile. The station is so big and I don't know which way to go so I ask one of the cops. He points me in the right direction and in a few blocks I'm on State Street. *Click.*

It's a cool, sunny day as I walk down the street admiring the shop windows. *Click.* Something grabs my attention, big department store windows with elaborate dark green metal frames. I take a closeup. *Click.* At the corner of Madison and State is this magnificent round entrance with circular openings so lush they look like they grew out of the ground before turning to iron. *Click.* I've never seen anything like this, even in New York.

The ornate patterns fascinate me and I have to take photos of them. *Click. Closer. Click.* I go through the revolving door and from the inside, the round windows look as if they're being overgrown by cast iron ivy. *Click.*

Inside, the store is luxurious, with dozens of crystal chandeliers covering the ceiling. *Click.* There are so many beautiful things to buy. I remember my suitcase is already full... but there's a glass case full of watches.

Rolex. Cartier. A mature saleslady with silver hair drifts over and smiles at me. "May I help you, sir?" Her voice is smooth but she has a funny accent.

"I'd like to see this," I point to a Rolex.

"Very good choice, sir, an Oyster, completely waterproof!" I put my Mickey Mouse watch in my pocket and try on the Rolex. It doesn't appeal to me, and I can't imagine a situation where I'd wear my watch underwater. I hand it back to her and move down the case.

I lean into the case because the Cartier watches are more interesting. Simple. Elegant. I point at a rectangular silver one with a woven metal band.

"This is a solid gold *Tank Normale* with a gold mesh bracelet. Very chic, sir."

I slide it on and like the way the metal band is cool on my wrist. "What is the price of this?"

She looks on the underside of the watch stand. "Five hundred and fifty dollars, sir."

I let my fingers run over the metal. It's beautiful, and if I really wanted to, I could buy it. But I didn't know what awaits in Hollywood. What if I want to buy a house or a car but I'd spent that money on a watch? I hand it back to her.

Then I see a watch so different I don't care if it costs as much as a car. It reminds me of my Leica—a silver rectangle, brushed, not shiny. Blank except for two small windows through which you can read the time. The top window shows the hour number, the bottom window, curved like a smile, shows 20 minutes with a pointer in the middle marking the current one. It's the simplest, most modern watch I've ever seen. "May I see this one, please?"

"*Tank à Guichets jumping hours* with an ostrich band. The only one we have or are likely to get now."

The watch feels cool and smooth, like my camera. I hold it up to my ear and listen—the ticking is so quiet I can hardly hear it. "What is the price?"

"Two hundred and fifty dollars, sir. All Cartier watches include free yearly cleaning and lubrication, and a lifetime warranty. A fine value for a fine timepiece to hand down to your son." She reaches out her hand to take it from me, but I don't want to give it back.

"I'll take it. Can I write you a check?"

"Of course, sir, it will be $255 including tax. You may make it payable to Carsons." She hands me a pen, then retrieves a red leather watch box from under the counter.

I take out my wallet, pull out a check and stop. This is a lot of money. I look at the watch again. This is too much money. I stroke the watch. This is what money's for, right? I spell out, "Two hundred fifty five dollars and 00/100s," sign it and hand it to her.

"Would you like me to set the watch for you?"

"No, I can do it, thank you."

She puts the box into a small shopping bag with handles. "You may set it to our famous clock outside or inside, they're reset three times a day. I've put my card in the box, Mr. Hamilton. Please call if you have any questions or issues, we here at Carson Pirie Scott & Co. are committed to your complete satisfaction."

I check the time. The top window shows an "11" while the bottom window shows 25. "Excuse me, ma'am, where do you recommend for lunch?"

"The *Men's Grill* on the 9th floor is a favorite for customers of a male persuasion. The elevators are right that way, sir." I nod in thanks and walk towards the elevators. I look at my watch. It's beautiful. The clock over the elevators says 1:15. I pull out the stem at the top of the watch and turn it, watching the hour numbers jump to 12, then 1 and the minute numbers spin. There, 1:15.

"Ninth floor, please," I tell the young operator in a blue suit with gold buttons. His cheeks are very pink and he smells of mint. More shoppers, all ladies, fill the elevator, smelling like different flowers, their big feathered hats poking at me. We stop at nearly every floor so they can get off like a flock of birds. *Click.*

"Ninth floor, Heather House and Men's Grill restaurants."

I get off into a very plush room, all cream and gold. "One for lunch, please," I tell the hostess, a pretty young woman in a cream dress, with her blond hair in a bun. She looks like part of the decoration.

"Of course, if you'd like. But might I suggest you'll be more comfortable in the Men's Grill where cigar smoking is allowed. It's to the right down the hall."

"Thank you, miss," I say then walk down the hall. The Men's Grill looks more old-fashioned, which I like. The bottom half of the walls are caramel colored from years of smoke. The top half are covered in antique murals of men and dogs and deer.

The formal host stands at his podium, "Good afternoon sir, how many will be joining us for lunch today?"

"Just me," I say, unable to resist looking down at my new watch.

"That's an exceptional watch, sir."

"Thank you, I just bought it here."

"You are clearly a man of discerning taste. Right this way." He guides me to a table by the window where I can look out on the city and hands me a menu. I look around at the other patrons, all men, all much older than me.

I'm torn between the "Luncheon Suggestion" of Fried Chicken à la Maryland or the Duke of Windsor sandwich of turkey, Virginia ham, Swiss cheese and thousand island dressing on rye. I like the name "Duke of Windsor" but would rather have fried chicken. The waiter appears so silently I jump when he asks, "May I take your order, sir?"

I order and he asks, "Would you prefer a salad or French fries with that, sir?"

That's an easy one, I ask for the fries. It's only after he leaves that I wonder if fried chicken with fries isn't maybe too much fried food since I'll be back on the train in a few hours... but it sounds good anyway.

I look outside and watch the sidewalks, full of people. There are so many people in the world. I don't know most of them, and I've left most of the ones I do know behind. I start to get choked up then feel embarrassed, I don't want to cry in a public place, especially one filled with men. I pretend to cough and tell myself, "It's OK, I have a return train ticket, I can always come back in two weeks and it'll be like nothing's changed..." except I know that's a lie. If I come back in two weeks it'll be because neither Kitty or Iris wants me. What if I decide I don't want them? Neither of them are the same people... maybe what I want is what I had and can't have again.

Luckily the food arrives and I don't have to think about it. The fried chicken is the best I've ever had. It's light and crispy, not greasy, and it has a lot of spices: pepper, garlic, chili powder, oregano... and is that allspice? It's delicious. The fries are definitely not too much—every bite is crunchy, I love that!

I look at my watch again. I love it, too! Maybe it's easier to love things than people. I guess I'll find out soon enough.

I finish and the waiter brings a dessert menu. I'm already full but hear myself reading the menu aloud, "Heather House Pie: Tempting ice cream meringue with graham cracker crust and a rum sauce," The waiter writes it down and I don't stop him.

I'd never had pie made out of ice cream, these Chicago people sure know how to eat! The top is a browned meringue covering deep gold vanilla ice cream, and on the side is a little silver pot filled with hot rum sauce so I can pour as much as I want, and I want it all!

It's so delicious but now I'm so full I feel like I could bust. I use a traveler's cheque to pay and the waiter gives me cash back, surprising because I thought he'd give me smaller travelers cheques back. Then I think about how much money I've spent and feel sweaty and dizzy but maybe that's because I'm too full. I look at my beautiful watch again, 2:30, and waddle out of the restaurant.

Back out on the street my watch looks even better in the sunlight! I'm so busy looking at it I run into a very tall man in a brown suit. Brown?

"Watch where you're going, asshole," he grunts, then looks down at me. All I can think of is, "Don't hurt my camera... or my watch... oh yeah, not me, either!"

He stops and looks... hungry. "I want that watch, kid."

I reach in my pocket and grab two silver dollars and throw them at him as I book it down the street as fast as I can which doesn't feel fast as my stomach sloshes. I'm sorry if he was hungry but he wasn't getting my watch. I stop around the corner and pant, I'm too full to run any farther. Maybe he was just being nice and admiring my watch and *I* was an asshole? I peek back around the corner and he's gone.

I keep walking in the opposite direction anyway, and then I see a building with columns and lion statues and a sign, "Art Institute of Chicago." Lionel told me about this. I walk up the stairs into the main hall and ask the lady at the information booth where the 'pressionists room is. She rolls her eyes and points to the left.

144 ➽ 'Pressionists

At first I only see black and white sketches but as I move down the hall they get more and more colorful, making me sad that I only have black and white film.

I'm stopped in my tracks by the color coming from a room on my left. So much color! Color that doesn't just speak to me, it yells. I look up and see "Impressionists" above the door.

I shuffle in, unable to take my eyes off the paintings, especially a wall-sized one of people, standing stiffly, in a park. It's dazzling, and sparkles in a way I've never seen before. As I get closer I see it's made entirely out of small dots of color. I'm transfixed and keep moving closer.

"Sir, please step back," the guard tells me.

"Oh, I'm sorry, I didn't realize..." noticing my nose was almost touching the painting.

The guard puts his arm between me and the painting, "Happens all the mother lovin' time."

I keep staring, unable to figure out how, at a distance, the dots come together as solid shapes and colors. Click (without color). I lose track of time staring at it. I read a card on the wall next to it. "Un dimanche après-midi à l'Île de la Grande Jatte (A Sunday Afternoon on the Island of La Grande Jatte), Georges Seurat, 1884 to 1886."

As glorious as this is, as I turn my head I see that the rest of the room is filled with mouth watering paintings, too. Up close, this one looks like a mess, but step back and it's sublime water lilies. Next to it... look at the card... another Monet, this one of haystacks. I wish I could get this kind of effect with my camera.

This one's a boring, fuzzy woman and parasols. Renoir. Eh. Wait, what is this one? A woman with a green face in the corner, behind her a woman with red hair, men in top hats. It feels dark but the color is still so strong... Lautrec, it looks both exciting and sad.

I am moved to tears by a painting of a man with a red beard and green eyes... Van Gogh... maybe because he reminds me of Sergei, but it's more than that. There's such swirling energy, sparks of red and touches of green on his face. His expression of weary distrust, as if he's saying I couldn't possibly understand him or what he saw. And yet, I can see how he saw, right there in that painting, and the one next to it —his bedroom with blue walls and a yellow chair. I can see what it was like to be in his head full of color and motion.

It's just paint and canvas, yet I can *feel* it. How can so much emotion be contained in paintings from 50 years ago? I wonder if my work will make people feel, now, much less in the far future of 1990.

All these paintings are talking to me in a language I don't yet understand. A language of emotion through shape and color.

The guard tells me the museum is closing. Already? I look at my watch, it's 5pm. I feel like I've only been here for five minutes, but it's been hours. I take one last look—not a photo—I want to remember them, in color.

Back on the street I ask another cop how to get to Dearborn station and he points down Michigan Ave and tells me to turn right on 8th.

I walk down Michigan, tall buildings on my right and a park across a wide boulevard. The buildings are apartments, hotels, offices and... a shoe store with Italian loafers in the window. Why not?

"Welcome, sir, and how may I assist you today?"

"I'd like to try on a pair of your shoes." I say, while wondering, "Why am I doing this? Nobody's going to think I'm a producer... but 'When in Rome...'" I don't want to look like some rube from the Bronx, no, I want to fit in!

"Please sit and I'll find your size." I sit and he pulls out a silver metal device with a lot of markings on it. He places my foot into the cold metal contraption, then slides some pieces to measure the length and width of my foot, plus one more whose job seems only to jab into my arch.

"Size 12," he announces, oddly envious. I look and he has very small feet. He's short, with dark hair and a five o'clock shadow. His sad expression reminds me of Van Gogh's. "We have many styles to choose from but I brought you the best we have, newly imported Salvatore Ferragamo, I hear they're all the rage in Hollywood." He opens three boxes, pulls a shoe from each, and holds them up for me.

One is tan with cream stitching, the next is a dark brown with black stitching. The third is black with red stitching. The red stitching gets me. I point to them, "I'd like to try these." He slips the black and red loafer on my foot. Why do I feel like Cinderella? Because it's just so beautiful. "Wow."

"Would you like to try on the left shoe?"

I nod, enthusiastically. He puts it on my foot.

"Walk around and try them out," he says. I do. "How do they feel?"

They are surprisingly comfortable. I've never had new shoes that weren't painful. Normally they're stiff and pinch my toes or dig into my ankle or cause a blister. Ma would insist I just had to break them in. She'd spray them with water and make me walk around the block six times. When I'd get home my feet were sore, even a little bloody, but eventually I'd get used to them. These are comfortable right from the start. "They feel like wearing slippers!"

"I'm sure you're aware of the new way to wear these."

"Which new way... there are so many..." I bluff.

"You put a penny in the slot in front. It adds a hint of flash."

Sold. Though I think I'll put dimes in because they're silver, and if I lose my wallet I can still make a phone call!

"I have two Canadian pennies for the man who desires the unusual."

That's me! I think about how I will put coins in from every country I visit... except I wasn't going to go to England now. "I'll take these, thanks." I'd forgotten to ask how much they cost. Did it even matter at this point?

"$24.50 sir."

I have more than enough cash in change from lunch. I hand him the money and he gives me change, then, separately, two Canadian pennies.

"Would you like to wear these now?"

"Absolutely!"

"I'll put your old shoes in the bag for you. May I put your other shopping bag in this one for your convenience?"

He was so nice—should I tip him? It never hurts. I give him two dollars.

Walking down the avenue feels different. I stand taller and take longer strides. I feel... more adult.

I look at my old shoes in the bag. I don't want them anymore. I see a bum sitting on the sidewalk. "Want a pair of shoes?" I ask. He reaches out and I hand them over.

I feel new from my wrist to my feet. Now I need a hat. But I don't know what kind. I'll ask June. I look at my sleek watch and supple shoes.

I'm gonna be a new man when I get to Hollywood.

145 ➽ Trading

I find the right track, and am shown to my car. As I climb into it, I trip and drop the bag with my watch box. I lean down to get it and as I stand, run smack dab into... a brown suit. I look up. Towering over me is the man who tried to steal my watch earlier!

My muscles tense and I'm ready to strike, when he says "Nice shoes," reaching into his pocket and handing me two silver dollars. "I think you dropped these."

I relax, embarrassed, "I'm so sorry..."

"I've never had anyone throw money at me. I liked it. Hello, I'm Abe Stoneman."

"Herb Hamilton. I just bought this new watch and I thought you wanted to steal it."

We shake hands and his grip is very firm. "I would absolutely steal it if I had a chance. I've been trying to find a Cartier Tank à guichets for ages. Where on earth did you find it?"

"Carson Pirie & Scott." I hold the watch up for him to admire.

"I would never have thought they'd have one in this hog town. No matter, how much do you want for it?" He wraps his large hand around my wrist and touches the watch gently with his other.

"I just bought it!"

"Good, then you aren't emotionally attached to it and will sell it to me."

"I'm not interested in selling it."

"Do you even know what you have? It's very rare, I know, I collect them." With his hand still grasping my wrist he displays his other wrist. "It's a platinum Cartier perpetual triple calendar moonphase tank. I'll trade."

I look at his, rectangular like mine, but with more dials, the day and month in little windows, then a hand pointing to the date around the edge, and the little moon phase at the bottom. Very fancy, but I like mine.

"Mine cost $950. Did you pay retail for yours? Of course you did. You'll still get the better end of the deal."

"I don't..."

"I'm not going to lie, yours is rare—only 50 were made and The Maharaja of Patiala has five. I only want one." He holds my wrist tighter. He's tall and I look up through his round tortoise shell glasses into his intense brown eyes.

"Abe, that's a very generous offer but..." I pull my wrist out of his grasp.

"Nice shoes, too, Where'd you get them?" He changed the subject.

Now he wants my shoes? I look at his, also Italian loafers, blue with red stitching, ooh, nice!

"I'll trade shoes if you want."

"Just tell me where you got them. I've never thought about shopping in Chicago. I go to the Ambassador East, take a bath, dine at the Pump room... Oh, well, next time. So it's a trade?"

"Sorry, no."

"Yours doesn't even say 'Cartier' on it so you're not going to impress anyone with it."

"I got it because I like it. Besides, it impressed you..."

"Nobody in Hollywood cares what something's actually worth, only how much someone else wants it. I'm the only one there who'll want yours because you can't wear it to the studio."

"Then where would you wear it?"

"To bed. I always wear a watch. Always. I wear one of my Rolex Oyster Perpetuals in the bath. I don't like being late."

"Let me think about it."

"We're going to be on the train for two days, you'll have plenty of time to change your mind."

"I don't think so. I like the way mine goes with my Leica."

His intense eyes crinkle into a smile. "I have three Leicas and no one coordinates their watch with their camera. It's simply not done. I can tell this is your first visit to Hollywood, right? Look, kid, I'm just trying to help you out. Here's my card. Abe Stoneman, head of production at 20th Century Fox, so it behooves you to be on my good side. What are you, a writer or an actor?"

"I'm a photographer for *Look* magazine."

"We're good to people in the press who are good to us, if you know what I mean. I hope you'll come to your senses before we reach Los Angeles. I'm in suite 3G."

He shakes my hand, again holding on too long while eyeing my watch before turning and walking down the hall. My hand is sweating.

146 ➻ Turquoise Room

"His name is Abe Stoneman." I tell June over a steak dinner in the exclusive Turquoise Room where she insisted we eat because "anybody who's anybody dines there and we want to be seen."

"Abe Stoneman? You told him about me, right?

"I didn't know I was supposed to mention you, I mean, he's a studio executive so I didn't think you'd be interested..."

"He's head of production! That's the top producer! Oh, my, you are so green."

"I'm sorry, I didn't know that. You didn't tell me that."

She looks around, feverishly, "Is he here?"

"He's in suite 3G."

"Good. I'll casually hang around outside his door and when he comes out I'll slip and fall. He'll have to pick me up and take me back to his room because my ankle will be too sore to walk and then I'll make things happen from there. Hmm... Fox. It's not MGM... But MGM could loan me out... I could get bigger rolls because they have smaller stars. Oh, wait, you said he was holding your wrist, maybe he'd prefer you."

"He was only interested in my watch."

"What does he look like? Just so I'll be prepared for the inevitable disappointment."

"He's tall. Kinda mean. Brown eyes. Round glasses. Little mustache..."

"Like Clark Gable. I loved his mustache... kissing wasn't itchy, and he knew how to use it in other ways... You done good, Herb, and you didn't even know you were doing good. Imagine how good you're gonna do when you're out to do good. You'll give him the watch, right?"

"No, I like it."

"Wise up, you can get another watch."

"I can't get another watch like this."

"No, what you can't get is another chance with a head of production at a major studio. You gotta get your priorities straight!" She holds up her knife, looks at her reflection and arranges her hair.

147 ➟ All Wet

I'm too excited to sleep. My roomette is like the previous one, but the upholstery is red mohair with an Indian blanket pattern of yellow and black. I pick up a brochure on the seat and read:

"Take Santa Fe all the way on the Super Chief —the train extraordinaire… Extra fine, extra fare, extra comfort… A space and time conquering service…. 60 miles per hour… swift…. sure… safe… Catering for people who are bred to gracious living! Meeting the epicure's every want and whim… Enjoy our PleasureDome observation car and experience glorious first hand landscapes from a reclining and swiveling balcony seat… Experience one of our three dining cars and exclusive Turquoise Room for relaxation, refreshment and superb food, exquisitely prepared. Before reaching your destination you might want to freshen up with a shower, shave and haircut at our barber for the men, or salon for the ladies. Such is life on Santa Fe's super chief…"

Wow, this is exciting! I walk down the hall. The porter hails me, "How'd ya do, Sir, I'm your porter, Jacob. Lemme know if there's anythin' I can do for you."

"Hi, Jacob. Actually, there is… I'd like to take a shower."

"The barbershop done closed right now," he looks around to see if anyone is listening, "But I gots a key and can let you in, just don't go tellin' nobody, OK?"

"Thank you, Jacob, that's very kind," I said, pulling a $5 bill out of my wallet.

"No, sir, you're the one who's too kind, follow me."

"You can call me Herb."

"Thank you, Mr. Herb, sir."

We walk through two cars of sleeper rooms and a dining car and reach a door that says, 'Greg Abbott, Master Barber.' Jacob unlocks the door and flips the lights on. "There's soap and shampoo and towels inside. I gotta go back to my post. I'll lock the door but you can still get out."

"Thank you Jacob, much appreciated!"

The room is a miniature barbershop with one big chair, mirror, and a lot of scissors and knives held in place with straps. In the back is a door labeled 'Shower' and next to it, a cabinet filled with white towels. I put my clothes and watch in a wicker basket.

The stall is small but the water is hot. For a moment I forget that I'm taking a shower going 60 miles per hour on my way towards California! What could be more modern!

Suddenly I'm thrown against the wall of the shower, lose my footing and land on my wet butt. I hear the squealing of brakes and scramble to my feet, wrapping myself in a towel. I step outside the barbershop to see what's the matter. It's nothing, we're just pulling into a station. I'll go back in and get dressed... but it's locked!

I'm dripping wet in the hallway as I hear the train car doors open! I run through the empty dining car, narrowly avoiding an aghast woman in a fur coat, then down the next car and finally to my car... only to run into Abe!

"Where's your watch?" he asks. "You wouldn't want someone stealing it now, would you?" he laughs, looking me up and down. "I think I'll head to the barber shop..."

"No!" I yell and he steps back, knocking into Jacob carrying a bag.

"Best to get back to your room now, sir," Jacob whispers to me, "I'll come and check on you in a bit."

I turn and take a step towards my room but my towel's stuck on something... Abe's hand! I try to yank it back but people are getting on the train so let go, cover myself, duck directly into my room... and worry that Abe will get to the barbershop before I can. I throw on some clothes and dodge passengers and porters on my way back to the barbershop... where Abe is calmly waiting.

"Are you kidding me?" I pant, exasperated.

"What?" Abe laughs. "Relax, I'm just fucking with you, Herb. But seriously, I want that watch. Don't worry though, I won't steal it." He takes off his fancy watch and drops it in my coat pocket. "Consider it a... gift. The nice thing about giving someone a gift in Hollywood is that then they owe you a favor. Now you owe me." He turns and saunters down the hall.

Jacob appears, shaking his head, "What 'cha doing running around all nekked like... sir?"

"I'm sorry, Jacob."

"Don't needs to apologize to me but I heard some ladies talking!" he laughs and unlocks the door.

I go inside, put on my watch and collect my clothes. I take another five from my wallet and hand it to him.

"Never you mind, it's all fine, sir. On this train, a good tip makes up for bad behavior. You have a good night, now, sir, and if you need me, press the little red button next to your reading lamp."

As I sulk back towards my car, I hear giggling behind me, pull up my collar, and keep walking.

148 ➥ Stone Man

I pull down the bed and climb into it, embarrassed and exhausted. I stare at the ceiling, watching shadows dart by, too fast. The click-clack of the tracks is soothing and I close my eyes...

...Suddenly a gigantic stone hand appeared outside the window of my room. It smashed through the glass and reached in, wrapping around me like I was Fay Wray in *King Kong*. Struggling was no use, the hand was too big and too strong as it tightened around me, pulling me through the window, dangling me above the landscape whizzing by at 60 miles per hour. It lifted me above the train and I noticed it was wearing a Cartier watch bigger than I was, each tick an explosion!

Up and up I went until I was faced with a massive mouth, smiling, exposing long, tall stalactite teeth. “Give it to me!!!” the giant bellowed, it’s foul breath stung my eyes. “I am the Stoneman and I will have what I want or I will crush you!” he yelled, tightening his fist, pushing the air out of me. I tried to scream but couldn’t breathe...

...I wake up, gasping for breath as the moonlit desert speeds by.

I hate Hollywood and I’m not even there yet.

149 ➳ Get Outta Dodge

The light wakes me as the train slows. A sign outside reads, “Dodge City, Kansas.” *Click!*

I jump out of bed, excited. I’ve seen this town in *Frontier Marshal* starring Randolph Scott playing Wyatt Earp. I bound down the stairs onto the platform. *Click!*

“Where ya goin, sir?” Jacob calls after me.

“I want to see Dodge City!” *Click!*

“Ya better make it snappy, cause in three minutes we’re gonna get outta Dodge!”

“Three minutes?”

He looks at his watch. “Two and a half minutes now.”

I look at the station, not much to see. Next to it are buildings that look nothing like the old Western town in the movies. As I get back on the train I notice Jacob shaking his head.

“What?”

“You young, aint’ you, sir?”

I get back on the train. There’s June. “I was looking for you—come with me,” her bright red fingernails digging into me. She opens the door to her room and pulls me inside. “I saw Danny outside Abe’s room which either means Abe is funny, and not in the fun way, at least for me, or Danny's trying to spread dirt, either way you've got to stop him."

"Me?"

"Of course, you know Abe."

"I only know he wants my watch!"

"And you've decided to give it to him, that's your pretext for going to his room."

"I have not decided…" I groan.

She slaps my face, hard, like in a detective movie. "I've decided for you, since you don't have the sense to figure it out on your own. You'll thank me later, I promise."

"Or what?"

"Or I'll give you head, what do you want me to say? Don't be a schmuck. You know what that guy can do to you if he doesn't like you? End your career in Hollywood."

"I don't have a career in Hollywood."

"Well, I do! And you'll want one once you get there, I mean, who wouldn't. Sunshine, orange trees by the swimming pool of your mansion. No more cramped studio apartments shared with three other chorus girls…"

"Look, June, I know I'm your knight in shining armor and all, but you're asking me to hand over part of my armor…"

"I'm not asking, I'm telling." She turns away, dramatically. "OK, so don't do it. But don't cry to me when you end up arrested for a crime you didn't commit because Stoneman fingered you… Oh, that sounds wrong, but good… I mean 'puts the finger on you'… You're too pretty for prison, trust me, I know. Not to mention *my* ruined life will be on *your* hands."

Everything she said sounds a bit too familiar, like I'm remembering it from a movie, but her tears look real enough. I don't want to be looking over my shoulder for Abe, I've only had the watch a day… and her fingernails are digging into me again as she sobs against my chest, quite convincingly.

"What am I supposed to tell him about you?"

"That my mother was a Dutch nun who gave up the order to marry my father, an Irish policeman, and I'm pure as the driven snow and the most talented singer/dancer you've ever seen in your short but sophisticated life."

"Is that true? I mean the nun and policeman thing?"

"It's a good story, that's all that matters. The truth isn't pretty. Eleanor Geisman, Jewish, the Bronx. You?"

"Herbie Horowitz, Jewish, Bronx, too."

"So you understand?"

"Fine, I'll give it to him, but I don't like it."

She stops sobbing and lifts her head from my chest, her makeup still perfect. "Nobody likes it but everybody wants it, that's how Hollywood works."

150 ➠ 3G

I stand outside his door and sigh. Almost knock. Sigh again. Knock. No answer, good, I can leave and say... the door opens and Abe's grin is almost as big as the one in my dream.

"I knew you'd come to your senses."

I close my eyes, undo the watch from my wrist and hand it to him. "Here. I hope you're happy."

"Ecstatic!" He stares at it like a starving man looks at a brisket and literally kisses it!

"You owe me," I say, trying not to sound as angry as I feel.

"Actually, I don't... why don't you come in and I'll explain how it works."

I roll my eyes and sit on his sofa.

"I gave you my watch, so you're not doing me a favor, you're returning one, we're even."

I pull his watch out of my pocket and hold it out for him to take. He doesn't.

"You keep it. Oh, I see, you want me to owe you. Fine, what do you want?"

"Ignore Danny Kaye, my friend June Allyson's mother was a Dutch nun who gave up the order to marry her father, an Irish policeman. She's as pure as the driven snow and the most talented singer/dancer I've ever seen in my short but sophisticated life."

He stares at me, then laughs. "That makes one thing clear—you're no actor... Wait, that's it? Really? Oh, please, Danny's a nudnik, and everybody knows June... biblically. I hear she's good, though, is she?"

"We're just friends."

"So you're a fairy?"

"I'm going to Hollywood to see my *girlfriends*."

"Girlfriends? Good for you. OK, so you did your duty for your friend, June. Look, kid, you've got a good eye and I admire your taste. So tell me what I can do for you. I'm being nice here, you won't get another chance like this in Hollywood." He kinda looks like a nice guy, now.

"What I want isn't something you can give me."

"You'd be surprised."

"No, you would."

"I rarely am—but you surprise me, Herb. It's not often that a young comer like you isn't asking something of me. Reminds me of myself at your age... which makes me *want* to do you a favor. You've got my card. Look me up if you need something. If anybody asks where you got your watch, tell them 'Stoneman' and that can unlock a few doors, too."

Other than being a greedy bastard, Abe seems like a pretty nice guy.

151 ➽ PleasureDome

I look at his watch, now on my wrist. It's beautiful. Better than anything I ever thought I'd have. All this is better than anything I ever even dreamed of. I forget how lucky I am.

I don't feel like being alone and remember the brochure said, "Visit the beautiful PleasureDome for fabulous vistas and the informal flow of social pleasantry."

I walk back four cars and climb the narrow stars to a car with windows on the ceiling. I settle into one of the swivel chairs and face the window, watching the cactus fly by. They look just like in the movies, only in color!

All the colors are wonderful, the reddish ground and hills, the green cacti, the gold brush... I could watch this for hours.

I sit back in my plush seat, the color swimming in my head mixed with the steady click clack of the track...

...I was sitting across the table from Kitty, as beautiful as ever. She was wearing the first thing I ever saw her in, pink and flimsy. She looked at me with love in her eyes, genuine love, and I reached my hand out to hers... She smiled, then snarled, revealing long, sharp teeth.

Her claws dug into my hand as she pulled it close and bit me, hard, her teeth going all the way through. I screamed in pain as she pulled me even closer and growled "I will kill you." I felt dizzy and faint and knocked over the vase on the table full of flowers... Irises... I apologized to the flowers, "I'm sorry I dragged you into all this," then one flower stood on its stem, walked across the table and smacked itself into Kitty's terrifying tiger nose. Kitty sniffed and shook her head... then sneezed, repeatedly, releasing my hand. The Iris leapt into the air and landed in my coat pocket and together we ran into the sunset...

...My eyes open—I'm panting, and my hand has marks from my own fingernails digging in. Outside, the sunset is turning the desert from pink and orange into dark red and purple. I'm shaking. Scared. And disappointed I can only capture the view in black and white.

152 ➟ Turquoise

The train slows again, this time at the nearly unpronounceable Albuquerque. Outside the train are Indians in their colorful clothes, holding trays of handicrafts, turquoise rings and pins and those western string ties.

As the train slows I ask Jacob, "How long do we stop here?"

"You gotta whole 20 minutes while we refuel and take on supplies, so it's OK to get off and buy something from these nice native folk, just don't leave the station. D'ya understand me this time... sir?"

"I'll check my watch and everything, promise."

The train stops and I'm the first out. I have never seen real live Indians before. *Click* They're beautiful! *Click*. Their brown skin and black hair glows in the setting sun. I want to look at what they're selling but I'm so distracted by their wondrous faces.

A short old woman who looks like Mother Nature herself, looks me up and down, then grabs my wrist with her tiny soft hand. "Come, there is something for you here."

She leads me away from the train to where a young woman waits, wearing a white dress embroidered with orange, yellow and red flowers. She is breathtakingly beautiful, more beautiful than any woman I've seen in the Westerns. Why is she not a movie star?

"May I take your picture?" I ask, and she smiles, turning the sunset into a sunrise. *Click*. Indians were always the bad guys in the movies, but these people are beautiful and serene.

She holds up a string tie with a large piece of turquoise surrounded by silver and speaks with the voice of a dove. "This is magical. It is calling for you. You must have it."

She hands it to me. As I take it, her fingers touch mine. I feel like I have jumped 100 years back in time into another life. The irregularly shaped chunk of turquoise is simultaneously cold and hot, with cracks of silver running through it.

The young woman turns the stone face down in my hand and closes my fingers around it. It seems to buzz. "It has been waiting... yes, it is yours. Take it."

Suddenly I can smell flowers, sand and the woman's skin. I can hear insects buzzing and the breeze blowing. I don't want to let this go...

"How much is this?" I ask.

Her face falls. "It is priceless. It wants to wear you. Take it."

Everyone else has gone and the train is starting to move. The old woman puts her hand on my neck and pulls me towards the train, the young woman whispering in my ear, "My name is Tsís'ná," as her hand slips from mine.

"I don't understand, Please, please take this." I pull out my wallet and hand the old woman a $100 traveler's cheque. She doesn't take it and I see it float away on the breeze.

The train starts to move faster and I run to catch it, grab for the handrail and jump on the step. The women smile, wave, and disappear into the distance.

I open my hand and it is empty. The train is picking up speed, and a cloud of red dust surrounds me, stinging my eyes. I feel my way up the stairs and into the train, looking out at the darkening desert.

I cough, and as I raise my hand to my chest, I feel the turquoise around my neck.

153 ⇒ Desert-ed

I sit in my room, half of me watching the moonlight desert fly by, the other half looking down into the turquoise stone shot with silver lighting. I suddenly feel sick as I question why I've come on this trip.

The turquoise is the earth, yet I ride in this machine, headed for more machinations. Towards glitz and glamour and maybe love, maybe, but how much of that is real and how much is just movie magic?

Do I love Kitty? Or do I just want to? Am I only pretending we're both in a movie with a happily-ever-after that hasn't happened yet?

I think Iris loves me, and I feel a bond with Myron. Has he always really been Iris or is he someone else now, a familiar stranger?

And what of this blue stone in my hand and the woman who gave it to me, whose name I couldn't pronounce and have already forgotten? I didn't know her but she seemed to recognize me on sight.

I inspect the stone. Touch it. Let the color penetrate me. I turn it over and see how the silver cradles this fragment of nature. The back and the front of the rock look similar, it's solid, not some superficial facade. Real—not paper thin, like photographs.

I see some scratches on the back, turn on the reading lamp and look more closely. It says "Tsís'ná Bitł'izh." Tsís'ná is her name. Below it... a series of numbers... a phone number.

I can call her once I get to Hollywood. But what will I say? All this is a question without an answer.

I hear a rumbling from deep inside me but it only tells me I'm hungry.

I walk to the Turquoise Room and look forward to a quiet meal by myself. I follow the maître d', trip and find myself falling. I grab a corner of a table and right myself, hearing sniggering. I look up to see Danny, his leg stuck out into the aisle.

"Very mature, Danny."

"Since when did we get on a first name basis... I can't remember *your* name."

"Just as well."

"Don't be rude, of course you recognize my dinner companion, Larry."

"Hello, Larry. Good luck with this one."

"You don't recognize me, do you?" Larry says in his English accent.

"Don't be offended, the little idiot doesn't recognize anybody."

Larry reaches out his hand, like a gentleman. "Larry Olivier, pleased to make your acquaintance..."

"It's a pleasure to meet a real gentleman, Larry."

Danny whispers, loudly, "Our friend here is playing by June's rules that one should never sleep with an actor."

Larry giggles, "Good thing you didn't tell me that sooner, my boy!"

I look at the patient maître d'. "I must be going, goodnight." He seats me at a small table at the end of the car. I study the other diners, well-dressed, respectable looking. But how many of them actually are?

There, in another corner, is June, sitting across from Abe. Good for her. They both see me and smile. I hope they're happy, even if it's just for tonight.

Maybe that's how it is. Maybe everything is just for today. Why not have the best. I order the Table d'Hote dinner: Mexican vegetable juice cocktail, Philadelphia pepper pot soup, Florida hearts of celery, chicken risotto Piedmontaise, new peas Francaise, California romaine and orange salad, New Orleans apple fritters glacee with chocolate sauce, and French Roquefort cheese.

I like being on my own, then I notice my thumb is rubbing the turquoise around my neck. I'm not alone.

The vegetable juice cocktail is awful, but then I hate tomato juice. Everything else is tasty. I'd never had risotto, I didn't know it was rice and chicken, it's so good. The peas are, once again, tiny—and are joined by tiny onions, too. I wonder if everything in LA will be miniature and only looks big on the screen... Oranges in salad? They sound weird but taste wonderful. I'm too full for dessert and eat it anyway because these are like big donut holes I can dip in chocolate sauce. Finally, cheese with blue streaks that look like it's gone bad. It tastes kind of bad, too, but luckily I still have chocolate sauce I can eat with a spoon.

The meal is $2.25 and I leave a two-dollar tip, then head upstairs to the PleasureDome and watch the stars through the ceiling windows. Windows in the ceiling remind me of the apartment with Kitty... no, I'm not going to think about that. I'm going to think about where I am, speeding through the Wild West in the lap of luxury.

I'm sleepy. I go back to my room and get in bed. We arrive in Hollywood tomorrow morning. The excitement has evaporated, leaving me feeling empty and sad and scared. I wish I knew what was going to happen. I do know that if all else fails, I'll be back on the train in two weeks going east.

Everything will be as it was, but nothing will be the same.

154 ➤➤ L.A. Times

The sun wakes me up. We come to a stop in a town called Barstow where there's nothing but a station.

I look at my watch... fancy, but it doesn't feel like mine. 5:30am. I'm too excited to go to sleep. I hear something hit the floor outside my door and open it to find the *Los Angeles Times* newspaper.

I bring it into my room and look at the headlines. "Nazis decree book purge for all Alsatian homes..." "28,739 Reservists called into Army..." "Liner Torpedoed: Western Prince, bound for England, sunk 410 miles from the Irish Coast..." If I'd sailed for London I might be at the bottom of the Atlantic right now...

I turn the page and an ad catches my eye, "Alexander and Oviatt Haberdashery Finest Men's Hats!" complete with pictures of some very Hollywood hats!

"Studio settles with Fanny Brice for $30,000." Seems 20th Century Fox (Abe!) made a picture called "Rose of Washington Square" that she says was based on her life but the studio claims it couldn't be true because "that nice Alice Faye looks nothing like Brice."

"Another Fine Mess? Stan Laurel Accused of Planning to Bury Wife in Backyard... Stan married Ida Ketiva (Kitaeva) Raphael, widow of an internationally known concertina virtuoso named "Raphael Raphael Raphael..."

"Mutterings: Studio heads who console themselves after flop previews with the fact that 'no one walked out' should remember that few people are sleepwalkers!"

"The police squad raided the stage production, 'White Cargo,' at the Beaux Arts Theater and arrested Patricia Sunders, 19, of 1126½ W. 17th St who rose from usherette to the leading role of Tondeleyo. She was booked in City Jail on suspicion of participating in an indecent show."

Los Angeles sounds as dramatic as the movies!

WAIT, WHAT?

On the third page is a gruesome photo of a dead man in a car. The caption reads, "Man found dead in stolen car." Something about him looks familiar. I read the story, "A dead man was found yesterday morning in the otherwise deserted Santa Monica beach parking lot. He had attached a hose to his car's exhaust and died of an overdose of phenobarbital and carbon monoxide poisoning."

"Society register member David Cooper was found dead of an apparent suicide. Rumors of late state that his wife, Heiress Clara Cooper of the Newport Coopers, had started divorce proceedings..."

Suddenly everything is quiet. I feel like I've stopped breathing. The paper slips out of my hands and I stare at the wall. It's getting lighter outside and I can't move. I feel sick.

The click clack of the wheels on the track is deafening. My face feels very hot. He had to have been there to see Kitty! Is she OK? What if he did something to her? I must find her.

There's a knock on my door and I hear Jerome say, "Next stop Pasadena, then we arrive at Union Station at 9am. I suggest you have breakfast now and I'll pack for you."

I can't even answer and hear him knocking on other doors, saying the same thing, over and over. I'm in shock and I'm hungry. I put on my dark blue trousers, light blue shirt and cream raw silk jacket, turquoise string tie.

I walk to the dining car, feeling dapper yet dazed. I'm seated and try to read the menu. Sirloin? Calves liver? This isn't breakfast. David dead in a car... Griddle cakes with bacon... Buckwheat cakes with little piggy sausages... Poached egg. They all sound sickening.

"May I take your order, sir?"

"I'll have the Kitty... I mean the corned beef hash."

All this is happening and it's like I'm on another planet where I can't get in contact with... I don't have her number anyway so how will I... I can't think about this now... I should have ordered the griddle cakes... Two men blown up in front of me, an arm dangling from a tree...

I'm overcome with dizziness. I hail the waiter, "I need orange..." I think about the lion in the car with the orange trees... I can't talk.

"Orange juice? Of course, sir."

It'll be all right. I'll be OK. Here's the orange juice. It's sweet and tangy and cold. I don't care that David's dead, that's what he deserved... that's a terrible thing to think but Hitler deserves to be dead, too and that's not terrible but David wasn't exactly Hitler but I hated him, too and that didn't cause him to die or Hitler would be dead.

Corned beef hash. Crispy. Greasy. Great. It'll be all right. I'll be OK.

155 ➠ Hollywood, USA

As we pull into Union Station I'm still dizzy with excitement and fear. Jacob is standing on the platform with the luggage. "Thanks again, and sorry!" I say, handing him a $5 bill.

"Thank you most kindly. The Beverly Hills Hotel driver will have a sign with your name on it. Enjoy your stay in the city of angels!"

The city of angels? From what I just read it's full of devils, too. But my angels are here, aren't they? I take a deep breath. I never thought I'd breathe the same air as movie stars, or see the palm trees here in person. It's bright and sunny, a far cry from the snow when I left New York.

A Red Cap takes my bags and I follow him down the train, down the stairs and into the large Spanish-style main hall, so different from Grand Central Station, warmer and friendlier. *Click.* There is a fireplug of a man in a black driver's cap holding a sign with my name. "Herbert Hamilton." *Click.* I'd almost forgotten when that wasn't always my name.

"I'm Mr. Hamilton," I tell him. "I need a minute to make a phone call, is that OK?"

"Of course, sir. Let me take your bags and I'll show you to the pay phones." I follow him to an entire wall of dark wood pay phone booths. I close the door and notice it has a little fan. I fish out a nickel and dial zero.

"I'd like to speak to MGM, please."

"You'll need to dial 113 for directory assistance, sir. Goodbye."

I hang up and the nickel falls into the return tray. I put it back in the slot on top and dial 113.

"Good morning, how may I help you?"

"I'd like to speak to MGM studios, please."

"The number is MGM-1111. May I connect you?"

"Yes, thank you."

I hear the ring tone. "MGM Studio answering service."

"I'd like to speak to Miss Kitty Rose."

"I'm sorry, sir, but the studio is closed. This is the answering service. I can leave a message if you'd like."

"Yes, please tell Miss Rose to contact Herb Horo... Hamilton at the Beverly Hills Hotel. Thanks."

"I've taken your message and it will be delivered on Monday during normal business hours."

Monday? "What is today?" I asked the driver.

"It's Sunday, December 15th, sir."

"Sorry, I got mixed up because of the long train ride."

"Of course, sir, it's very common. Please follow me to the front and I'll bring the car around."

Out in front of the station the sunlight is so bright my eyes are watering. Was it ever this bright in New York? I wipe my eyes and it feels like I've been crying, which I could be, because it's so exciting and terrifying at the same time.

It's hard to see through the squinting. I see why they all wear sunglasses, I will get some today. And a hat.

A big black car pulls up. The driver puts my bags in the trunk... He opens the door for me and I get in, relieved to be out of the glare. It's such a nice car... oh, a Cadillac! The brown mohair velvet upholstery is as nice as any sofa I ever sat on.

The city rolls by outside the windows and cool air is pouring through a vent. A car with air conditioning? I am living in the future.

"Excuse me..." I say to the driver.

"What is it sir, am I driving too fast for your taste?"

"No, not at all, I just wanted to know your name."

"Bob, sir."

"Thank you, Bob, you're an excellent driver."

"Thank you, sir. Is this your first time in Los Angeles?"

"Yes, it is."

"I would be pleased to show you around if you'd like."

"That's so kind, thank you!"

"I was going to take Sunset for speed, but how about I show you Hollywood Boulevard? Sid Grauman's famous Chinese and Egyptian Theaters."

"I'd love to see those!"

Bob turns right and we head... I don't know what direction is what here, towards some mountains. Everything looks so new and clean! We turn left and when I look up at the hillside I can hardly believe it, I see the famous "HOLLYWOODLAND" sign! *Click! Click! Click!* I hear "Hooray for Hollywood" in my head.

"Hooray for Hollywood!
That screwy ballyhooey Hollywood!
Where any office boy or young mechanic
Can be a panic, with just a good looking pan

And any barmaid can be a star maid
If she dances with or without a fan"

"There on the left is the Egyptian thea-ter, it's got genuine mummies and stuff carved on the walls... on the right is the famous Chinese thea-ter. If you have time I can stop so you can see the footprints of the stars."

"Oh, yes, please!"

He pulls to the curb, gets out, comes around the back and opens my door. "I'll wait here for you, my cousin's a cop, we'll be fine."

I step out and I'm in another world, one I've only seen in the Movietone newsreels. There's the famous Chinese palace, and in front, all these squares with the actual footprints of actual movie stars. *Click.* I think about all the movies I've seen and these people were in them! There's Mary Pickford and Douglas Fairbanks! *Click.* Not just their feet, but their handprints and signatures, too! Harold Lloyd, Groucho Marx, Bing Crosby, Myrna Loy and William Powell of the *Thin Man* movies! Clark Gable, Tyrone Power, Fred Astaire! Mickey Rooney, Judy Garland... *Click. Click. Click.*

I put my loafers into the footprints to see how I stack up... My feet are bigger than Tyrone Power's! About the same size as Gable's. A lot bigger than Astaire's. I put my hand in their handprints, too, and think about how I'm touching the very same thing they touched. I'm so happy!

I feel dizzy again, probably from leaning over, but then I remember David and Kitty and Iris and the worry returns. I see Bob, chatting with a movie-star handsome policeman who slaps him on the back. *Click.*

Again the sun is so bright! I squint back to the car and Bob opens the door. "I need some sunglasses!"

"I'd be happy to take you to Bullocks Wilshire if you'd like."

"Yes, I'd like that, thanks, Bob."

It's all so different from New York. Very few tall buildings, instead, everything's spread out. So many vacant lots, sometimes the only thing filling a block are rows of billboards for cigarettes (Chesterfields!), and soap and toilet paper. *Click.* We drive past a beaut of a modern building with green copper trim and then around the back. I almost ask why we're going to the service entrance, and then I see the entrance is in the back for the cars.

The doorman in a long navy blue coat with gold buttons, opens my door. "Welcome to Bullocks Wilshire, sir."

"Thank you, I need sunglasses and a hat... And some presents for ladies."

He waves to a woman in a navy blue striped dress with a white lace collar. "Hello, sir, I'm Amy and I'll be happy to assist you." She leads me through a tall room covered in cream colored marble, punctuated by vertical bands of chrome surrounding frosted glass panels of light. *Click.*

The walls of men's accessories are alternating horizontal bands of dark wood and chrome, and there are big clubby chairs in case one suffers exhaustion from shopping! *Click.*

Amy offers me a pair of Persol sunglasses in tortoise with dark green lenses, "They're what Cary Grant wears." Sold.

The choice in hats is so extensive I can now see how a man could become exhausted. Fedoras, homburgs, trilbys, western, porkpie, Panama, flat caps, even bowlers and top hats. One of the top hats is spring-loaded so it can be pressed flat, then pop up to full height.

"I'm from New York so I don't know what's appropriate in Los Angeles," I explain.

"California is decidedly more casual, but one still needs to strive for elegance. For your raw silk sport coat, might I suggest wearing a fine Panama."

"Would that be the right thing to wear to a movie studio?"

"I see, in that case, the man about town would do well with this ultralight Knox Foxhound Pinched Crown. Both dignified and sporty, it's like two hats in one! Perfect for a day at the office or a day at the races. All the features of a fedora in a trimmer, more au courant size." She hands me the hat and it feels smooth and soft. "That's the luxurious Kasmir Finish, hand made and felted by master craftsmen. The fashionable dove gray goes with all colorways. Do you know your hat size?" I didn't. "May I measure your head, sir?"

I feel chills as her warm hands touch my temples where she holds the measuring tape. "7 3/8, I'll get your size." While she's gone I try on a few others, including the collapsible top hat which is too big but still looks very Fred Astaire.

She returns with the hat and places it on my head. There's a three panel mirror on the counter so I can see three angles of myself at once. "It looks quite dashing on you, if I may say so," she says. It does look good, even with the raw silk sport coat.

"I'll take it. Now I need a gift for two lady friends."

We go back into the marble hall, past a life-size weeping willow tree made entirely from feather boas. *Click.* Down a bright and fragrant aisle of perfumes and jewelry. "May I ask your relation to these ladies?"

"They're... friends."

"Not rings then. I would suggest necklaces, bracelets, brooches, scarves, gloves or perfume."

Then it hits me, "Oh, for one, something with a cat on it, for the other, an iris."

Amy walks to a nearby case and pulls out a tray of pins. "New from Schiaparelli, very a la mode." At first I think "ice cream," but the tray is filled with animals made of gold and crystals. A red crystal lobster catches my eye, but I see something more appropriate: a shiny black cat with a silver chain joining it to a gold canary. *So* Kitty!

No irises here... but in the next case, a perfect one! Two tone blue and green enamel flower with rhinestone dewdrops. "I'll take both these."

"Shall I have them gift wrapped?"

"Yes, please."

She rings a bell and a skinny young blond woman in a black dress with a white collar springs into action, taking the items and disappearing with them.

"Is there anything else I can get for you today? Amy asks. She's so nice.

"That's all, thank you. May I write a check?"

"Of course, sir, Let me total this for you. Sunglasses, $12.50. Hat $7.95. Cat and canary brooch, $16.50. Iris pin $11.25. That totals $48.2, and with 2.5% sales tax, it comes to $49.40."

I write the check and hand it to her. I realize I've never noted the checks I've written and have no idea how much is left in my account. I'll call the bank tomorrow.

"Thank you, Mr. Hamilton. It's been a pleasure serving you. Here are your sunglasses and hat," she says, handing them to me along with a bright red hat box. "I've placed your wrapped gifts in the shopping bag."

I put on the hat and sunglasses and see myself reflected in a large mirror. I don't even recognize myself.

156 ⇒ Miracle Mile

"I'll take you down the Miracle Mile," Bob announces proudly, as we drive slowly down a wide street that only occasionally has anything at all, much less anything of interest. "There's the Brown Derby restaurant, lots of movie people eat there!" he says, pointing to a giant brown derby hat with a neon sign on top. *Click.*

There's nothing but billboards in empty lots and the occasional church. *Click.* I've never seen this much space in my entire life. Finally, a modern green building that looks like it came from the *Wizard of Oz.* "That's the *Wiltern* theater named for the corner of Wilshire and Western." *Click.* Then empty lots again.

"Here's the Miracle Mile!" Bob says, excitedly. There are a few buildings but it hardly seems miraculous to me... except for one small storefront that looks like a building-sized camera with a sign above that says *The Darkroom.* I love that, wait till Glenn sees it! *Click.*

"Bob, can we stop at The Darkroom, I need to pick up a light and some more film."

"Sure, boss."

The car glides to a stop, Bob dashes around and opens my door.

Inside, The Darkroom reminds me of Glenn's shop with boxes of cameras and film and paper floor to ceiling. Otherwise, it's empty, until a man with a hang-dog face slowly rises up behind the counter and drones, "What do you need?" like he couldn't care less.

"I'm here shooting for *Look* magazine and I need a compact light, something like a Bell and Howell Luxite."

He stands a little taller. "*Look* magazine, huh? I just got the latest thing, the Luxite 2. Whole thing, including stand, folds into a black leatherette case you can carry with one hand."

"Perfect. I'll take it."

"You sure? It's $39." Then I see him looking through the window at the Cadillac. "Yeah, you're sure." He opens the box and plugs in the light to make sure it works, then closes it back in the case. "You gotta let it cool for at least 10 minutes before you close the case or it could burst into flames, otherwise use it like your regular fill or kicker."

"Give me a case of *Kodak Panatomic X* and one of *Kodak Super-XX.*"

"You should get yourself a polarized filter for the California sun."

"I don't know what that is," I admit.

"It cuts the glare. I'll sell you one with a pamphlet about it," he says, smiling.

"OK, sure. Anything else I need here?"

"Loads of stuff. Like a better strap for your Leica, don't want that dried out leather cracking and your camera getting smashed up. I got the newest thing, a genuine 100% man-made never-fray Nylon strap. Even got one of the last black leather cases to come out of Germany. You'll need that, too."

Black nylon strap and black leather case? Yes, I do need those! $62.50, OK! I write him a check. He puts the new strap and case on my camera. "I put your polarizer in the filter slot of the case. Thanks for shopping at The Darkroom. If you need anything just call!" He hands me their card, shaped like a tiny camera with a hole in the middle where the lens goes.

My camera feels both sleek and protected around my neck. I carry out the Luxite case and Bob opens the trunk. I put it in. He opens my door and puts me in.

Now something smells bad. I wonder if Bob farted... but outside the window, the vacant lot is covered with an ooze of bubbling black tar. *Click.* "What's that?"

"That's the tar pits. Got a few of 'em around here. So much oil it bubbles up from the ground. That's why there's all those oil derricks, pumping oil for the cars here."

I expected a land of palm trees and it's an alien world of bubbling black tar and oil rigs! *Click.*

We continue west and things get better. There's a modern building with a shiny four-story gold cylinder at the corner and a sign that says "May Co." *Click.*

"This here is Beverly Hills, we're almost at the hotel."

Suddenly, it's all hitting me at once. David. Kitty. Iris... Thankfully I'm distracted by Beverly Hills, a quaint little town with shops and restaurants, then mansions!

"I'll point out the movie star houses," Bob explains. "I know 'cause I pick 'em up and drive 'em home when they drink at the hotel. There's Oliver Hardy's house, he's a sweetheart..." an English Tudor. "Carole Lombard, pretty as a picture and drinks like a fish..." Spanish style. "Dick Powell, kinda quiet and a big ladies man..." White brick. "Boris Karloff, not at all scary..." I couldn't see the house behind the tall hedges. "Joan Crawford... the less said the better." A big white house like in *Gone with the Wind.* "Marlene Dietrich, oh, she's a card!" French chateau. I am so excited I forget to take pictures!

157 ⇒ Beverly Hills Hotel

Up ahead is a big white Spanish building with three domes. We pull up a long driveway under a green and white striped awning. A doorman in a green coat that matches the stripes in the awning opens my door. "Welcome to the Beverly Hills Hotel!" he greets me with a smile full of perfect teeth.

"Thank you, I'm pleased to be here." Bob gets my bags out of the trunk and hands them to a bellboy. "Thanks for the tour, Bob," I hand him a five dollar bill.

"My pleasure, sir, please ask for me by name and I'll be happy to show you around."

I follow the bellboy up the green carpet into the lobby, decorated in a Spanish moderne style. Everyone is dressed so casually, light or bright colors, even shorts and sandals in December!

Behind the front desk are three handsome, nearly identical men with slicked back hair. They're wearing matching green vests with a palm leaf embroidered on the left side.

"Good afternoon, sir, welcome to the Beverly Hills Hotel," says one with the name "Rodrigo" embroidered on his vest.

"Hello, I have a reservation, the name is Hamilton."

"Yes, sir, Bungalow number 7, one of our finest. I see Chesterfield has provided an open tab for you and your guests, so please do take full advantage of our fine mixologists and world-famous chefs. Archibald will be your butler."

"Thank you, Rodrigo," I say while wondering what to tip Rodrigo. Two dollars?

"Thank you, Mr. Hamilton, the bellboy will show you to your bungalow."

The bellboy looks like he's all of 12, suddenly making me feel old. I can see the pool outside, empty, while people in various shades of brown and red lie on lounges in the sun. *Click.* We walk through a veritable tropical garden of palms and fragrant flowers to the front door of a small house. *Click.*

Archibald stands by the front door in his formal green coat. "Good afternoon, Mr. Hamilton, it's a pleasure to welcome you to your home in Beverly Hills," he says in a posh English accent.

My home. That sounds... permanent. I can imagine living here. The bellboy puts down my bags and I give him two dollars.

Inside, the room is decorated in modern jungle. Cream colored walls, except for one covered in a bold pattern of green palm leaves, rounded furniture including a pink sofa and two chairs in a palm leaf fabric that match the wall. The rest of the furniture is so modern it's almost invisible: a free-form glass coffee table, sinuous glass lamps, a glass dining room table and six chairs with glass backs.

"I'll unpack for you, sir." Archibald asks.

"May I call you Archie?" I ask, timidly.

"Of course, sir."

"I've never had a butler before, so do I tip you now or at the end of the day?"

"At the end of your *stay*, if you so desire, sir."

"Thanks. I need a phone book, is there a phone book here?"

"Of course, sir, it's in the drawer of the phone nook right here, sir."

"Please call me Herb."

"Of course, Mr. Herb."

I get the phone book out and look under R, then under RO... there are a lot of "Rose"'s but no Kitty, no Iris, no Katherine, no Myron. I'm startled by the phone ringing. I pick it up. "Hello?"

"Hello, I'm Diane Singleton, I'm sure Jerry mentioned me. I'm *Look* magazine's west coast advertising manager. I trust you had a good trip. I need to come by and give you a shooting schedule for the Chesterfield campaign. Is this a good time?"

"Of course."

"I'm at the Crossroads of the World and can be there in about 10 minutes."

"That would be fine. I'm going to order lunch, would you like something?"

"I like their salad Niçoise."

"I'll order that and see you in a few minutes." She hangs up.

"What would you like for lunch, Mr. Herb?"

"A salad Knee-saws and... is there a menu?"

"Of course, but you can also order anything you'd like and the chef will be happy to prepare it."

"What's good?"

"Everything. The steak tartare is a particular favorite."

"OK, I'll have that."

"Excellent, sir... Herb."

"Thanks. I'm going to clean up a bit."

The bathroom has wall to wall mirrors. It's a little too much. It's a lot too much. But I guess movie stars need to be able to see every bit of themselves.

I decide to take a quick shower. The soap package says "Gardenia" and smells like tropical flowers. I dry off, wrap myself in my towel in case Archie is about, and go to the bedroom to get dressed.

My clothes look all wrong here. Too heavy. Too dark. Except my raw silk jacket, which reminds me too much of Sergei, and my Myron suit... no, my *Iris* suit, which feels too fancy. I'm going to need different clothes. I put on blue gabardine pants and my bright blue shirt from Saks—that color feels right here. Nobody in the lobby was wearing a tie, so I leave the collar open, which feels both weird but good.

So far, that's how LA feels, uncomfortably comfortable.

The only part of my outfit that feels right are the shoes, and even they're too dark. I take a quick look around the bungalow—my bedroom is mint green with pastel peach. The wall behind the bed is more of that palm wallpaper, busy yet soothing. The bedspread is green velvet that matches the wall, with the palm motif quilted in it. The room has big windows that are actually doors. I slide one open and let the warm California breeze blow into the room. Heaven. I can see the pool from here, sparkling aquamarine, the reflections creating ripples of light on the ceiling.

There's another bedroom next door, peach with green accents. Its bathroom is pink tile with mercifully fewer mirrors.

There's a kitchen, all blond wood with clear green knobs. A door opens to the outside and Archie enters carrying a tray of fruit.

"I thought you and your guest would enjoy this until the food arrives," he says. "Would you prefer to dine inside or al fresco?"

I don't know who Al Fresco is so I say, "I'd rather eat here," and he puts the tray down on the glass dining table.

The doorbell rings and Archie answers it. "I'm Diane Singleton, here to see Mr. Hamilton."

"Right this way, miss."

Diane is quite tall, and what my mother taught me to call "big boned." Short dark hair, dark eyes, very red lips and fingernails. Her dress is lightweight blue fabric with a profusion of white flowers. She has shapely legs and her white shoes match her white collar.

She puts out her hand, "Good to meet you, Mr. Hamilton. I was impressed with your work in the Fair/Unfair issue. Very persuasive."

I shake her hand, "Thank you, Miss Singleton."

"Call me Diane. Nice room."

"Yes, thank you."

"Don't thank me, thank Chesterfield. I find it all too bourgeois," she says, looking disgusted.

"Oh, I didn't ask for it..."

"I know. I'm sorry, I'm being dreadfully forward, but I've been doing this job too long and I'm used to dealing with Jerry."

"He's very direct."

"He's a horse's ass," she blurts out.

I had to laugh. "You're certainly direct, too."

"I'm hoping to get fired which will force me to get serious about my screenwriting." She blushes. "I'm sorry once again, I don't know you and I shouldn't be this free, but you have a sweet face and I'm fed up."

"Thanks. Why don't you just quit?"

"Because the money's too good. Why don't you quit?"

"Because I love the work," I reply, honestly.

"You're clearly not a communist and have no problem profiting from pushing cigarettes on the people."

"I had my qualms but Jerry convinced me."

"The devil can do that. If you're not going to get me fired then we should get on to business."

Archie arrives with lunch. Her dish is a salad with tuna on top. Mine, a round pink disk of rare meat with a raw egg on top. I thought I'd ordered steak... but don't want to be rude.

"Thank you for lunch, Mr. Hamilton, this is one of the more palatable aspects of capitalism."

I'd never eaten raw egg, so I push it to the side and put some meat on my fork. I prefer my steak well done, but Diane is enjoying hers. I take a bite. It's cold! Did they forget to cook it? I think about spitting it into my napkin but my fork is already out of my mouth, so I chew and it actually tastes good. Meaty, peppery, mustard, onions, capers, and even a little lemon.

"I couldn't eat raw meat," Diane says, clearly enjoying her salad.

"I couldn't either," I reply, each bite tasting better.

"But you are!" she laughs.

"Excuse me, ma'am, sir, I couldn't help but overhear. Steak Tartare is not technically raw, as our chef steams it for 10 seconds."

"Thank you, Archie," I say, gratefully. Diane looks at him and rolls her eyes.

"If you really want, I can tell Jerry you're very rude and try to get you fired."

"Oh, would you really, please? That would be swell. I've been doing this job for four years and it's destroying my soul."

"That's settled, then. What's the schedule look like?"

"Wall to wall assholes." She laughs again. "I already feel so free! I've typed up the schedule. You have Mickey Rooney and Judy Garland tomorrow, followed by Cary Grant and Katherine Hepburn on Thursday, Jimmy Cagney and newcomer Ronald Reagan on Friday. Finally, Errol Flynn on Saturday."

I realize my mouth is hanging open and clasp by hand over it. "Wow... that's a lot of..."

"Assholes."

"I was going to say 'stars.' Are they really all assholes?"

"Out of that list I've only met Flynn who's a drunken asshole but a great lay. Oh, did I shock you?" She dabs her lips with the napkin, very ladylike.

Now it's my turn to laugh. "Not at all, but I don't know how you haven't gotten fired long before this!"

"Right? Something snapped inside me as I typed up this list. All these talented people whoring themselves out for cigarette money... I didn't mean you, of course."

"Of course. I came here to follow..." I thought about it carefully, "A... girl."

"That's completely different. Even communists approve of love. Oh, my. This is an elegant hotel and lunch. Makes me temporarily forget about the proletariat and fall happily into the bourgeoisie. In fact, I thought about giving up communism when Stalin had Trotsky shot in August. But no, I must be strong and write screenplays with messages that encourage the workers to unite."

I like how animated and frank she is. "I respect your convictions."

"I feel like a fraud any time I enjoy myself. Like now."

"I imagine even communists like a good time. I'm starstruck myself. I've seen these people in movies since I was a kid and I can't believe I'm going to meet them in person."

"They're just people." she says, between bites.

"I know that—but they're literally larger than life!"

"Aren't you sweet?" she says, her elbows on the table. "If I was into boys I'd want to fuck you."

I suddenly wondered if my queerness was obvious. "But you... and Errol Flynn!"

"He's Errol Flynn."

"Yeah, even I'd f him."

"I knew I liked you," she said, reaching over and putting her hand on my arm. "Here's my card. if you need anything while you're here just give me a buzz."

"I hope you'll stick around long enough to help me, if that's OK."

"Sure... Oh, God, I really am a whore."

"I'm not paying you."

"Then I'm just a slut and that's OK! Especially when Errol's here."

"Was he good?"

"No, too drunk, but I just lay there, looking at him naked, and that was fun."

"You're a very interesting girl, Diane. Wait, you are a girl, aren't you?"

"Last time I looked."

158 ⇉ Palladium

Archie finishes tidying up. "If you don't require anything else I'll be going back to my rooms."

"I'm fine, Archie, thanks. Where do you live?"

"In the main building. If you need me, simply dial 117 and I will be here in three minutes."

"I don't want to bother you."

"It's no bother," he looks at his watch. "But I must go. It's 6am in London and the circuits won't be busy so I'll be able to get through to my mum."

"Is she OK?"

"The building next door to hers was bombed last week. She was upset, but unharmed. Moved in with her sister in Tottenham Hale, a ways from the center of town but I still worry. I wired money for them to go to the country and need to make sure she received the funds," he says, stoically.

"How awful!"

"I am worried, but at the moment it's all I can do. Goodnight, Herb," he bows, and leaves.

Americans need to know about this! We need to get involved! I should have gone to London when Pat asked... But I made my decision.

I go outside to the private patio, complete with a bubbling fountain. It's like a summer night but in December, the sky clear, the stars bright.

So quiet it scares me, or maybe it's being someplace new. I used to feel at home wherever I went, but this is different. I'm alone with 3,000 miles between me and the people I know.

Kitty and Iris are here... somewhere. I'm so confused. I feel like they're one person when I know they're two very different people... girls...

I sit in a lounge chair, listen to the fountain and look at the stars. My eyes close...

...Suddenly searchlights swept across the sky. I was in the black Cadillac, riding down Hollywood Blvd to a premiere at the Chinese theater. I passed throngs of people waiting to catch a glimpse of stars. The searchlights grew brighter, shining on me so starkly it hurt, the blinding glare, the searing heat.

I tore myself away from the light and looked around at a bombed out city. The searchlights swept the sky, but now for war planes, as anti-aircraft guns shot into the night like fireworks. The theater's marquee said "London Palladium." I heard the whistling of bombs and ran for cover.

Two men were standing in the street until a deafening explosion caused them to disappear, an arm dangling from the marquee which now read "Hollywood Palladium." The title on the sign: "Lost in Wonderland, starring The Rose Sisters"

The marquee went dark. The dismembered arm fell to my feet. I screamed…

…I see something move in the corner of my eye. Something in the flowers, pink by day but glowing blue in the starlight. A bee.

I find myself back on the lounge chair. Alone in paradise. Suddenly cold.

I go to the bedroom and crawl under the covers, shivering.

159 ➻ If the World Survives

I wake to a knocking a the door. My eyes are dry and I open them a bit to see Archie, in full regalia, next to the bed.

"Good morning Herb. I noted your shooting schedule for today and felt it was prudent to awaken you so you had time to fully prepare for the day." He holds a tray with orange juice. "I squeezed it myself from the orange trees on the property."

"Thank you…" I think I say but I feel I've only mumbled. I take a sip and it's like I've never tasted orange juice before. It's so fragrant and sweet I not only feel awake, but like all my senses have kicked in. The room is warm and smells of flowers. I hear birds singing, and the sun streams through the glass doors. "Thanks, Archie," I say, this time making actual words. "Is your Ma OK?"

"Thank you for asking. I was unable to get through last night. I'll try again tonight."

"I wish I could do something," I say, guiltily.

"Very kind of you. As for something I can do for you, shall I draw you a bath?"

"I'd love that, thank you."

He disappears and I sit up. People are suffering there and I am here, so I must do what I can to help Kitty and Iris. I find my watch and look at the time, 8:30. I put on the thick white terry cloth robe at the end of the bed and go to the phone nook. I remember the number, MGM-1111 and dial.

"Good morning, MGM studios, how may I direct your call?"

"I'd like to speak to Miss Kitty Rose, please. No, wait, Miss Iris Rose."

"I'll connect you, thank you."

I hear the phone ringing. "Hello, costume department, this is Rory speaking."

"Hello Rory, my name is Herb and I'm calling for Iris."

"Iris is swell!" says the young voice at the other end of the phone.

"She sure is, may I speak to her?"

"You could, but she's in a meeting with Adrian and LB. I can leave a message if you'd like."

"Thanks, please have her call Herbert Hamilton at the Beverly Hills Hotel, thanks."

"Will do, HH!" he answered cheerfully. "Bye now!"

I felt less alone already.

"Your bath is ready sir. I took the liberty of choosing bay rum bubbles."

"A fine choice, Archie, thank you."

"What would you like for breakfast?"

Having a butler felt wonderfully normal. "Scrambled eggs, bacon, crisp, hash browns."

"Coffee or tea?"

"Can I get hot chocolate?"

"You can get anything you'd like sir. Would you like Kahlua in that?"

"I'm not sure what that is."

"It's a coffee liquor. Quite popular for aperitifs."

"In that case, no thank you, I don't drink."

"Of course, a bit early in the day. Might I make a suggestion, sir. Drinking is an important social lubricant here. So even if you do not drink, I would suggest you at least pretend you do. I can write up a list of cocktail names and if you discreetly add the word 'virgin' after them the bartender will know what to do."

"I'm not a virgin, Archie."

"I'm sorry, no offense intended, that's the technical term for a drink without alcohol."

"Oh. No offense taken. I appreciate you telling me of the ways of the world here."

"You're most welcome, Herb. I am happy to help."

The lights in the bathroom seem even brighter this morning. The mirrors are certainly more intriguing—mirrors facing mirrors making endless reflections. I take off my robe and look at myself, front and back. I look OK. But pale, I will get a tan.

I sink into the big bath tub. It's the perfect temperature and smells delicious, rich and spicy. I almost fall asleep again when I wonder— what if Iris calls? I jump up, covered in bubbles, turn on the shower and rinse off, then pull the plug and watch the tub drain into a whirlpool.

I don't even need to dry off, I put on the robe and it's like wearing a big towel. Archie is setting the table on the patio. "Any calls?"

"Not this morning. Are you expecting one?"

"Yes, from Iris Rose —when she calls please find me, no matter what else I'm doing."

"I took the liberty of setting the table al fresco this morning with the bougainvillea in bloom."

Oh, so that's what "al fresco" means. "Thanks, Archie, good idea."

There's a knock at the kitchen door, then a waiter enters with a tray. Archie takes it from him and places it on the table.

"Thanks, Arch." Here I am, outside, in a bathrobe, under sunny blue skies, at Christmas time. Who could ever leave this place? He lifts the silver dome from my plate and everything is still steaming hot.

It couldn't be better, except the hot chocolate tastes different. Good, but bitter... It makes my tongue feel funny and my throat especially warm. But the more I drink the tastier it is. I drink it all.

I unfold the newspaper on the table and read the headline: "FDR FEARS WORLD CHAOS!" I put down my fork and read the article.

"Warm Springs, Georgia: On a gloomy, wet Sunday the President ate turkey, shook hands with discombobulated Helen Cothran, 4 (who shifted her sticky candy to her left hand just in time), with Wade Cothran, 3 (who had cake in both hands, put most of it in his mouth and said "Glmph!" to the President), and with 90 other polio patients. In a gay little speech he said deliberately: "I hope to be down here in March, without any question, if the world survives."

I remember my dream last night and watch my food get cold. The phone rings—I spring up and sprint to it, but Archie has already answered.

"Just a moment, I'll get him for you," he says, handing the phone to me and whispering, "Miss Rose."

Miss Rose? Which one? "Hello?"

"Hi, Herbie! I was so happy to hear you're in town, why didn't you tell me?"

I'm smiling and crying at the same time. "I'm so glad to hear your voice. I'm sorry, it was very last minute. I'm here shooting for *Look*... and to see you."

"That's so sweet! Come down to the studio and we'll have lunch at the commissary. Lots of movie stars, you'll love it."

"I really want to! Hold on, I have to look at my schedule. Wait a sec."

I find the paper Diane gave me. "I'm shooting Mickey Rooney and Judy Garland today at 2."

"Perfect, I just met with Judy for the Ziegfeld picture. Oh, sorry, Adrian's calling and I must go. I'll leave your name at the gate—see you at noon!"

I'm not sure if I heard kissing noises or if it was just me sniffling.

I dial the number on Diane's card. "Hello, Diane? Hi, this is Herb. Where am I supposed to shoot Mickey and Judy today?"

"Hi, Herb. At your hotel, that's where all the shoots are scheduled."

"Can you call and change it so I can shoot them at MGM? I think that would be much more interesting."

"Sure, I have nothing better to do. Oh, sorry, I don't have to have an attitude with you. It's actually a good idea, I'll call them right now and handle it."

"Thanks, Diane!"

I'm happy but feel hot. I'm not used to this weather. "Archie, there's been a change in plans for today. I'll be shooting at MGM instead of here. Can I walk there from here?"

"It's possible, but I imagine it would take several hours. I'll arrange a car."

"Thanks... oh, I need to get some new clothes, what do you recommend?"

"Previous guests have found that kind of advice at Saks Fifth Ave on Wilshire."

"Saks. Perfect." I put on the same clothes I wore yesterday—doesn't matter since I'll be wearing new clothes to lunch. I look in the mirror and see something's missing. The turquoise string tie. I put it on. Better, though why do I look slightly out-of-focus?

160 ➺ Quicksand for the Rich

Bob is waiting at the entrance. "Good morning, sir, I'm glad to be able to drive you again."

"Hi, Bob! Thanks, I appreciate it."

"Are you feeling OK, sir? You look a little peaked."

"I'm tired... and warm. Not used to this weather."

We drive down the quaint little streets of Beverly Hills. My cheeks feel hot, so I open the window and stick my head out for the breeze. It feels like a village, then we turn onto a big street... Wilshire, and there's an imposing white moderne building with the familiar words "Saks" over the door.

"I'll be waiting. Just have them call the garage and I'll meet you in front here." Bob explains as he opens the door for me.

"I can open the door for myself, Bob, but thank you."

I am starting to feel... bad... about feeling good—too good at a time like this when so many people are suffering. But will my suffering help them? I can't see how. I feel quite relaxed.

The inside of the store feels like a glamorous movie set, I expect Fred and Ginger to come dancing through a doorway at any time. Except the carpet's too thick to hear tap dancing and my shoes sink into it like quicksand for the rich.

"May I help you, sir" a blond woman asks me. I'm dazzled by her beauty, her perfect skin and hair. What is this creature doing in Saks? Why didn't someone lasso her and put her in the corral of stars at MGM or Fox or Warners or anywhere? Who do I call to make this happen? That guy on the train, what was his name?

Then I realize I've been staring at her for too long without answering. "I'm sorry, I just got here from New York and I'm..."

"I understand, sir, how may I assist you?"

Her teeth are perfect. She smells like the love-child of roses and soap. I'm not used to so many attractive people all together in one place like this, it's overwhelming.

"I'm going to MGM this afternoon and want to wear something... Hollywood," I say, stupidly, my cheeks hot.

"Follow me," she says, walking briskly towards silver elevator doors that look like streamlined Greek columns surrounding the view of a moderne village. The whole place feels like set designer Cedric Gibbons took a break from *Metropolis* and worked with Lyle Wheeler from *Gone with the Wind* to create a vision of futures past.

Why is it hard to focus? The blond woman's backside, complete with perfectly straight seams down her stockings is gloriously unsettling.

"Third floor, menswear," the elevator operator announces. We get out and an unusually attractive man bows.

"Mr. West, this gentleman is looking for suitable studio attire." She bows and returns to the elevator, disappearing between the silver doors as I stare.

Mr. West clears his throat, "That Rhonda's quite the looker, isn't she... who do I have the pleasure of assisting today?" Mr. West could be Clark Gable's younger brother.

"Hamilton. Herb... Hamilton."

"A pleasure to serve you, Mr. Hamilton."

"I'm from New York and am going to MGM and I want... I want something..."

"That's a fine watch, sir, and shoes. Are you a producer?"

"Maybe someday, right now I'm a photographer for *Look* magazine."

"*The* Herbert Hamilton? Such a pleasure to meet you! I love that publication! Your recent issue about the World's Fair floored me. I'm getting my master's in psychology at UCLA and I decided to write my thesis about it."

"I... I'm impressed."

"I wish I had my issue here for you to sign, Mr. Hamilton. You took the photos of that beautiful girl... what was her name... Kitty, that's it. I'd be surprised if she didn't have a studio contract by now."

"She surprised me, too..."

"That center spread of the explosion, that single image encapsulates the duality of our times... it inspired my thesis title, '*Modern Barbarism, the effects of technology and mass media on modern warfare and mating rituals.*' It's long, I know, but not for a thesis title... Oh, wait... you took the pictures of the boy and the duck!"

I thought I'd come in to buy a shirt and some pants but now I wasn't sure where I was.

"I'm sorry sir, I hope I'm not boring you," Mr. West said, kindly.

My knees felt woozy. "I need to sit down for a minute." He put his hand on my back and led me to a big leather chair. It swallowed me up.

"I apologize, Mr. Hamilton."

"No, it's not that, I like that you liked it..."

"*Like* is an understatement, it was utterly illuminating. I felt as if... Please forgive me, I so want to return the favor and help you."

"Thanks. I'm just not feeling quite right."

"I'll call Doctor Jacobson, he's very good. His vitamin shots are especially popular. He'll have you right as rain in no time. While you wait, I'll pull some selections for you... you look like a 36 regular... I'll be right back."

I'm sweating, yet there's a cold breeze on me from the air conditioning. I must have caught a bug. Except I actually feel good, so relaxed, just a bit dizzy and things don't entirely make sense.

"The doctor will be here shortly. In the meantime, I've selected some lighter fabrics for our California weather, linen and seersucker. Personally, I recommend the Haspel Seersucker, made in New Orleans. Unlike linen, it always looks crisp while feeling cool. The new Haspel suits can be laundered—you can even shower in one, that's what the advertisements show, though I'm not sure why you would, but maybe in some tropical place where a laundry isn't handy. I took the liberty of selecting navy and white to compliment your complexion."

"You are so nice, Mr. West... what's your name, I mean your first name?"

"Charles. Charles Montgomery West."

"Thank you Charles Montgomery West. You look like a movie star, did you know that? You must know that. You and that glorious creature who brought me up here. You should have babies together. But first, you should both be in the movies."

I don't know if I said that out loud. I do know I'm drooling. I'm relieved that he's gone over to talk to a man who might be the doctor so he can't hear or see me.

"Hello, Mr Hamilton, I'm Doctor Max Jacobson. I hear you're not feeling well."

"It must be... the weather. I'm not used to summer in December. I said that out loud, didn't I?"

"Yes, it can be disconcerting for our Eastern visitors. I have just the thing for you, my own special formula, in fact. Very popular with the studio folk who I visit to give regular booster shots. Roll up your sleeve, please."

I roll up my sleeve and close my eyes once I see his big silver syringe. I feel him pinch my upper arm, then a short, sharp pain, then warmth spreading through my muscle.

"That wasn't so bad, was it? It only takes five minutes to kick in, then you'll be feeling as good as new... better!"

"Thank you, doctor! How much do I owe you?"

"Nothing, son, the first one is free. I've got to run to shoot up a recalcitrant actress at Republic, holding up the entire production. Here's my card, call me anytime day or night. I make house calls. Ta ta!"

He disappears and the fog in my mind is clearing. I see the salesman... what was his name, nice guy who liked my photos... three names... North... no, West, Charles somethingorother West. What a nice suit he's wearing, I didn't even see it before, a brilliant blue.

"Feeling better, Mr. Hamilton?"

"Yes, thank you, Mr. West. I like your suit."

"It's the same one I chose for you, the Haspel seersucker in Royal Blue. I need to wear it with a white shirt because that's the rule here, but as an artist I thought you'd like to pair it with a Haspel canary yellow shirt, a bold ensemble."

I feel so much better! My head feels clear—and sharp. I'm noticing everything again. The colors are brighter, the textures more defined. Mr. West holds up the suit and the intense color tickles my eyes. "Yes, I love it, I'll try it on."

I feel like there's less gravity now as I spring up, take the clothes from his hands and dash to the dressing room, dark paneled wood with a wing chair and crystal vase of bright red dahlias. I shed my clothes like a snake and slip into the seersucker. It's light as a feather, with a slightly bumpy texture. The canary shirt is smashing and makes the turquoise pop. The royal blue suit is sensational! Everything is fantastic!

I look at myself in the mirror. I feel taller. There's color in my cheeks. There is nothing I can't do.

"How does it fit?" Mr. West asks from outside. I open the door and show him.

"It's perfect. It's glorious. It feels like Superman's cape!"

Mr. West smiles, "I'm so glad you like it! Now you need shoes to complete the look. I've taken the liberty of bringing a few selections for you."

He holds up a pair of royal blue loafers with gold stitching that make me positively giddy. I am breathless. I am speechless! I slide them on and they not only fit perfectly but make me feel like I'm levitating! "I'll take them all, and if I didn't have a lunch appointment I'd get more, so please give me your card and I'll come back." Mr. West's smile is so wide, so white, so dazzling. "Has anyone ever told you that you should be in the movies?"

"You did, very kind of you."

"Did I? Then I must be right. You get to work on that right after you write this up so I can pay you."

The air tickles my skin in a most delightful way. Mr. West hands me the bill. I write the same numbers on a check, sign it and hand it to him. "Thank you, Mr. West, you shall be my personal haberdasher!"

I turn to leave and he calls out, "Wait, your old clothes!" He hands me a Saks shopping bag with them in it. Oh, yes, I like that blue shirt and those black loafers, I'd forgotten.

"Thanks, Mr. West! Ta ta!" I have no idea why I said "ta ta" but it felt good. I am going to start saying it now. The thick carpet now feels springy as I practically skip over it. I exit the front door and the car isn't there. I remember, go back inside and ask a saleswoman to call the garage. I wait out front, the sun feels good on my skin.

Bob pulls up in the Cadillac. I open my own door and fall in, laughing. "I love Saks, Bob. Just love it. I feel so damn good!"

"Where to, sir?"

"To Oz! Follow the yellow brick road!"

"Do you mean MGM?"

"That's what I said!"

161 ➻ Oz

The warm air caresses my face. The city smells like pine trees and flowers and tar. Everything is new here. I feel so happy—like I have soda pop in my veins. The low-slung city speeds by. *Click.*

And there it is. A gleaming white colonnade an entire block long with a wide opening that reads, "Metro-Goldwyn-Mayer-Studios" next to the famous lion head surrounded by the words, "Ars gratia artis." *Click!*

We pull up to a guard in a black uniform with gold trim. "Good afternoon. What is your name and who are you here to see?"

I roll down the left window. "Herb Hamilton, here for Iris Rose."

The guard checks his list, salutes and opens the gate. "Costume department straight ahead then turn right. Welcome to MGM studios."

We glide into oz. I stop breathing. This is where so many great movies were made. I remember seeing a short that said MGM had, "More stars than there are in the heavens." *I'm* here. I can't sit still. I can't stay in the car. "Thanks, Bob, I'm going to walk from here."

"OK, sir, when you need me, call the hotel and I'll pick you up."

Everywhere I look there are pretty girls and handsome men in costumes of all eras, *Click.* Egyptian outfits, Grecian togas, Knights in armor, Wild West cowboys and showgirls, 1920s flappers and dandies. *Click.*

I am in heaven. *Click!* I'm also confused. Where am I? I stop a Roman centurion, "Excuse me, I'm looking for the costume department, Mr. Adrian's office."

"I dunno, I'm just an extra," he sounds like a farmer. I hold up my camera, he holds up his shield and makes a face like a warrior. *Click.*

"Excuse me, ma'am" I say to a woman in a fancy pink dress with very tall white hair. "Which way is the costume department?" She sees my camera, smiles and poses. *Click.*

"I'm on my way there, come with me," she says, taking my hand. "My name's Lila. I'm a dancer. I've been shooting costume tests for Mr. Berkeley's new musical 'Viva Les Girls,' about famous vamps throughout history. This is Marie Antoinette's costume, the skirt tears off to reveal panties with velvet cakes on them, you know 'let 'em eat cake,' it's very dirty so it'll probably get nixed but I like it. Do you?"

Her hand is warm and a little moist. Her voice is gravelly and she walks faster than I do, pulling me along. The colors seem especially bright. *Click, unfortunately in black and white!*

Then it hits me and I stop, her hand sliding out of mine. The yellow brick road is somewhere here. I must find it!

"Why'd ya stop? Come along," she takes my hand again.

I am now absolutely sure this is what heaven will be like. Absolutely, positively, 100% sure.

"We're here. I gotta change, I'm Nefertiti next. I hope I see you later, handsome!" she says.

I'm standing in front of a green building with white trim that looks like a cross between an army headquarters and a southern mansion. *Click.*

The door says, "Costuming —Adrian" in silver script letters. The handle feels electric as I turn it. Inside, the lobby has shiny white walls with silver trim, reflecting men and women rushing around, carrying mountains of material. *Click.* A young blond man sitting behind a large round counter looks up and smiles.

"Hello, how can I help you?"

He sounds familiar. "Rory?" I ask.

"Yes, how do you know my name?"

"We spoke yesterday on the phone, I left a message for Iris..."

"Oh, hi Herb! She's been talking about you nonstop! You're a photographer for *Look* and have known her since you were both kids in the Bronx and she made you a very special suit... but that doesn't look like what she described."

"Her suit is my favorite, but it's a bit warm for this weather. I just bought this at Saks."

"It's very smart. And I like your hair, is it natural or a perm? I'm sorry, I'm sure Iris is waiting for you. Right this way." Once out of the lobby, the showplace becomes a warehouse: two stories of open shelves and desks, bolts of colorful fabric and a small army of people cutting, sewing and draping. The tailoring reminds me of when I first met Myron... and Iris.

Rory gestures to a fluted glass door with silver lettering that reads, "Iris Rose, Assistant to Adrian." I knock, shyly because I don't want to break the glass.

"Come!" I hear her voice. Kitty... Iris... they sound simultaneously the same and completely different. Softer, yet more sure.

I open the door, and there she is, backlit, a glowing vision in white. Her hair perfectly done up, her narrow waist accentuated with a silver belt, matching her shoes silver. Her office is white and silver, too and I want to dance up to her, take her in my arms and kiss her. But I don't. Instead my hands are shaking.

"Hello, Herbie," she says, and I feel deliciously weak. She gives me a peck on the cheek that feels like an explosion of butterflies.

She walks around the office, "I've done pretty well for myself, haven't I?"

"You're amazing,"I say, unable to move anything but my arms, which are flailing.

She smiles, "And look at you, that watch, those shoes, why people will think you're a producer! I approve of the Haspels seersucker, too. Good choice, too warm for the suit I made you. You always had exquisite taste. The bolo tie is a good eccentric touch." My hand is shaking as I look down and touch the turquoise. "Are you OK, you're trembling. Come, sit, let's talk." Her voice is mellifluous. I sit in a low white satin club chair. She perches on the edge of her chrome and glass desk.

"I'm a very lucky girl. Adrian says I'm the only person he knows who can truly understand what a woman wants to look like and what a man wants to see."

"You look beautiful! I'm so happy to see you!" I blurt, effervescently.

"I'm happy to see you, too," she says, calmly while I feel like I'm going to pop. "Let's go to lunch, I'm famished," she says. So many memories flash in my head, from our very first, very confusing first kiss, to watching her walk away.

Her hand feels small, soft, and cool. "I want Adrian to know about you." She knocks on the wall, opens a hidden door, and gestures for me to come to her. She pulls my arm until my head is through the door into another office, this one much grander with a distinguished man in a gleaming white suit sitting behind a chrome and glass desk.

"I told you he was real—and adorable." she tells him, simultaneously breezy and pointed. I feel her breath on my ear and goosebumps run down my arm. "He's taking me to lunch. Later!." She pulls me back in and closes the door. "There, now he's met you, let's eat."

She introduces me to people she passes in the hallway, "Hello, Wylie, this is my friend Herb I was telling you about... Hi, Leslie, yes, this is Herbie... Hola Pedro, este es mi amigo Herb."

"You speak Spanish?"

"Un poquito, a tiny bit, I'm learning. Oh, you must meet George. George! I want you to meet my dear friend Herb."

"Hello, Herb, nice bolo," he says, extending his hand which I shake. He's a small man with big glasses and an unusually precise and cultivated way of talking, pronouncing every word distinctly, "Dear Iris has told me absolutely everything, we have no secrets among friends. I'd love to chat but Kate is waiting and you know how *he* can be. I do hope you'll come to my home on Saturday for luncheon and a dip with the boys. Ciao." He waves and scurries off.

"He seems nice, what does he do?" I ask.

Iris laughs, sweetly, "Why that's George Cukor, my favorite director. He's shooting a charming piece with butch Kate and mary Cary called 'The Philadelphia Story.' Adrian and I have made Kate the most sophisticated clothes, very modern. I came up with the classical corset design for her on-screen wedding dress, but don't you dare ever say that to the great man as he designs absolutely everything himself," she laughs, genuinely pleased.

I marvel at her happiness. She wears it well. Outside in the sunlight she positively glows.

A tall woman with short curly hair approaches and takes Iris' hands, "You're a wonder—absolutely right about the rose crepe de chine, I was the bell of the ball and caught his eye... and the rest of him, too." She kisses Iris's cheek and looks at me, "This must be the famous Herbie, hi, doll, I'm Eve."

"Hi, Eve, it's a pleasure..."

"Sorry, darlings, but I really must run!" she says, running.

"Eve's a lot of laughs. Here we are."

We enter the commissary, a big pale green room with dozens of tables filled with men and women, mostly wearing street clothes, a few in terry cloth robes. *Click.* "Why're they in robes?" I ask.

"We give them hell if they eat in their costumes. Kate dropped some ice cream on a one-off dress and Cukor slapped her. She deserved it!" We walk past the tables to the cafeteria at the far end.

"There's an executive dining room I sometimes go to with Adrian, but I usually eat here, you meet more people this way and it's all about who you know."

The place is abuzz with activity, men and women, young and old, carrying their trays of food. I stop to watch Rita Hayworth and Ronald Coleman eat fried chicken.

Iris pulls me along. "Here's a tip I learned about meeting people in Hollywood. Doesn't matter how famous they are, you just march right up to them, put out your hand and say, 'Hi, I'm Iris... or in your case, Herb... good to meet you,' like *you're* somebody, too, because you are! It's that easy." I charge towards Rita and Ronald then feel Iris grab me by my belt. "But not while they're eating, nobody wants to be caught with their mouth full."

The cafeteria food looks good, and so cheap. 25 cents for meatloaf and mashed potatoes and a roll and butter. Or lasagna. Or fried chicken. Or baked cod. There's cherry pie, apple pie, chocolate or vanilla cake, pudding or jello all for a dime. Iris chooses a green salad, with vinegar, an apple and a cup of coffee.

I'm especially hungry, so I go for the fried chicken, and french fries and a piece of cherry pie, chocolate cake and a glass of milk. I pay for both our meals, 55 cents.

"You're eating like a bird, do you want some of mine?"

"You men are so lucky, you can just loosen your belt, but I've made myself a lot of nice dresses so I need to keep my girlish figure."

"Aren't you hungry?" I ask.

"No, because my life is so full."

I'm happy for her. I'm also happy with the fried chicken, Rita and Ronnie know their food!

"Sometimes I do splurge on a nice dinner, hint, hint." She says, reaching out and tickling my chin.

"You should come to my bungalow at the Beverly Hills Hotel, they'll make us absolutely anything."

"As appealing as that sounds, it's also a bit forward, don't you think? Us, alone together?"

"My butler, Archie, will be there."

She stares at me, incredulously, then laughs, "Oh, my Herbie, how far we've come. Mind you, I don't have a butler, but I do have my own apartment not far from here, and my life here—as me."

"The world is a wonderful place, Iris."

"That it is, Herbie. With storm clouds on the horizon."

"I know. Pat wants me to go to London to cover the war there. I feel guilty about not going, but I feel like I can do something important here, with you."

"That's very sweet, and I do think what we do here is important for morale. Sometimes it seems worlds away from the real world, but it's the perfect place for me because it's where people come to reinvent themselves. Underneath the beautiful costumes, we're all just normal, insecure people who are especially good at pretending."

I look around. The movie stars look smaller in real life, but they still don't look normal. Then again, nobody working in Saks looked normal, it's as if the entire city is populated with beautiful people.

"I'm so glad you're doing so well. How's Kitty?"

There's a silence as Iris' face momentarily turns into Myron's. "She's not here."

"What happened?"

"What always happens with Kitty," she says, looking like Iris again.

"A man?" I ask, more out of disgust than jealousy.

"Frank. Dead. So, of course, Kitty conveniently disappears." Iris says, stabbing the last piece of lettuce on her plate.

"What? Frank, too?" I ask, incredulously. "I read about David. The man she was seeing when I met her. He was found dead in his car. I was worried that something might have happened to her... And you."

She snaps a carrot in half and bites into it, angrily. "So you were worried about *her*..." then dismissive, "I'm sure *she's* fine, *she* always is. Nine lives and all," then disappointed, "I thought you were here to see *me*."

"I am! You're the one I called, not her!"

"Then let's talk about me. And you. You may know me better than anybody, but that was the old me...."

"I want to know the new you, the real you."

She relaxes and daintily lifts a cherry from my plate with her red fingernails and places it on her tongue. "You always were a sweetheart. OK—Let's go to Michael Romanoff's for dinner. It's the hottest place in town, impossible to get into but he and Adrian are friends so we can get a table. Harry's a Brooklyn boy passing himself off as a count, you'll love him."

"Who's Harry?" I wonder, aloud.

"Michael."

"Maybe I should change my name, too," I say, "Oh, wait, I already did! I fit right in here."

"I have no doubt that you will, Herbie." She looks at her small silver watch with a tiny face. "Oh, look at the time, I have a fitting with Kate and you've got your shoot with Mickey and Judy."

"I'd almost forgotten!" I jump up, frantic, my hands shaking again. "Oh, no, I left my light back at the hotel!"

She teasingly tells me, "I'm sure your *butler* can bring it to you. Are you sure you're OK? You seem so anxious."

"I feel great! Never better! I felt off this morning, but Dr. Jacobson gave me an injection and..."

"Dr. Feelgood? That's what we call him around here. How wonderful. He's giving me experimental estrogen shots. Everyone swears by him. Gotta run. I'll get us a table for tonight and leave the time with—your butler!" she laughs, giving me a big wink walking off... a sexy walk that nearly knocks me off my feet.

I head to the pay phone booth in the corner and call the hotel, explaining the situation to Archie.

"Are you OK?" he asks.

"Why does everyone keep asking that? I'm fine, but I feel dumb forgetting..."

"...It's my fault, I'm so sorry, Herb, I'll make it right. I'll have Bob drive me right over. Diane called to say your shoot will be on Stage 3. I'll meet you there."

I float out of the commissary, and the next thing I know I'm back in New York, at least it feels like that with a perfect street of brownstone stoops. *Click.*

"CUT!" I hear someone yell. "Get that idiot off the set!"

I wonder who the idiot is until an older man in a dungarees runs up and grabs me by the arm. "Get outta here, ya dope!"

"SORRY" I yell as I wander off towards the Eiffel tower around the corner. I take a walk around the world and through time. Paris, ancient Rome, the Old West, the Exotic East. It reminds me of the World's fair, only smaller. *Click.*

I need to find Stage 3. I march up to a man with a clipboard, thrust out my hand and say, "Hello, I'm Herb Hamilton. Good to meet you!"

The man looks surprised. "Do I know you?"

"No, but you will. I'm a photographer for *Look* magazine and have a shoot at stage 3, can you direct me to it?"

He shakes his head, "You're standing right in front of it," pointing to the right.

"You're too kind, thanks!" The gigantic stage looks like an aircraft hangar I'd seen in "Dawn Patron" with Errol Flynn. A sliding door, as big as a house, is open and I walk in.

162 ➻ Mickey & Judy

Inside, the darkness is blinding. I take off my sunglasses and it's still too dark to see.

I feel a hand on my shoulder and hear a familiar friendly voice ask. "Hey, are you Herb?"

I look down to see the one and only Mickey Rooney, only as high as my shoulders. He thrusts out his hand to me and says, "Hi, I'm Mickey, good to meet you!"

I shake his hand, "Hi, Mickey, I feel like I already know you."

"Yeah, I get that a lot. It's nice. Judy's not here yet, but she's always late. Don't worry, once she shows up she'll be dynamite."

"That's OK, I'm waiting for my equipment." Just then I see a black Cadillac pull up outside. Archie gets out carrying the box with my light. "Oh, here it comes."

"Ain't it great having a butler?" Mickey asks, like everyone does.

Archie arrives, winded. "My apologies, Herb, we would have been sooner but there was traffic and..."

"It's fine. Archie, this is Mickey."

Mickey sticks out his hand, "Hi, I'm Mickey, good to meet you, Arch!"

Archie tentatively shakes hands, "My pleasure, Mr. Rooney."

"Aw, nonsense, my friends call me Mickey, or Mick."

"Excuse me... Mickey, I'm sorry to intrude, but it's terribly important that I speak with Herb privately for a moment."

"Take your time!" Mickey says while strutting out into the sun.

"I must humbly ask for your forgiveness, sir..."

"It's fine, Archie, and what's with this 'sir' business?"

Archie looks at his feet, then stands straight again. "I'm afraid that in being too familiar with you I became lax, and thus it's all my fault."

"You don't have anything to apologize for, Archie."

"But I do, sir. For the hot cocoa this morning."

"It was good..."

"I neglected to specify that it was to be a virgin drink and the bar man just assumed... It had alcohol in it, despite you specifically telling me you did not drink. I didn't realize the error until I was cleaning up and by that time you'd left. I'm terribly ashamed and will, of course, resign immediately."

"No, Archie, it was just a mistake. And I liked it. I like you. I'm glad you told me, it explains why I felt funny this morning but that all turned out for the best." I patted his arm. "Hey, really, it's OK."

Another butler approaches and speaks with an accent that sounds just like Archie. "Excuse me, sir, but have you seen Mr. Rooney?"

"Clarence Cox?" asks Archie.

"Archibald Tentrees?"

Recognition lights up their faces and they hug each other like old friends. "I haven't seen you since... Where'd you land?" Clarence asks.

"The Beverly Hill Hotel bungalows," Archie answers.

"That must be lovely, always new faces instead of just the same grumpy one! I'm preparing high tea for Mick, come with me you old ponce!"

"You sure?" Archie asks, concerned. Clarence grabs him around the waist and they walk away. I hear Archie say, "I'm so sorry. I made the most dreadful mistake today, with alcohol in hot cocoa..."

Clarence nods his head, "Not enough? I hear that every morning!"

Mickey wanders back in, "All the limeys around here know each other, you'll get used to it. Where to, chief?"

"I want to show you in your element."

"In that case you should follow me to a cathouse!" Mickey roars with laughter. "And Judy to a pharmacy. Naw, just joking, she's swell, I never met another performer who could show up at the last minute and deliver the goods the way she does. She works her ass off, though she doesn't have much of an ass, not at all my type, but I love her like a sister. Me, I've got a thing for Ava Gardner, she's got the most beautiful bicuspids."

This is not at all the Mickey Rooney I knew from the movies. "What do you do for fun, Mick?"

"Besides cattin' around? Golf, I'm crazy about it. Pretty damned good, too. I got a putting green in my dressing room, wanna see?"

"Absotively!"

He reaches up and puts his arm around my shoulder like we're pals. His dressing room looks like a fancy country house—lots of stone and wood. "Nice place you got here!" I say. *Click.*

"It's pretty sweet. I loved what the art director, Van Nest, did in 'Bringing up Baby' and had him design this for me." We pass Archie and Clarence laughing in the kitchen.

"This is my baby here," he says of an especially bright whitewashed room, empty other than a strip of grass down the center of it. "Clarence keeps it watered and mows it with scissors. I got special lights to make it grow. Even Bing doesn't have anything like this!" *Click.* "Hey, wait till I putt!"

He holds up his putter, looks with one eye, then plants his feet, takes a swing, and the ball rolls perfectly into the cup. He raises his arms in triumph. *Click!*

"Drat, I forgot to have you smoking!"

"No problem, boss, I'll do another take!" He lights up a Chesterfield and does the same shtick as the first time. Exactly the same. "How's that?"

"Perfect. Now, do that thing you did with the stick and one eye."

"You mean the *club?*" Mickey laughs.

"Yes, the club." He follows directions perfectly. *Click.* "OK, don't move." He freezes. I take the club from his hands and replace it with a Chesterfield. *Click.* His expression changes and becomes like a puppy dog begging for a bone. *Click.*

He freezes again, "How was that?"

"You're a pro!"

"Don't I knows it. Can I move now?"

"Sure. Would it mess up the grass if you laid down on it?" I ask.

"Naw, besides Clarence can get on his hands and knees and fluff it up when I'm done."

He lies on his back, his legs crossed, takes a long drag then lets out a big puffy cloud of smoke. *Click.* He turns so his face is right next to the grass. I lay down on my stomach and get a shot of the grass, and a happy contented look on his face. *Click.*

He hands the cigarette to me, "Want a drag?"

"Oh, I don't smoke cigarettes."

He breaks into gales of laughter, joyfully rolling on the grass, *click,* spewing smoke, *click,* until he's back on his back, what's left of the cigarette between his fingers. *Click.*

"Hey, I'm sure you'll like smoking this!" He leaps to his feet in a single move and disappears for a moment, coming back with a tall fancy green glass thing that looks like a Genie's bottle, all decorated with gold. He takes the long hose from the side, puts it in his mouth and inhales. His eyes roll and he exhales a sweet smelling cloud. "Here, give it a try," he says, handing the hose to me.

"I don't know what to do," I tell him.

"Just put your lips together and suck." I put the tip of the thing in my mouth and suck... and cough, and cough and cough. He laughs and laughs. "OK, big sucker! Try it again, champ—just a little this time."

I've only just stopped coughing and don't much like the idea, but his face is so excited I don't want to disappoint him. I draw in a little breath and taste the smoky flavor in my mouth. I start to feel light headed.

"Woah, there, partner, you'd better sit down." He guides me to the window seat. "Feels good, don't it?"

It did feel good, or might when the room stopped spinning. "What's in that crazy genie bottle?"

"Hash."

"Doesn't taste like corned beef," I say, the room slowing.

"Hashish. Just the thing on a long stressful day. Calms me right down."

"Teatime, Mick!" Clarence announces at the door. Mick holds me up and we go to his dining room next to what looks like a roaring fire but doesn't feel hot. I lean down and stare at it.

"His first time with hash!" he laughs.

I can't take my eyes off the fire that looks like it's made of sparkling rubies.

"I'm afraid he's had too much excitement for one day," Archie says, pulling me away gently and sitting me down at the table. "You should eat something, Herb," he hands me a little sandwich with the crusts cut off. I take a bite and it tastes like butter and cucumber.

"Somebody forgot to put meat on this sandwich, but it's still OK," I say, grabbing another, this one pink and tasting like the lobster I had on the train, another one egg. "These taste *so* good!"

"He's on cloud 9," Mick says before stuffing a tiny strawberry tart into his mouth.

"My old family recipe," Clarence says, gently placing a tart, and a finger into Archie's mouth. Archie smacks his lips and licks the cream off Clarence's finger. They sure got friendly fast, maybe that's what you're supposed to do!

I pick up a cream puff and stick it and my finger in Mick's mouth. He spits both out. "What'ya doing? I'm no fag."

"I saw them do it and thought... no pun intended... I mean, no offense taken."

"It's OK, loopy boy," Mickey puts his hand on my shoulder. "You don't know what you're doing. You'll feel better after a nap."

"But I have to shoot Judy..."

"She won't be here for a while. I'll show our high-flying friend to my bed and wake him when Miss Judy honors us with her presence." He takes my arm again. I reach back to get one of those tarts and stuff it in my mouth. Yummy!

Mick has a big fluffy bed and I plop down on the chenille cover. "Get a load of this!" he says, pressing a button next to the headboard. The lights dim and suddenly it's raining outside. "My own personal special effects weather machine..."

...My eyes close and I'm standing in the rain getting soaked to the skin. A big black Cadillac pulls up, splashing me with even more water. Iris steps out, the rain clouds part above, glowing gold in her own beam of sunshine.

She floats towards me, her arms reaching out. I run to her, then stop at the curb and look down. There, under water in the gutter, her face all blue, is Kitty. I look up at Iris, then down at Kitty.

"Oh, look, you've found her!" Iris says, dreamily.

"Help me!" I cry. "Help me get her up."

Iris looks sad. "You know there's no helping her, Herbie."

Leo the MGM Lion bounds in, picks up Kitty, limp in his mouth, and lopes off with her.

I shiver from the wet and cold. Iris reaches out and touches my hand and the sunshine hits me...

...My eyes open. It's raining outside. I press Mickey's magic weather button and suddenly it's sunny here, too. I sit up, feeling better, but hungry again. The others are still at the table, only a few treats left. I reach in and take another tart, look up, and there's Judy in the doorway, ravishing in a glamorous bottle green gown.

"You're gorgeous!" I gasp.

"I like this one," she says, pointing to me, drifting over, gently extending her hand and saying, "Hi, I'm Judy, it's a pleasure to meet you."

"The pleasure is all mine," I manage to say, mouth full of tart.

"When you boys are quite finished stuffing yourselves, maybe we could finally get to work."

"I'm so sorry to keep you waiting Miss Garland," I say, sincerely, hearing Mickey snicker.

"I accept your apology. Now let's lose these cretins, shall we?" she says so deliciously that the tart is tasteless in comparison.

I'm surprised how tiny she is since she looks so big on the silver screen. I follow her across the massive sound stage to her dressing room, a white metal trailer. Inside it's all built-in furniture and knotty pine. "Mickey gets the Taj Mahal and I get the Taj Ma and Pa—Kettle. But, as Mr. Mayer tells me, daily, I'm just lucky to be here."

"I think *he's* lucky *you're* here."

"Sweet of you to say. I'm sorry I'm late. I'm just so tired. I can't remember the last time I slept."

"Not at all?"

"I go into stupors," she said, "they don't feel like sleep anymore." She seems so sad, yet everything I'd seen of her in the movies was so bright and full of life.

"I'm sorry."

She smiles. "Huh. I can't remember the last time someone said 'I'm sorry' to me." She stares off, in a daze.

Uncomfortable, I look around and see a small movie projector at the end of the trailer. "What do you like to watch?"

"Do you want the truth or a good story?"

"Whatever you want to say."

"Gee, you're nice, so I'll tell you the truth. I like to watch my own movies because I look and act like a happy person. I see that girl and imagine I'm her. Crazy, isn't it?"

"Not crazy, Judy. Can I call you Judy?"

"I've been called worse."

"You bring happiness to millions of people. Why shouldn't you bring happiness to yourself, too."

She smiled. A very pretty smile, like in the movies. "That was more helpful than all the shrinks they've inflicted on me. If you're not busy I'll pay you to stick around and be nice to me."

"I'm nice for free."

"I'm not used to people being nice to me, especially not handsome young men, so we better get to work or I'll start to cry."

"I didn't mean to make you..."

"Never mind me, it's just my sense of humor. Time to tell me what to do."

"I have a crazy idea, but then I'm a little bit crazy..."

"seems we have a lot in common."

I find the switch on the projector and turn it on, "I want to see both sides of you at once. The real, sleepless Judy, and the happy Judy who thrills the world. Stand here, please."

"Nobody ever says 'please,' I could get used to this." She stands where I point.

"May I touch you to get you in just the right position?"

I see a tear forming in her eye. "You can touch me any way you want, dear." I gently move her shoulders into place, then lightly touch her chin and feel her shudder.

"I'm sorry, I didn't mean to…"

"No, it felt lovely, go on." I guide her chin so the film being projected aligns with her face, her black and white eye in the film matching her real glistening brown eye. I hand her a cigarette which she barely puffs. The happy movie Judy dances on her own pensive face. *Click. Click. Click. Click. Click.* Even though she's completely still, each shot is totally different because the image projected on her keeps changing.

"That's perfect, hold that." I go to the projector and rewind a bit, then when it hits an especially beautiful smiling closeup of her, I stop the projector reels from moving to hold that image. *Click. Click. Click.*

The heat of the projector lamp is too much for the film and it starts to buckle and melt, making horrible but beautiful patterns on her face. *Click. Click.* Then simply strong, pure light. *Click.*

"Thank you. I'm sorry I ruined your film."

"There's always more where that came from." She gives me a peck on the cheek which feels electric. "You might have captured the real me. Do you think people will be disappointed?"

"I hope they'll see the depth of your beauty."

"Oh, Lord, boy." She sighed. "Marry me and take me away from all this."

"Don't you think it might help to get to know each other first?"

She puts her hands on my shoulders and draws me towards her, "What if it's better not to know?" She whispers, looking entreatingly in my eyes, not like she wants to kiss me, but like she wants me to see her.

I look into her eyes, "That's a good question and I don't have an answer, so you're right, maybe that's better."

She breaks my gaze, lets go of my shoulders and sits, a long piece of cigarette ash falling onto her dress. She leaves it there, like a dead, gray worm. *Click.* "You're wonderful," I whisper.

"If you say so. You've been awfully nice and made me feel good, which makes me feel bad. I wonder if Mick will let me at his green glass pipe, what'd ya think?"

"I'll ask for you if you'd like."

"Yes, that's good. You go ask him and I'll stay here. I feel a stupor coming on."

"I'll bring it to you."

"Such a sweet boy." She notices the ash on her dress, and looks sad again but doesn't brush it off.

"I'll be right back," I tell her.

"I bet you actually will be," she says, lying down, shoes still on her feet.

I dash over to Mickey's house. "She hit it out of the park, didn't she? She always does."

"Yes—but I need to borrow your magic green pipe so she can sleep."

"Naw, buddy, I don't think that's such a hot idea." Mick said, having his shoulders massaged by Clarence.

"But she needs it," I protest.

"That's the last thing she needs, my friend."

I run back across the soundstage to her trailer. The door's open. She's gone.

163 ➺ Buttling

I pick up the light I never ended up using and head for the car. Archie is still gabbing with Clarence. I hate to interrupt them, and besides, there's one more little egg sandwich on the table. I stuff it in my mouth and wait until Archie sees me.

"Are you finished, Sir?"

"Yes, if you are. I need to develop these rolls and make some contact sheets."

"Of course. Excuse us, Clarence. Will I see you later?"

Clarence straightens Archie's tie and winks.

We walk to the car. "I need a darkroom," I tell Archie.

"There's a one back at the hotel in the publicity department. I'll arrange for you to use it."

"Thanks, Archie, you're swell." We get in the car.

Archie was very formal again, "Sir, After what happened earlier today I believe we should observe our traditional roles of master and butler."

"If that's what you want, but I'd rather be pals. My other pals are 3,000 miles away." I stick my head out of the window—the warm air feels so fresh.

"I'd like that very much, Herb, thank you."

I pull my head back in the car, "Since we're pals, what's up with you and Clarence? You guys seem awfully chummy." I can't figure out the expressions that flash across Archie's face—a smile, a grimace, a tear, a sigh, a cough, another smile.

"Much as I would like to share this with 'a pal,' I fear I cannot tell you as you might disapprove and my position here could be in jeopardy."

"I understand better than you might think. Were you... close... even..." it's hard for me to say, "romantic?" Archie's face turns red. "Oh, I'm so sorry I offended you."

"I have never talked about this," he whispers so quietly I'm not sure if I heard him right. I roll up my window.

"Never?"

"In my field it's quite common but always very hush hush. It's not something that's acceptable in polite society... even though polite society is filled with it, oh, the stories I could tell but of course never would, part of the Buttling code." He dabs his eye with his pristine handkerchief as his back slumps.

"You don't have to tell me if you don't want to..."

"...We were *very* close friends at the British Butler Institute. But I was young and stupid and made a grievous error."

"I'm sorry..."

"It's a relief to talk about it. Rence had a chance to open a florist's shop at the Savoy. Wanted me to run it with him... But I was afraid of what people would think. So afraid that I left for America... without even telling him." Archie's tears soak into his black coat.

I put my hand on his shoulder. "We all make mistakes. I fear I made one when I was much younger."

"I hope it's not too late to say I'm sorry." He asks, sitting stiffly upright again. We drive in silence the rest of the way.

Back at the hotel Archie takes me to the darkroom. I develop the film and it's fine. I make contact prints, they're better than fine. I make a double exposure of Mickey holding the golf club overlaid with the cigarette. It's fun, especially how his expression changes.

The ones of Judy are so striking. Happy on the surface, yet I know what's underneath, and, I suspect, so will women who see it.

There's a knock at the door. "Herb, are you in there?" It's Archie. "Just finishing up."

"I received a call from Miss Rose, she made reservations at 7 and it's almost 6. It's a short drive from here but I wanted to make sure you time to clean up and change.

"6? I completely lost track of time, thanks for getting me." Back at the bungalow I take a quick shower and change into the beautiful blue suit Iris made, paired with my sky blue shirt, turquoise bolo and black loafers.

"You look very smart, Herb. The car will pick you up out front at 6:45."

"Thanks, Archie. What're your plans for this evening, seeing Clarence?"

The usually straight-faced Archie turned pink. "As a matter of fact..."

"I hope you two will feel free to use the bungalow while I'm out—I expect to be out late."

"That's very kind, sir... Herb. I don't feel it would be appropriate..."

"Nonsense. You boys order whatever you'd like and enjoy yourselves! I should be going." I leave before he can protest.

The suit feels so good, like my lucky charm. As I walk through the lobby I see people looking at me. Bob is waiting at the car. "Good evening, sir, those are some swanky threads you got on!"

"Threads?" I look down to see if there's a seam loose.

"It's hip lingo music folks are saying, I drive a lot of 'em." he says, opening my door. "But this is the first time I've dropped anybody at the prince's place. Nobody can get a table. You must be important."

"I don't think so, Bob, I just know the right people."

"That's what matters in this town. I hope you'll remember me when you need a driver, or a fix."

"Sure, Bob, if I'm ever in a fix."

The night air is warm as we drive past the mansions, lit from within. We cross a narrow park, a wide street and are in the Beverly Hills village again. Bob turns right, then left and left again so he pulls up at the curb of the sleek restaurant, waiting behind a line of other Cadillacs.

164 ➻ Romanoff's

A flock of women in candy colored evening gowns emerge from jewel tone Cadillacs. We creep forward until a doorman in a bright red coat and a Russian black fur hat opens my door. "Good evenink, sir, velcome to Romanoff's," he says with a heavy accent.

I emerge into the warm night in front of a modern low-slung building one long white wall with "ROMANOFF" in impressive gold letters, the R looking like a royal crest with a crown. Another man in a red coat and fur hat opens the shiny red door. Inside it's dark and moderne, with birch trees spotlit against the rich burgundy walls.

The maître d' quite obviously sizes me up and looks stern.

A bit daunted, I tell him, "I have reservations for two, under the name of Iris Rose."

He checks his book, smiles slightly, "Ach, lovely, Miss Rose is alveady here, I shall show you to your tahbul," in another heavy accent.

The room is stuffed with stars. Cary Grant, looking just as handsome in person, sits at a table with the equally handsome Randolph Scott. Imposing Clark Gable is lighting glamorous Carole Lombard's cigarette.

And there, glowing in the soft candlelight, is Iris, radiant in red. Sipping a drink, she looks up to see me and smiles. The maître d' pulls out my chair and I sit.

"You're stunning." I say, transfixed.

"You look quite elegant. That's a beautiful suit."

"Made by beautiful hands," I say, taking her hand.

She looks across the room and waves at a man, oh, it's Adrian. He nods. "It's good for him to see me out with you so he doesn't think I'm just waiting around..."

A distinguished looking man appears, his blazer emblazoned with a big gold crest. He's wearing spats and carrying a silver-tipped walking stick. "Prince Michael Dimitri Alexandrovich Obolensky-Romanoff," he says, with a mysterious accent. "We are so pleased to have you as our guest this evening." He kisses her hand, straightens and commands, "Enjoy!" before bowing, clicking his heels together, and turning to go.

We watch him ooze to his table where two large dogs sit on a red velvet banquette. A waiter brings three plates to his table, one for each of them and even the dogs eat elegantly.

"That was quite the floor show!" Iris exclaims.

"He sure seems like a real prince."

"Harry's a real prince of thieves, I've no doubt, though Gilbert and everyone else in town finds him charming.

"Who's Gilbert?"

"Adrian, originally Adrian Adolph Greenburg. Fakes of a feather..." she says, pointing around the room, then at herself and me.

"We're not fakes."

"You're telling me you're still lil ol' Herbie from the South Bronx? You, with your Swiss watch, Italian shoes and English butler? I'm certainly not... I don't ever say his name... But you're right, we're not fakes, we're just new people."

For a moment I don't even recognize her. Or myself. Everything feels like a dream again. I expect a lion to walk through the doors and sit down with us... what I don't expect is to see a familiar face, not across from me, but across the room—another Kitty? But she turns around and all I see is a small man in a pinstriped suit.

"Roving eye already?" Iris asks.

"No, sorry, I thought I saw somebody I knew."

"Not likely, is it? And isn't it wonderful?" She takes another sip of her drink. "How do you like my gown?" She gestures to her red, clingy dress that exposes one shoulder while the other arm has a sleeve down to her wrist.

"It's incredible, like you."

"That's sweet. I designed and made it myself. Adrian says, 'A woman must look as she feels and not try to feel as she looks.' This is how I feel now."

"You must feel beautiful," I say, because she does.

"I was cursed, or blessed, with wide shoulders like Garbo. So, like Adrian does with her, I don't try to hide them, I accentuate them, make them my style. But you didn't come to dinner for a lesson in fashion, now, did you?"

"I came here for you..." I momentarily forget her name, "...Iris. I'm so..."

"...confused, I know *you* are. But *I'm* not. I knew how I felt about you, Herbie. I loved you."

"I love you, too!" I declare.

Her eyes well up and a tear runs down her cheek, making a black line from her makeup. She dabs it with her napkin before it can land on her dress. "I've longed for you to say that... but you're confusing me with someone else."

"No, it's you! I loved you the moment I saw you... change."

"How I wish that was true."

"It is true!" I protest.

"You loved Kitty. You still do."

"No, I don't..." I stop. I don't even believe myself so I try to remember, "She was awful."

"Always. Yet you still love her, don't you?"

"No, I don't, I don't... know."

"I know. You look at me and you see her. How could you not? But I'm not going to be a consolation prize."

"You're not! You know I've always been fond of you."

She freezes. I study her image, like a still photo.

Her mouth moves again but the rest of her face is fixed. "Ah, 'fond.' Yes, that I believe. And kind, Herbie, you've always been kind. I will always remember that."

I don't know her. I knew someone who looked like her. No, I thought I knew someone who looked like her.

"I'm not being cruel, Herbie... neither are you, but we're not the same people anymore. You know I'm right, don't you?"

"I don't know anything, Iris. But I know I have feelings for you."

She gasps, "Feelings. Oh, dear." then takes a long, deep breath, puts down her napkin and stands, sad and strong. "Find me again when you know exactly what those feelings are."

"They're good feelings, Iris, good feelings..."

She puts her hand on my shoulder and looks me in the eye. "I can get feelings from a dog," then walks away.

My face is hot, my hands cold. I'm sure Cary and Randolph and Clark and Carole are all looking at me. I want to run but can't move.

Across the room I see the man in pinstripe. He turns, and for a moment there's Kitty, again. Then he turns away and laughs with two large men and three sparky ladies. Are they laughing at me?

I stand up slowly and walk to the door. The maître d' stops me. "Nobody leafs Romanoff's mitout dining."

"Miss Rose was feeling ill and I'm going to make sure she's OK."

He moves close and whispers, without a trace of accent, "I don't think so. She told me to tell you to enjoy your dinner."

I slink back to the table. I look around. I'm the only one alone at a table. Even the prince has his two dogs.

The waiter approaches, sheepishly. "Dinner for one?"

I'm ravenously hungry. "I'll have the green salad, onion soup, double lamb chops bearnaise with mushrooms, French peas, French fries, baked potato and sour cream… and a chocolate souffle." I look at Iris's glass. It's half-empty. I swallow what's left. It tastes like medicine. "And another one of these drinks, make it two."

165 ➻ Ruined

If there was music, I didn't hear it. If the food had flavor I didn't taste it, just a touch of salt as a tear landed on my lips.

I've ruined everything. How strange to be living a nightmare in this place of dreams.

I'll finish the shoots here and go home. But where is home? Glenn's filing room? He'll probably move in with Pat, or her with him. No place for me. I don't have a job at *Look*. Maybe I can do more shoots for Jerry, or try to get work at another magazine. I can go to London, nobody will care if I die…

I let out a long, uncomfortable burp just as the waiter arrives with a silver platter holding Romanoff's famous chocolate souffle. It looks beautiful but I instantly feel sick and rush past him to the bathroom, all burgundy tile, and dive into a toilet stall to throw up.

166 ➻ Jimmy

I splash water on my face and drag myself back to the table. The souffle is still there, flat. I take a bite just to get the bad taste out of my mouth. I hope it will be sweet. It isn't.

I stop the waiter and ask for the bill. "The lady already took care of it."

That makes me feel worse. I leave $5 for the waiter. Now I have to get past the maître d'. Luckily he's busy with a man who's clearly a producer, with two young female starlets hanging on his arms, their low-cut dresses displaying their talent.

Outside the night air is still too warm. An endless line of Cadillacs keeps pulling up, disgorging happy, colorful occupants but where's Bob?

Everybody's having a good time in this stupid city except for me.

I wander down the street looking for where Bob might have parked. Or maybe he went back to the hotel and I was meant to call him. I feel like walking anyway. I head up the street in the direction of the hotel.

In two blocks I find myself in the land of movie star mansions. These people aren't idiots like I am. They're rich and famous so they must all be happy.

My feet feel heavy. I'm sweating. I take off my jacket. Where am I? Where am I going? I don't know. The hotel, yes, but where is that? I have no idea. I can only shuffle along.

All I want to do is lie down on this lawn. Lie down and sleep and wake up and find that this was yet another dumb dream. Wake up back at Glenn's or the Ansonia or... No, not the South Bronx. But they're all 3,000 miles away from Beverly Hills. I wish I could go home but don't have one.

I lay down on the cool, wet, sweet-smelling grass. This feels good. I like the dewy dampness against my cheek. I lay here, panting, trying to remember where the day started. It feels like I've been here a month.

Do I still have feet? I can't feel them.

What did I say to Iris that was so awful? I can't remember anything but the movie stars and waiter's hats and the toilet, a burgundy toilet.

I close my eyes...

...I squinted in the sun and I looked up at a blue sky filled with puffy clouds shaped like Bugs Bunny being chased by cartoon lions and tigers and bears, oh my! I heard Iris's voice calling, "Wash up for lunch, boys!" as two young boys ran past me. I got to my feet, barefoot, wearing shorts. The house looked like a cute English cottage. Life was perfect. Then I froze. I didn't know what to do.

"Cut, CUT!" a man's voice shouted. There was a loud BUZZ and the lights went out with a clang. A director in jodhpurs marched up and smacked me with a riding crop. "Wrong, wrong, wrong, wrong, wrong! You're wasting everyone's time. Get it right this time, moron! Now, back to the top."

The boys blew Bronx cheers at me and taunted, "you blew it, you blew it!" I looked around, disoriented. The director marched back up to me, "God, you really don't know what you're doing, do you? Get in your starting position, you dolt!" I laid back on the grass the way I started...

...I feel something tap my shoulder. My eyes open, it's dark. I see a plaid slipper nudge my shoulder and hear a familiar voice. "Hey, buddy, you can't sleep on my lawn. You gotta go or I'll hafta call the cops and I don't wanna do that. I'm tryin' to be nice here."

I look up. It's Jimmy Cagney. "Oh, I'm sorry, I'm so sorry, I got lost on the way back to the Beverly Hills Hotel."

"You tried to walk? You must be from New York!"

"South Bronx."

"Lower East Side!" he says, reaching down and pulling me to my feet.

"Oh, Mr. Cagney, I'm so sorry to bother you. My name's Herb, I work for *Look* and Chesterfield and have a shoot with you on Friday."

"You're a little early, ain't ya?" he says in a friendly way. "You look like hell, kid, come on inside."

I'm wobbly. He puts his arm around my waist and guides me into the big brick house. "Look what the cat dragged in," he says to a surprised looking curly haired woman in a nightgown.

"Jimmy, I've asked you before..."

"Naw, Billie, this kid's supposed to take my picture for the Chesterfield ad and got lost on the way back to the Beverly Hills Hotel."

"He's taking your picture at, what time is it? Midnight? Heavens, young man, I don't know how they do things where you come from but this is not how it's done here."

"I'm so sorry, ma'am, my girl walked out on me at Romanoff's... I got sick and couldn't find my driver and thought I'd walk..."

"Walk? In Los Angeles? Where're you from, New York?"

"South Bronx," Jimmy said for me.

"Well, I'm from Des Moines, Iowa where we know better. Lord, you look awful. I'll get you a bicarb and call the hotel to pick you up."

"What day is this?" I ask Jimmy who looks at me with concern.

"Thursday, kid."

"Wednesday was a very long day... Thursday, I shoot Cary Grant and Katherine Hepburn," I remember.

"I've wanted to shoot Hepburn myself. And that pansy Grant, real name Leach. Bunch of phonies out here. Ya don't see me changin' my name."

"My name's always been Herb..."

"...Good for you, don't you go changing it for nobody."

My face feels hot again. My pants are damp from the lawn and I start to shiver.

Jimmy stares off, "As a kid, I slogged through the snow without a coat. In Hollywood, the thermometer drops below 70 and we're all chilly." He throws a crocheted blanket over me. "My nana made that with her own hands, don't you go puking on it."

"I've got nothing left to throw up. I've got nothing left."

"Yeah, I know how that feels. Been down in the dumps myself many a time. The trick is to keep gettin' back up. You're a hearty lad, you can do it."

The woman in the robe hands me a glass of bubbles. "You drink this all up. The hotel's car will be here in a minute."

I drank it, fizzy, salty, bad. I cover my mouth but couldn't stifle a long burp.

"Workin' already, you'll feel better in the morning, lad." Jimmy says.

"I'm so sorry to bother you, so sorry to bother everybody..."

Jimmy leads me back out front. "So your girlfriend dumped you?"

"How did you know that? Does everybody in Hollywood know?"

"You told me, kid. Few things hurt a man more. Ah, there's your Caddy. I'll be interested to see if you remember any of this on Friday. Go on, get in."

A driver I don't know rushes around and helps me in.

167 ➻ Just Kids

I drag myself through the lobby, feeling like a bum. It's dark in the bungalow. I run into a chair, "Damn it all!"

The lights in the second bedroom come on and Archie, wearing a white hotel robe, leans out through the door. "Oh, Herb! The lobby was supposed to call me when they sent a car for you. I didn't mean for you to see me this way."

I hear another voice and the door opens wider to reveal Clarence, also in a hotel robe. "Oh, hello, Herb." He speaks softly to Archie, "He looks like hell, you got your work cut out for you. I'll get dressed and go."

"You don't have to go, Clarence. Just because I'm miserable doesn't mean you have to be."

Clarence and Archie look at each other, their eyebrows raised. Clarence retreats, closing the bedroom door behind him.

Archie looks concerned "I take it dinner didn't go well."

"She left me, again. This time for good."

"For good can be for the best."

"Is that how Clarence felt when you left?" I hiss. "Oh, God, I'm such an asshole!"

Achie sits down with me on the sofa, laying his warm hand on top of mine. Neither of us say anything for a while until he says. "I'm sorry, Herb, that was thoughtless of me."

"No, you were being nice and I was being mean. I'm the one who's sorry. I don't know what happened, Archie. She looked pretty, she told me she loved me and I told her I loved her, too, but then I said something and she got hurt or mad and left. I'm such an idiot I don't even know what I said."

"That happens when you drink," Clarence says, fully dressed in his butler's suit.

"I don't drink..." I say at the same time as Archie says, "He doesn't drink... until this morning."

"I'd best be going now, we'll talk tomorrow Arch."

"Please don't go on my account, Clarence. Please, I'll feel even worse if I mess things up for you, too."

Clarence sits on my other side and puts his hand on my shoulder. I feel safe with these men by my side. I let go and start sobbing, sniffly, snotty. Clarence hands me a handkerchief. "You kids like Mickey and Judy... seem so professional but you're just kids. You should see Mickey bawling like a babe when he loses a girl."

Archie adds, "I remember what it was like to be a kid..." I see the two men exchanging a glance and it makes me feel better. I may have had a lousy father but I've been lucky with Sam and Max and Glenn and now Archie and Clarence. There are good men in the world and I want to be like them.

"Thank you, guys. I'm so tired but I need some air..."

Archie takes my chin in his hand and looks me straight in the eye, "What you need is to go to sleep, young man. You march right off to bed. I'll wake you in the morning and make sure you get plain cocoa."

I shuffle slowly to the bedroom, dropping clothes along the way. Archie pulls back the covers, and opens the windows. I slide into bed and he tucks me in. I reach up and touch his face, feeling the stubble on his chin. "Thank you, Archie. I wish you'd been my dad."

Archie smiles, tears in his eyes, as mine close.

168 ➤➤ Tomorrow's Another Day

I smell jasmine. The room is full of light. The world is OK again... until I remember last night. The jasmine withers, the light fades. I'm so hot under the covers I have to throw them off.

There's a knock at the door. Archie opens it and looks in, unusually chipper, "Ah, up, I see. Good. It's 11am. You've got your shoot today at 1pm at MGM. Rise and shine, Herb."

"Thanks, Archie. I hope you and Clarence had a good night. Is he here?"

"We did, thank you. He left early this morning because Mickey needs him to get ready for the studio. Before he left he asked me to send his regards to you."

"I appreciate you both being so kind to me last night."

He sets down a tray with two white pills and a glass of water. "Aspirin, take it now." He waits while I do. "What would you like for breakfast this morning?"

"I don't know. Surprise me?"

"Banana pancakes to settle your stomach."

My head feels like it was stuffed with cotton. I hear buzzing. I stand up, unsteady and hold the wall as I shuffle to the bathroom. Oh! I see myself in the mirror, eyes puffy... Why is there dirt on my face? I try to remember. Restaurant. Iris. Oh. Then? I don't remember.

I get in the shower, it's hot, steamy and the soap smells very strong and makes my stomach feel queasy. I watch the dirt sliding off me down into the drain. How did I get so dirty at dinner? I hear buzzing and see a spot out of the corner of my eye, but then it's gone. I towel off, feeling a little better.

I put on the white robe and see breakfast setup outside. Six golden, plate-sized pancakes await with three kinds of syrup in glass bottles with their names on chains around them: maple, boysenberry, strawberry. I've never heard of boysenberry. I pour it over a pancake and take a taste, tart-sweet, almost making my tongue tingle. The slices of banana in the pancakes make them sweet even without syrup.

I hear buzzing again and see something move. How'd that bee follow me from New York? It lands on my plate and seems to enjoy what's left of the syrup. I watch it crawling around the plate and hope it's happier than I am.

I'm angry with myself. I'm in the lap of luxury in a place where it's summer even in winter and I'm meeting movie stars. There's no reason for me to be unhappy. Oh, yeah, Iris.

The bee flaps its wings but is stuck in the syrup. I use my knife to gently pick it up, then look it in the eye. "Go back to work, little fella." It flies off.

That's what I need to do, too, go back to work. I'm good at that even if I'm not good at love.

I hear the phone ring. Archie answers, then brings it to me, "Glenn Fine, calling collect, I accepted the charges."

I grab the phone, "Glenn! Boy, am I glad to hear from you!"

"Are you OK? You said you'd call, I've been worried, Pat's been worried. I was afraid you fell off the train or took a wrong turn at Albuquerque!"

"I'm sorry to make you worry, Glenn. It's been crazy."

"When we woke up today and still hadn't heard from you I finally said I was gonna call."

"I'm glad you did, Glenn. It's good to hear a familiar voice."

"I'm relieved. Pat, he's OK..."

"Wait a sec, 'when *we* woke up?'"

"Yeah, I'm staying at her place in Tudor City." Glenn said, then I heard some tussling and Pat came on the line, "You're a naughty boy, Herbie. Glenn was so worried he could hardly eat his pizza last night."

It made me smile to think about them together. "I'm sorry, Pat. I'm kinda having a hard time... not with the photos, they're good, but..."

"Kitty?" She asked.

"It's hard to explain."

"I'm sorry kiddo," she says, sounding like she means it. "Hold on, Glenn wants to talk to you again. Tell Diana to get proofs to editorial, too. I hope she's being helpful."

"Diana. No, she's terrible. I'd fire her if I were you."

"I'll see what I can do. Here's Glenn..."

"So... Kitty?"

"Let's just say 'she's changed.'"

"Sorry, boychik. When you find the right one it'll be right, like with Pat."

"I'm gonna focus on my work for now. I met Mickey Rooney and he's a pip. Judy Garland, such a doll. And Jimmy Cagney... wait, I haven't taken his picture yet, why do I remember..."

"Hey, I got a surprise for you. Pat's sending me to Hollywood to photograph that radio guy, Welles. I hear you got an extra room so we can roomies again!"

"That's great, but I could have taken that..."

"I told her that but you don't work for her no more and Orson won't do cigarette ads, says they're... doesn't matter. I'm flying out and will be there tomorrow."

"Flying?"

"They need it for the next issue so it's a rush. I'm scared about the aeroplane but excited, too."

"I'm so happy you'll be here, Glenn!" Archie points at his watch—noon. "Sorry, I gotta go or I'll be late. When do you get here?"

"Tomorrow, can you believe it? It's only a 19 hour flight! OK, you go, we can talk in person tomorrow night!"

The phone clicks. I take a deep breath. It will be a relief to have Glenn here, but it feels funny him taking pictures I could have taken.

I don't have time to think about it. I get dressed, putting on the blue seersucker suit and loafers. I'll wear my new hat and sunglasses.

"Knock knock!" Diane says.

"She didn't give me time to announce her, Herb."

"That's OK. Hi, Diane. I just talked to Pat who says you need to send her proofs of my shots. I made extra copies and they're on the table by the door, in the hotel envelope with your name on them. Oh, and I told Pat to fire you."

Diane kisses me on the cheek, rather roughly. "You're a peach. Penury here I come!"

"You're welcome. Hey, I heard that Osron Welles says cigarettes are bad for you, can that be true?"

"Funny you should ask—I have new copy to show you in case it inspires something for the shoot."

I read the typed page:

"A medical specialist is making regular bi-monthly examinations of a group of people from various walks of life. 45 percent of this group have smoked Chesterfield for an average of over ten yars. After ten months, the medical specialist reports that he observed... no adverse effects on the nose, throat and sinuses of the group smoking Chesterfield. Much milder, CHESTERFIELD IS BEST FOR YOU!

"Oh, that's good," I say, relieved.

"It's bullshit," Diane says out of the side of her mouth while lighting a cigarette. "These things'll kill you. Chesterfield sent over some research papers by mistake, linking smoking with the epidemic of lung cancer."

"I don't believe it. They couldn't have all these ads saying it was good for you if it wasn't. Besides, if it's so bad, then why do you smoke?" I ask her.

"Clearly, to punish myself. That, and they also kill my appetite so I lose weight. Any more questions, nosy Ned?"

"Nope. Except if they're that bad for a person I want to start." I add.

"Yes, a hard day snapping pictures of movie stars and ordering room service will do that to a person. I told you, capitalism is for suckers, so you might as well suck on this." She hands me a cigarette. I put it on my mouth and she leans in and lights it from the end of hers.

I remember the green pipe and just take a little puff. I still cough. "This is awful."

Diane grins, "That's the whole point, baby. You just gotta hate yourself a little bit more. By the weekend you'll be a regular nicotine fiend."

The cigarette tastes less bad and I'm feeling better.

"By the way, I'm coming with you today. Apparently Mr. Hepburn hasn't signed her release yet."

"You mean 'Miss.'"

"You heard me," she said, letting out a puff of smoke that engulfed her head.

I collect my gear and take Archie aside. "I'm sorry to tell you this but a colleague from *Look* is coming tomorrow and he thinks he can stay in your bedroom."

"That's fine. We weren't planning on staying here again, it's unprofessional. Besides, Mickey has a yacht he never uses—poor thing gets seasick." Archie's gray eyes sparkle.

I put my Leica around my neck and carry the Luxite light case. Diane and I get to the car and Bob is waiting.

"Sorry I missed you last night, Herb. Pedro told me..." He looks at Diane and stops. "Just sorry."

"Thanks, Bob, I don't remember much."

"Then you musta had a good time!" he says from behind the wheel.

I watch Diane stroking the mohair upholstery. "Yes, I like the damned car, so kill me. I either need to start a revolution or marry rich." She lights up two more cigarettes and hands me one. I feel very sophisticated blowing smoke out of the window and watching it drift into the sunlight.

169 ➣ Eye eye eye

MGM already feels old hat. The guard's uniform is missing a button. There's paint peeling from the brown buildings. The hordes of people in their fancy costumes look tired.

We pull up in front of Stage 6 which looks exactly like Stage 3 yesterday, a big aircraft hangar-like building with massive sliding doors.

Bob gets my light out of the trunk, "Call when you need me," he says, tipping his driver's cap.

It's bright inside the stage, with a wide expanse of lawn and the back of a big white mansion. Katherine Hepburn, in white dress with silver sequins up the neck and down her arms, runs up to us and throws her arms around Diane. "What kind of trouble are you going to get me in this time you darling girl!"

Diane whispers something in her ear and she turns to me, "Ah, Diane tells me I was terribly rude, do forgive me." She thrusts out her hand, strongly, and says, "I'm Katherine, it's a pleasure to meet you, Harve."

"Herb," Diane whispers.

"Herb, of course, I'm at sixes and sevens, quite in a mad rush to finish a shot. I have to enter a room, look around and smile. Oh, the acting challenge involved! The lighting alone has taken hours." She turns to Diane, "You were right, he's adorable in an unbaked baguette kind of way."

Diane looks at me and shrugs.

"I'm really more half-baked," I insist.

Miss Hepburn laughs, "You're OK, kid!"

A voice shouts, "Miss Hepburn on set, please."

"Bad timing, my darlings. I must run. No time today. Come to Kook's on Saturday for a swim and we'll have more time then." She floats off towards the set.

"She likes you," Diane says.

"We we need to shoot today!"

"She'll be more relaxed at Kook's. I'll be there, too."

"Why at some kook's place?"

"Kook. Cukor. George. Her director on this picture. They adore each other. She lives in one of his guest houses. His pool parties are great fun, you'll enjoy them, even if you do like girls."

I think I see Iris out of the corner of my eye but when I turn to look she's gone. I rub my eyes. Diane hands me another cigarette and walks towards the set. I follow her.

The lights are so bright I put my sunglasses back on and there, in front of me, is a man in the same sunglasses. We glance at each other with a start, and simultaneously slide them down our noses to get a better look. I lean in.

It's Cary Grant. I reach out my arm, "Hello, I'm Herb Hamilton from *Look* magazine, and I'm through with love."

"I like your sunglasses," he says, removing his. "And that was the most original introduction I've heard in ages. Good for you! Hmm, I have no idea what Kate was going on about, you look completely baked to me. "

"What?"

"Your eyes, quite red, dear boy," he says, nicely.

"I just started smoking, maybe that's it."

"Wacky weed? I could use some. Kate's a dear, but she has boundless energy that can make a person pine for some dope."

"I'm a dope. They're Chesterfields."

"Don't smoke 'em myself, but... wait, this is the shoot for the advert, isn't it? Sorry, mate!" He becomes like a character, "Yes, I *love* them. Truly. Makes my day." He relaxes, "Was that at all convincing?"

"You don't have to convince me," I tell him, "you just have to look handsome."

"Where's my stuntman when I need him? You cannot imagine how trying it is to have to work my face into this 'Cary Grant' creature," he says, with a mischievous grin. "Where shall we go for this latest exertion of handsomeness, Herbert H. Hamilton the third?"

"What's your favorite place on the lot?"

"My car, driving off it," he said, rather unconvincingly as I follow him to his dressing room that looks like something from an English manor house. He sinks into a wing chair and crosses his legs.

I hand him a cigarette. "Are you sorry that you have to play this part?"

He cocks his head and looks me straight in the eye, "You have got to be joking. How can there be any better part to play than the dream of what one could be?"

"That's what I've been doing, but not very well," I said, bitterly.

"Feeling sorry for yourself, are you? Believe it or not, I have had my share of lost loves. When that happens it helps to have a good mate to cheer you up, like Randolph Scott does for me."

"My friend, Glenn, is coming."

"Love is fleeting. Friends are forever. I read that in a fortune cookie, so it's got to be true."

"Glenn's solid. But otherwise, I've got nothing left."

He takes me by the shoulders. "Don't be an arse! How many chaps your age, or any age, get a photo credit in an advert?"

"You've seen one?"

"It's hard to miss on the back cover of *Look* magazine, right here." He hands me this week's issue with a photo of Vivien Leigh knitting 'Bundles for Britain' in front of a very Sergei starburst background of radiating red, white and blue.

I flip it over and a Chesterfield ad fills the back cover, with a big photo of Cole Porter. A big, *bland* standard-looking headshot that's not what I gave them! Under it, in small but clearly readable type, 'Exclusive portrait by Herbert H. Hamilton III.'

"FUCK!" I blurt, shocking myself as I'd never said that word aloud before.

"Impressed with ourselves, are we?"

"No, this picture is crap. I didn't take it, or if I did it was just a throwaway. I had this great image of him and his shadow. This makes me look like a hack!"

"That's the business we're in, kid, it's all up to the editor."

"Who's this Herbert *H.* Hamilton, eye, eye, eye?" I spit.

"I imagined it was you, the third, after your father and grandfather."

"The 'H' is completely made up!" I protest.

"My entire name is made up," Cary says. "But at least I made it up myself."

"I'm the *first* Herbert Hamitlon!"

"Has a good ring to it, HHH."

"I'm going to kill Jerry!"

"That's the patriotic spirit!" he says, cheerfully, "We all want to kill the Jerrys."

"But first, I know exactly how I want to shoot you."

"That's what Cagney said to me when I pulled a prawn from his salad."

"Since you're tired of being handsome, how about you don't even try. Mess your hair. Look as bad as you can possibly look."

"Why, my boy, would I do that?" he says, squinting, handsomely.

"Because, this time, we're gonna show those assholes!"

His eyebrows raise, "I'm not in the habit of showing that part of my anatomy to just anyone. Not in my best interest, kiddo. Yours, either. What *have* you been smoking?"

"We'll take some handsome ones first, I imagine you can do them in your sleep. Smoke a cigarette and look longingly into the distance, remembering your many lost loves."

"I didn't say *many.*"

"I'm directing here," I say with authority. He follows directions perfectly. *Click.* He looks every bit a movie star. *Click.* "Give me some different angles." He does, even his smoke looks elegant. *Click, Click, Click.* I move his reading lamp to change the light, not even bothering with my photographic light. *Click, Click, Click.* "That's all they need. Now, for some fun."

"Oh why not, like 'I just went gay all of a sudden!'"

"Your line from 'Bringing up Baby,' I saw that three times."

"Why not, let's go wild!" He says, screwing his face up into Quasimodo.

"That's very pretty!" *Click.* "But your hair still looks good." He musses it and the Brylcreem makes it stand on end like a crazy person. *Click!* He sticks out his tongue and drools. "Perfect!" *Click.* Finally, he pulls a big, bug-eyed open-mouth face like I remember from 'Arsenic and Old Lace." *Click!*

Now we're both laughing so hard I can't take a sharp picture, so I close down the f-stop and take a long, blurry exposure of him laughing.

"That was fun, Herbet H. Hamilton, eye yi yi!"

It only now hits me that I'm face to face with *the* Cary Grant and it wasn't just business, we shared a laugh. I sit down and put my hand over my face, then uncover my eyes to make sure it's really real. It seems to be. "Thank you, Mr. Grant."

"I'm not your father, for heaven's sake, call me Cary, naw, Archie Leach, old chum."

"I have another friend named Archie."

"Now you have two," he says, shaking my hand, then patting me on the cheek.

170 ➤ Beat the Devil

Back at the bungalow I hear the toilet flush and Diane comes out of the bathroom, my bathroom, why couldn't she use the second bathroom?

"I'm so fucking mad!" I yell.

"I'm so fucking mad all the time." she says, not sounding mad.

"I want to kill Jerry."

"Join the club," she says, eating a lobster taco Archie thought we'd like.

"I see why you want to quit," I say to her, finally understanding.

"I will miss the lobster, though," she says, her mouth full.

"I can live without lobster but I can't live without my artistic integrity!" I say, mouth full of lobster. Diane laughs so hard a little piece of food flies across the table and hits me in the forehead, which normally I'd think was funny but I don't want to laugh and undermine my rage!

"What made you think you'd get 'artistic integrity' Herb?"

I put down the taco and remember Pat. She always appreciated my work. She warned me about Jerry and I ignored her. Defied her! My face turns red with embarrassment. Glenn's going to be here tomorrow, how can I even face him?

Diane reaches over to take the taco off my plate but I channel my anger into a death dagger stare and she recoils. "Aim that at Jerry, and make sure to tell him that I hate him, too."

"Oh, I will, I so *fucking* will. I've said 'fuck' twice today, three times if you include that last one, and I'm gonna say it a dozen more on the phone to that... fucker!"

"Gotta tell you, Herb, it doesn't sound quite right when you say it. You gotta hit the "Fff" and "K" sounds harder."

"FffucK!"

"Better. Before we get fired, let's have Archie order some dessert. I have a hankering for something flaming."

"After I call Jerry. What time is it there now?"

"Six. He'll have left at 4, 4:30 at the latest."

"FUCK!"

"The good news is I have his home number and he hates it when I call there, so that'll make your call even worse!"

I jump up, lean over and kiss her on the cheek, then grab the phone. I'd rather express my fury in private, so I drag the long cord into my bedroom. I feel a little queasy, maybe I shouldn't have eaten before I called, but I was hungry and Archie had it all ready...

Archie. I exhale like a deflated balloon. I'm going to miss him. I'm going to miss making a lot of money. I dial the number Diane gave me. It rings. And rings. And rings. Fuck—I think that word again, it's getting easier and even thinking it I hit the "F" and "k" harder.

"Jerry here," he finally answers.

"You worthless fffucKer!" I yell.

"Who is this? It could be anybody I know," he says, unfazed.

"It's Herbert ffucKing H Hamilton the fucking third!"

"Aw, you saw the ad. I thought you'd like that."

"I hated it and I hate you. You ruined my photo!"

"I thought it looked nice. And you got your precious credit," Jerry says, still calm, fuck him!

"It's not my photo, asshole."

"You took it"

"I didn't take *that!*" I say, punching the bed pillow.

"Yes, you did. It wasn't very good, we had to do a lot of retouching."

"I sent you the final double exposure!"

"Half of it was enough."

"No, it's not, you cut out the personality!" I actually spit.

"No, I cut it down to what was important—the celebrity's face. That's what the advertiser is paying for. That's what draws the reader's attention. Everything else is just fluff."

"FLUFF?" I almost throw the phone but I wouldn't be satisfied unless it hit him. "You can't do this."

"Did you read your contract? Of course I can. Your credit's right there, under the photo, that's what you asked for. You didn't specify anything about editorial control, which I can guarantee you'd never have gotten." Jerry puffs like he's smoking.

"You said I'd never get photo credit, either."

"Yeah, that surprised me, but I can sell anybody anything."

"Anybody could have taken that picture." I protest.

"Exactly. So aren't you the lucky little asshole."

"What? I'm embarrassed to have my name on it."

"But you insisted, Herbert. Besides, Diane will have a nice check for you that'll make it all better."

"No, it won't. Speaking of Diane, she hates you, too."

"Of course she does, probably asking you to get her fired, right? That's cute."

"Everybody hates you, Jerry."

"I can live with that. But, can *you* live without your bungalow at the hotel? How about your butler, Archibald?"

"Yes, Jerry, I can, and I will, because I quit."

"You can't quit, you have a contract."

"I don't care."

"You will care when Chesterfield's lawyers sue you for every penny you have and stop you from ever working as a photographer again."

"Bullshit."

"No, business. Calm down, you ungrateful little bastard." Jerry laughs. "I own you for the next three years..."

"That's not possible."

"I guess you really can't read."

"Of course I can read, but why would you do this to me?"

"Boo Hoo. Good news! I got you signed up to shoot for Schlitz, "the beer that made Milwaukee famous." When you're done in tinsel town you're off to Omaha to shoot rodeo clowns."

"I will not."

"OK, you dumb fucker, be thankful people want to pay you for pressing a little button which, as you yourself said, anybody could do. From now on, I only want to hear the words, 'Yes, sir, thank you, sir' come out of your illiterate little trap. Otherwise, I'll put your name on pictures so bad you'll wish the camera was never invented. Your reputation will be ruined. I *can* do that, because *you* asked for it."

I feel a tear roll down my cheek but don't want him to hear it. "No! Please, Jerry, you don't understand..."

"All you lensmen are the same, whining 'I'm an artist,' and then the checks roll in and the clients tell you what to do and you do it... till the next dumb shutterbug kid comes along, just like you did."

"Diane was right, you're the devil."

"HAHAHAHA. I love her! God, I love my job!"

He hangs up, the sound of his laughter ringing in my ear. I slink back into the gilded cage of a living room and throw myself onto the sofa.

"He owns your ass, doesn't he?" Diane says, somehow soothingly.

"I don't know what to do."

"Yeah, I understand all too well," Diane sighs.

"I told him you hated him."

"He already knew that."

"That's what he said." Neither of us say anything for a while. It's so sunny outside and I feel like I'm in the dark. "At least I took terrible pictures of Cary Grant. He won't be able to use them."

"He'll find a way. He always does. Look at the bright side, at least we're both in his hell together!"

Archie enters carrying a silver tray with something that looks like a small white mountain. He places it in front of us, lights a match and makes the mountain erupt in flames.

"What the fuck!" I say, stressing the "f."

"That was good, Herb, the 'f' was very expressive." Diane compliments.

Archie sounds disappointed, "Baked Alaska. I thought you'd enjoy it."

"I'm sorry, Archie, it looks... hot."

The flame dies out quickly. Archie uses a large silver knife to cut into the mountain, then gently lifts it onto a plate. Under the white is a layer of brown, then pink, then white at the bottom.

He slides the plate in front of me and I taste it... Oh—it's meringue and ice cream and cake! Yum! This is so delicious that for a moment I forget how desperately unhappy I am. Can I live without Archie now? I must be able to. I must... but I will miss him, the way I miss Sam and Max... I set down my fork and stare out into the cloudless blue sky.

The ice cream starts to melt. "Do you not like it, Herb?"

"I love it, Archie. I love you."

"Thank you, the feeling is mutual."

"I love you both, too," Diane adds.

"I hate Jerry... and myself."

"Have another bite, it'll pass," Diane says, mouth full.

171 ➡ Marco, Polo

I sleep without dreams and wake up feeling good, until I remember, then I feel angry and trapped. I'm going to get out of this somehow. First, I need to know how much money I have. I call The First National Bank's downtown Los Angeles branch. I ask for my balance and they don't know. "We'll have to wire the New York office for your records," the man tells me.

"Do it, then!" I snap, immediately feeling bad. "I'm sorry, you didn't do anything wrong, I'm in a very bad mood. I'm sorry."

The bank man calls back, sounding timid, "Mr. Hamilton, your current balance is $2,245.56, minus any outstanding checks."

"How do I know what checks are outstanding?"

"The latest check number we have processed is 121. You'll have to refer to your own checkbook to see what check number you are on, then deduct any other checks from that total."

I check my book and #122 is $62.50 from The Darkroom. I didn't write down #123. What was that for? Saks. How much was that? I don't remember. I'll say $50.

So I've got about $2,133.06. I won't starve, in fact, maybe I'll just stay here on my own. "Archie, do you know how much this room... and you... cost?"

"I believe the rate is $100 a night, Herb, why do you ask?" He says, laying out a breakfast of French toast, bacon, and hash browns.

I couldn't even stay here for a month! "No reason, just wondering," I reply, sweating. Am I really going to have to go to Omaha? I don't even know where that is, but clowns scare me!

I call Diane, "Do you know any good lawyers?"

"As a matter of fact, I'm sleeping with the best lady lawyer in all of LA."

"Can she get me out of my contract with Jerry?"

"Doubtful. Rick St. Dennis, the photographer before you asked the same thing. Went to three lawyers and spent all his money and still ended up having to shoot scorpions in Truth or Consequences, New Mexico."

"Who's Rick St. Dennis?"

"Exactly. I got a postcard from him, he's raising angora goats in Taos. But hold on, I'll check with Gretch." I hear her yelling across the room, "Gretchen, you sexy thing, do you think my pal Herb can get out of his contract with Jerry, you know, the devil?" I hear someone else speaking but it's muffled. "Gretch says it's unlikely, and she should know since she's looked at my contract and yours is surely worse... but she's happy to take a look at yours for $100 per hour."

"That's good, I mean, it should only take an hour, right?"

"She says it'll be a minimum of 10 hours, probably 20." I do the math. I'll end up raising goats!

"Tell her thanks for me, 'As God is my Witness, I'll find a way somehow!'"

"That's *not* what Scarlett said. Besides, it didn't work out very well for her, so might as well just get used to it like I have and learn to drink. Oh, by the way, I canceled Cagney and Reagan for today. Cagney said he wasn't surprised, whatever that means. Reagan whined. Nobody's heard from Flynn since Monday so he's either on a bender or dead. I'll reschedule should he turn out to be alive. I'll see you tomorrow at Kooks... Cukor's, might as well enjoy it while you can. His address is 9166 Cordell Dr. above the Sunset Strip."

I hang up, my stomach in knots. "Archie, can you get me a hot chocolate like you did before, I mean with booze in it."

"Of course, though I fear I have created an inebriate..." he shakes his head as he leaves.

What am I going to do with myself today? Hell, what am I going to do with myself for the next year or the rest of my life? Does it have to be goats? My life is over.

An inflatable beach ball soars over my patio wall and hits me in the head. I'm either cursed, or it's a sign. Or it's just a beach ball, but it feels like a sign. I carry the ball out of the gate and look around on the other side.

"Anyone lose this?" I yell?

A little girl with red hair approaches. "It's mine, give it back!"

"Can you say 'thank you'?"

"I don't have to do what you say!"

A fair woman with curly black hair rounds the corner. She's wearing a white two-piece bathing suit covered in sequined pineapples. I can see a sexy bit of stomach between the top and bottom. "Vivian, there you are," she says to the little girl

"He won't give me my ball!"

"I just asked that she say 'thank you,'" I say, starting to hand the girl the ball.

"Thank you—don't give it to her until she says it, she's so spoiled."

I hold the ball too high for the girl to reach and finally she angrily says, "Thank you, God Dammit!"

I'm so shocked I drop the ball, but the woman catches it before the girl can. "Oh, no, you do not, missy, you know better than to say that."

"Dada says it!"

"We have talked about this, young lady. Your pool time is done. Over. You will go back to the room and think about what you have done." She turns to me, "I'm so sorry, her parents let her do whatever she wants and this is what happens."

I reach out my hand, "That's OK. Hi, I'm Herb, it's a pleasure to meet you."

She shakes my hand. "Nice watch. I'm Esther, the pleasure's mine. I'm always the designated nanny for family friends while they're in town. This deplorable couple is taking their little brat to Santa Barbara for a wedding, so I'm free after one. Room 414, call me." she winks, grabs Vivian's hand firmly. The girl sticks her tongue out at me, Esther sticks hers out at the girl, and I stick mine out at both.

The pool looks inviting. I go back in the bungalow. "Archie, I need some swim trunks."

He shows me to the hotel's shop, just off the lobby. "Don't buy the monogrammed towels, or robe, you can take them from the room and I'll get more from housekeeping," he whispers conspiratorially.

There are all sorts of tchotchkes, like snow globes with a little model of the hotel inside, as if it ever snows here. I shake it anyway and it's not snow—it's glitter! I want one and it's only $2. I'm going to have to start minding my pennies, but I'll do that tomorrow. I see the men's swimsuits and choose one with big red crabs on it. Archie shakes his head. "Why not?" I ask him.

"Crabs? Do I have to explain?" he says tilting his head down making me not want to ask, so I put them back. I gingerly pick up a pair covered in flamingos and look at Archie to see if they're OK. He nods. $5 seems like a lot for swim trunks, but I don't have any and I like the flamingos.

Back at the bungalow I put on the trunks and look at myself in the mirror. I'm pale compared with the other people I see. I need to get a tan today. I grab a towel and go to the pool which is empty except for a few kids. The adults are all lying in the sun.

The pool is surrounded by sand, like the beach. I like the feeling of it on my feet. I put my towel on a lounge chair and wonder if I should swim. No other grownups are swimming, but I want to, so I dive in. The water is warm and enveloping.

"Hey, Mister, you're too old to be in the pool," a plump kid yells.

"I'm not all that old, I just feel old."

"You wanna play 'Marco Polo?'" he asks, filling his mouth with water and spraying it at me. I do the same back to him, though the water doesn't taste very good and I remember peeing in the pool as a kid and think putting water in my mouth was yet another in a long string of very bad ideas.

The kid, Sammy, explains the rules and I'm "it." I close my eyes and hear the kids get out of the pool. "That's cheating!" I yell at them. But now the pool is mine. I go to the edge, hold onto the coping, slide underwater and kick off, crossing the pool in a single breath, my favorite thing to do because it feels like flying.

When I emerge for air I hear, "You stopped calling Marco!" I reach out and grab the kid's leg standing by the end of the pool.

"You're it," I say.

"That's not fair. I'm gonna tell my mom." Like I care. He runs off. I swim the length of the pool underwater again, only occasionally thinking about how to murder Jerry. When I come up for air on the other side I realize that even if Jerry was dead the contract would still be there, so I need to focus on that. A large woman in a pink and orange muumuu stands above me, her gold-sandal foot and red toenail polish heading for my head. I dive, so she misses. I come up in the center of the pool where she can't reach me.

"Putz, my son says you're a cheater."

"Lady, your son is the one who cheated."

"My Sammy would never..."

"Your Sammy did. Marco Polo. Gotta stay in the pool. He got out. Take it up with him." Her head swivels to Sammy who runs faster than a pudgy little kid should.

The world is nothing but rules.

The other kids cannonball back into the pool, jump on me and try to drown me, at least that's how it feels. Time to get out. I spread my towel on the lounge chair like the other adults and lie down, the sun feeling warm on my skin.

I'm feeling hot when I see the woman next to me roll over on her stomach and that seems like a good idea so I'm not tan on just one side.

I fall asleep.

172 ⇛ Esther

"Excuse me Herb," Archie says, stabbing me in the shoulder.

"Ouch, that hurts."

"I saw that you were turning somewhat pink and felt it was best to get you out of the sun."

I feel like I'm burning up. Yup, I'm officially in hell.

"I've prepared an ice bath and arranged for a quantity of Calamine lotion." He helps me up, ow, it hurts to move. I waddle back to the bungalow and get in the bath. "This is freezing!" I cry. Burning, or freezing, are those my only choices now?

I stay in the bath until I'm so cold I feel like I'm on pins and needles. "Lay on the bed, Herb, and I'll put on the Calamine." Archie says. I feel the heat rising from my body in waves. Archie gently applies the lotion. "Once again I feel I have let you down, Herb, I should have been watching."

"I'm not a child!" I bark, like a child. "I can take care of myself."

"I'm sure you can, Herb," he says, deftly applying more cool lotion. "But I feel protective of you."

"That's nice, I'm sorry. You're nice. I'm an asshole."

"You're upset. I don't care for this Jerry person, but, sadly, feel powerless to help you."

"I'm not going to be your problem for much longer, Arch. They'll either throw me out or send me to Omaha. Do you know where that is?"

"Nebraska." he explains.

"Where's that?"

"Somewhere... else," he says, sadly.

The phone rings. Archie answers, then carries the phone into the bedroom. "It's a young lady named Esther, says she met you earlier." He hands me the phone.

"Hi, I'm free and wondered if I could show you around town," she says. I like her sultry voice.

"I would love that, Esther but I stupidly got a sunburn and..."

"...I know just the thing, I'll be right over." She hangs up.

"I guess we're going to have a guest..." I say as the doorbell rings. Archie answers and I watch Esther's sequin pineapples enter the room.

"Oh, you poor thing. I'm an expert at this, kids get sunburns all the time, and I know what to do. Butler, Call the kitchen and request four cups of oatmeal, a cup of schmaltz and a cup of honey."

"Very well, ma'am," he says.

"Wait, butler, four aspirin, too, right away. We'll put you in an oatmeal bath, it draws out the pain and soothes the skin... a little schmaltz, nature's moisturizer... a light layer of honey to keep the air off. You'll feel better in no time.

Archie puts the pills and water down on the nightstand. I turn to take them and get a better look at her. She reminds me of a girl I liked in school, Goldy Goldbaum. And a bit of my Ma. "This is very nice of you, but you must have better things to do."

"Sadly, no. What do you do to merit an entire bungalow?"

"I'm a photographer for *Look* magazine... I *was* a photographer."

"An artist! Penniless. How romantic. What are you now?"

"Your guess is as good as mine."

"A lion tamer? Fuller brush man? Ventriloquist?"

"Unemployed, I guess."

"Oy, all the cute ones are."

"But I might end up raising goats."

"Kosher, my mother would approve. If you raised shellfish it'd be a deal breaker."

Archie arrives with the supplies. Esther instructs, "Put some cheesecloth over the drain so it's easier to clean up later, which housekeeping will do if you leave them a good tip. Pour it in the bath, fill with cool water. We'll soak him there like a Mikvah, then I'll take care of the rest, Butler."

"His name is Archie," I tell her.

"Thanks, Archie!"

"You're welcome... Miss Esther."

"Archie is so nice," I tell her.

"You lucked out, the German butlers are antisemetic SOBs. Once you're feeling better I'd like to drive you around, show you the beach, get you liquored up and have my way with you."

"What is it with the girls out here, all so direct."

"We're getting older by the minute and can't afford to be coy. Plus, there are so few cute boys. The bellboys are infants. The desk staff are pretty triplets but homos. My best friend, Adam, is a homo. I like them but they're no good in bed, at least not with me. Oh, I've done it again, I didn't ask, are you a homo? It's fine if you are, I'll still show you around because you seem nice but we'll have more fun if you're not."

"Everyone asks me that and I don't have a good answer."

"Ah, very sophisticated of you. Hedging your bets in case you meet the right producer. I respect that."

"No... wait... you really don't mind?"

"Eh, it's just sex," she says, and I flash back to Kitty and wonder if this is another big mistake. "At Bryn Mawr we all experimented. Let's get you into that bath now." she says, and I stand up slowly and painfully, feeling the dried Calamine crack off and fall to the floor.

"It's best without your swim trunks, allow me" she says untying the cord in the front and pulling them down.

"Ow!" I cry, as they slide painfully down the back of my legs.

"Don't be a baby, I just wanted to make sure you're Jewish," she says, following me and patting my butt as I walk to the bath. I sink into the milky, lumpy bath which immediately feels good. "20 minutes, then I'll get you out."

As I soak I hear her and Archie laughing, with the occasional shout of "Gin!" A while later she appears at the door, "Rinse off in the shower and meet me on the bed." I do as I've been told.

I lie face down on the bed. She comes in, closing the door behind her. I feel her cool hands rub something greasy and comforting into my skin.

Then I feel something cold drizzled on my back, and her hands gingerly rub it around. "Much better, you're only a pretty shade of light pink now."

I jump, surprised, as I feel her straddling my butt, then feel her blowing on my back. "I don't do this for the kiddies, but you have a much nicer ass than they do."

I feel her run her fingertips along the side of my body, giving me goosebumps. She reaches under me and wraps her hand around my hard cock. "Turn over," she whispers, and I do, getting a good look at her delicious naked curves. "I hope this doesn't hurt too much," she says, sliding down my shaft. Nothing hurts anymore. Nothing else matters.

It's so simple yet electric. I forget everything except her body, and her smile. We're Adam and Eve in our own garden.

The pleasure courses through me, the sunburn making my entire body feel passionately on fire. She leans in, grips my wrists above my head and kisses me, sticking her tongue deep in my mouth, and that's it. The pleasure and pain reach a crescendo and I tense from my toes to my scalp—exploding over and over again. Warmth spreads through my body, and I look up at her as she tenses, then goes limp and lays on top of me as we pant, together.

She rolls next to me. "Thank you, I needed that... I got nothing since Purim with a student moyel who I figured would be good with his hands."

I start to cry and can't stop.

"Oh, not again. You looked like you were enjoying it."

"I was. I did. It was the best I..." I couldn't talk for the crying.

"Happy crying is good," she says, kindly, nuzzling her face against mine.

"It's happy," I sob, "and sad at the same time."

She kisses my earlobe. "That's sweet, I like sensitive boys. You're feeling 'gamuty.'"

"I don't know what I am."

"'Gamuty' is a word I made up for when you're feeling the full gamut of emotions at the same time. I'm a writer and couldn't find an existing word in English."

"I'm lucky. I'm cursed. I'm so happy right now and so sad about... you don't want to know this."

"Ah, baby. I like you. You've got a girl's emotion in a man's body. That's the best of both worlds."

I remember thinking that about Iris and the tears come again, which isn't so bad, but the sniffling and sobbing are embarrassing.

She caresses my cheek and I feel better. "I'm sorry." I swallow.

"No need to be. It's lovely to meet a man who cries rather than making me cry." She puts her arms around me and squeezes tight. I relax.

"I wish I understood," is all I can get out.

"Understood what?" she asks, softly.

"How the world works."

"I'll tell you. It's a lot of mishegas, and occasionally we get moments like this which make it all worthwhile." She kisses me on the mouth, tasting like licorice and smelling like vanilla.

"Thank you," I whisper.

"My pleasure," she replies. "I like it when a boy thanks me after we fuck, it's good manners."

It feels so sweet to be next to her. Her eyes close. My eyes close. When they open again she's gone. Was this all a dream? I sit up and feel my back sticking to the sheet, still, it feels better. She comes in, hair damp, wearing a butter yellow dress with orange triangles around the neck that remind me of the Chrysler building.

"OK, Rip van Winkle, let's roll while we still have the light!" She looks through my closet. "All these solid colors are going to stain... but don't worry, I'll get you something from the shop. I'll be right back."

I put on shorts and wait.

"She seems like a lovely young lady," Archie says, smiling.

"She's ... surprising."

"Indeed. Since I sense you will be otherwise engaged I was wondering if I could have the afternoon and evening off. It's not something I would normally ask but Clarence has time off..."

"... Yes, of course, Archie, I want you both to enjoy yourselves."

"Thank you. Before I go, I need to remind you that Glenn arrives this evening around 7pm. Burbank Union Air Terminal. I've scheduled a car to meet him. I hope you have a fine day with Miss Esther and I'll see you in the morning."

"I hope you have a fine time with Clarence, and you don't need to be here bright and early, OK?"

"I'm glad you're feeling better."

"Funny how that works."

173 ⇻ Picnic

Esther arrives carrying a stack of shirts. "I wanted to give you some costume choices."

One shirt is blue with boats sinking while the sailors drink beer. I shake my head "no." She tosses it aside. The next has big green leaves with scary monkeys drinking beer. Nope. A third features an erupting volcano and screaming natives. I must look horrified because she laughs and says, "I wanted to see if you had bad taste. You passed."

The last has a black background covered with red crabs. At the top, a giant crab is pinching the "H" of the Hollywood sign which seems like a sign. "I like this one," I say, thinking I'll hide it when Archie comes back since he doesn't seem to approve of crabs for some reason.

"That's the least offensive one they had and won't show grease stains," she says, rubbing more schmaltz into my back, followed by a light layer of honey. "I'll return these to the shop. Meet me in the lobby." She picks up the ugly shirts, kisses me on the cheek and dashes off with them.

I put on my watch and hold the shirt next to the bolo, but no, crabs and turquoise do not mix. I put the shirt on. It's cool and light. I put my camera around my neck but the strap feels like it's made of fire. I'll leave it here.

I feel more at home in the lobby now with the other guests wearing similarly bright if questionable clothes. Esther takes my hand, "Come on... oh, Lord, do I even know your name? Yes, you told me when you did that studio handshake thing... Herb, that's it. Let's go."

Waiting out front is a sleek butter yellow convertible with a red leather interior. "Wow, that's gorgeous."

She jumps behind the wheel. The front of the car is so streamlined it doesn't even have headlights. Rows of long chrome strips wrap around the front, intersected by two shining chrome tubes that run from the engine to the fenders.

Inside, the steering wheel is the same yellow as the body, the seats and doors are red leather, and the dashboard is metal engraved with circular patterns that look like the front of the Spirit of St. Louis airplane.

"What is this?" I ask.

"A Cord Phaeton. E.L. Cord is our next door neighbor. He gave it to dad to use in "Damsel in Distress" with Fred Astair and Joan Fontaine, then never asked for it back." The engine roars to life and we take off so fast my head snaps back. She drives fast down a wide street, lined with mansions. "This is Sunset Boulevard," she tour guides. "I live just up to the right but mother is home so we wouldn't have any privacy. Besides, you'd rather see the beach."

The road is curvy and as she corners the wheels squeal and I'm thrown to the left and right. She stops fast and I put my hands on the dash to keep from running into it. "This is like a ride at Coney Island!" She doesn't let other cars get in the way, weaving around them. The wind feels good on my face and neck.

We head down a hill and I see the ocean sparkling up ahead. I can smell it, too, salty and fresh, cleaner than at Coney Island. The car heads straight for the sand and she drives right onto it towards the water, then stops. She turns off the engine and it's quiet with just the waves.

"December isn't a good time for the beach, but everyone who visits wants to see the Pacific, so I figured you would, too."

I get out of the car and walk on the sand, like the sand at the hotel pool but deeper so it gets into my loafers. I take them off and dig my toes into the sand. "Let's go swimming!" I yell, excitedly, as I run towards the waves.

"Not a good idea..." I hear her say just as my feet hit the water and freeze. I run back onto the sand.

"What's wrong with the water?"

"Nothing, it's always cold," She says, laying a blanket on the sand. "But the sand is nice, and nobody's here on weekdays so I had Archie pack us a picnic." She opens a wicker basket and sets out plates with cheese, olives, sandwiches, potato chips, and a bottle of wine. I sit next to her on the blanket. She leans in and kisses me. I place my hands on her cheeks and kiss her deeply. This goes on for a long time until the wind kicks up sand in our faces.

"Must be a sign from God it's time to eat," she says, handing me a sandwich.

"Do you believe in..." I ask.

"Signs? Yes. God? Yes. You?"

"Signs, I guess. God... I didn't used to but I was in this church..."

"Wait a second, church? I thought you were Jewish."

"Why'd you think that?"

"Curly hair and circumcised."

She pours some wine which is a little bit yellow. I take a sip. It tastes like grape cough syrup. Not great. "I'm learning how to drink," I tell her, proudly, taking another sip which tastes less bad than the first.

"It's an acquired taste, like chopped liver, but you'll grow to love it... like chopped liver."

"This is so nice, Esther, you're so nice, thank you."

"Again with the manners. You're a keeper Herb... what's your last name?"

"Hamilton."

"Real last name?"

"Horowitz."

"Mom would love you if she ever met you, but she's not going to," she says, laying her hand on my thigh. I sit there, smelling the ocean and her, salt and spice. I take a bite of the sandwich, ham and swiss with mayo, mustard, and just a touch of crunchy sand.

"Ah, ham," she says, "I can never eat this at home. We're not exactly kosher but there's never ham. Sometimes bacon, which, conveniently, nobody questions because we're expected to have that when we hold a brunch." She takes a surprisingly big bite of sandwich and washes it down with an entire glass of wine. "At Bryn Mawr I did anything and anyone I wanted. But I graduated this year and my parents insisted I come home and act like a lady. God it's boring."

"It's nice your parents care."

"Yours don't?"

"They can't afford to care, I think that's it." I stare at the waves.

"Where'd you go to college?"

"I haven't gone to college."

"You're a bad boy bohemian artiste and don't need college. Makes you even more exciting— forbidden fruit."

"I don't think I'm a fruit, really."

Esther laughs. "But you are funny. I like you. How long are you in town?"

"I don't know. A week. Maybe two. I have to finish shooting some movie stars at MGM.."

"Not 20th Century Fox? Too bad."

"I might have to go to Omaha if I can't get out of my contract."

"I could ask my father, he has a lot of lawyers working for him... except I don't know what I'd tell him about you."

"Thanks, but I don't want to get you in any trouble."

"It would be messy."

The waves sound soothing. "I'm sleepy."

Esther pats her leg and I put my head in her lap. She strokes my hair. I want to remember all of this. I don't want to fall asleep, but I do...

...I see a sudden flash of a clown's painted face, it's big red mouth open wide and moving towards me....

I feel Esther shake me, "You were having a bad dream, Herb. What about?"

"Clowns."

"The world is chock full of 'em" she says, stroking my head again.

174 ⇒ Adam

The wind kicks up again, sand flying in our faces. We grab the basket and blanket and dash to the car. I help her put up the heavy convertible top. We drive off the beach and head north on the Roosevelt Highway, the ocean on our left.

She turns on the radio and holds my hand. Artie Shaw's swingy *Frenesi* plays. Perfect driving music in rhythm with the tires. It feels like we're in a movie. "So how come you don't work for *Look* magazine anymore?"

"Artistic differences."

"You're an artist and they only care about business?"

"How'd you know?"

She laughs. "Story as old as the sea. I'm afraid my father is one of those businessmen. For him it's all about numbers."

"But you said he's in movies?"

She gives me such a look, then reaches down and yanks a lever on the floor while turning the steering wheel. It feels like slow motion as the car stops and spins 180 degrees and we're headed back from where we came. For a second I think I'm going to lose my lunch.

"Barney Oldfield taught me that when he was shooting the chase scene in 'Johnny Apollo.' For a second I thought you were only interested in me as a way to get to dad and I got angry... it's happened more than once. But then I remembered I seduced you, so nevermind."

It takes me a while to calm down as we continue to speed down the highway. She pulls over onto the sand. "I've been kind of emotional lately, what with the wedding and all."

"Who's wedding?"

"Mine."

"What, but we...?"

"I love him... but marrying him is a mistake." A single tear rolls down her cheek.

I hand her my handkerchief. "Then why do it?"

She dabs her eyes. "Because it will make everybody else happy."

"You don't seem like that kind of girl."

"I've tried so hard not to be. Like today's wild abandon with you. But deep down I've always been the good girl."

"You could have fooled me."

"Thank you."

"Look, if you want more wild abandon, I'm going to George Cukor's pool party tomorrow and hear they're fun. Want to come with me?"

"That's a sweet offer, but I've got wedding plans with Adam. Being a homo he's very good with colors and flowers and all that."

"It's nice he's helping."

"He's also the groom," she says, starting the car and squealing back onto the road.

"Why are you marrying him?"

"We've been best friends since we were six. We laugh a lot. That's more than I can say about my parents. He has great taste and I won't have to worry about other women."

"What about other men?"

"I told you, it's just sex. He's kind, like you are, and I know he's not marrying me for my money or connections. Let's get ice cream!" She turns up a steep hill and we're back on Wilshire Boulevard. The car stops in front of *Thrifty Cut Rate Drugs* and she strides into the store. I grab a nickel in my pocket and put it in the parking meter.

"Two Chocolate Malted scoops," she tells the pimply teenager in a paper hat behind the counter. I suddenly feel like an old man. He uses an odd device that punches into the ice cream and comes up with a slab-sided cylindrical scoop which he places on stubby cones. She hands him a dime and we walk around the store.

"We should buy some condoms... except, wait, you look a lot like him and I should start having kids. I love this ice cream!"

I lick it, and it is good, but I can't figure out what's going on in her head. I seem to have that problem with all women, and men.

"You'd love Adam," she tells me between licks. "You could be friends and... given that you're AC/DC, maybe more. That could work out."

"Are you... crazy?"

"I don't think so... Doctor Levy keeps trying to convince me to take lithium but I refuse to be like mother." She walks up to the pharmacist. "We'd like a box of Trojans, please."

He looks at us both and smirks, "You two married?"

She grabs my shoulder and pulls me close. "Of course we are, why else would we be..." now she gets very loud, "*fuck-ing?*" He scowls, turns red, hands her a box and retreats to the back.

"That was fun," she says, setting the box on a shelf next to crown-shaped 'Prince Matchabelli' perfumes.

We get back in the car. "Help me put the top down and let's go to the planetarium." We unlatch the top and put it down. I yelp as it pinches my finger. "Poor baby," she says, kissing it then driving off.

I watch the city speed by. This is a strange place. I wonder if Omaha is less strange, then I remember the clown from my nightmare. Probably not.

Maybe I'm what's strange.

Glenn Miller's 'Song of the Volga Boatmen' plays on the radio, slow and somber. Even the screaming trumpets sound sad. I'm taken back to the Bronx where I heard this song before, one with men singing in low voices. I remember Pa, listening, crying at the kitchen table. He never liked me. I never liked him.

I snap back to the present as a sharp turn uphill throws me against the door. We come to a stop in front of a big white Art Deco building with three domes overlooking the city. "I like to come here to put things in perspective," she says, taking my hand. We walk to the patio and watch the sun set, the city lights flickering on. "We're all so small, even Dad who's a big shot. Doesn't want me in 'this dirty business.' Eventually he'll have to relent and produce one of my screenplays. See, I *do* want something. What do you want, Herb?"

"I want to help people see.."

"Really?" She says, excitedly. "Not to be rich and famous?"

"I like having money. But that's not why I take pictures." I thought about it and spoke slowly, "I love discovering... something new... different perspectives. And showing them to other people."

"That's why it hurts so much when you're reminded it's all just business."

"But it doesn't have to be!"

"I'd love to hear you tell my dad that."

"Since I have nothing to lose I wouldn't be afraid to."

"Maybe I will introduce you, after all," she says, starting to shiver from the breeze. I pull her closer. I want to kiss her again. I do.

175 ➤ Crazy Kids

"Thanks, Herb," she says, giving me a kiss on the cheek as she lets me off at the hotel. "I'd better be getting home. Maybe I'll see you around." She blows a kiss as she speeds away. Do I want to see her again? Doesn't matter, I don't even know her last name.

Back at the bungalow the lights are all on and music is playing. I open the door and there are Glenn—and Pat, swing dancing on the patio.

They look so out of place here, yet perfectly in sync with the music and each other. The music stops and I applaud. "I'm so happy to see you!"

"Surprise!" Pat says, dryly while smiling. She's wearing a pink skirt that only comes to her knees, a pink blouse and a fuzzy sweater which she takes off, fanning herself.

"We decided to make this our honeymoon!" Glenn exclaims.

Archie comes in carrying a tray holding four glasses with frosted edges, a big pitcher full of pink liquid, and a small one filled with orange.

"Honeymoon?" I ask, astonished.

Pat takes a glass from Archie, "Just what I needed!" Archie fills her glass and she takes a sip while I stand, stunned. "I joined Glenn to write a feature on Orson, then we decided to have the pilot of the plane marry us—over Kansas, isn't that right, honey?"

Glenn looks different, too. His hair is shorter, he's got a goatee, and he's wearing the exact same Hawaiian shirt with crabs I have on. "Sure thing, bubbala, just before we landed to refuel. Flying is fantastic, I got some great aerial shots!" They kiss.

"I'm... so happy for you!" I am happy, but shocked. "You guys didn't waste any time, did you?"

"Our first real date, after the housewarming party, was to meet my mother," Glenn says, dreamily. "She loves Pat as much as I do."

"Your mother's a doll, honey. She raised you right!" they kiss again.

Archie pours me a glass of the orange drink and whispers, "It's virgin, just for you."

"You should enjoy the bungalow here, and I'll get another room," I say to be nice, but not exactly happy about it.

Glenn speaks up. "We wouldn't put you out, Herbie,"

Archie adds, "The rooms are completely soundproof, Herb."

Glenn looks at Pat and says "Unless he'd rather spend the night at Kitty's?"

Hearing her name made me feel gut punched.

Pat shakes her head at Glenn, "Are you OK, Herb?"

"Yeah, I... you should... I'm gonna leave you two love birds alone for the night."

"Let's get together for breakfast," Pat hugs me. Glenn hugs me.

"I really am so happy for you both," feeling like I'm going to cry. "I'll see you tomorrow," scooting for the door before Glenn and Pat notice.

Archie follows me outside and hands me a key. "My room, 117. I'll bunk at Clarence's." He puts his arms around me and holds me tight. I curse myself for crying, yet again.

"I'm sorry, I'm like a babe in arms," I sniff.

"You're a babe in armor," He pats me on the back. "Sweet dreams, Sir Herb. I'll see you in the morning."

As I walk away I think, I *am* happy for Glenn and Pat. I *am*. I'm also jealous, not because I wanted to marry either of them, but because they found each other so easily and I've been jumping from one impossible person to the next. I'm 18 years old and feel like I'll never meet the love of my life!

I wander around looking for room 117 and finally find it, on the ground floor in the back of the building. I use the key and turn on the light. Archie's rooms are classy, like him, old-fashioned and warm! The walls are covered in books. The dark wood floor is covered with Persian carpets in rich reds and browns. There's a brown leather tufted chesterfield sofa and two chairs covered in the same dark brown plaid as the drapes. There's a small patio outside with a view of the pool.

Off the living room is a ship-shape galley kitchen with stainless steel counters and white enamel cabinets. The bedroom has a big wooden four-poster bed, with brown curtains covered in small red flowers. I pull back the covers, sink into the fluffy mattress and fall asleep...

...I was in a dark room, the only light coming from under a door. I heard people on the other side, laughing, music playing, the smells of roast chicken and freshly baked bread.

I felt around for the doorknob but couldn't find it. Over the music, I heard the sounds of two people having sex. "It's only sex!" the woman says. "Oh baby!" the man cries. I back away from the door and into something fuzzy and warm. It felt nice, with its big furry arms closing in on me. Then it was suffocating, it's long sharp claws digging into me.

I felt hot breath on my neck. A growl shook the room. Its hot fangs pierced my neck, I couldn't move, the teeth tightening, crushing.

I couldn't breathe.

I found myself in bed with my face buried in a thick feather pillow. I turned over and gasped for air. My back was itching and I didn't feel good. I slid out of bed and went to the bathroom. The room was covered with blood red tile and I looked green in the mirror.

I scratched my back and it hurt. I got in the tub but the water was hot and it hurt worse. Still, I was so sleepy. I slipped under the water and started choking.

I couldn't breath...

...I wake up, coughing. I go to the bathroom. The tile is white. I call room service, ask for four cups of oatmeal and fill the tub with cool water. It feels good.

I remember Glenn and Pat are here and I'm happy to see them. Now I don't feel alone... just ashamed.

176 ➻ Sorry's Not Enough

I wish I'd brought a change of clothes but I have to put on the same shirt with the crabs on it. I pick up the phone to order breakfast, then remember Pat asked me to have it with them. I look at my watch, it's 8am. I should let them sleep in. I try to make the bed as perfect as it was before I slept in it but it looks lumpy.

I peruse Archie's books. Most of them are about flowers. 'Flora and Fauna of England;' 'Blooming Love;' 'The Sword and the Rose.' On the coffee table is a big leather-bound book titled 'The Forbidden Garden.' It has color photographs. I've never seen a book with color photos. They're glued in separately. I really want to shoot in color.

The phone rings. It's Glenn. "Hi, Herb, you up? We didn't want to bother you too early, but with the time zone it's kind of late for us so we're up and hungry. Archie told me he knows what you want, so come on over."

It feels weird going back to *my* place which doesn't feel like my place now. I forgot that it was never actually mine.

The bungalow door is open. Pat is dressed more like she did at work, a long sky blue skirt and blouse and jacket. Glenn is wearing a blue seersucker suit exactly like mine. "I saw it in your closet and Archie told me you got it at Saks, so we made a quick trip there." I knew Glenn meant it as a compliment, but now even my clothes didn't feel like mine.

"Good morning, Herb,' Archie says, patting me on the back, "Oh, I'm sorry, how is your back today?"

"Much better, I took an oatmeal bath... oh, I forgot to call housekeeping for the tub..."

"I'll take care of it. Breakfast is served on the patio."

Archie set the table complete with a bowl of red and white carnations. I know which breakfast is mine: corned beef hash, hash browns and hot chocolate. Glenn has a tortilla with scrambled eggs and small circles of sausage—a Mexican breakfast pizza, and orange juice. Pat has an eggwhite omelette, grilled tomatoes and a side of fruit salad and coffee.

Glenn pulls out Pat's chair for her. "Bon Appetit, my darling. So, Herbie, how's it going?"

"It's been good, great! Mickey and Judy were swell, and Cary Grant..." I drink some juice and choke on my words.

Archie smacks my back, hard. It hurts. He leans in and whispers, "They're your friends. Tell them the truth.

I put down my fork and take a deep breath. "It's been terrible... Kitty's missing, David's dead, Frank's dead, Iris walked out on me, I nearly threw up on Jimmy Cagney... I'm so unhappy..." I trail off.

"You sounded funny on the phone," Glenn says, kindly while still eating. "I'm sorry it's rough but we're here now..."

"Who's Iris?" Pat wonders aloud.

"I quit working for Jerry."

"I was wondering how long it would take," Pat says, dabbing her lips.

"He won't let me out of my contract for three years and is sending me to Omaha to shoot rodeo clowns and I may have to raise goats."

The silence is filled only by the sound of children laughing in the pool.

"I wish I could help, Herb, but I have no sway over Jerry," Pat takes a sip of coffee.

"You can't talk to Clive?"

"I know Clive and he won't interfere with advertising."

"Did you explain it? Can you try to convince him?"

"I can't Herb. That's not how business works."

"You don't care!"

Glenn put down his fork, "I was so mad when I saw what he did to your photo I told Pat I wanted to kill Jerry for you."

"He did say that, Herb."

"Pat said she didn't want me to go to prison."

"I don't want you to go to prison, either, Glenn, but thanks. I made my cake, now I have to lie in it. It's only Omaha, not London."

"Speaking of the war, Herb, what is your draft number?" Pat asks, looking concerned.

"I forgot to sign up."

"Then *you* could be the one going to prison, Herbie," Glenn says, seriously.

"Maybe that would get me out of my contract," I joke, only nobody laughs. "I'll do it on Monday, it's not like I have anything to live for," I say, digging into the perfectly crispy hash.

Suddenly I feel Pat's hand grab my left arm and Glenn's grab my right. "Herbert H Hamilton the third," Pat snaps. "How dare you speak like that—how dare you. There are boys your age dying in Europe. They'd give their eye teeth to be where you are."

I thought I couldn't feel worse, but I do.

Pat looks me in the eye, "What's gotten into you? *You* used to care about doing the right thing. You're acting like a selfish brat."

Glenn puts down his fork, "We're trying to look out for you, Herb."

"You have each other, you don't need to worry about me."

Pat clears her throat, "Look at the time, we've got to meet Welles at RKO." Glenn pulls out her chair. "Thank you, honey." They kiss. It's sweet and sickening at the same time.

As they leave, they stop to thank Archie for breakfast. Once they're gone he comes back and stands over me, "The draft?"

"I know!" I sigh. He shakes his head. I go into the bathroom and close the door. The mirrors reflect me, endlessly, there's no way to avoid myself. Me, me, me, me me. I flick off the lights so I don't have to see, but then I can't find the door knob in the pitch blackness. I feel trapped, in the dark, clawing at the walls until the door opens.

"Are you having some difficulty?" Archie asks.

"I was in the dark," I tell him but don't add 'and still am.'

177 ➽ Kook & Kate

Bob drops me off at Cukor's address. From the street there's only a tall white brick wall broken by a shiny black door with the words "Gardens of Honor" above it in bronze letters. I knock and a familiar face opens the door. It's Alvin, the Asian dancer I shot at Sergei's.

"Hey, Herb! Funny meeting you here!" He gives me a warm hug.

"It's good to see a friendly face," I tell him.

"The gang's all here. Come on in! Jack took one look at your photos and sent for us all. We owe you, Herb, and let me be the first to show my appreciation!" he says, squeezing my butt.

The garden is elegantly manicured with a wide green lawn and a riot of roses. We walk around a large house with rounded windows to a bright blue pool filled with men, laughing, swimming, splashing, naked.

Alvin yells, "Guys, look who the cat dragged in!"

It's suddenly silent as everyone freezes for a moment. They shout, "Herb!" jump out of the pool and surround me in a group hug, all talking at once, "Hi, Herbie!" "Allo, Herbert!" "Thanks, Herb!" I'm so surprised and happy I feel myself tearing up again till I remember Archie's words, "Babe in armor," and smile.

The chatter fades. The group parts. A lithe man with dark hair and sharp features saunters up and silently sizes me up. A subtle smile slowly spreads across his face, his arms reach out gracefully, he gives me a tight hug and whispers in my ear, "How lovely to meet you at last, master of the lens."

His slight but steely body doesn't let me loose. "Lovely to meet you, too..." I whisper back... but I don't know who he is.

"Jack Cole. I'm indebted to you for how beautifully you portrayed my dancers."

"It was my pleasure."

"So I've heard from Alvin and Bobby," his smile widens. "Come, join our merry band." He takes my hand and leads me to Cukor, the only one clothed, wearing a linen suit and Panama hat. "George, I'd like to introduce you to..."

"...Hello, Herbie, I'm so glad you came," he says, with genuine kindness.

"This is the talented chap who took those photos I showed you." Jack explained.

"You have a vivid imagination and a superb eye, young man," George says to me, then turns to Jack, "He'll make a fine director."

"Thank you, sir."

"I'm just George here, Herb."

"Thanks, George."

"Lunch will be served shortly, make yourself comfortable, won't you?"

I take off my shirt and am getting ready to drop my drawers when I see Katherine Hepburn, wearing trousers and a striped sailor shirt, waving from a lounge chair on the far lawn. I grab my green camera bag and walk over to her.

"Hello, kiddo! I've trowled on the old pancake and am all ready to be shot, stuffed and sold to the highest bidder!" she intones in her inimitable way. I laugh. "You get my sense of humor, so few do. I like you."

"I've enjoyed all your pictures."

"How sweet."

"You're so different."

"I'll take that as a compliment."

"Miss Hepburn..."

"Call me Kate, all my friends do."

"Kate, I'd like to take your picture, but I'm not working for Chesterfield anymore."

"Good. It's a filthy habit I can't seem to shake myself. Still, I've fixed my face and need to publicize my new picture, so I'm game. The light out here is awfully harsh, though, let's go inside."

I follow her into a cozy house, whitewashed with nautical blue and white striped furniture. I like her style. "You have a lovely home," I say.

"It's Yar," she says, sweeping through. I don't know what that means. I follow her into the bathroom, like mine at the hotel, every inch covered in mirrors. "This room is too ghastly for words, why anyone would want to subject oneself to this kind of scrutiny I'll never know."

Her reflection reveals so many angles. I catch one and say, "Freeze." She doesn't, instead, turning to me with a quizzical look. *Click.* "Look straight ahead please."

"I hope you know what you're doing." She turns her head and tilts it up. *Click.* She has a fine profile, and the mirror shows her straight on as well. The image reminds me of a painting I saw in the Chicago Art Institute of a woman seen from different angles all at once.

"Turn away from the camera, please."

"The back of my head has always been my best angle," she says slyly. *Click.* I capture her cropped hair in the foreground, profile in the left mirror and full face in another mirror. *Click.*

"You look wonderful from all angles."

"You dear little liar."

"Now put your cheek right against the mirror." *Click.* I take a closeup that makes her look like twins. I gasp.

"That bad, brother?" She says, not moving.

"That good, sister," I say, moving to the other mirrored wall, facing away from her. I shoot into the mirror, reflecting her over and over and over again. *Click.* "Keep that position but move away from the mirror." Now there are even more of her. *Click.* "Thank you."

"That was relatively painless," she says, relaxing.

"Oh, if you don't mind I'd like to take one more, just in case the advertiser wants to sue me."

"Hopefully not for malpractice."

I laugh again. "I might have to raise goats, but before I do I'd like to send them a Bronx cheer." Kate sticks out her tongue, her eyes wide and blows a big raspberry. *Click!* We both laugh. "Thank you, Miss Hepburn. You are a dream."

"And *you* are charmer. Now I've got to take off this makeup with one of my wonderful Vic washcloths. They feel like sandpaper, the very best thing for one's skin." The doorbell rings and Kate goes to answer it. It's Diane! "Hello darling, just in time. Our mutual friend just finished. We shot in the bathroom of all places."

Diane kisses Kate on the mouth. "He's very good, I'm sure it'll be wonderful."

"I took a shot that's guaranteed Jerry-proof!"

"I wouldn't be so sure," Diane says, tossing me the latest issue of Look. On the back cover is Cary Grant—the picture I took as a joke where he's bug-eyed and open-mouthed. The headline reads, '*WOW! I can't believe how mild Chesterfield is!*' Under the picture my credit reads, "Exclusive portrait by Herbert H. Hamilton IV."

"The fourth?" I choke.

Diane rolls her eyes, "Jerry says this was your best shot yet!"

"He took one of me with my tongue out. I'm not sure the world is ready for that," Kate says.

Diane who responds cheerfully, "I am!"

Kate hugs Diane, "What you do to me, dear. Sex is a funny thing, isn't it? Once shorn of my fancy facade I'm practically transparent. Lying there, naked, with another soul, there's no place to hide. I love it and I fear it. Honestly I do."

Kate notices me, "Be a good boy and go play with your little friends, Herb."

"We'll talk on Monday," Diane tells me. I go outside and when I turn around they've drawn the curtains.

178 ➡ The Deep End

"There you are!" Alvin grabs my hand. "I've been looking for you!"

"Sorry, I had to shoot Kate,"

"That bitch?"

"I like her."

"Oh, look, fish tacos!"

There's a long table covered with platters overflowing with food. I pile food on my plate, three tacos, potato salad, pasta salad, corn on the cob, vanilla pudding with bananas and vanilla wafers. Alvin has a single fish taco on his. The other guys also carry mostly-empty plates. I think about taking things off my plate but I've already touched them.

George comes up behind me, "I like a man with an appetite. How did you find Kate?"

"I turned left at your pool?" I joked.

"Very droll."

"She's wonderful, very funny and nice."

"Is that right? If you brought that out in her you can get along with anybody... It'll serve you well in this business." George waves to Jack who comes over. "I believe Herb might be the solution to your problem, Jack."

Jack raises his eyebrows, "I was thinking that same thing myself. But first, a question. Herb, how would you shoot a dance sequence in a movie?"

"The way Fred Astaire does, where the camera shows the dancer's entire body so you can see them dance."

Jack and George look at each other and nod. "Have you ever shot motion pictures?" Jack asks.

"No, but I consider contact sheets as a form of that—showing progression and action."

George adds, "I see, like storyboards."

"Herb. I have a proposition for you. I've choreographed three numbers for 'Moonlight Serenade," with Betty Grable at Fox. The director, who shall remain nameless, is famous for his westerns and doesn't know jack about musicals. He told me he wants to see the entire tango number on horseback, and if that isn't bad enough, he wants to shoot in mostly closeups—no doubt of the horses. I've got my boy dancers and some of the top girls, like my Gwenny, and I will not have them take a backseat to some horse's ass."

I'm distracted by a fly on my taco so I'm not sure what this has to do with me. "Sorry, I'm not a fan of Westerns, they always seem hot and dusty."

"George suggests I talk to Stoneman and request a separate director for the musical numbers and..."

"Abe Stoneman?"

George interjects, "Head of production at Fox. Real SOB."

"I know... I mean I know him," I say. "He owes me a favor. I could talk to him for you."

Jack and George look at each other again. "You would do that?"

"Sure, anything I can do to help."

Jack continues, "If you can get him to agree, you can direct the dance numbers."

"Wow. What? How? I've never directed a picture."

George explains, "The cinematographer knows all the technical things, your job is to have the vision."

"After the boys sent your photos, I saw what you've been doing for *Look* and it's inventive—fresh—That's what I want... no, that's what I *need* for my dances." Jack explains. "We'll work together, Herb. I'll show you the dances and we'll storyboard camera angles and movements."

I *have* seen a lot of movies. I am always looking for new ways to show things. "I've got Stoneman's card right here, should we call now?"

"No, no, no. I don't think Stoneman's orthodox, but it's still not Kosher to work today. I'll telephone Cedric and you three can meet tomorrow, plan it out with some sketches and have visuals to show Stoneman because those studio guys have no imagination."

"We'll meet at my dance studio tomorrow, 10am."

George warned, "Pack a lunch, Herb, Jack doesn't believe in eating."

"I do so eat. I thoroughly enjoyed your buffet."

George gives him a blank stare, "You ate a pickle."

"That's a green vegetable!" Jack protests.

My mind is far away. On a lake, under the moonlight. I'm wearing jodhpurs and carrying a riding crop like a real director. I am making dreams come true. I'm shaken out of my reverie by Alvin. "Hey, Jack, can Herb come and play?"

"Yes, boys. George and I have some plotting to do."

Alvin pulls off my bathing suit and I dive into the deep end.

179 ➽ Dancing on Water

I get back to a dark bungalow, excited and wanting to share my news, but there's nobody there. Archie is with Clarence... but where are Glenn and Pat? I see a flashing red light and follow it to the telephone.

I pick up the receiver and a woman's voice says, "Hello, Mr. Hamilton, there is a message waiting for you. Would you like me to read it or would you prefer to have it delivered?"

"Please read it," I tell her.

"'From Pat Whyte, 5:54pm. Orson is eager to give *Look* an exclusive feature on a day in his life so Glenn and I are staying at his guest house tonight. Let's meet for dinner on Sunday before we fly back Monday.' End of message."

"Thank you."

I leave the lights off and go outside. The moon is bright and blue. The pool is empty, smooth as a mirror, reflecting the moon like a twin. One is real, the other isn't, but they look the same.

I go back to my patio and lay on a lounge chair, staring up at the sky, basking in the moonglow.

Everything fades out...

...I saw the moon reflected on water, this time a lake. Alvin delicately stepped onto the water and created ripples. He reached out for a girl dancer who took his hand. Together they danced onto the water—not in it—but on it, their bodies reflected, like a mirror.

More dancers joined them. They skimmed the surface, kicking up water. In a single beam of moonlight, Alvin leapt into the air, dove into the water, and disappeared into the deep, followed by the other dancers who did the same. The water became a mirror again, reflecting the moon.

I raised my arms and floated off the ground. I flew over the lake, over the hotel, over MGM, over the city. This was how I felt swimming underwater, but now I was high in the sky. I wanted to feel this forever...

...A noise startles me. I see a fedora, then a face with a pencil mustache—familiar yet strange—peering over the patio wall. I leap up to chase him but I can't get the gate open as I hear footsteps running away.

I trip my way through the dark bungalow and out the front door, but it's too late. I go back inside and lock the front door, patio door, my bedroom glass doors. I make sure the windows are bolted, too.

I pick up the phone and call the front desk, "There was somebody creeping outside my room."

"We'll send security right over, sir."

I turn on all the lights and sit on the sofa, listening. I hear footsteps approaching the front door and pick up a heavy sculpture of a leopard and brandish it like a weapon.

There's a knock at the door and I'm ready to strike when I hear, "Hotel security, Mr. Hamilton."

I put the leopard down close by in case I need it. I look through the peephole and there's a man in a security guard uniform. I put the chain on the door and open it a crack.

"Hello, sir, we've checked the grounds and haven't found anyone. I'll keep watch here tonight to make sure nobody bothers you."

"Thanks," I say, closing the door and bolting it.

I go to the bedroom and as I close the curtains I see the palms rustling. Maybe the wind, maybe that person...

I go into the bathroom, turn on the light and lock the door. I lay down in the dry bathtub, my eyes wide open.

180 ➳ Blossoming

I don't think I've slept a wink when I hear a knock at the bathroom door and Archie's voice. "Herb, are you in there? Are you alright?"

I get out of the tub, cold and stiff, "Yeah, I... musta fallen asleep." I open the door.

"What's going on? Have you been drinking?"

"No, I swear I saw someone."

"Hotel security told me they didn't see anything unusual."

"Thanks. Maybe I'm just not used to being alone."

"What do you feel like for breakfast this morning?"

"You know. Oh, I have such exciting news! Please have breakfast with me so I can tell you about it!"

"It will be my pleasure."

I smell like chlorine and tacos. I get in the shower." The water reminds of a dream I had... but I can't remember it. I'm excited and nervous.

I put on the robe and breakfast is waiting on the patio, bacon and eggs, hash browns, toast and orange juice. Archie pulls out my chair, then sits next to me with his breakfast, fried eggs, sausages, bacon, beans, mushrooms and fried bread. "It's a full English breakfast," he tells me.

"It looks great—and I have great news!" I tell him what happened yesterday and how I have a meeting today.

"That's excellent news, Herb. I have news of my own. Clarence and I have decided to open a florist shop here at the hotel. I spoke with Douglas, the general manager and he agrees we would provide a vital service to guests and events in the hotel, as well as a select local clientele."

"That's wonderful!" I say, getting up to hug him in his chair. "I am so happy for you."

"Thank you, we're delighted. Sometimes life gives you a second chance, after all," he says, dreamily.

181 ⇛ Diorama

Bob drops me off at the address on Jack's card. I look up to see a building that reminds me of Oz—a shiny blue-green tower shooting into a bright blue sky. It's the Wiltern theater again. Around the side is an awning that says, "Jack Cole Dance Studio" and I enter a large space lined with mirrors and watch Jack, dancing, leaping, spinning. He sees me and stops.

"Right on time, very professional," he says to me, putting a towel around his neck. "I don't know what's keeping Cedric, we need him to do sketches. You and I can get started without him. Let me show you my choreography for the big rodeo wedding finale. Don Ameche has just proposed to Betty Grable and they're having a shindig. The cowboys and cowgirls are all dressed up in their finest duds. Alfred Newman and I talked out the music, a swinging polka..." He proceeds to sing, "la la la da da, la la la la da da," while he dances up a storm, stomping and turning. At first I stand still, then I walk around and get closer to him, then walk back.

When he stops I clap like crazy. "That's terrific, from every angle! I wanted to get right in there and feel like I was one of the dancers. What do you think about the dancers spinning around the camera instead of just in front of it?"

Jack closes his eyes and spins around, "Yes, I can see that! Breaking the fourth wall—I love that."

"And if it's a wedding party they're going to need lots of flowers, right? The horses could be covered with them like that Rose parade in Pasadena. I know these two English flower guys.

"Yes, the horses draped in bowers of flowers, the girls can wear crowns of flowers, and Grable can have an entire bouquet as a hat! Now for the *Moonlight Serenade* number..." he starts humming and dancing.

"I just remembered a dream I had about this..." I tell him the dream of dancing on water, ending with, "The water becomes a mirror again, as if this was all in our imagination."

Jack stops dancing and throws his arms around me, "I love it! That's exactly the kind of fresh take I want! It will look visually arresting—and expensive. Grable's their number one star and they want to compete with MGM, so Stoneman should love it."

Just then the door slams and a distinguished middle-aged man stomps in. "That motherfucker. I'm going to chop off his head, mount it like a stag and hang it on my bedroom wall where she can see it every night!"

Jack takes Cedric to a chair. "Now, now, now, dear, why don't you tell us all about it."

"Why's it so damned hard to buy a machete on a Sunday?" he fumes.

"Cedric, whatever it is, I'm sure we can help you."

"If you want to help, bring me motherfucking Welles' head on a platter! I have the platter in my trunk, I just need a machete. A gun would work for now, I can chop his head off later."

"Orson Welles?" I ask.

"That baby-faced son-of-a bitch. Can you believe he had the gall, the unmitigated gall to come to *my* home, my *home*, and tell me he was going to marry my wife—my *wife*! I went into a blind rage, I literally couldn't see or I would have grabbed the prop swords from above the fireplace I designed and stabbed him through the heart! 'I've loved her since I was a teenager' he tells me, as if I give a shit. I thought, 'this man must be insane, I know my wife, she loves me!' Later, when I found Dolores in the bedroom, packing her suitcase I told her in no uncertain terms, 'Lolita Dolores Martinez Asúnsolo Lopez Negrette, you love *me*!' She couldn't look me in the eye as she left, so I'm sure she still does! I swear, he's got her under some kind of Martian spell!"

He bursts into tears, reaching into his pocket for a monogrammed handkerchief. Jack pours three glasses of whiskey, "Here, drink this Ced." Cedric downs his, and Jack's, and mine. "No woman's worth all this upset."

"Dolores is perfect. When I find things I like I see no reason to change them. Except women."

Jack suggests, "Perhaps you'd feel better if you made a few sketches..."

"I can't think much less draw, I don't even know why I stopped here except I thought they might carry machetes at Woolworth's next door, but would you believe it, no!"

Jack looks at me. I shake my head and shrug.

"I'm going downtown, They must have machetes there. Failing that, a baseball bat. No, I don't want to damage his head if I'm going to stuff and mount it like an animal. I am simply at a loss for what to do, but I cannot stay here." He grabs the whiskey bottle and storms out.

"Poor dear. Now what are *we* going to do?" Jack asks, sullen.

"Maybe... Come with me," I tell him. He follows me into the Woolworth's next door. I hand him a basket and hurry up and down the aisles. I grab two black cloth napkins. I toss a dozen gray lead toy soldiers standing, and toy soldiers on horseback into the basket. Two handfuls of delicate pink wax flowers. A round mirror. An extra-large white shell button. All for $1.50.

Back at Jack's studio I lay one black napkin on the table, the other on the wall behind it. "Stick the flowers to the horses," I instruct, arranging the horses in a semicircle. "More flowers, on the heads of the figures." We pepper the last remaining flowers on the background napkin.

I arrange the gooseneck lamp to light the scene from the side, giving it depth, and put the camera on the table, focusing as close as I can. *Click.* I stop down the aperture for a deep depth of field. *Cliick.* I rotate the camera as I *click*, for a long exposure full of motion. *Cliiick.*

I move the camera in closer, so the semi-circle of horses surround the lens. *Click.* I move the camera up a bit, shooting down like the crane shots I've seen in movies. *Click.* I review the shots and angles in my head. "OK, clear the set," I tell him and he snorts.

We brush aside the horses and flowers. I put the mirror on the black napkin. I take each standing lead soldier and pry off his gun. Jack joins me to finish the rest. "Stage them like dancers," I tell him, and he does.

I snap two of the lead soldiers in half and position their bottom halves on the mirror, feet up. I reshape a wax flower to look like a splash as they dive into the "lake" and stick the big white shell button on the background napkin like the moon.

I adjust the lamp so its light is straight down. I put the camera back on the table, making sure I can see both the moon and its reflection. *Click.* "Hold your hands under the light to make the light dappled," I tell Jack. *Click.* It's missing something... I move two of the soldiers right in front of the lens, framing the shot. Looking through the viewfinder I see a bee land on a soldier's head. *Click.* I look up and the bee is gone and I don't hear any buzzing.

I see another shot in my head and tell Jack, "Move the lamp in an arc from desk level, then over the top, back to the desk on the other side, that'll give us a wide variety of lighting angles." *Click, click, click, click, click.* I stop down the aperture again, "One more for motion" and this time I hold the shutter down as the light moves. *Cliiick.*

"There's still a third number—A pas de deux with Grable and Amichi. He's not much of a dancer so I'm going to stage it as a dream ballet, with Gene as Amici and Gwen as Grable."

"If it's a dream then I can see an expressionistic set, weird angles, smoke..." I suggest.

"And color, deeply saturated red and blues."

"Color?" I ask, excitedly.

"First-class all the way."

Color, at last! My stomach rumbles. "Darn, I forgot to bring lunch."

"I'm a bit peckish myself, haven't had a bite today. Let's go to the Farmer's Market."

He jumps into his tiny sporty red car without opening the door, "Do you like my new car? It's a Jaguar SS100. I love the proportions, it's quite phallic," he says. *Click.* We zoom off. "The power of 125 horses, it'll hit 100 miles per hour, can you believe it?" His driving isn't as scary as Esther's but the car is so much smaller it feels like the pavement is only inches away and the other cars tower above us. *Click.* We zip into a parking space in front of a white clock tower that says, "Farmer's Market."

Inside, rows of green and white awnings shade elaborate displays of colorful fresh fruits and vegetables. *Click.* "I know what I want," Jack says, "Go get what you like. I'll meet you at this table under the tree in five minutes."

Rows of stalls offer food of all kinds, Mexican, Italian, Greek, Burgers. It's a veritable wonderland of food! I don't know where to start, but a cloud of smoke and the smell of Barbeque draws me in.

Four cooks work the grill full of hamburgers, ribs, chicken, and slabs of brisket. It smells so good my mouth is watering. The sign says, "Try our world-famous brisket burger."

"What can I do you?" the man behind the counter asks.

"I'll have the world-famous brisket burger, well done, fries and a coke."

"Fifty cents."

I pay him and a lady to his right hands me a tray. "Condiments around the corner," she says, pointing. I ladle on catsup, mustard and sweet pickle relish, then find my way back to the table to meet Jack.

He's already seated, patting his stomach. "I'm stuffed. Absolutely stuffed!"

"What did you eat?" I ask, setting down my tray full of food.

"Not just one mind you, I had two. Two whole peaches. I made a pig of myself!" He looks at my food, "What are you going to do with all that?"

"Eat it," I reply.

"All of it? Yourself?"

"Do you want some?"

"Lucky you to be behind the camera where no one will see you become a blimp."

He stares at me as I eat, but I don't care, I'm so hungry and it's so good! I devour every last morsel of it.

"You'll need to walk that off, my boy," he says, charging off and haggling with a farmer over a head of lettuce. "Is it made of gold? I'll give you 7 cents and not a sou more." The farmer shakes his head, Jack hands him a dime and claims his prize. He proceeds to juggle three lemons from the next stand, tossing them in his bag, one, two, three and handing the proprietor another dime. "Dinner sorted."

I longingly eye luscious pies: apple, cherry, lemon meringue, coconut cream, as Jack practically sprints towards the car. I chase after him, barbeque sloshing in my stomach. "You get those photos blown up and I'll work on the dances. We'll meet, 11am sharp at the Fox lot."

He drops me off at the hotel and I use the publicity department darkroom to develop the film. The negatives look good, but the 8x10 glossy prints are a little fuzzy. Nothing I can do about that now except call them "atmospheric" and pretend they were meant to be that way.

"Herb, Diane called and said it was most urgent you call her back," Archie says as I enter the bungalow. I call her.

She answers, "Herb, I imagine that you, like me, have been wishing for Jerry's demise."

"Yes, lotta good that'll do."

"Of, ye of little faith! Our wishes are coming true—Jerry's in the hospital in Jamaica."

"Queens?"

"No, Jamaica, the island. He went there for a holiday, got stung by a swarm of bees on his patio and went into anaphylactic shock. I can't imagine how a beehive could find it's way right outside his room, but It couldn't happen to a nicer guy."

I felt bad, then remembered it was Jerry and didn't feel so bad. "Is he going to die?"

"They don't know, but if there's a God... and I'm an atheist, we can hope," she exclaims.

"That's a terrible thing to say."

"I know, I'm so happy! I'll postpone the rest of your shoots till we hear one way or another. What's the worst that can happen, we'll get fired?" She laughs as she hangs up.

I feel guilty and sleepy and go to the patio to breathe. There's a bee in the magenta flowers on the patio, "Did you guys do this for me?" I ask. It buzzes away. Maybe I'm going crazy.

I hear, "Herb..." and jump.

"I talk to flowers, too," Archie says, "Makes them grow bigger."

"I wasn't... I mean..."

"Bougainvillea. Stunning, aren't they? They bloom all year. Pat and Glenn called, they'll be here for dinner at 5. Would you like me to order you something to tide you over?"

"I'm still full, and sleepy. I'm going to lie down for a bit." I take off my shoes but don't get undressed as I lay on top of the covers and fall asleep...

...I was the size of a lead soldier and everything was in fuzzy black and white, including me. Jack was normal size, his gigantic hand hovered over me as he moved the soldiers around, then picked me up, too. He dropped me on top of my camera, which was the size of a house.

I kept trying to focus my eyes but it didn't help, the edges of everythings were soft. I tried to focus the lens with my feet, but it was too big and hard to turn. I slid down the back and looked through the viewfinder, the only place things were in color.

The bee sitting on a soldier's head was the size of a St. Bernard. Its buzzing made my teeth rattle like Morse code dots and dashes which tapped out, "Y O U A R E W E L C O M E" before it flew away.

I'd be happy if Jerry died. That wasn't nice. I sat on the mirror, looked at my own reflection and didn't like what I saw...

182 ➻ Rain & Flowers

I wake up and see the palms moving outside my window again. It must be the breeze. Archie put yellow sunflowers in a vase on the inside dining table, and white orchids floating in a bowl on the patio table. He's wearing an orchid in his lapel.

I don't want Glenn to be wearing the same thing I am, so I put on my older blue pants and bright blue shirt from saks, and my turquoise string tie. Each blue is different but I like it.

"You look quite natty, Herb." He pulls a small puffy sunflower from the vase, snaps off the stem, and places it through the button-down hole in my collar. "A dwarf teddy bear sunflower makes for a perfect contrast to your blues."

Archie smiles, he's so happy that it makes me happy and I feel myself starting to cry. "I'm sorry, Arch," I say, escaping to the bedroom to sit on the bed till it passes.

Archie comes in and puts his hand on my shoulder, "You don't have to hide your feelings, Herb."

"Good thing, because I don't seem to know how!" I laugh and cry at the same time. "Things just set me off lately. Just now I felt so happy for you and Clarence... and myself, yet selfishly alone... then, waterworks."

Archie sits down beside me, "I stopped myself from feeling for too many years. It only made me feel worse. You know what Clarence and I did our first night back together? We held each other and cried. Years of having it all bottled up—it had to come out. Frank Lloyd Wright stayed here last year and admired the way I arranged the hollyhocks. He told me, 'Art is the flower of the human soul.' You're watering your flowers, Herb."

I hear the doorbell ring and pull myself together, squeezing Archie's hand. "Thank you," I whisper.

"Hi, Arch!" I hear Glenn say. I go to greet him and he's a mess, sporting a shiner and wearing a suit that's too big.

"What happened to you?"

"Orson hit me! Isn't that great!"

"Are you OK?"

"I'm fine, and Pat gave him a good right hook!"

Pat enters, also sporting a black eye. "Hi, Herb, we're famished."

"I forgot to eat, can you believe it?" Glenn says. Archie hands him a piece of raw steak to put on his eye, sees Pat and goes back to the kitchen.

"What is going on with you two?" I demand.

"Orson's a genius!" Glenn gushes!

"He really is, Herb," Pat says, placing a steak on her eye.

Archie brings out a tray with little bits of food on it. "Canapes, goat cheese and fig, prosciutto and black olive tapenade."

Glenn pops one in his mouth, "Mmm, so good, you've got to try this, love," he says, guiding another into Pat's mouth. I promise myself there will be no more tears tonight. I take a deep breath.

"Pure heaven," Pat says, biting into a red rose made of ham.

"Archie, I'd love to get the recipe for this," Glenn adds. He and Pat sit on the sofa, devouring the canapes with their free hands.

"OK, Joe Louis, I've heard Welles has a temper but what the hell happened?"

Pat swallows, "He's practicing pugilism for his physique and offered to teach us. That's all. Great fun."

I stare at them while they scarf down what's left on the tray. "He clearly didn't knock some sense *into* you!"

"What're you talking about? It's the best possible souvenir. How many people can say they were beat by the great Orson Welles?" Glenn takes the last canape and gently places it in Pat's mouth.

"He's the most charming man I've ever met." Pat says, rearranging the steak on her eye. "He literally charmed the pants off Glenn!" she laughs.

"This is the suit Welles wore when he made 'War of the Worlds.' I admired it and he said, 'I want you to have it.' I'm over the moon!"

"It doesn't fit, Glenn."

"I'd be jealous, too, if I were you, Herb."

"Dinner is served on the patio," Archie announces.

Glenn pulls out Pat's chair and she sits between us and she rhapsodizes, "Orson's such a flirt, it was utterly delightful."

"I was afraid he'd take Pat away from me..."

Pat finishes his sentence, "...Until Dolores, who didn't know we were there, emerged from the shower wearing nothing but a towel."

"She can't hold a candle to you, honey," Glenn kisses her on her unbruised cheek.

They are talking to me but it feels like I don't need to be here.

"You should see the storyboard for his new picture, *Citizen Kane*! Revolutionary angles..."

I'm silent, not even paying attention to what I'm eating.

"This is a heavenly sauce, Archie," Pat says, satisfied.

"It's herbed hollandaise, Pat."

"Herb-ed!" Glenn laughs.

"Tarragon, chives and chervil, with a touch of cayenne," Archie explains.

"I met Cedric Gibbons," I say, wondering if anyone will notice.

"Who's that?" Glenn asked, between bites.

"Dolores' *husband.*"

"Poor man, he didn't stand a chance," Pat shakes her head.

Glenn puts his arm around Pat, "That's why I'm taking you back to New York before he tries to take you away from me!"

"What did you do this weekend, Herb?" Pat asks.

"Nothing nearly as exciting as getting beat up by a genius, I'm sure."

Pat reaches over and holds my chin in her free hand. "Feeling sorry for yourself isn't like you at all."

"This is me, now."

"I'm disappointed in you," Pat says like a left hook to my heart.

"Thanks for the delicious meal, Archie, but we must get back to Orson's, he's having a little going away party for us with a few of his movie star friends. I heard him on the phone with Joe Cotten, they're all going to blacken one eye with makeup so we won't feel out of place —talk about charm!"

"He's a hoot!" Glenn gives me a hug. "I'm sure we'll be back here, soon, boychik."

"Don't bother. I thought you were *my* friends."

"Herbie?" Glenn pleads.

Pat gives me a look. "Let's go, Glenn."

"Just go. Go!" I yell.

They leave and the room feels very quiet. Archie breaks the silence, "What was that about Herbert?"

"I'm fine. Fine. Really. Fine. Really fine. I need to go to bed now because I have a big day tomorrow. I'm fine."

I'm not.

183 ⟫ Favors

"Rise and shine, Herb," Archie says, chipper.

"Leave me alone, Pa!" I yell. I open my eyes and see Archie. "Sorry, sorry, sorry..."

"It's 9am. You've been sleeping for 12 hours. Your studio meeting is at 11. Come on, up we go," he tries to pull the covers back but I grab them so he can't see I'm still in my clothes.

"I don't want to do this—I *can't* do this."

Archie signs, "I'm disappointed..."

"Why do you and Pat have to sound like my Pa?"

Archie puts his hand on my shoulder. "Carpe Diem, Herb."

"What do fish have to do with it?"

"'Carp-ay' means 'seize' and 'diem' means 'day.' Seize the day, Herb."

"I can't do this when *everybody's* disappointed in me."

"We're not disappointed in *you*, just the way you're acting. If you want to be grown up, then you have to buck up."

I'm disappointed in myself, too. Why am I scared of Stoneman? What else is he going to make me give him that I don't want to give?

I take a shower, and Archie has a full English breakfast waiting for me on the patio.

"Eat hearty, lad!" Archie says, sitting down with his own breakfast of corned beef hash. I take a bite of the English breakfast. Beans for breakfast? I don't love it. Archie switches plates with me.

Bob drives me to the Fox studio gate and the guard directs us to the executive offices. I walk down the long hallway to a door that reads, "Abe Stoneman, Head of Production."

I look at my watch, formerly Abe's watch. It's 10:55, I'm five minutes early. I force myself to open the door. The walls are paneled in striped wood and at the center is a shiny black desk with two secretaries, one blond, one redhead, both talking on the phone.

I stick out my hand, "Hi, I'm Herb Hamilton, pleased to... have an appointment with Mr. Stoneman." Neither secretary so much as looks up.

The blond speaks into the phone, "'That's impossible, Miss Crawford. Impossible. Mr. Stoneman is a very busy man. Goodbye.' Well I never!" The redhead rolls her eyes as she listens to a voice on the phone, "I'm sorry but we must cancel your 3 o'clock with Mr. Stoneman. Yes, as a matter of fact, I do know where to 'stick it.' Good day, sir."

Jack is sitting, cross-legged, breathing deeply, his eyes closed. I sit next to him on the built-in black leather sofa.

"Stoneman *owes* me a favor." I say to myself, but aloud. "*He* owes *me* a favor."

"That's the spirit, Herb! We're doing *him* a favor by creating a top quality production that surpasses MGM. If he wants to keep bedding Betty he's got to keep her happy—we can make her happy."

I don't hear what Jack is saying, I just keep repeating "He *owes* me a favor." I need to make this work. If I'm not going to have a girlfriend—or any friends—then I need to have work.

The blond tells us, "Mr. Stoneman will see you gentlemen now. He only has 10 minutes until his next meeting..." The redhead finishes, "So make it snappy," opening the tall, stainless steel doors to Stomeman's office. The room is the size of a hotel lobby with windows on three sides overlooking the lot. Stoneman stands, at the far end, gazing out on his domain.

He doesn't bother to turn around and speaks commandingly, "Yes."

"We're here to explain why..." Jack starts.

"Whatever it is—yes." Stoneman intones.

"Moonlight Serenade. Bryce Byrd is fine for the talking scenes, but he wouldn't know a musical number from a horse's ass..."

"...So Betty tells me. Tell me something I don't know."

I pipe up, "I can direct the musical numbers."

Stoneman's body remains motionless while his head turns slowly towards me, "You."

I look at my watch and confidently say, "I've been a photographer for *Look* magazine. I'm enough of a name that Chesterfield is giving me credit in their ads, which is unheard of..."

Stoneman turns his entire body towards us. "Did you putzes not hear me say 'yes'? Betty loves your dances, Jack. Leon's shooting so her legs will be well lit... the kid can't fuck it up. Go. Do."

"I want $250 a week..." I tell him.

Stoneman laughs. "Is that all? You coulda asked for a grand, but you only get what you ask for—lesson for today."

I cross the room and hand him his old watch. "Thanks. Take it."

"What's this for?" He grabs it, greedily. "You got your favor, now we're even."

"OK, give it back then," I hold my hand out for the watch. He drops it in his pocket and chortles. "You still owe me," I smile, gesturing for Jack to follow me out before Stoneman changes his mind.

184 ➠ Apple Pan

"That was too easy," Jack says, nearly sprinting for his car.

"Stoneman's simple, you just give him what he wants," I say, my green bag feeling heavier as I try to keep up.

"We didn't even have to sell him on the numbers."

"Those aren't the numbers he cares about."

"This calls for a celebration!" Jack says, screeching off the lot.

"Peaches or pickles?"

"Cheeky bastard!"

The city sparkles in the sun and smells of oranges as we drive west on Pico Boulevard. It feels glorious until Jack slams on the brakes and my head hits the windshield with a thud.

A rabbit hops across the street, all traffic having come to a screeching halt. The moment the bunny reaches the other side of the road, traffic roars to life again.

We stop at a white cabin with green trim. A neon sign flashes, "The Apple Pan, Quality Forever." Inside, the small room is taken up by a U-shaped counter that surrounds the smoky grill. The place is packed with men, women and children eating hamburgers and piles of French fries.

We sit on built-in chrome stools covered in red leather. The waiter tosses a one page menu in front of me: Steakburger, Hickoryburger, Ham & Cheese, Egg Salad, Tuna Salad, and Pies: apple, banana, pecan, peach, chocolate and coconut cream.

I look at Jack, "What exactly are *you* going to eat here?"

Jack waves to the waiter, "Hi, Hector, the usual. The kid'll have a Hickoryburger with cheese, fries, coke and apple pie, thanks."

I'm about to protest Jack ordering for me but it's exactly what I wanted. "Sounds good to me," I tell him, imagining his usual must be iced tea with *two* entire wedges of lemon! I laugh to myself. Hector pushes a burger in front of me. It's wrapped in paper and dripping sauce. He slides a big pile of fries on a paper plate and squirts catsup on the side.

I look over at Jack and he's already chowing down on a burger with cheese, while another sits, waiting next to his pile of fries. He takes a swig of coke from the bottle, gives me a look and says, "What? It's got pickles," then continues to eat, finishing his first burger before I've even started mine.

I take a bite—it's great, crispy, salty, with a quarter head of lettuce, pickles and a smoky sauce I lick off my fingers so as not to miss a drop. The fries are perfectly crunchy on the outside and soft inside.

I'm still working on my fries when I see that Jack's finished. Hector slides pies in front of us. Mine's fragrant apple with a lattice top, creamy vanilla ice cream melting down it. Jack has apple *and* pumpkin!

I polish off the pie and feel stuffed like a Hanukkah goose. Jack's perusing the menu again! "A little something for the road?"

186 ➽ Golf Ball

Jack pulls up in front of my hotel. "I'll set up a meeting for you with Leon Shamroy, the cinematographer. He's the best in the biz. Show him your concept photos, he'll get it instantly, Consider him your teacher and listen closely."

"Will do... um... Jack. Thank you for... this."

"Thank *you,* Herb. Let's make something beautiful together!"

He speeds off and I trip over the curb, dizzy, the doorman catches me. I stumble to the bungalow.

"How'd it go, Herb?" Archie asks.

"I'm getting a headache. What did you ask?"

"Are you OK?"

"Uh, I don't remember. I had a hamburger. Why is everything sparkly?"

"What did you drink?"

"A coke, and pie," I say, tripping on the sofa.

"You better go lie down, I'll call the house doctor."

I lie down on the sofa, feeling like one of those cartoon characters with stars circling my head.

"Hi, Herb, I'm doctor Zanger. Archibald says you're not feeling well."

"Who?"

"Doctor Zanger, the hotel physician. What happened to you?"

"I have a headache and I ate pie."

"Do you know what happened to him, Archibald?"

"No idea, he had a meeting with Stoneman at Fox and he came back like this."

"That bastard turns grown men into whimpering babies."

"Stoneman took my watch," I say.

"What's your name, son?"

"Herbie... uh... Horowitz."

"Are you sure?" the doctor asks.

Archie says, "His last name is Hamilton."

"I know my name."

"What year and month is it?" The doctor asks, annoyingly.

"It's December Monday. I want to go to sleep."

"We can't let him fall asleep," I hear doctor whateverhisnamewas say.

The next thing I know two men in white pick me up and put me on a stretcher and carry me into an ambulance. "Stay awake, Herb," Archie says, sitting beside me.

"I like the sound of the siren. I'm gonna throw up now," I say, then do, marveling at the pieces of French fries among the mess. "Pretty." I try to read the sign as they carry me in but it's fuzzy and upside down. "Where am I?"

"Cedars of Lebanon Hospital, Herb, they'll take good care of you."

They put me in a dark room and lower a buzzing machine to my head. "Please lie still, sir," a voice says which makes me want to move but I'm too tired. Click. Buzz. The click reminds me of my Leica. The buzz, of a bee.

I hear men whispering. "We need to keep him here tonight for observation." Archie looks worried.

"I'm OK, I remember now, I hit my head on Jack's windshield after our meeting with Stoneman. Oh, I'm gonna direct a movie, Archie. Can that be true? That's what I remember."

They move me to a room on the 4th floor. I can see the "Hollywoodland" sign from my window. Jack arrives carrying a bunch of white flowers.

"He's going to live so lilies are hardly appropriate," Archie says.

"It's what they had downstairs."

"I'm OK, Jack."

Archie explains, "He's had some temporary memory loss but he's doing better." Archie leads Jack into the hallway but I can still hear them. "The doctors said it's OK for him to sleep now, so let's give him some quiet. I'll call you if there's any change."

I hear Jack's shoes clicking away. Archie closes the blinds. "I want to see the Hollywoodland..." I trail off, falling asleep...

...Color! Giant bunnies and tigers and stone men, oh my. Cars and oranges. Watches. Melting. Life in fuzzy black and white. Contact sheets. My blue suit has a black eye. Busby Berkeley dancing machetes. Button moons and mirrors. The 20th Century Fox fanfare and searchlights and bees flying in formation, spelling "Hollywood!"...

...I open my eyes. It's dark out. Archie is asleep in a chair by the bed. My headache has gone. I have to pee. I slide out of bed but my arm is attached to a metal stand holding a bottle of water. I drag it with me to the toilet and pee so much I don't know where it all was. I get back into bed. The sheets are rough.

The sun hits my face. Archie is arranging yellow flowers. "Morning, Herb. How are you feeling today?

"My head feels better and I remember everything that happened."

"A pale young man with a mustache brought you these yellow roses but didn't want to disturb you. He didn't leave his name."

An older man with a sagging face enters wearing a white coat and carrying a large manila envelope. "Hello, Herbert, and...?"

"Archibald, I'm Herb's... friend." That makes me smile.

"Pleased to meet you both. I'm Dr. Shienman, the head of neurology here at Cedars. You're a very lucky man, Herbert. If you hadn't been in that accident you might not have known about this..." He pulls the biggest negative I've ever seen out of the envelope and holds it up against a lightbox on the wall. He points to a circle above my right eye. "This appears to be a haemangioblastomas in the frontal cortex."

"What is that?" Archie asks, which is good because I'm having a hard time hearing above the pounding in my ears.

"A tumor. It might be cancerous, it might be benign, but we have no way of telling without surgery."

"I feel fine," I tell him.

"It's possible to have no symptoms. For now. But the location suggests it could cause hallucinations, meaning it could make you see things."

"Seeing things is what I do."

"Herb means he's a photographer, doctor, so seeing things is his job."

"I understand, but when I say 'seeing things' I mean things that aren't there."

"They aren't there until I take the picture and make them be there," I explain.

"This does not sound good." The doctor is very serious. "We need to perform surgery to remove it."

"But, doctor, if it's benign..." Archie starts.

"*If*. Even then, it could cause problems over time. If it's malignant, and it might be, it will grow and be fatal. I'll schedule surgery and remove it myself. Before I do, I am legally obligated to inform you that there are risks of adverse effects."

"Like what?" I ask, not liking anything I'm hearing.

"They include problems with speech, memory, muscle weakness, balance, vision, coordination, and other functions. These may last a short while or be permanent. You could develop a blood clot or bleeding in the brain. Seizures. Stroke. Coma. Infection. Blindness."

When I hear 'blindness,' I get out of bed and yank the needle out of my arm, "No."

"Please, sir, I must insist you get back in bed."

"No. I'm not going to go blind." I put on my clothes.

"Sir, you cannot leave until you're discharged."

"Watch me."

"Herb, please listen to the doctor," Archie says, quietly.

"No. If we hadn't stopped for that rabbit you'd never know. I'm going to go on with my life like I would have without a bunny."

"How big was the bunny and did it talk to you?" the doctor asked.

That makes me mad, "About your height and he said the most unbelievable things.... Like you."

"It's natural that you're upset, but you need to understand that this could kill you." the doc says somberly.

"So could crossing the street."

The doc doesn't have a sense of humor. "But we have no idea when this might be fatal."

I stop tying my shoes, "Till the very day she died, my grandma said, 'you never know when you're going to die.' So, Doc, do you have any idea when you will die?"

"I'm not sick," he protests.

"That's what I thought when I woke up this morning. So I'll ask again, do you know when you're going to die?"

"No, nobody does."

I stand up, not letting a little dizziness stop me. "Exactly. I'm done here."

"But you're more likely to die," he emphatically points to the dark spot on the negative. I've seen enough dark spots on negatives. It doesn't scare me.

"More likely than *who?* Everybody dies eventually, right? I'd rather take my chances. If you don't take chances you end up like my father." I say, storming past him.

"Herb, come back," Archie says. I keep walking. I get in the elevator and Archie rushes in. "Herb, there's something wrong with you."

"What if what's wrong with me is what's right about me?" I ask him. "What if my hallucinations are why I see things other people don't? That thing is part of who I am, Archie. I'm not going to lose it." The elevator stops, we get out and exit the lobby. I get in a cab. "What if it gets removed and I lose my vision? Not just my sight but my vision? What's left?"

We ride in silence the rest of the way to the hotel. Archie gets out and holds out his hand to help me out of the car.

"Thanks, Arch. I'm fine." We get back to the bungalow and I eye the phone, wondering who I should call. Nobody. "It means the world to me that you care, Archie. Someday I hope I can do something for you."

Archie looks exhausted. He sits on the sofa and speaks so quietly I can't hear him until I sit beside him. "You don't know what you've already done, do you? You helped me stop feeling like a servant and start feeling like a friend. You led me back to Clarence and our dreams together. I heard Glenn and Pat talk about how you brought them together. That's what you do Herb, you go around pollinating people and ideas like a busy bee."

I exhale and put my head on his shoulder. I feel him lean his head on mine. Even the light pressure of his head makes me wonder what's going on inside mine.

The dark spot on the negative means it is actually light—a light inside my brain. I imagine it, shining out through my eyes like a movie projector, showing the world what's inside of me. Eventually the projector gets turned off. The movie ends. You go back home to the real life you were able to forget while that light was shining.

The movies are part of my memories, sometimes more real than real life. I want to be able to give that gift to other people the way it was given to me. Even if it's the last thing I do.

187 ➤ Cinema Secrets

"Leon Shamroy is here to see you, Herb. Do you feel up to it?" Archie asks.

"I'm fine! Please show him in."

A distinguished man with salt and pepper hair enters wearing a dark suit, white shirt and bow tie. He reaches out his hand, "Hello, I'm Leon. I hear I'm going to be working with you and you don't know bupkis."

I shake his hand, it's soft. "Hi, Leon, I'm Herb. I'm a photographer myself. I've seen a lot of movies. But you're right, I do know bupkis. Teach me."

"I end up having to teach every director I work with anyway—at least you asked. I've seen some of your photos—they're good. You're very visual, which is more than I can say for most directors who only care about the talking."

Archie places a tray of small pastries on the coffee table. "Excuse me, may I get you something to drink?"

"Russian tea with raspberry jam."

"I'll have the same, Archie, thanks."

"I can make any image possible. That is what I do. It's your job to have a vision to show me."

"I can!" I say, finding my green bag and removing the photos I took with Jack. "These are rough and fuzzy..." I start to say.

"...Atmospheric. I like that, though in film we must be sharp or the audience will yell at the projectionist. Now I will tell you the secrets to being a good director. Listen up."

I pull a pen and pad out of my bag, ready to take notes.

Archie arrives with two half-filled cups with tea bags steeping, two carafes of steaming water, and two bowls of raspberry jam. Leon pours a little water from the carafe into his cup, then two spoonfuls of jam, mixes it.

I follow his lead. The tea is very strong, and I'd never thought of putting jam in tea—it's tasty.

"Number 1: Be the first one on set. If you're not 10 minutes early, you're 10 minutes late. This shows everyone else you care so they get to work right away. The only reason to be late for a call is being dead. "

"Dead, hopefully not. I always arrive early," I tell him, which is true.

"Number 2: Be the happiest guy on set. The crew expects you to be an asshole. If you're nice, they'll be caught off guard and be afraid you're nuts so they'll do anything you ask."

"Check."

"Number 3: Know what you want to get before you get on the set. See it in your head. Shot by shot. Storyboard it. Doesn't matter if you can't draw, show me stick figures and I'll get it, like this," he takes my pen and draws six boxes on my paper. "'Each of these is a shot."

"Like a contact sheet."

"Yes. Except here you're showing the order and movement. First, an establishing shot so the audience knows where they are, the geography and time of day. Next, the master, showing everyone in the scene at once—you always need a good master for the editor to cut back to. Then the wide, showing the actors in relation to their environment—are they big or small, in a crowd, by themselves. You're writing this down?"

"Yup."

"A full—meaning a full body, head to toe. Medium—waist to head. Get closer with a single. Push in for a two shot, showing two people. An over-the-shoulder is just that, the camera looks over one actor's shoulder to another actor. Finally, there's the closeup, which is just how it sounds, when you want an actor's face to fill the screen so the audience is drawn into their emotion. In our case we'll only have closeups on Betty's beautiful face and legs, nobody else is that important in one of her movies."

"This is exciting!"

"Number 4: Be as bold as you want. I can see from your atmospheric photos that you have an eye, that's good."

"I know what I want."

"Perfect. Which leads me to Number 5: Listen to your gut instinct and believe in it. There will be a half dozen studio execs hovering like flies. They will tell you what they think you're doing wrong. Nod. Thank them. Ignore them. They are mostly accountants who don't even go to the movies themselves."

"I always go with my gut."

"Number 6: Don't act like you know what you're doing if you don't. If you're not sure, ask. People will respect you and you'll learn. *Listen*, because all good ideas reflect well on you."

"Thank you."

"Number 7: Don't be afraid to fail. The best work can feel like a mess till you call 'action' and it magically comes together. If it doesn't, do more takes until it does. If it still doesn't, try something else."

"Number 8: I put this last because it's most important for you to remember: Always do what I tell you. Always. I have shot 42 pictures so far. It is my job to make you look good. Let me do my job or I'll call Stoneman and he'll kick your baby ass off the lot faster than you can cry 'mama.'"

"Yes, sir. You only have 8 commandments?"

"I'm not God—except on the set. These cookies are delicious. Did I mention that you have to make sure the crew is well-fed? That doesn't count as a commandment, just common sense."

"Thank you, Sir."

"Leon."

"Sir Leon."

"Leon will suffice. Finally, I want you to know this: I *want* to work with you because you don't yet know what's impossible."

188 ➽ Falling or Flying

My mind is stuffed with new knowledge—it fills every corner so there's no room for fear.

I look over my notes. I'd started using the contact sheet because I couldn't shoot motion. Now I see how those little boxes help me visualize it. It's so exciting and yet I'm so sleepy. I lay down on the bed for a nap...

...The contact sheet was like a skyscraper. Each frame was a different room. I walked into a frame and saw a scene unfolding. Night time. A young guy named Guy was making out with his girlfriend. She disappeared. In her place was a man. They started making out. The man disappeared, too, and Guy was left alone. He went up the fire escape made up of the sprocket holes in the film, and used them as footholds to climb up, row by row, floor by floor, until he was at the top of the contact sheet building.

The sun was setting, a golden glow. Guy saw the girl again, naked. She dressed herself in dungarees and a t-shirt and became a boy. Guy stepped back on the fire escape and fell, watching the contact sheet rooms blur by.

We pulled back, and in the middle of the contact sheet we see Guy, frozen—falling or flying? ...

189 ➻ The Rabbit Died

It's morning. I'm startled awake by the phone ringing in the other room. Archie doesn't answer. I jump out of bed, a little dizzy, and dash to the phone. "Hello? Herb here."

"How're you feeling?" I hear Jack say.

"I'm OK, really, Jack, what's up?"

"Production meeting today, Stage 7, 10'clock."

"Thanks, see you there!" I hang up and look around for Archie. There's a note on the coffee table that reads, *'Sis cabled. Mum is doing poorly. Must see her while I can. Had to rush to catch the flight to New York, then Yankee Clipper flying boat to London. Your friend, Archie.'*

I close my eyes and send him my best. My eyes snap open when the front door does, and in comes a tall skeleton of a man in a formal cutaway jacket. "Good morning, sir. I am your butler," he rumbles, sounding like distant thunder with a German accent.

I'm only wearing my boxers and feel embarrassed.

"I will get you a robe so you are decent," his voice so low it gets under my skin. He returns with a hotel robe and stands, completely motionless, holding it out for me to step into.

I wrap it tight around myself. "Thank you... what is your name?"

"Call me Butler, befitting mine station."

"Thank you... Butler," the word sticks in my mouth. "I have a meeting today at Fox, I can take care of myself."

"But your brain is damaged..."

"I don't know what you heard but you were misinformed. I am fine and will be taking care of myself. I will call you if I need you."

"Certainly, sir," he says, clicking his heels and practically goose stepping away, muttering, "Take care of himself, ha!"

I lock the front door and shake it off like a dog. Without Archie, the place feels colder, impersonal. I take a shower, call for breakfast and eat it alone on the patio where the table is dusty. I draw some storyboard boxes and fill them with stick figures of what I remember from my dream. The camera in the middle, the dancers spinning around it. I draw another page of the lake scene and imagine the camera coming up through the water full of fish at the start and sinking back down into it at the end.

I wonder if I'll need a special outfit for directing. I'll wear my blue seersucker today as it's yet another sunny, warm day. I put my drawings and camera and film in my green bag. I want to take pictures of everything but don't want to offend Leon by having a competing camera.

Bob drives me to the lot. The guard directs him to Stage 7 which looks like the ones at MGM. It's 12:30. I'm plenty early. I look around the giant space and see lines of tape on the floor. This must be where the dancers will stand. I close my eyes and imagine this place full of the energy of hundreds of talented people.

"Good student, you're early" I hear Leon say behind me.

"I made some storyboards."

"Show me," he says, inspecting them. "I see. What are those squiggles?"

"Fish, the camera comes up through the water..."

Leon laughs. "Impossible already, wonderful!"

Jack arrives, along with a serious brown-haired woman wearing a brown dress with brown shoes and carrying a brown clipboard. "Hi, boys, this is Agnes, she's the production secretary. Agnes, you know Leon, of course." Leon bows slightly to her. "And this is Herb."

I freeze, staring at her, my mouth agape, speechless. She reminds me of my Ma. "Hello... I'm... happy to see you... meet you." I see her eye Jack as if to say, 'who's the half-wit?'

She smiles at me, dryly, and shakes my hand in a single up-and-down motion. "Pleasure."

"Let's get to work, boys," Jack sits.

"Herb's been showing me his storyboards. I'll have my artist, Wylie, redraw them to clarify for the crew." Leon explained.

"Joe Wright has preliminary set plans," Agnes says, handing drawings to Leon as if I wasn't there.

"Thank you, Agnes," I say, nicely. "The color of your dress really sets off your eyes."

Leon nods imperceptibly. Jack raises his eyebrows.

Agnes smiles, "Thank you, Herbert."

Jack gets up and starts to move. "I'm going to run through Betty's part in the dances to give you an idea of the movement, designed to flatter her legs, of course."

"Of course," the three of us say, in unison.

The graceful movement of his arms and the swaying of his hips makes him instantly feminine. We're mesmerized, but the spell is broken for me when I see a familiar figure walking by the open stage door. I jump up and run to her.

"Esther, what are you doing here?"

She's surprised, "Me? What're *you* doing here?"

"I'm in a production meeting with Jack Cole and ..."

"Leon Shamroy. Midnight Serenade," she says.

"Yes, how did you know?"

"I saw the name Herbert but I didn't piece it together. Oh, dear."

"What's wrong?"

"Come on, I should tell you all at once." She walks briskly to the table. Jack is still nearly floating through the air. He ends, arms up in a final flourish!" We all applaud.

Jack, breathing hard, says, "Esther, what a pleasure to see you!"

"The pleasure is mine, Jack. But I wish I was here in happier circumstances. It's Betty. The rabbit died."

Leon's hand reaches for his forehead. Jack sighs dramatically. "She just found out this morning."

I think about the rabbit in the road, he seemed fine when he hopped away.

She continues, "Dad is arranging for her stay with her mother in Missouri."

"How soon?" Jack asks, concerned.

"Tomorrow. It's all very hush-hush, you're not to breathe a word of it."

"Of course," I say, thinking everyone was going to say it, but no it's only me.

"This means that *Moonlight Serenade* is shelved, as of today. Sorry, gents. Leon, you've been reassigned to *Little Old New York,* Jack there are dances for you in *Lillian Russell.*"

"And for me?"

She reads off a piece of paper, "It just says, 'tell him that's the way the Cartier crumbles.' Doesn't make sense to me, but maybe you'll understand it. I'm sorry, Herb."

Jack and Leon shake hands with each other, then with me. Their mouths are moving but all I hear is a high-pitched noise. They leave and I'm still standing there.

"Hey, you OK?"

"Dissa...pointed," I manage to say. My mind is screaming, 'This isn't how this is supposed to be! None of this is right!' but I only say, "Goodbye Betty, hello Clowns."

"So many clowns around here. Let's get lunch," she says, gently. I follow her down long beige alleys to a blue and white striped awning.

"Did the rabbit really die?"

"Yeah, that's how the test works."

"What test?" I wonder.

"Pregnancy test. You didn't know?"

I shake my head. We walk through the main dining room into a door marked "Private" where the tables are covered with white linens and crystal glasses. I pull out Esther's chair and she sits. "Always the gentleman."

I watch her take a compact from her purse and powder her nose.

An elderly waiter approaches the table and stops at Esther's side. "Good afternoon Miss Stoneman, what can I get for you today?"

"We'll both have the Chinese chicken salad, thanks Ralph." The waiter hobbles off. "Chef Wong invented that salad here, knowing how much Alice Fay loves..."

"...Stoneman? That's your dad?"

"It's my cross to bear. Do you know him?"

I gulp down an entire glass of water. "We met on the Super Chief. He made me give him my watch."

"Ah, 'Cartier crumbles,' now I get it. The one with the little windows for the time?"

"That's the one."

"I particularly liked that one. He was very happy. He must owe you a favor."

"This was the favor."

"That's tough."

"How're the wedding plans?" I ask.

"I lobbied for cornflower blue but Adam is partial to dusty rose. What's your preference."

"I was looking forward to shooting in color, but up till now I've thought in black and white."

"Black and white would be very cinematic, I'll bet Adam would go for that. With some silver to make it sparkle."

"I don't know what I'm going to do now. It must be nice to have your life all planned out."

"It's utter hell."

Ralph places two large salads in front of us. "Thanks Ralph. Give my regards to Edna and the kids."

"My grandson Zeb just got promoted to focus puller!" he huffs.

"That's wonderful. I remember when he and I were kids running around the lot," she holds his hand, sweetly before he leaves. "Ralph's a fixture here. Been here forever. He's a sweetheart. Now, pour the dressing over the salad and toss it lightly. Then sprinkle the fried wonton noodles on top."

I follow her lead and take a bite. It's sweet and I've never had peanuts in a salad before.

"It's my favorite. So, what's all this talk about clowns? I thought you were going to raise goats?"

Despite how tasty the salad is, I put down my fork and explain it all to her. "That was a long story, wasn't it? I'm sorry I rambled on."

"It was a good story, I enjoyed it, Herb. I know something we can do to take your mind off it."

"Did I tell you I have a brain tumor, only my rabbit didn't die."

"Are you serious?"

"Yup."

"Are you afraid?"

"Nope."

"You're very brave."

"I'm not going to let it beat me."

"That's the spirit." She takes a few more bites of salad. "Does it affect your erections?"

"Not that I know of."

"Then let's go back to your hotel and fuck." she smiles, her hazel eyes twinkling.

"You're so nice. I like you."

"Ralph, please box up our salads to go."

190 ➤➤ South of the Border

I pay attention to every little detail. To the feeling of her skin on mine. The light diffused by the peach fuzz on her ass. The beautiful curves of her full breasts and the salty taste of her nipples. The smell of peanuts on her breath. The soft sounds of pleasure we both make. The sweat that makes us slippery against each other. The way we hold tightly to each other, as if it can stop the world from spinning out of control. To the tears, this time, hers.

"Oh, no, I didn't mean to make you cry?"

"Gamuty. Happy tears, being with you. I don't want you to go to Omaha."

"I don't have a choice," I moan. "I don't want you to marry Adam."

"I don't have a choice," she cries, more tears flowing.

I take a breath, "I want to marry you."

"You've only known me two days."

"I want to marry you before I die." Now both of us are crying, and laughing. "This is ridiculous, isn't it?" I dab her tears with the sheet.

"Totally," she laughs. "Let's drive to Tijuana and do it right now." She wraps the white sheet around her and hums the 'wedding march,' "Here comes the bride!"

I get down on one knee, naked, and take her hand. "Esther, will you marry me?"

"I can't. I want to. Fuck it, yes!" She pulls me to my feet and we kiss.

"FffucKK, yes! Let's go!" I say.

She looks into my eyes, "You're serious."

"You weren't?"

"I was. I am. But..."

"But what? When we first met you told me, 'We're getting older by the minute and can't afford to be coy.' I don't know how long I... What are we waiting for?"

"It's just that... I'm..." Her eyes dart around as she thinks. "I have no idea."

The drive down the coast is beautiful with the sun setting over the sea.

Tijuana is exotic, with donkeys painted like zebras and Mariachi music and twinkling gaslight on the buildings. We drive to the coast.

"There it is, the Hotel Cortez, we used to come down here for the races."

The hotel is small and quaint covered in those familiar pink flowers glowing purple in the moonlight. "Miss Esther, it's been too long, my how you've grown," the owner kisses her cheeks.

"Dear Jose! This is my fiancee, Herbert. We can't wait for the big wedding at home..."

"...I understand. I'll call mi amigo Judge Carlos, he can marry you tonight! Alejandro will show you to the bridal suite!" He rushes off, "Juanita, Nuestra pequeña Esther se va a casar! Llame al juez Carlos..."

"How long will I have you before you die?"

"I have no idea. When are *you* going to die?"

"I have no idea!" we fall into each other, almost crying becoming outright laughing. Uncontrollable laughter. We gasp for air, the laughing subsides, then it starts up again.

A large man in a white linen suit and Panama hat arrives and watches us. "Good evening, I am Judge Carlos." We try to be polite but start laughing again. "Ah, the sweetness of love," he says, wistfully.

Jose and Juanita are all in white, too. "Come, come my children," Jose says, carrying a guitar and leading us to the beach where there are torches lit. We are sore from laughing and finally stop, holding each other and looking into the night sky ablaze with stars.

For a moment there's only starlight and the sound of the surf. "I always ask if you are both certain. This is a lifetime commitment."

"Till death do us part," I say, kissing her hand. I look up and see the stars reflected in her watery eyes.

"Hopefully not soon," she whispers into the warm wind.

I hear his voice. I feel her heartbeat in her hand. I say, "I do."

She squeezes my hand and says, "I do, too."

We forgot to buy rings, so the Judge ties pieces of seaweed into little circles. It's sandy and wet as I put it on her finger. Her hands are warm as she slips one on me.

"I now pronounce you husband and wife. You may kiss the bride, as if you haven't already done that!" he chuckles.

We kiss. The warm breeze picks up around us and I feel lighter than air.

Jose plays his guitar and Juanita sings. I have no idea what they're saying but it's happy music. We dance on the sand, in the moonlight.

"Goodnight, you two lovebirds, I only hope you are as happy as Juanita and I have been all these years."

We sit in the sand, water lapping at our feet, our heads resting on each other.

We try to make love on the beach but it turns out to not be such a great idea. We laugh it off, go back to our room, get in the shower together and do it there, wet, warm and smelling like flowery soap. We get in bed, naked, and hold each other.

I wake up, not knowing where I am. I look over and see Esther, angelic. I remember Kitty in bed in the mornings. I was crazy about her, or maybe I was just crazy. Maybe I still am. 'Stoneman is my father-in-law' I think. He wanted her to marry Adam and she comes home with the snake? I can't even imagine what he will do. I wonder if she only married me to get out of marrying Adam.

Esther's eyes flutter open. "Good morning, my love," she kisses me sweetly.

I want to ask her why she married me, but I'm afraid of the answer, so I don't. "Good morning, love." Saying the word makes me know that 'love' isn't enough for what I'm feeling. I *adore* her. "What shall we do today, love?"

"I've got to get home to plan the wedding," she says. I freeze— literally feeling myself get cold.

I mutter, "Of course. This was just for fun, I didn't think..."

"Right, this was fun, but it's not the real thing."

"Don't worry, I won't get in the way of you and Adam…"

"What're you talking about? I mean a real wedding for *us,* with family and all."

"Are you sure?"

"Aren't you sure?"

"Your father won't be happy."

"He's never happy. Besides, he's not the one getting married. At least you're a *nice* Jewish boy. Or, after what you did last night… a Jewish boy," she purrs.

There's a tray of fruit and baked goods outside the door. We eat off each others' bodies, savoring life's sweetness.

191 ➽ Driving Lessons

I give Jose a $100 tip before we leave, "Thank you, mi amigo," I say to him.

I hold Esther's hand, even as she shifts gears. "I'd like you to drive me," she says, pulling to the side of the road.

"I don't know how."

"I'll teach you!" she says excitedly! "Hold down the brake. Press the clutch in, just past where you feel pressure… like you did with me this morning," she giggles. My left foot presses down and I feel the spot where there's pressure and push down past it. "Release the clutch then press it in again and move the stick, the pattern is etched right on top." It's an H-pattern, with a 1 in the upper left, a 2 below it, a 3 up to the right and an R on the bottom right. "Now, let up on the clutch…"I pull my foot back, the car jerks then stalls. "I should have told you to release the clutch *slowly.*"

I try again and it stalls again. "It's OK, It helps to press on the gas as you release the clutch." I try again, this time the car starts to lurch forward, I give it more gas, and am pushed back in my seat as the car speeds down the road, the engine getting increasingly loud.

"Shift, shift!" she yells. "Clutch in, move the stick to the center, clutch out and back in again, shifter down, clutch out," I do, there are awful grinding noises, the car slows then speeds up. "Good, you'll get the hang of it." The car is moving very fast and I'm focused on steering then she again yells, "Shift, shift!" I do the whole clutch/stick thing, this time without the grinding. "You got it!" she beams, her face luminous in the sunlight.

After a while I don't even have to think about it, my feet and arm know what to do and I can look at the instruments. "What do these dials do?"

"That's how fast we're going, that's how fast the engine is going... water temperature, oil pressure... and gasoline level... almost empty! We need to find a gas station! There, there!" she points off to the right. I turn off the road. "Brakes, brakes!" she squeals and I press the middle pedal hard, the steering wheel keeping me from hitting the windshield again. I look over and Esther has braced her hands against the dashboard. "Whew, that was fun!"

I maneuver next to a gas pump. It's harder to drive this thing slow, I have to work hard to turn the wheel.

Three attendants in green jumpsuits spring into action. One is washing the window in front of us, which is good because it's covered in bugs. The next leans down to the tires. There's a loud hissing noise as he connects a hose to the tire. The third looks confused. "He needs the key for the fuel door, it happens all the time," she takes the key from the ignition, gets out of the car and opens a little flap in the rear fender.

When he's done he says, "20 gallons at 18 cents a gallon, comes to... $3.20."

I give him a $10. "Keep the change!" I say, hoping to make a graceful getaway and only stalling once.

I feel like a pilot flying up the coast with Esther my gorgeous copilot. Then I remember she's my ladywife, like in "The Adventures of Robin Hood," with Erroll Flynn and Olivia de Havilland and yell. "Hi ho!"

"Hi ho!" she yells back.

We stop at "Anthony's fish Grotto" a little shack by the water, and have fish and chips, then I drive some more, thoroughly enjoying it.

As we get closer to Los Angeles, the traffic gets busier and a blue car cuts right in front of me. Esther reaches over and smacks the center of the steering wheel, setting off the car horn.

"Asshole!" she yells, sticking up her middle finger.

"Me? I ask.

"No, the jerk in the Buick! I'll drive now, honey," she says, as traffic gets busier.

All I hear is "Honey."

"Come, on, pull over, baby."

All I hear is "baby."

She pinches my leg. "Come on, let me drive." I pull to the side of the road and we switch places without getting out of the car. She races back on the road, zooming up and cutting off the blue Buick, then thrusting her finger into the air again, laughing. God she's gutsy!

When we pull up in front of the hotel it almost feels like we never left. "What now?" I ask.

"I hadn't thought that far ahead. Let me go back home and tell my mother. If she doesn't drop dead on the spot, then she can tell dad. If he doesn't kill me then I'll call and you can come over."

I joke, "If he kills me, well... it was only a matter of time!"

She doesn't laugh. "I forgot about that, Herbie. She puts her warm hands on my cheeks. "I need you to know that's not why I married you, OK? I fell in love with you the first time I looked into them there eyes," she sings. She gives me another serious kiss, simultaneously sweet and sad. "I want to be married to you till the end of *my* life," she says, teary eyed.

"I do, too," I tell her, hopefully. She drives off, waving. I get to the bungalow, excited to tell Archie but of course he's not there. Maybe I should have gone with Esther to protect her from her father? I would go right now but I don't know where she lives!

I touch the piece of seaweed tied around my finger. It's dry and falls off. I'd better get us some real rings!

I go to the jeweler's shop just off the lobby. Mordecai Goldsmith, Goldsmith. A round man wearing magnifying goggles is mounting a diamond into a ring. He finishes, then looks up at me. "Good afternoon, what can I do for you?"

"I need wedding rings made. Two of them."

"Two is the best number for wedding rings." He pulls out a case of simple gold bands. "I got yellow gold. I got rose gold. I got white gold. I got ⅛th inch for her and ¼ inch for you."

"I want something special."

"A man after my own heart. I do custom work. Ropes. Lattice. Diamond cut. What is that piece of dreck on your finger?"

"It's seaweed, we got married on the beach."

"The beach? With the sand everywhere? Oy, no thank you. But this seaweed has a nice shape. I could cast this in green gold should you want it green."

"I love that idea."

"You would. I mean, 'you're good.' I can set some tiny green diamonds like seawater sparkling. I'm a genius—now even I like this idea. Let me get your size here... an 8. What is your wife's ring size?"

"I don't know."

"Oy, the first lesson for a long happy marriage is to know her ring size so you can buy her more jewelry. I can make a cast of this and size it when she comes in with her pretty little hand."

"Thank you. How much do I owe you?"

"Money money money, is that all you think about? Think about how this is the symbol of your love for eternity. $200 for hers and $300 for yours, 50% deposit upfront.

"Can I write you a check?"

"Is the Pope Catholic?"

192 ➤ Cry Uncle

"I'm a married man," I think, looking through the kitchen drawers for a bottle opener, a cold bottle of coke in my hands. I'm ready to give up and go to the pool bar when I see an opener mounted to the side of the refrigerator. Snick, fizz, I take a long, cold drink. The bubbles tickle the roof of my mouth.

Being married is a surprise—a pleasant one. Maybe we could even have a baby before... nope, I'm not thinking about it. "I am a *happily* married man," I say out loud.

There's a knock on the door and I'm the only one here to open it. I look through the peephole but can only see a hat. I open the door anyway and a man pushes past me, closing the door behind him. I pick up the heavy statue which is still lying on the floor by the door.

When the man turns around I recognize him, it's William, the British spy from the Cloud Club. "Hello Herbert. Your photos of Noël were very amusing," he says, unamused.

"I'm surprised to see you here," I say.

"Good, I like to keep people guessing. I could use a coke, with some vodka." He sits on the sofa, his legs crossed.

"My butler is... nevermind, I'll get it for you." I grab another bottle from the fridge and open cabinets looking for vodka.

"Look in the freezer," I hear him casually say from the other room. I do, and there's a bottle of vodka. "Short glass, cabinet to the right of the refrigerator." He's right again. "Opener's on the side of the fridge. Jigger's in the middle drawer..." I don't know what a jigger is. "...give me two... oh, you have no idea what a jigger is, do you... quarter glass vodka and the rest coke." I carefully eye what looks like a quarter glass of vodka and fill the rest with coke. I start to open the freezer again to get some ice and I hear him call out, "No ice."

Back in the living room, I hand him the glass and he takes a sip, "Excellent for your first attempt, but that's what you do."

"How would you know that? And how did you know where everything was in the kitchen?"

"It's my job to know. Just like I know that best-wishes are in order for you and your charming bride, Esther Hamilton nee Stoneman."

"I didn't know 'nee' was her middle name."

"Ah, to be 18 again. A blessing and a curse. Speaking of curses, I saw your x-ray. Bad luck, old chap."

I'm feeling angry but take a deep breath to stay calm. "I'm fine, Mr. Stephenson, and yes, I know things, too, like your last name. What I don't know is what you want from me. I do know you want something, or you wouldn't bother keeping tabs on me. I'm right, aren't I?"

"You are. You've always been a bright young man, which is why I'm here."

"I'm waiting for a call from Esther, so please get to the point."

"You won't hear from her today. Abe is too angry and she doesn't want to subject you to that."

"You can't know what hasn't happened yet."

"It's already happened. I have ears everywhere. But I'll get to the point. I have an assignment for you."

I remember his last assignment and respond bitterly. "You want me to take pictures of more men being blown up?"

"In a fashion, yes."

I stand up, fling open the patio door and go outside to breathe. Birds are singing. Children laughing.

"I want you to work for your country. Not Oma-ha, Uncle Sam. I turn to look into his cold, gray eyes. Wrinkled around the edges. Serious. Inscrutable.

"What do you want?"

"First, everything I tell you must be kept in the strictest confidence. Trust me, I will know if you tell anyone, even your bride."

"Cross my heart."

"Britain needs America to get into the war, soon, or we could lose. The Germans know how to move armies, but the English and Americans know how to move hearts and minds. We're launching an all-out propaganda campaign designed to call Americans to action as you have as much to lose as we do should Hitler prevail. You saw with your own eyes how the Nazis are already infecting America."

"I'm proud to help in any way I can," I say.

"Except going to London, yes, I know everything about you, lad. Though now, in your condition even the army wouldn't take you now."

"I'm fine."

"Stiff upper lip and all that rot. Good for you."

"What do you want?" I demand.

"A picture."

"What kind of pictures do you want me to take?"

"Not pictures, *a picture*. A movie."

"Why, when you know I've never done that." I say, swigging the last bit of my coke.

"Of course I know that. I also know that Leon is ready to work with you."

"How? Did you bug this place?" Then it hits me and I have to sit down. I remember Archie always being there. "Archie?" I gasp.

"I never reveal our agents."

"You don't have to. He just happened to leave in the middle of the night for England without saying goodbye..."

"Not his decision, lad. He was quite fond of you. Too fond, I felt."

"Fond..."

"He spoke most highly of you. As did Pat."

"You'll have to excuse me because, as you went out of your way to remind me, I'm just a kid, and not right in the head, but why me? There are dozens of good British directors in Hollywood. They would make more sense."

"Normally, yes, which is why I initially approached Hitch. But he's too high-profile, no way to keep this quiet."

"And too big of a target?"

"I see I have not overestimated you, Herbert. Yes, you understand the problem. If the SS killed him it would be all over the news."

"But if they kill me, a first time director... People die in Hollywood every day. I know at least two myself."

"Exactly."

"Were you responsible for David and Frank?" I ask.

"No."

"Would you tell me if you were?"

"No. But I'm not. Mob business doesn't interest us."

"Do you know where Kitty is?"

"I'm not in the habit of answering questions."

"Where's Kitty?"

William takes a moment and looks even more serious. "Unfortunately I don't know, and that concerns me. No more questions. Back to you, Mr. Director. I would be remiss if I didn't mention that you will have a target on your back."

"I already have one on my head."

"We want you to be creative—but you must also do what we tell you."

"I want Esther to write it."

"Fine, though she will work with our people to make sure the message gets across. Huxley's already written a scenario under an assumed name."

"When do we start?"

"Now. Stage 7 is open at Fox after news of Betty's bundle of joy."

"Did you arrange that, too?" I wonder, aloud.

"You know the adage about curiosity and the cat?"

"It hasn't killed me yet."

"'Yet' being the operative word. One more thing to make your decision easier, we can get you out of the draft which you haven't even bothered to register for yet. So do what I tell you or go to jail."

"Hmm... difficult decision," I mocked his threat. "But you already knew I'd agree."

"Precisely. I'll drop by and tell Stoneman what's what. I might even put in a good word for you, just so he doesn't strangle you before we're done. After, well, that's your problem. Say nothing around Otto, the skinny Butler from next door. We have our eyes on him."

"I didn't like him."

"Good instincts. You've already know your direct contact, Diane. Despite being a lesbian communist her heart's in the right place. And so, I am sure, is yours. Thanks for the drink. Learn what a 'jigger' is.." With that he sweeps out, leaving me to wonder if the pounding in my head is normal, given the circumstances.

193 »→ Huxley

"Did you know about Archie?" I ask Diane when she arrives, dressed to the nines wearing a mink stole.

"Know what?" she says, checking her lipstick in the mirror.

"That he was working with William."

"I don't know who or what you're talking about, Herb and I don't have time to gab, I'm meeting Kate for supper in Chasen's back room, she refuses to eat in public. I'm just here to drop off Huxley's scenario for the film."

"Do you really hate Jerry?"

"Fuck yes."

"How is he?"

"Who cares?"

"And you didn't quit because..."

"Breakneck said you asked too many questions." She applies a dab of perfume to her neck and mink.

"Who's Breakneck?"

"See?

"By the way, in case he didn't tell you, I'll be working on this screenplay with Esther to make sure the message remains clear. If you don't like that you can take it up with Breakneck."

"I don't know who that is!"

"Yes, you do, he was just here."

"Oh."

"You should call your bride, I hear she's had a tough time. Better yet, pick her up and take her somewhere nice like the mensch I know you are."

Diane breezes out, leaving a trail of lilac perfume in her wake.

I call the number Esther gave me. A slow voice with a southern accent answers, "Good evening... Stoneman residence."

"May I speak to Esther, please."

There's a pause. "Miss Esther is... indisposed. Good... bye..."

"... Wait—tell her Herb called..."

I hear her say, "Belvedere, give me that phone this instant! Oh, Herb. I can't talk here..."

"What's your address?"

"875 Nimes Road... no, wait, it's better if I meet you at the service entrance, 800 Bel Air Road. Take St. Pierre to St. Cloud to Bel Air."

"I'll be right there."

"I'll be waiting," she says, with a kissing sound.

I press the hook twice and the hotel operator answers. "Hi, this is Mr. Hamilton in Bungalow 7, I need a car, ASAP. Bob, if he's available. No, wait, anybody but Bob. Thanks."

The car is waiting and the driver is Otto. I tell the doorman I want a different driver. He waves Otto away and another car pulls up with a driver I've never seen before, dark hair, strong dimpled chin, movie star handsome. I get in. "800 Bel Air Road, please, and make it snappy. Take St. something..."

"St. Pierre to St. Cloud, The Chartwell estate, I know," he says, doffing his cap.

The car glides gently out of the hotel, but once we reach Sunset he takes off, "Hold onto your hat, sir."

I'm not wearing a hat, why didn't I bring a hat? I hold onto the leather strap next to the window and bounce on the springy seat as we wind around narrow roads to a street with tall walls and trees trimmed like lollipops.

We pull up to a fancy iron gate. Esther emerges from a hedge and jumps in the car.

"GO!" she says, and we drive off.

"Where to?" the driver asks.

"The Original Pantry Cafe downtown," she says breathless. "Dad would never deign go there and be with the riff raff who pay to see his movies!" She's shaking. I put my arm around her. "He says you're a gold-digger."

"I'm not a gold digger."

"That's what I told him."

"You came after me."

"That's what I told him. But he says you've been trailing him since that first meeting on the train."

"I'm sorry, love."

"It's not your fault, he's horrible. I escaped when his friend Stephenson arrived. I don't know why but he'll drop everything for that man. I think he's a blackmailer."

"He's..." I stop myself. Did the driver's head just move to the right so he could listen? "You don't have to go back there. Come stay with me in the bungalow. Then we'll find a nice apartment." She puts her head on my chest and cries. "Ah, baby, I'll take care of you."

The driver drops us off at "The Pantry" where we get in the long line outside. The motto on the wall reads, "Never closed, never without a customer since 1924." Everyone in line is chatting loudly above the traffic, so I feel it's safe to whisper to Esther.

"I'm on a secret mission."

"A frequent mortician?" she says loudly.

I move closer and speak more slowly, "You're finally going to get to write a movie at Fox."

She's shouting now, "Airworthy cocks? You're not making any sense."

I kiss her cheek and hold her close as we wait in line. Once inside it's not only loud, but we're seated across from each other at a long table with 10 other people! The waiter, who's 100 if he's a day, drops off plates heaping with coleslaw, a fresh loaf of sourdough bread, and a big steel bowl of carrots, celery and radishes.

Esther points to the menu written on a chalkboard. "I like breakfast for dinner but you can't go wrong with the open-faced hamburger steak." She flags the waiter and orders, "I'll have the French toast and bacon. He'll have..."

"I'll have the hamburger steak with cottage fries..."

"...And two pieces of peach cobbler," she adds, turning to me, "What were you trying to tell me outside."

"I know what Stephenson was talking to your dad about."

"Is that thing in your brain an antenna? Do you think you're a mind reader now?"

"Why are you being mean?"

"I'm sorry, I'm still in fighting mode... but how could you know."

"All I can say is Stephenson wants me to direct a movie at Fox and I said I'd only do it if you write it."

Esther looks concerned and puts the back of her hand against my forehead. "You don't seem to have a fever." She shakes her head and takes a big forkful of coleslaw. "Oh my God, this is the world's best coleslaw, you have to have some."

I look at the coleslaw but can't even lift my fork, "Maybe I'm crazy, because if you don't believe me then I don't believe myself."

"It just doesn't make sense, love."

"I know, and I'm not allowed to tell you why."

"Who's going to know, Herb? What, are you suddenly a spy or something?"

I see a crayon on the floor from a kid at the next table who was drawing on the paper placemat. I pick it up and write as quickly as I can, "Stephenson=spy. We make movie to get US behind UK. You write it. I direct." I point to it and she reads and looks surprised. I scrawl, "It's true" then tear the placemat into tiny pieces.

She takes the crayon and writes on her placement, "Why can't we talk?" and hands me the crayon.

I write, "Stephenson has bugged my room and your house." I see her read it, then I cross it out. We look at each other, frustrated. I write, "He's always listening," then cross it out. I shrug. The food arrives on plates that qualify as platters. Even I couldn't eat the pile of pancakes on Esther's plate and my hamburger steak looks big enough for all 12 people at the table. We eat what we can, about ¼ of what's on the plate. The waiter brings paper boxes for the rest. I pay at the cashier's cage and leave a big tip.

There's nobody else on the street but I still feel like somebody's listening. "I don't know where we'll be able to talk."

"I do," she says confidently.

Back at the car she tells the driver, "Take us to Bullocks Wilshire." Once there she I follow her into the ladies "Foundation Garments" department where it's all bras and strange contraptions that look like torture devices. She chats with a mature saleslady and gestures for me to come over. The woman says, "Newlyweds, how sweet. Please follow me to our VIP changing room." She opens the door to a mirrored room with two chairs and a table with fresh flowers and closes the door behind her.

"My mom took me here for my first bra. She said it was soundproof so nobody would hear me cry. We fought all the time and she was tired of me embarrassing her so she took me in here to give me a spanking."

"That's awful."

"No, I was awful and she was right. Anyway, I know it's safe to talk here. Besides, Stephenson couldn't know we were coming here, so talk."

"We'll be helping the war effort."

"Dad will never let you do anything at Fox."

"Stephenson will make him. I think it has something to do with Betty's baby. Jack said... no, I don't want to say it."

"Jack said what? Say it."

"Jack thought your dad was schtupping Betty and I think it was his baby."

"A blackmailer, I knew it!"

"Back to the movie... oh, I can talk to you about that openly, you're just not supposed to know *why* we're making this movie."

"That's stupid."

"I agree. Diane... she works at *Look* magazine advertising but also for Stephenson, she's in charge of the message part of the picture and you write the rest."

"She can get 'story by' but I want full screenwriting credit."

"I'll tell Stephenson that."

She holds me tight and kisses me deep, "I don't even care if this is true or not, it's exciting and I feel alive! I'm so happy, Herb. I love you."

"I love you, too."

Our kissing grows more intense and we're groping each other all over when there's a knock at the door. "How does that fit, miss? Would you like to try another size?"

We stop, cold. She speaks to the door, "You were right, it's a perfect fit. I'll get dressed and be right out."

"Take your time, dears," the saleslady says.

We take our sweet, sweet time.

194 ➻ Love is Blind

Back at the bungalow we look at the pages Diane dropped off. Esther reads aloud:

> Title: The Retrograde, By Aubrey Huxtable.
>
> The Nazi's have discovered another dimension of time called 'The Retrograde". They plan to use it to change history. It has to be destroyed or they will control the future. The Hero, Martin, must go into the Retrograde with a bomb and blow it up, even if it means blowing himself up in the process.

Esther drops it like a hot potato, "This doesn't make sense. How will it get Americans to..." I put my hand over her mouth. "...to buy tickets?"

I call Diane. There's no answer. "Operator, connect me with Chasen's restaurant please."

"Chasen's, how may I help you?"

"I need to speak to a woman named Diane, dining there with Katherine Hepburn."

"Hold please." I hear clicking on the line.

"Who is this?" Diane says, testility.

"It's Herb, and we need to talk."

"I will talk to you tomorrow."

"Now. Or do you want me to call Breakneck?"

There's a pause, and she replies, "You bastard, I'll be right over."

I take Esther's hand and we go out to the patio. I lean close and whisper in her ear. "I love you."

"Don't make a secret of it!" she says, turning to kiss me.

The doorbell rings. It's Diane. "Kate was most displeased with you, Herb. She never eats alone."

"Silly me, I assumed that the future of the world was more important than a dinner date."

Diane lights a cigarette. Without dinner dates there is no future."

"Speaking of the future, did you read the Huxley story?"

"It's strange, but I thought that your clever bride could make something of it."

"She can't." I say.

"But I do have an idea," Esther says.

"Esther, you'll need to go into the other room." Diane says, patronizing.

"I already told her everything." I announce.

"Did you hear that, Breakneck? I'm sure he heard that."

"I can't write something effective if I don't know what the point is," Esther adds.

"This isn't a game," Diane blows smoke in my face. "Millions of lives are at stake. If you can't take orders then Breakneck will... I don't know what he'll do."

"Huxley's is too intellectual. Not commercial. Let me tell you my idea," Esther says. "Sit down. It's called *'Love is Blind.'* It's about Sarah, an English nurse and Henry, an American in the ambulance corps. That part's from 'A Farewell to Arms' and you know how popular that was. I've changed enough so we won't have to buy the rights. Henry's wounded and Sarah takes care of him. He falls for her and pursues her but she doesn't like him because he's a cocky Yank. I happen to love cocky Yanks myself..." She looks at me and smiles.

"Back to the story, Sarah's house is bombed and she's shell shocked so she can't see or hear, but we'll use voiceover so we know what she's thinking. Henry picks her up in his ambulance and helps her through her recovery. She falls in love with him not knowing who he is. Her sight and hearing return and they live happily ever after."

I'm amazed, "That's a beautiful story, love, I love it."

Diane is unmoved, "How, exactly does it further our goal here?"

"An American steps in and helps a Brit," Esther explains.

"We're not going for subtle, we're going for effectiveness," Diane disagrees.

"It's about love and that moves people. How was 'The Retrograde' going to call people to action?" Esther argues.

"That's for you to figure out."

"You're right, there are no Nazi's in my story other than the ones bombing the shit out of Jolly Old England! Fine, you want more Nazis, I can add Nazis.... Um..."

"I photographed a big rally in New York where 20,000 Americans thought the Nazis were just swell," I remember.

"That's it," Esther continues. "The happy couple comes back to the US and the Nazis have already converted tens of thousands of Americans. We can use a little of Huxley's time travel, and go to the year 1945 when Democracy is dead, freedom is history, and we see life under Nazi rule."

"That's not very happy," Diane says.

"But Roger and Sarah are part of the Underground and lead a revolution of democracy!"

Diane takes a long drag on her cigarette and answers in smoke, "I don't hate it.

"Said like a true studio executive."

"Start with the Nazi takeover, then flash back to Roger meeting Sarah and all that."

"I don't hate it," Esther says.

"Breakneck, did you hear that? We'll have to get his approval…"

The phone rings. It's Stephenson. "Story works. Write it. Breakneck out." he hangs up.

"I'm going back to Chasen's, I might just be in time for dessert. If you call me again tonight I will… ug, I don't know what I'll do."

"You need to work on your threats, Diane," I say, mockingly.

"This isn't a joke, and if you treat it as one… Oh nevermind." Diane breezes out.

I put my arms around Esther. "How'd you come up with that story so fast?"

"Because I wrote that story four years ago, set in World War I. Dad said, 'Nobody wants to see war movies, we had the 'war to end all wars,' it's ancient history.' In my original story she has a big facial scar but he was right about no actress wanting to look ugly, so I didn't mention it in this one."

"Let's go to bed," I say, kissing her cheek.

"I thought you'd never ask!" she replies, sliding her hand into the back of my pants.

195 ➻ Mother Earth

"What if Henry…" she asks as I unbutton her blouse.

"That could work," I answer, as she unzips my pants.

"It needs more of a patriotic angle," she says before slipping her tongue in my mouth.

"But not flags or old-fashioned stuff," I try to say, with her tongue in my mouth.

She pulls back. "It needs a spiritual angle."

"But not religious," I add.

"Because if we choose one religion everyone else will feel left out and that's the opposite of what we're trying to say." She's sitting up, naked, her eyes darting as she thinks. "We need to get to the heart of the land."

"Native people!" I say, remembering them from Albuquerque.

"Yes! Mother earth herself!"

I hop out of bed and get the turquoise string tie. "A beautiful native woman gave this to me in Albuquerque."

"Prettier than me?" Esther teases?

"Not possible."

She has a flash of inspiration, "She can lead the underground and inspire Henry and Sarah to save America itself!"

I kiss her. "The native woman's number is scratched into the back," I show her.

"Did you call her?"

"No."

"But you thought about it?"

"No, I forgot it was even there till now."

"I forgive you."

"I didn't do anything!"

"I'm just kidding. Let's see," she reads the name, "Tsís'ná Bitł'izh." First thing we'll have to do is change her name, nobody can pronounce that."

We are up all night, tossing ideas back and forth. I call the front desk and have them send over a typewriter. She types very fast. We laugh. We argue, "It's good for couples to argue so things don't get built up. My parents have barely exchanged 10 words in 10 years so who knows what's festering inside them... Mom told me once 'when you're married you never want to go to bed angry.' Her solution to that was to stop giving a damn. About anything. We're not going to be like that," she says, brightly, slapping my cheek.

"Ow!" I howl. "We're not going to be like that, either!" I protest.

"Is bondage out, too?"

"I don't know what that is," I tell her.

"We'll give it a try later. Oh, look, it *is* later."

The sun is rising. I yawn and see she's sitting up, asleep. I put my head in her lap and fall asleep too...

...We were on the movie set—a painted desert that's literally painted, peppered with paper mache cactus. Tsís'ná stood on a rock, arms up to the heavens, a spotlight shining down to illuminate the turquoise in her hand. "Oh, great father, protect us, guide us to victory against the evil Nazis, they are not of this land, they are not of our hearts!"

Lightning! Thunder! Torrential rain, yet she is miraculously dry.

Henry and Sarah's car skidded off the wet road and stopped at Tsís'ná's sandal shod feet. They stared at her, awe-struck.

"We must save our country, our land, together!" she pronounced!

The music swelled. There wasn't a dry eye in the house....

196 ⇒ Father sky

Esther wakes up when she smells the coffee, toast, eggs and bacon. "Breakfast! You're a mind-reader" she exclaims.

It's noon and too bright to sit on the patio so we eat inside in contented silence. When we're all done I take the empty plates back to the kitchen. "Shall I draw you a bath, madame?" She laughs. "I learned from a master!"

"I'll have to give Archie my regards if we ever see him again."

That makes me feel sad as I fill the tub, sprinkle in bubble bath, and pour in Gardenia bath oil. I stop being sad as I watch her, naked, sinking into the water like Venus.

The phone rings, "Breakneck here," he says.

"Hi William... Breakneck."

"Good job on the script last night. All the more necessary as the production schedule has been moved up. Parliament was bombed last night and reports from London express concern about making it through the winter. We need to get the film out as soon as possible.

Stonefox says with all hands on deck it can be finished in 4 weeks once the script is complete."

"Are you watching or just listening?" I ask, a bit concerned.

"Finish the script tonight. Oh, and Merry Christmas." He hangs up.

Christmas? Did I miss Hanukkah, too? When was it this year?

The phone rings again. "Hello. Is this Mr. Hamilton?"

"Yes, who is..."

"This is Charles Montgomery West calling from Saks to send you the warmest Christmas wishes. And ask if there might be anything I can do for you for this festive day."

"Thank you, Charles, and the same to you. How's your thesis?"

"I'm almost done thank you for asking. And, on another personal note, Rhonda and I are spending Christmas together."

"All the best to you both! I got married, myself."

"This is a joyous season! I thought you might have some last-minute shopping that I could do for you."

"Actually, I'd like to buy my wife a surprise, a locket," I whisper while she's still safely bathing. "But I don't know how to keep it a secret."

"I can pull a selection and bring them to your hotel. We can meet surreptitiously in your lobby, all very undercover," Charles whispers.

"Simple. Modern. Gold."

"Got it. I'll call from the lobby. Charles out!"

I wonder if there's anyone else I should get a present for. If Archie was here I would buy him cufflinks or a watch. I wonder if I'll ever see him again. Pat and Glenn... I don't know. Diane, no. Ma! I call the bank and have them send her money.

I call the operator. "Can you tell me when Hanukkah was this year?"

"It starts today, Mr. Hamilton. Would you like a menorah sent to your bungalow? We offer a special Hanukkah dinner, brisket, latkes with sour cream and applesauce, kugel, a selection of sweets and a bag of Hanukkah Gelt."

"Perfect, can you send it around 5pm?"

"Of course. Happy Hanuakkah sir."

"Happy Hanukkah to you, too."

I hear the shower stop, my surprises are just in time. She emerges with a towel around her hair and nothing else, looking like the most beautiful mermaid in the entire history of mermaids. She presses her damp skin against me and gives me a big kiss, then pads into the bedroom.

I count the pages... "Love, you wrote 46 pages, how many do we need?"

"Around 90."

"We're over half way there—we can finish tonight, then!"

She puts her arm around my neck. "What's the hurry, sailor?"

"Breakneck called. Production's been moved up. They need the movie complete in four weeks, tops."

She laughs and I notice how pretty her perfectly straight teeth are. "Dad must be livid."

There's a knock at the door. I hope it's not Charles, we were supposed to...

The knocking becomes pounding. The pounding becomes yelling, "Open this door you little shit!"

"It's dad!" Esther exclaims.

"Should I call security and have him thrown out?"

"I would pay to see that!"

I pick up the phone, "Hotel security, there's a madman pounding on my door."

"We'll send someone right over."

The pounding stops.

Esther and I look at each other. "Maybe security nabbed him."

I look through the peephole. There's nobody there. I hear Esther scream!

Stoneman has come in through the patio doors, his face dark red. He holds out the Cartier watch I bought in Chicago. "Here, take this.

I'm taking her." He grabs Esther's arm, she struggles. "You're a very clever con man. I'll give you that."

"Take your hands off her!"

"You *just happened* to bump into me on the street? Right. You're so shrewd you were made for the movie business. If it weren't for... Breakneck, I'd call J. Edgar Hoover personally."

Esther struggles. "You're hurting me daddy—Let go of me!"

"You're not going anywhere young lady. Your mother is in tears."

"Like you've ever cared about that," she hisses at him.

I grab her other arm and try to pull her from him, "I love Esther."

"You love my money!" he roars.

"I have enough money."

"You can never have enough money."

"I love him, daddy." she cries.

"Love was made up for the movies," he smirks.

"If you honestly believe that I feel sorry for you!" I say.

"I'm not gonna feel sorry for you when you find yourself locked up by the FBI."

"I pity you. I wouldn't want to live inside your head."

"And I don't want you inside my daughter!"

"Ew, dad, shut up!" She hits him, pulls away and backs towards the kitchen.

I stand nose-to-nose with him and speak quietly, "*Your* daughter, like you *own* her! Have you met Esther? Nobody owns her. You don't even care about her. If you did, you wouldn't have wanted to marry her off to a homo rabbi."

"Watch your mouth, kid."

"You knew and you didn't care. You bastard."

He smashes his forehead into mine—my skull feels like it's splitting open. I see flashes of light, take a step back and hold onto a chair to keep from falling. He takes a swing at me, misses, trips on the leg of the sofa and falls on the floor.

I lean down, which makes my head hurt more, and whisper, "Imagine what your wife would do if she found out the truth about Betty's baby."

He grunts. Esther approaches, carrying a kitchen knife. "I've been scared of you my whole life. But no more. Now you're gonna do what I want. Got it?"

There's a knock at the door. "Security. Are you OK, Mr. Hamilton?" The front door opens and the security officer enters. "Looks like you've already subdued him. Good job. I'll take him to our holding cell and call the Beverly Hills police. They're tough on intruders here."

The guard puts his foot on Stoneman's neck and pulls out his handcuffs.

"That won't be necessary. This is my wife's father. He's a mean drunk. But he's OK now, aren't you, *dad*?"

Stoneman fumes and pulls himself to his feet and looks at me with loathing. I move to pick up the watch he dropped but feel dizzy and steady myself as he grabs it.

"Once Breakneck is done with you, I'm gonna break your neck," he grunts.

The phone rings. "Put Stonefox on."

"It's for you," I say, handing him the phone.

He grabs it from my hands, "What now, you limey bastard?"

Stoneman looks angry but says nothing. "I'm sorry, Mr. President. Yes. Yes. Yes. Of course." He hangs up and turns to me, calm on the surface but still seething. "I'll see you on Monday when we commence production." He stands tall and walks out.

As he leaves, the security man shakes his head, "Wow, I've heard that Stoneman guy was an asshole but this takes the cake!"

I sink into the sofa, my head throbbing. Esther takes my hand, "My hero."

All I can do is laugh. Once I've caught my breath, I say, "I've got a surprise for you."

"I don't know if I could take another one today," she jokes.

The phone rings again. I get up, my knees weak. It's Charles from Saks.

"I've got to meet with Breakneck... no.. I'm never going to lie to you. This is part of your surprise. I'll be right back. Lock the doors," I say, kissing her gently.

I feel unsteady and have a headache behind both eyes, but I'm not going to let that stop me. I recognize Charles in the lobby, even though, or maybe especially because, of his trench coat, fedora, sunglasses and briefcase attached to his wrist with a chain. I motion him over and ask Renaldo, one of the triplets at the front desk if there's somewhere I can have a private meeting.

He unlocks a small meeting room for us.

Charles and I sit at a desk. "You can take your disguise off now," I tell him.

"It's good I wore it, though, there was a madman in the lobby."

"That was my father-in-law."

Charles looks concerned. "I'm sorry."

"I am, too. But she's worth it."

He unlocks the chain from around his wrist and opens the briefcase. Inside, a series of lockets hang from the midnight blue velvet lining. "I selected the most modern pieces."

They're all hearts except the one that stands out immediately—A golden egg with two rows of diamonds around the widest part. I flip the tiny latch and inside one half is a yellow enamel yolk surrounded by the white. The other side has space for a photograph.

"This is it, Charles, thank you."

Charles blushes. "That's our most expensive piece, sir. It's $350."

"You can't take it with you," I say, writing him a check. "Thank you, Charles." I hand him a $50 tip.

"That's two months rent, it's much too generous."

"I've been very lucky. It feels like I've laid this egg myself. Merry Christmas, I hope you and Rhonda will be very happy together."

"Thank you, Mr Hamilton. Please call me if you need anything. Any time. Merry Christmas."

Back at the bungalow I do a "shave and a haircut, two bits" knock on the door. Esther opens the door and I slip in quickly, locking the door behind me.

"All clear on the western front," she whispers. "Are you OK?"

"Better than OK. You and I are doing something important here, and I want to commemorate the occasion, and wish you a happy Hanukkah."

"Oh, honey, you're the only thing I need." She kisses me so sweetly I feel dizzy.

"Close your eyes." She does and I place the necklace around her neck. She feels it with her fingers. "You can open them." She looks down at the golden egg and gasps. "This is gorgeous, fit for a tsarina! But it's too extravagant, Herb."

"What're we saving for?"

"The future, hopefully.

"Oh yeah, that."

"And you're unemployed!"

"Oh, yeah, that."

She takes it off and puts it in my hand. "I love it. You should take it back."

I feel her warmth radiate from it. "I'll only hide it and give it back to you later. You might as well wear it now." I put it back around her neck and kiss from her mouth, down her chin, neck, and around where the egg sits. She kisses the growing lump on my forehead.

"Come with me," I take her hand and lead her to the Goldsmith's shop.

"Herb, what else have you done?"

"You'll see." Mr. Goldsmith measures her finger.

"Come back tomorrow, little lovebirds, tweet tweet," he tells us.

Walking back to the bungalow she holds my hand so tight. We've just gotten there when there's a knock at the kitchen door. "What now?" she asks.

"'Wait in the bedroom," I whisper, then let the waiter in. "Just set it down in the kitchen, I can serve it." I tip him.

"Something smells good!" she says.

"Surprise number two! —Happy Hanukkah." I say, bringing plates of food to the table outside. "Our first holiday together!"

"And hopefully not our last," she says wistfully.

"I'm sorry we can't spend it with your family."

"I'm not, are you kidding me?"

"I didn't mean your father."

"Mom'll be fine as long as there's wine. Mmm, this is delicious, almost as good as our cook at home!"

I feel a drop of something hit my head. I hope a bird hasn't pooped on me. Then another, and another plops on the table, making a dusty ring. It's raining. We grab our plates and go back inside, watching the rain hit the window like it's playing percussion.

197 ➻ All Through the Night

After dinner, my headache turns into a dull pain.

Esther and I talk through the scenes, standing up and playing the parts, making it up as we go along. She's very good, especially in the scene where Sarah finally gets her vision and hearing back and sees it's been Henry taking care of her all along. Esther slaps me clean across my face. "You!" she cries.

"What? What have I ever done except love you?" I say.

"Is this what they call love in America?"

Then she whispers in my ear and I repeat what she says, "Yes. We call it taking care of the people and things that mean the most to us. This land. This country. Family. Democracy. The American way of life! That's what we call love!"

She rests her head on my shoulder, "I needed your help and you were there for me. You yanks are good eggs, our countries like kin!" She looks up, patriotically. I put my hand over my heart.

"That was really good, Esther."

"That's because you helped me get into it."

Her fingers pound the typewriter. I go through what she wrote last night and draw storyboard boxes and stick figures to show how I see it. In the part where she can't see or hear, I draw fuzzy black boxes, with little spots of light that get bigger as she gets better. I want the audience to be able to see what she sees, or doesn't, and I make a note below them that the sound should be muffled, too, like a steady buzz that obscures what Henry is saying.

Esther calls out, "Can you help me, Herb, I'm stuck here on your *beautiful* Indian girlfriend."

"She was never my girlfriend."

"But she was *beautiful!* The only Indians I've ever met were on movie sets and most of them weren't real Indians so I don't know how they talk."

"I had a dream about that part. The Indian princess...

"Princess?"

"Medicine woman..."

"...Better..."

""Oh, great father, guide us to victory against our enemies—the evil Nazis! They are not of this land, they are not of our hearts!'

"Lightning! Thunder! Torrential rain. Henry and Sarah's car skids off the wet road and stops inches from her. She proclaims, "We must save our country, our land, together!" I strike a pose I imagine Tsís'ná would take and freeze, for dramatic effect.

Esther stares at me and squints. "Is that how they really talk? Too on-the-nose."

"She's trying to make a point!" I tell her.

"It's... OK, it's good, thanks, you gave me some ideas, I'll take it from here."

I go back to my storyboards. For the moment when Sarah becomes shell shocked, I draw an extreme closeup of her face, in terror, moving even closer towards her eyes... Leon said he could do anything... right into her eyes—and the blindness inside. We stay there, seeing nothing but pinpricks of light and hearing only muffled buzzing

—until we quickly pull back and see her from the outside, in the bombed out house, with rescue workers shaking her—then back in through her ears—silence! Back out—cacophony!

I show the sequence to Esther. "I love it, very dramatic—like we're inside her head!"

"Exactly!"

"I need a name people can pronounce for whateverhernameis princess medicine woman... something like *pocahontas*... but not."

"Why not just use her real name, but shorten it, so it's Tsís'ná... Tina... no, doesn't sound Indian... Stina?"

"Too much like Chris-tina."

"Sisna?"

"Kinda like *sister*—we're all related, yeah, that's good!"

My eyes are tired as I draw more storyboard frames. I rest my head on my arms to take a little break...

...The rain pounded harder, the wind was a hurricane. The porch wall was blown away like Dorothy's house in *Wizard of Oz*. I could see the pool as it overflowed. The flood moved in waves towards the patio windows. I turned to tell Esther we needed to go to a higher floor but I couldn't find her. I ran from room to room, there were at least 20 rooms, each with less and less color until they were just black and white.

The flood lapped at my feet, ruining my suede loafers. I called out to her and heard a growl louder than thunder—a tiger—a real, live, striped tiger strutting through the water towards me. I locked myself in the bathroom, as water poured in from under the door and the room filled with water up to my neck so there was scarcely room to breathe! I heard the scratching of claws on the other side, and one long, sharp claw pierced the door. Now I had to choose, drown in here, or open the door to the tiger...

...I wake to thunder and look around, Esther is right there. The floor is dry.

Esther stops typing, "The end! I don't know if this is any good but at least it's finished!

198 ⮞ Canter's

"Let's go out and celebrate!" she exclaims.

"It's 1am and raining!"

"So?" She grabs her coat and purse. "Let's go!"

It's pitch black and pouring. The only saving grace is that there's nobody else on the road because they're all sane! After the terror subsides, the neon signs stream by like blurred rainbows. *Click...* damn, I need to get some color film! The swaying of the car feels like being rocked in a cradle. My eyes are getting heavy when—we're there!

"Best place to eat in the middle of the night, especially Christmas eve" she says, running from the car to the restaurant. Inside *Canter Brothers Delicatessen* it's like being back in New York City, a narrow room with black and white tile floors.

The place is packed with people talking loudly, laughing, eating. It smells like corned beef, comforting. The waiter arrives with a bowl of dill pickles. "I'll have a half corned beef, extra lean, half chopped liver sandwich on marbled rye with sauerkraut."

"Sounds good, I'll have the same." The waiter leaves. "This joint is jumpin'!"

"You should see it at 4am, there'll be a line outside."

I take her hand. "I'm so proud of you."

"Thank you, darling, that means so much to me. My dad has never read anything I've written. He has someone else read it and write up a paragraph synopsis to which he can say 'no.' My mother started out as a writer but gave it all up to be married and have my brother and I."

"I'm sorry. My Pa... nevermind."

"Please tell me."

"He hardly even acknowledged my existence. When he did, he called me a 'burden,' and 'the thing that ruined my life.' He was always unhappy. Worked in the shmata business, a cutter for knockoff ladies dresses. Hated it. When he got drunk he'd tell the same story of how he was ready to join the merchant marine and see the world but no, Ma was pregnant with me, 'the destroyer of dreams.' Instead, for the past

17 years his hands had to cramp from holding scissors all day to feed the two of us."

"I'm sorry, love."

"Doesn't matter anymore, does it? Ma was sweet, but quiet. Didn't want to cross him. She and I would sneak off to the movies whenever we could, like at night after he passed out. Sometimes it was so late it'd just be her and me in the movie theater—our own private world where everything was beautiful. We had little code words we used so we knew what the other meant, like "Grapefruit" for when we wished we could punch Pa. It's from that scene from 'Public Enemy' where Jimmy Cagney smashes a grapefruit into Mae Clarke's face. I got older... she got sadder... and the movies weren't enough to make up for her real life."

It surprised me that I wasn't crying, but it all seemed so long ago... even if it was only a few months. Remembering it felt like another life— someone else's life. "I left one day when I met... Kitty. A girl... never went back home. Never will. But I also don't forget what Ma did for me. I send her money every month in hopes that she'll take it and leave Pa. In my imagination that's what she's done. I don't want to know if it's not."

She leans in and kisses my hand.

"I never told anybody that stuff. But I wanted to tell you."

"Thank you, sweetheart. Who was this Kitty girl?"

"You don't have to be jealous of her."

"I'm not, I'm just curious."

"She was a showgirl. I thought I loved her but I didn't know what love was until I met you."

She kisses my hand again. "That's a wonderful line, I'm writing that down for the movie."

"It's true, I never heard it in a movie or anything like that." She rests her head on my hand. Her cheek is warm.

"I told you earlier I always want to tell you the truth. So the truth is I came out to Hollywood to find Kitty... or her brother... sister, Iris. It's so complicated even I don't really understand it myself."

"I understand. My brother... sister, Noah, likes to dress up in women's clothes and put on shows. A 'female impersonator' he calls it. He hasn't told our folks, of course, but I saw one of his shows and he's a marvelous singer. Beautiful voice. And when he's all done up, he's much prettier than I am."

"That's not possible," I say, and mean it. "Maybe he could sing for our movie."

"A theme song, under the credits, yes!" The waiter arrives with the sandwiches. "No matter what happens, love, I..." her eyes are watery and she can't speak, trying to wave it away, finally giving up and biting into the chopped liver, a single tear rolling down her cheek and landing on the rye bread. "It needed salt," she smiles.

I take it all in. The noise. The steam. Her hand. The pickle. The laughter. The tear. In the past, happiness came with excitement, even anxiety. Now I'm relaxed as the feeling flows through me. Esther is delicious. The sandwich is delicious. Every moment is momentous.

I think about all the things that have happened to me in the past few months. *It was like I was watching a movie of my own life, but I was behind the camera. Now I'm starring in it...* Feeling her knee rub against mine. Smelling the rye in the bread before I take a bite, tasting the saltiness of the beef as the flavor floods my mouth. Esther's face reminds me of Merle Oberon, but no, it's better, because it's *her* face. I try to count her eyelashes. Our eyes meet, her hazel eyes looking gold. I stop eating and take it all in.

"What're you thinking about?" She asks.

"Everything."

"Me, too, all at once."

"All at once."

I feel the wind as the door opens and smell the rain and wet leather. A woman wearing a hat with pink feathers sits down behind Esther. It looks as if Esther has sprouted bunny ears. *Click.* "I need to take more pictures of you."

"I'm right here."

"That's exactly why."

The waiter places a piece of carrot cake between us. Esther points to him, "They know me here. It's the best." She presses her fork through the white frosting down to the plate, pulls off a piece and holds it at my mouth. The frosting is creamy and sweet and the cake coarse, sweet but with that earthy tang of carrot I taste on the front and sides of my tongue. She puts more on the fork and as she guides it to me I take another picture. *Click.*

Now it's my turn to put cake on the fork and guide it to her luscious lips. "The best," she says. "The cake, and you."

I'm jolted out of the moment when a plate smashes to the floor. Then there's a familiar smell I can't quite place. A small man walks by, his hair slicked down. He passes Esther then turns to look at me.

Green eyes.

Kitty?

Thin mustache, that same man from Romanoff's... and the one who ran away from my patio. I jump to my feet.

"What's wrong, honey?"

"I don't... someone I... he looks... familiar."

"Go say hello, then, networking is everything in this town. I'll be right here."

I follow him, pushing my way through the crowd, into the black kitchen door with its porthole window. The kitchen is crowded and steamy and I see him slip out the back door. I try to get by waiters carrying trays full of food but the floor is slippery and I feel my foot sliding from under me. I grab the only thing I can, a waiter, and he and his tray of sandwiches come tumbling down on top of me, my head cushioned by a Reuben sandwich yet still hitting the floor with a crack.

"I'm sorry, are you OK, I'll pay for all the food," I say to him. Two more waiters pull us to our feet. "Here, please excuse me, I'm so sorry," I say, handing him a $20 bill. I brush myself off, and eat the piece of corned beef that's stuck to my lapel. I go out the back door and look around. There's nobody there.

Back at the table I tell Esther, "I want to go."

"Why are you wearing sauerkraut?" she asks, stifling a smile.

On the drive home I keep seeing the face. Her face? But more like Myron. Except Myron is more like her. My head hurts. What if the doctor was right?

"So who was that friend of yours?"

"I musta been confused. I thought... but who knows..."

"...who knows where or when..." Esther sings.

"Hey, your brother's not the only one with a beautiful singing voice."

She keeps singing, "Some things that happened for the first time
Seem to be happening again
And so it seems that we have met before
And laughed before, and loved before
But who knows where or when."

The song ends and I listen to the sound of water on the tires.

"That bad?" she asks.

"Beautiful, I told you, I just..." I watch the rain slicked city rush by. "Maybe it's all in my head."

199 ➻ Zephyr

I sleep dreamlessly. Fitfully. Each time I wake up I check to make sure Esther is really there. She is. Then I wake up and she isn't. But I smell coffee.

"Good morning, sleeping beauty. I ordered breakfast. I hope you like Belgian waffles."

I'm more of a pancake person but the waffles are so good I might change my mind. These are the biggest I've ever seen, square with deep indentations that fill with butter and syrup.

After breakfast we go to Goldsmith's. He hands me her ring, green gold that looks like seaweed with little diamonds, and I place it on her finger. "Always," I kiss her hand.

"I... you..." she starts to cry. She kisses me.

Goldsmith hands her my ring, which looks like hers only wider and without diamonds. She slips it on my finger. "Forever," she whispers in my ear.

"They're beautiful, sir, thank you." I tell him.

"I wish you a long happy life," he says as we leave, hand in hand.

Back at the bungalow it feels very quiet as we sit close together. "I'm a very lucky girl," she says.

"No, I'm a lucky boy."

"Let's fight over who's luckiest," she laughs.

"I don't want us to ever fight."

"I want to fight. Otherwise it gets all bottled up, unsaid."

"No—my folks fought all the time, I didn't like it."

"Look, our first fight! It was good."

"It wasn't bad."

"We'll need to continue the fight, or at least the make-up sex, later. I've got to run errands and see my brother and talk to him about writing a song for the movie. I'll be back around lunch." She kisses me, so sweetly I don't understand it. It's like my brain stops and there's nothing but the feeling in my lips. It's a long kiss, and when she finally pulls away it feels like I've returned from another planet.

I push the dishes aside and work on my storyboards again. There's a knock at the door. I check the peephole to make sure it's not Stoneman. It's Diane.

"Good morning, Herb. Could you order me some breakfast, I'm famished, Katie's not much of a cook. Nevermind, I'll do it myself." She picks up the phone and orders something called a 'breakfast burrito.' She hands me a check, "First things first, here's a check for $2,000."

"Wow, what's that for?"

"Cole, Noel, Gene, Ethyl, Mickey, Judy, Cary and Katie."

"That'll come in handy," I think aloud.

"Money so often does. And now the good news," she sings, "Ding dong the witch is dead..."

"What?"

"He's gone where the goblins go, below, below, below..."

"...who?..."

She says "Jerry," then sings again, "yo ho, yo ho, yo ho, let's sing and ring the bells out!"

"That's terrible." I say.

"But is it? Really?"

"I feel bad for not feeling bad."

"Look at your check, you'll feel better. Everybody dies sometime," she says, lighting up a cigarette. "We're free!"

The word "dies" bounces around inside my head. "I still have a contract."

"No you don't."

"But, Jerry said..."

"Jerry lied. That's what Jerry did. Did you ever sign anything?"

"Was I supposed to?"

"That's how contracts work."

"You sure?"

"I'm very sure. I checked—there's no signature on file. To quote Samuel Goldwyn, "A verbal contract ain't worth the paper it's written on."

The doorbell rings, it's her breakfast. She sits at the table and eats while I sit on the sofa, the words, 'die' and 'free' playing tennis in my head.

"Clive offered me Jerry's job. I'm moving to Manhattan."

'Die' and 'free' are still duking it out in my brain.

"I cleared it with Breakneck. He said I would have made a lousy Communist and he's right. Herb? You don't look happy. Did you hear me?"

"What did you say?"

She proceeds to talk for five minutes about how excited she is. She'll miss Katie, of course, but she can tell Katie's getting tired of her, as is her way. She wants a penthouse with a terrace and a view and a butler.

"Speaking of which, I've got to run, so much to do. Your new handler will be here shortly." She kisses me on both cheeks. "All the best to you and Esther. She's probably too good for you—all women are too good for men. Then again, you might be an exception." she says, patting my ass. She breezes out.

I take a deep breath. No contract with Jerry. No rodeo clowns or goats. Freedom! Die!

I think of the motto, "Life free or die," and decide I'll live.

"Yoo hoo!" I hear Esther say as she comes in. "I've got a couple of surprises for *you* now!"

"I've got another one," I tell her.

"Mine first. My brother and I wrote a song for him to sing in the movie! Wanna hear it?"

"Yes!"

"Imagine Dinah Shore singing this, because that's who Noah sounds like." She sings,

> *"I could feel your love across the ocean*
> *Our worlds colliding like two ships, adrift*
> *Drawn together through intense emotion*
> *War takes away and then it gives this gift*
> *Sometimes when we're feeling far apart, dear*
> *We are closer than we'll ever know*
> *Close your eyes and follow with your heart, dear*
> *When love is blind the truth will always show.*
> *America must help each friendly nation*
> *Democracy our common precious bind*
> *Or we risk complete annihilation*
> *Love's our weapon, when that love is blind.*

I'm stunned. "I don't know what's better, the song or your singing, you should sing it!"

"No, my brother is better, you'll see. Besides, it's what he wants. I'm doing what I want now, thanks to you."

"You're so talented it takes my breath away."

"Breathe, baby, breathe," She says, leading me to the parking lot.

"My surprise is that I don't have a contract with Jerry, after all."

"Perfect! Since you're going to be staying in Tinseltown, you need to be able to drive. And, voila!" she says, pointing to a curvaceous vehicle, navy blue with a white convertible top. "It's a Lincoln Zephyr, V12. 120 ponies under the hood." She drops keys into my hand. "It's all yours, love."

I see myself reflected in its shiny paint. Inside, the seats are white leather. The dashboard is streamlined. I run my fingers along the vertical chrome strips.

"That's the speaker for the radio," she says, sitting next to me.

"A radio? In a car?"

"It was an option, like the clock."

"A clock and a radio in a car?"

"Yes, and then there's the car itself," she says, turning the key. The engine sounds so smooth compared to her car. "Take her for a spin. It works just like mine."

I release the break, push in the clutch pedal, move the shift lever to the upper left... and the car stalls. Clutch back in, turn the key, *slowly* release the clutch and we're off!

I turn onto Sunset boulevard and drive west. At a red light we jump out and put down the top, then breeze down the road. I keep my right hand on the shifter and she puts her hand on mine.

"Turn left here," she tells me, "There's a wonderful little taco place in Westwood." Are pedestrians staring or is it just my imagination? I feel like we're movie stars. "There's a space," she points to a gap in the curb between cars. I pull the front of the car into the space but it doesn't fit. "You have to parallel park," she explains.

"I don't know what that is or how to do it."

She proceeds to explain it to me, and I can imagine it in my head but the car won't go where I think it's going. "Turn it all the way to the left, then put it in reverse."

I'd never put a car in reverse. With her hand on mine on the sifter, she shoves it far to the right then down. I let go of the clutch and the car jolts backwards—crunch!

"Stop, stop, stop, just stop," she turns the key and the car goes silent. She gets out and looks at the back of the car. "Not bad for your first attempt," she says, nicely, but when I look I see the back of my new car smashed in, and the front of someone else's car with a broken headlight and grille.

"I guess I shouldn't drive anymore," I tell her.

"Nonsense. It's your first time, everyone smashes their car the first time, I know I did. I'll leave a note under their windshield wiper with my number. This is why we have insurance, they'll sort it out. I'll finish parking, then we'll have lunch."

I watch as she effortlessly guides the car into the space. I feel embarrassed and hope the driver of the other car doesn't see me.

"Los Tacos Del Sol is very authentic, that's why there's a pig outside." she explains. The tacos are good, but I keep thinking about the car.

"Will you drive back to the hotel?" I ask her.

"You've got to get right back on the horse," she tells me. I'm nervous all the way back to the hotel.

Esther checks her watch and gets in her car, "Noah and I have an appointment with a musical arranger at 1 so I've got to go. I'm thinking we'll start with violins and move into horns for the patriotic part. Back in a jiff," she says, giving me a kiss. I watch her drive away like a race car driver.

Back at the bungalow I stop when I see the door is open. I look inside and hear, "Hello, Herb."

"Archie!" I say, hugging him, before remembering I'm mad at him. "You were spying on me!"

"Not spying, Herb. Watching over you."

"Are you really a butler? Is Clarence really your friend? Are you really opening a flower shop?"

"Yes, I was buttling here when Breakneck asked me to work for my country. I have to do my part, you understand that. Yes about Clarence and the flower shop. I'm not a spy, just a patriotic butler."

"Can I trust you?"

He looks me in the eye, "You heard Breakneck say I'd grown *too* fond of you."

"He did say that. I really missed you." I give him a long hug. "How's your mum?"

"I'm sorry I had to make up that story. She and my aunt Belle moved to Tonypandy, Wales, where we have cousins. She should be safe there."

The phone rings, Archie answers. "It's Leon at the studio for you, Herb," he hands me the phone.

"Hi, Leon. Yes, I can be there in a half hour." I hang up. "When Esther gets back let her know I'm at the studio."

I put on my blue seersucker so I look professional and slide the storyboard sheets into my green bag. The only watch I have left is my old Mickey Mouse so I put it on. I still like him.

200 ⇒ Toast

I've got a headache but I've had a lot of those lately. I can keep going. The keys jingling in my pocket sound especially loud. I have a beautiful car! Sparkly. It's hard to believe. I rub my eyes. Everything's sparkly. I smell something burning... toast... rubber... I'm suddenly dizzy and grab the door handle , feeling myself sliding down the side of the car... pain, sparkling, smell...

Blackness.

"Herbie? Herbie? Herbie? Can you hear me?" says a low but familiar voice. Somebody I used to know? My head is full of light. Opening my eyes makes it worse, so I keep them shut tight.

"What the..."

"You don't look so good," the voice says.

"Where am..."

"Help me get him in my car!" the voice shouts. I hold my head. I'm lifted from under my arms and ankles. I try to open my eyes but it's too bright.

Blackness.

I can feel the movement of the car. "I'm taking you to the hospital," the voice says.

I squint through my left eye and see a small man in a gray suit... thin mustache... green eyes.

"Who are..."

"An old friend."

I force myself to look at the face like I was a camera. I know those eyes.

No, no, no, no, no, no, no, no, no.

201 ➺ Tiger Thorne

What a beautiful man.

I don't believe my eyes. "Kitty?" I ask, weakly, my head splitting.

"Tiger." the low voice answers.

"Kitty Rose," I insist.

"Tiger Thorne."

"You *were* Kitty, weren't you? Like Iris was Myron?"

"We're not at all the same."

"But you're twins."

He/she turns to me with a hard expression, "Light night and day."

I feel tears rolling down my cheeks from the pain and confusion. "I thought you were dead."

"Kitty is. I killed her."

"Did you kill David and Frank, too?" I ask.

"No, they had plenty of enemies—probably DiMorte. So it was time for Kitty to go, too."

"You left me."

"Kitty did, stupid bitch!" he laughs, not her laugh. Deeper.

"I don't understand," I say, closing my eyes so I can hear this new person.

"Oh, Sweet Herbie, I'm sorry. All Kitty ever had was ambition—that's poison for a woman, but manna for men. You were right when you said I used men to get what I wanted. I finally figured out I had to stop acting like a man and start being one."

"I'm not sure you're real."

"Real is what you make it, boychik."

I flash to all the swashbuckling movies where men get stabbed and I know what it feels like. I've got one dagger in my forehead, another in my heart.

We careen through the street and I try to hold on, but everything goes black, then flashes into white again. I feel his arm guide my head down to his lap, his hand stroking my hair.

"I thought becoming a man would solve everything, but men are so afraid of each other. You were never afraid. I learned from you."

"I thought I loved you."

"You still do."

"I love Esther."

"She's the next best thing to me. But she isn't me."

"You're not you."

"You're wrong, I finally am. I know what I want."

"What?" I ask.

"You."

Everything stops. No sound. No movement. I can't see or hear.

"Why???" I cry, about everything.

"Because I don't *need* you... I *want* you," Tiger says.

I don't understand anything. I swallow hard but it feels like trying to swallow sand. "I *want* Esther."

"What you *want* and what you *need* are two different things. You *need* me."

He kisses me, and at last, I finally know her.

Pain. Noise. Everything dissolves into light.

I wake up as three big orderlies put me on a bed. They strap down my wrists, and tighten a leather belt around my forehead so I can't move.

The old doctor who showed me the negatives stands by the bed, "Mr. Hamilton. Your symptoms indicate you may be having a stroke. We need to perform this surgery—now—for your own good. You will most likely feel better, or you'll feel nothing at all, but either way you'll be out of the pain you're in."

202 »→ I Can Still Do That

I can't move, can't even turn my head to see if Esther and Archie are here. All I can see are the square ceiling tiles filled with holes. I can still do that. I wiggle my fingers and toes. I can still do that. I feel air enter my head through my nose, go down my throat and into my lungs. I can still do that.

I stop fighting and see a storyboard in my head.

Box 1: the doctor is holding a saw.

Box 2: He saws off the top of my skull.

Box 3: He reaches in and pulls out chunks of my brain.

Box 4: He screws the top of my skull back on and sews up my scalp all around the edge, like Boris Karloff in Frankenstein.

Box 5: Blackness, with specs of light, like Sarah after being shell-shocked. There's a note under it saying, "All he hears is buzzing."

Box 6: Esther is standing at the altar with Adam, Stoneman smiling.

Box 7: Kitty is wearing the white dress with red cherries, working as a cocktail waitress as a customer pinches her ass.

Box 8: Archie and Clarence in their flower shop.

Box 9: Pat is shaking hands with FDR while Glenn takes her photo.

Box 10: Ma on the beach in Florida.

Box 11: I am still in this room. Unable to move or see or hear.

Box 12: Nobody misses me.

Tears flow down both sides of my face and I can't move to wipe them away. At least I can still cry.

203 »+ Light

Light.
Sound.
Breath.
A warm kiss on my cheek.
I turn my head and see Esther. She's fuzzy.
Beeping.
"Doctor, he's..."
Blackness.

204 »+ Buzz

Dark.
Buzzing. Loud.
Sweet smell.
I can't see—I know others by their smell and the vibrations in my antennae.
I feel my way along the six-sided tubes,
I am inside a beehive.
I dance in the dark to tell the others where to find pollen.
I mate with the queen.
I die.

205 ➤➤ Nothing

206 ➤ Look

Ow, I feel a sting on my hand.
Buzzing.
Inhale. Yes.
Eyes. No.
Fingers? Maybe.
Clicking. Beeping.
Buzzing.
"Why doesn't he..."
Buzzing.
Pinpricks of light.
My head hurts.
Frankenstein?
Can't move my arm or feel.
Struggle. Nothing...

...I was back in the bungalow but it had no roof. I was lying on the sofa with everyone I loved around me. Ma, Kitty, Myron, Pat, Glenn, Sam, Max, Iris, Archie, Esther. They wrapped me in the palm frond bedspread, lit me on fire and sang:

"Forget your troubles c'mon get happy,
the lord is waitin to take your hand.
shout hallelujah c'mon get happy,
we're going to the promised land.

We're headin' across the river
wash your sins away in the tide.
it's all so peaceful on the other side.
Get ready, get ready, get ready—for the judgment day!"
I smelled smoke. It was hot all around me...

...I cough. It feels like my throat is being pulled out of my mouth. My eyes snap open, it's blindingly light. "Look!"

207 ➠ Fuzzy

Fuzzy people.

Buzzing "Herb. Herb? Can you hear me?"

I talk but the sounds coming out of my mouth don't make sense. "Where she."

Buzzing "What is he saying?"

I want to say, 'where am I, what's happening, where's Esther?" but it comes out "She, she?"

Buzz. "...not an uncommon side effect. It may be temporary. Or it may be a permanent disorder."

Crying.

Ammonia.

I move my left arm.

Buzz "Look!"

"...hemiplegia, paralysis on the right side of the body."

"Me what!" I say.

"...Sedative..."

Sting in arm.

"Click!" I say.

Darker. Quieter.

Hand? Touch?

Blackness.

208 ➠ X-ray Hearing

Breathing. I can still do that.

Eyes, opening.

Seeing... fuzzy, but I can make out shapes. One looks like Esther.

"You you!" is all that will come out of my mouth.

"Calm yourself, Mr. Hamilton," the not-Esther voice says.

I try hard but can only say, "Es... Her..."

"There were some complications but you're alive, isn't that nice?" the not-Esther says.

"N.. N... ice," I manage to say after some struggle.

The not-Esther leaves the room. I still can't move my head. My left arm is hot, my right is cold.

I hear traffic and see reflections occasionally darting across the ceiling.

I hear voices arguing outside the door, then the door opens. "I am his wife and I have a right to see him!" says the real Esther. Hearing her voice makes me cry. She stands to my right and leans over me, backlit like an angel. Her tear lands on my cheek, she kisses it. "I've been so afraid!"

"You. You!"

"Yes, I'm here."

"You. Dad."

"I'm not speaking to him, but don't you worry your sweet... head about it." EstherKitty touches my cheek.

I try to touch her with my right hand but can't move it. "Can't." I cry more, trapped in my own body.

"I brought your camera, I thought you'd want it." She pushes it into my right hand but I don't feel anything. "Here it is, hold it. Can't you..." I see tears in her eyes which makes me cry more.

"No. I. Bad. Go."

"I'm not going, Herb. I am here for you." She leans down and I feel her soft, warm cheek against mine.

"Tiger."

"What? You need to rest," She kisses my cheek. "I'll be right here by your side." She sits. I can't turn my head to see her but I hear paper.

"Read?"

"You want me to read the script to you. Good idea. Then you can get out of here and direct it. Here we go. 'Interior. Day. Henry's POV. Henry's eyes open on a very bright hospital ward. Everything is white. A nurse leans over him, glowing in the late afternoon sun. HENRY:

Where am I? SARAH: St. Pancras Hospital, London. HENRY: Why? SARAH: You were injured by a German Bomb.'"

I grunt, too tired to even try to talk.

"You like it, Herb?"

I grunt again, not remembering what she just said. My eyes closing.

"I'm glad you like it. You look tired. You sleep now. I'll be right here." ...

...I was in Stoneman's office. I turned and saw Tiger, stuffed and mounted on the wall. I screamed...

..."ARGH!" I scream.

"I'm right here, darling. Do you need something?"

I want her to stay but I say "Go."

"I'm not leaving..."

"Go!"

She kisses my cheek. Warm. Sweet. "No." I sob. I close my eyes, too tired to see.

I hear her leave the room, then raise her voice. "Get away from me, you monster, you did this!"

"Don't be absurd, I didn't plant a tumor in his head, Esther.." Stoneman's voice says.

"He would have been fine if you hadn't head-butted him!"

"You're being hysterical, I'm here to support my little girl, is that a crime?" Stoneman intones. I can almost hear the ticking of his watch.

"Why the sudden concern?"

"You're my daughter, I want to be here for you."

"When did you learn about normal human emotions?"

"Esther, I will not have you talk to me that way."

"Get used to it, Dad. No, get used to it, *Abe*."

"You're hysterical. I'm going to have them give you a sedative."

"I'm going to kick you in the balls."

"You're clearly overwrought. Doctor? Doctor, my daughter... UG!" I hear a thud, then Stoneman screams in pain.

"I'm sorry doctor, my father suffers from kidney stones and seems to be having one right now. He clearly needs a lot of morphine."

"Orderlies!" the Doctor yells. I hear feet run down the hallway.

Footsteps coming into the room. Esther. I can tell from the way she walks. I feel her holding my left wrist and putting something on it.

"Here," she says.

"What?"

"Abe's watch... no, *your* watch. I took it off him."

"I. Can't. Read it."

"I will do everything I can to make sure you can."

"I feel. Bad. You taking. Care of. Me." I admitted.

"I feel good getting to take care of you. Once dad disowns me I can get a job at any other studio to support us."

I laugh/cry at the same time. She showers me with kisses. "My. Love." I can still say that.

209 ➻ Wheels

"Come on, Mr. Hamilton. Time to sit up and do our exercises!" the chipper young nurse in a pink and white striped dress says.

"Esther?" I ask.

"Your pretty wife is in the waiting room while we do our exercises."

"We? You, too?"

"I'm here to help you do yours."

A commanding woman strides into the room. "Good day, Mr. Hamilton. I am Mrs. Morris, the physical therapist assigned to your case. I will be assessing your muscle strength, working on a series of what we call 'passive movements,' and then we shall begin what will most likely be a very long and slow re-education of your muscles. I trust you will do everything I tell you, as it is in your best interest to do so."

"Yes. Thank. Mrs..."

"Morris. As in 'more' and 'is.' Say it again, please."

"More-is."

"Fine, just fine. Now Miss Lee and I will help you out of bed and into this wheelchair."

"No, I..."

"I understand you may have some trepidation but, as I explained, it is in your best interest to do everything I tell you. Do you understand?"

"Yes. Thank."

"Thanks—with an S on the end. Repeat after me, 'thanksss'."

"Thank-sss."

"Very good. A strapping young man like yourself should be able to look forward to at least a partial recovery and use of a wheelchair. Let's begin. His ankles, Miss Lee."

Miss Lee puts her arm around my ankles. That feels nice. Mrs. Morris reaches around my chest quite firmly, less like a hug and more like a vice. She smells like tar.

"And three, two one," Mrs. Morris says as they lift me and lower me into the wheelchair. "Into the hallway, Miss Lee."

Miss Lee wheels me into the hallway. She smells like radishes and soap.

"Today's goal is to get your wheelchair to the end of the hallway and back, if possible. Can you raise your right arm?"

I try. My hand shakes but I can't get it to do anything else.

"That's fine, just fine. The fact that there was a tremor is a good sign, you might possibly regain some use of it. Raise your left arm."

It feels heavy, but I can raise it.

"That's wonderful, Mr. Hamilton," Miss Lee gushes.

Miss Morris looks at her sternly, "We never want to get a patient's hopes up, dear, as that can lead to disappointment and depression. In a case like this we simply say, 'Fine' or 'Good,' nothing more."

"Fine. Good, nothing more, Mr. Hamilton." Miss Lee says, looking down at her hands.

"Now, Mr. Hamilton, place your left hand on the chrome wheel to the left of the rubber tire. Can you feel that?"

"Yes. Ma'am."

I struggle to push. The wheelchair turns to the right.

"Miss Lee, I told you to engage the cardan shaft."

Miss Lee looks flustered. "I thought I did." She reaches down but Mrs. Morris swats her hand away. She presses down a lever until it snaps.

"Please try it again, Mr. Hamilton."

I push as hard as I can with my left hand and the wheelchair inches forward.

"Yay..." Miss Lee trails off.

"Please push yourself to the end of the hallway, then wait for us there. Take all the time you need."

Each push is a struggle. Each propels the chair forward just a bit, but I'm so excited I keep pushing, almost running into a doctor who sees me just in time. At the end of the hall I'm drenched in sweat but I raise my left arm, triumphantly.

Mrs. Morris approaches. "Fine, fine. To turn you will reach down, flip this lever, turn the left wheel until you have rotated a full 180 degrees, flip it back and push back down the hallway. Got it? Go."

I struggle to pull the latch and almost pinch my fingers. I push the left wheel and turn to the right so I'm facing the other direction. I flip the lever back down until it snaps and push myself back down the hall, getting slower and more exhausted with each attempt. Miss Lee stands behind Mrs Morris and claps, silently, then jumps up and down until Mrs. Morris turns around, at which point Miss Lee pretends she was still all along.

"Fine, Mr. Hamilton. That is all for today, you may feel tired but that is normal. I will see you again tomorrow and probably for the next four months."

"Four?" I ask.

"Maybe six. Good evening, sir." She leaves.

Miss Lee pats my hand, "That was excellent for your first attempt, you should be proud of yourself. I'll get Mrs. Hamilton for you."

"Thank. You. Miss. Lee."

"Four words in a row—you are doing so well, so very well!" she gushes, leaving the room.

Esther enters, wearing the yellow dress with the triangles she wore the second day I met her. "I saw you racing down the hall!" She smiles and kisses me.

"I was. Thinking. Of. You." I feel her cheek against one side of my face. "You smell." She makes a face. "Good. You. Smell. Good. Please. Read me. Script." She sits in the chair next to my bed and reads more. "Makes me. Cry."

"Good, love, that's what it should do."

210 🐝 Tsís'ná

The days repeat till I lose count.

Wake. Right arm still not working. Tasteless food. Pushing the wheelchair further. Trying to walk while Bjarke, a big red haired orderly, holds me up because I can't hold myself up. My right side doesn't work and I'm more and more frustrated.

Esther sneaks in lunch, often corned beef. We eat and I can talk more. Archie brings in a vase of fresh flowers and tells me about the progress on his and Clarence's florist shop at the hotel. "We've named it 'Buds' because that's what Clarence and I are," he tells me.

They leave me for a nap, but mostly I cry because I am so happy they came, but also so sorry to be such a burden. I ask them to only come for lunch so I don't waste too much of their days. I heard them talking about how tired I must be, but I'm not. I'm angry. Sad. Scared.

Nobody will tell me about Tiger or Kitty.

Mrs. Morris has Miss Lee wheel me outside for some "Sun and much-needed vitamin D." I like to feel the breeze and watch the leaves move. I wheel myself further and further, almost all the way back to the room before my left arm cramps.

Tasteless dinner. Watching light from headlights play across the ceiling. Sleep.

I feel like I have been here forever. I ask Miss Lee, "How long. Have I. Been here."

"Just two weeks, Mr. Hamilton, and look how well you're doing?"

I don't feel like I'm doing well.

"Your wife said she'll be a little late today and will meet us outside. Won't that be nice?"

I wonder why she's late. Maybe she's getting tired of me. After a long session of wheeling myself, including up and down a ramp, Miss Lee wheels me to a bench under a large oak tree. "I'll leave you alone with your guests."

Esther kisses me on the lips, not the cheek. "Wow," I say.

"Wow, is right. The doctor said I shouldn't do that, lest I expose you to germs, but I couldn't help myself."

"Don't help yourself. Help me!"

I brought this, she says putting the turquoise string tie around my neck. I try to touch it with my right hand. I can't.

"I brought someone special to see you, Tsís'ná?" she waves and the native woman walks from behind a tree.

"I found them, Esther," Tsís'ná says. She is wearing a dark blue dress with a heavy silver necklace. "Hello again, Herbert."

"Oh. You." I try very hard to say her name, "Sis... na."

"That is close, very good, Herbert." she says, kindly. "Thank you for remembering me."

"Thank you. Why?"

"Why, what, Herbert?"

"Why you. Give me. Turq... Blue rock. Why?"

Tsís'ná looks at Esther who nods at her. "Honestly, it was my grandmother's idea at first. She saw your shoes and watch and thought... but that doesn't matter. I saw you and saw more."

"More. What?"

"Tsís'ná. That is my name. It means 'bee.' One was flying above your head—a sign."

"You saw?" I choked.

"Bees are fierce warriors who can slay larger foes. I knew we must meet."

The air suddenly feels different in my lungs, warmer, easier to breathe. "I see. You saw."

"Yes. Even the strongest warriors need protection from the Gods."

"And women,"Esther says.

"Yes, us, too. I sensed the Nádleehi in you."

"Nad... what?"

"Male and female spirit, together. Seers."

"I see. I see."

"That's what I told her, Herb," Esther says, "She has come to help."

"I am more of a guide," she says. "Come with me," she says, wheeling the chair. "Esther, please stay here for your own safety." Tsís'ná wheels me off the path and into a grove of trees. "They have been waiting for you," she says.

I hear buzzing and see bees flying in and out the hole in a tree.

"You must call them. Knock on the tree—welcome them. Do not be afraid to accept their gifts. Remember, 'feeling is healing.'" She walks away.

I can feel the warmth of the hive and smell it's waxy sweetness. I knock on the tree with my left hand. "Hello. Friends."

The buzzing gets louder. I see a single bee float in front of my face. I close my eyes and send it a message from my heart. "Thank you."

The buzzing gets even louder. I can feel a slight breeze from their wings. I keep my eyes closed and remember my time in the hive.

I feel a tingle in my right arm and leg. I hadn't felt anything there and now, something. I open my eyes and gasp. My right arm and leg are covered in bees, stinging me.

The tingle gets sharper until I feel the pain. I want to cry out but I stay silent and feel it—Tsís'ná said, 'feeling is healing.'

"Thank you," I say to them as they struggle to pull themselves from my arm, "THANK YOU!" I scream.

Tsís'ná returns, brushes the remaining bees off me while chanting, "ahéhee', ahéhee', thank you, dear friends. Thank you for your gifts. We shall always be grateful. May you be at peace."

My arm and leg are burning hot. "I can feel them."

"Their medicine is working."

211 ➥ Feeling is Healing

The burning is becoming unbearable.

"It hurts so much."

"Feel it, Herbert."

"I don't want to, make it stop."

"Don't fight, accept the gift."

"Ow, how is pain a gift?"

"Because you *can* feel it. That's better than not being able to feel."

She is right, though it's hard to be thankful for this gift when it hurts so much. My arm and leg are red and swelling. Tsís'ná wheels me back to Esther who looks alarmed.

"What happened to him?"

"Medicine," I grunt.

"Yes, we must get him medicine," Esther says.

"No," Tsís'ná says, calmly. "We must keep him away from other medicines for at least an hour."

"I can't!" I cry.

"Give up and you will lose the feeling in your arm and leg again. Is that what you want?" Tsís'ná says.

"No!"

"Don't fight, feel. Feeling is healing." Tsís'ná repeats.

Esther looks worried, "Are you sure about this, Tsís'ná?"

"Very sure. You and I will pull the stingers out while Herbert accepts his medicine."

Tsís'ná hands Esther a pair of tweezers and she pulls stingers from my legs which already hurt so much I can't feel any more pain. Tsís'ná pulls them from my arm, whispering words I don't understand.

"Prayers," she says.

"I don't believe," I tell her.

"*You* don't have to. *I* do."

I focus on the pain, "It's interesting," I explain, "At first the pain was like 1,000 hot needles, but now, it's not so much pain as intense heat."

Esther stops and looks at me, surprised, "You sound better already."

"The medicine works fast," Tsís'ná says.

I thought the heat was burning, but the more I feel it, the more it's like a hot bath—not scalding but penetrating."

"Look, your fingers are moving!" Esther exclaims.

"He'll be swollen for a day, so movement will be limited, but after that he will return to normal."

I am surprised and ask, "How can you be so sure when the doctors and Mrs. Morris say I might only regain partial use of... oh, it is easier to talk. I used to think all these things but only a few words would come out."

"They didn't tell you because they didn't know."

"Thank you for seeing me," I tell her.

"We seers can see each other."

"I think I've removed them all," Esther announces.

"I will check his leg, you check his arm," Tsís'ná tells her.

Esther inspects from my hands to my shoulder, and when her face is close to mine, I whisper, "My hero."

"Tsís'ná is the one who did this."

"But you knew to bring her here." I kiss Esther's soft lips and inhale her scent, like black cherries.

"What're you feeling now, Herbert?" Tsís'ná asks.

"Very hot, in a good way. Swollen. Relaxed."

"He should sleep now, probably until tomorrow. That is to be expected." Tsís'ná covers my arm and leg with the blanket and the two of them take me to my room where I'm able to pull myself into bed.

"I won't leave your side," Esther kisses me.

"Neither will I," Tsís'ná adds.

"How did I get so lucky?" I ask, falling asleep before I can hear the answer.

212 ➠ Reality

I sleep for 24 hours straight without a single dream. I wake up, feeling better than I have in weeks. I think about moving my right arm and leg—and they move! It takes a lot of effort because they feel stiff and weak, but they move and I yelp with joy!

"You're awake!" Esther gasps, putting down her book and touching my right hand. "Do you feel this?" I wrap my swollen fingers around her sweet hand. "Tsís'ná, look!"

Tsís'ná tickles my toe and I laugh. "Our friends did their work well."

"I want to get up, I want to walk, I want to dance!"

"Patience, my friend."

Esther comes back with the doctor. "Look, Look!"

I proudly move my arms and legs and fingers and toes for him. "I'm glad to see my operation was such a success," he says. Esther, Tsís'ná and I roll our eyes.

"You have Tsís'ná to thank for this, doctor," I explained.

"What? I performed the surgery brilliantly."

"But it was her native medicine that..."

"I don't believe in that mumbo jumbo. It was probably a matter of time until you regained some use of your limbs."

I am determined to show him how well I am doing, so I slide out of bed and stand up, unsteadily and holding onto the bed, but still up. "I can stand up!"

"You were very lucky I was your surgeon," is all he says on his way out. As soon as he's out of the room, I'm saved from falling by Esther who helps me back in bed.

Later, Mrs. Morris announces, "My physical therapy has worked wonders for you, young man," as Bjarke helps me walk up and down the hall, the big toe on my right foot still feeling numb.

Esther brings a veritable feast from Canters for dinner. She turns off the overhead light and we dine by the glow of city lights and of the Hollywoodland sign.

Tsís'ná has never eaten corned beef or chopped liver, both of which she said she likes but didn't finish, claiming to be full. She does, however, manage to eat two chocolate covered coconut macaroons and an apricot hamantaschen before leaving to commune with the coyote she heard bark outside.

"What happened to Tiger?" I asked.

"What tiger?" Esther asked.

"Not what, but who."

"'Who tiger' doesn't make sense, darling."

"Tiger, who brought me here."

"I thought Archie brought you here, dear."

"Did he tell you that?"

"No, I just assumed because you were at the hotel."

"Can I tell you what I remember without you thinking I'm crazy?"

"Hopefully a little crazy."

"I remember a man in a gray suit—oh, you saw him at Canter's, remember?"

"The friend you went to see before you knocked down a waiter?"

"Yes, but I didn't know who he was." I said slowly.

"A friend you didn't know?"

"He said his name was Tiger but I recognized him as Kitty, and he told me that he'd decided to be a man."

"Who just decides that?" she asked, gently.

I turn over in bed, away from her and look at the Hollywood hills and sign. Maybe I'd imagined all of this. Maybe I was still imagining all this.

I'd never told her all about Kitty and Myron, so now I do... "That's why Kitty could be Tiger."

Esther takes her time thinking about it. "I studied Greek mythology in college, so I know about Hermaphroditus, child of Hermes and Aphrodite, the gods of masculinity and femininity. In the myth, Salmacis was so besotted with Hermaphroditus that she prayed to be united with him. The Gods answered her prayer by melding them into one, a hermaphrodite... So you're saying Kitty and Myron are both male and female?"

"Yes. Kitty was my first so I didn't know any of that."

"And you know this was true and not just..."

"It isn't my tumor talking if that's what you mean. She's in my photos in Look magazine!" I say, furiously.

"I'm sorry, Herbie. I haven't seen the magazine but it doesn't matter—I believe you."

"I need to see the magazine. I need to know what *was* real, what *is* real."

"The library should have a copy, I can check tomorrow..."

"No, I have a copy in my suitcase. At least I think I do. Please ask Archie to bring it here now."

"OK, honey, please, calm down." She calls and talked to Archie. "He said he'll look for it and be right over."

The wait feels endless. What if everything I remember was just a hallucination. It all felt so real. Just as all this feels so real. Then again, my dreams feel real, too... So how do I know if anything's real? "Please, hold my hand, I need to feel you," I tell her. "I can feel your hand. I can feel it. You are real, aren't you?"

"Yes, Herbie, I am real."

"How do I know?"

"Because I'm telling you, that's how."

"But if I'm imagining you, you'd say you were real." I was breathing hard and fast and starting to feel dizzy. I squeeze my eyes closed, then open, then closed and she is still there. I'm breathing faster and faster, feeling lightheaded, as the room starts to spin...

213 ➻ What's My Name?

It's sunny when I wake up again.

Esther is gone.

There's a copy of *Look* magazine in her chair. There's the cover photo I took... Did I take it? I am too scared to look inside to see the photo credit. What if none of this was true?

I turn the pages and there's Kitty, pointing at the Perisphere. She's real. The caption reads, "Our All-American Girl, Miss Kitty Rose, invites you to join her in the world of tomorrow *Photo: Herbert Hamilton/LOOK*!"

Yes! It's true! It happened!

But—what if I'm not Herbert Hamilton? I know that's not my real name, or wasn't my real name but now is...

"Nurse! NURSE!" I yell.

Miss Lee enters in her pink and white striped dress. "What's wrong, Mr. Hamilton?"

"I'M MR. HAMILTON!" I cry triumphantly!

"That's the name on your chart."

"Are you sure?" I ask, worried again.

"It's on your chart, they're very careful about these things."

"But how do they know? Who told them my name?"

"I did," Tiger says, sauntering into the room.

"I'll leave you two alone," she leaves, looking relieved.

"Are you real?" I ask him.

"As real as a brain tumor," he laughs, sounding Kitty-ish.

I feel the bandages on my head. "I don't know what's real anymore."

"Yes you do, Herbie. I'm real," Tiger said. "And you have the magazine—look! I'll always remember that day..."

"...the day I lost you..."

"...the day I found myself." Tiger takes my hand. I feel chills.

I pull my hand away, "No, I can't."

"Can't what?"

"Where's Esther? Is she real?"

"She went to get coffee."

"You talked to her?"

Tiger smiled, his green eyes the only thing unchanged from Kitty. "I've been coming every day but she didn't know who I was. Yesterday she saw me and we talked. She really loves you."

Just then Esther enters the room carrying muffins. "Who loves who?"

"Tiger said you love me."

She kisses me on the lips. "Of course, no matter what."

"What does that mean?" I asked her.

"You told me who you were when we first met and I told you I was OK with it."

"I don't remember what I said."

She hands a muffin to Tiger who hands it to me. She hands him another and he takes a bite. "Blueberries, ug."

Esther takes a bite of hers. "Chocolate?" Tiger nods. She switches with him and says to me, "You told me I had nothing to be jealous of," winking at Tiger.

All I can do is stare.

For a long time.

"You don't think he's having another stroke, do you?" Tiger asks Esther.

I laugh/cry.

"No, both sides of his face are moving." Esther inspects me.

"He's always been a very sensitive boy." Tiger adds.

Esther smiles, "I love that about him."

"Me, too," Tiger says, leaning in and kissing me on the mouth.

"Hold on there, Tiger!" Esther says. "We still need sound ground rules, here."

"Who made you the boss? Tiger asks.

"Me," I say firmly, and they both stop and look at me.

Esther continues, "Good. If this is going to work, I need more time alone with Tiger at the bungalow so we can see how we get on."

"Intimately?" Tiger smiles. Esther smiles back.

214 ➤ I See

Two days pass. I don't see Esther or Tiger. Archie brings lunch and tells me he's heard a lot of laughing between Esther and Tiger. I ask him what else he heard but he says, "A butler never divulges such things."

I'm getting stronger. I can walk down the hall by myself now, with a cane. Esther had a custom one made in clear Lucite, the top hand-carved to look like a bee. It's classy, like Charlie Chaplin. I can imagine it becoming my trademark as a director.

I get back from a walk and Esther and Tiger enter my room, holding hands. She looks smashing in his gray pinstripe suit, and he looks dashing in a short suede bomber jacket and khaki pants.

"I see what you saw in her—in him," she says, simply.

214 ➤ Pre-Production

I'm raring to get going on the movie, but Tsís'ná reminds me to be patient—nature doesn't work by the clock and takes its time. I can wait, I'm not alone. Esther and Tiger are here together with me at the hospital every day. Esther manages visitors and Tiger mans the phone, rarely handing it to me, but this time, he does.

"Hey, brother, Diane just told us—are you OK?" Glenn asks. I'm so happy to hear his voice.

"Yeah, I'm great! I mean, honestly, I'm doing OK, getting better."

"I'm sorry Pat and I were so wrapped up with Welles when we were there."

"You were here?" I say, figuring I now have a good excuse for my bad behavior.

"Pat, he doesn't remember! You do still remember me and Pat, right?"

"Always, brother... and sister-in-law?"

Pat gets on the phone, "Herb, we're so relieved—and proud of you. Is there anything we can do?"

"Hi, Pat. Knowing you guys are there for me is all I need right now, thank you."

"We know you're busy and don't want to get in the way, but the minute you're done shooting, Glenn and I are coming out to the coast to do a piece on your film, the war effort—and you."

"Not me. I'm strictly behind-the-camera."

"We love you!" I hear them both say and I really don't want to cry in a room full of people but there's no stopping it.

"You OK, love?" Esther asks.

"I'm so happy."

"We've got a lot of people coming in today for meetings, you ready?" she asks.

I take her hand. "Ready, willing and able!" I salute.

Leon visits to go over the storyboards. At first he blurts out, "Impossible!" then "that will be a wonderful challenge!"

Lyle Wheeler, the art director, shows me sketches of the costumes and sets. I asked Iris to do the costumes but she happily claimed that Adrian wouldn't hear of it. Besides, given the time constraints, Lyle has to repurpose things they already have on the lot. He explains that they often do that anyway and audiences don't notice. I don't tell him I recognize the staircase from *The Mark of Zorro* I saw earlier this year, because it all looks great to me!

Lisa, the head of casting, shows me headshots, explaining that due to the time and budget she could only use contract players. I haven't heard of them but am glad they'll be getting their big break like I am. I hear Esther rehearsing the actors in the hall, then she brings them in to do their scenes for me and I applaud.

Breakneck convinced his pals, Laurence Olivier and Vivien Leigh, to play small but pivotal roles (he, a British general, she, the head of the nurses corps). Tiger, working at the William Morris talent agency, convinces Jimmy Cagney to play the American general for one day's shooting.

Doctor Shienman makes a big show of shooing the production people out of the room. I insist Esther and Tiger stay.

He unwraps my head like a mummy. Esther nods, Tiger looks unsure. Esther hands me a mirror—my head is mostly shaved with a big scar running down the side. Tiger calls it "virile" and Esther says, "It adds character."

I feel the long scar and say, "Argh!" like a pirate. Esther takes off her scarf and wraps it around my head, tying in the back, completing the look. "Ahoy, ye maties!"

Tiger scoffs, "Don't encourage him."

I pull my hand into my sleeve and grab a fork like a hook, "I'll make yer walk the plank!" I growl.

"Spoken like a true director," "Esther adds, dryly.

The doctor says, "I'll discharge you, but only if you promise to stay quietly at home for the next three months,"

Esther, Tiger and I say in unison, "We promise," and have absolutely no intention of doing any such thing. As soon as the doctor leaves, Esther says, "Studio tomorrow?"

"Bright and at least 10 minutes early!" I say, with effervescent relief.

Esther drives me back to the Bungalow. Archie has filled the place with flowers: gardenias, tulips and roses in white, pink, orange, yellow and red.

"You're a doll, Archie," Esther hugs him, "and isn't the smell divine!" I feel enveloped in a floral cloud of love.

I give Archie a big hug, and he smells good, too, like leather and tobacco and freshly cut grass.

"Corned beef hash, Herb?" He knows me so well and I savor the crisp, oily, salty flavors and rye toast.

Esther eats a peanut butter and chili pepper sandwich, "I was craving it."

I'm excited and scared about tomorrow. I go over the schedule and storyboards with Esther. "You got this," she tells me.

Later Tiger comes over with a real leather whip he can flick to make a loud cracking noise. "Use this on the set if somebody messes up," he says, spending the next half hour teaching me how to use it until my arm is tired.

Tiger is sleeping in the second bedroom while Esther gets in bed with me. "Why are you being so nice to Tiger?" I ask.

"At first I was jealous," she says. "But he saved you, and in a way, me, too. Look, I was going to marry Adam. We would have been friends but I wouldn't have had love. Now I can love two people. That's wonderful. I never believed it was reasonable to expect one person to be your everything in life. Together we have more love to share."

I stroke her cheek, warm and fuzzy like a peach in the sun. I lean in and smell her, like licorice and lavender. "But how does this work?" I ask.

""We're the perfect trio," she whispers, "You, the director, me the writer, Tiger the agent—we're an unstoppable trio. Nobody in this town cares what you do as long as you make money for them. Look at Lunt and Fontanne and Noel Coward—just a few years ago he came right out and wrote a play about their threesome. Look at Cary Grant and Randolph Scott, they even go to parties in drag. We'll just get a house with a guesthouse, like George Cukor."

"Knock, knock," Tiger opens the door.

Esther says, "Come on in, the water's fine." Tiger gets in bed on one side of me, Esther on the other.

I feel warmth and love all around.

215 **↠** Raising the Moon

The next morning, Esther drives me to the studio. I still need my cane and use it proudly. We get there a half hour early, yet Leon is already there, lighting the set single-handedly until grips and gaffers join him, looking ashamed for being late when they're actually early.

"Come take a look at this," he says, helping me on the tall crane he's using today for a sweeping shot from the ground up into the heavens. He pulls a level and we're lifted nearly to the roof. "This'll be a hell of a shot!"

The set looks like a bombed out Gothic church, bursting with white flowers that Archie and Clarence are still arranging.

"It'll look even better when it's lit," he says, as we float back down to the floor. He rushes over to the grips who are manning the moon. I told Leon I wanted the wedding shot in actual moonlight, which he said was impossible, even for him, but that he would make it look like real moonlight. Leon works with the grips to position the large glowing object.

My assistant director, Bruce, arrives with binders of schedules. He speaks in a swift whisper "Here's today's shot list, we got 10 pages to get through today so I'm going to ride everybody hard. I'll be the Mutt to your Jeff. Tell me what you need and I'll get it done."

"Thanks, Bruce. Please, please tell me if I'm doing anything wrong, or if you know a better way to do it. I need your help, OK?"

"You got it, boss!" he says, softly, smiling, and rushing off.

We're shooting the last scene first, where Sarah and Henry finally get married. I knew this was coming, but it still feels strange to shoot everything out of order.

The stand-in bride wears a white wedding dress similar to the one Sarah will wear. The stand-in groom is in a black tux. Leon holds his light meter next to them and complains about the contrast. I have a flash of inspiration.

"How long 'till the actors are on set?" I ask Bruce.

"At least two hours. First shot usually takes three hours to set up. The actors'll be in costume and makeup, want me to get them?" Bruce has already started to dash away until I stop him.

"No, no, it's OK. I just had an idea. Is the actor playing the minister a real minister?"

Bruce checks his cast list, "Let me see... Aaron Vigran... he's a Rabbi, is that a problem?"

"No, it's perfect. Where's Mr. Thorne?" I ask. I've made Tiger a producer so he can be another pair of eyes helping me out on the set.

"Last I saw he was schmoozing the talent."

"Tell him to get his ass onto the set and bring the Rabbi with him." Bruce sprints off like a bunny.

I whisper my plan to Leon who laughs, "Weren't you supposed to stop being crazy when they took that thing out of your head? OK, let's do it."

I find Esther, consulting with the script girl. "Sorry to interrupt. Esther, I need you."

She asks, "What's wrong?"

"Nothing. Everything's right. I've got an idea."

Tiger brings the Rabbi in. I huddle with them and Esther and tell them my plan. Esther lets out a hoot and Tiger smacks me on the back.

Bruce tells the bride and groom stand-ins to take a break and take off their costumes.

I get on the crane with Esther and raise us both into the air. I hold the director's megaphone to my mouth and say, "Attention, please." Nobody stops working. I yell, "ATTENTION, PLEASE." Nobody stops working.

Down on the floor, Bruce foghorns, "QUIET ON THE SET!" Everyone stops. Complete silence.

"Hello, I'm Herb, the director, and this is Esther, the screenwriter. We want to thank each and every one of you for helping with this project, so important for the war effort. This isn't just about entertainment, also about the future of freedom."

The crew applauds.

"This story is ultimately about love, for each other and our fellow man. So, to show you how serious I am about love…" I take Esther's hand, "Esther and I are going to get married here on the set, right now."

Back down at the floor, Bruce is waiting with the bride and groom costumes. "How did you arrange this?" Esther asks.

"You know me, I don't plan, I just take advantage of what happens."

We change clothes behind a flat. The tux is tight, but I squeeze into it. Esther's dress is too big, but Celeste, the costumer, safety pins it up the back.

Archie hands Esther a spray of white flowers and puts a gardenia in my lapel. He kisses her cheek and shakes my hand until I bring him in for a hug.

Tiger watches, "What am I, chopped liver?"

"We love chopped liver," Esther laughs as Archie takes out his own boutonniere and puts it in Tiger's lapel.

Leon gives me an "OK" gesture, then there's a loud clunk sound and the lights go off, except for the large glowing moon.

Esther and I ceremoniously place our rings on Tiger's fingers.

We stand under a flower-covered Gothic arch. I whisper to the Rabbi, "Make it snappy, sir." He nods and proceeds.

We glow in Leon's moonlight: Esther on my right, Tiger on my left. I see the Rabbi's mouth moving but only hear the blood rushing in my ears. Tiger takes Esther's ring off his finger and hands it to me, our fingers touching. I put the ring on Esther's warm hand and say, "I do." Tiger takes my ring off his thumb and hands it to Esther, their fingers touching. She puts the ring on my hand and I hear her say, "You bet your ass I do."

I feel Tiger lean in behind me and whisper, "I do, too."

Esther looks around, "We need to break a glass."

Leon puts a large light bulb into a paper bag and places it on the floor. Esther takes my hand and together we step on it with a satisfying crunch.

The rabbi says, "You may kiss the bride." We step towards each other and kiss. She laughs, looking behind me. I turn and see Tiger giving us both air-kisses.

The crew cries, "Mazel Tov!"

Bruce says, "We gotta get moving!" Esther and I go back behind the flat to change clothes. Tiger follows. I kiss Esther. Tiger kisses her, then me.

I'm glad that thing was removed from my brain so that I know this is real.

216 ➻ Action!

I sit on the crane with Leon and watch the cast hit their marks.

The floor is a beehive of activity. Bruce yells, "Quiet on the set!" The set is hushed.

I take a deep breath, letting myself feel everything in the moment. Everything in my life. Life, itself.

My head feels clear for the first time. I see Esther, Tiger, and the whole crew waiting to work together—for good.

We are making a movie!

No-one moves. It's silent and still. Leon nudges me.

I call "ACTION!" and the world comes to life.

➻ *The End... for now.*

➽ About the Author

An internationally-recognized best-selling author, MoMA has called Daniel's work "truly unique." He's developed plays with the *Kennedy Center Playwriting Intensive, Naked Angels Theater,* and *The Actor's Centre* in London.

His 8 books have sold over 300,000 copies, he has three produced screenplays to his credit, and he's written over 600 short stories currently featured in his popular story podcast.

Daniel created and wrote the book on his *Write in the Now* writing practice. He teaches writers and artists to discover endless ideas, eliminate writer's block, find passion in their projects, and get to the very heart of their work.

See all his work here:
WWW.WILL-HARRIS.COM